PROGENY

FOURTH EDITION

R.T. KAELIN

ISBN-13: 978-0-615-42103-2

Book Design by Donna Overall
donnaoverall@bellsouth.net

Cover Design by R. T. Kaelin

Terrene
O.
Press

Columbus, Ohio
www.RTKaelin.com

ACKNOWLEDGEMENTS

I can think of hundreds, perhaps thousands, of other things I would have thought I might do in my life before writing acknowledgements for a book I had written. Nevertheless, here I am.

I would like to thank my wife for supporting me through this effort. I cannot imagine what she thought when I told her one day, "Hey, I'm going to write a book." Lisa, you are a terrific wife and wonderful mother.

Thank you to my two children, whose spirit and love inspire me every day. As you grow older (and learn to read), I hope you enjoy the story you helped contribute to without knowing.

To my first editor who must have gone through quite a few red pens to kill my love affair with semicolons—especially in the beginning—thanks, Mom.

Thank you to all the friends and family members who took the time to read some early versions for their feedback and encouragement.

Thank you to a pair of sisters, Diane Kistner and Donna Overall, for hearing my call for help and being infinitely patient with their advice and guidance.

Thank you to anyone reading this book. I hope you enjoy reading the story as much as I did writing it. Let us see where our travels go.

NEW EDITION ADDENDUM

Thank you to all of the wonderful readers who have embraced my work. Thank you for the encouragement and kind words. I love writing the stories as much as you do reading them.

Thank you to the numerous authors I've met in the past year. You have all been invaluable to my evolution as a writer.

Thank you to a trio of readers who have been wonderful in their support and proof-reading services. Chris, Caleb, Nate, Lee, Uriah, Jim…thanks.

CONTENTS

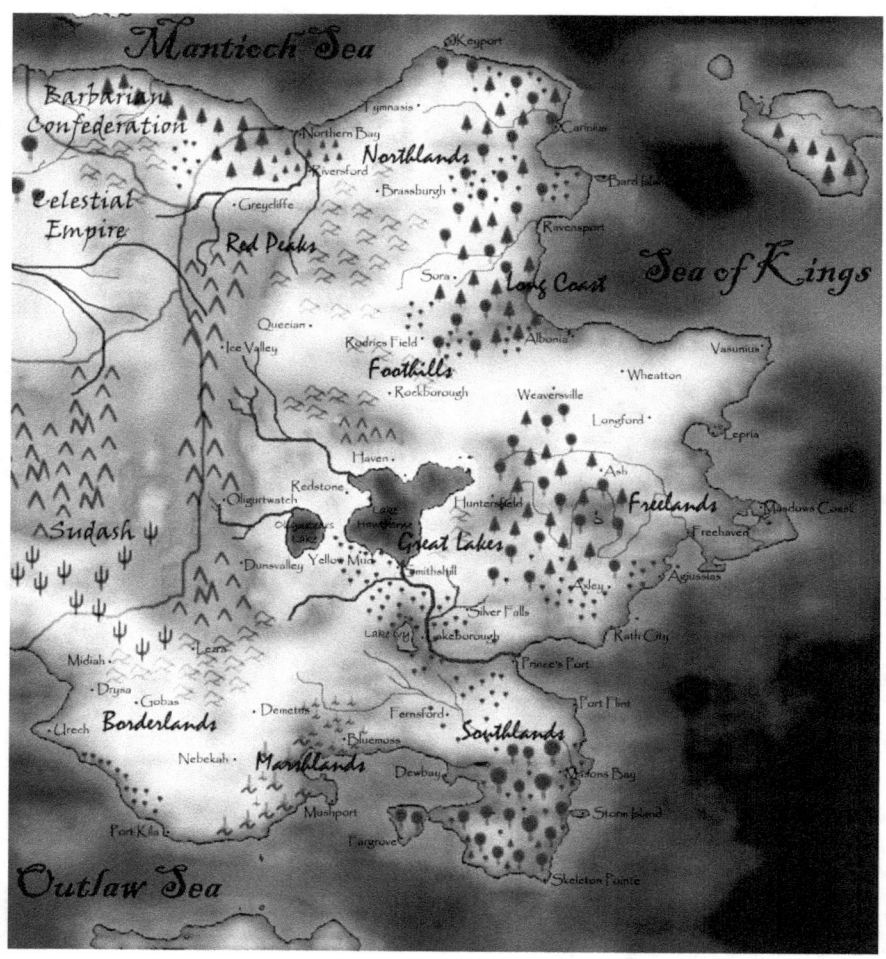

THE OAKEN DUCHIES

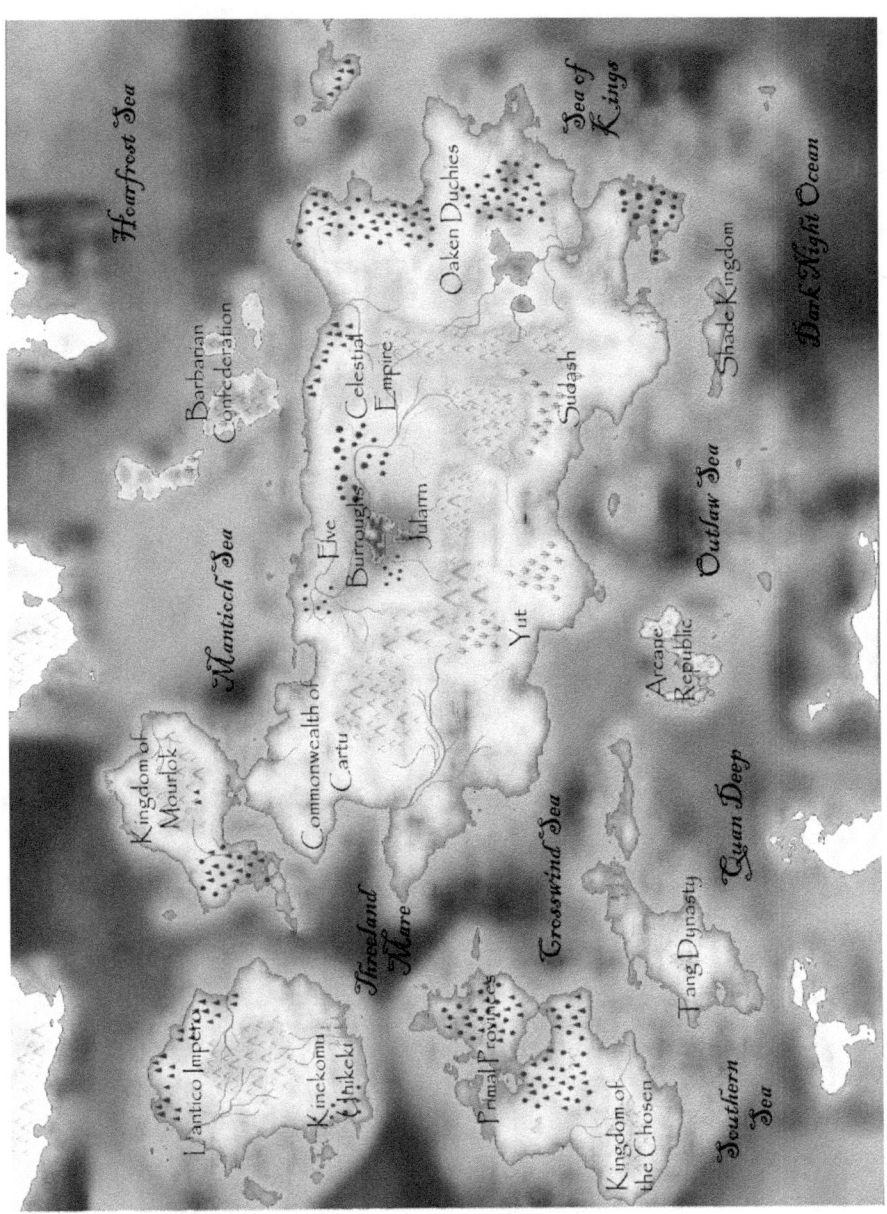

TERRENE

The roar of the Lions will drive back the spawn,
And the lines of men, strong once again, will be redrawn.
Yet that which drives man's soul will fray at the seams,
While the strength of the Lions will fade as do last night's dreams.

Torn apart by deceit and distrust,
One will perish and One will be lost.
One will leave, while Another will stay.
And Two shall find each Other one day.
Against his will, one must fight,
While it falls upon the Half-man to unite.

Chaos will rise again, unraveling what has been made,
With Strife, Pain, and Deception in tow, lending aid.
Hidden, then found,
Willingly come around,
The Progeny must rise to lead the fight,
Along with new and old, seek to make it right.

– As recorded by High Priest Ensul, First of Indrida
3rd day of the Turn of Lamoth, 4639

PROLOGUE

24ᵗʰ of the Turn of Maeana, 4744

Jhaell awoke lying on his back, wet and shivering. A wave of icy water rushed up to cover his legs, shocking him with its chill. His eyes snapped open as he drew in a quick, hissing breath. The sky stared down at him, a solid slate of gray. A soft, mumbled croak slipped past his numb lips.

"Syra…?"

He dug his elongated fingers into the soupy wet sand and pushed himself up into a sitting position. Looking to the right, he scanned the beach, the winter wind whistling in his ears. A lone gull strutted through the breakers' edge, the only sign of life on the otherwise empty shore.

He croaked again, "Syra?"

The scene to his left was the same, only no gull. Barren beach—a mix of sand, jagged rocks, and waves of frothy surf—stretched clear to the horizon where the silhouette of the academy's towers waited. The wind surged, blowing his long white-blond hair forward so that it smacked his cheek and stuck, plastering itself to his pale skin. After clearing his throat, he tried calling for her again, a bit louder.

"Syra?"

His mouth tasted of saltwater. Grains of sand crunched between his teeth.

"Syra!"

Another wave rushed over him. Gasping against the cold, he scooted back from the tide and rose on wobbly legs. His blue robes, soaked heavy with seawater, clung to his thin frame. He spun around, searching.

"Syra!"

Wanting a better view of the area, he stumbled toward a boulder several dozen paces away, shivering uncontrollably. Upon reaching it, he grabbed hold of the rough stone and attempted to scale the rock but his numb, wet fingers slipped from the rock, prompting a sharp curse.

"*Beelvra!*"

He tried again, but the result was the same. His long fingers were weak and unresponsive to his wishes. Frustrated, he reached for the Strands of Air in order to craft a quick Weave and lift himself atop the rock. That failed, too, the white strings of magic quickly falling apart before he could complete the pattern. Prolonged exposure to the elements was affecting his ability to concentrate. He slouched forward to lean against the rock, taking a moment to try to remember what had happened.

Ignoring academy rules, he had brought Syra to the shoreline to help her prepare for her final trial of the semester. Preceptors were restricted from providing individual instruction, but he had made an exception for Syra. In her six turns here, the pair had grown close. Very close.

He rested his forehead against the cold, pockmarked stone and stared at his sand-covered boots. As he stood there thinking, a few drops of crimson appeared on the toe of his right boot. He looked at his hand and discovered a deep gash on his palm. He must have cut it on the boulder, but the numbness had muted the pain. Now that he saw it, it began to throb.

He turned around, back to the sea, thinking he might gauge the tide's position and determine how long he had been unconscious. He stared up and down the beach, looking for the meandering line of dead seaweed that marked high tide, but it was gone. It was as if something had swept it away.

His eyes opened wide.

"Gods…"

He remembered.

Perhaps in an effort to impress him, Syra had reached for far too many Strands of Water. She was a talented mage, but an acolyte, and her inexperience showed. Her Weave had become increasingly tangled, yet Jhaell had stood back, giving her leeway to fix her mistake. She failed.

He shut his eyes and cursed himself. Had she been any other student, he would have unraveled the twisted mess, admonished her for overreaching, and made her start again. By the time he realized what she had wrought, it was too late.

A thirty-foot wall of water had risen from the sea and washed over the shore. Jhaell tried to craft a protective barrier of pure Air around them, but the wave had moved too fast. He remembered Syra screaming reaching out to grab his arm as the water struck. The torrent ripped them apart in an instant.

He spun around and hurried inland, scanning the beach, praying the wave had released her before rushing back into the sea. Dozens of newly formed tide pools littered the sand. He tripped over his robes, fell into one, but rose from the icy water immediately. As he stood, he spotted a gray lump in another pool a hundred paces away. The robes were a shade darker, wet from the seawater, but Jhaell marked them as acolyte garb in an instant.

"No…"

He began sprinting toward the pool, his elongated arms swinging as he ran. Perhaps she was simply unconscious, as he had been. Halfway there, as he splashed through another pool, that hope died. Syra was lying on her stomach, her face submerged in the water. The only speck of color in the pool was a lone ribbon in her blond hair: crimson, her favorite color.

"Gods, no….please, no…"

He leapt into the pool and dropped to his knees, showering Syra with seawater.

"No, no, no…"

He grabbed her shoulder and flipped her limp, lifeless body over. Her head flopped to the side as he turned her, revealing a red, bloodless gash running from her left temple to her chin, marring her once beautiful face.

An icy numbness filled Jhaell, thrice as cold as the winter wind slicing through him, sucking away what little heat remained in his body. He squeezed his eyes tight, shutting out Syra's pale, slack face. There had been plans for her to come back to Immylla once she completed her studies at the remaining academies. Jhaell was going to petition the registry for Syra to join him as his assistant, a request he was certain they would have granted. Apparently, fate had other plans for them.

Cradling her body in his arms, he opened his eyes, stared into hers, sightless though they were. He hoped the viscous head wound meant her death had been a swift one. The thought of her drowning was unbearable. Tracing a numb finger along the side of her face that was still pristine, he whispered a short prayer. "Khirlorn raecil erian elrict, Maeana."

"Wrong god, Jhaell."

Jhaell's head snapped up. A black-robed saeljul stood a dozen paces away, his hair the same white-blond as Jhaell's own, but pulled tight and bound with three black cords.

"Who are—" Jhaell stopped short, his brow furrowing. "Wait…what did you say?"

Folding his hands before him, the saeljul stepped forward a few paces. "You asked Maeana for aid, yes? To perhaps spare your friend's life? Sorry, Jhaell, but Maeana will not answer your plea. She has rules, rules she does not break. And this?" He nodded at Syra's body. "This is one of her more important ones."

Jhaell's eyes narrowed. "How do you know my name?" He was certain he had never met this person.

A sly smile spread over the stranger's lips. "Tell me, Jhaell. Do you believe in fate? Or is your life your own to live?"

Jhaell was in no mood for riddles. "Whoever you are, please leave me be."

"I'd rather stay, if you don't mind."

Anger joined Jhaell's growing bewilderment. "I mind. Go away!"

The stranger nodded at Syra's body. "How do you plan on explaining this to your superiors?" He shifted his blue-eyed gaze to Jhaell. "Preceptors getting students killed? That's not good, Jhaell. Not good at all. I expect there will be an investigation, followed by some sort of unpleasant discipline."

The saeljul was right. There would be an investigation. Accidents were common at the academy, but deaths were rare. Jhaell did not care about that, though. Looking back down to Syra, he shook his head. "It doesn't matter what happens to me. Not now."

"I see," said the stranger. He approached and stopped at the pool's edge. "If you would like, I could help you."

"Help me?" asked Jhaell with a derisive huff. "I don't see how."

"I could show you. Would you like that?"

Jhaell pulled his gaze from Syra and stared up at the saeljul. The wind whipped at the stranger's robes. "Who *are* you?"

The corners of the saeljul's mouth curled up a fraction. "The answer to that question is…complicated. Now, would you like my help or not?"

"What help?! What are you talking about?"

The stranger nodded at Syra. "I can bring her back to you. I can save her."

Jhaell remained quiet for a moment, baffled by the saeljul's claim. "Are you mad?"

"Not anymore," answered the stranger, his grin growing a little wider. "So, are you going to let me help her?" He twisted around and stared back to the academy's silhouette on the horizon. "Or shall I find another?"

"You can't help her!" shouted Jhaell, his voice strong enough to cut the wind now. "She's dead!"

The stranger faced him, gave a tiny shrug of his shoulders, and asked, "So?"

Jhaell wondered if the water and cold had so addled him that he was imagining this conversation. "'So?' *So?!*' She is *gone*! Dead! In Maeana's realm!"

"At the moment, yes."

Furious and bewildered at the same time, Jhaell screamed, "Whoever you are, just go! Leave me be!"

The saeljul let out a small sigh, shifting his attention away from Jhaell and to the empty air above the pool. The familiar crackling of magic filled Jhaell as hundreds of pulsating gold and silver threads appeared overhead. The stranger began directing them, weaving them into an impossibly intricate pattern with such speed and skill that in the span it took for Jhaell to gasp in shock, the saeljul had completed a single, massive Weave.

Staring with wide eyes, Jhaell muttered, "How is it—?"

"Quiet," interrupted the stranger, his tone terse. His face a mask of concentration, the saeljul looked to Syra's corpse, directing the web of gold and silver around her. "This will not last long. I am meddling and Maeana does not like meddling."

Jhaell gaped at the stranger. "What won't last—?" He cut off as Syra stirred in his arms.

He looked down just in time to watch her take in a deep, gasping breath as though she were bursting free from the depths of the sea. Fresh, red blood began to seep from the wound on her face. Her eyes, alive and alert again, briefly darted about before locking on his face. She smiled. "Jhaell…?"

At first, all Jhaell could do was stare. This was impossible. No mage, no matter how skilled, was capable of doing this. Wondering if this was an illusion, he reached down to touch Syra's face. As he did, her gaze drifted to the gash on his palm. A look of concern flashed over her face.

"Oh, Jhaell, you hurt yourself! How did that—?" She cut off, her eyes opening wide. "The wave! Gods! I am so sorry. I thought I could—"

"Hush," said Jhaell, a joyful smile on his face. "It was an accident."

"I so wanted to impress you." She shivered. "I wanted you…to be…" She shivered again. "…to be…proud…" She trailed off and began shivering uncontrollably, her teeth chattering. Her eyebrows drew together. In a quiet, bewildered voice, she mumbled, "I'm cold, Jhaell. Why am I so cold?"

He began to lift her from the chilly pool when the glittering Weave around her fell apart. The Strands unraveled, fading in an instant, and Syra went limp in his arms. Her head lolled to one side, her unfocused eyes staring back out at the white-capped sea.

Jhaell lifted his head to stare at the stranger, pleading with his eyes and voice. "Bring her back."

The saeljul shook his head. "I cannot. The Weave is too difficult to maintain."

Fury swelled in Jhaell as he shouted, "Bring her *back*!"

A dark and wicked shadow passed over the saeljul's face, bringing with it a fear so deep, so complete, and so cold that Jhaell wanted to flee and never look back, leaving Syra to the scavengers.

"Do *not* make demands of me! Not now! Not *ever*!"

As much as Jhaell wanted to run, terror kept him rooted in place.

The stranger glowered for moment longer before shutting his eyes and taking in a deep, steadying breath. After exhaling slowly, the saeljul reopened his eyes and offered an apologetic smile. "Pardon my outburst."

Jhaell's terror faded, allowing bafflement to return tenfold and drown out every other emotion. "Who *are* you?"

"Again, the answer to that is complicated." A slight smile spread over the saeljul's face. "But you may call me Tandyr."

CHAPTER 1: WATER

7ᵗʰ of the Turn of Sutri, 4999

The day was hotter than a pot-stove at eveningmeal.

It was the high point of summer, the days as long as they were muggy, when flocks of redbirds huddled in the cover of shade trees rather than fly in the sweltering air. From horizon to heat-shimmering horizon, the cerulean sky was clear, marred only by Mu's great, shining orb.

Two people braved the heat, treading up a hill along a path that ran parallel to a stream too straight to be a natural creek. Countless bushes littered the trail's side, their yellowing, crispy-edged leaves yearning to taste the water that flowed so near.

A lad in his seventeenth summer led, two dozen paces ahead of a girl a year or so his junior. Tall and lanky, but with broad shoulders hinting at a powerful build in the near future, his close-cropped, sandy-brown hair stuck up as stubborn as a bristle brush. His skin was fair, but the years spent in the groves and vineyards had provided a rich tan. He wore simple-spun, drab brown field clothes and leather boots.

The girl behind him, scurrying to catch up, called out, "Nikalys! Slow down!"

Nikalys ignored her pleas and continued to stride ahead, a slight smile on his face.

"Blast it, Nik!" shouted the girl. "My legs aren't as long as yours!"

As ordinary looking as the boy might appear, the girl trailing him was anything but. More than two years from her Matron's Day, her beauty already rivaled that of most women in Yellow Mud. Golden hair the color of harvest straw cascaded down her back, straight at the top, wavy in the middle, and curly at the end. She, too, wore simple clothes: a dusty tan summer skirt—a little over knee-length—a pale lavender blouse, and sturdy leather sandals.

"Nikalys! Slow down!"

Nikalys halted his ascent and, keeping his back to his sister, called over his shoulder, "Slow enough for you?"

As she caught up to him, her breathing rapid and heavy, Kenders gasped, "You're a lout, you know that?"

Turning around, Nikalys looked down—he was a full head taller than his sister—and smiled. "If your legs weren't so short, you wouldn't have a problem keeping up."

She stared up at him through narrowed eyes. As the siblings stood in the sun, Kenders' irises flashed hazel. Had Nikalys stopped a few paces up the path in an old oak's shade, they would have appeared a rusty brown.

He waited for a retort, but none came. Instead, her gaze swept past him, focusing on something further up the hill. "That's odd…"

As Nikalys turned his head to see what had drawn Kenders' attention, she reached out, grabbed his arm, and yanked, pulling herself past him and breaking into an immediate sprint.

"Race you to the lake!"

Nikalys stumbled down the hill a few steps, regained his balance, and spun around, catching sight of Kenders off the path and darting through the trees. He smiled, paused a moment to give her a small head start, and then moved into the thick brush, his boots crunching on leaves as he ran.

Their destination was Lake Hawthorne, the largest body of freshwater in the Oaken Duchies, a lake so massive that it took rafts a week to cross at its widest point. Dozens of villages and towns dotted its coast, farming communities that leveraged intricate irrigation systems to sustain their crops during the region's blistering summers and mild winters.

Their village, Yellow Mud, was just such a place. A remote settlement that supported only a few hundred residents, the town was named for the ochre-colored soil that was perfectly suited for growing olives and grapes. The groves and vineyards were communal, worked by the town as a whole, their bounty shared equally amongst everyone each harvest. Families kept what they needed and sold the rest in Smithshill, a city to the east. While spring and harvest were the busy seasons, summer was slow and lazy, with little to do but wait for the grapes and olives to fatten.

Today was Seventhday, when people worked in the morning and took the afternoon to relax with family and friends. Nikalys and Kenders typically had light chores on Seventhday, but this morning their father had relieved the pair of any responsibilities, sending them sprinting down the street while good-naturedly teasing their older brother, Jak, who was headed to the fields with their father.

As he now dashed through the forest, Nikalys realized he was catching fewer glimpses of Kenders. Regretting the large head start he had granted her, he increased his pace to close the gap.

He was still twenty paces behind when Kenders dipped into a shaded gully, slipping from view. Cresting the edge of the gulch, he careened down the leaf-strewn side, burst into a small clearing, and nearly collided with a stationary Kenders, rooted in place like one of the oaks.

He skidded in the leaves and dirt, grabbing her arms as they both shuffled forward a few steps and stopped. Somehow, they avoided falling to the ground. Staring down at Kenders, he asked, "Why'd you stop?"

Kenders lifted a finger to her lips, motioning for him to be silent, and glanced around the forest, her brow furrowed.

Confused, Nikalys scanned the underbrush, looking and listening. Thickets of bushes and tree trunks—mostly elm and oak—surrounded them, but nothing else. Looking back to his sister, he found her facing the opposite side of the gully, where the lake waited.

Kenders whispered, "It's coming from there."

Nikalys stared north. "What's coming from there?"

Kenders did not respond. She stood motionless, peering northward, her face etched in concentration as if she were trying to hold onto the final note of a song that had just ended.

"Hey," prompted Nikalys. "What is it?"

With a slow, wondering shake of her head, Kenders muttered, "I thought I heard…" She trailed off, paused a moment, and then looked at him. "You know the sound straw makes when you crumple it in your hand?"

Nikalys blinked, his confusion deepening. "Yes?"

"It was like that," she mumbled, a frown spreading over her face. "Only, it was more like I *felt* what crushing straw sounds like." Her face scrunched up. "Only that's not right, either. I just don't know how else to—" She cut off, whirling to face the lake again. "There it is again!"

Wary, Nikalys stared north, too, eyeing the lip of the gully. "There what is?"

"You don't hear—feel it?"

Nikalys held his breath and remained perfectly still, trying to see if he heard or felt anything. Eventually, he shook his head. "I don't hear anything. Come on." Looking back to her, he saw an earnest expression on Kenders' face and began to worry. "You aren't jesting, are you?"

"I wish I were…"

He peered up the gully, through the staggered tree trunks. "Well, let's go see what 'it' is, then." He began to step forward when Kenders reached out and grabbed his hand, stopping him.

"We need to be careful."

"Why?"

Kenders' gaze danced north again. "We just do. And don't ask me how I know, because I have no idea."

Reaching up, he gave Kenders a brief, reassuring pat atop her head. "Fine. We'll be careful."

Kenders slapped his hand away. "I'm not a barncat." She began walking toward the gully's northern slope. "Let's go."

Nikalys followed.

*　*　*

Jak leaned against the sun-bleached oak door, waiting for his father to emerge from the barn's dark interior. He had yet to decide if he wanted to spend the afternoon napping under the ash tree outside the Isaac home or head to the lake for a swim. While he had told Nikalys and Kenders he would meet them, the hike was a few miles, uphill. A trek like that in today's heat almost negated the lure of cool water.

A few inches over six feet, Jak had a dark tan complexion, black wavy hair, and deep brown eyes. His muscled arms were strong enough to lift a full bushel of olives in each, and his quick smile brought color to the cheeks of young women in the village. While he bore almost no resemblance to his brother and sister, he was, until recent years, a balanced mix between his mother and father. Lately, though, friends and neighbors remarked how much he was looking like Thaddeus Isaac, his father.

A bang echoed from the heart of the barn, followed by a stifled curse.

Jak turned his head and called inside, "Need some help?!"

A muffled voice drifted from within. "I'm not that old!"

An affectionate smile touched Jak's face as he sighed, "No, but you are that stubborn."

As he waited for his father in the barn's shade, he carefully examined his dirty field clothes. His mother hated when he came home with new holes for her to sew.

"All done!" called his father.

"About time," muttered Jak. Standing tall, he turned toward the door as Thaddeus trudged into the light of day, squinting against the bright sun. Jak's father had celebrated his fifty-third yearday only a few weeks ago, but looked a decade younger. Recently, though, his hair had begun to gray, his curly black locks turning salt and pepper. His eyes were a brilliant blue, bluer than the cloudless sky above. Women of Yellow Mud would frequently comment to Jak's mother just how beautiful Thaddeus' eyes were. Marie's typical response was a slight smile and nod, reacting as one might when someone mentioned that grass is, in fact, green.

Eyeing his father, Jak asked, "Everything in its place?"

"You're mocking me, aren't you?" asked Thaddeus in his deep, gravelly voice.

Jak smiled. "A little."

"So I like an orderly barn. What of it? Makes it easier to find things when I need them." Thaddeus pointed into the barn's interior. "If I asked you—right now—where the iron long-spade was, could you tell me?"

"Of course," said Jak with confidence. "Without doubt."

Thaddeus' eyes narrowed. "Fine, then. Where is the iron long-spade?"

With a wink and a grin, Jak said, "Easy. It's in the barn. Wherever *you* just put it."

Thaddeus shook his head, chuckling. "Practicing to be a playman again?" He gave a lighthearted slap to Jak's head—having to reach up to do so—and headed down the dirt road. "Close up. And hurry, please. I'm hungry."

Jak slid the double doors shut, secured the latch, and then jogged down the road to catch his father as the pair settled into a relaxed walk home.

Back in the sun again, baking under its rays, Jak made a decision on his afternoon. "I think I'm going to head up to the lake after all." Peering skyward, he added, "That sun is blasted hot."

Thaddeus glanced up, too, shading his eyes with his hand. "Yes, it is." He had left his straw hat at home—something about which Jak had teased him all morning. Wiping the sweat from his face for at least the fifth time since leaving the barn, he muttered, "If the lake were a bit closer, I might join you." He glanced over, a single eyebrow raised. "And try leaving the hard words in the fields, son. Your mother will be all over you if you use them at home."

Jak nodded. "Yes, Father."

They strolled through town, exchanging quick pleasantries with friends and neighbors. Most people in Yellow Mud got along well enough with one another, although the occasional minor dispute arose. Last spring, the town thatcher had accused his neighbor of stealing a new tool he had purchased from a traveling peddler. The accusation had the town talking for a full week and nearly led to a formal inquiry by the village council before the thatcher quietly apologized to his neighbor, admitting he found the tool wedged between two bundles of straw.

Yellow Mud's buildings were simple structures: wooden walls made from stacked oak logs topped with pitched roofs of yellow straw thatching. Homes had small, limestone pipe chimneys sticking from the roof, allowing smoke from the stove-pots inside to escape. The area's climate allowed for open-air windows in buildings, letting a breeze flow through should one ever occur. Every so often, a rare cold snap visited during the winter turns, forcing residents to jam straw pads in the holes. None in Yellow Mud was prosperous enough to afford a luxury like glass as in some of the larger towns.

Father and son were halfway home when Jak caught a strange scent on the air, a whiff of wet metal. Thinking he had imagined it, Jak sniffed the air twice. Each time, the odor was a little stronger. Curious, he turned to look at his father.

Thaddeus, already wearing a perplexed expression, was glancing around, sniffing the air, too. "I smell rain…"

"So do I," muttered Jak, confused. They both stopped and turned in a circle, searching the heavens for signs of a storm that should not be coming, not at this time of year. "How is that possible? The sky is clear." When Thaddeus did not respond, Jak glanced over. The creases in his father's weathered face seemed deeper and longer than normal. "Father? What's wrong?"

Rising above nearby neighbors' chattering voices—others had marked the impossible smell of rain—was the sound of a strong wind blowing through the boughs of the forest. Jak's bafflement deepened. The only thing rarer than a shower this time of year was any sort of breeze. As he faced north, the sound shifted, changing from the wind rustling trees into something that made even less sense.

"If I did not know better," muttered Jak, "I'd say that was a waterfall."

He turned to see what his father thought of his assessment and found himself alone in the road. While other folks had stopped whatever they had been doing to stare north toward Lake Hawthorne, the patriarch of the Isaac family was sprinting down the road toward home.

Thaddeus glanced over his shoulder and shouted, "Move it, Jak!" His eyes were as round as the moons. "Now!"

Without knowing the reason for the rush, Jak ran after his father, his confusion and worry growing with each pounding step of boot on dirt.

CHAPTER 2: LAKE

Nikalys stood motionless beneath the boughs of an old oak, staring north through the tree trunks, spotting little glimpses of sunlight on the lake's shimmering surface. A roar, distant and oddly familiar, drifted from the lake.

"Tell me you hear that," muttered Kenders.

Not only did he hear it, he thought he recognized it. Bewildered, he whispered, "It sounds like a waterfall." The problem was there were no waterfalls anywhere near Yellow Mud. The closest—and only—one of which he knew was in Smithshill, a week's travel east. "Have you 'felt' anything else since the clearing?"

"It comes and goes." She hesitated, opened her mouth to say more, but then shut it quickly.

Nikalys prompted, "What?"

She shook her head. "Nothing. Let's go." She went to take a step forward when, this time, Nikalys reached out, wrapping his hand around her wrist to stop her.

"Hey." He gave her wrist a gentle, reassuring squeeze. "You can tell me."

She dropped her head to stare at old leaves and a rotting log. After a moment, she sighed and peered up at him. The worry in her eyes matched the anxiety growing inside him.

"You'll laugh if I tell you," she whispered.

He would be thrilled if that were the case. "Try me."

"I feel…" She trailed off and dropped her gaze again, a stray lock of blonde hair falling over her eyes. "I…feel colors."

Unsure he had heard her correctly, he asked, "You feel…colors?"

Her cheeks flushed. She looked up and nodded once. "Actually, just one. Blue."

That was little consolation. In fact, her words only fueled his worries. They had grown up hearing the same stories. She must be thinking the same thing as he was. "Perhaps you've had too much sun?"

Kenders' typical stubborn determination set in. "That's *not* it, Nik. And you know it."

Nikalys ran a hand over his forehead, dropped it down to rub his eyes, and then finally scratched his chin. After letting out a quiet sigh, he said, "No…I suppose it's not…" He went quiet, staring north, afraid to give voice to what he—and most likely she—was thinking.

After a few moments, Kenders looked toward the lake. "I say we get a closer look."

"Are you sure about that?"

Kenders stepped away, toward a break in the trees. "No. But I need to know what this is about."

Nikalys shook his head and followed. When Kenders made her mind up to do something, there was no use arguing with her.

The waterfall's roar grew as they neared the lake. Upon reaching the edge of the tree line they stopped atop a rise that sloped down to the shore's edge, a sand and mud beach littered with smooth tan or gray stones. Nikalys peered north across the water's surface, clear to the horizon. The lake's vastness never failed to awe him. Spotting movement to the northeast, he turned his head. What he saw sent a spike of pure fear into his chest.

Far beyond the point of a nearby land jetty, about a mile offshore, a massive wave crested on the lake's otherwise serene surface. A fine mist, almost like an early morning spring fog, coated the pair, cooling them from the heat of the day. Grabbing Kenders' arm, Nikalys opened his mouth to shout the obvious need to run. The warning, however, never made it past his lips. He stopped, frozen in place, and stared. The wave was not moving.

Judging the crest of the impossibly stationary wave to be nearly as tall as the most mature oaks onshore, Nikalys asked the obvious. "Why is it—*how* is it not moving?" Not that he expected an answer from Kenders, but he looked at her anyway. She was staring across the lake, her eyebrows together and forehead furrowed like a freshly tilled spring garden.

"You know why," whispered Kenders, her voice barely audible over the water's distant roar. "We both do."

A sick, hollow sensation swelled inside him, threatening to envelop him. He gave a firm shake of his head. "No, there *must* be another reason."

"Truly?" huffed Kenders. She pointed at the wave. "You can think of another reason for *that?*"

He stared back to the water. The wave was even bigger now and still implausibly in the same place. As he spoke, even he could hear the wishful tone in his voice. "It might not be magic."

"Nik. There's a wave the size of Yellow Mud out there, just sitting on the blasted water. Going *nowhere*. And that crackling straw feeling?" She arched her eyebrows. "That *blueness?*" She nodded at the wave. "I can feel it out there. I *feel* the crackling, I feel the blue." Squinting through the mist, she muttered, "Hells, I swear I can almost see it..."

He opened his mouth to protest, but she lifted a hand, halting him. "Don't, Nik. Just don't. *That* out there is magic. Plain and simple. And if I can feel it…that means that I…that I am a…" She trailed off, tilted her head to the side slightly, and added softly, "Well, you know what it means."

He wanted to tell Kenders she was wrong, that there were a hundred rational explanations for this. Only there were not. His mind struggled to come up with just one and failed. Kenders was right. He simply did not like what that meant. After letting out a long breath, he muttered, "We can't tell anyone about this."

Kenders gave him a tiny, brave smile. "Wasn't planning on it."

"I mean it, sis. Not Mother, Father, Jak. *Nobody.*"

Her grin faded. With a short nod, she whispered, "I know."

Under Oaken Duchies law, anyone having anything at all to do with magic was a lawbreaker, an outlaw. Should the Constables discover that Kenders was a mage, they would take her and, if the stories were true, she would never be seen or heard from again.

Nikalys sighed and opened his arms to her. "Come here." She fell toward him and he embraced her, resting his chin atop her head. "How about we make this another one of our secrets? Like where Mother's grape tarts go when she gets done baking them?"

A weak chuckle slipped from her. "You're the thief there, not me."

"And you've kept my secret. Now I get to return the favor."

She tilted her head back and looked him in the eye. "Thank you."

"What'd you think I was going to do? Turn you in?" He took a deep breath, stood straight, and stared back to the lake. "So. It's magic. Why here? Why now?"

Kenders shrugged her shoulders. "How should I know?"

Nikalys was about to point out that she was the mage, not him, when the water's roar surged. The wave began to change shape, growing taller and thinner, taking a new form that was both unnatural and familiar, almost like a torso with arms fused to the chest. In short order, the wave creature towered over the tallest trees along the shore. A misshapen, nebulous head now sat atop its odd, neck-less torso. An enormous pyramid of swirling water spread outward at the wave's "waist," stretching over the lake's surface.

Kenders whispered, "What's that near the bottom?"

Tearing his eyes from the water creature, Nikalys looked near the wave's base. There, for the first time, he noticed five figures—nearly obscured by the swirling mist—wearing dark gray robes and lighter gray cloaks. All five stood facing the creature, their backs to Nikalys and Kenders. Nikalys blinked twice when he realized the figures were standing on the lake's surface.

The water's roar suddenly ceased, the unexpected silence startling them both. A sixth figure, wearing crimson robes and a black hooded cloak, appeared from the opposite side of the water creature, also striding on the lake's surface.

"*Six* mages?" muttered Kenders. "What in the Nine Hells are *six* mages doing here?"

It was a valid question. They had lived their lives lucky enough never to have encountered even one—save Kenders, apparently. Now, here were six, standing on a lake. Nikalys did not answer his sister, however, so intrigued was he by the figure in red. Its arms seemed too long for its body, swinging back and forth like the submerged reeds in the oscillating waves along the lake's shore. After a few moments of watching the figure, he said, "I think that's an ijul."

Kenders stared at him. "You're jesting."

He shook his head, never taking his gaze off the red-robed individual.

Looking back over the lake, Kenders asked, "An ijul? Here?" Her surprise was justified. Ijuli were as rare in the Great Lakes Duchy as rain in the summer.

"Look at his arms," whispered Nikalys. "The way he moves."

There was a long pause before she responded. "Perhaps…" She sounded unconvinced.

"And how would you know if it is or not?" asked Nikalys. On his annual journeys to Smithshill with his father and Jak, he had seen a few ijuli. Kenders had never been out of Yellow Mud.

The figure halted before the looming wave creature, reached up and slid back its hood to reveal bright, white-blond hair that shone brilliant in the sunlight. Now Nikalys was doubtful. The ijuli he had seen in Smithshill had darker skin with brown or black hair. Yet the figure's long arms and graceful movements were impossible to ignore.

The ijul approached the five gray-clad figures, moving slightly closer to where Nikalys and Kenders stood huddled in the trees. Afraid they might be spotted, Nikalys dipped behind their tree trunk only to feel foolish a moment later when he realized that the forest's clutter concealed them.

A heartbeat later, the massive water creature began to move over the surface of the lake, crawling at first, but quickly gaining speed.

"Bless the gods," whispered Kenders.

The creature's lower half was a mass of tumbling waves, as though a huge storm had churned up giant whitecaps. When the wave crashed upon the shore, it ripped century-old oaks and elms from the ground as if they were three-year old saplings. Water from the lake fed the wave, flooding the land behind it.

Nikalys glanced back to the mages on the water and was surprised to see four additional gray-cloaked figures who had been hidden by the creature's mass.

"Do you think we're safe here?" asked Kenders.

"Here? Of course. That thing is a mile away. Can you imagine being in front of—" He cut off, his eyes going wide. He looked back to the open swath forest, where the wave had gashed through the trees like a cleaver through a grape.

Without saying a word, Kenders pushed away from the tree trunk, turned, and began sprinting south, crashing through the forest's undergrowth. Nikalys was a step behind.

CHAPTER 3: HOME

Thaddeus threw open the front door, letting it bang against the inside wall. Like most of the homes in Yellow Mud, the Isaac house had only a few rooms, the center of which was sparsely furnished with some rustic chairs and a single table. Seeing the empty room, he began shouting. "Marie! Where are you?! Marie!"

A voice drifted through the cracked-open back door. "Thad! I'm out back!"

He rushed across the room, opened the back door, and stuck his head outside. Marie stood beside the Isaac's summer vegetable garden behind the house, her back toward him as she stared northward. She turned at once.

Marie Isaac was an uncommonly beautiful woman, rivaling women twenty years her junior. Her sleek, black hair was pulled back tight and bound in a ponytail. Her high cheekbones, full lips, and dark brown eyes typically combined to give the impression of permanent mirth. Except for now. Now, her eyes were wide and fearful. "Thad?"

He reached her in a couple of strides and grabbed her arm. "I know. We need to move." He might not know for sure what was rushing toward their home, but he could guess. Marie probably could, as well.

Jak's voice rang out from inside the house. "Father?! Mother?!"

"Stay there!" shouted Thaddeus. "We're coming!" Pulling his wife behind him, Thaddeus rushed back into the house.

Jak stood in the front doorway, a bewildered expression on his face. "Father, what—"

"No time for questions," interjected Thaddeus. The roar was steadily increasing. The scent of water hanging in the air was not only stronger, but now carried with it a hint of old fish and rotting algae. Locking eyes with his son, he ordered, "Go to the kitchen and get the beltpurse in the larder. Quickly!"

Jak hesitated for only a moment before sprinting to his right and through one of the two doorways.

Thaddeus gave his wife's arm a reassuring squeeze. "Wait here." He released her and moved toward their room. "As soon as I get the bundle Aryn gave us, we're leaving."

After entering their room, he moved to the couple's straw-mattress bed, dropped to his knees, and lifted the bed. He shoved it against the back wall of the house, knocking over Marie's carefully arranged display of pottery jugs. He dragged his fingers along the floorboards, searching for the small slit in one of the boards. Digging his thumb into the hole, he pried a long board loose. He winced as a splinter jammed under his fingernail.

Tossing aside the board, he reached into the dirt depression below and grabbed a tightly wrapped leather package. Four feet at its longest point and skinnier than his thigh, the case had a bulge at one end, a tip at the other. After lifting it free, he brushed away the thick layer of dirt that coated it. Fifteen years had passed since he had last laid eyes on this.

Gripping the package tightly, he repeated the four words Eliza had told him to use should something like this happen. "Chaos has found us." He waited a heartbeat or two, expecting something to happen. Nothing did. At least, nothing that he could sense.

Shaking his head, Thaddeus muttered in disgust, "Blasted magic." With a burst of energy he seldom showed any more, he leapt up and ran back into the main room. Jak and Marie were waiting for him. Eyeing Marie, he asked, "Kenders and Nikalys?"

Marie grasped the silver teardrop pendant that had hung from her neck for the past decade and a half, shut her eyes, and then opened them a moment later, a tiny smile on her face. "They are unhurt."

Thaddeus nodded, relieved. "Good." Noticing Jak staring at them both, a question forming on his lips, Thaddeus shook his head. "No time. I'll explain as we run." He took two steps toward Jak and shoved the bundle he had retrieved into his son's arms. "There are straps that will fit over your arms like a backpack. Put it on!"

Appearing equal parts baffled and worried, Jak took the package and began strapping it to his back.

"No matter what happens—" implored Thaddeus, "—*no matter what!*— keep this bundle close! Do you understand?!" Jak nodded, questions brimming in his eyes. Thaddeus cut them short, asking, "You have the beltpurse?"

Jak held up the small leather sack, silent.

"Good. Now, move!" After ushering—almost shoving—his family out the front door, Thaddeus led them south down the street at a run, away from the lake.

* * *

Zigzagging through the trees, Nikalys overtook his sister and passed her without saying a word. He aimed southwest, back toward the irrigation stream that ran from the lake, through the groves and into town. As he burst from a thicket, he found himself sloshing through inches of dirty water, yellowed from the soil and spotted with floating leaves and sticks. He slowed to a walk and looked down to his boots. The water was already up to his calves and they were still a quarter mile from the stream that would lead them home.

"Hells."

He turned around just as Kenders emerged from the trees. She stopped short, her gaze fixed on the shallow river of water running down the slope. She looked at him.

"Now what? We can't get home that way."

Nikalys splashed through the water, back to where his sister stood. "We'll go south and cut over when we get closer."

Nodding her agreement, Kenders started to jog down the hill, breaking into a run after a few steps. Nikalys followed.

* * *

Thaddeus and his family sprinted past dozens of people standing motionless, mouths agape, looking northward. Others, far too few, were running south along with the Isaac family. Some ran against the throng, screaming for their loved ones.

As they neared the center of Yellow Mud, Thaddeus looked ahead to where Jak was easily outpacing his parents and shouted out an order. "Jak! Go right!"

Jak listened, turning west and slowing to wait for Thaddeus and Marie. When he glanced northward, he halted in his tracks, his eyes opening wide.

The fibríaal was moving fast then, faster than Thaddeus would have hoped. He twisted to see where Marie was and cursed. "Blast."

Spry and athletic in her youth, the years had robbed his wife of the speed and stamina necessary to keep up such a frantic pace. As Thaddeus silently urged his wife to hurry, he also stole a glance northward. "Bless the gods…"

The fibríaal was as massive as it was swift, looking like the torso of a giant slate-blue man towering over the treetops. Judging the wave already in the northern groves, Thaddeus looked back to his wife.

Back to the fibríaal.

To his wife.

"Hells…"

Marie was moving much too slowly. His mind drifted back to his old smoke-filled smithy, to the promise he and Marie made fifteen years ago. In an instant, he made an impossible, heartrending decision. Shoving aside his feelings, he turned, sprinted to Jak, and grabbed his son's arm. "Jak! I need you to listen to me!"

Jak did not respond, his gaze fixed on the wave of water, his eyes wide and mouth agape.

Gripping Jak by the shoulders, Thaddeus shook his son, shouting, "Jak! Listen to me! You need to survive. You *must* survive. Do you understand? You must *survive!*"

*   *   *

Jak tore his gaze from the impossible spectacle, looked at his father, blinked a few times, and then unwittingly glancing back to enormous wave chewing through the forest.

"Blast it, Jak!" shouted Thaddeus. "Pay attention!"

Jak winced as his father's fingers dug deeper into his arms. "What is that!?"

"There's no time to explain. You need to find Nikalys and Kenders! Do you understand? Find them and keep them safe! Change your name and—"

Marie arrived at that moment, interrupting Thaddeus. She took one look at his face, briefly stared over her shoulder, and then faced Jak wearing a mournful yet determined expression. She reached up to slip her leather cord and silver pendant necklace over her head, stepped forward and, standing on her toes, looped it over Jak's. "Hold it in your hand and picture their faces. You'll know where they are and if they still draw breath."

"I don't understand."

Marie patted his chest and, in a strained voice, said, "You will." She kissed his cheek. "Now, go."

"Go? What do you mean go?"

"I mean go!" said Marie, her voice firm. A lone tear ran down her cheek. "We'll only slow you down."

"I'm not leaving you here!"

"You must!" exclaimed Thaddeus. "I'm sorry, Jak. We should have told all of you the truth years ago."

"The truth?" asked Jak, his eyes darting between his parents. "The truth about what?"

Thaddeus spared a quick glance over his shoulder before looking back to Jak. "Promise to keep Nikalys and Kenders safe. They are important!"

"Important? What does—?"

"Blast it, Jak!" shouted Thaddeus, shaking Jak once, hard. "Promise me! Promise me, now!"

Shocked by his father's intensity, Jak swallowed his question and mumbled, "I promise."

With tears flowing freely down her face, Marie wrapped her arms around him and squeezed tight. "I love you."

Too stunned to return the hug, Jak simply stood there.

Embracing them both, Thaddeus said, "Tell them we love them. We *love* all of you, you understand?" He pulled back—his eyes were tear-glistened now, too—and gave Jak a gentle shove. "Now, go."

Jak shook his head, baffled. "Why are you—?"

Marie cut him short by placing her hand on his chest and pushing even harder. "Go, Jak."

"No! Just come with—"

Using both hands, Thaddeus shoved Jak hard enough that he lost his grip on his mother and stumbled backwards. He stopped and stared at his parents, shocked and numb inside, as dozens of people rushed past them, screaming in terror. Thaddeus and Marie were like statues.

Jak shook his head. He could not—would not—not leave them to die. He took a step back toward them, a step matched by Thaddeus and Marie as both backpedaled.

"Go, Jak!" shouted Thaddeus. An expression of absolute resolve filled his face. Jak looked to his mother and found a matching one on hers.

Sick at what he was doing, Jak took a slow step backward. Then a second. And a third.

He shut his eyes, turned his back on his parents, and started to jog. After a few paces, someone bumped into him, forcing him to reopen his eyes. Tears blurred his vision. He wiped them away as he sprinted down the street, joining the stream of people fleeing south.

He never looked back.

* * *

Kenders was doing her best to keep up, but still trailed Nikalys by several dozen paces. As hard as she tried, she could not match her brother's speed. She had never seen him run so fast.

Hot, sweaty, and exhausted, she pushed past her discomfort. The crackling of magic was still rolling toward her home.

Dread sat in her stomach like a lump of cold lard.

* * *

Jak turned a corner and came upon The Lout and The Witch. Garry, the tavern's portly owner, stood in front of his establishment staring north, frozen with fear. As Jak ran past the man, he grabbed Garry's arm and began to pull. Garry stumbled along with Jak a few steps, but was reluctant to move.

"Let's go, Garry!" shouted Jak. He yanked the large man's arm. "Now!"

Garry finally looked down at Jak, his eyes glassed over. "My inn…everything…"

Jak tugged even harder on the man's arm. "Forget the inn. We need to run!!"

Garry pulled his arm free. "I'm too big to run." In an even, disturbingly calm tone, he said, "I think I'll go have one last drink. Good memories behind." He patted Jak on the shoulder and began marching up the inn's steps.

Leaving Garry to his fate, Jak turned to start running again and noticed the horse and cart in front of him. The ruddy brown horse was whinnying, stomping at the ground, its eyes wide with fear.

Jak drew his knife from his belt sheath and sliced through the horse's harness, thinking he might be able to gallop out of town on horseback even though he could count on one hand the number of times he had been atop a horse. Soldiers might ride the beasts, but not farmers. In Yellow Mud, horses pulled carts.

The moment the horse was free however, it bolted forward, bucking as it turned in a wild half-circle. Then, for reasons unknown, it shot northward down the street, back in the direction from which Jak had come and straight toward the oncoming wave.

As Jak's gaze followed the horse, his eyes went wide. The water figure towered over the trees, its roar punishing his ears. A sick sense of inevitability gripped him. There was no way he could outrun this. Nothing could. Had the horse run in the right direction, even it would be doomed. Jak turned to the cart, rested his head against one of the ale barrels stacked in the back, and accepted his fate.

"I wonder if drowning hurts."

He pulled his head back and banged it on the wooden keg. He did it again, harder. He felt, rather than heard, ale sloshing inside. He banged his head a third time—harder, still—and winced. The keg was solid as a rock.

Lifting his head, he stared at the barrel's wood grain. These kegs were solid as a rock. And full.

"If these are full…"

Jak stood tall, rushed around the cart, and ran to the rear of the inn. Skidding around the corner, he spotted a dozen empty barrels stacked neatly near the back door. Choosing the largest, sturdiest-looking barrel of the bunch, he turned the massive cask on end and tried to open the lid, cursing when he found it stuck. Pulling out his beltknife, he dug the tip between barrel and lid and tried to pry it open. It would not budge.

Glaring at the name seared into the lid, he exclaimed, "Blast you, Wembly Brewery!" Screaming, he threw all his weight into the effort and, with a pop and a crack, the lid burst free.

Jak removed the bundle his father had given him, tossed it into the giant barrel, and climbed in after. It was a tight fit, but he somehow managed to fold himself inside. He reversed the lid, gripping the handle meant for the outside and accidentally dropped his knife to the ground. He stared at it, lying there in the dirt, when the shrieks of cracking wood drew his attention north. The water creature was in Yellow Mud.

Forgetting the knife, Jak crouched down and pulled the lid as tight as he could. His breathing was quick and heavy, each lungful of air reeking of warm, stale beer. He jammed his right foot against the hole where the tap had been, blocking the last bit of daylight, and waited in the hot and damp dark.

Outside, the water's roar grew louder. Wood groaned, popped, and cracked. People screamed. Jak closed his eyes, trying to shut out the cries. He wanted to cover his ears, but he dare not let go of the lid.

A short prayer seemed in order, but before he could settle on which god to beg for aid, the wave arrived. With a violent thrust, the barrel went tumbling.

Jak started to scream.

CHAPTER 4: HIDDEN

Nikalys reached the edge of the forest ahead of Kenders and rushed into the open. Dodging one last yellowed-leaf bush, she lunged after him, burst from the trees, and stopped beside her brother atop a ridge overlooking Yellow Mud, still a half mile away.

The water creature was in their village, thrashing about, shattering everything. Buildings lifted up and smashed against one another, leaving jagged shards of wood in the water's froth. The massive waves, muddied with dirt and debris, acted against the laws of nature. Whenever a breaker reached the village's outskirts, it shifted direction to rush back through buildings, horses, and people rather than disperse into the countryside. It was as if Yellow Mud was trapped in a giant, invisible bucket.

With her heart in her throat and the taste of sick in her mouth, Kenders choked out, "Nik?"

Nikalys put his arm around her, pulled her close, but said nothing. There was nothing to say.

Kenders stood there, feeling utterly helpless as she watched the devastation of their home, their family, their entire life. Throughout it all, the cursed crackle of magic surged and waned, surged and waned. A single, muttered word slipped from her lips.

"Why…?"

Still, Nikalys remained silent, even as his grip on her grew tighter, so tight that her shoulder started to hurt. The pain helped push aside the feeling of helplessness, of anguish and sorrow, allowing fury to creep in and take root.

Angry now, Kenders repeated her question. "Why? Why is this happening?" She glanced at her brother. His eyes burned, muscles rippled in his neck and jaw.

He shook his head once, growling, "I don't know."

Then, as though it were a flame snuffed by a stiff wind, the crackling sensation disappeared, the feeling of colors halted and the creature stopped thrashing. Water fell to the ground and rushed outward, no longer bound by the invisible bucket. The flood flowed south, depositing whatever it carried: crushed houses, barns, field carts, timbers, furniture, barrels, horses, and people. The scene sickened Kenders, but she could not look away.

Swallowing back a bit of bile, she said, "We need to get down there."

"And what about the mages?"

"Mother, Father, or Jak are down there, Nik. Forget the blasted mages."

Nikalys pressed his lips together and nodded. "Fine, let's go. South, though. To the road. It'll be faster."

The pair turned and resumed running down the hill. Rocks and bare roots jutted from the path they careened down, providing firm footholds for those intent on treading carefully, but treacherous obstacles for anyone in a hurry.

As they ran, Kenders began to wonder at the wisdom of rushing toward the ruined village. Nikalys was right to worry about the mages. The group from the lake, obviously intent on destroying Yellow Mud, would surely inspect things afterwards. One did not plant a squash seed and not wait to see it grow.

Nikalys was a full two dozen paces ahead of her now, dashing through shin-high grass and around oak trees, when he suddenly took a sharp right turn and scurried up the western rise. Kenders watched in disbelief, wondering if her brother had gone mad. The crest of the slope up which he sprinted was clearly visible from the village.

Kenders skidded to a stop, wrapping her arms around an old oak trunk to help stop her descent. The rough bark scraped the soft skin of her forearms as she whipped around the tree. Peering up the rock-infested slope, she hissed, "Nikalys!" He did not stop. Raising her voice a fraction, she tried again. "Nikalys!"

This time, he glanced back, lifted a finger to his lips, and continued climbing.

Kenders glowered, boring a hole in Nikalys' back with her stare. "What in the Nine Hells are you doing?"

A dozen paces from the top, Nikalys halted, dropped to his stomach and crawled the remaining distance. Kenders breathed a sigh of relief. Nikalys was not brainless.

She looked around the forest, scanning every tree, every bush for movement. A pair of redbirds burst from a nearby ash, startling her as they chased one another into the sky. Restless, she glanced back up the hill to her brother. He was gone. Her already quick-beating heart thudded even faster.

"Nik?"

Movement atop the rise drew her attention to a bushy yellow-leafed shrub under which she spotted the bottoms of Nikalys' muddy, grass-covered boots. She began to breathe again. "Oh, thank the gods."

With her brother safely hidden, she suddenly felt very exposed. Pushing away from the tree trunk, she began to climb the grassy slope, intending to join Nikalys. After only a few steps, he spun around, glared at her, and motioned for her to stay in place. She continued, however, ignoring him. Nikalys did not get to make rash decisions and then dictate orders to her.

The higher up the slope she climbed, the more violent Nikalys' gestures became. His eyes as wide as those of a spooked horse, he jabbed a finger in the air, pointing north.

Realizing what he was trying to convey, Kenders stopped. Whipping her head around, she peered northward, through the summer-fried forest. She spotted a flicker of gray, then a flash of pale skin and red hair. It had to be one of the mages.

Her instinct was to drop to the ground, but she worried the sudden movement might draw the mage's attention. So, she stood motionless, petrified. Already halfway up the hill, she could still try to reach Nikalys and hide with him, but dismissed the idea an instant later. The gray-robed mage would easily spot her movement or hear her hurried climbing. She would give away both her own and Nikalys' position.

She could sprint down the hill, run away, and perhaps save her brother. Yet again, she immediately dismissed the idea. If she ran and the mage came after her, Nikalys would leap up to help and they would both be caught. Or, more likely, killed.

Staring through the tree trunks, she saw the flicker of gray again and marked the mage as a man. And he was getting closer.

Absent any good idea, Kenders slowly crouched to the ground, stretched her legs out, and lied down, hoping the sparse grass would hide her while seriously doubting it would. If it were spring and the grass thick and green, it might conceal her. In the middle of summer, however, the grass, while tall, was dry and thin. Kenders closed her eyes and said a quick prayer to Ketus, god of Luck and Shadows, pleading he could spare a bit of both while wondering if even he could hide a girl in a lavender shirt on a bare, sunny hillside.

She held her breath and stared into the clear blue sky, listening to the mage's shuffling steps get closer, crunching on leaves and grass. She wished Nikalys were beside her. Or her father. Or Jak. Or anyone, for that matter.

Suddenly, the crackling and colors—new ones this time—returned, startling her.

White. Silver. Gold.

The sensation of colors surged, throbbing and pulsing. Swelling around her. Filling her insides so, that it overflowed like a cup trying to hold a bucketful of water.

She opened her eyes a crack and tilted her head, chin to chest, staring back to the old oak beside which she had stopped, somehow certain that the colors were coming from there. A gold filament hovered in the air a few paces from the tree, faint and translucent, truly visible only if she did not look directly at it. If she focused on it, the string disappeared. She tried to lock onto to it, but it was like chasing a black moth on a moonless night.

She felt rather than saw the colors fly up the hill and settle over her, hanging in place like an invisible gold, silver, and white spider's web.

Hearing footsteps, Kenders momentarily forgot about the colored net surrounding her and looked to her left and down the hill. Approaching the oak was the gray-robed mage, skinny and pale, perhaps a few years older than Jak, and with reddish-blond hair. It surprised her that he looked so ordinary. Had he been wearing field clothes, she might have thought him a neighbor on a woodland stroll.

He meandered through the trees, turning his head back and forth, scanning the area. As his gaze drifted up Kenders' hill, every muscle in her body reflexively tightened. She bit her lip so hard that she tasted blood. When his stare reached where she was lying, she nearly leapt from the grass and charged him, thinking she might be able to surprise him and perhaps crack his head against the tree. Yet she remained still, frozen to the ground, as his gaze skipped over her and continued to sweep the grassy hillside.

He had not seen her.

Stunned, she watched the mage trek southward, down the hill and away from her and Nikalys. Once he dipped out of sight, she propped herself up a little, twisted around, and looked up the hill. Nikalys was already sitting up and staring down at her, looking as befuddled as she felt. He mouthed a single, silent word. "How?"

Kenders' answer was a silent, astounded shrug of her shoulders.

After several quiet, stunned moments, Nikalys lowered himself to the ground again and peered west. He immediately looked back to Kenders and waved, indicating that he wanted her to come up.

She took a quick look around to ensure there were no more wandering mages and realized she could no longer feel the colors. They were gone.

Deciding that it was safe to move, she climbed the ridge in a crouch and lowered herself beside Nikalys, lying in dirt and leaves. Kenders breath caught in her throat upon seeing the wet ruins of Yellow Mud waiting below. The devastation was as complete as it was cruel, a mess of broken timbers, tumbled stones, matted straw, and shattered furniture. Twisted, wrecked bodies lay in the mud and debris, some of them half-naked, their clothes ripped from them by the rushing water. The summer air, hot and overly moist now, smelled of fresh mud and lake water.

Nikalys mumbled, "How did that mage not see you?"

It took Kenders a moment to respond. When she did, she started and stopped twice before muttering, "I...I don't know." She could not taker her eyes off the remains of their village.

"I tried to warn you," whispered Nikalys. "I saw the ijul all alone and wondered where the rest were. I swear, as soon as I thought it, that one came over the ridge."

"Where is he?" asked Kenders. "The ijul?"

Nikalys pointed northwest. "Up there."

She looked to where Nikalys indicated and spotted the bright crimson robes at once. The ijul stood all alone atop a bluff, staring down into the remains of the village.

"And the rest?" muttered Kenders.

"Out here, I guess."

Kenders shook her head. "You realize how lucky we are? If we had kept running, we would have come out down there." She pointed to a clump of oaks just as the reddish-blond mage emerged from the trees. She looked back to the bluff and saw the ijul staring down at the gray-robed mage. .

"Gods," muttered Nikalys. "You're right."

She turned her head to look at Nikalys, scraping her chin against the dirt. "What made you come up here?"

Nikalys shrugged. "It suddenly seemed like a good idea."

"Have any more? We need to get down there."

"We wait until they leave."

"And if they don't? Our family needs us, Nik."

Nikalys stared at her, eyebrows climbing to his hairline. "Are you mad? You want to go now?" He jabbed a finger at the bluff. "If they see us, Kenders, they *will* kill us. It's hard to help anyone when you're dead."

"But they—"

"But nothing!" hissed Nikalys. "Will you think before you act for once?!"

She tried to dig her fingers into the ground but ended up scraping her nails against the rock-hard, bone-dry dirt. It took all of her self-control not to rush into their village. "Fine. We wait." Her nose twitched.

"Thank you," sighed a relieved sounding Nikalys. She waited for him to look away from her, but he did not. After a few heartbeats, he asked, "Any more…feeling colors?"

"No," lied Kenders. "None."

He stared back to the bluff. "Good."

They watched in silence as one gray-robed mage after another rejoined the ijul atop the distant bluff. When all nine had returned, the willowy ijul turned and began speaking to them.

"What do you think they are saying?" whispered Nikalys.

"I don't much care," murmured Kenders. "Why does it matter what—" She stopped short. The crackling and colors were back.

Blue. White. Silver.

Coming from the bluff.

Despite not wanting to admit what she sensed, she muttered, "Nik?"

"Yes?"

"Something's happening."

Moments later, the gray-robed mages began to grasp their throats and stumble about the bluff. One by one, they collapsed to the ground until the crimson-clad ijul stood alone.

CHAPTER 5: TEACHER

Jhaell stared at the town's ruins below and frowned. Streams of muddy water drained south, following the natural slope of the land. Debris and bodies littered the ground, deposited haphazardly by the ensuing flood after he had released the fibríaal. Of the people he could see, none appeared alive.

The destruction was complete, yet something taunted him. He shook his head slowly, frustrated. "This was too easy."

Had this been the correct place, there would have been some sort of resistance. It seemed he had found yet another false lead. Making things worse, he had acted on it.

Grinding his teeth, he hissed, "*Beelvra!*"

A few days past, he had ported himself and nine acolytes to a secluded courtyard in Redstone. The ten of them had then traveled via cart along the Southern Road, disembarking a few miles southwest of Yellow Mud and continuing the rest of the way on foot. Upon reaching this very overlook this morning, he had observed the village for a time, trying to determine if this was the correct place or not. Short of going through the town and knocking on every door, he had no real way of knowing.

After decades of waiting and searching, Jhaell made a rash decision. Recalling the map of the area, he knew that a large lake lay to the north. The opportunity had been too tempting.

He had left the weaving of Water to the acolytes, intertwining additional Strands that only he could touch. Fate had seen fit to gift him an entire class who could touch Water, yet not a single acolyte could reach Will or Soul. To Jhaell, it had been a sign he was destined to do this.

Once the Weave was complete, he instructed the fibríaal to follow the irrigation ditch the townspeople had so kindly dug through the middle of their town.

Now, he regretted it all. He had created a spectacle, one that could not be easily explained away, especially in a country where magic was outlawed. He pressed his lips together. "This was foolish."

He gazed at the surrounding hillsides, the almost too-quiet forest. The acolytes had reported no witnesses. He prayed they were correct.

Sighing, he turned to face the bodies of his students and released the Weaves binding their airways. Water spilled from their noses and mouths. After a quick search of the students to ensure nothing would identify them, he crafted a few simple Weaves of Air, lifting the bodies off the ground. He started down the bush-lined path leading from the bluff, directing the acolytes ahead of him, accidently bumping some against rocks as he went. When he reached the edge of the dissipating flood, he stopped. No reason to get his sandals muddy.

He studied the ruins with a cold, unfeeling stare. Bodies hung from trees and bushes, random bits of stone and wood lay half-buried in the yellow mud. A horse lay draped over a black metal pot-stove. The frown that had been affixed to Jhaell's face for some time now deepened. It would take two lifetimes to come up with a rational explanation for this. All he could do was hope Tandyr never learned of this indiscretion.

Twisting the Weaves' pattern, he tossed the limp, lifeless bodies of the acolytes into the mess. All but one landed in the mud with a soft, squishing sound. The last body stuck amidst the stripped-bare branches of a fallen oak. Explaining the acolytes' disappearance would be a challenge.

He stood in place, listening for anything that might indicate life. All he heard was running water as countless, spontaneous streams carried away the last of the fibríaal.

After glancing around one last time, he effortlessly called forth the glowing white Strands of Air, then strained to summon the requisite number of deep, midnight-black ones. Once he had what he needed, he stared into the air and set to crafting the correct pattern. As he neared the Weave's completion, he closed his eyes and drew forth the image of his office at Immylla. The sound of thick parchment being torn in two filled the wilderness.

He opened his eyes and spotted the telltale slit of a port, hanging in midair before him. He reached out with a hand to touch the slit's edge—an icy chill ran along his arm—and pulled it to the side, much as one would a curtain. Concentrated blackness waited for him inside. With one last look around— fixing the scene in his mind should he need to return—he stepped through the opening and disappeared into the void. The flap of reality fell back into place.

A few moments later, the slit vanished with a small pop.

CHAPTER 6: DISCOVERY

The road leading into Yellow Mud was a thick, mucky mess that reminded Kenders of over-churned, too-creamy butter. The sloppy mud significantly slowed their pace as she and Nikalys slipped in some places and got stuck in others.

Getting to this point had taken longer than she would have liked. Once the ijul had taken the slaughtered mages—aided by crackling white magic—from the bluff, she and Nikalys resumed their descent, stopping to hide in a bush when Kenders felt a surge of black and white. Since then, Kenders had not felt any more magic.

A half-mile from the edge of town, they began to encounter debris. Muddied bundles of wet straw lay scattered about, the remnants of roof thatching. Splintered timbers and tree branches blocked parts of the road, forcing the siblings to go around them. Unripe olives and bunches of tiny green grapes littered the ground. The wave had brought the harvest to town a few turns early.

Dirty pools of water were everywhere, some large enough to be considered ponds. Household furniture—broken chairs, tables, dented pot-stoves, chests cracked and missing their drawers—jutted out of the mud. Kenders spotted a child's crib on the side off the road, almost went to it, but turned her head and kept walking. She listened for an infant's cry, but there was none.

She had walked this path countless times before, but the destruction around her made it seem as if she were treading upon it for the first time. She was in a state of perpetual shock, her head slowly shaking from side to side, never pausing.

Once they finally reached what had been the eastern edge of town, Kenders pointed to an empty plot of land. "Widow Johns' house is gone."

Nikalys looked over. "All the houses are gone, sis." They stood in the mud, quiet for a few moments. Nikalys sighed, clenched his jaw, and said, "Let's go. We shouldn't linger." He continued west, down the road. Kenders followed.

A short time later, they found the first body, stopping a few paces from the corpse and staring in silence. The poor soul lay face down in the mud, covered in yellow, slimy muck, oak leaves, and grass clumps.

Fighting back the urge to get ill, Kenders asked quietly, "That's not Father, is it?" She could tell that it was a man, but that was all.

Nikalys hesitated—worrying her—before answering, "Father's taller."

"Jak?"

He shook his head. "The hair is wrong."

"Who, then?"

Nikalys was quiet for a few heartbeats before moving away, sloshing down the road. "I don't want to know."

Kenders knew if they turned the man over, they would have recognized him. Because of that, she was glad they let him be. Not knowing his name somehow made the death easier to accept. The anonymity of the dead did not last long, however.

Mrs. Bodsworth—her eyes wide and blank—lay slouched against a dented pot-stove. She had been the unofficial teacher in Yellow Mud, instructing children in their numbers and letters if their parents wished. All three Isaac children had spent four afternoons a week with Mrs. Bodsworth, even during the busy spring and harvest seasons.

Kenders bent down in order to close Mrs. Bodsworth's eyelids. It took her three tries before she could bring herself to touch the corpse. Tears that had begun falling at some point now dripped onto Mrs. Bodsworth's ruined dress.

"Maeana welcome you with open arms."

It was said that Maeana, the Final Friend and goddess of death, waited for every soul who passed from this life, kindly welcoming them into her hall. In Kenders' opinion, it did not matter much who welcomed you when you died. You were still dead.

As they wandered the ruined, lifeless hillside that used to be their village, the tears eventually stopped flowing. The overwhelming sorrow she felt morphed into the numbing throb of hopelessness.

At one point, Nikalys reached up to retrieve an old leather satchel hanging from an uprooted tree. Soon after, he picked up a hunting knife still in its sheath and dropped it in his scavenged bag. Without looking over, he said, "I need you to search the bodies and see if you can find any beltpurses."

Kenders stopped short and stared at him. "What? Why?"

"Just do it," ordered Nikalys. His officious tone earned him a sharp glare from her, one he did not see as he was peering about the mud. Even so, he said, "And please don't argue."

"We are *not* thieves, Nik."

Tossing something he had retrieved from the mud back to the ground, Nikalys replied, "It's not stealing if they are already dead."

She stared at him, open-mouthed. His callousness shocked her. "Do it yourself. I'm not stealing!"

Sounding more than a little exasperated, he said, "They don't need the coin, Kenders. We do."

"No!"

He stopped what he was doing, dropped his chin to his chest, and stayed that way for a few moments before muttering, "Fine." He half-turned his head back to her. "At least try to find things that might be useful if you were going into the woods for a time. Knives, flint, any sort of tools. Waterskins, too."

Kenders eyes narrowed. "Why?"

"Because we're leaving," said Nikalys. He kicked over a plank of wood, exposing a chest of drawers lying on its back.

"Nine Hells we're leaving!" She hurried to Nikalys, avoiding muddy puddles as she went. "We're here to look for Mother, Father, Jak…anyone."

Ignoring her, Nikalys scooted around to one side of the toppled chest. "Here, help me tip this up."

"No! Leave that blasted chest alone and help find our family!"

Nikalys' visage of calm crumbled. He slammed his hand down on the chest so hard that the wood cracked. "Blast it, Kenders! Look around you!" Gesturing in all directions, he shouted, "There is nothing left! *Nothing*! Our home is gone! Yellow Mud…is gone!" Even though he was yelling, his voice wavered. "Everyone—*everyone*—is dead!" His words voice echoed in the empty hills.

Kenders stared at her brother's wild-eyed face and then dropped her head. She was angry, bitter, heartbroken, and a dozen other emotions she could not hold onto long enough to name. "You don't know that…"

Nikalys let out a long, weary sigh. Squishing in the mud, he walked to her and wrapped his arms around her. "Hey. I didn't mean to yell." His voice was softer, but still carried an edge sharper than any knife. "I'm just so…so…" He trailed off, never finishing the sentence.

"I know," whispered Kenders. "Me, too."

He held her for a long moment, then pushed her back to arms' length and stared at her. "I know you don't want to hear it—Hells, I don't either—but there's nothing left for us here. No one could have survived this. Mother, Father, and Jak—" his voice caught "—they're gone. In Maeana's hall. Happy and free, yes?"

Kenders' tears threatened to start flowing again.

Nikalys continued, his tone gentle. "I know it hurts…Gods, I know it hurts. But we are alive, Kenders, and we need to get moving. That mage—that blasted mage—might come back. And I doubt he'd let us live if he found us here."

She knew he was right, but she could not bring herself to leave. Not so soon. "People might still need help."

Nikalys let out a long, anguished sigh. "Kenders, the only help we can offer anyone—and I do mean *anyone*—" his voice caught "—is to dig graves and bury them. But there's no time. We need to get far away from here as quickly as we can. Mother and Father would want us to stay safe."

She wanted to protest more, to insist their parents and brother were alive. Yet she did not. Nobody could have survived this. She wiped away her tears with both hands, leaving streaks of ochre clay on her face. "Fine. Let's go."

Nikalys gave her a final, almost reluctant squeeze, then released her and stepped back. Without meeting her eyes, he moved back toward the chest of drawers he had been trying to open. "Now, let's get this up and see if there is anything inside worth taking."

Kenders tamped down her emotions as best she could and helped Nikalys lift the chest and go through the drawers. They found ruined knitting supplies, old rags, and a change of clothes for them each. Nikalys stuffed everything into his satchel. The bottom drawer held a pair of boots that looked as if they might fit Kenders. She grabbed them and moved off to see what else she could scavenge.

Spotting a quick glint of sunlight flash from a toppled stone pile—she thought it might have been a chimney—she slogged through the mud and retrieved an oaken tinderbox with a silver plate on one side. Save for a chipped corner and some mud, it seemed intact. Upon opening it, she was surprised to find the firesticks inside were dry.

While most people still used flint and steel to start a fire, some preferred the simplicity the firesticks offered. Strike the head of a stick on the lid's rough interior and it would light. Even though the wagon merchant who had brought them had worked hard to convince the townspeople that they were not magic, only a handful bought them. The rest thought the firesticks might earn them the interest of the Constables.

As Kenders sealed the box and dumped it into Nikalys' leather sack, a screech from above pulled her attention upward. Squinting against the day's glare, she spotted three birds circling overhead, their silhouettes black against sky. "Nik? Blood vultures." She looked over. Nikalys was staring up at them, too.

"We should leave," he said. "We've lingered too long."

After a bit more hurried scavenging, they collected a small sum of coins—three silver ducats and seventeen copper—as well as some snare wires, a leather sling, and a pair of waterskins. Nikalys found and removed the second waterskin from the mangled body of a boy with whom Kenders had danced during Horum's Leisure Time festival. The celebration, just last week, now seemed like it was years ago.

A blood vulture's shrieking cry pulled Kenders' eye up just in time to see two birds swoop down and alight on the face-down body of a woman. As horrifying as it was to be standing in a muddy field filled with dead neighbors, the thought of watching the carrion birds pick the corpses clean was worse.

Ready to go now, Kenders looked to where Nikalys had been rummaging through a dead horse's saddlebag. The horse was still there, but Nikalys was not.

"Nikalys?"

"Over here."

She scurried around a large pile of rubble and found him standing beside a muddy pool with another body, staring upward at a lone tree that had somehow survived the raging torrent. Its leaves were all gone, some of its boughs snapped off, but it was still standing.

Never taking his gaze from the tree, Nikalys spoke, his voice quiet, his tone somewhat detached. "Our house was here." He pointed at the stubborn tree. "There's the ash." He turned west and gestured to a pile of stones. "There's the water basin between our house and the Turners."

It took a moment for Kenders to get her bearings, but once she did, she realized he was right. "Gods, Nik..." Not a single log of the Isaac home remained.

A few quiet, utterly surreal moments passed after which Nikalys faced her and muttered, "We need to get moving." He reached out, took her hand, and led her east, away from their home and back to the road.

Their trip leaving Yellow Mud was a silent one with neither sibling uttering a single word. Kenders stared long and hard at the destruction as they left, burning every morbid detail into her memory, determined to find justice for Yellow Mud, for her family. The mage in the red robes would answer for what he had done.

CHAPTER 7: LOSS

The road out of Yellow Mud ran east for a few miles through carefully tended vineyards and olive groves before giving way to wilder, more natural terrain. Upon reaching the pinnacle of Baldtop Hill, the way swung south toward the well-traveled Southern Road. Nikalys trailed Kenders, one eye on her and the other searching for any sign of danger, his mind churning. They needed a plan.

In town, instinct told him they needed to move. Now that they were out of immediate danger—or so he hoped—he had no idea what to do next. There were no grandparents, cousins, uncles, or aunts to whom they could run. The entirety of the Isaac family had been five people.

Thaddeus had been an orphan and Marie's parents had died in a massive fire in Fernsford, a city in the Southlands, less than a year after Nikalys' parents had married. The young couple left Fernsford and headed north to Lakeborough where Thaddeus worked as a blacksmith and Marie as a tailor. All three children were born there. With Kenders less than a year old, the young family left Lakeborough, came to Yellow Mud, and had lived a good life ever since. A life that was gone now.

Nikalys sighed and looked ahead to his sister. "I think we should head to Lakeborough."

Sounding surprised, she answered without turning around. "Lakeborough? Why Lakeborough?"

"Perhaps somebody there will remember us. Or at least Mother and Father."

Kenders glanced over her shoulder. "And how does that help us?"

Nikalys shrugged his shoulder. "Perhaps we could find work there? Day laborers, I guess? You could see if—"

Kenders halted in the shade of an oak and wheeled around to face him, her eyes burning hot. "What's wrong with you?! Someone just killed our family! Killed everyone we've ever known! And you're already turning the page!"

Suddenly angry himself, Nikalys fired back. "No, I'm not! Trust me, I'd like nothing more than to see that ijul hang!"

"And how is running off to Lakeborough going to accomplish that?"

As much as he wanted to shout at her—to scream and yell—he pressed his lips together, muffling his rage. Kenders did not deserve his anger. He shook his head, stepped around her, and started to walk down the road. "Forget I said anything."

Kenders hurried and fell in beside him, staring at him. "I'm sorry, but I can't do that. I cannot believe—"

He cut her off, snapping, "Leave it be, Kenders. I'll think of something—"

Ten paces away, a rabbit burst from the brush, startling them both. Kenders grabbed Nikalys' arm as it dashed across the road, a blur of brown fur, and reentered the forest on the other side. Nikalys stood motionless, staring where the rabbit had vanished into the brush, his heart pounding. After a few moments, he tilted his head back, stared at the blue sky, and let out long sigh.

Kenders released his arm. "Gods, that scared me..."

"Yeah," mumbled Nikalys. "Me, too." A rabbit—a tiny, harmless rabbit— had terrified him.

Realizing he had just missed an excellent chance at securing food for this evening, he dropped his gaze and dug into the satchel draped on his shoulder. Upon finding the leather sling, he pulled it free and unwound it. He felt Kenders' gaze on him as he bent over to look for a smooth, mostly round stone. After selecting one, he armed the sling and with eyes straight ahead, set to walking again. He made it two steps before Kenders snapped at him.

"Nikalys!"

He drew to a stop, scuffling his feet in the dirt, and dropped his head, chin to chest. The mud from the village was drying, coating his boots with crusty, cracked crud. "What?"

"We're *not* done talking about this."

"I was sort of hoping we were."

"Well, we're not. Are you *truly* ready to just run away?"

The answer to that was no. There was another path to take, one that would have made all the sense in the world before today, but one he did not want to mention. He knew Kenders too well. Impulsive, stubborn, a little short-sighted. The moment he gave voice to the idea, she would latch onto it and race ahead without ever looking back. He should keep his mouth shut.

"Nik! Answer me!"

Lifting his head, he turned to face her. "There's another option, but it's sour. So sour that I've decided against it."

Kenders jammed her hands on her hips. "Oh, *you've* decided, have you? Well, seeing how you don't get to make decisions *for* me, I'd like to hear what that option is, *Lord* Nikalys."

Her sarcasm scraped away the ever-so-thin layer of calm he had so far managed to maintain. Annoyed, he shot back, "Fine! We could go to Smithshill, tell the Constables what happened, and let them deal with those mages!"

Kenders nodded her quick approval at the idea. "That sounds better than hiding in Lakeborough."

Vexed, Nikalys took a step closer to her. "Kenders, if we go marching into the Constables' office and tell them what happened, there will be questions. Lots of them. Questions about what we saw. Questions about who we saw. Questions about *mages and magic.*" He watched as the anger and determination drained from her face.

A heartbeat passed before she muttered, "Oh."

With raised eyebrows, Nikalys nodded. "Exactly. 'Oh.' If they get too curious—which I'm sure they will once we tell them about the giant water creature and people *walking on the lake*—they just might discover things we don't want them to. I've already lost my mother, father, and brother today. I would like to keep my sister safe."

Kenders looked up to him, her eyes—brown at the moment—full of contrition. "I hadn't thought of that…"

He let out a long sigh. "I know…" He reached out and patted the top of her head. "It's fine. No matter."

She pulled back a bit, ducking her head an inch or two. "Still not a barncat, Nik."

Nikalys withdrew his hand. "Right. Sorry."

The pair stood in the road for a few moments, surrounded by trees and the gentle rustle of leaves teased by a breeze only they felt.

Nikalys nodded east and said, "Come on, let's keep moving." He turned and continued down the slope. Kenders followed, silent.

As they walked, Nikalys kept alert, alternating his gaze forward and behind, looking for rabbits or the ijul in red robes. His luck evened out, no rabbits and no mage, either.

Upon cresting a small rise, Nikalys spotted the Southern Road below, still a half mile away, its russet brown line meandering through the hills. He stopped, as did Kenders beside him, and stared at the road. He could not see it, but he knew an old wooden sign was down there, staked at the Southern Road junction with "Yellow Mud" painted in faded black letters.

He looked over at Kenders. "I don't think we should go down there. If we meet someone this close to home, stories could travel."

"Makes sense, I suppose. What then? We need to keep moving."

Nodding at the tree-choked side of the road, Nikalys said, "We head into the forest and move east."

Kenders stared into the woods. "And what about wolves?"

Wolves were common in the hills surrounding Yellow Mud. Widow Johns had become Widow Johns because of one.

"We stay close to the road," said Nikalys. "Just not on it. Wolves don't come close to the road. It smells too much like people." He spoke with a confidence he did not feel. Wolves concerned him, too.

After a moment's hesitation, Kenders nodded. "Alright."

Happy they had at least a short-term plan, Nikalys said, "Good. Let's go." He turned and began walking to the roadside. "And keep your eye out for rabbits or we're going to sleep hungry."

"Oh, I'll find them. You just make sure you hit them."

Glancing back, he spotted the tiniest of smiles on Kenders' face and was surprised how good it made him feel. He gave her a slight grin in return, faced forward, and stepped from the sunny, wheel-rutted road into the shade of the forest.

CHAPTER 8: PLAN

Kenders sat against the trunk of an oak, the ridged bark digging into her back and head as she peered upwards, through the leaves and into the night sky. Both moons were visible tonight. White Moon was nearly full, a bright orb hanging high overhead, while her smaller sister, Blue Moon, was a thin cobalt crescent.

Eveningmeal had been a lone rabbit seasoned with a bit of foraged hillsage and then roasted over the fire. Nikalys had buried the carcass and guts so no scavengers or wolves would be drawn by the smell. There was no need to leave an open invitation.

Their tiny campfire crackled and popped in the dark, sending up wispy curls of white smoke. The fire could use another log, but they had decided to let it die. The night would not be cool enough that they would need the warmth.

Kenders was exhausted and had tried to sleep, but every time she closed her eyes, images of Yellow Mud's devastation greeted her. After a time, she had given up, scooted over to this particular trunk, and had not moved since even though the gnarled tree roots made for an uncomfortable perch.

Their sack of scavenged items sat next to her. She flipped back the leather flap and began digging inside, seeking something to occupy her mind. Spotting the tinderbox, she pulled it out, pried open its lid, and withdrew a firestick. She had used one to start the fire, but had paid it little notice. Now, she held up the finger-length, red-tipped stick and studied it.

The Isaac family had never owned firesticks. Father had always refused to buy them, but not because he feared the sticks were magical as many said. In fact, he called such claims "the most backwards thing" he had ever heard. He simply preferred the feel of flint and steel.

Kenders dragged the firestick against the rough pad inside the lid. The stick's tip flared and ignited with a small puff of smoke that smelled, oddly enough, like rotten eggs. She stared at the little flame, watching it slowly consumed the stick.

"Don't waste those," grunted Nikalys. "We're going to need them."

Looking over, she found her brother staring at her through cracked eyelids. He was leaning against a fallen oak trunk, his legs outstretched and hands folded across his chest. He looked like he was taking a Seventhday afternoon nap, save for the unsheathed hunting knife resting on his belly. People did not take naps with knives at the ready.

Without saying a word, Kenders tossed the remainder of the firestick into the campfire's meager flames and closed the tinderbox with a sharp clack. Nikalys watched her for a moment before shutting his eyes again.

Kenders stared at him for a long time, thinking. Not long after their brief confrontation in the road, she had made a rather important decision. Since then, she had spent almost all of her time trying to figure a way to tell her brother.

"Nikalys?"

With his eyes still shut, he muttered, "Yes?"

"Remember the year you threw a fit when Father and Jak went to Smithshill? You stomped about the kitchen, insisting you were old enough to go, too?"

A wistful, embarrassed grin spread across Nikalys' face. "Sure. I was what? Ten?"

"More like thirteen."

"I was not."

"Yes, Nik, you were. I remember because it was the harvest before my Maiden's Day."

Girls in the Oaken Duchies marked their thirteenth yearday with an intimate family celebration, marking when a girl was no longer considered a child, yet still was not a woman. When her eighteenth yearday arrived in a few years, a much larger celebration—Matron's Day—would have denoted her entrance into womanhood.

Nikalys cracked open his right eye and looked across the dying fire. "Are you sure you are remembering that correctly?"

Kenders cocked a single eyebrow. "It was a Firstday, Mother was making bread dough, I was chopping summer squash at the table. Father stood in the doorway with his arms crossed, frowning at you. Jak nearly fell over because he couldn't stop laughing at your tantrum."

Nikalys gave a conciliatory shrug and shut his eyes. "Fine. I was thirteen. What about it?"

"Do you remember the small package Father brought from Smithshill?"

He opened both eyes now and stared at her with curiosity. "I do. You thought it was for you. A gift for your Maiden's Day."

"That I did," admitted Kenders. "I snuck it from their room and opened it." She smiled, recalling how pretty the painted glass dove had been. The colors had been brilliant, like a rainbow after a spring shower. "It was so beautiful. I held it up to the sun, just to see it sparkle."

"And then you dropped it."

Kenders winced, remembering the horror she had felt as the figurine slipped from her fingers. Upon hitting the floor, the dove broke into three solid pieces. "I wrapped it up quickly and put it away. No one knew I had broken it."

"Remember the look on Father's face when he gave it to Mother? He was so disappointed."

Their father had spent the rest of the evening crestfallen, wondering aloud how it had happened. Kenders had excused herself and gone to bed early, hoping to escape the incredible guilt she felt. It had not worked. Remorse had gnawed at her for a week, growing worse by the day.

Nikalys was quiet for a few heartbeats, his brow furrowed. Sitting a little taller, he asked, "What made you think of that now?"

"Do you remember what you said when I told you I had broken the dove?"

His eyebrows drew together even closer. "Vaguely..." The worried expression he wore betrayed him. She guessed he knew exactly what he had said.

Kenders leaned forward, brushed a few strands of hair from her face, and said, "You told me that I needed to tell them what I had done. That I shouldn't let my fear of what would happen to me stop me from doing what was right."

Nikalys sat up quickly. "No! We are not going to the Constables! They will—"

She interrupted him, rushing to get out what she wanted to say. "You were right, Nik! It *was* the right thing to do! It was hard and I was afraid, but I did it! With you standing at my side, I did what was right!"

Nikalys stood, agitated, his face angry. "This is different, Kenders! Much different!"

"How exactly? The right thing to do here is to tell the Constables what happened!"

"Kenders! You are a *mage*!"

While she was fully aware of that awful truth, hearing the words aloud was like a slap to the face. Shaking it off, she shouted, "That changes nothing! We have to report this!"

Nikalys began pacing about the campsite, his mud-encrusted boots kicking sticks and leaves. "No! No we don't! If the Constables find out you're a mage...they'll...they'll...Hells! We don't know what they'll do, do we?!" He stopped and glared at her. "But you know the stories as well as I do!"

"Perhaps they won't be able to tell!" shot back Kenders. "Hells! Perhaps all that stuff at the lake was my imagination!"

"Your *imagination*?! You felt colors *before* we saw the blasted thing!"

Kenders pressed her lips together, wanting to refute his point, but unable.

Nikalys walked around the fire and stopped at her feet. "Kenders, if we go to the Constables, they *will* take you."

"But—"

"No 'but!' No nothing!" He shook his head vehemently. "We aren't going!"

Undeterred, she pressed on, "It's the right thing—"

"I don't care!" shouted Nikalys, waving his hands before him once, cutting her off. "They'll take you, Kenders! They *will* take you. And then I'll be all alone!" His words and sharp emotion filled the small grove, sudden out of place against the backdrop of the quiet night. His eyes were wide and cheeks flushed, his lips tight and drawn. Her brother was angry, yes, but mostly he was scared.

Kenders rose from the ground, stepped close to him, and laid a hand on his shoulder. In a voice as soft and restrained as his had been loud and uninhibited, she whispered, "Hey, I love you, too."

He glared at her, defiant, for another moment before dropping his head and sighing.

Kenders reached under his chin and directed his gaze back to her face. "But we *are* going to the Constables. We owe it to our family, to everyone. It's the right thing to do."

He ran a hand through his hair, pulling at his bristly locks, dropped his arms to his side, and mumbled, "I know…"

Hopeful, Kenders asked "So we'll go, then?"

He remained still for a long moment, his eyes locked on hers, a tortured expression on his face. After a few heartbeats, he squeezed his eyes tight, nodded once, and sighed, "Fine. We'll go."

Kenders wrapped her arms around him, placing her cheek on his chest, and embraced him. He returned the hug, gently at first, but soon, he was clasping tight, so tight she wondered if he ever intended to let go. He was stronger than she remembered.

"Umph…I can't breathe, Nik."

He relaxed his embrace some, but did not release her. "Sorry."

They stood that way for a while, like two statues locked in a perpetual embrace, lit by the lattice of moonlight filtering through the oak leaves overhead. Eventually, it was Nikalys who broke the somber silence.

"One condition, though."

Without moving, she asked, "What's that?"

"I get to talk to the Constables alone."

Kenders smiled and shook her head, her cheek scratching against Nikalys' rough-spun shirt. "Sorry, but we stay together."

He let out a long sigh, his breath tickling her hair. "Gods, you're stubborn."

"Yes, I am."

As she stood there in her brother's arms, listening to the crackling of the fire and subdued sounds of the forest at night, she noticed Nikalys' breathing change. It slowed at first, then turned irregular. After a few tiny shudders and a sniffle she knew he tried to hold back, a drop of wetness struck her forehead.

She closed her eyes, held him tight, and remained quiet as more tears followed the first.

In the distance, a lone wolf's howl cut the night.

Chapter 9: Escape

8th of the Turn of Sutri

Letting out a low moan, Jak slowly opened his eyes. Utter blackness greeted him. The odor of moldy barley and rotten hops filled his nose, permeating each breath.

He laid at a slight upwards slant, his right arm pinned beneath him, his legs curled up and painfully stiff. Something sharp was sticking him in the right ribs, he had no room to move, his clothes were soaked, and he could feel every heartbeat thud in his head. Propping himself up with his left arm, he freed his right. A thousand tiny pinpricks stabbed at his forearm and hand as blood rushed back into his limb.

His thoughts felt jumbled and slow, swimming around in his head like a fish in a vat of grape jam. He tried to stretch, but could not. Tired and weary, he lay there for a while, waiting for his arm to stop throbbing and his muddled thoughts to begin making sense.

He remembered getting into the barrel, but try as he might, he could not remember anything past that point.

Running a hand along the back of his head, he found a large knot, wet with either blood or water; he did not know which. As there was water sloshing in the bottom of the dark prison, it could reasonably be either.

Needing to do something about the sharp point sticking in his ribs, Jak felt around and grabbed the leather package his father had shoved in his arms. With a great deal of effort, he pried it loose and moved it so it was not jammed into his side.

Lifting his head, he spotted the small tap hole near his left knee. A ray of soft white light streamed through the cutout. His jumbled brain reasoned that it was moonlight.

"Gods…how long have I been in here?"

His voice was scratchy, his throat raw. He seemed to recall screaming as he rode the wave, holding the lid as tightly as he could. Reaching over his head with his left hand, he felt the lid still in place above him and pushed.

It did not move.

He pushed again, slightly harder. The barrel lid still did not budge.

"Hells!"

He took a moment to rest, taking a few deep breaths, then braced his legs against the bottom of the barrel and pushed upward. He grunted and shouted as he strained to pry the lid open. The effort made his head swim as a wave of blackness washed over him.

*   *   *

The air in the barrel was warmer now, staler somehow. And thicker, almost as if it had weight. It was like he was breathing old beer.

His head still hurt, but less so. It felt like a horse was racing across the back of his head, from one temple to the other. Earlier, it had been an entire wagon team. Cracking open his eyes, he found the barrel's interior much brighter than before. Daylight streamed through the hole.

He was sweating profusely. Thirst demanded that he cup handfuls of the foul water at the bottom of the barrel to his mouth. It was gritty, tasted like dead fish and waste, but he needed to drink something. He choked on the water, swallowed as much as he could stomach, and then set to assessing his situation.

He needed to get out of this barrel now. If today's heat were anything like the past few weeks', he would roast in here. He was surprised he had survived yesterday.

He tried the lid again and found it as unyielding today as it had been last night. Something on the other side was holding the lid shut.

"Blast it."

Once, when he and Nikalys were in Smithshill with their father, they had seen three short-statured merrymakers stuff themselves into an apple barrel. When their father had told his sons the small men were tombles, Nikalys and Jak had shared a knowing look. Thaddeus Isaac was known to tell tales. Tombles existed in playman's tales, not in the real world. At the moment, Jak wished they were not only real, but that he was one.

A sudden, cool draft pushed its way into the barrel, giving Jak a brief respite from the hot, rank air he was breathing. A moment later, he felt the entire barrel gently sway one way, accompanied by the sound of creaking wood. He and the barrel slowed to a stop and then slowly moved back in the other direction.

"Hells...I'm in a blasted tree."

Puzzling things out, he supposed the wave had deposited him here, jamming his barrel in such a position where the lid pressed against branch or trunk.

As another puff of a rare summer breeze sent him swaying again, he thought through his limited options. The air in the barrel was heating up quickly; he needed to take action soon. Thirsty again, he stared down at the brown, rancid water at the barrel's bottom, shuddered, and croaked, "I'd rather die…"

His mumbled, offhand comment brought his parents to mind and the fact that they were truly dead. He tried to shake off the sorrow and guilt swirling inside him; he needed to focus on his own predicament, something he could not do when thinking about what might have become of his family.

His family.

Nikalys and Kenders.

The thought of his brother and sister jolted through him like a lightning bolt. He reflexively tried to sit and ended up cracking his head on the keg. A hollow thud filled the barrel.

"Hells!"

Wincing, he laid his head down and rubbed what was likely to become a bump in the front to match the one in the back.

Ashamed that he had forgotten about his siblings' well-being, he grabbed the silver teardrop pendant around his neck. Remembering his mother's instructions, and with less trepidation than he would have expected, he pictured Nikalys and Kenders in his mind. At once, a sense of perfect calm washed over him. Without knowing how, but knowing nonetheless, he knew they were alive and well.

He caught a muted, musical tone dancing just beyond his range of hearing, teasing him. Curious, he tilted his head and tried to focus on it. Instantly, the tone faded. He opened his eyes and stared at the silver pendant.

"That was…odd."

He shut his eyes and pictured Nikalys and Kenders again. Immediately, the tone returned. The more he focused on his brother and sister, the tone grew louder, more distinct. Turning his head, he sought the sound's origin and found that if he looked to where his right elbow rested, the ringing was strongest. He released the pendant and the tone stopped.

He assumed the feeling of wellness coupled with the musical tone meant that his brother and sister were alive and well and located in a general "right elbow" direction.

Opening his eyes, he looked around the stifling barrel and frowned. "It doesn't matter where they are if I can't get out of here."

Jak examined the unusual leather package his father had given him, wondering if it contained something he could use to free himself from the barrel. There was enough light shining in from the tap hole for him to note the package was four feet at its longest, had a slight bulge at one end, and a tapered point at the other.

He repeatedly turned the case over in his hands, looking for some way to open it but he could not find a seam anywhere. There were no laces, holes, flaps, or anything of the like. Other than the two leather strips that allowed someone to strap the case to his or her back, the leather appeared to be a single, unbroken piece.

With his face twisted in confusion, he muttered, "What in the Nine Hells?"

Concluding the package was not going to help him with his barrel problem, he released it, letting it splash into the water at the barrel's bottom. "Useless."

Unfortunately, Jak could only think of one way out of this situation, yet was as worried the idea might work as he was it might not. By rocking side-to-side, he thought he might be able to dislodge the barrel enough to open the lid. Too far, however, and the barrel might fall. If he was only ten feet up, he might get hurt a little. Any higher than that, and he would likely break something when he landed.

Wiping sweat from his brow yet again, he muttered, "Or I can stay here and roast like a Year's End lamb."

Settling on his imperfect, potentially dangerous plan, he took a deep breath and offered a short prayer to the Cold Twister of Fate. "Greya, I place myself in your hands." He thought it ironic that he was invoking the name of the goddess of winter and fate. The fate part certainly seemed appropriate, although the sweltering barrel was nothing like winter.

Jak lurched left first, followed a moment later by heaving right. Repeating the process, he felt the barrel shifted ever so slightly as wood scraped and creaked. Jak stopped, pushed at the lid, and found it still sealed. He sighed. "Because that would be too easy."

He started again, rocking side to side, each jerk more violent than the last. After a particularly forceful shove right, the barrel began to roll. A shout of joy leapt from his raw throat.

"Ah-ha!"

His exuberance was cut short and when the barrel did not stop moving. A moment later, he felt weightless, like he was swimming. In a panic, he shoved the lid upwards. It opened easily and fell away. He willed his legs to extend but they refused to respond.

The barrel slammed into another branch, and tipped upside down, sending the fetid water spilling over him. The leather package slipped out and cracked him hard in the chin before bouncing off the branch on its way to the ground below, spinning end-over-end. Jak and the barrel teetered in place for a moment, giving him a glimpse of what waited below. He was still twenty feet in the air.

The barrel toppled over and resumed its inevitable crash to the hillside. Reaching out with his left arm, Jak grabbed the tree branch, slicing his hand on a bit of sharp bark in the process. As the barrel tipped, Jak tried to free his right arm to reach the branch as well, but his body's position made such a move impossible.

Holding on with one arm only, Jak and the barrel swung downward like a door on a hinge. When the barrel was below him, it slipped off and fell, cracking on the soft muddy ground. Now free, he grabbed the branch with his right arm and hung suspended.

The relatively cooler air felt glorious and smelled impossibly clean. Extending his legs for the first time in a day was wonderful. Jak enjoyed the sensations for only a moment, though. He was not of out danger yet.

He tried to pull himself up, but after a single, feeble attempt, he realized he did not have the strength to do so. Surveying the area below, he figured that his feet were only twelve to thirteen feet off the ground, a height from which Jak had made numerous jumps in his life. Of course, those had been from a barn loft into a large pile of hay.

With his strength ebbing with each ragged breath, he let go and fell to the mud below. His legs, rubbery and useless, did not respond when he landed, and he collapsed in a heap, sinking into the muck with a soft squish. Somehow, he had managed to avoid landing on the barrel or the leather bundle.

He remained motionless for a few moments, taking a quick account of his body and concluding that nothing hurt any more than it had when he was folded in the barrel. A shocked laugh leapt from him as he rolled onto his back and stared up into the leaf-bare tree. A redbird sat on the branch, peering down at him. It chirped once.

"It's all yours, bird."

With some effort, he sat up and looked around. His mood sobered in an instant. "Bless the gods…"

The destruction around him was unimaginable. Bodies, timbers, animals, furniture, carts, baskets, clothes, thatched straw, and all other sorts of remnants of the town lay strewn everywhere, some wedged in trees and bushes like he and his barrel had been.

A patient crunching drew his attention to his right. Swiveling his head, Jak spied a blood vulture standing on the chest of a naked body not thirty feet away. Two feet tall, black and mottled gray feathers covered the carrion bird except for its bare, muddy-green skinned neck and head. The vulture stared at Jak with beady yellow eyes. A piece of flesh dangled from its hooked beak.

Jak abruptly realized the air was not as crisp and clean as he had first thought. A nauseating mixture of mud, stagnant water, and the sickly sweet odor of rotting flesh assaulted him. He rolled over to his hands and knees and retched, but nothing ever came up. Once he regained control of his stomach, he closed his eyes and took a few breaths to steady himself while making sure not to breathe too deeply.

Gathering his strength, he stood on wobbly legs and tried to fix his position. Based on the terrain around him, he figured he was a half-mile southwest of Yellow Mud. He considered heading back to see if anyone might still be alive, but the devastation was so complete, he knew the search would be futile. Besides, he knew two people who needed him for sure.

Jak gripped the muted silver teardrop necklace and thought of his brother and sister. Again, the sense of calm rushed over him, along with the faint ringing. He spun in a circle, listening. It seemed strongest when he faced east.

"East it is."

Nikalys and Kenders most likely thought him dead. If they had been smart, they would have run immediately, giving them a full day's head start on him. He glanced upwards and found Mu's orb high in the sky, meaning the day was a little more than half spent. He bent over, retrieved the leather case, and strapped it to his back. "Let's get on with it, then."

Glancing north, he said a quick prayer to Maeana for the souls of his parents and neighbors and then turned his back on the ruins of Yellow Mud. He stumbled toward the blood vulture and swiped at the bird as he passed. "Shoo!"

With an annoyed screech, the carrion bird took to the air.

CHAPTER 10: STRANDS

9th of the Turn of Sutri

The wave creature was coming fast, tearing up trees and bushes, roaring with the strength of a thousand waterfalls. Kenders sprinted past Widow Johns' small house, hoping the old woman had fled, having no time to stop and check. Her sandaled feet slapping against the hard dirt road, she glanced behind her, looking for Nikalys. The way was empty. Odd as she did not remember passing him. Nevertheless, she pressed on without him and raced into Yellow Mud proper.

Chaos reigned around her, people running and screaming, shouting for wives, husbands, sons, and daughters. Some carried household items: tools, sacks full of one thing or another, clothes, oil lamps. It looked as if they had grabbed whatever was nearby and ran. One man was carrying a squealing piglet.

Dodging her fleeing neighbors as she ran, she made for the Isaac home. She doubted she could reach the house before the water did, but she had to try. Upon rounding a corner, she skidded to a stop in the middle of the road, baffled by what awaited her.

"How...?"

Her house was a few hundred paces away when only moments ago she had been on the far edge of town. She had no time to make sense how that was possible when a quick glance north revealed the water creature was almost in Yellow Mud. She ran.

Upon reaching the front of her home, she burst inside, letting the oak door slam against the wall. The center room was empty. All four doorways to the other rooms were empty.

"Mother! Father!"

There was no response.

"Jak!"

She moved to the kitchen first, then the other rooms, frantically searching. Nobody was here. Noticing the back door ajar, she hurried over and shoved it open. Her parents stood by the vegetable garden in the back, locked in a quiet embrace.

"Oh, thank the gods..."

The pair seemed to be enjoying a loving moment, hugging one another as Kenders had seen countless times before. Neither acknowledged Kenders' sudden arrival nor the approaching wall of water. Mist sprayed the back of the Isaac home, water thundered, wood shrieked and cracked, but Thaddeus and Marie Isaac appeared oblivious to it all, wholly content to stand there and await the inevitable.

"Mother! Father! Let's go!"

They seemed to ignore her. Thaddeus leaned down and whispered something to her mother. Marie looked up, gently stroked his cheek, and smiled back.

Panic gripped Kenders. In a matter of moments, the wall of water would be on top of them. She needed to do something. Staring at the looming wave, she screamed.

"Noooo!"

The thundering roar shifted in tone, deepening. Trees no longer cracked and popped with the suddenness of a snapped twig, but creaked and groaned as a too-small chair would under the weight of a heavy man. Peering north, she saw the wave still moving toward her, but at an impossibly slow pace. A bird hung in the sky, wings outstretched, like a fly caught in tree sap. Baffled, Kenders looked back to her parents. Her mother's eyes closed slower than a slug crawling up a barn door, then reopened at the same glacial pace.

"What in the Nine Hells is—?"

She cut her murmured question short when a glimmering, glittering white string popped into view before her, hanging in midair, just beyond arm's length.

The filament dangled there, light and airy, waving as though teased by a soft breeze. Pulsating with bright white light, it fluttered and danced, almost beckoning Kenders to reach out and take it. It appeared only a few feet long, although when she tried to judge the true length, she could not. As her gaze traveled up and down the twisting thread, the part she had just surveyed would diminish, weakening and fading from sight. She could not say whether she ever saw its start or end. More flickering beyond the lone strand pulled her attention to the yard.

Her eyes opened wide. "Bless the gods…"

Dozens upon dozens of the strings hung in the air. Most were white, like the first, but there were other colors, too. Vivid hues of blue oscillated like waves on a lake. Ruddy, earthy-brown ropes hovered near the ground, somehow sturdier and firmer than the white and blue ones. Every string radiated a powerful, otherworldly energy. They were as beautiful as they were terrifying.

She reached out to touch the nearest wispy white filament, but her hand passed right through it. A crackling, tingly feeling ran up her arm, reminding her of the sound straw made when it crumbled.

Without warning, the wave's pounding roar resumed. She snapped her head up and saw the water surging toward them again, muddy, frothy, and laden with uprooted trees.

Staring at the wave now, she saw countless glimmering strings tumbling and roiling within water and debris. Instead of hanging haphazardly like those in the yard, however, the strands within the creature were arranged in an intricate, impossibly complex pattern, like a blanket's weave. The bulk of the strings were blue and white, but she also caught flashes of brilliant, glorious silver and gold within the pattern.

Without knowing why or how, she reached out with her mind and began to pluck the loose strings from around her—white and brown only—weaving them together clumsily, blindly. Soon, she had a misshapen tangle of strings that she directed toward her parents moments before the water struck them.

The wave rushed into the Isaac's yard and buffeted Kenders' pattern of strings. For a moment, it held against the onrushing force before, with a resounding crack that she felt more than she heard, the tangle of strands gave way, bending, breaking, shattering.

Her parents screamed as the oncoming wall of water engulfed them, driving them to where Kenders stood in the doorway. She threw her arms up to cover her face and shouted as the wave slammed into her.

"Noooo!"

Still screaming, she opened her eyes. It was dark. Firelight flickered. The odor of fired pinecones filled the air. She was sitting up, her arms held in front of her face. Her brow and neck were damp with sweat, her breath quick and ragged.

"What?" hissed Nikalys "What is it?"

Whipping her head around, she found him crouched over and scrambling to her side, the hunting knife in his hand gripped so tight that his knuckles were white. He was scanning the woods, his eyes wide.

She looked around again, her disorientation already fading. The campfire was still going strong; Nikalys must have been adding logs as she slept.

"What was it?" asked Nikalys again, his voice an anxious whisper. "Did you hear something? See something?"

Kenders closed her eyes and, putting her fingers to her temples, tried to rub away the images of her parents' faces caught in the wave. "No…sorry. It was…it was just a nightmare. An awful, terrible nightmare. I was in Yellow Mud as the water came, looking for Mother and Father. I found them in the back of the house, just…standing there. I tried to help them, but I couldn't get the…" She trailed off, wondering what she was about to say.

She had no idea what she had seen, what she had been doing, other than it probably had something to do with magic. Opening her eyes, she stared at her brother and shook her head. "You know, I'm already starting to forget the details." She forced an embarrassed, tired smile, hoping he would accept her lie.

He did, lowering the knife to his side and slumping to the ground next to her. "Gods, you stopped my heart. I thought the wolves had finally come."

Kenders' eyes narrowed. "Why would the wolves come? You said they wouldn't come near a fire."

Nikalys tilted his head and gave weak shrug of his shoulders. "Actually, I said that I *heard* wolves would never come near a fire."

"From who?"

He dropped his head, poked his knife at an unremarkable tree root and replied somewhat sheepishly, "William Holder."

"William Holder!?" exclaimed Kenders. "William Holder says lots of things! Most of them are mad!" The man had once run naked through Yellow Mud's streets screaming that "the lions are coming for us!"

"It makes sense," snapped Nikalys, his tone defensive. "Wolves don't like to be burned, right?"

Kenders rolled her eyes. "So? I don't like getting burned, but I don't hide from fire because of it."

Nikalys opened his mouth—most likely to say something smart—but stopped short as a lone, haunting howl echoed through the hills. Kenders turned her head side-to-side, trying to determine from where the cry was coming. The forested hills played havoc with sounds, however, and she could not. It seemed close, though.

As the howl slowly tapered off, a second, slightly deeper yowl answered. Brother and sister spun around as one, facing west. There was no doubt from where that one came. A third, higher pitched whine joined the first two.

As the trio of howls faded, one by one, Kenders glanced at Nikalys and spoke in a quiet, subdued tone. "There's three now."

Nikalys nodded, his eyes scanning the dark forest past the fire's glow. "Don't worry. We're fine."

Kenders shut her eyes and muttered a short prayer to Thonda, the god of Beasts and the Hunt, begging him to send his creatures away from here.

Late this morning, they had heard the first wolf call, but shrugged it off. After midday, another howl had pierced the relative quiet of the forest. Kenders had been about to ignore it when a second cry answered. Throughout the remainder of the day, the wolves' calls had periodically echoed back and forth, drifting through the hills.

The Isaac siblings had again discussed the wisdom of traveling through the woods rather than on the road. There had been a brief yet intense argument when, through the trees, they spotted a patrol of soldiers on the Southern Road.

Kenders suggested they tell the soldiers what had happened in Yellow Mud, but Nikalys insisted they continue to avoid everyone.

Kenders looked to her brother. "I told you we should have traveled on the road."

"We agreed not to."

Kenders hissed, "I only agreed because you said a fire would keep us safe!"

"I still don't think they'll come close," replied Nikalys, firelight glinting in his eyes as he stared around the glade. "I'm not worried." The timbre of his voice said otherwise.

Another howl cut through the night, raising the hairs on the back of Kenders' neck. She glanced at her brother. "Perhaps you should be."

Nikalys remained quiet, staring into the dark. He slipped his hunting knife in the sheath on his hip, stood, and crept to the fire. He grabbed the unburned end of a log jutting from the flames and scooted back to her, holding it over his head like a crude torch. When Kenders gave him a questioning look, he shrugged his shoulders.

"Just in case."

"In case of what?"

When he shrugged his shoulders again, she sighed and stared into the forest.

Tonight's campsite was nestled in a small clearing between three large trees—two oaks and one ash. A tall thicket of fingerprick bushes with inch-long thorns ran between the pair of oaks. Nothing but small, eminently passable bushes surrounded the rest of the clearing.

Hearing soft scuffling of leaves, across the fire and to her right, she stared into the blackness. The moonlight filtering through the canopy of leaves should have illuminated the forest, but the fire—while turning their camp bright—made it difficult to see much beyond the reach of the flames' light.

When a low huff, wet and throaty, drifted from the forest, Nikalys grabbed her hand, pulled her to her feet, and guided her so their backs were to the fingerprick bushes. He leaned close and whispered, "Do you see anything?"

Kenders could not, having made the mistake of glancing at the fire, wondering if she should get a torch, too. Now, leftover, ghostly images of the fire danced in her vision everywhere she looked. "No. Nothing."

To their left, a low, guttural growl slipped from the dark. Staring into the nighttime forest, Kenders watched as a pair of yellow eyes emerged from the night, reflecting the fire's light. They were only thirty paces away.

A sharp pinch in her calf triggered a quick, startled cry—part pain, part surprise. Without realizing it, she had backed into the fingerprick bushes. At her exclamation, the wolf's growl picked up and a second throaty rumble joined the first. Kenders looked to the right side of the clearing to spot another set of yellow eyes. "Nikalys...?"

"I know." He moved his right hand to his sheathed knife, gripped the handle, and slid the blade free. With his left, he held his improvised torch out to Kenders. "Take it."

"Why?"

"Just take it."

Shifting her gaze between the wolves, she reached up and took the torch from her brother.

Displaying remarkable calm, Nikalys spoke in hushed tones. "I'm going to charge the one on the left. When I do, the other will probably come after me. The moment it does, run."

She swiveled her head to stare at her brother. "No! I'm not—"

"Don't argue!" hissed Nikalys. "It's the only chance you have. If they chase you, climb a—" He cut off, his gaze snapping to the center of camp. His eyes went as round as silver ducats. "Bless the gods...."

Kenders looked across the clearing and spotted a third wolf—the largest she had ever seen by far—slinking from the blackness and into the firelight's circle. Standing four feet tall at the shoulder, the wolf was covered in shaggy, dark gray fur except for what would have been white paws were they not coated with dirt. Its ears were pointed, alert and twitching, its lips drawn back to expose yellowed teeth and blackened gums as it growled.

Nikalys' chances against a single wolf were terrible. The idea of him taking on two was preposterous. Against a pack of three, he would be dead in moments.

Kenders murmured, "Now what?"

Her brother remained silent.

She wanted to look over, but could not stop staring at the center wolf as it padded closer. "Nik?"

"I'm thinking!" he hissed. The steady calmness from before was gone.

The massive lupine approached the fire and, appearing wholly unconcerned by the flames, circled the fire, its yellow-eyed gaze fixed on them. It issued a quick snarling growl which seemed to prompt the other wolves to creep closer, low to the ground.

Kenders stood, rooted in place, her heart pounding. She lifted the torch and waited, waiting for one of the wolves to charge or pounce. She was determined to get off one good blow before being torn apart.

Suddenly, the lead wolf paused in its approach, stood a little taller, and raised its snout to sniff the air. Its ears flattened and a strange, almost worried whine slipped from its throat.

A moment later, the unusual crackling sensation she now knew was magic surged in her, around her. She had no trouble distinguishing the colors.

Green. Silver. Gold. And something else, something that was not a color.

Thinking the ijul was here, she reached out and grabbed Nikalys' arm just as a monstrous roar exploded from behind the fingerprick thicket, filling the forest night and rattling Kenders' bones. Before she could react, the growl shifted, inexplicably soaring over their heads. She glanced up, cringing, expecting another wolf to come flying into the glade. Instead of lupine gray, however, a dusty gold streak flashed over their heads. With nary a sound, a mass of golden fur landed ten paces in front of Nikalys and Kenders, directly between them and the wolves.

Kenders stared, wide-eyed and stunned. A lynx the size of a horse cart crouched in the forest clearing.

While she could see only the back of the cat, what she saw was spectacular. Its coat was a glossy, golden brown with two lines of mahogany spots straddling its spine. A short, stubby black tail stuck up from atop its muscular haunches. Thick claws extended from its massive paws—all four of which were the size of Kenders' head—and dug into the dirt when the cat flexed them. Black-tufted ears lay flat against the lynx' enormous head as it stared at the closet wolf. Its loud snarl faded into a low, growling rumble.

A single, whispered word of awe fell from Nikalys' lips. "Gods…"

Kenders silently concurred.

The lead wolf hesitated, glaring at the lynx, seemingly annoyed that the cat had dared to interrupt its pack's hunt. Whether driven by bravery or hunger, the wolf moved forward, loping the few feet separating it from the lynx, let out a snarl, and leapt for the cat's throat.

With lightning speed, the lynx swept its right front paw through the air and batted at the wolf. An audible crunch filled the clearing when the cat's paw struck the pack leader's side. The wolf went tumbling thorough the dirt, rolled out of the firelight and into the underbrush. A soft, whimpering sound drifted from the dark. Kenders guessed it had numerous broken ribs.

The lynx faced the next closest wolf, tilted its head and stared as if daring the lupine to move. The remaining wolves were silent now, and motionless. After all of the growling and snarling, the quiet of the forest was pronounced, interrupted only by popping firewood and the soft whining of the injured pack leader.

The nearest wolf dropped its head and looked backward, as though it were weighing its options. The lynx loosed another bone-rattling roar that reverberated through the hills and, ultimately, made the wolves' decision easy.

Tucking their tails between their legs, the pair immediately scampered away, kicking up dirt and leaves as they ran from the clearing. Kenders heard the whimpering pack leader running away as well, but not nearly as fast as the others were. The lynx padded to the far side of the fire and looked in the direction the wolves had run. It tilted its head, listening.

Nikalys whispered, "That thing is thrice the size of any lynx I've seen."

Kenders nodded her agreement, paused briefly, and then asked, "What if it means to have us for its own eveningmeal?"

The lynx swiveled around, turning toward them and giving the pair the first good look at it from the front. Its face had an almost wise look to it. A clean, white ruff hung under its neck and long whiskers draped from its maw, glinting in the firelight. White tufts of fur sprouted from the inside of its ears. Staring at the two of them with deep, dark brown eyes, the cat began to saunter to where they huddled by the thicket.

Nikalys stepped forward, waving his hands over his head, and called out, "Hey! Over here!"

The cat stopped and stared at them both, its gaze dancing between them.

"Nik, what are you doing?"

"Getting its attention," murmured Nikalys. Raising his voice, he called, "Over here, you overgrown tuft of hair!"

The lynx instantly shifted his gaze to rest solely on Nikalys.

Continuing to wave his arms at the cat, Nikalys looked over at her and hissed, "Kenders, Run!"

Now, the lynx turned its full attention to her.

"Go!" ordered Nikalys. "I'll distract it!"

Kenders shook her head once. "No. I'm not leaving you."

As the massive golden-brown cat resumed its approach, padding around the fire toward them, Nikalys yelled, "Blast it, Kenders! Go! Now! I'll be right behind you!"

She took a single step away from him and immediately stopped. Nikalys would not be right behind her. He would stay here, fight the lynx to give her a chance, and die.

In that moment, the soul-draining events of the past few days caught up to her and a flood of emotions exploded inside her.

Anger. Grief. Hopelessness. Frustration.

Yellow Mud was gone. Mother, Father, and Jak were dead. She was not going to run to save herself and let a giant cat kill her only remaining family. Clenching her fists and gritting her teeth, she turned back to glare at the cat with burning eyes.

She wanted the giant lynx to leave them alone.

She wanted the blasted cat to go flying into the forest like the wolf.

She desperately wanted something—anything—to keep her and her brother alive.

Abruptly, a pattern of colored strings popped into existence before her, hovering in the air above the campsite. Brilliant, pulsating white ones intertwined with sizzling yellow strands.

The giant cat's eyes widened in surprise as it stared straight at the pattern. Nikalys ignored it entirely, continuing to wave his arms and shout at the lynx.

She released the tangle of strings, urging it at the golden-brown cat. The moment she let go, a searing pain ripped through her head, accompanied by an exhaustion that was deeper and more complete than any she had ever experienced.

With a soul-wrenching scream, she went limp and collapsed, unconscious.

CHAPTER 11: SHAPECHANGER

A blinding white flash filled the clearing, paired with a concussive boom that slammed into Nikalys, throwing him back into the fingerprick thicket. He screamed out as hundreds of sharp thorns scratched, tore, and punctured his flesh. The bushes grabbed hold of him, suspending him in the air, trapping him in its brambles.

He lay that way for a few moments, groaning and moaning, his back, arms, and legs aflame with pain. He forced his eyes open, but could not see anything. The flash had blinded him. He tried to move, but only succeeded in pressing the thorns deeper into his flesh. He yelled for Kenders and was surprised when he could not hear his own voice. A tinny, persistent ringing filled his ears.

He blinked furiously, trying to clear the cloudy blackness blocking his eyesight. Slowly, his vision returned and he spotted the campfire's soft glow. Whatever just happened in the glade had left the flames untouched.

He looked left—sending sharp, shooting pain through his body—and spotted Kenders sprawled in the brambles beside him, her body a twisted heap. Dark crimson patches covered her shirt and skirt, growing larger by the moment. Blood trickled from the countless scratches lining her arms, neck, and slack jaw. Her mouth hung open, her eyes closed. She looked dead.

"Noooo!!"

His anguished cry cut through the night, a cry that made him realize that he could hear again. Hearing a soft mew of discomfort from near the fire, he turned his head and gasped in pain as the fingerprick thorns dug deeper.

The lynx stood there, shaking its head as though something was caught on its whiskers. When it stopped, the cat tilted its head to the side and looked at Nikalys. It blinked once, slowly, and then turned its gaze to Kenders. The cat padded forward, striding unhurriedly to her.

Nikalys shouted, "Leave her alone!"

The cat glanced at him but did not stop walking. When it reached Kenders, it brought its nose down to her bloody body and sniffed.

Glaring at the lynx, Nikalys screamed, "Go on! Get out of here!" Not about to let this overgrown barncat eat his dead sister, Nikalys tried to stand, but pain wracked his body every time he tried to move. He collapsed back into the tangle of fingerpricks and cried out in agony again. He was stuck here, helpless. Despair washed over him, overwhelming and complete. Lifting his head, he stared at the lynx and muttered in defeat, "Fine. Go ahead. Eat us. It doesn't matter. Everyone else is dead, anyway." At least he would get to see his family in Maeana's hall.

The lynx turned its watchful, brown-eyed gaze to Nikalys. After a moment or two, it sat on its haunches, tucked its chin to its chest, and began to shimmer, to shift. Its white-tufted ears retreated into its head. The ruff of fur along its neck shrunk as if growing in reverse. The giant paws twisted and morphed, the toes thinning as they grew longer. Its lithe front legs turned muscular as they quickly took the shape of a man's arms.

Legends about Shapechangers—people who had lived in the wilderness, away from civilization for so long that they took on the form of their natural surroundings—abounded in Yellow Mud. Nikalys had enjoyed the stories as a child, but had stopped believing them years ago, believing them the fancy of a playman's imagination. It seemed he was wrong. Very wrong.

In the span of a single heartbeat, the largest lynx Nikalys had ever seen transformed into the largest man he had ever seen, bent over and crouching in the forest clearing. The moment the shift was complete, the man stood upright.

Nikalys gaped, his eyes wide and round. The man had to be a full seven feet tall.

The giant's hair was the same golden-brown hue as the lynx's fur; his dark brown eyes matched the cat's eye color, as well. He was bare-chested—his skin a rich, bronze tan—but wore a pair of hide breeches. A large, sturdy leather bag rested on his right hip, hanging from a thick strap that was draped over his left shoulder. Small turquoise and ebony stones dangled from the string used to tie the sack shut. A white stone pendant carved in the shape of a lion's head dangled from a leather thong around his neck.

The giant spoke, his deep, rumbling voice vaguely reminiscent of the lynx's growl. "I have no intention of eating you, uori." A slight smile crept over his lips. "I do not think you would taste very good."

Nikalys opened his mouth to ask or say something, but no words came out. He was speechless. Were it not for the searing pain from the thorns carving up his flesh, he would have thought he was dreaming.

The man reached into his bag and withdrew a light-colored jute shirt. He lifted the sack over his head, set it on the ground, and then pulled on the shirt. Taking a step closer to Kenders, he glanced at Nikalys and rumbled, "Does this happen often?"

Nikalys had no idea what the man was asking. "Pardon?"

"When she uses magic, does she normally faint?"

Realizing what the man was implying, Nikalys asked, "*Kenders* did that?"

The Shapechanger peered at Nikalys, his eyes narrowing slightly. "You are surprised?"

Nikalys gaped at the man, stunned into silence. Kenders had summoned lightning from a clear, moonlit sky. Surprise did not begin to name what he was feeling now.

The massive man looked to Kenders, then back to Nikalys, a slight furrow splitting his brow. "Let us get you two free and have a look at those thorns. I am sure they must hurt."

"Why bother?" muttered Nikalys. "She's dead."

"No. She is not."

Nikalys winced as he stared back to his sister. "But all the blood…"

"You should see what *you* look like, uori. The thorns make it look worse than it is. They are painful, yes. But lethal? No. Once we get her out and clean her wounds, she will be fine. You as well."

A surge of hope filled Nikalys. "Truly?"

"Truly," rumbled the Shapechanger. "You will both recover."

Nikalys smiled wide as a relief so joyful, so complete spread through his body, it nearly chased away his pain.

The Shapechanger reached out a giant hand to Nikalys. "Good days ahead, uori." He studied Nikalys carefully as he added, "My name is Broedi."

Pulling his arm free of the brambles, wincing at every burst of pain, Nikalys took Broedi's offered hand and managed to complete the traditional greeting through gritted teeth. "And good memories behind."

Broedi grasped Nikalys' hand, engulfing it. "Now, this will hurt." Without a moment's hesitation, he pulled Nikalys from the fingerpricks.

Nikalys' eyes went wide and he drew a hissing breath, sucking air through clenched teeth. Emerging from the thorny thicket hurt thrice as much as falling into them. Once free, he stood, hunched over, and tried not to move, doing his best to ignore the countless stabs of pain dancing along his back, arms, and legs.

Broedi eyed him as he stood there. "Will you give me your name?"

Wincing, Nikalys answered, "Nikalys."

"And the girl? She is your sister?"

Nikalys eyed the stranger, filled with sudden suspicion. "How could you know that?"

"You look alike."

Deciding the answer was plausible, Nikalys started to nod, but stopped as his neck and back cried out. Holding very still, he answered, "Yes. She is my sister."

"Where are your parents?"

Nikalys glanced up at the odd question, hissing at the pain. "Pardon?"

The man's brown eyes bore into Nikalys. "Your parents, uori? Where are they?"

Nikalys dropped his gaze. Droplets of blood dripped from his hands onto the dirt below. "Dead."

Broedi was quiet long enough that Nikalys looked up, curious. He had thought he might get a bit of condolence. The large man's face was a mask of restrained sorrow and confusion.

"You are sure?" asked Broedi.

Irritated, Nikalys snapped, "I'm quite sure." He glanced over at Kenders. "Can we help her now?"

The Shapechanger looked to the fingerprick thicket and nodded. "Of course." He moved to the brambles, bent over Kenders, and pulled her free. After laying her on the rocky dirt, he kneeled beside her and began inspecting her scratches, cuts, and piercings. After a few moments, he placed one of his massive hands over Kenders' forehead and closed his eyes. His hand around her head looked like Nikalys' around an egg.

Worried, Nikalys asked, "What are you doing?"

"Ensuring she sleeps peacefully for now." After a few moments, he opened his eyes, and looked up to Nikalys. "Stay here, uori." He stood and moved across the camp to grab Nikalys' waterskins.

"You're leaving us here?" called out Nikalys. "What about the wolves?"

Broedi stopped, sniffed the air twice, and then said, "They are gone. You will be safe for now." With a few giant, loping strides, he strode from the glow of the fire and disappeared into the forest making nary a sound, leaving Nikalys staring in the dark after him.

For a brief moment, Nikalys considered grabbing Kenders and running. He took a step toward her and stopped at once, hissing in pain. He could barely move. There was no way he could carry her. Frowning, Nikalys let out a long, weary, pain-filled sigh. He had no choice but to wait for the Shapechanger to return. Grinding his teeth, Nikalys decided that he would take the man's help only as long as necessary.

Pushing past the agony, Nikalys moved to Kenders and sat beside her. She, like him, had countless scratches and dozens of puncture holes, some with broken-off thorns still in them. Despite her horrid condition, Kenders seemed to be sleeping peacefully, her breaths slow and deep.

Grimacing as he stretched his legs out, he muttered, "Lucky you."

While waiting for Broedi to return, he wiped the excess blood from Kenders' face, marveling at the fate Greya had handed him: his family was dead, his home gone, and his sister a mage. And now, he was at the mercy of another mage, a Shapechanger at that. A weary, worried sigh slipped from his lips. "Gods...what else could go wrong?" Using his shirtsleeve, he dabbed at a cut on Kenders' chin that would not stop bleeding. As he did, the Shapechanger's deep voice filled the quiet campsite.

"Do not worry. She will be well."

Startled, Nikalys looked up, the thorns in his neck cruelly reminding him of his own condition. Broedi stood on the opposite side of the clearing, holding two full waterskins. The giant had not made a sound during his return.

"How can you be sure?" asked Nikalys.

"She will because she must."

Nikalys' eyebrows drew together. "What does that mean?"

Broedi stared at him, but did not respond as he moved around the fire and crouched before Nikalys. "I will treat you first, uori."

"Stop calling me that. My name is Nikalys. And I can wait. Help her first."

Broedi glanced at Kenders. "She feels no pain. You do."

Nikalys shook his head. "No. Her first."

With a nod, Broedi said, "As you desire."

Turning his attention to Kenders, the Shapechanger used water to wash away blood and dirt, searching where thorns were stuck in flesh. Nikalys watched the ministrations closely to ensure Broedi was truly helping.

Once the wounds were wiped clean, Broedi placed his large hand over a hole on Kenders' arm where one of the thorns had broken off, its woody nub buried below the skin's surface. He glanced over at Nikalys seemingly to say something, but after pausing for a moment, he pressed his lips together and stared back down to Kenders. A couple heartbeats later, he pulled his hand back and turned it over. The thorn rested in Broedi's palm.

Nikalys gaped at him. "How in the Nine Hells did you do that?"

Broedi stared at him, dropped the thorn to the dirt, and remained silent.

Nikalys supposed the answer was obvious: more magic. More blasted magic.

Broedi continued tending to Kenders' wounds, removing one thorn after another, using magic to coax out the thorns that he could not pry free with thumb and forefinger. Throughout the entire ordeal, a scowl rested on Nikalys' face.

Once Broedi had removed all of the thorns, he retrieved his leather satchel from which he pulled a small pouch. After loosening the drawstring, he turned the pouch over and dumped a few sprigs of a dried, green plant covered with small white flowers into his hand. He ripped a bit off and rubbed it between his fingers. A bitter, crisp scent tickled Nikalys' nose.

Broedi opened Kenders' lips and placed the crushed plant in her mouth.

Concerned, Nikalys asked, "Wait…what is that?"

"Mesingervo." Broedi glanced up. "You might call it meadowsweet. It is to help blunt the headache she will have when she wakes."

Nikalys had no idea what meadowsweet was. It surely did not smell sweet.

Holding up her head a little, Broedi poured water into her mouth. Kenders choked a bit as she swallowed the plant and water, but remained asleep. Then,

Broedi laid her flat again and placed both of his hands on the center of her chest. The mammoth man sat that way for a few moments, not moving, eyes closed.

Nikalys was about to ask what Broedi was doing when he noticed the more superficial scratches on Kenders' skin begin to smooth over as new skin grew, sealing the cuts and scrapes. The more serious gashes and punctures diminished or faded, turning less red and angry but not healing completely. After a little while, the Shapechanger pulled his hands back, peered up to Nikalys, and sighed. "Now it is your turn, uori."

Nikalys eyed Broedi warily. The thought of having the Shapechanger use magic on him was not a pleasant one, but he could not travel in his current condition. He stared down at Kenders—she looked a hundred times better than a short while ago—then peered at his own bloody, thorn-strewn arms. After a long, drawn-out silence, he muttered, "Fine."

"Your arm, please."

Nikalys extended his right arm and endured the same inspection Kenders had undergone. When Broedi came across the first thorn that could not be removed by simply pulling it out, he placed his hand over the hole, and murmured, "This may feel strange."

Strange was a wholly inadequate term to describe what happened next. It felt like his flesh was pushing the thorn out while something else was gently tugging at it. A moment later, Broedi pulled back his hand, opened it, and dropped an inch-long thorn to the ground. As Nikalys stared at the bloody barb, an exclamation of quiet surprise slipped from his lips. "Huh."

Broedi resumed his examination wearing a slight smile. After a few more extractions, he glanced up at Nikalys. "This is unusual to you, then?"

Nikalys flinched as another thorn extruded itself. "If you mean Shapechangers, summoned lightning, and…" He nodded to the giant's hands over his arm. "Whatever you're doing here? Yes. This is 'unusual.' In fact, 'unusual' is too mild of a word."

Broedi frowned and turned his attention back to Nikalys' wounds. For as long as it took, Nikalys patiently tolerated Broedi's treatment. Neither of them said anything, although Broedi seemed on the verge of breaking the silence a number of times. Nikalys was glad he did not.

Once Broedi had removed all of the thorns, he rumbled, "Lie down now, please."

Nikalys complied and Broedi laid his hands on Nikalys' chest. A few moments later, a slight warming sensation filled his entire body. His heart began racing as though he had just run from one end of Yellow Mud to the other and back again. He watched in pure wonderment as the shallow scratches on his arms sealed and faded. Wounds that should have taken more than a week to heal were soon gone. The deep punctures closed, but were not fully healed when Broedi withdrew his hands.

The Shapechanger said softly, "The rest you do on your own."

Nikalys only managed to grunt in response. He was suddenly exhausted.

Broedi reached into his leather satchel and pulled out a cloth pouch, different from the first. Upon opening it, he withdrew a few green bundles that looked like small, soft pinecones. Selecting one, he handed it to Nikalys. "Place this in your cheek. Do not swallow it."

Nikalys stared at the herb and muttered, "Why?"

"It will help you sleep better."

Fighting back a yawn, Nikalys said, "I don't want to sleep." He was not about to pass out now, leaving himself and his sister helpless.

"Take it. Please."

Nikalys glared at the giant, frowning and fighting off another yawn. "No."

Broedi let out a long sigh. "Uori, if my intentions were to harm you, I would have done so already. I am here to help you. Truly."

Nikalys stared into Broedi's eyes, searching for deceit. Seeing none, he reluctantly took the small pinecone and jammed it between his gum and cheek. Twisting his face in disgust, he said, "Gods, that tastes awful."

"Its taste is irrelevant," rumbled Broedi. "Now, please, sleep. I will watch over you both."

Nikalys dropped his head back and closed his eyes, intending to pretend he was asleep.

Within moments, he was snoring.

CHAPTER 12: ROAD

10th of the Turn of Sutri, 4999

The dust cloud kicked up by the wagon train stuck in Jak's eyes and coated his tongue, crunching between his teeth. Jak tried to draw spit to clear his mouth but failed, forcing him to take a sip from his nearly empty waterskin. He sloshed the water around, turned his head, and spat it on the road.

Six wagons rattled past him, varying in size from a small, two-wheeled cocking cart with a single horse to a four-wheeled carriage pulled by a team of bays. Crates and barrels filled every wagon, the sides of which bore faded green script letters spelling out *Southern Porters Company*. Not a single man glanced in Jak's direction as they rattled past.

Under his breath, Jak mumbled, "Blasted Porters."

The Southern Porters Company had a reputation for being dependable but ruthless. The merchants who contracted them to transport goods were happy to pay the Porters' high fees as the company always delivered on schedule. The Porters' competitors had fewer kind things to say about them. None, in fact.

On Jak's last trip to Smithshill with his father and brother, in the inn where they were staying the night, he had sat at a table with a group of men from a rival company. A local merchant had just awarded a large contract choosing the Porters over Hayle and Sons. Bitter and drunk, the men were happy to share tales of the Porters.

One in particular was when men from both companies had stayed overnight at the same crossroads inn. Overnight, all of the Hayle horses came down with colic, yet, not a single Porters' horse took ill. As the Porters drove off the next morning, they laughed uproariously at the "misfortune" of the Hayle men.

During the Isaacs' return journey to Yellow Mud, Jak went on about the Porters' wickedness. At one point, his father had interrupted him, cautioning Jak—and Nikalys—not to rush to judgment, to question words spoken by the slighted. Jak knew his father was right, but had already formed his opinion of the Porters, and opinions were often no match for logic and careful thought.

As the last wagon rolled past, rattling and bouncing along the rutted road, Jak stared after it hoping the jostling would dislodge a crate or barrel. Yet by the time the carts rounded a bend, slipping back into the forest, nothing had fallen off.

Jak's frown deepened. "Well…Hells." Letting out a disappointed sigh, he turned east and resumed plodding down the road. The occasional weak chirp of one bird or another flitted through the quiet forest.

The sun was high in the sky, hot and glaring, seemingly intent on roasting Jak. The simple head covering he wore—made from a rag he had scavenged yesterday—was soaked through with sweat but Jak was too tired to wring it out. If sweat dripped into his eyes, so be it. Whenever the Southern Road turned north or south for a stretch, Jak rejoiced, welcoming the brief respite of shade provided by the oaks lining the roadside.

After escaping the barrel yesterday, he had washed himself off as best he could—he had reeked of ale, after all—and made his way south, searching only the bodies that were lying face down. He had collected additional coin, a large waterskin, a rucksack, and a spare change of clothes hanging from a bush. His prize find had been an unstrung ash bow, arrows, and dry sinew sealed inside a watertight case. The case was strapped to his back now, next to the leather package his father had given him.

"One foot in front of the other," muttered Jak, ordering his body to keep going. "One blasted foot in front of the other." He received and unexpected response in the form of a stomach grumble. He glanced down. "Quiet, you."

He had skipped morningmeal the day of the attack planning to catch and eat a few halock at the lake later. When roasted with just a little salt and hillsage, the fish turned into a delectable, flaky, white treat. At the thought of food, Jak's stomach rumbled even louder. He frowned, knowing that if he did not find sustenance today, he would grow weak and his pursuit would slow. And he could not slow down. Not now. He needed to find his brother and sister.

Last night, as he sat against a tree trunk in the dark, he had used the teardrop pendant to check on Nikalys and Kenders. Expecting the same calming feeling to which he had already grown accustomed, he instead was shocked when countless pricks of pain danced along his neck, back, and arms, ripping the breath from his lungs. Releasing the pendant, he had pulled back his shirtsleeves, inspected his arms, and found nothing.

Bracing himself, he had grasped the silver teardrop again and focused on their faces, ignoring the pain. The muted ringing was still east and noticeably louder than before. He figured that meant he was closer. Worried that something might have happened to them, he had gotten up and continued walking in the dark, despite his weariness. He had traveled most of the night, taking only short breaks when he was afraid he might topple over.

While his waterskin was almost empty, Jak was not worried. For the last five harvests, he had traveled with his father to Smithshill so he knew the road well. There was a bridge running over a creek not too far ahead.

When Jak had been young, Thaddeus had always spoken as though the excursion to Smithshill was a terrible chore, going on about how much work was involved. When Jak was thirteen, he was allowed to go along for the very first time. After dreading the journey for weeks ahead of time, Jak soon discovered his father's lamenting was nothing more than a ruse, a jest he had been setting up for years to play on Jak. The actual four-day ride to Smithshill had been quiet and relaxing, a welcome relief from Jak's normal duties in Yellow Mud. His only task during the trip was to shoo the bodflies that tried to land on the crates.

When they had arrived in Fallsbottom—the lower section of the dual city—he had been further surprised as the men at the delivery point unloaded the crates while Jak and Thaddeus watched. He could still remember the smile and wink his father had given him as the men hauled away the grapes and olives. That evening, father and son had enjoyed a large meal and played knuckles with the locals.

When Jak returned home, he, too, had talked up the difficulties of the trip to Nikalys. Then, two years later, he had delighted in watching Nikalys go through the same series of revelations he had. To this day, Kenders still thought their trip was an onerous task.

So lost was he in happy memories, Jak did not hear the sound of a wagon approaching from ahead until the rattle was impossible to ignore.

Looking up, Jak spotted a pair of horses pulling a small, four-wheeled cart driven by a lone man. Bandit crimes were rare in the Great Lakes Duchy, making it commonplace for people to travel the Southern Road alone. Even so, brigands were not nonexistent, which explained why the man in the wagon pulled his horses to a stop upon spotting Jak and scanned the forest and edges of the road.

For the briefest of moments, Jak had the inkling to scream out "To arms, brothers!" and charge the man. As the reality of his current situation kicked in he sighed and muttered, "Too much sun, Jak…" Instead of launching a one-man bandit assault, he held up his arms and called out, "Good days ahead!"

The cart's driver hesitated and, after taking one last glance at the trees lining the road, snapped his reins, urging the horses closer. Wearing a blue shirt and yellow straw hat, the man appeared to be the same age as Jak's father and wore a beard, a fashion favored by Southlanders. Summers in the Great Lakes Duchy were much too hot to have hair covering one's face. Stepping to the roadside to allow the horses and cart to stop, Jak reached up to his chin and felt some fledgling stubble. He needed to get a razor when he could.

Once halted, the man stared down at Jak, still wary, and nodded once. "Good memories behind, traveler." His gaze left Jak, darting to every tree, large rock and bush nearby. "Don't see too many people traveling alone out here.

Besides me, that is." His slight accent confirmed Jak's suspicion the man was a Southlander; his "oh" sounds came out more like "ew."

"Relax, good man," said Jak reassuringly. "I'm no bandit."

"That's something a bandit might say."

Lifting a hand to his brow to shield his eyes from the sun's glare, Jak peered up at the man. "Trust me, stranger. Look." He lifted his other arm to give the man a clear look at his belt. "No sword. No knife."

The man nodded to the bow casing on Jak's back. "An arrow in the heart is as deadly as any blade."

Jak glanced over his shoulder. "Ah...well, I suppose you have me there." He looked back to the man and smiled. "I'm a rather poor shot, though. When deer see me coming, they lie down and take a nap."

The man continued to study him. "So you say."

Jak could claim he was not a bandit all day long and the man might never believe him. Rather than tell, he would have to show. "I do thank you for stopping, sir. Most people would not."

"If you are not a bandit, then they are ruder than I. However, if you *are* a brigand, then I am a fool."

Jak grinned wide. "At least you'd be a polite fool."

The jest brought a smile to the man's face and he visibly relaxed, his shoulders slumping a bit. He leaned back in his seat, looped the reins around a wooden peg, and rested his hands in his lap. "The name's Ropert, Ropert Paulson. From Hollowstone."

Jak nodded as if he knew where Hollowstone was. He did not. "I'm Jak. Jak Isaac of Yellow Mud."

The moment the words tumbled from his lips, he wished he could grab them and stuff them back into his mouth. Sharing his name and home was a sour idea. Word of what had happened in Yellow Mud was bound to spread. Jak had concluded the attack had been magical in nature and doubted the perpetrators would be happy to hear some had survived their treachery.

Pushing past the moment, hoping Ropert might not care or remember his name, Jak quickly asked, "Have I convinced you I'm no brigand?"

Ropert smiled. "Any respectable bandit would have sprung the trap by now. So, Jak Isaac of Yellow Mud—" Jak winced inwardly "—for what reason have you waved down an honest trader?"

Jak stared at Ropert, caught off guard by the question. He had kept such a singular focus, to stay alive and to find his brother and sister, that he had never considered coming up with a plausible story for just such an occasion. "Well...you see, I..."

Ropert's eyes narrowed a fraction, his earlier suspicion returning for a repeat performance.

Using the moment's hesitation to his advantage, Jak mumbled, "Truth be told, it's a rather embarrassing story." Jak launched into a false tale about how he had argued with his father, how he was tired of rural farm life and wanted to make his fortune in the city. After a nasty shouting match, he had left in the dead of night but had not been thinking clearly, forgetting to bring proper supplies—namely food. However, he did have some coin with him, and would be happy to buy something to eat from Ropert if he could spare some.

As he finished his yarn, Ropert leaned forward, the wooden carriage seat creaking. "Son, I'll be happy to sell you a bite to eat. But my price isn't a few copper ducats."

Jak was hungry, but if this man was going to charge him silver for a meal, Ropert was the highwayman. "Sir, I don't have much to spare. I could only—"

"No," interrupted Ropert, shaking his head. "I don't want coin. The going rate for a young man in your position is to listen to some advice from a father with two sons himself." With a hard glint in his eye, he said, "Jak, if you don't want to be a farmer, so be it. But leaving things the way you did with your father will haunt you. Go back and talk it out with him. If he's any sort of a man, he'll respect your decision. If not, well, then you're a better sort than him and you can live your life free of regret."

Ropert's words caught Jak off guard. He stared at the Southlander and, for the first time since leaving his parents standing in the middle of Yellow Mud, truly felt the permanence of their absence.

His mother and father were gone. Forever.

Jak spent a few moments gawking at Ropert before finding his tongue and mumbling, "Thank you, sir…"

Ropert nodded once and then turned to reach into a compartment on the back of his seat. After pulling out a small parcel wrapped in a light tan cloth, he tossed it down. "There's some salted Southlands boar side. Best in the duchies. Enough to tide you over for a few days."

"Thank you," murmured Jak. "I appreciate the generosity."

"Your thanks are welcome but unnecessary." Ropert stared west, down the way from Jak had come. "I need to be going, Jak. Have to get my yellowberries to Redstone before they're brown berries." He looked back to Jak and cocked an eyebrow. "If you'd like, I can give you a ride."

Jak knew the Southlander was offering him the chance to reconcile with his father. Shaking his head, he replied, "There's nothing for me back there…"

Minor disappointment flickered over Ropert's bearded face, but he smiled anyway. "One day, you'll feel differently, Jak Isaac of Yellow Mud. And when that happens, I expect your father will welcome you back with open arms. Nothing can trump the love a parent has for a child. *Nothing.*"

Jak nodded, but stayed silent, afraid that his voice would crack if he responded. He prayed Ropert could not see the tears pooling in the corners of his eyes.

Ropert said his goodbye and with a snap of the reins, drove the horses into a quick trot. Jak faced east and started walking, shoving the package of dried meat into his sack. He was no longer hungry.

* * *

The remainder of the afternoon was uneventful.

Later in the day, after his sorrow had passed somewhat, he pulled the boar meat from his sack and ate a good portion. The saltiness of the dried meat made him extremely thirsty, but he drank his fill of water at a creek and filled his waterskin.

Jak encountered other travelers as he walked and kept his head down every time. Beyond the meal, the advice, and sad memories gained from his meeting with Ropert, he had learned to be careful of what he said.

Twice more, he checked the teardrop pendant. Both times, he found he was closer to his brother and sister. He was happy that was the case, yet was puzzled how he could be making up so much ground. In addition, each time he checked, the painful prickling sensation lessened. Jak hoped that was a good thing.

Tired though he was, Jak walked into the early evening and was considering marching through the night again. There would be plenty of light as White Moon was nearly full. However, a few wolf howls made him think he should stop and build a campfire. According to Nikalys, the flames would keep wolves away.

Mu's orb had just dipped below the western treetops behind him when Jak caught a whiff of wood smoke. His next breath brought with it the inviting aroma of something savory and meaty cooking. Upon rounding the next bend in the road, he spotted a large camp of men in a meadow and instantly stopped short. "Uh-oh."

Canvas tents were perched on both sides of the road with little black and red pennants hanging from their peaks. Eight campfires roared, five on the left and three on the right. A few dozen horses were lined up, picketed and trying to eat what little green grass they could find.

The men were all dressed the same: red undershirts, black tabards that fell halfway to their knees, and dark gray cloth pants tucked into calf-high, black leather boots. From his trips to Smithshill, Jak recognized the soldiers as Red Sentinels, the army of the Great Lakes Duchy. Were he any closer, he would see Duke Everett's crest on the right breast: a red sword crossing a white and black quartered shield. Random bits of evening sunlight filtering through the trees glinted off the rounded silver helms atop some of the men's heads.

Jak stood in the road, wondering if he should attempt to pass through the soldiers' camp or retrace his steps, go off path, and travel through the woods to avoid their scrutiny. A commanding shout made his choice for him.

"Hold!"

Two of the soldiers were already striding toward him, both with their hands resting on their sword hilts.

Jak whispered, "Hells." Running seemed like a bad idea, so he instead forced a friendly, almost goofy smile on his face and stepped forward, stopping two paces later when the soldier on the right shouted at him.

"I said, 'hold!' That means you are *not* to move!"

Jak halted, put up his hand indicating he understood, and waited. The soldiers stopped in the middle of the road, fifteen paces away, and studied him. Jak reciprocated. The man on his right looked exhausted, scraggly blond hair sticking out from underneath his helm, matted with sweat and grime. The other soldier appeared much more alert, his dark eyes sharp and peering over a long, hooked nose.

Thickening what little rural accent he had, Jak said, "Good days ahead, good sirs."

The tired solider spoke, his voice flat and uninterested. "State your business, traveler."

"Headed to Killis Post, good sirs," said Jak, giving the name painted on a sign at a turnoff a day east from here. "My father sent me to pick up some things from there."

"By yourself?" asked the more alert man. "With no cart?" The other guard stared up into a tree and yawned. Perhaps he was bored, not tired.

Jak shrugged his shoulders and lied. "We're too poor for a cart, good sirs."

"Stop calling us that," said the alert man.

The bored soldier spoke up. "Speak for yourself, Holb." He looked to Jak, a smug smile on his face. "You may call me 'sir.'"

Turning to his companion, the man called Holb said, "As long as you are wearing that uniform, *Footman* Haynes, you will call me Corporal Holb. And nobody will call you 'sir.' or anything of the like. Do you understand?"

Footman Haynes glared at Corporal Holb for a long moment, the resentment in his eyes clear, before answering through gritted teeth. "Understood."

Corporal Holb continued staring at the soldier, seemingly waiting for something. After a few tense moments, Footman Hayne's eyes narrowed. "Understood, *Corporal*."

At once, the corporal turned back to Jak. "So, what are you buying in Smithshill?"

Jak smiled on the inside, proud of himself for recognizing that the soldier was trying to catch him in his lie. "Not Smithshill. Killis Post."

"Ah, yes," muttered the soldier. "My mistake" He studied Jak's dirty clothes, the sack he carried, and the packages strapped to his back. "What's your name, friend?"

Without hesitating, Jak answered, "Edward. Edward Hardtak." He had worked on the false name for some time. He liked it.

"Fine, Edward Hardtak, I'd appreciate it if you would accompany us back to camp."

Jak bit down hard and put on a smile he did not feel. "Of course."

Corporal Holb glanced at the footman. "You lead."

Footman Haynes scowled at the corporal, but still turned and began walking back to camp.

"You next, Edward," said the corporal.

Jak fell in behind Footman Haynes, wondering what about his story had led the soldier to bring him into camp. As they strode between the tents, an uneasy Jak looked around with legitimate curiosity.

Every soldier was busy doing something. Some tended to the horses, checking hooves, rubbing them down, or feeding them what smelled like sweet oats in cloth bags hooked over each horse's head. A handful of men were skinning and dressing a deer, apparently planning to roast the animal. Two groups of soldiers patrolled the northern and southern rim of the clearing. Jak eyed them, wondering why they were bothering. There had been no war in the Oaken Duchies for well over two centuries. The worst threat the soldiers might face was a squirrel and rabbit invasion.

Hearing the repeated clang of metal, Jak looked over and spotted a dozen soldiers in the midst of practicing with their swords. He slowed his pace a bit, fascinated by the swordplay. He was disappointed when they fell out of view, hidden behind a line of tents.

At one point, Corporal Holb moved past Jak and took the lead from his partner, snorting with impatience at Footman Hayne's leisurely pace. He glanced at Jak as he passed. "Don't try to run."

Jak shook his head, happy to show that he, Edward Hardtak, was quite sensible and would never do such a thing.

Corporal Holb led them to a group of three men standing in front of a tent. As the trio was engaged in a quiet discussion, the corporal halted a dozen paces away and waited. Jak took the opportunity to study the three soldiers.

The two younger men—not much older than Jak himself—held their helmets under their arms and listened with interest to everything the third was saying. The older man stood a couple inches over six feet, had long, dark brown hair pulled back in a single bunch and held in place by a thick, red leather band. Like Ropert, he had a thick growth of brown hair on his face that was bushy yet meticulously trimmed. Jak estimated him to be in his late thirties, perhaps older, yet young looking the way that some people are blessed. He was strong and stout, his wide shoulders filling out his uniform where a pair of white symbols was sewn: a square and a diamond. Curious, Jak looked at Corporal Holb's uniform and noticed a single white circle on each shoulder. Footman Haynes had nothing besides the sword and shield emblem of Duke Everett.

Not long after Jak arrived, the bearded man dismissed the two younger soldiers who then put on their helmets and headed away, into the camp. Jak watched them go, envying them.

"Let's go, *Edward*," muttered Corporal Holb. The sarcastic twist he added to Jak's false name was worrisome.

Nevertheless, Jak kept his grin wide. "Yes, sir."

As the three strode forward, the man obviously in charge turned toward them and looked Jak over, taking in every detail, scrutinizing and evaluating.

The few days' growth of a pitiful, wispy beard.

The bow case.

The leather package from his father.

The dirty work clothes.

The sweaty rag on his head.

The satchel and waterskin.

After a few moments, he said, "Corporal." The single, crisp word was a greeting, a question, and an order all in one.

"We spotted him coming from the west," said Corporal Holb. "Your orders were to bring any travelers that seemed out of the ordinary to you."

"Those were my orders," mused the man. "Did you get his name?"

"He says it is Edward Hardtak."

"Edward Hardtak, huh?" The man's gaze danced over Jak a second time.

"Sir, yes, sir," said Jak. "On my way to Killis Post, sir. To get supplies for my—"

Footman Haynes took a sudden step forward, interrupting Jak. "Look, this is a waste of time. He's just some brainless farmer wandering the roads. Let him go so I can get something to eat."

Jak sensed Corporal Holb stiffen as, for the first time since Jak had arrived, the bearded man even acknowledged Haynes' existence. The expression on his face changed in an instant, going from amused curiosity to restrained tolerance. "You now get to eat after everyone else is done."

"But I'll get the bottom of the pot!" protested the footman. "I won't eat that crusty muck."

"You will if you're hungry enough."

Footman Haynes glared at the bearded soldier. "My father—"

The soldier took a quick step forward, interrupting the footman. "Is not here at the moment, *footman. I* am." He jerked his chin westward. "Go. Return to your post." When the footman did not move, the bearded man's voice grew firmer still. "*Now.*"

Footman Haynes spun around and tromped west, heading back to where he and Corporal Holb had been guarding the road. As he skulked away, Jak caught the corporal muttering something about a "useless, spoiled noble's broodling."

The bearded soldier's gaze shifted back to Jak and immediately softened. "So, then. Headed to Killis Post, are you?"

Jak grinned even wider, committing to his lie. Nodding his head up and down, he said, "Yes, sir. That's right. My father sent me to buy supplies."

The soldier's gaze bored into him. "What sort of supplies?"

Jak's smile slipped a fraction. "Pardon?"

"Your father sent you to buy supplies. What's on his list, son?"

Jak shifted from one foot to another, uneasy, as the man's eyes picked him apart. He had not worked out this detail. "Well, sir, I...don't—"

Keeping his eyes on Jak, the bearded soldier interrupted him, asking, "Corporal, what bothers you about young farmer Hardtak here?"

Jak glanced at the corporal, wondering at his misfortune. The Red Sentinels he had seen in Smithshill had seemed lazy and dull-witted. Somehow, he had managed to stumble upon one of the few groups of capable soldiers in the duchy.

"Well, Sergeant," began Corporal Holb. He stared at Jak, shrugged his shoulders. "Let's just say that if he were a playman, he would not be a successful one."

The tiniest hint of a smile touched the sergeant's lips. "Thank you, Amiles. You are dismissed. Go tell Lord Haynes's son that I have changed my mind about his assignment. I want him to do five sweeps of the northern glades. Alone. Then he can eat."

"It'll be dark before he gets done," said the corporal with his own slight smile.

"A shame, isn't it?" asked the sergeant. "Go, Amiles. I'd like to speak with young Edward for a moment."

The corporal gave Jak one last look before heading west, following Hayne's path. Jak watched him leave, again wishing he were the one walking away. As he stared, the sergeant approached Jak and stopped several paces away. Jak looked back to the sergeant and waited, wondering what might happen to him.

"You aren't going to Killis Post, are you?"

Jak did his best to feign confusion. "Yes, sir, I am. I just couldn't remember what—"

"Two things, son," interrupted the soldier. "First, call me Sergeant Trell or Master Sergeant. Not 'sir.' That title is reserved for men wiser than I. Or people like Haynes who happened to be born to the right parents and need to be constantly reminded how important they are."

Jak smothered a grin.

"Second, end the show. Amiles said it perfectly: you are an absolutely awful playman. And should that be your true profession, I would kindly suggest a reevaluation of your life's goals."

Deciding that it was pointless to continue with the act, Jak sighed and said, "Thank you, Sergeant. I'll take that under advisement."

Sergeant Trell nodded. "Good. Now, one look tells me you are no brigand, no danger to anyone traveling the Southern Road. Why you felt the need to try to swindle your way past us is your business, young man, not mine. I'm tasked with keeping the roads safe for travel, not free of atrocious playmen pretending to be farmers."

Jak let out the giant sigh of relief. "Yes, Sergeant Trell. My apologies."

The man continued to look long and hard at Jak. "What's your real name, son?"

Jak considered giving a new made-up name, but decided Sergeant Trell deserved the truth for treating him so honestly. Moreover, Jak was afraid the soldier might see through his second fake name and rescind the pardon he seemed poised to grant. "Jak Isaac."

"And from where do you hail, Jak?"

Jak sighed before answering, "Yellow Mud."

"Well, Jak Isaac from Yellow Mud, stop by the cookfire and grab a bowl of whatever they're serving tonight. Smells like rabbit stew to me. And be sure to scoop from the top. Haynes was right; the bottom turns to sludge. Also, if you'd like, you are welcome to stay with the camp this evening. In fact, I recommend it. I heard wolves in the hills today."

"Thank you," replied Jak politely. "That is very agreeable of you. Both concerning the meal, as well the offer of a safe night's sleep. While I welcome the former, I must turn down the latter."

Sergeant Trell cocked his head then shrugged his shoulders. "Your choice. Ketus be with you on the roads, son."

"Thank you, Sergeant," said Jak, grateful for the good-luck wish.

The sergeant studied Jak one last time before turning his back and walking away, toward a group of soldiers. After a few steps, he called over his shoulder, "Good days ahead, Jak Isaac!"

"And good memories behind, Sergeant Trell!"

Jak stood in place for a moment, full of relief mixed with chagrin. Since leaving Yellow Mud, he had spoken at length to but two people and on both occasions had shared his true name and that of his home. If he had some paint and a board, he could make and carry a sign proclaiming "Jak Isaac of Yellow Mud" to save time.

With the immediate crisis averted, Jak's stomach took the opportunity to remind him that he was hungry. Following the stew's aroma through camp, he went looking for the cook fire and his promised eveningmeal. A quick glance at the sky revealed he still had some daylight in which he could put some distance between himself and the Red Sentinels' camp. Should anyone else come from the west carrying tales of Yellow Mud's fate, Sergeant Trell—a smart soul for sure—would want to speak at length with Jak.

Jak peered eastward, down the Southern Road, anxious to be on his way. He needed to find his brother and sister.

* * *

Ropert sat atop his driver's bench, staring into what he assumed had been the village of Yellow Mud. "Gods…"

A small breeze stirred the still air around his cart, forcing Ropert to cover his mouth and stifle a gag as the stench of death filled his nose. Both horses whinnied and pranced, as disturbed by the odor as he was.

He pulled on the reins, muttering through his hand, "Whoa, girls. Whoa…"

After one last glance at the destruction, he turned the wagon around and headed back down the road on which he had just come.

When he had seen the sign for Yellow Mud on the side of the Southern Road, he made a snap decision. If one of his own sons had run from home as young Jak had, Ropert would want to know he was safe. He had turned down the way to Yellow Mud, hoping to find Jak's father. The yellowberries were still green; his delivery to Redstone could wait a day.

Now, as he whipped the horses, driving them twice as fast as he had on the way to town, his wagon bounced and rattled along the uneven road. He knew he should slow down else risk a broken axel, but he wanted to put Yellow Mud far behind him.

Whatever heartless catastrophe had happened back there, it seemed impossible to deny that magic had something to do with the devastation. He had to get to Redstone as quickly as possible. The Constables needed to know what he had seen here.

As he snapped the reins, studying the oaks and ashes around him with a cautious eye, the image of the beaten-down Jak Isaac flashed through his head.

Ropert prayed the young man had nothing to do with this. He shuddered and snapped the reins again, spurring the horses to run faster.

CHAPTER 13: TRUST

A chill was in the air, something wholly unexpected for a summer night in the Great Lakes Duchy. Shivering, Nikalys rose from the ground and shuffled to a small woodpile, intent on retrieving another log to add to the fire. As he started to bend over, a series of sharp pains shot up his back and neck and he stood upright immediately, wincing through a sharp intake of breath. He tried again, ignoring the pain, gathered a log, and dropped it on the fire, sending a flurry of glowing orange embers into the air.

A deep voice rumbled through the clearing, gently chastising him. "Be careful, uori. You are still recovering."

Nikalys looked over at the giant man.

Broedi sat on the ground, smoking a long, white pipe, the first of its kind Nikalys had ever seen. The pipes used in Yellow Mud were short and wooden whose function trumped form. However, the ornate creation Broedi held was as much a work of art as it was a smoking-leaf pipe. Engravings of animals, leaves, and trees lined the sides of the pipe that, to Nikalys' eye, appeared to be made of bone. He had tried puzzling out to what type of animal it might have belonged, but had so far failed. He simply prayed it was from an animal.

"Yet again, my name is Nikalys, not 'uori.' Why do you keep calling me that?"

The Shapechanger eyed him for a long moment before replying. "It is a word my kind uses that means…" He hesitated a moment, pensive, before saying, "Young one."

Lifting an eyebrow, Nikalys said, "A word 'your kind' uses?"

"Yes. 'My kind.'"

"And what 'kind' is that?"

The Shapechanger stared at Nikalys, puffed on his bone pipe twice, and then lifted his gaze to the night sky.

Nikalys knew no answer was forthcoming. Their savior was a man of maddeningly few words. He had pressed Broedi at length about a number of things, but the giant's responses were always short and uninformative. Eventually, Nikalys had clamped his own mouth shut, stubbornly deciding he would match the man's reticence.

Shaking his head, Nikalys moved back to where Kenders slept and— wincing again—sat beside her. After checking that she was sleeping peacefully, he laid his head back against the trunk of an oak tree and shut his eyes.

"You should sleep, uori. You are tired."

Nikalys opened his eyes and stared across the fire. "Pardon?"

Broedi pointed the bit of the bone pipe at him. "I said you should sleep." He looked to Kenders. "You must be alert when she wakes. You have a long journey ahead of you."

Nikalys' eyebrows narrowed. "You have no idea what we have ahead of us."

Again, Broedi peered at Nikalys for a long moment before slipping the tip of the pipe between his teeth and returning to his study of the stars.

Frustrated, Nikalys glared at the Shapechanger and muttered, "Blasted know-everything." The words were quiet enough that Broedi should not have heard. Nevertheless, the giant glanced back at him, the corners of his mouth upturned slightly.

Nikalys seethed in silence. This exchange was like every other the pair had shared today: ending with him upset and Broedi infuriatingly calm.

When Nikalys had awakened earlier, Mu's orb had already crossed halfway across the sky. The soft, green pinecone that Broedi had given him last night had turned into a mushy, gritty mess stuck between his cheek and gum. After sitting up and spitting it out, Nikalys had smacked his lips while grimacing; his mouth tasted like bad ale.

Nikalys had found Broedi in the same position he was now: relaxed against a tree, staring at them through the smoke curling from his pipe bowl. Broedi's lone acknowledgement that Nikalys was awake had been a silent, stoic nod.

Upon checking Kenders, Nikalys had been stunned by her vastly improved condition. Only the particularly grievous wounds remained while everything else had healed. Upon inspecting his own body, he had found that he was in the same shape.

Broedi had cleared his throat, drawing Nikalys' attention, and pointed in the direction of the fire where a veritable feast—three small rabbits and two quail—was roasting over the flames. Ravenous, Nikalys set to eating and, before he knew it, had consumed both of the tiny quail and two of the rabbits.

He happened to look over at Kenders as he was wiping the juices from his mouth, and immediately felt guilty for not leaving much of anything for her. Broedi finally spoke at that point, assuring Nikalys that he would hunt for more. That being the case, Nikalys had finished off the remaining rabbit. Broedi had left a short time later—giving Nikalys time to change from his bloody clothes—and had returned as evening fell with more rabbits and quail. The giant had not taken a sling or any other weapon with him, but then again, Nikalys suspected Broedi did not use such tools to hunt.

Nikalys had prepared the rabbits and quail, set them to roasting over the fire, and then sat down. More than a few times, he had braved a close inspection of Broedi, his gaze repeatedly returning to the white stone lion pendant hanging from the Shapechanger's neck. Something about the white lion was intimately familiar, yet he could never place why he felt that way. He strained to remember, but it was like trying to remember a dream from last year.

With a heavy sigh, he now stood to check once more on the roasting game and found the meat nearly over-cooked. He had wanted to keep the rabbits and quail warm for Kenders, but if he did not remove them now, she would be gnawing on blackened, charred lumps.

As he pulled the sticks from the ground, he felt Broedi's eyes on him, observing. He tried to ignore the man's gaze, but Broedi's constant, silent watching was growing increasingly irritating. Standing there, with skewers in his hand, Nikalys glared at the man, unable to hold his tongue any longer. "At least tell me this: you're a Shapechanger, aren't you?"

Broedi pulled his pipe from his mouth, parted his lips, and let a long curl of gray smoke drift out, all the while peering at Nikalys. "Are you asking if I am someone who has spent so much time with nature that I have somehow become a part of it? Whether I've given my soul over to Lamoth to help guard her forests?"

Nikalys nodded slowly, unsure that he wanted an answer now.

A slight smile touched Broedi's lips. "No, uori. I am not that."

Exasperated, Nikalys asked, "Then what are you? *Who* are you? And as long I'm asking questions I know you won't answer, what were you doing in the middle of the forest last night?"

In a calm, deep baritone, Broedi rumbled, "I could ask *you* the same thing."

"I asked first," shot back Nikalys.

Broedi nodded slowly, his eyes narrowing as he shifted his gaze to Kenders. "I will answer your questions when she wakes."

"Why not now?"

Broedi stared at him, stoic. "Patience, uori."

Nikalys pressed his lips together and shook his head in disgust. Upon returning to Kenders' side, he jammed the skewers into the ground and sat next to his sister, purposely putting his back to Broedi. He stared at Kenders' sleeping face, wishing she would wake up so they could be on their way. A lock of her golden hair had fallen across her lips that, with each breath, she drew into her mouth before blowing them again. Reaching down, Nikalys brushed the stray hair aside.

"You care very much for your iskoa," rumbled Broedi. "That is good."

Nikalys looked over his shoulder. "Iskoa?"

"It means 'sister.'"

Nikalys nodded and looked back to Kenders. "Of course I care for her. She's all I have left."

"I would like it if you shared some of your story, uori."

A sly, sardonic smile spread over Nikalys' face. Again, he half-turned to examine Broedi. "You want my story?"

Broedi nodded. "Very much so."

With narrowed eyes, Nikalys said slowly and with purpose, "I will answer your questions when she wakes."

Broedi's faint smile returned, carrying with it a sense of familiarity that made little sense. With an accommodating nod, he said, "As you desire."

Nikalys swiveled around to face Kenders. He was done with Broedi.

CHAPTER 14: WEAVER

Kenders now knew what a nail felt like when struck by a woodworker's hammer.

She lay on her left side, stretched out on uneven, rocky ground with something soft under her head. She cracked open her right eye, caught the flickering campfire a few paces from her, and immediately squeezed her eyelid tight. The light made her head pound even more. She attempted to speak, but all that came out was a low groan.

Behind her, someone scurried close, kicking up what sounded like leaves and rocks. Feeling a light touch on her right shoulder a moment later, Nikalys whispered with evident concern, "Kenders?"

"Mm-hmm?"

Keeping his voice soft, he asked, "How are you feeling?"

She was ever so grateful he was whispering. The fire's cracking and popping was already too thunderous for her liking. It took her a moment to respond, but she managed to scratch out, "What happened?"

Another voice—a composed, deep baritone—rumbled, "Give her a moment, uori."

Confused, she opened her eyes, but only halfway to keep the jabbing firelight at bay. It was still nighttime, but the air was much cooler than she had remembered it being when the lynx had arrived.

She wanted to sit and see the owner of the deep voice, but her head vehemently protested against the proposed movement. Through lips that felt thick and wooden, she managed to eke out a question. "Is the cat gone?"

After an unusually long pause, Nikalys answered, "In a manner of speaking."

The baritone voice reverberated again, relaying instructions. "Uori, get her some water, please. I will get some more meadowsweet for her. Perhaps a larger dose, this time."

Kenders shut her eyes again, wondering both what meadowsweet was and what the man meant by 'this time.'

She listened as Nikalys stood and hurried from her, dirt, leaves, and stone crunching beneath his boots. The owner of the baritone voice also moved about the campsite with long, almost silent steps. Nikalys retrieved the waterskins and started moving back to her. Upon hearing the sloshing of the water, she realized how thirsty she was.

The stranger sounded as if he were rummaging through a bag or satchel. After a small grunt of satisfaction, he tossed the bag to the ground and approached where she lay. The pair arrived at the same time and the man rumbled, "I think it wise if you give this to her, uori."

Hearing the unusual word again, Kenders wondered if a third person was here.

Kneeling beside her, Nikalys asked, "Do you think you can sit? I have some water for you. And herbs. Broedi says they help with the headache."

While she was grateful that something might stop the thudding inside her head, she was a little anxious as to exactly who this Broedi was. "I'll need some help."

Nikalys slipped his hands under her and helped prop her against a tree trunk, still with her eyes shut. Once situated, he placed the waterskin in her hands and she raised it to her mouth. The first sip was glorious. She tipped the skin back and drank gulp after gulp, relishing the wetness soaking her scratchy throat.

The deep voice cautioned, "Slow down, uora."

"Yeah," agreed Nikalys. "Take it easy. Your stomach may not take too kindly to so much water at once. You've been asleep for nearly a day."

With that revelation, she stopped drinking, lowered the waterskin to her lap, and opened her eyes, squinting against the brightness. Nikalys was crouched beside her on her left, a concerned expression on his face. Small red marks covered his face, neck, and arms.

"Asleep for *a day*? How in the—" She cut off as her gaze drifted right. A pair of thick, muscular legs stood before her. Her gaze traveled upwards to sienna-brown hide breeches that started just above the knees. Further up was a wide chest with two bulging arms crossed over it. Her stare lingered on a white stone lion pendant that hung around the man's neck before continuing to the stranger's face. "Oh my…"

The man who towered over her had to be at least seven feet tall with golden-brown hair and sun-bronzed skin. He peered down at her, his brown-eyed gaze so intense, it was if he were trying to see inside her. She stared into those eyes, curious why it felt as though she had done so before.

"Good days ahead, uora," rumbled the giant. "My name is Broedi."

Her mouth hanging open, Kenders managed a quiet and impolite, "Uh-huh."

Nikalys chuckled softly. "You should see your face, sis."

The stranger glanced at Nikalys. "Yours looked no different yesterday."

Nikalys stared up at Broedi for a moment before turning back to Kenders. "As long as your mouth is open, eat this." He held out the crushed remnants of a dried plant with tiny, white flowers. A bitter scent came with it.

She accepted the herb silently, held it in her palm, and returned to gaping at Broedi. "Who are you?" Looking back to Nikalys, she added quickly, "And what do you mean I've been asleep for a *day*? What happened?"

The giant gave Nikalys a long, solemn look with purpose behind it.

Kenders grew worried. "Nikalys, tell me what happened."

Her brother sighed and stood tall. Crossing his arms so that he looked like a smaller, skinnier version of the stranger, Nikalys spoke, his tone both somber and sober. "Take that and sit for a moment. Then we can talk." He glanced at the giant. "We all have questions we would like answered."

*   *   *

Kenders sat in the clearing, munching on her quail, chewing without truly tasting the meat, trying to grasp everything Nikalys and Broedi had shared with her. Her gaze alternated between her brother, the dark forest, and the giant man sitting across the fire from her.

A Shapechanger. A blasted Shapechanger.

If her brother had not sworn three times to all of the gods, she would have called them both pretenders. After Nikalys' third affirmation, she had demanded the Shapechanger prove it to her. Broedi had politely refused her request, asking if she would ask a bird to prove it could fly.

Eventually, she had come to accept the claim. Nikalys had no reason to tell a tale, and it certainly explained the lynx from yesterday and Broedi's presence now.

After swallowing a mouthful of quail, she fixed her gaze firmly on Broedi, cleared her throat, and said, "I suppose I should thank you for saving us, Mister Broedi."

"Please, just 'Broedi,' uora."

Broedi had yet to call her by her name, repeatedly using the strange term instead. After the first few times, Nikalys had quietly explained that—according to Broedi—he was 'uori,' she 'uora,' and the terms simply meant 'young one.'

"Thank you, *Broedi*, then."

The giant man inclined his head. "You are welcome."

Glancing between the pair, she asked, "So what happened after you chased the wolves away?"

With a worried frown on his face, Nikalys asked, "What do you remember?"

Kenders took a deep breath and exhaled. "Well, the lynx—sorry—Broedi was walking around the fire." She looked up at Nikalys. "You told me to run and...I started to, but stopped. Then..." She trailed off, her eyebrows drawing together as she strained to recall what had happened next. Try as she might, she could not. "Sorry, but that's it. That's all I can remember." Turning her head, she stared at her blood-soaked, balled-up skirt and blouse a few feet away and muttered, "Although something obviously happened." Looking back to Nikalys and Broedi, she asked, "Why was I covered in blood?" She lifted her arm to indicate the red marks all along it. "And bodfly bites?"

Nikalys looked at Broedi, his worried frown morphing into open unease.

Broedi ignored him, his gaze firmly fixed on Kenders, his brown eyes awash in curiosity. "Tell me, uora, what do you know of the Strands?"

A moment skipped past before Kenders responded, confused. "The strands? The strands of what?"

A faint smile settled on Broedi's lips. "You have nothing to fear. You may tell me."

Kenders glanced at Nikalys—who shrugged his shoulders—then back to Broedi. "I'm sorry, but I have no idea what you mean. What are 'the Strands?'" This time, she put the same emphasis on the word as Broedi had.

A slight furrow appeared in Broedi's forehead. He stared at her for a few moments before looking back to Nikalys.

Shaking his head, Nikalys said, "Don't look at me."

The crease in Broedi's forehead deepened and he dropped his gaze to the fire. As he remained that way for a while, quiet and unmoving, Kenders and Nikalys shared a series of glances with one another, having a silent, wordless conversation that consisted solely of facial expressions. The gist of their 'talk' was that neither one of them had any idea about what Broedi was asking.

Finally, Broedi pulled his attention from the fire and focused on Kenders, a slight frown on his face. She held the giant's weighty gaze, expecting him to say something—he certainly looked like he wanted to—but he simply stared.

She was beginning to think the man odd when the crumbling straw sensation filled her. A surprised gasp slipped from her lips as colors swelled and swirled inside her: a hot, coppery reddish-yellow hue mixing with a brilliant, honey color. Her eyes grew round as she caught the faintest flicker of the two colors above the campfire. In quiet, wondering tone, she whispered, "Orange and gold."

For a fleeting moment, the colors turned opaque. Pulsing, bright strings twisted together quickly to form a simple, clearly defined pattern, and then dropped to the campfire. The flames flared tall, leaping a foot higher than normal. While Nikalys jumped back a step, staring at the surge with wide eyes, Kenders was unsurprised. She was as certain that Broedi had used the strings to manipulate the fire, as she was that the sun would rise tomorrow. Her stomach lurched at the additional confirmation that she was a mage.

The fire fell to a normal height and the crackling of magic stopped. Broedi looked at her and then Nikalys, his stoic expression giving away nothing.

Anxious, Kenders stared up at her brother. Nikalys was glancing back and forth between her and Broedi, an almost accusatory glint in his eyes when he looked at her.

Shaking her head quickly, Kenders said, "Nik, that wasn't—" She cut off as the crackling returned. This time, she felt a crisp, pure white coupled with the golden honey from a moment before. Whipping her head back around, she spotted the glowing threads in the air, hovering in place as they arranged themselves into a woven pattern. Her eyes opened a little wider as she whispered, "White and gold..."

A firm breeze swept through the camp, whipping up dust and fanning the campfire's flames. Lifting a hand, Kenders covered her eyes to protect them from the grit blowing in the air. The gust only lasted for a heartbeat or two before fading. The crackling stopped but her anxiety grew. Dropping her hand, she stared at the Shapechanger. Broedi was staring at Nikalys, his gaze searching and seeking.

"Anything, uori?"

Mute, Nikalys shook his head.

Broedi frowned a little, turned to Kenders, and said, "What you are feeling is the weaving of the Strands, uora. It is incredible that you are able to distinguish among them so quickly without knowing what they are. And use them without training." He paused and then added a quiet afterthought. "To be certain, you have *not* had training?"

Wide-eyed and silent, Kenders shook her head.

Wearing a slight frown, he peered at her, his gaze intense. "So all of this is new to you?"

"Of course it's new to me. I've *never*—" She stopped short as the entirety of Broedi's statement hit her. "Hold a moment...you said 'use them.'" Her heart pounded in her chest. "What do you mean by that?"

The giant man pressed his lips together and turned to Nikalys. "Perhaps it would be best if you tell her."

Kenders' worried, almost panicked gaze shifted to Nikalys. "Tell me what?"

Nikalys stared at her, shuffling his feet. He almost looked ill.

Growing more nervous by the moment, Kenders muttered, "Nik? Please..."

Despite his obvious discomfort, he scooted back to her and knelt in the dirt. Leaning over, he reached out and took her hand and spoke, his voice wavering. "After Broedi chased the wolves off, you..." He paused a moment, bit down hard, and took in a short breath. "Well...you sort of called down lightning."

Kenders stared at him, her expression blank. She was certain she had heard him clearly, but the words did not make any sense. She began to shake her head. "No...no...I—"

Nikalys continued, saying, "The blast tossed us into the fingerpricks. Gods, did it hurt… And you…you looked terrible. Honestly, I thought you were dead." He pointed to the bumps on her arms. "And these? They aren't bodfly bites. They're puncture marks from the thorns."

Numb inside, Kenders looked at her arms. "That's impossible. They're too small—"

"Strands of Life," rumbled Broedi. "I used them to help you heal."

Horrified, she stared up at the giant. "You used magic on me?"

While the Shapechanger did not react, his face remaining a blank mask, Nikalys squeezed her hand. "He helped you, sis. He helped us both." With a half-hearted, teasing smile, he said, "And to be fair, you used magic on him." He paused. "Me, too, if we're making marks."

She dropped her gaze and stared at a nearby stick, certain she would have remembered doing something that horrendous.

"Strands of Charge are yellow, uora," rumbled Broedi. "Air is white."

Kenders stared up at Broedi. "Why are you—" She cut off, her eyes going wide as pieces of last night bubbled up from the depths of her memory.

The buzzing strings.

The wispy white ones.

The pattern that had popped into existence, right before her eyes.

One image after another rushed through her head in quick succession. She suddenly remembered everything, right up until the moment she threw the pattern toward the lynx. Dropping her gaze, she stared into the heart of the campfire, unable to deny it any longer. She was a mage.

After a few moments of quiet, she looked up at her brother. "Nik, I am *so* sorry. I didn't mean to hurt you."

"I know, sis," said Nikalys, shaking his head. "It's no matter." He flashed her a brave, understanding smile, but the uneasy look in his eyes told a different tale.

Looking up at the large Shapechanger, she added, "You, too, Broedi. I'm terribly sorry. It was an accident."

"There is no need to apologize," rumbled Broedi. "As you say, it was an accident." The slight smile he wore was supportive, true, and without reservation.

"But how?" pleaded Kenders. "How did I do that?"

Broedi's smile fell away as a shadow passed over his face. "I am…uncertain. Every Charge and Air mage I know must work for years to do what you did. There is—" He stopped a moment and let out a sad sigh before continuing. "There *was* only one other I knew who had such an affinity for the Strands."

"Who?" asked Kenders.

Broedi remained silent for a few heartbeats, staring intently at her, then Nikalys, and back to her. "Truly? All of this is unfamiliar to you?"

"Magic and mages?" huffed Nikalys. "Shapechangers? Lightning from a clear sky? If *this* is 'familiar' for you, I don't want to know what you think is odd."

Broedi reached a hand—Kenders marveled at its size—to his face and rubbed his chin. After drawing in a deep breath and slowly exhaling, he said, "Can you tell me of your parents?"

Kenders glanced at Nikalys, surprised. The question seemed rather out-of-place.

Meeting her gaze, Nikalys said, "He asked about them last night, too. A few times, in fact." He glared at Broedi. "Why are you so interested in our parents?"

Broedi appeared on the verge of saying something when he stopped suddenly. His eyebrows drew together and he stared into the fire. After only a moment or two, he looked up to them both and said, "Their names. What were your parent's names?"

Nikalys asked, "Why should we tell—?"

"Thaddeus and Marie Isaac," interjected Kenders. Her interruption earned her a dirty look from Nikalys. Holding his sharp gaze, she said, "Oh, come on, Nik. He helped us, healed us, and didn't kill us in our sleep. What harm is there in telling him Mother and Father's names?"

Nikalys scowled but remained silent.

When she looked back to Broedi, she found the giant man distracted again, staring at nothing in particular. Excitement, hope, worry, and a touch of sadness mussed his stoic, pensive demeanor. She swore she could hear him thinking.

Suddenly intrigued, Kenders said, "Why do you ask?"

Broedi looked up quickly and stared at her long enough to make her uncomfortable. "I need to think on this, uora. Please excuse me." He immediately strolled away from them, moving to the edge of the campfire's glow to stare into the dark forest.

Kenders gave her brother a searching look. Nikalys shrugged his shoulders and stepped away as well, making a show of tidying the campsite. He was either pouting that she had given up the names of their parents so readily, or he was giving her time to come to terms with what she had just learned. Regardless, she was grateful for the silence, at least until she began to think about what had become of her life.

Her parents and eldest brother were dead, her home was gone, and now she had incontrovertible proof that she was a mage. None of this was fair. None of it. Why Greya had felt the need to twist her fate in this manner baffled Kenders. The longer she deliberated the more confused, frustrated, and angry she became.

Playmen's sagas told of a time when mages had not always been persecuted, when great heroes had used magic to save the duchies from utter destruction and ruin. Most people in Yellow Mud had ridiculed the tales. The only exceptions had been their parents.

Whenever one traveling entertainer or another would regale the village with such a tale, Thaddeus and Marie would speak quietly with their children afterwards, telling them magic was not something to fear, claiming that it was a tool, no different from a spade. You could use the spade to cultivate, or you could use it to smash in a man's head. Either way, the spade was a spade. The person who wielded it was what mattered.

As Kenders sat alone against the tree trunk and her initial shock faded, she realized something. While she might be a mage, she remained the same person. As long as she never, ever did what she had done last night, nothing needed to change. If she did not want to do magic, she simply would not do it. It was a simple matter of choice.

She looked over at Broedi, still staring into the forest. He was a mage and seemed a decent soul. Perhaps he could teach her how to control these Strands. Not for her to use, but rather so she could suppress them.

Sitting there in the glow of the campfire, still holding the stick to her half-eaten quail, Kenders decided she would like Broedi to stay with them, regardless of where they were headed. She wondered if he would be interested in accompanying them. Unfortunately, they had almost nothing with which to pay him. She frowned, wishing now she had looked a little harder for coin in Yellow Mud.

As she stared at the Shapechanger, Broedi's head snapped up and turned to the southwest. His nostrils flared as he took two quick sniffs of air, reminding Kenders of a barncat when it caught the scent of a mouse. His eyes narrowed and his lips twitched. His entire body went rigid. Kenders was tense just looking at him.

The Shapechanger turned, strode back to the fire, and sat across from her. In a quick, almost brusque tone, he said, "I require answers now." He glanced at Nikalys. "Please, join us, uori."

Nikalys was standing a few paces away, leaning against the trunk of an oak tree. She watched him closely as he came over and settled next to her.

Without preamble, Broedi rumbled, "Tell me exactly what happened in Yellow Mud."

Kenders threw an accusing glare at her brother. "Nik!"

Broedi lifted a quick hand. "Your kaveli has told me nothing. He refused to speak until you were awake."

She stared at Broedi, her mind reeling. If Nikalys had not said anything, then Broedi should have no way of knowing from where they hailed. Full of new worry, she kept her mouth shut, as did Nikalys.

"I see you are both wary to speak," rumbled Broedi. "Normally, that would be a good thing. But not now." His gaze flicked over her shoulders, out into the darkened woods behind her. A moment later, he looked back to them and forward. "Fine, then. I will tell you what I know and you correct me if I go astray. Someone unleashed a terrible Weave on your home, a massive fibríaal of Water, it would seem." He looked directly at Kenders. "You are not the mage responsible, uora. While I suspect you have the power to do so, you do not have the control."

Kenders held his gaze, her uneasiness growing as Broedi continued.

"Whether by Greya's grace or Ketus' luck, you two were not in town when the wave struck. You did come into the ruins afterwards—*not* wise at all, by the way—but quickly fled." His eyebrows drew together as his gaze shot over their heads, out into the nighttime forest.

Something in the forest had him worried. And if the Shapechanger who had faced down three wolves was anxious, Kenders figured she should be as well. She glanced over her shoulder, but could see nothing beyond the campfire's glow. A nervous chill danced up her spine.

"Uora, you will listen to me." Broedi's insistent tone drew her attention back to camp. "You headed east, avoiding the main road, which was a wise choice, were it not for the wolves. Am I correct so far?" He paused, waiting for any corrections although Kenders got the impression he did not expect any.

After a few moments, Kenders muttered, "Amazingly so."

Nikalys glared at her. "Kenders!"

"What? He seems to know everything that's happened so far."

"You're right." Nikalys turned his glowering stare to Broedi. "How is that exactly?"

Broedi tilted his head, his eyes alert and intense. "I have but one question for you." It was not lost on Kenders he did not answer Nikalys' question. "Do you know *why* your village was attacked?"

A derisive laugh slipped from Nikalys, paired with a bitter scowl. "You have no idea how many times I've asked myself that question."

"Truly?" asked Broedi with forced calm. "Those who raised you, they told you nothing?"

Nikalys glared at the Shapechanger, his grief raw and plainly exposed. "Those who 'raised' us? You mean *our parents?*"

Broedi closed his eyes and shook his head. "That is not what—"

"And tell us what, exactly?" interrupted Nikalys. "That one day, a giant wave would flood our home, killing *everyone we know?*! No, Broedi! I am sorry!

They neglected to tell us *anything* like that before they had the audacity to drown."

Kenders muttered, "Nik, calm down..."

He shifted his hot glare to her. After a moment, he pressed his lips together, shut his eyes, and exhaled slowly.

Bowing his head, Broedi rumbled, "I do ask your forgiveness, uori. My words were callous. Two people important to you are with Maeana now. I am sorry for your loss."

Nikalys' eyes shot open. "Try three! Our brother died, too! No, you know what?! More than three! The entire blasted town was important to us, Broedi, not just our family!"

Broedi sat up a little taller. "You have another kaveli?" He seemed taken aback by the information.

"Hah!" exclaimed Nikalys. "There's something you didn't know, Shapechanger! Yes, we had another brother. His name is—" He cut off, squeezed his eyes tight, and then reopened them before continuing. "His name *was* Jak. And he was in the village, too, when the wave...when...when it..." Nikalys trailed off and looked away, the anger draining from his face.

Inexplicably, Broedi let out a sigh of relief, a reaction that seemed entirely out of place considering the tenor of the conversation. "It seems there is at least one thing I know about that day's events that the two of you do not. Something I could not make sense of until just now." He looked over their heads and he called into the night, "Please! Join us!"

Alarmed, Kenders spun around and peered into the dark forest. A few moments later, she heard steps coming through the brush.

* * *

After leaving the Red Sentinels' encampment with a full belly, Jak had traveled east long after the sun had vacated the sky, using the light of White Moon to travel. Once at what he judged to be a safe distance from the Sentinels' camp, he had checked the teardrop pendant, bracing himself for the pain he experienced earlier in the day. Instead, a calm feeling had come over him with only a hint of unpleasantness. What commanded his attention now was the sound of the ringing bell, clearly resonating, but no longer straight away east. Turning, he had searched for its strongest point and decided it was northeast, in the forest.

He knew that once he left the road and headed into the wild, travel would be slower, more difficult, and treacherous. White Moon's glow was sufficient for moving along a dirt road at night, but in a forested area, its stark light and the sharp shadows it cast, a curse. One hidden hole and Jak would have a broken ankle.

Nevertheless, the decision to veer from the safety of the road was easy. Nikalys and Kenders were near.

The acrid scent of wood smoke was the first thing he had noticed. Cresting a small rise, he spotted a tiny campsite, its light flickering through a screen of tree trunks. Elated, he was set to rush down to his brother and sister when he spotted three figures sitting about the fire, not two.

Worried, Jak had crept closer to discover a stranger sitting with them. Jak swore his eyes were playing tricks on him as the man looked to be a full head and a half taller than Nikalys.

He sneaked closer still, moving from trunk to trunk as quietly as he could manage. The giant man seemed to stare in his direction once or twice, freezing Jak in mid-step. When the man looked away, Jak would resume his approach. When he was a hundred paces away, he stopped behind a large oak to decide what to do. He had only been standing there few heartbeats when the giant looked right at Jak and, in a deep, baritone voice, boomed, "Please! Join us!"

Jak had been so careful on his approach. No one should have been able to hear him.

He briefly considered shooting the man with an arrow, but he was not entirely sure the giant was a threat. And if the stranger could see Jak—however implausible—he would most definitely notice Jak readying the bow, giving him plenty of time to reach out to Nikalys or Kenders and snap a neck.

Drawing a deep breath, Jak moved out from the tree, walked the remaining hundred paces to the edge of the camp, and stepped into the fire's glow.

Chapter 15: Hillman

A week ago, Broedi had arrived in the region and wandered aimlessly, restless. He knew something was going to happen soon, something important. He knew it to be true as much as he knew the sky was up. The problem was he did not know what. Or why. Or how. Or when, exactly. That was the problem with this part of Thonda's gift: Broedi's sixth sense was never specific.

He had been sitting on a log beside Oligurtears Lake, smoking his pipe, staring at the water's surface when Eliza's beacon had called to him. Within moments, he had been in the air, soaring east.

Upon reaching Yellow Mud two days past, he stood among the ruins, both saddened and angered by the senseless slaughter. Dreading what he might uncover, he had nonetheless searched the area, sifting through collapsed buildings and piles of rubble. After a thorough, heartrending investigation, he had come away knowing three things.

The first was that a pair of individuals—related, according to the commonality of their scent—had headed east two days prior. Second, the scent of another fortunate soul appeared beneath an oak tree and traveled south not long before Broedi's arrival, along with the echoes of Eliza's beacon. Finally, the surprising yet unmistakable scent of an ijul covered an outcrop west of town and led to the edge of the devastation where it suddenly disappeared.

Without hesitation, Broedi raced east, after the brother and sister. If the destruction around him was any indication, they were in grave danger. He would worry about Eliza and Aryn's package later.

As Jak emerged from the forest's gloom, Broedi noted the leather casing peeking over the young man's shoulders and breathed a quiet sigh of relief. The mystery—and problem—of who had the beacon was solved. A flash of silver drew Broedi's gaze to the necklace hanging around Jak's neck. A wistful smile crept over Broedi's lips even as his confusion deepened.

Shock held Nikalys and Kenders in place for only a moment before both shouted for joy and ran to embrace Jak. Broedi sat and watched in silence, letting them have their happy reunion. After what they had endured so far, they deserved a cheerful moment.

As the trio rejoiced, Broedi closed his eyes and drew in a deep breath, hoping nothing—or nobody—had followed the boy here.

Smoke from the fire.

The scent of oak and ash.

The spicy mint of grannok bush.

Minerals and mud from a nearby creek.

Musty fur of a rabbit in the bushes.

Finding nothing out of the ordinary, he shut out the young ones' jubilance and listened to the world around him.

The soft rustle of the leaves.

The clicking of a squirrel's tiny claws as it ran along a tree branch.

Water flowing in the creek.

Trees creaking as they swayed in the night's gentle breeze.

Broedi opened his eyes and allowed himself a quiet sigh of relief. They were alone for the moment and safe, although he doubted that would last.

The three children were now speaking in hushed tones, evidently trying to conceal their words from Broedi. He, however, heard every word spoken.

Nikalys and Kenders asked how Jak had survived.

Eyeing Broedi suspiciously, Jak whispered, "Later."

They asked if anyone else was alive.

Jak whispered, "Later."

They wanted to know how he found them.

Exasperated, Jak hissed, "Later!"

The young man appeared wary to speak before a stranger. That was good.

Broedi rose from the ground and stepped forward, eying the trio. They seemed so young to him. Kenders was more girl than woman, and he wondered if either boy could grow a proper beard.

As Broedi approached, Jak slid his arms around the others and stared up at Broedi, his eyes full of defiance, distrust, and only the barest flicker of fear.

Broedi had to choose his words carefully. As much as they needed to know the truth, now was not the right time. After what they had been through, he could not risk shocking them further. He let out a short, inaudible sigh. This was going to be harder than he had hoped.

Eyeing Jak, he rumbled, "Good days ahead, uori. My name is Broedi."

Before answering, Jak glanced at his brother and sister. Their relatively relaxed attitude seemed to ease some of his anxiety, so he looked back to Broedi and replied, his tone surprisingly steady. "Good memories behind. I'm Jak."

Broedi indicated the leftover rabbits and quail next to the fire. "If you are hungry, please eat."

Jak barely glanced at the roast meat and sticks. "Thank you. It is kind of you to offer." He did not move.

Broedi motioned to the fire. "Please, come sit and rest. I expect your iskoa and kaveli are anxious to speak with you."

Jak's brows furrowed. "My what?"

Nikalys clarified, "It means sister and brother."

Jak nodded slowly. "I see." He remained in place, unmoving, staring at Broedi with eyes full of distrust.

After a few tense moments, Kenders tugged on his arm. "Come on. It's all right. Broedi won't bite, I promise." She glanced at Broedi, a tiny smile on her lips. "You won't, will you?"

Broedi appreciated the small jest, yet showed no reaction. "No, uora. I will not."

Jak reluctantly allowed Kenders to drag him to the fire where he began removing the gear he carried, never taking his gaze from Broedi. As Nikalys selected a roast rabbit for Jak and Kenders fetched him fresh water, Broedi turned to retrieve another log for the fire while watching Jak out of the corner of his eye. The young man removed the leather case Broedi recognized from years past and slid it behind him, then quickly tucked the silver teardrop pendant inside his shirt. Broedi found both actions intriguing.

The four settled around the fire, Broedi on one side and the three children on the other—Kenders, Jak, Nikalys, left to right. As Jak nibbled on his cold rabbit, he quietly inquired about Nikalys and Kenders' wellbeing. The pair was deliberately vague with their story, sharing almost nothing of their journey before Broedi's arrival. As both took great pains to talk around what Kenders had done with the Strands, Broedi concluded that young Jak did not know of Kenders' gift. Considering Nikalys' reaction to the lightning, that was not surprising.

Broedi listened to their tale with quiet amusement, surprised to hear that he was a trapper from Dunsvalley who, while returning from Smithshill, just happened to be nearby when wolves attacked the pair. According to them, Broedi had leapt to their defense and beat off the wolves with his bare hands. Broedi did his best not to smile at their fictitious account.

Throughout their story, Jak's gaze repeatedly returned to Broedi. His glances were hesitant at first, but he slowly grew bolder until he was openly holding Broedi's own level stare. The suspicion in his eyes was as clear as the moons in the sky.

Broedi sighed inwardly. The thing he needed the most right now was the same thing he utterly lacked: their trust.

He reached into his satchel, retrieved his pipe, and set to packing it with a special blend of smoking-leaf. When he was done, he stuck a short stick into the fire, waited for it to catch, and then pressed its flame into the pipe's bowl, puffing gently. He could have just as easily used a small Weave of Fire, but figured this was safer based on the others' unfamiliarity with magic.

He smoked quietly, the cloying aroma of the Sweetbush cut wafting through the camp as he waited for the inevitable questions to begin. He had taken but two draws on the pipe when Jak leaned forward.

"Mister Broedi, sir—"

Broedi held up a hand to interrupt. "As I told your iskoa, it is just Broedi. 'Misters' and 'sirs' are for people who need to feel important."

A faint smile touched Jak's lips. "So I've heard. Fine, then. Broedi, I would like to ask a question of you."

"Then ask."

Jak hesitated a moment before speaking, the words bursting from his lips like cream from a squished pastry. "Who in the Nine Hells are you?" Kenders and Nikalys stiffened and turned to stare at Jak as a roaring river of inquisitiveness poured forth from the young man. "Your accent is odd, your words even odder. Uori? uora? Iskoa and kaveli? I suppose they are from a different tongue, but not one I've heard." He pointed at Broedi's pipe. "And please tell me that's made of wood, because it looks like bone to me."

Broedi attempted to answer. "Actually, it is—"

"And, Hells!" exclaimed Jak. "If you aren't the largest man in all the duchies, I don't want to meet the one who is. You know, perhaps the better question to ask is 'What in the Nine Hells are you?'"

Nikalys and Kenders had dropped their gaze during the short interrogation, apparently ashamed by their brother's brashness. Now their eyes slowly crept back to Broedi, their inquisitive stare nearly matching Jak's own intense gaze.

Broedi allowed himself a slight smile. Looking from face to face, he spoke, keeping his voice soft and soothing. "Have any of you heard of aki-mahet?"

All three stared at him blankly. Only Jak responded with a muttered, "Pardon?"

"Aki-mahet," repeated Broedi. "Have you ever heard the name before?"

The trio shook their heads indicating they had not.

Broedi took a short draw on his pipe and spoke with curls of smoke accompanying his words. "In Argot, the name roughly translates to 'Men of the Hills.' Most lowlanders—people like you—simply call my kind 'hillmen.'"

A triumphant smile spread over Jak's lips. He seemed as pleased as a festival patron after figuring out a merrymaker's riddle. "I knew it! The moment you stood, I knew it!" He glanced between Nikalys and Kenders as though looking for congratulations. He received none as the pair both stared at Broedi through narrowed eyes.

"Hillmen are a myth," said Nikalys. "Everyone knows that."

"Who is 'everyone?'" rumbled Broedi. He took another draw on his pipe.

"Everyone in Yellow Mud, at least," answered Nikalys. The mention of their village drew a sharp stare from Jak that Nikalys did not notice.

Broedi cocked an eyebrow and blew out a long stream of white smoke. "Then everyone in Yellow Mud was wrong." Pointing the pipe's bit at the three children, he asked, "Did you live there all your lives?"

"Mostly," said Kenders. "We were born in Lakeborough."

"You were?" asked Broedi. He was surprised to hear that.

Kenders nodded. "None of us remember it, though. At least I don't. We left right after I was born." She glanced at her brothers. "They were a little older."

Broedi shifted his gaze between the young men. "Do either of you recall anything of your time there?"

As both shook their heads, indicating their memories were likewise blank, Broedi pressed his lips together, disappointed. They knew nothing of the truth. Nothing.

Leaning forward, he said, "Please understand, Yellow Mud is a single village. A single village in a single barony in a single duchy in a single country. What is 'myth' in Yellow Mud is almost certainly accepted truth elsewhere. If I shared but a handful of the things I have seen in my life, you would call me a liar. Or worse."

The three children stared at him, quiet and thoughtful. After a moment, Kenders asked, "Then you truly *are* a hillman?"

"That is not the name we use for ourselves, but yes, I am."

She nodded as if accepting his answer even though the incredulous frown on her face said otherwise.

Broedi bit down on the tip of the pipe, quietly frustrated. They were utterly ignorant of the world outside their village. Worse, they were overtly suspicious, almost afraid, of magic. Feeling a quick, familiar flash of anger at what the people of the Oaken Duchies had become, he frowned and adjusted his legs to ensure he was comfortable. Their education was long overdue.

After pulling his pipe from his mouth, he said, "The origin of aki-mahet is a topic of some disagreement. Some believe we are nothing more than men and women who wandered into the mountains ages ago, growing in both size and stature to match our surroundings. Some believe we are the child race of two of the Celystiela."

"Pardon me," said Jak. "Celystiela?"

"The gods and goddesses, uori."

"Gods can have children?" asked Kenders.

Broedi shrugged. "Honestly, uora, I never thought to ask them."

The three children smiled at what they assumed was a jest.

"Our earliest history is lost for we were nomads, letting the seasons guide our path. We avoided other races, preferring to coexist with our neighbors from a distance. Time passed, our numbers swelled, and our tribe grew too large to move on a whim. As is common with large groups, there were disagreements. Divisions were natural."

"Some headed north, to the shores of the sea. Others left and traveled west and south, over the mountains. Those who stayed called themselves Totta

Kotiv-aki." Seeing the question in their eyes, he answered it before they could ask. "In Argot, it means 'the True Tribe.' To this day, they consider themselves purebloods and the descendants of those who left to be lesser tribes."

"Aki-mahet who moved south and west found dry lands over the mountains, as well as creatures vastly different from us. Oligurts, mongrels, and nascepel—perhaps you know them as 'razorfiends'—lived in the highlands. In order to survive, Tuhka Kotiv-aki—the Dust Tribe—was forced to fight. They have seen much hardship."

"Those who traveled north soon forgot what it meant to be aki-mahet. Greed wormed into their hearts, pushing out harmony and benevolence. They called themselves Vahva Kotiv-aki—the Strong Tribe—and attacked their neighbors, choosing brawn and blood over words and peace."

Broedi paused to take a long draw from his pipe, pleased to see all three children listening intently. While he was quiet by nature, he enjoyed telling a story to an appreciative audience. After exhaling the pipe smoke, he continued his tale.

"Not all of the Strong Tribe hungered for conquest, however. Many wished to return home, but were ashamed to crawl back to Totta Kotiv-aki. So, they built great boats and sailed the seas. Saewyn's winds took them south and east to a land the maps call Ursus where Titaani Kotiv-aki—the Titan Tribe—found a kinship with the primal creatures who lived there."

"Generations passed, yet our nomadic nature could not be suppressed. Some of Titaani Kotiv-aki set to the seas again, sailing east to an island full of men and strange beasts. There, they tried to carve out a life and failed. Kotiv-aki ei Mitaan—the Tribeless—left and continue to this day to search for a home they might never find." Gazing at each one of their young faces, he quietly concluded, "And that is the tale of aki-mahet. A story that, I assure you, is not myth."

He placed his pipe in his mouth and puffed once. The chronicle of his people seemed to have had the desired effect. The children appeared more relaxed than when he had begun.

A few moments passed before Kenders asked, "Which tribe is yours?"

"I am originally Totta Kotiv-aki.," rumbled Broedi. He shook his head slowly. "No longer, though." His thoughts drifted back to another time, one full of tragedy that rivaled what the trio across from him was experiencing now. Staving off the old memories before they came, Broedi focused on Kenders. "Now, uora, I am without kotiv-aki."

"You are one of the Tribeless, then?" asked Nikalys.

"No, uori. I have no tribe. I am unique, I am…alone." Unintended sadness must have slipped into his voice, for when Kenders spoke a moment later, sympathy filled her voice as well as her eyes.

"I am sorry, Broedi."

Forcing a slight smile, he said, "Do not be. I have recently begun a journey to remedy that." Shifting his gaze to Jak, Broedi pointed his pipe at the young man. "Your turn."

Jak's eyebrows drew together. "Pardon?"

"I answered your question, uori. I told you my history. I would like to hear yours now." He glanced at Nikalys and Kenders, but continued addressing Jak. "I know what happened after they left Yellow Mud, but what of you?"

Jak glared at his brother and sister. "What did you two tell him?"

"Nothing," said Nikalys, holding Jak's accusatory glare.

When Jak looked at Kenders, she shook her head. "He's telling the truth. We didn't tell him a thing."

Jak turned his narrowed-eye stare on Broedi and scowled. Broedi had thought his story had helped relax the young man, but it was apparent now that Jak's suspicion had never left.

With a firm, resolute nod, Jak said, "Thank you again for helping my brother and sister. I'm sure you wish to resume your journey home." He glanced at Nikalys and Kenders and began to stand. "Let's go."

As he reached his feet, Kenders stared up at him. "Go?"

"That's what I said," affirmed Jak. "We're leaving."

Nikalys leapt up immediately, the relieved smile on his face indicating his apparent approval of Jak's plan.

Kenders, though, remained sitting, staring at Broedi with a disappointed frown on her face. After a moment, she looked to Jak. "Why now? Shouldn't we wait until morning?"

"No," said Jak, his tone firm.

Broedi eyed the two young men standing across the fire from him. The pair trusted him as much as a rabbit trusted a wolf. Considering things from their point of view, he could certainly understand why. As much as he needed their trust, it was not a requisite at the present. He did not intend to let them leave. Not now. Not ever.

After placing his pipe on the ground, he rose from his sitting position and, upon reaching his full seven-foot plus height, rumbled, "If possible, I would like to travel along with you."

Jak glared at him. "Why?"

"The woods are not safe, uori. I would worry if I left you alone."

Jak shook his head, refusing the offer. "Thank you, but that is not necessary." Jak's eyes burned with a certain intensity Broedi interpreted as an earnest desire that he would have the decency to go away.

"I believe it is," rumbled Broedi. He had no idea how the Cabal had found them, but they had and that was all that mattered. He could not, would not, leave them alone.

As Jak and Broedi held one another's gaze, both of them silent and unrelenting, Kenders stood, walked around the fire, and stopped beside Broedi. The top of her head did not even reach his shoulder. "I say if he wants to come, we let him."

Broedi, Jak, and Nikalys all stared at her, clearly surprised, perhaps Broedi most of all. He had not expected to have an ally in this discussion.

Kenders looked at Nikalys alone. "He showed how useful he can be by chasing away those wolves."

"Are you mad?" asked Nikalys. "We can't walk into Smithshill with a blasted—" He stopped short, giving Jak a quick, sidelong glance. Broedi wondered if "mage" or "Shapechanger" had been Nikalys' next intended word.

"Wait," said Jak, looking over at Nikalys. "What's this about Smithshill? Why are you going there?"

The revelation both surprised and concerned Broedi. Surely, they knew of the Constables.

As Kenders and Nikalys exchanged a quiet look, he frowned. The pair had apparently arrived at some course of action of which he was not yet aware. He was about to protest when it occurred to him that an excursion to Smithshill might provide the time necessary to gain their trust. Deciding that a little push was necessary to get them to do what he needed, Broedi combined some of what he knew with a logical guess and answered Jak's question.

"I would assume they mean to go to the Constables and tell them of the water fibríaal that destroyed your village."

Disbelief washed over Jak's face. Glaring at Kenders, he asked, "You told him what happened?" He whipped around to face Nikalys. "Blast it! I thought you two had more sense than that!"

Wheeling on his brother, Nikalys exclaimed, "We didn't tell him anything! He figured it out himself!"

"Did he?" huffed Jak.

"Truly, Jak," insisted Kenders, "we didn't tell him a thing."

Jak's eyebrows climbed high. "You expect me to believe that a hillman trapper from Dunsvalley who was *heading west* figured out that a giant wave destroyed a village that is still nearly two days *ahead* of him? I'm not a fool, Kenders."

Jak's astute observations impressed Broedi. His opinion of the young man was steadily increasing. Eyeing Jak, he rumbled, "Your *kaveli* and *iskoa* have not been entirely truthful about me."

After the trio exchanged a flurry of accusing looks and uneasy glances, Jak asked, "What does he mean by that?" When neither Nikalys nor Kenders responded right away, he pressed them both. "One of you had better tell me what is going on here."

As nothing but sore feelings would come from Jak interrogating them, Broedi drew the attention to himself. "Uori, you wish to protect them, do you not?"

Jak turned his harsh glare on Broedi. "Of course. That's all I want."

"Then tell me, should the wolves come again, how will you chase them away?"

"We'll fight them off."

"How?"

"I have a bow," shot back Jak.

"And how fast can you string a bow, draw an arrow, and nock it, aim, and then fire? Faster than a wolf can run you down?"

"You managed," snapped Jak. Peering at Nikalys and Kenders, he added with a hint of sarcasm, "Apparently with nothing more than your bare hands." The young man, rightly so, seemed to have a few problems with Nikalys and Kenders' made-up story.

Broedi sighed. There was no time plead or reason with them, to beg and cajole. The longer they stayed in one place, the more likely they would be discovered. Making a decision he hoped would not be a bad one, he crouched to the ground and began reaching for the Strands. Kenders let out a quick gasp and looked to him with wide eyes.

The pattern he wove was so familiar by now that he needed to think about its design as much as he did about drawing his next breath. Pulling at the verdant Strands of Life, golden Strands of Will, and the silver Strands of Soul, he arranged them in the proper pattern, overlaying, intertwining, and twisting. When the Weave was nearly complete, he added a unique piece from within himself that only he knew how to find and grasp.

As his body began changing, the stench of the smoke from the fire overwhelmed him, its acrid blackness briefly blocking out the finer scents in the area. He could still smell the three young ones, however, each one's odor as distinguishable as ice is from fire. The woody perfume of the forest, dominated by the piney scent of cypress and the freshness of oak, wafted through the air like waves on a wind-teased pond. The musky, meaty smell of rabbits swelled, prompting a longing for the taste of raw, red meat.

Nearing the final form—he had chosen the lynx as Nikalys and Kenders were already familiar with it—he prepared himself for the final moment when he went blind. For reasons he still did not understand, when he shifted, his sight did not slide from his prime form's vision to the animal's like the rest of his senses. Instead, after a brief, vulnerable moment of total blindness, the world popped into view through the eyes of his new form.

The moment of blindness came and went, revealing a world with a significantly muted color palate compared to just a moment ago. He had difficulty distinguishing between reds, greens, and yellows, but he could suddenly see deep into the dark forest with extraordinary clarity.

The shift complete, he sat on his haunches, twitching his short, stubby tail, watching the three children through the eyes of a lynx. All three remained motionless and silent, staring at him. Nikalys appeared to be only mildly surprised. After all, he had seen the shift before, albeit in the opposite direction. Kenders eyed him guardedly, her face a mixture of worry, wonder, and a hint of curiosity. Jak simply gaped, his mouth slightly parted and eyes wide.

Broedi expected the palpable odor of fear to seep from the young man but none came. He watched closely, wanting to be sure to catch the first emotion Jak experienced beyond blind astonishment. It would tell him a lot about the young man.

After a few moments, Jak's eyes narrowed some and his mouth closed, the corners curling up ever so slightly. It was Broedi's turn to be taken aback. Of all the possible reactions Jak could have had, he appeared to be amused.

Broedi waited patiently. Someone had to say something and it was not going to be him. For all of the fantastic abilities he gained while in an animal's form, he also suffered the limitations. A lynx could not talk.

Jak finally broke the silence, muttering, "So *that's* how you fought off the wolves. You're a Shapechanger." Arching his eyebrows, he added, "A very big Shapechanger."

Kenders lifted her arms, pointing to the red spots along her arm. "He helped with our injuries, too. These used to be fingerprick punctures."

Jak glanced at her arms. "I was wondering how you got those."

Without pause, Kenders lied, "We tried to run from the wolves, tripped and fell into the bushes."

Nikalys frowned, but did not contradict her. Neither seemed to want Jak to know what she was. Broedi wondered how long they were going to be able to keep the truth from him.

Jak stood there, his hands on his hips, looking between his sister, brother, and Broedi. After spending a few moments quietly frowning, he stared at Broedi alone and let out a long sigh. "Alright. You can come."

Broedi was surprised. He had expected more discussion on the matter. A moment later, he got it.

"Are *you* mad?" exclaimed Nikalys. "He's a blasted *mage!*"

Kenders glared at Nikalys, evidently taking exception to his tone.

Jak's gaze never left Broedi, though, so he missed her consternation. In a surprisingly even tone, he said, "I don't care right now. If the wolves show again, I'd rather have him with us than not." He peered at his brother. "Remember what Widow John's husband looked like when they found him, Nik? His throat was gone. I like my throat. You?"

As Nikalys stared at Broedi, a deep scowl on face, Jak looked to Kenders. "And you're fine with this?"

Kenders nodded while eyeing Broedi with clear trepidation. "I think so."

With an air of finality, Jak said, "It's settled, then." He stared into the lynx's eyes. "Broedi comes with us. For now."

Broedi was content. It was a start.

CHAPTER 16: STUDENT

12th of the Turn of Sutri

A shaft of sunlight broke through the bulky gray clouds, illuminating the galley's sails billowing in the wind. A short, mid-morning squall had pushed through earlier, leaving behind a cool breeze and wet deck before slowly marching northwest over the Outlaw Sea.

Nundle Babblebrook stood on that wet deck, staring upward, examining the ship's masts. The main post held three wide yardarms and two sets of square sails, one of which had the sapphire blue symbol of the Academy at Immylla on it: a triangle encompassing three wavy lines. Drafting at only thirteen feet, the galley was a coastal ship, one meant to stay within sight of shore. Nundle was grateful for that tiny blessing.

Nundle's nausea worsened as he stared upward, prompting him to drop his gaze to his sandals instead. Ship and sea were conspiring against him, his stomach lurching with each swell and roll. He loathed boats.

During his oversea journey to the Arcane Republic, he had sworn that once he reached land he would never set foot on a ship again. When he had made the seasickness-inspired oath, the semester he would spend studying Strands of Water—this semester—had seemed a lifetime away. The time had come, though, and now found the tomble standing on the deck of another blasted ship.

Prior to leaving home, Nundle had been excited to travel here in order to study at the greatest magical universities and colleges in all of Terrene. Then he had looked at a map. There were a few places throughout Terrene further from Deepwell than the Arcane Republic, but not many.

His family and friends had not understood what he was doing nor knew where he was going. He kept things a secret for good reason. All they knew was that Nundle was giving up more than seemed sensible, leaving behind one of the most successful mercantile enterprises in the Five Boroughs.

Years ago, he had inherited his great-uncle's thriving business and promptly went about inadvertently ruining it. In a few short years, he had managed to whittle the once great company down to a single stall in the back row of the Deepwell market.

One day—on the brink of failure—he was negotiating with a Cartusian trader over a shipment of Sweetbush smoking-leaf. As usual, the give and take was mostly Nundle giving and the other merchant taking. Nundle had grown upset and glared at the man, silently willing him to accept his offered price.

When he saw bright, golden strings dancing before him, his first thought was that he had gone mad. He flailed about, panicking, and accidently arranged the golden threads into a pattern. He flung the gold knitting away, striking the longleg with it who showed no reaction whatsoever as the pattern melted into him. When negotiations resumed, Nundle was shocked when the longleg stopped haggling and gave Nundle his asking price.

That was the beginning of Master Merchant Nundle Babblebrook of Deepwell, one of the most respected and successful traders in the Five Boroughs. He never used what he called 'twisting the strings' to ruin another dealer or take advantage of anyone. Nundle just tilted the scales in his direction.

While he rebuilt and expanded his great-uncle's trading empire with help from his secret trick, he began a discreet search for more information on what he was experiencing. Some tombles were practitioners of magic, but society treated them as outcasts. He worked at collecting old books and texts whose subjects focused on magic, gathering an impressive private collection on the details of the Strands, as they were called.

Unfortunately, the books focused on the theory behind what the Strands were, not how to use them. He had learned, however, that the best place to study the craft was at the Strand Academies in the Arcane Republic. Nine different schools spread throughout the nation, each with a singular focus on a specific type of Strand.

He sold off controlling interest in his business and set off, traveling through the provinces of Gobberdale, Sweetbush, and Alewold before crossing into Jularrn where he stopped for a week and visited with a saeljulan friend, Lynnya.

Lynnya had tried to convince Nundle to turn around and return home, warning him of the excessive discrimination he would face in the Arcane Republic. The dual-island nation had been founded by three races—longlegs, saeljul, and divina—all of whom had low opinions of most anyone else.

Nundle's desire to learn was too strong to let this new information dissuade him. Seeing her friend so determined, Lynnya gave him the name of an old acquaintance who could help him gain entrance into the Academies. While open to all citizens of the republic, a non-citizen needed sponsorship by a preceptor or a government official.

Nundle had thanked Lynnya and continued south, through slate gray mountains and into the nation of Yut, where he skirted the eastern edges of the Great Shakti Desert. Prior to leaving, Nundle had read about deserts, but before

Yut, he had never seen one. After Yut, he decided he did not ever want to see another.

In the port of Yusi, he secured passage on the *Bhika's Maiden*, a trading ship headed to the City of the Strands. They were taking pigs and goats to sell and were going to purchase magical artifices.

Nundle wondered if his hatred for the sea came from the constant rolling and pitching he endured while on the ship, or from being cooped up on a ship full of pigs and goats for three weeks. The winds had been nearly non-existent—common for the time of year, according to the captain—resulting in both a longer voyage and a stench that had seeped into Nundle's soul.

As *Bhika's Maiden* approached the City of the Strands, Nundle had stared, flabbergasted by the nine twisting spires that stretched into the sky, sparkling in the sunlight, almost glowing with the hues of the Strands they represented. Beneath the towers sprawled an enormous city dominated by marble columns and granite domes.

His meeting with Lynnya's contact had been underwhelming and short. The ancient, white-haired saeljul had smirked at him and immediately named a price for sponsorship. It was a hefty sum, but Nundle had it and plenty more. He had carried a weighty purse with him on his journey without fear of robbery. With his trick, he could bend the will of those around him; brigands found targeting him a mistake.

For the most part, Nundle enjoyed his studies. He had traveled to the longlegs' Academy in Golden City first where he spent six turns further exploring the properties and capabilities of the Strands of Will. Nundle had excelled in his time there, actually earning praise from the preceptors, begrudgingly though it was given to a 'mainlander.' When he moved on to the other Academies, his studies became much more difficult.

Nundle had success working with the Strands for Life, Charge, and even Air, but Fire, Stone, and Soul were untouchable to him. Those semesters he studied a Strand to which he was deaf were terribly frustrating. He spent most of his time reading and studying while watching others excel.

A turn ago, Nundle had come to Immylla to begin his semester focusing on Strands of Water. Like every other class he had taken, this one included nine acolytes, a tradition based on the fact there were nine types of Strands. This class was made up entirely of Arcane Republic citizens, all of whom had a low opinion of their mainlander classmate.

One in particular, a female saeljuli named Landor, had made it a point to ensure Nundle's life was difficult at every turn. The pair had studied together at Golden City when Nundle had excelled at weaving Will. Landor had been deaf to the honey-colored strings and had not hidden her frustration that a mainlander—in his first semester, no less—had outshone her. She spent every day here at Immylla doing her best to embarrass Nundle.

However, even Landor was tolerable compared to Nundle's teacher.

Nundle had decided that Preceptor Myrr was the most unpleasant person he had ever met. The saeljul was constantly on edge. Nundle often wondered why the preceptor did not simply stop teaching. Most of the time, Preceptor Myrr's mind seemed to be elsewhere. Often during lessons, he would stand, staring at nothing for long periods in perfect silence.

Now was such a time.

Preceptor Myrr had been leaning on the deck's railings for a while now, staring at the rolling sea in perfect silence. As today's lesson on Water Strands was not going well for Nundle, he was hoping the preceptor might stay quiet until it was time to sail back to shore.

"Perhaps our tiny mainlander would like to try now."

The words cut into Nundle's reverie, causing him to look up so quickly that he nearly sprained his neck in the process. Nine pairs of eyes were on him, eight of which mattered not, even the strange iris-less stares of the divina in his class. The squall's leftover breeze whipped at Nundle's shaggy, bright red hair, forcing him to reach up, pull it back, and hold it in place so he could see. With great reluctance, he regarded his teacher.

Preceptor Myrr stood a full two inches over six feet, twice as tall as Nundle. Like all ijul, his features were stretched out, his face and nose elongated, his lips and eyes wider than any longleg or tomble. Willowy arms hung at his sides, reaching several inches lower than seemed normal. His hair was straight and blond, almost white in the sunlight. Most hung past his shoulders, but the sides were pulled back, held in place by a single crimson cord that matched his out-of-place robes.

Typically, preceptors' robes matched the shade of the Strand taught at their academy. When Nundle had arrived at Immylla, he had been greeted by a yard full of blue-clad preceptors, acolytes in gray, and a lone red-robed figure: Jhaell Myrr.

"So, mainlander," called Preceptor Myrr over the wind. "Will you try or not?"

The question was a holdover from earlier today and one Nundle had hoped he would not need to answer yet again. Sighing, he replied in his normal, high-pitched voice. "No, sir. I'll just wait here until class is over. Thank you, sir." That was all he was willing to venture. Things went best when the students said the least.

Preceptor Myrr eyed Nundle for a moment, his hair and robes rippling in the wind, and then shook his head as he turned away. Placing both hands on the railing, the ijul stared back out over the sea. The elongated fingers—they reminded Nundle of spider's legs—wrapped around the wood and squeezed.

Nundle and the other eight acolytes waited patiently, silently.

After a time, the quiet got to Nundle and he began to look around, staring about the boat again. His gaze fell upon the stairs that ran up to the deck at the boat's rear. He wondered if those had a special term, too. It baffled him that everything on a ship had a different name than it did on land. Nundle did not know his fore from aft or port from starboard. Nor did he care. The ocean was for fish. Not tombles.

"Mainlander?"

Nundle turned back to find the preceptor staring at him.

"This is your last chance."

Nundle winced inwardly, wondering what exactly the preceptor expected from him. Asking Nundle to try to touch Strands of Water was akin to asking a trout to fly.

Today's lesson had been a disaster up to this point. They were supposed to be working on a pattern of Water Strands that would bind liquid water together into a hard surface. When the preceptor told them to think of it as making ice without the cold, Nundle had made the mistake of asking why they just did not make ice. The resulting glare from his teacher certainly was cold enough to attempt the feat.

To demonstrate the pattern, Preceptor Myrr had ordered the gangplank lowered to the ocean's surface, walked down, and stepped onto the water. For a three-foot radius all around him, the sea's undulation ceased, the little waves frozen in place reminding him of a seascape painting.

The preceptor explained how the pattern was crafted and what it looked like, describing the requisite loops and hooks necessary in the Weave. The acolytes who had an affinity for Strands of Water were able to see the Weave while those that could not—Nundle included—were left standing around, staring at the ocean.

All four saeljuli in the class had easily grasped the lesson and joined the preceptor on the water. Smirking, Landor had extended the area of hard water a solid ten feet around her. Neither divina had been able to weave the pattern effectively and both fell into the sea, quickly lifting themselves back out with a Weave of Air. One of the longlegs had joined the divina in their impromptu swim while the other had made a mistake in the pattern, resulting in a geyser of water shooting him thirty feet into the air.

Nundle had simply refused to try. There was no point. Since arriving at Immylla, he had not sensed the tiniest flicker of blue.

It was not unusual by any means. Most mages showed proficiency with only two, sometimes three types of Strands. Fewer could touch four. It was rare when someone could effectively use five. After eight different academies, Nundle had discovered he could work four types of Strands and was proud of that accomplishment. If he could not touch Water, so be it.

His original refusal had prompted the preceptor's first long period of quiet. Nundle sensed that would not be the result this time.

"Still?" muttered Preceptor Myrr. "You still will not try?"

With the eyes of the entire class on him, Nundle answered, "No, Preceptor, I will not."

The longleg who had shot himself into the air earlier audibly gasped at Nundle's defiance.

Preceptor Myrr nodded slowly and, folding his arms behind him, took a few steps toward Nundle. "Tell me, mainlander, have you ever heard of the needleteeth shark?"

Nundle's eyes narrowed a fraction. "No, sir."

"Wondrous creatures, they are," said the preceptor. "Smallish, like you, perhaps only two feet long, but they have these long, spiny teeth with sharp barbs at the end. When they bite, their teeth break off, sticking in your flesh. Painful, I would expect, although that is not the end of it. You see, the teeth secrete a poison, a poison so potent that it paralyzes you within a few breaths yet it leaves you entirely aware as the sharks start to nibble away at you. Death is a race between being eaten alive and drowning."

"That sounds rather unpleasant, sir."

"It does, does it not?" mused the preceptor. He turned to stare out at the ocean. "I am surprised we have not seen any today. These shoals are infested with them."

A flicker of white was the only warning Nundle had before being abruptly lifted off the deck, whisked over the ship's rail, and dangled over the water. Believing that he was about to be some shark's next meal, he reached out for the Strands of Will and quickly knit the pattern that would make Preceptor Myrr susceptible to suggestions. It was forbidden to use a Weave against a preceptor, but Nundle was happy to make an exception in this case.

Yet when he directed the pattern at the ijul, it unraveled, the golden Strands swiftly falling apart before fading away.

"I read the report on you, mainlander!" called Preceptor Myrr. "And *that* was incredibly predictable!" If a mage could see a Weave, he or she could unravel it if they knew where to pull. Apparently, the preceptor knew exactly where.

Nundle did not answer as he was too busy panicking over being eaten. Or drowning. Or both.

As the preceptor lowered him to the water's surface, Nundle readied himself to start swimming, his mind racing for a way out of this. He was surprised when he thudded onto something solid rather splashing into the sea. Righting himself, he looked around and found a three-foot diameter circle of hard, unmoving water surrounding him. Curious, he bent over and touched it. It looked like ice, but it was warm. A lone word of wonder slipped from his lips.

"Huh."

The preceptor's voice cut through the air. "Back to the docks!"

Nundle's head snapped up. "Wait…what?" He looked on with growing anxiety as sailors rushed about the deck, readying the ship for sailing. Some stared out at him with worried expressions, yet none made any effort to toss him a rope.

Preceptor Myrr leaned over the galley's railing and called out, "When you have figured out the pattern, walk to shore. If you are not in class tomorrow morning, I may send someone for you." The ijul then turned and walked away, his long arms swinging freely by his sides.

Nundle stared at his fellow acolytes, foolishly hoping they might help him somehow. Most of them seemed unconcerned about him. Landor wore a wide smile.

As the ship sailed away, Nundle had no choice but to stand there and watch. After a time, he sat down cross-legged on the not-ice and, rising and falling with the swells, stared at the white sails as they shrunk to a dot on the horizon.

"Wondrous."

As he let out a long sigh, a shark's fin pierced the water's surface nearby.

"Uh-oh…"

CHAPTER 17: RESEARCH

Jhaell lifted a hand and absentmindedly scratched his nose, his gaze traversing the words written in the book that lay open before him. On the corner of his desk sat a jar of sand in which a Yutian incense stick burned, its curls of peppery smoke coiling up from the glowing tip to join the thick haze hanging near the ceiling. Beeswax candles clasped in tall bronze stands illuminated the room with a soft, quivering glow.

He was trying to plan tomorrow's lesson, but try as he might, he could not concentrate on the pages before him. He glanced to another book on his desk, a faded blue, canvas-bound tome from Quan that contained one of the most promising passages of text he had found in years. It was nothing to bring to Tandyr yet, but if he could find corroboration in the library, he certainly would.

Tilting his head back, he stared at the ceiling and sighed heavily, his exhalation causing the incense haze to twist and spin. With each passing semester, his restlessness increased. Over two hundred fifty years had passed since Syra's death. At times, he had difficulty remembering her face. Yet the ache of loss was as potent as it had been that day on the cold, sandy shore.

When he had agreed to help Tandyr, he had never expected things to take so long. He had met some success—finding the first for which Tandyr was searching—but the going was interminably slow. He was only a third of the way through the academy's massive library.

What made things worse—what he had made worse—was the chance it was all for naught. If the Progeny were not found, Tandyr's plan could fail and Jhaell's promised reunion with Syra would never come.

He sighed again, quietly cursing, "Beelvra..."

The sound of metal striking wood issued forth from his office door, the crack reverberating through the room. Jhaell's melancholy mood fled in an instant, his long fingers balling into fists. If another one of the acolytes was coming to complain, Jhaell just might kill him or her.

Reaching over, he picked up the blue tome, opened a front drawer, and slid the book inside. Shutting the drawer, he shot a quick glance around the room, confirming that he had not left anything else out. Tables stretched the length of the walls, covered with stacks of maps and yellowed parchments. Seeing nothing important in plain sight, he looked to the door.

"Enter."

When the door swung open, a slight frown spread over Jhaell's face. It was not a student.

The ijul standing in the doorway wore robes of cobalt silk lined with ornate, teal ribbing at the cuffs and neckline. A sapphire the size of Jhaell's thumb was sewn into the robe at the neckline's inverted peak. Ensconced in the robes was an old saeljul with long, white hair so thin that it reminded Jhaell of threads hanging from a sleeve after being caught on a stray splinter.

While Jhaell was nearly four hundred years old, he was still several decades from his first wrinkle. This saeljul's face was a web of them. Lines spread across his pale skin like the roads on a city map. Contrasting the ijul's feeble appearance were his bright green eyes, sharp and alive.

As the saeljul shuffled into the room, Jhaell rose and gave a small bow. The elder ijul looked out of place, his bright blue robe clashing with the plush crimson rug that covered the office's stone floor.

"To what do I owe the pleasure, Distinguished One?"

Distinguished One Hovathil studied the room, taking in the closed shutters on the three arched windows, the candles, and the sparse, crimson-heavy décor. When his gaze rested on Jhaell and his red robes, Hovathil frowned, reorganizing the age lines on his face. Letting out a wisp of a sigh, he scanned the room again. "Do you not have a chair so I may rest?"

Jhaell had removed the chairs from his office decades ago. They encouraged people to sit and stay when Jhaell would much rather that they had never come in the first place.

"No, Distinguished One, I do not."

Hovathil glared at Jhaell for a long moment, saying nothing. Jhaell met his stare with a quiet, tolerant confidence.

"Preceptor Myrr, we are a patient race, are we not?"

Jhaell nodded once. "We are."

"Would you say that we here at the Academy have been patient with you?"

Jhaell kept his face a blank mask. "Pardon, sir?"

"Your behavior and attitude have been...let us say 'challenging' for others to deal with over these last few decades. Centuries, even." Hovathil paused, seeing if he would get a response. He would not.

Jhaell clasped his hands together and stared in silence, curious as to why the Distinguished One had come. Visits to his personal office by the registry were rare.

After a few moments, Hovathil gave a tiny, wondering shake of his head. "What has become of you, Myrr? You were one of our best instructors. Acolytes requested you. Now you are temperamental. Irritable. 'Cruel' is a word many whisper."

Jhaell replied in an even, unassuming tone. "I have modified my teaching methods through the years. That is all."

"For the worst, it would seem," muttered Hovathil, strolling over to one of the tables covered with maps and parchments.

Jhaell stiffened, praying the Distinguished One did not start shuffling through the table's contents. "Why are you here, Distinguished One?" The question served its purpose, pulling Hovathil's attention from the papers and placing it back on Jhaell.

"One of your classes—all *nine* acolytes—quits the Academy, leaving nothing more than letters of notice in their quarters, and you have to ask the reason for my visit?" He began to advance on Jhaell's desk, his eyes burning. "We have *never* had that happen at Immylla, Myrr. *Never.*"

It had been difficult, but Jhaell had managed to arrange things to appear that the nine students had quit the Academy on their own accord. He continued to regret his indiscretion in Yellow Mud, but the acolytes' disappearance had proven to be a boon of sorts. He had more time to research for Tandyr now.

Inclining his head, Jhaell said, "They will be missed, sir."

"I doubt by you," muttered Hovathil. He leaned forward, letting his thin hair hang before his wizened face like dead, moss from an ancient tree. "You *will* modify your tutoring methods, Myrr. Do you understand? Else your position here at Immylla will be terminated."

Jhaell tried hard not to glower at the ijul, but could not be sure he succeeded. "I under—"

"Do you still wish to teach here, Myrr?"

In all honesty, the answer was no. Yet in order to continue searching the library's dusty tomes and parchments, seeking any mention of the Locking and—more recently—anything that might lead to the Progeny, Jhaell needed to retain his position of preceptor. "

The Distinguished One leaned even closer. His breath smelled of onions and fish. "I am waiting for your answer, Myrr."

Along with patience, humility was a quality Jhaell had ceased to practice over the centuries. It took him a moment to summon some, bow his head, and say politely, "Yes, Distinguished One, I value my place at Immylla."

"Excellent to hear. Because that means I shall *never* again hear of you doing something as brainless as leaving a Water-deaf acolyte alone in the middle of the ocean! Should you ever perpetrate such idiocy again, you will be removed from your position here. Is that understood?!"

Jhaell finally understood what had prompted Hovathil's visit. "I was merely trying to teach the mainlander today's lesson."

Hovathil's green eyes opened wide. "Oh! By all means, teach. Impart. Demonstrate. Educate. Lecture. Elucidate…Pontificate if you must!" Smacking his palm on Jhaell's desk, Hovathil hissed, "But *never* put the acolytes in mortal danger! Mainlander or not!"

Jhaell dropped his head, stared at the open book on his desktop, and swallowed his pride. "Understood, Distinguished One. I apologize."

"You are incredibly lucky, Myrr. Had the tomble not been particularly clever, he would most likely be dead. And we would have had to cancel *another* one of your classes."

That had actually been Jhaell's hope. Looking up, he asked, "May I ask how he returned, sir?"

"He adapted a Weave coastal mages use to aid fishermen and charmed the needleteeth to pull him to shore—without biting him. He arrived on shore a while ago, dripping wet, but none the worse for wear."

Jhaell lifted an eyebrow, forced to acknowledge the tomble's ingenuity. "And then he ran straight to the registry and reported me, did he?"

"Actually, no," replied Hovathil. "Preceptor Filaeril spotted him on his way back to the dormitory and asked why he was sloshing seawater all over the halls. The tomble claimed he had tripped and fallen off the docks, but—as the mainlander is *your* student—Preceptor Filaeril suspected something else had occurred and brought him to me. The tomble refused to reveal what happened until I threatened to expel him."

"So everything is fine, then? The tomble is alive, no harm was done, and class may continue." He was less than thrilled with the outcome.

The already deep creases around Hovathil's eyes turned to canyons. "You would be wise to spend time thinking on what we have spoken of today, Myrr." He turned around and began walking back to the office's open doorway. After a few steps, he halted, looked back, and pointed a long, bony finger at Jhaell. "By the way, we continue to disapprove of your choice in fashion."

"And I will continue to wear it," replied Jhaell evenly. Crimson had been Syra's favorite color. "The Academy's bylaws allow it."

Hovathil pressed his thin, dry, and cracked lips together and sighed. "I suppose that is the least of my concerns." He glared at Jhaell's robes a moment longer before lighting his gaze to Jhaell's face. "I will be observing your class tomorrow, Myrr. Do you have any objections?"

While Jhaell could think of quite a few, he shook his head. "None, sir. It would be an honor."

Hovathil nodded once and exited the room, leaving the eight-paneled oak door open behind him, Jhaell suspected on purpose. Moving from behind his desk, Jhaell strode across the plush rug to shut it himself. As he grabbed the door's edge, he felt a black, crackling vibration in the air. His eyes widened as panic rushed through him.

Poking his head out of the door, he ensured that Hovathil continued striding down the hall. When the Distinguished One did not turn back, Jhaell closed the door and hurried to the table over which Hovathil had been hovering. He retrieved a bundle of ten parchments from a stack's bottom and, after taking them to his desk, fanned out the blank sheets and waited.

Moments later, a long, flowing script began to appear on the fourth from the left. He pulled the sheet free and stared. The individual at the other end was writing as quickly as a snail crawled. Jhaell squeezed his eyes shut, impatient. "Write faster, blast it."

These parchments had become invaluable in his search. A preceptor from the Academy at Hollow who possessed superior control over Strands of Void had made them for Jhaell ages ago. A unique Weave, bound to two sheets of parchment, allowed someone to write on one sheet and the letters would appear on its mate, regardless of distance between the pair. With a simple weave of Air, the parchment could be cleared and reused indefinitely. The pairs to these ten were spread across Terrene—most in the Oaken Duchies—with different Tandyr loyalists.

Jhaell slowly counted to twenty, opened his eyes, and read the now complete message, his anger mounting with each sentence. This parchment's counterpart belonged to an erijul currently investigating an area around Greycliffe in the Duchy of the Red Peaks. According to the message, an official of Duke Thomas' court had visited him, curious about the odd questions he was asking.

"Blasted fool," muttered Jhaell.

After clearing the message with a tiny Weave of Air, he dropped the parchment on the desk and stood there, thinking through how he should handle the situation. After a few moments, he decided he needed to visit Greycliffe personally and learn exactly what the foolish erijul and duchy official had discussed.

A long, frustrated sigh seeped from him. He had hoped to spend the evening in the library. Instead, he would be thousands of miles away, fixing someone else's mistake.

CHAPTER 18: LUCK

Nundle strode down the cool, gray granite hallway, walking through alternating strips of light and shade as Mu's orb shined through the tall arched windows on his left. The smack of his sandals against the stone floor was the only sound echoing within the cavernous passageway.

He had been lying atop his bed, contemplating different ways he could manage to hide for the remainder of the semester when the idea to go speak with Preceptor Myrr had popped into his head. Suddenly determined to ask his teacher that he be allowed to either study independently for the remainder of the semester or be moved to another class, he had hopped up, slipped on his sandals, and began wandering the academy's maze of halls. He doubted the preceptor would be receptive to his requests, but, amazingly, he had not turned back.

He sighed and shook his head. "Perhaps I've gone mad..."

Ahead of him, Distinguished One Hovathil exited the hallway that led to the preceptor's office, his blue robes swishing as he walked. Nundle halted in place and almost dove into a nearby alcove. He had no desire to speak with the saeljul again.

Luckily, the Distinguished One seemed preoccupied and did not notice Nundle. He turned left and shuffled away from the tomble, passing through the patches of sun and shade farther down the hall.

For once, Nundle rejoiced in his small stature. At three and a half feet tall, he was much shorter than most everyone in the Arcane Republic. In fact, he had come across but one soul his size while studying, an atarkas named Kemir during his semester near the Ciyriel volcano. The pair had become fast friends, finding solidarity in being two short people in a tall persons' world. Unfortunately, their paths had not crossed again once they both finished at Veduin.

Considering todays' events, Distinguished One Hovathil coming from the direction of Preceptor Myrr's offices most likely meant he had visited Nundle's teacher, something Nundle had begged the elder ijul not to do.

Nundle let out a long, weary sigh. A visit from the Distinguished One would not have improved the preceptor's mood. Still, Nundle resumed his path down the hall. He had come this far already.

Upon reaching the intersection, Nundle turned left, having been down this corridor only once before when he had come to introduce himself to his new teacher. He hoped today's visit would go better than that one.

On his first day at Immylla, Nundle had knocked on the preceptor's door. A few moments passed, then a voice from within told him to enter. Nundle shoved the heavy wooden door, pushing it into the room, and began to introduce himself at once. He had only gotten out his name when he had felt a soft, white crackling of Air. With a great gust of wind, the giant oak door had slammed in his face forcing Nundle to leap back quickly to avoid his foot being crushed in the doorjamb. The preceptor had barely glanced up from his desk.

Now, that same eight-paneled oak door waited ahead, beckoning him. He shook his head, muttering, "This is madder than a goose napping in an oven."

He was still a dozen paces from the door when the familiar crackling and crinkling of the Strands filled his chest and the air around him. While it was common to feel weaving inside the walls of the Academy, the Strands he sensed stunned Nundle. His eyes opened wide.

"Oh, my…"

The sparkling white of Air was clear and familiar, but the thick, throbbing, black Strands rushing through the walls, past him, and into the preceptor's office were new. He had never before sensed them. Ever.

"It can't be…"

Nundle was astounded. The ebony Strands of Void were as clear to him as the gold of Will. He spun in place, gaping at the air in the hall, watching the inky black Strands whip past him.

Few ever showed proficiency with Void. The Academy at Hollow, where Void was taught, was the smallest and least attended of all of the schools. Often, they did not even have the requisite nine acolytes to teach a lone class there. Most students simply skipped the semester at Hollow. Even Nundle had considered not going, scheduling things so it was the last remaining Academy on his list.

A wide, joyous smile spread over his lips. He, Nundle Babblebrook, was one of only a handful of mages who could touch five types of Strands. He almost giggled with excitement.

Suddenly, the Strands stopped flying past him and he sensed that the Weave—whatever its purpose—was complete. Moments later, the sensation of the Strands disappeared altogether.

Nundle looked up and down the hallway. It was empty. He was almost disappointed; he wanted to share his good fortune with someone. Not that anyone would have cared.

"Well, I am *certainly* going to Hollow now."

With a renewed sense of confidence, he hurried down the remaining dozen paces to Preceptor Myrr's door. He was about to knock when he halted, his fist hovering inches from the wood.

It was time for eveningmeal, meaning most everyone was in the dining hall, most everyone but Preceptor Myrr. Nundle had not seen the saeljul attend a meal there yet, which meant the odds were high that the preceptor was responsible for the Strands of Void, something the saeljul had never mentioned. In fact, it seemed he had purposely concealed it. On day one of the class, Preceptor Myrr had proudly listed his proficiency with the Strands: Water, Will, Air, and Soul.

The great oaken door stood before Nundle, taunting him. Taking a deep breath, he rapped his knuckles against the wood and waited. There was a bronze knocker affixed to the door, but he was too short to reach it.

After a long period of silence, he knocked again, harder this time. The crack of bone on wood echoed down the empty hallway.

He waited again, expecting a command to open the door. Or at least one telling him to leave. However, only silence met him.

With a frown, he mumbled, "You can't ignore me." Reaching up, he pulled the latched handle and pushed the door open a crack. The heady scent of peppery, spicy incense drifted from within. "Preceptor Myrr, sir?"

Silence.

He pushed open the door further and peeked inside. The office was empty.

Confused, Nundle stepped into the office. With all three windows shuttered, the room was darker than the hallway. A dozen candles burned unattended on tall, bronze candelabras.

Nundle shook his head. "Now that's just reckless…"

Having read more than most on Strand theory, he reasoned Preceptor Myrr had crafted a port. It certainly explained the Void and Air Strands and the fact that his teacher was not here. He was about to turn and leave when his gaze fell on the shelves of books built into the wall behind the preceptor's desk.

"Ooh! Books!"

Curiosity overrode good judgment. Nundle strode across the crimson rug and around the desk, his gaze running over the rows of colorful volumes.

Sliding the heavy desk chair closer to the shelves, he climbed atop the seat and studied the bottom row. The leather-bound covers were various shades of browns, blacks, and grays, while the canvas books were a mix of bright blues, reds, and greens. Titles were stamped or embossed on the spines with gold, silver, or black lettering. The books so enthralled Nundle that he forgot he was standing in Preceptor Myrr's office, uninvited and alone.

One book grabbed his attention, *Amamene's Study of Will*, a brown leather-bound volume by an author he had never read. As he reached his hand toward it, a colorless crackling rustled inside of him. His heart leapt into his throat as he spun around, expecting to find the preceptor standing there, ready to deal with him harshly for the intrusion.

The office, however, was still empty.

Nundle shut his eyes and muttered in relief, "Oh, thank the gods…"

After taking a quick, steadying breath, he reopened his eyes and focused on the sensation of magic. They were ebony Strands of Void, but much fainter than before.

Eyeing the open door, he quietly called, "Hello?"

There was no response.

Out of the corner of his eye, he caught a flicker of movement on the desk. Other than a few books and some sheets of parchment spread in a haphazard fan shape, it appeared empty. Curious, he hopped off the chair and scooted to the desk. Standing on his toes, he peered over the edge. Reaching out, he slid the top parchment to the side and froze.

Handwriting was appearing on one of the sheets as though by an invisible hand, the script rushed and agitated. Apparently, the invisible hand was in a rush.

"Well, that's a nifty trick."

It suddenly occurred to him he was in a rather untenable situation. Should Preceptor Myrr return from wherever he had gone and found Nundle rummaging through his belongings, he would not be happy. "I should go."

He was about to replace the top parchment when a particular phrase in the message's text made him stop. Eyes narrowing, Nundle slid the scrawled-upon parchment from those on top of it and read from the beginning. He reached the last word a moment or two after the writing stopped.

Heart thudding, he re-read the entire message again.

"Not possible…"

Staring at the parchment, he wondered if he had actually fallen asleep in his room earlier and this was a dream. Reaching to a burning candle on the desk, he stuck his right index finger over the flame.

"Ouch!"

Whipping his hand back, he shook his finger in the air. This was no dream.

He looked back to the parchment, shaking his head. The words did not make sense. The preceptor was an impatient soul and an awful teacher, but Nundle could not believe he would involve himself in something as insidious as this message implied.

He stood there a moment, considering what he should do. Deciding this was more trouble than it was worth, he shook his head. "Forget you ever saw this, Nundle."

He slid the parchment back in its original place and scurried around the desk. Halfway across the plush rug, he stopped. Turning slowly, he stared back to the massive desk. If the words on the parchment were true, he could not ignore it. Against his better judgment, he hurried back, pulled the parchment free, and read the message a third time. Shutting his eyes, he folded the parchment and jammed it in the pocket of his cloak.

"Gods…what am I doing?"

Scampering from the office, he quickly and quietly shut the door behind him and rushed down the hall, heading back to his room. He had to pack. His semester at the Academy at Immylla was finished.

CHAPTER 19: BROTHER

The unseasonably cool weather had lasted for only a day, leaving the three Isaac siblings and Broedi to travel overland in heat more typical for the summer. For three long, arduous days, the party moved east, hiking up and down countless hills while continuing to avoid the Southern Road. The shade of the oak and ash trees provided some relief from the burning sun, but it was negligible.

Every day, the group used the same walking order. Broedi led, followed by Kenders, then Jak, with Nikalys at the end of their short column. When the hillman had insisted on the sequence, no one had argued. Personally, Jak thought it unwise to argue with a giant Shapechanger mage.

Broedi had proven himself a useful if near-silent traveling companion, rarely saying more than a few words a day. He did stare, however, focusing most of his attention on Nikalys and Kenders, although Jak occasionally caught the large man studying him as well.

Every evening when they stopped for the day, Broedi would tell them to set up camp and leave for a short while. He would return later with enough rabbit and quail for them all to eat their fill. Jak was tiring of hillsage-roasted rabbit and quail, but the alternative was to eat nothing.

As of yet, Jak had not chanced talking to his brother and sister about what had truly happened in those final, confusing moments with their parents in Yellow Mud. The only occasion he had alone with them was the limited time each evening when Broedi hunted. Nikalys and Kenders had quietly pressed him, but he put their questions off, afraid to speak freely in front of Broedi. Jak did not trust the hillman. Something about him did not ring true.

This evening, however, Jak needed to take the chance. Smithshill was less than a day away and he had to persuade Nikalys and Kenders to alter their plans. Jak had no interest whatsoever striding into the Office of the Constables with a magical necklace around his neck.

He had tried to order them not to go last night, claiming he was the head of the family now and they should listen to him. The both dismissed his demand outright, Nikalys with rolled eyes while Kenders laughed aloud at him. She was determined to seek justice for Yellow Mud. Jak respected his sister's resolve, but she was basing her decisions on incomplete information.

Jak reached up, scratched his still-wispy beard, and glanced back through the trees at the orange sky. Mu's orb had already set. Frowning, he stared back ahead, still waiting for Broedi to call for a halt. The past two nights, they had already made camp by this time of day.

It was some time later when the hillman finally held up his hand, saying in his deep baritone voice, "We will stop now."

Jak scanned the area. They stood amidst a cluster of small trees where the ground looked slightly less rocky than the rest of the forest. A small spring bubbled up fresh, clear water, filling a small pool and feeding a creek that trickled down the hillside. Broedi had chosen a good site for camp.

Kenders began looking for fallen deadwood to build a fire while Nikalys began washing the grime from his face and hands in the creek. None of them had had a proper bath since before the tragedy. Jak sniffed his dirty clothes and wrinkled his nose. He reeked.

Uneasy and apprehensive, Jak meandered about the camp, waiting for Broedi to leave, making a show of stretching his sore muscles and mentioning how hungry he was. After the third time he announced his ravenous appetite, Nikalys—squatting by the spring and filling the waterskins—stared up at him. "Are you feeling alright?"

Jak stopped, looked down at Nikalys, and silently chastised himself. He was acting like a guilty child who had stolen a tart from the kitchen. "Yeah. I'm just hungry." That made four times. "And sore. You know, from all the walking today."

Broedi—who had been drinking from the pool—looked up to stare at Jak, his brown-eyed gaze curious, evaluating.

Nikalys said, "If you're so tired, stop walking around. Sit. Rest."

Jak nodded. "You're right. I will." He did not sit down, though.

Broedi bent over, took another long drink of water from the spring, and then stood, wiping the leftover drops from his chin. His gaze settled on Jak again and stayed there. Jak did his best to appear calm. After a few moments, the hillman turned to Kenders.

"Have the fire ready, uora. I will be back shortly."

Kenders nodded as Broedi moved off to the north side of the clearing, giving Jak one last interested look. Jak smiled wide and offered an overly friendly wave.

"Good hunting, Broedi." As soon as the hillman stepped into the cover of the trees, Jak turned his hand on himself and smacked his forehead lightly. "Idiot..."

After counting to twenty—slowly—he scurried over to where Kenders had set up the logs. She was crouched by the unlit wood and dry brush with a firestick in her hand. Jak scanned the trees where Broedi had left and, seeing or hearing nothing, looked over to Nikalys and called in a hushed whisper, "Nik! Come here!"

In the midst of refilling the waterskins, Nikalys looked up at his brother's call. "Why?"

"I need to talk to you."

"Can it wait a bit?"

Kenders struck the firestick against the rough lid. The tip flared bright and sent a sharp, hissing puff of air through the clearing, startling Jak.

Trying to calm his nerves, Jak stared back to his brother. "No, it can't. I need to talk *before* Broedi gets back."

Looking up, Kenders asked, "Is this about home?" The dry, shredded kindling under the thicker logs was already beginning to catch.

Jak nodded quickly. "There are some things you need to know before we go marching into Smithshill."

Nikalys shared a quick look with Kenders, placed the waterskin he had been filling on the ground, and moved to stand next to Kenders. "Go on."

Unwilling to waste even a moment—Broedi was a fast hunter—Jak reached into the neck of his shirt and pulled out the silver teardrop necklace he had been sure to keep hidden.

Kenders gasped the moment she saw it. "That's Mother's necklace…" She reached out a hand as if to touch it, but stopped short. After dropping her arm to her side, she asked, "Does this mean you…that you found their…?" She trailed off and peered at Jak with wide eyes.

Realizing what they must think, Jak shook his head quickly. "No…no! Gods, no! Mother gave this to me before—" He stopped short. He needed to tell the story from the beginning. "Just listen. *No* questions. I want to get this done before Broedi gets back."

He relayed the story of his last moments with their parents, his time in the barrel, and subsequent escape from the tree. When he revealed how he had used their mother's necklace to find them, both Nikalys and Kenders remained oddly silent. Considering that the necklace was obviously magic, they should have been upset or at least surprised.

Nikalys, his gaze fixed on the silver pendant, asked, "Can I see it?"

Jak lifted the necklace over his head and gave it to his brother.

Nikalys turned it over in his hands, examining the silver teardrop. "And you are sure this is magic?" He sounded dubious.

Jak nodded. "Oh, it's magic. How else could I have found you? The forest is too blasted big for me to just trip over you."

A worried scowl crept over Nikalys' face. "How'd you say it works?"

"Close your eyes and picture the person you want to find."

Nikalys shrugged his shoulders. "Sounds simple enough." Pointing to one side of the campsite, he instructed, "Jak, over there." He indicated the trunk of an old oak on the other side. "Kenders, there."

Understanding at once what Nikalys wanted to do, Jak hurried to where Nikalys had pointed. When he turned around, he found Kenders still standing by the fire and staring at Nikalys. Shaking her head, she muttered, "I don't think this is a good idea."

"Perhaps not," conceded Nikalys. "But we need to know what we are dealing with. We can't go marching into the Constables' office with this around one of our necks if it's magic, can we?"

Jak was glad his brother saw things the way he did.

Kenders gave a reluctant sigh, turned, and moved to stand beside an old oak. Twenty-five paces separated each of them from one another, the fledgling campfire burning in the center of an Isaac siblings' triangle.

Nikalys closed his eyes, wrapped his hand around the silver teardrop pendant, and stood still for a few moments. With his eyes still shut tight, he murmured, "Are you sure it's magic, Jak?"

Jak's eyes narrowed. "What? Why?"

After opening his eyes, Nikalys looked at his brother. "I thought of you and nothing happened."

Confused, Jak nodded to their sister. "Try Kenders."

Nikalys glanced at her, shrugged his shoulders again, and closed his eyes. A moment later, he let out a startled yelp, dropped the necklace to the dirt, and took a quick step back, staring at the silver pendant.

Jak stared at the talisman as well, thoroughly bewildered. "I'm guessing it worked that time?"

Nikalys' gaze remained locked on the pendant, his brow lined with deep concern. "Oh, yes. It worked."

As the three of them eyed the necklace in silence, a baffled frown spread over Jak's face. He wondered why it worked on Kenders but not him.

After a few moments, Kenders spoke up, her voice uncharacteristically timid. "Toss it here, Nik. I'd like to try."

Nikalys peered across the clearing at her. "Are you sure?"

Kenders gave a quick nod. "Just one time."

Nikalys hesitated before retrieving the necklace from the ground. After brushing the dirt from the silver, he lobbed it to his sister. Kenders caught it, held it in her open palm, and stared at it, her expression a nervous one. Jak was surprised. Kenders was the fearless, impetuous soul of the family.

After another moment's hesitation, Kenders wrapped her palm around the talisman and closed her eyes. Jak expected some sort of reaction from her, similar to Nikalys' start and shout. Instead, her anxious expression slowly melted away, morphing into one of curiosity, confusion, and wonderment.

Kenders opened her eyes and hand to stare at the necklace. "It only works on me and Nik." She looked over at Jak. "I thought of you, and nothing. But with Nik, I felt that sense of calm you mentioned. And I heard the bell, too." Glancing between them, she added, "Out of curiosity, I thought of Broedi and—" she paused and peered back to the necklace "—there was nothing." A few golden curls fell before her face.

Walking toward her, Nikalys asked, "Why would Mother have a necklace that only worked on two of us? And where in the Nine Hells did she get it?"

Looking to Jak, Kenders asked, "Where's the package Father gave you?"

Jak moved to where he had put his traveling gear down and retrieved the long leather bundle. Hurrying back to Nikalys and Kenders, he held the package out.

"What is it?" asked Nikalys. "A bow case?"

"I don't think so," said Jak. "Have you ever seen it before?"

"Sure."

Surprised, Jak peered at his brother. "When?"

With a tiny, lopsided smile, Nikalys said, "I've been following you for three days, Jak. All I have to look at is trees, bushes, rocks, and your back."

"That's not what I meant," said Jak. He looked to Kenders. "You?"

Kenders looked over the leather package and shook her head. "Sorry, no."

Nikalys stepped closer and studied the bundle in Jak's hands. "What's inside?"

"I couldn't tell you." Jak began rotating the four-foot long package. "I can't find a way to open it. There are no seams, laces, holes...nothing."

"Make this plain for me," said Kenders. "After Mother gives you a forbidden necklace, Father hands you this leather case, and they tell you to run away...you just *did*?" Her eyes and voice betrayed open disbelief.

"Well, in a manner of speaking, yes. But—"

Reaching up, she smacked him in the arm. "What in the Nine Hells is wrong with you?!" She struck him again, harder this time. "You just left them there?!"

"You weren't there, Kenders! It was madness. People screaming, buildings cracking, the roar of the water!"

"You left them to die, Jak!" shouted Kenders.

"I did what they told me to do!" snapped Jak. "They told me to run! That I had to keep you two safe. 'Promise to keep Nikalys and Kenders safe. They are important.' were father's exact words right before he shoved me down the road!"

Some of Kenders' anger drained away. "Why would he do that? Why say something like that?"

A deep baritone voice rumbled through the clearing. "Is not every child important to their mother and father?"

Jak spun around to find Broedi leaning against an oak tree at the edge of the clearing, watching the three of them. He did not have any rabbits or quail with him. Dropping the case to his side, Jak asked, "How long have you been standing there?"

Broedi stood tall and strode into camp, straight for them. He stopped before Jak and looked to the bundle Jak held. "May I see that, uori?"

Jak slid the case behind him. "No. This doesn't concern you." Broedi was not family. Broedi was not a friend. He was simply something to keep the wolves away at night.

The hillman fixed Jak with an appraising stare. After a long moment, he sighed, put his arm around Jak's shoulders, and rumbled, "Come, I would like you to hunt with me tonight." He began to march back to the edge of the forest, dragging Jak with him.

After a few stunned steps, Jak pulled away. "No!"

The hillman turned and glared. His voice dropped low as he growled, "I am asking nicely."

Jak took a step backwards and shook his head. "I don't much care. I'm not going."

Broedi's gaze flicked back to Nikalys and Kenders. He remained that way for a moment, intense and pensive, before pressing his lips together and stepping close to Jak. Stopping a pace away, he leaned down and whispered so only Jak could hear, "I need to speak to you. *Alone.*"

Confused, Jak peered at the hillman. "Why?"

"Because they are not ready."

"Ready for what?"

From behind, Nikalys asked, "Jak? Is everything alright?"

Broedi looked over Jak's shoulder. "One moment, uori." Shifting his stare back to Jak, he whispered, "I can tell you what is inside the case. But I need you to come with me." His eyes flashed wide, insistent. "Now."

"How could you know what is—?"

"*Now*, uori. You must trust me."

Frustrated, Jak hissed, "Just tell us all—"

With an urgent, passionate earnestness, Broedi muttered, "*Please.*"

Jak glanced over his shoulder to Nikalys and Kenders. They were staring at Broedi with apprehension. Looking back to the hillman, he set his jaw and shook his head. "No."

Broedi's deep brown eyes turned hard. "Come with me now and learn the truth, or you will *never* leave this clearing. I will *not* let you impede what must be done."

While the hillman's threat triggered a certain sense of panic, Jak found himself intrigued. "What does that mean? 'What must be done?'"

Broedi's stony expression softened a fraction, from granite to sandstone. "Come with me and I will tell you."

Jak eyed the hillman, surprised that he was actually considering the offer. Broedi was offering answers. Whether or not they were legitimate or the mad imaginings of a Shapechanger mage, Jak decided that he had to risk it. "Fine."

Relief flooded Broedi's face. "Thank you." Standing tall, the giant peered over Jak's head and said, "Uora, uori, we will return in a while. Please stay here. Do not worry, we will not go far." With that, he turned and began to move toward the northern edge of the clearing.

Kenders asked, "Can we come?"

Without slowing, Broedi rumbled, "No."

Jak looked back to his brother and sister, summoned a smile, and then turned to follow the hillman. After a few steps, Nikalys called out, "Jak, you forgot a sling!"

Broedi, already standing at the clearing's edge, said, "He will not need it."

As Jak reached the hillman, Broedi placed a firm and heavy hand on his shoulder and led him into the forest.

Chapter 20: Travel

Nundle glanced west while adjusting the canvas sack slung over his shoulder. The setting sun was enormous, a glorious half-circle falling into the ocean, painting sky and sea alike with layers of orange, red, and soft lavender.

He frowned and increased his pace, but was careful not to go too quickly. As much as he would have liked to take the stone steps to the docks two at a time, it would most likely result in him rolling down the stairs.

Three wooden piers jutted out into the academy's harbor, lined with over two dozen ships, most of which were the style favored by Arcane Republic longlegs: sweeping curves, triangular sails, and figureheads of animals on the bow. Longlegs manned nearly every ship in the nation. Few saeljul or divina sailed.

As he stepped onto the docks, he noted with disappointment that the decks of all but a few ships were empty. Hurrying to the first one with sailors still aboard, he chatted with the longlegs, asking them to point out the fastest ship in Immylla Harbor. Their answer was quick and unanimous. A cutter, *Morning's Mist*, held the title.

Praying the ship was not tied for the night, Nundle rushed to the where the *Morning's Mist* was moored. The ship was long and narrow with tall, spindly masts—smaller than Nundle had expected—and a massive, carved wooden goat's head mounted at its front. He wondered what a goat had to do with morning mist.

Longleg sailors moved about the deck, talking loudly as they tied ropes, pushed crates around, and did whatever else it was seamen did on boats.

He stood on the jetty for a moment, eyeing the ship, a frown on his face. Greya, goddess of Fate, certainly had a cruel sense of humor. For as much as he loathed ships, here he was about to voluntarily board one yet again.

Stepping to the edge of the knot-holed wooden dock, Nundle called out in his high-pitched voice. "Pardon me!"

A blond longleg with long, thick sideburns stared over the railing at him. Surprise flashed over his face. "Can I help you, little acolyte?"

Apparently, Nundle's gray robes had given him away. Offering the sailor a friendly smile, he called, "I don't suppose I might come aboard?" He reached up to hold his hair from his eyes. The breeze blowing through the harbor was strong. He had lost his favorite hat while in Veduin during a harrowing experience when a classmate lost control of a Weave of pure Fire.

The sailor stared at him for a moment, shrugged his shoulders, and said, "I don't see why not." He lifted an arm and pointed down the dock. "Plank's down there."

Nundle nodded, hurried down the dock and up a ribbed wooden board to the ship's deck. Nearby sailors who noticed Nundle's arrival stared at him with open curiosity. The blond sailor with the sideburns met him at the top of the plank. He was dressed in tan breeches and a sleeveless shirt, although with the grime and dirt covering his arms, Nundle almost did not notice.

"How can I help you?" asked the sailor.

"This is the *Morning's Mist?*" inquired Nundle, looking at the rigging and sails.

"She is. Why do you ask?"

Nundle shrugged and lied, "I am a lover of the sea and ships. I find sailing absolutely fascinating."

"You here to mark your name for a haul, then?"

Nundle stared at the man and tried not to look terrified at the idea. He would rather swim naked in a vat of leeches. "Ah…Perhaps I will do so after my studies are complete, mister…?" He trailed off, hoping the man would give his name. The sailor complied.

"Abiv. Just Abiv. No 'mister.'"

"A pleasure to meet you, Abiv." Smiling, he glanced around the ship again with fake admiration. "I was hoping you might be able to give me a quick tour of the second fastest ship in Immylla."

A number of nearby sailors slowed whatever activity on which they were working and looked up.

"Second fastest?" repeated Abiv, his eyebrows raised.

Nundle nodded, saying, "That's what everyone says in the meal hall." Another lie. Nobody ever mentioned a word about ships in the meal hall.

One of the other sailors—another longleg with sideburns—said, "You heard wrong, mainlander. The Mist is easily the swiftest ship in the harbor."

"This ship?" asked Nundle. He looked around again, shaking his head. "I don't see how. It looks as if a stiff wind would sink it."

Every sailor within earshot stopped what he was doing. Any chatter died. The whistling of the cool sea wind whipped exposed canvas and shook the rigging.

Nundle swallowed the lump that had popped into his throat. Perhaps this was the wrong approach.

Abiv grumbled, "Were you a sailor, words such as those would earn you a knife in the back. Or at least a swim in the sea." His eyebrows drew together. "However, as you are not, I will grant you a pardon. But watch your tongue. Do *not* speak ill of the Mist. She *is* the fastest ship here."

Nundle held the man's glare and said with more gumption than he felt, "Prove it."

The longlegs all stared at one another. After a moment, Abiv said curiously, "Prove it?"

Nundle turned and pointed to the distant mouth of the harbor to the west, straight into the sun. "If you can sail to the rocks and back before dark, I will give each of you a gold arcan."

The offer did not have the intended effect. Nundle jumped, startled, when the entire deck of longlegs erupted into laughter. Spinning around, he stared at the sailors, confused.

Abiv stepped close to him and said with a wide grin, "That was an excellent jest. Who put you up to this? Was it Enes? Randa? Perhaps Hof?"

Nundle shook his head. "I don't understand. Is one gold not enough?"

"A gold arcan?!" exclaimed the longleg. His bushy eyebrows lifted so high they might as well be sails on the mizzenmast. "Hells, I'd sell my mother to the Pirate Lords for a gold arcan."

It dawned on Nundle that they must think he could not satisfy the proposed bet. "How many of you sail this ship?"

"Eleven. Why?"

Looking down to his beltpurse, Nundle pulled the string, reached inside and pulled out eleven gold coins. Extending his arm, he opened his palm. "You're losing daylight."

Nundle had never seen people move so fast. They were away from the dock within moments.

Now, as they approached the harbor mouth, Nundle glanced over his shoulder to stare at the academy's stone walls and towers, bathed in dusk's fading light. He prayed they were far enough away for what he was going to try next.

Abiv began to call out commands and the longleg sailors scurried about the deck, preparing to turn the ship about and race back to the docks. Noticing the blond longleg repeatedly looking back to shore, Nundle strode over him. "Worried you will not make it?"

The sailor glanced at him and shook his head. "Oh, we'll make it. I'm just hoping the captain doesn't come out before we do."

Nundle's already nervous stomach soured further. "You aren't the captain?"

"Me?" replied Abiv. He shook his head vigorously. "Gods, no."

Nundle looked around the deck and counted the men. Besides Abiv, there were only nine others. He had made a poor assumption. Sighing heavily, he asked, "So where is the captain?"

"His sister studies here," said Abiv with a nod of his head back to shore. "He went to visit this evening."

Nundle dropped his head and stared at the deck planks. Too deep into the hole already, he had no choice but to keep digging.

Reaching for more golden Strands than he had anticipated needing, Nundle set to crafting the same, small Weave he had used countless times during his time as a merchant. He held it in place, looked to the longleg, and asked, "What's the fastest a ship could get to the City of the Strands from here?"

"With decent wind?" asked Abiv.

"With conditions as they are now."

The sailor scratched his right sideburn, staring at the sky. After a few heartbeats, he shrugged his shoulders. "I'd say two and one half days."

Nundle directed the Weave over the man, waited a moment for it to take effect, and then said, "If you can bring her into port in under two, each of you gets two gold arcans."

Without a moment's hesitation, Abiv said, "Done."

A nearby sailor's head snapped up. He stared at Abiv and hissed, "Are you mad?"

Abiv pointed at Nundle. "He's the mad one, Itan, not me. He's offering two gold arcans! *Two!*"

"How are you going to spend it when you're dead?" growled Itan. "The captain will murder us if we take the Mist to the capital!"

An argument broke out and quickly escalated, turning into Abiv versus everyone else.

Sighing, Nundle began to knit nine additional Weaves, one after another. He kept them small, hoping that the allure of coin was a motivation nearly as great as their fear of their captain. He did not want to get them into trouble, but he had little choice. He needed to get to the Oaken Duchies as quickly as he could, and this was his best path for doing so. He should be able to find someone in the capital who knew both the Weave for a port and had also been to the distant nation.

After directing the Weaves atop the sailors, he asked, "Pardon me? Could you all listen for a moment?"

The sailors did not hear him over their shouting and continued to argue. Two men began to shove one another.

Clearing his throat, Nundle shouted, "Quiet!"

The chatter died down in an instant.

When all of the sailors were staring at him, he said, "Stop the arguing and get sailing. To the City of Strands, please. As quickly as you can manage."

To a longleg, the sailors returned to their duties, conversations starting up about what they were going to do with all of their gold.

Nundle shut his eyes and allowed himself a tiny smile of relief. Facing east, he reopened his eyes and stared at the academy. His smile grew. He had made it. He was free.

A moment later, he thought of Preceptor Myrr returning to his office and discovering the missing parchment. His smile fell away. "Gods, I hope he doesn't figure out it was me."

Chapter 21: Siblings

15th of the Turn of Sutri

The light from a waning White Moon filtered through the oak boughs, trying to illuminate the forest floor but struggling to get past the rustling leaves. Blue Moon was only a sliver, its soft glow unable to assist. Kenders sat in the moonlight, warmed by the campfire's flames, waiting. Broedi and Jak had been gone for a long time. A very long time. So long that her stomach had given up growling.

When Broedi had more or less dragged Jak into the forest, Nikalys had wanted to go after them, afraid the hillman was going to hurt their brother. Kenders stopped him by pointing out that Broedi had been nothing but helpful so far, that he deserved the benefit of the doubt.

That had settled Nikalys down for a time, but he was up again, pacing back and forth across the campsite. She had asked him to stop a few times, but he had either not heard her or was ignoring her requests. The scraping of his feet shuffling across the rocky soil was growing increasingly irksome.

"Nik? Will you *please* sit down?"

He did not.

On his next pass, she stuck her leg out from her skirt. His foot caught on her ankle and he tumbled to the dirt, slamming hard on the ground. Lying prone, he glared at her. "What in the Nine Hells was that for?"

"I asked you to sit down four times! You're wearing a blasted trench in the ground!"

Nikalys turned over and sat up, drawing his knees halfway to his chest. After brushing dirt from his legs and shirt, he inspected his hands for any scrapes. Seeing none, he frowned at his sister and draped his arms over his legs, baring his forearms. Kenders noticed all of his injuries from the fingerprick bushes were gone. Hers were, too.

Nikalys let out a long sigh and stared into the forest. The flames from the campfire lit up one side of his face. "I'm worried, Kenders."

"Jak will be fine."

"How do you know that?"

"I don't. But I trust Broedi, even if you and Jak don't."

Shaking his head, he looked back to her. He had a twig and a dry oak leaf stuck in his hair, both gained during his fall. "What was all that whispering about? Why did Jak go off with him?"

As Kenders could not answer either question, she did not try.

Seeing the twig dangling before his eyes, Nikalys reached up and pulled it from his hair, leaving the oak leaf.

With a tiny smile, she said, "There's a leaf, too."

Nikalys rolled his eyes up as if he might be able to glimpse the top of his head. He felt around for the leaf and, upon finding it, took it, and tossed it to the forest floor. "Thanks."

"You're welcome."

As Nikalys went back to staring into the dark, Kenders looked back to her lap. Their mother's pendant rested in a little depression where her dress dipped between her crossed legs. She wanted to tell Nikalys something about the necklace—preferably before Jak got back—but was hesitant, which only served to irritate her. Since discovering she was a mage, she had not felt like herself; acting timid and cautious was alien to her. She did not like it. Making a conscious decision to be impulsive—if that were possible—she pressed her lips together, eyed her brother, and spoke.

"Remember those Strands Broedi mentioned?"

Nikalys expression turned wary in an instant. "What about them?"

"When you used the necklace, I saw some. Silver ones. They led from the necklace straight to me."

Nikalys' uneasiness grew. He grimaced and shifted positions but remained silent.

After a moment, Kenders added, "And then when I thought of you, they led to you."

His frown deepened as he eyed the necklace in her lap. "So it is magic, then?"

"Is water wet?"

Frowning, Nikalys shook his head. "We shouldn't have used it. It was a mistake."

"You were curious, Nik. I certainly was. Jak, too, I think."

With a dry chuckle, Nikalys said, "Being curious about magic is not a good thing."

That was the biggest part of Kenders' problem. She found herself increasingly curious about magic now. The silver Strands had been beautiful, sparkling and glittering like morning sun dancing off a thousand tiny waves.

Nikalys looked over and nodded at the necklace. "We should leave it here tomorrow. Just leave and forget about it."

"What? Why?"

"Because nothing good can come from it, Kenders. Nothing."

Kenders let out a derisive huff. "You certainly have a short memory. Like Jak said, without the necklace, he would have *never* found...us..." She trailed off, her eyes narrowing as a moment from her past revisited her. With a note of mild surprise, she muttered, "Huh."

"What?"

"Remember when I fell out of the tree in the north grove and broke my leg?"

"Sure. Mother ordered you to stop climbing trees."

"I remember lying in the leaves and grass, crying my eyes out. Gods, my leg hurt." She looked to her brother. "I couldn't walk, Nik. I was terrified. I didn't know how I was going to get home."

"You're lucky Mother and Father found you. Ketus was with you that day."

"Was he?" asked Kenders. "Because I'm thinking luck had nothing to do with it."

She had only been lying there for a short time, curled up at the base of the tree, when Thaddeus and Marie had come running through the forest. Her father had scooped her up and carried her home where the village healer set her leg.

Peering at Nikalys, she said, "I always wondered how they knew I was hurt. And why they came looking for me there. I asked Mother a few weeks later while we were making tarts. She looked at me with this funny smile on her face and said 'A mother knows, dear.'"

Nikalys' gaze returned to the silver teardrop pendant, a frown on his face. "You're suggesting they used that?"

Kenders shrugged her shoulders. "Perhaps magic can be a good thing?"

He looked away, took a deep breath, and exhaled. "It doesn't matter. Magic's outlawed, Kenders." He glared at her. "*Outlawed.* You use it, the Constables take you. No questions asked."

Kenders dropped her gaze back to the necklace. "You don't need to remind me, Nik. I'm the one who disappears if we get caught."

Nikalys sighed, scooted closer, and reached his arm around her shoulders. She tilted her head, resting it on him, and stared into the fire. After a few quiet moments, she said, "Please don't ever tell Jak about me. I don't want to scare him."

He gave her a gentle squeeze. "I won't."

So far, Jak remained ignorant of what she was. Neither Nikalys nor she had told him, and Broedi was as talkative as a tree. Whatever the reason for his silence on the subject, Kenders was grateful to the hillman.

Lifting her head, she looked up to Nikalys' eyes. "I've been thinking. When we get to Smithshill, I think I should stay with Broedi while you and Jak go into the city."

He pulled back a little to stare down at her. "Why?"

"Think about it. You said how dangerous it would be for me to go to the Constables, yes? Now I don't have to. You and Jak go. I will stay with Broedi."

Nikalys shook his head, murmuring, "I don't know."

"You want me to go with you?"

"Of course not."

"You want me to stay with Jak and you go alone?"

He grimaced. "Not so much."

"You want me to wait outside the city by myself?"

"Fine," grumbled Nikalys. "You've made your point." His expression hardened. "Just be careful while we're gone. You were right earlier. I don't trust Broedi."

"I'll be fine." She smiled up at him. "You worry too much."

The deep frown Nikalys gave her prompted her to reach up and playfully slap his cheek. "Stop that. You look like Father when you scowl." She froze the moment the last word tumbled from her lips. She had just referred to their father as though he were still alive. The sorrow that she managed to keep at bay most of the time returned, swift and unrelenting.

With a bittersweet smile, Nikalys said, "You know, it's my job to look after you now. Mine and Jak's. Father would want us to."

Fixing him with a steady stare, she cocked a lone eyebrow. "Who says it's not my job to look after you?"

His eyes narrowed a touch, and the wistful smile turned into slight frown. "You know what I mean."

She sighed and decided now was not the time to remind Nikalys that she was perfectly capable of taking care of herself. "I know, Nik." She dropped her gaze, rested her head on his shoulder, and whispered, "I know..."

The two fell into a comfortable, melancholy silence, waiting for Jak and Broedi to return. They did not have to wait long.

A rustling to the north brought them both to their feet. Broedi entered the camp carrying four rabbits and tossed them at Nikalys' feet without uttering a word. Jak emerged from the forest a few moments later, carrying two quail, the tan leather bundle strapped to his back. He, too, remained silent.

Kenders searched both of their faces, hoping to puzzle out what had happened. She discerned nothing from Broedi's typical stoicism. Jak, on the other hand, looked a mess.

Physically, he was fine. His expression, however, was a stew of emotions, so many playing across his face that Kenders had a difficult time placing them. She glimpsed anger, disbelief, fear, betrayal, and something else she could not name. Kenders met Nikalys' eyes and saw that he was reading their brother the same way.

Nikalys looked to the pair and smiled. "So, how was the hunting? Took you long enough." His tone was jovial, but forced.

Without looking at them, Broedi rumbled, "It took longer than I had hoped." He eyed Jak. "The prey was uncooperative."

The comment drew a sharp look from Jak. Broedi held Jak's glare, unflinching. Finally, Jak broke away and shifted his gaze to Nikalys and Kenders. He still hovered at the edge of the campsite, over twenty paces from them.

"Jak?" muttered Kenders, his whispered name carrying a dozen questions with it, the most important being if he was all right.

He stared a moment longer before mumbling, "Go ahead and eat without me. I'm not hungry." He tossed the quail on the ground and scuffled over to where his gear was. He took off the leather case and lay down with his back facing them.

As Kenders started to walk across the campsite, Broedi intercepted her, resting a strong hand on her shoulder, engulfing it. "Leave him be, uora. The hunt was hard on him." He nodded in Nikalys' direction. "Perhaps your other kaveli would like some help?" His eyes and voice both were gentle but the message was firm: leave Jak alone.

She nodded and with one last searching look at her eldest brother, walked to where Nikalys was already preparing to skin rabbits. He was staring across the camp at Jak, obviously concerned.

As Kenders settled next to him, he leaned close and whispered, "What happened out there?"

"I'm not sure, Nik," muttered Kenders. She glanced back at the prone form of Jak again, worried. "I'm not sure…"

CHAPTER 22: HILLTOP

Nikalys dropped one last handful of dirt onto the campfire coals. Once he was sure the fire was extinguished, he moved to collect his belongings, staring up at a pair of tiny yellow-feathered arause fluttering about from bough to branch, chirping like mad. The birds had been twittering since before dawn, but were using the sun's arrival as an excuse to sing even louder.

Broedi had awakened them when the sky was first shifting from black to gray, urging an early start. He promised that if they pushed hard this morning, they would reach the outskirts of Smithshill by midday.

Standing at the eastern edge of the clearing, Broedi rumbled, "Are we ready?"

The three Isaac children nodded.

"Then let us go." The hillman turned and began to walk east. Kenders, Jak, and Nikalys followed.

Jak's dark mood from the night before continued throughout the morning. Nikalys tried making idle conversation, but received only short, clipped answers for his efforts. After a few single-word responses from Jak, he stopped trying. If Jak did not want to talk, Nikalys was not going to beg.

Summer's typical, sweltering heat returned as the sun climbed higher in the sky, doing its best to pierce through the tree canopy. Birds that had been singing noisily at dawn went silent and hid in the shade. Even the insects buzzing about the forest seemed to lose some determination in the heat.

Near midday, when Nikalys noticed a gentle roaring mixed with the normal hum of the forest, his eyes opened wide. It sounded like the water creature that had destroyed Yellow Mud. Alarmed, he asked, "Does anyone else hear that?"

"It is the White Falls, uori," rumbled Broedi without stopping. "We are nearing Smithshill."

Relief flooded Nikalys. Of course it was. He wondered if he would react that way every time he heard a waterfall now.

The roar steadily increased as they followed Broedi's sure step up another hill. Upon cresting the top, the four of them emerged from the trees and stared down at the dual cities of Smithshill.

"We are here," announced Broedi.

The Southern Road was on their right, looping around from the southwest and leading to a fork a half-mile below them. The left branch ran east along a flat plateau, straight into the upper half of Smithshill. Known as Hilltop, the upper city rested on Lake Hawthorne's shores and overlooked the White Falls. The right fork twisted down the side of a steep cliff face, into the valley and through the lower city of Fallsbottom. Traffic heading from Hilltop to Fallsbottom was laden with crates, barrels, and stuffed bags, while the uphill cartage consisted mostly of empty wagons, carts, and bare packhorses.

The two halves of the city were very different from one another. Fallsbottom was for workers, laborers, or skilled artisans such as blacksmiths or carpenters. Inns and taverns catered to a rougher type of soul and were a good deal cheaper than the nicer establishments in Hilltop. Goods that were floated over Lake Hawthorne arrived at the docks in Hilltop and moved by cart into Fallsbottom. There, the items were stacked onto river rafts and floated down the Great White River to the distant coast.

Fallsbottom sat just far enough away from the White Falls that the river was no longer churning and choppy from the falling water. Yet it was close enough that a constant mist bathed everything, turning the entire town into a soggy, dripping mess. A tarry substance coated the buildings below making the dark-stained wood resistant to the constant moisture.

Every time Nikalys and Jak had been to Smithshill with their father, they had headed straight to Fallsbottom to trade their grapes and olives. Nikalys had asked once if they could go to Hilltop and his father had shaken his head, saying, "The air in Hilltop reeks." When Jak and Nikalys asked Thaddeus what it reeked of, their father had answered "Conceit."

Hilltop was full of rich merchants, government officials, diplomats, minor nobles, or anyone with a large purse or important title. Free of the persistent mist of the falls, the buildings consisted of expensive limestone with flat, oak-plank roofs painted tan or some other light color to refute the sun's heat. The city, with Lake Hawthorne sparkling beside it, was picturesque.

Curious at Kenders' reaction, Nikalys turned to eye his sister. She had never come with them during the annual harvest trip. Fallsbottom was no place for an attractive young woman.

Kenders stood on the overlook's crest, her eyes a fraction wider than normal, her mouth hanging open. Nikalys could not help but smile. She looked like a rock lizard lying in wait for an unfortunate, wandering insect.

"Trying to catch a bodfly, sis?"

While Kenders did not respond immediately, a low grumbling sound caused her—along with Nikalys and Jak—to stare at Broedi. The normally taciturn hillman was actually chuckling.

After a few moments, he glanced over, noticed their stares, and raised a single eyebrow. "Yes?"

Kenders tucked a stray lock of hair behind her ear. "I was starting to think you couldn't laugh."

Broedi turned to stare east, back to Hilltop. "Until now, none of you have said anything humorous."

Nikalys grinned a bit at the small jest, as did Kenders. Even Jak, still sullen and distant, cracked a reluctant smile. Catching Nikalys staring at him, Jak tilted his head to the side and studied his brother for a moment before looking back to the city.

Nikalys frowned. As much as he wanted to know what had transpired last night, his questions could wait a little longer. He and Jak were heading into Smithshill alone.

After returning last evening, Broedi had wanted to discuss today's plan with Nikalys and Kenders. Jak stayed on the camp's edge throughout the conversation, his back to them. He pretended to sleep, but Nikalys knew better. He had shared a room with Jak for years; he knew when his brother was sleeping.

Kenders and Nikalys shared with Broedi their proposal: Nikalys and Jak go to the Constables while Kenders stayed with him. Nikalys was a little surprised when he agreed to the plan, no questions asked.

While the brothers went to Hilltop, Broedi and Kenders were to head into Fallsbottom and straight through, doing their best to remain unnoticed. Nikalys wondered exactly how the seven-foot-tall hillman planned to move clandestinely through the city. The pair would travel south and, after a few miles, head off the road and wait for Nikalys and Jak.

The brothers were to go straight to the Constables and report a slightly modified version of what had happened at Yellow Mud. After, they would hurry down to Fallsbottom, purchase traveling supplies—including three horses—and head south. Once they were a few miles out of the city, they would use Marie's necklace to find Kenders. Broedi promised them it was perfectly safe, explaining that the magic of the necklace was only noticeable from close by and while in use.

If everything went smoothly, they would all be back together by evening. There had not been much discussion about what would happen after that, although Nikalys' plan started with asking Broedi to leave. They had not heard a wolf in three nights. The Shapechanger's presence was no longer necessary.

The quartet stood on the slope west as Broedi reviewed everything one last time before everyone said his or her goodbyes. After Nikalys gave Kenders a hug and kissed her forehead, he looked at Jak. "Ready?"

Jak stood a few paces away, his gaze locked on them both. He had done a lot of staring this morning.

With a decisive nod and quick sigh, he moved to Kenders, wrapped her in a long embrace, and gave her a quick kiss on the cheek. Taking a step back, he looked her in the eye, and said, "I love you more than you know, Kenders." His voice was husky, his words choked with emotion.

Kenders appeared a bit perplexed by the sudden display of affection—Nikalys certainly was—and, with mock seriousness, she said, "I love you, too, dearest brother of my heart." Giving him one of her dazzling smiles, she smacked him on the chest. "Now, go. I'll see you later."

Jak's expression lightened some, and with a soft pat atop her head—which she playfully slapped away—he turned to face Broedi. While neither of them spoke a word, the grim, serious look that passed between the pair said quite a bit.

The brothers set off down the hill, aiming for the fork in the road. Broedi and Kenders were to follow a short while later on their own, a suggestion made by the hillman. He had pointed out that two people emerging from the woods when a perfectly good road was so near might draw less attention than four would.

Nikalys and Jak picked a careful path down the hillside, avoiding loose dirt and rock. Halfway down, Nikalys noticed that Jak was not carrying the long, leather case. Curious, he turned around and saw it slung over Broedi's shoulder. Kenders waved, apparently thinking that he was looking back at her. He waved back, but was left wondering about that case.

Neither of them said a word as they made their way to the road. They slipped into the line of traffic moving toward Hilltop, walking behind a creaking, four-wheeled wagon drawn by a team of bays. Thankfully, the dust kicked up by the wagon was blown south, over the cliff, sucked down by the waterfall's cooling effect.

As they walked, Nikalys glanced at his brother a number of times, worried. Jak was the jester of the family, even more so than their father had been. This dark, silent mood was unnatural. It was like watching a hawk trudge down a road. Hawks were supposed to fly.

Hoping to start a conversation, Nikalys asked, "So, do you think the air in Hilltop will smell different?"

Jak turned to regard Nikalys with haunted eyes. "What do you mean?"

"Remember what Father used to say about Hilltop?" Imitating father's voice as best he could, Nikalys said, "'The air in Hilltop reeks.'"

A rueful, sad grin spread across Jak's lips. "Yeah, I remember." His gaze shifted forward, affixing itself to the empty wagon in front of them.

Nikalys sighed and stared ahead, too, as the uncomfortable silence returned, broken only by creaking wagon wheels, thudding horse hooves, and mumbled chatter of cart drivers.

After a while, Jak broke the silence. "You loved Mother and Father, didn't you?"

Nikalys might have stopped in the middle of the road had there not been a moving horse cart behind them. "What kind of brainless question is that? Of course I did. I still do."

Jak nodded, his eyes filled with anguish. "Sure, I mean, I knew that. I just…" He trailed off and let out a deep sigh, running his hands through his hair. Reaching over, he put his hand on Nikalys' shoulder and squeezed tight, so tight that Nikalys winced. "Hey, I'm sorry if I've been a little glum since last night."

Eyebrows raised, Nikalys gave his brother a lopsided smile. "A *little* glum?"

"Yeah, I know," sighed Jak, releasing Nikalys "I'm sorry."

"No matter," said Nikalys, waving away the apology. He waited a few steps before looking over. "So what exactly happened last night, Jak?"

"Ah…Broedi just wanted to give me some hunting tips."

"Hunting tips? That's the story you're going with?"

Jak stared to the north and the shining surface of Lake Hawthorne. "It's the truth."

Nikalys shook his head. "Come on, Jak. You're a terrible liar."

When they were younger, any time their parents had caught the brothers doing something mischievous, they would question Jak, knowing the quickest way to the truth was via Jak's fibs.

Staring at the back of Jak's head, Nikalys asked, "What did Broedi say to you to get you all upset?"

Jak remained quiet, continuing to peer northward at the lake. A pair of ships was drifting closer to the Hilltop docks.

"Jak!" pressed Nikalys. "Answer me!"

Still with his gaze north, Jak mused, "How many ships do you think come here in a day?"

Nikalys let out a frustrated sigh, faced forward, and dropped the topic. Yesterday, Jak did not trust Broedi. Today, he seemed to be choosing the hillman over his brother. It was baffling.

They walked the rest of the way in silence.

When the wagon ahead of them slowed to a stop, Nikalys peeked around the left side to discover the line of traffic had halted. A hundred paces ahead, two men in red and black uniforms stood on opposite sides of the road, stopping everyone trying to enter the city.

"Hells," muttered Jak, staring at the soldiers as well. "Broedi didn't mention there would be guards."

"Perhaps he didn't know?" suggested Nikalys.

Jak looked over his shoulder, frowning. "Do we turn around?"

"No," said Nikalys quickly. "We need to report this."

The wagon rolled forward. Nikalys and Jak followed.

"What do we say?" asked Jak, his voice hushed.

"I don't know." Nikalys peered at his brother. "Any ideas?"

"None. But whatever we come up with, you get to do all the talking."

"Me? Why me?"

"We both know it's for the best." Nodding down the way, he added, "I'll say three words and they'll mark me a liar."

The line was moving quickly. Nodding in agreement, Nikalys said, "Fine, I'll talk. But about what?" Facing forward, he eyed the Red Sentinel guards.

"I have no idea," muttered Jak.

Nikalys scooted a few more steps forward while trying to come up with a credible story. "Hey, what was the name of that soldier who stopped you on the road? The nobleman's son?"

Jak thought a moment before answering. "Haynes, I think."

Only one wagon separated them from the guards. Lowering his voice, Nikalys murmured, "Agree with whatever I say. And look threatening."

Jak looked over, his eyes filled with uncertainty. "Look threatening? Why?"

"Just do it," mumbled Nikalys. "Pretend you're like the men in The Brown Horse and Cart." The inn had been where they stayed during their annual trip to Smithshill.

Jak appeared doubtful, but nodded nonetheless. "Rude and crude. I can manage that."

They went quiet as the wagon in front of them reached the checkpoint. The driver showed a well-worn parchment to the guard on the left who barely looked at it before waving the wagon past.

Nikalys and Jak shuffled ahead and stopped when the Red Sentinel on the left told them to halt. The man was in his mid-twenties, with deep-set eyes and reddish-brown hair sticking out from under his silver domed helmet. He spoke, his tone emotionless and bored. "Passes, please."

Nikalys did his best to assume the brutish attitude of a Fallsbottom tough and shook his head. "No passes."

The soldier looked them both over, frowned, and said, "Well, then, you aren't getting in. Get back to Fallsbottom and wallow in the mud."

Nikalys frowned inwardly. This was not off to a good start. Nevertheless, he committed to the show, taking a step closer to the soldier and lowering his voice. "Look. I need to get into Hilltop."

The soldier wrinkled his nose. "I hope to visit a bath house."

Ignoring the insult, Nikalys said, "We need here to talk to someone. A Sentinel by the name of Haynes. You know him?"

The soldier's eyes narrowed a bit. "Perhaps."

"Yeah, well, he owes us some coin. And he hasn't paid up."

"He owes *you* coin? How?"

"He thinks he's better at knuckles than he is."

A smirk spread over the soldier's face. "That sounds like Haynes. He is—" He cut off and shook his head once. "Not my problem, that's what. Take your business to him."

The other guard was crossing the road, a curious expression on his face. He motioned to the traffic behind the brothers to wait, prompting the driver of the next horse-cart to shout something unpleasant in response, earning hard looks from both soldiers. Shutting his mouth, the man settled lower in his seat while muttering to himself.

The second soldier stopped beside the first and asked, "What's this about?"

The first guard pointed at Nikalys and Jak. "They want to see Haynes. Says he owes them a gambling debt."

The new arrival beamed. "Does he now? I didn't know the brat had the guts to gamble with Fallsbottom folk."

"He's got the guts to think he doesn't have to pay when he loses," said Nikalys. "He's had over a turn to pay, and today we intend to collect."

The second soldier said, "Well, as much as we'd like to watch that, Haynes is on patrol. Come back in a few days. They'll be back then."

"Not good enough," said Nikalys with an emphatic shake of his head. "I told him that if he didn't pay up by today, I was going to his father to get what's mine!"

A grin as large as Lake Hawthorne spread over the second Red Sentinel's face. "You want to go to the baron to collect on his son's gambling debt?"

Crossing his arms over his chest, Nikalys gave a single, emphatic nod. "I sure as the Nine Hells do."

The guards glanced at one another, chuckled, and then stepped aside. "Go right on in," said the first. "Just stop by when you leave. I want to know how red the baron's face turned."

"Agreed," said Nikalys. He glanced at Jak. "Let's go."

With a grunt and a nod, Jak followed Nikalys past the clearly amused Sentinels. Once they were out of the guards' earshot, he looked over. "Hells, Nik. You're a much better playman than I."

Nikalys glanced over and smiled. "A dead cow is a better playman than you." As Jak chuckled at the jest, Nikalys added, "You know, perhaps I *should* become a playman."

"Sour idea," said Jak. "You wouldn't be very successful."

"Why not?"

Jak winked at him. "Because every playman I've ever seen is handsome."

Nikalys grinned and slapped his brother's back as the two headed into Hilltop proper for the first time.

Two dozen steps in and Nikalys felt like a duckling in a nest of redbirds.

The men bustling about Hilltop wore dark, loose-fitting pants, shiny leather boots, and brightly colored shirts that were billowy at the shoulder, pinched at the elbow, and tight along the forearm. The women walked about in long, lightweight dresses, the sashes around their waists a contrasting color to the dress they wore: yellowberry yellow on cobalt, sky blue on ruby red, vineyard green on evening-sun orange. The vivid colors were incredibly garish against the bright white backdrop of the limestone buildings.

Jak tilted his head close and muttered, "Quite colorful, aren't they?"

Nikalys chuckled.

They drew stares and sneers as they walked the stone-paved street, something neither of them had ever seen. Every road they had ever traveled had been dirt, grass, mud, or some combination of the three.

Most buildings were single-story with large, multi-paned glass windows and signs hanging over bronze-handled doors. Nikalys eyed the signs as he passed.

Tena's Herbalist Shoppe.

Bredon and Sons Bronze

Pep's Clothiers.

Yellow Mud had never needed signs. People had always known where to go for something.

Peering down the smaller streets that intersected with the one they walked down, Nikalys spotted taller stone structures, two and sometimes three stories high. While topped with flat plank roofs like the rest, these larger buildings had gaudy, ornate, colored-glass windows and oaken double doors.

Farther along the main street, they came across the largest building Nikalys had ever seen. Standing at least six stories high, the edifice had five towering, white square columns propping up a domed roof. Stairs that ran the length of the building's front led up to a fifteen-foot-tall set of stone doors carved to resemble bookshelves holding giant books.

The brothers paused to stare at the monstrosity.

"It looks like it should fall in on itself," said Jak.

"Do you think that's the Constable's Office?"

"Gods, I hope not. I don't want to get near that thing."

Men and women sat on the steps or strolled around a small plaza, all wearing the same flowing light yellow robe. Every man was bald while the women had their hair cut close.

"Temple?" suggested Nikalys.

"Probably," replied Jak. He smacked Nikalys' arm. "Come on. Let's go find the Constables."

They strode down the main street, following it north toward the lake, away from the cliff's edge. A short time later, they stepped onto a sprawling plaza filled with a teeming throng of people. A gentle wind drifted from the north, bringing with it the aroma of roasting meats and herbs along with the sweet, intoxicating fragrance of fresh flowers. A white stone fountain of a woman cradling a wolf pup stood in the middle of the plaza, water flowing from the animal's mouth. Dozens of stands filled the space, each with a colorful cloth awning. Street performers and playmen entertained the crowd, juggling, dancing, reciting poetry, singing songs, and playing instruments.

A few individuals in the crowd stood out from the others. Nikalys spotted three ijuli standing together, their long arms, spider-leg-like fingers, and elongated faces impossible to miss. He felt a quick flash of anger, thinking of the saeljul from the lake, but he realized these ijuli were of a darker complexion.

Getting Jak's attention, Nikalys whispered, "Look. Tijuli."

Jak glanced over, shrugged his shoulders, and said, "Interesting, but not why we're here. Let's ask where the Constables are."

Nodding, Nikalys looked to the nearest stalls and, after picking the least-unfriendly looking peddler, suggested, "How about him?"

Jak looked to where Nikalys was staring. "As good as any, I guess."

The brothers approached the man's stand and asked for directions. The rotund man—who was selling fresh-cut, blue honeybells and white tumbleshoots—gave them a queer look, but answered them nonetheless. With a quick word of thanks, they left.

As they walked away from the flower stall, Jak shook his head. "Flowers? Truly? What a waste of coin."

Nikalys shrugged. People who had more coin than they needed often found pointless things on which to spend it.

Following the flower vendor's directions, they crossed the plaza and moved down the flat-stone road on the other side. A short time later, they came to another limestone building, three stories tall with a sun-faded black sign proclaiming "Office of the Constables" in painted white letters. The brothers strode to the single oak door and opened it. As they stepped through the entrance, Nikalys checked that his mother's necklace was tucked inside his shirt. He prayed Broedi was right about its magic not being detectable.

Inside, they found a sweltering, well-lit room. Windows along the building's front were propped open to let in fresh air, but it was of little help. The furnishings were sparse. Six simple wooden chairs, a few of which were occupied, lined the wall to Nikalys' right. Across the room, on the opposite wall, was a single table on which a blue vase full of white tumbleshoots rested. Nikalys caught Jak eyeing the flowers and shaking his head.

Two men in gray tunics stood behind the counter that ran the length of the room, each one speaking with a separate group of people. Behind the men was a stone wall with two open, wood-framed doorways. Nikalys hoped the sweet odor of incense and fresh flowers hanging in the air would cover up his own unique "traveling in the wilderness for days without a wash" scent.

As the brothers walked to the counter, one of the men in gray eyed them with obvious distaste. Without saying a word, he pointed to the chairs placed against the wall. Taking the man's meaning, they moved over and sat next to an older woman in a yellow dress with a light green sash. Nikalys offered her a friendly smile as he collapsed in his seat and received a haughty frown in return.

A short while later, one of the men behind the counter finished with the man and woman with whom he was talking. As the couple left the counter, the now-free man in gray called, "Next, please."

The old woman in the yellow dress, her white hair pulled into a tight bun atop her head, stood and strode to the counter, stopping before the balding man.

The Constable gave the woman a polite smile. "And how can we help you today, Lady Uberts?"

In a voice as crisp and firm as a perfectly ripe grape, the woman announced, "I am here to report the dastardly use of magic near my home last evening."

Nikalys' ears perked up. Sitting taller, he exchanged a worried look with Jak.

Oddly enough, the man behind the counter did not seem to share their concern. In an almost bored tone, he said, "I see. And what happened this time, my Lady?"

"Yesterday afternoon, I was supervising my seedsman in the garden as he attended to my shortbud roses—I swear that man has horse hooves for hands—when Lady Therrbur wandered by and commented that my roses seemed to be wilting. I was quite polite to her, I assure you, but that woman was born sour. She is still jealous of my roses besting hers in last festival's show."

Nikalys wondered what this had to do with dastardly magic use.

"Then, this morning," continued Lady Uberts, "when I went to check on my roses, I found every bud withered and brown!"

"How terrible for you, my Lady," said the Constable. His tone, while sympathetic, was not very believable. Lady Uberts did not seem to notice, however. "Now, how does this concern us?"

"It concerns you because Lady Therrbur came by in the cover of darkness and, using *magic,* withered my roses! I demand you detain her and investigate!"

Nikalys bit his lip in order to stifle a laugh. Jak tried to hold in his amusement, too, but when he saw his brother struggling against a smile, a small chortle escaped. In the quiet office, Jak's outburst was as noticeable as if someone had dropped a clay pot.

As both Lady Uberts and the man in gray turned to stare at them, Jak covered his mouth with a hand and stared out one of the windows. Trying to appear contrite, Nikalys raised a hand in apology and tried to stop smiling.

After looking back to Lady Uberts, the Constable said, "Thank you for bringing this to our attention, my Lady. I will record your account and provide it to one of the Trackers." He pulled out a small piece of parchment and began to scrawl on it. "They will follow up with you."

Lady Uberts stared at the paper on which the man was scribing. "Do you need my place of residence?"

The man glanced up. "Ah…no. We have it from your other reports, thank you." Looking back down, the Constable continued to write—especially slowly, it seemed to Nikalys—while Lady Uberts watched every word he scribbled. After a moment, he looked back up. "I believe I have everything I need."

"Hmm?" muttered the noblewoman. "Ah, well. Yes. Of course. See to it that something is done this time."

"Yes, my Lady. Of course."

With a curt nod, Lady Uberts spun around and exited the office, giving Nikalys and Jak a disdainful look before walking out. The quick burst of fresh air when the door opened was welcome.

The moment the door shut, the man behind the counter uttered, "Next."

Nikalys and Jak stood and approached the counter, stopping opposite the man who was crossing out whatever he had written on the parchment during his talk with Lady Uberts. While the clerk had appeared bald from across the room, he had hair, albeit only a long, thinning wisp combed from left to right. His eyes seemed small for his face while his bulbous nose seemed too large.

Looking up from the parchment, he asked, "How can I help you young—" he paused, running his gaze over their dirty clothes, and wrinkled his nose "—gentlemen?"

Jak said, "We'd like to report a magical event of sorts."

"How lucky for you that you found your way into this office, then." His sarcasm was thicker than Fallsbottom mud. "What is your report?"

Jak looked to Nikalys. "I think it'd be best if you tell it."

After taking in a long breath to steady himself, Nikalys launched into a revised version of what had happened at Yellow Mud, changing the story so that Jak and he had been the ones at the lake. He never even mentioned they had a sister.

As he shared the tale about the crimson-robed ijul and the nine other mages, the attendant wrote, peering at him with incredulous eyes throughout. Jak stared at Nikalys as well, appearing nearly as dubious as the Constable was. This was the first he had heard what had happened on the lake. With Broedi around, Kenders and Nikalys had never shared the full story with Jak.

When Nikalys was finally finished, the bald man said, "Thank you for bringing this to our attention, gentlemen. I will provide your account to one of the Trackers. If they wish to follow up, where might we find you?"

Thinking quickly, Nikalys said, "The Brown Horse and Cart."

The man looked up, a phony smile resting on his face. "A fine establishment."

Nikalys knew the man was mocking them. The inn's only redeeming feature was its cost.

Smirking, the Constable dropped his head and resumed writing, his quill scratching against parchment.

The two brothers stood still, waiting.

After a few moments, the man looked up. "If there is nothing else?" He nodded at the door of the office.

Nikalys and Jak stared at the man, then each other, and then back to the man.

"That's it?" asked Jak.

"What did you expect?" asked the Constable. "For one of the Trackers to run out to your village right this very moment?" The man sighed and leaned on the counter. "Honestly, your story is interesting—one of the better I have heard in a while—but had something like this happened I am sure we would already be aware of it."

Suddenly very angry, Nikalys slammed the counter with an open palm, causing the other Constable and group with whom he was speaking to turn and look. "It *did* happen!"

Jak murmured, "Nikalys, perhaps you—"

"People died!" exclaimed Nikalys. "*Hundreds* of people died! Our mother and father died!" Jabbing a finger at the Constable, he growled, "You need to do something about it! *Now!*"

"Let's go," said Jak, his voice firm. He grabbed Nikalys' arm and started toward the door, pulling Nikalys with him. Calling over his shoulder, he said, "Thank you for your assistance, sir! Good memories behind!" Upon reaching the oaken door, Jak opened it, yanked Nikalys through, and closed it quickly.

Facing his brother, Nikalys exclaimed, "What'd you do that for?"

Jak positioned himself between Nikalys and the door, his arms crossed. "He doesn't believe us, Nik. Shouting at him was unlikely to change his mind."

"You don't know that!"

"Hells! *I* barely believed you! And I lived through it!" He nodded to the door behind him. "They hear stories about wilted roses all day long, and then we bring them *this*? Nothing we say will convince them."

"But they need to—"

"Nik!" interjected Jak. "This path is at an end. Yelling and screaming about it will only get you time in the stockades."

Nikalys glared at his brother. He wanted to argue the point, but knew Jak was right. Fists balled, he spun and walked away from the building, back toward the street. "Now what?" He felt defeated. The one group he had believed could mete out justice was as interested in his tale as a fish was in a bird's nest.

Jak walked up from behind, put his right arm around him, and led Nikalys down the street slowly, back toward the plaza. "First we get out of Hilltop and down to Fallsbottom. We get our supplies and horses, then find Kenders and Broedi."

"Then what? What are we going to do, Jak?"

Jak let out a long sigh, paused, then said quietly, "I have a feeling Broedi might have a few ideas."

Surprised, Nikalys glanced over. "Pardon?"

Jak hesitated for a moment before saying, "I think Broedi might be able to help us."

"Help us do what, exactly?"

Jak looked over, held Nikalys' gaze for a moment, and then stared ahead. "Supplies first. Then we can talk."

"Jak? How can Broedi help us?"

Jak evaded the question thrice more by the time they reached the plaza, each time turning the subject back to what supplies they needed to purchase. Giving up for now, Nikalys promised himself that when they found Broedi and Kenders, he was going to get some answers.

Supplies first. Then a talk.

CHAPTER 23: HISTORY

Kenders was miles south of Fallsbottom and her hair was still damp, the ends curling up more than usual. Her clothes, too, seemed determined to cling onto every last drop of moisture.

The valley at the waterfall's base had been refreshing and cool compared to the heat atop the Smithshill ridge, but she could have done without the constant, pervasive mist. She welcomed it at first, but by the time she and Broedi had made it into the city she had been soaked through.

It did not take long for her to conclude that Fallsbottom would be a miserable place to live. The ground was a soupy mud, the roofs of the tarred buildings dripped water constantly, and people squished as they walked. The lone benefit of the mist was the effect it had on the vegetation. Atop the ridge, dust had coated a sun-cooked, tan landscape, yet in the valley everything was a rich, verdant green.

Broedi had drawn a fair number of long stares as they had moved through town, as had she but for different, less respectable reasons. At one point, when a filthy, unkempt man shouted something inappropriate at her, Broedi had stared at the man and loosed a rather lupine-sounding growl. Eyes wide, the man had started running down a nearby alley before tripping and falling into the mud.

As they had made their way past all sorts of people—fishmongers, smiths, tanners, carpenters, masons—she spotted a sign naming the Efrern Warehouse and Pressing Shop. Recognizing the name, she looked away at once. The old wooden building was where her father had brought the Isaac family's share of the harvest every year.

For the first half-mile or so out of Fallsbottom, the road had remained full of people heading in both directions. Farther south, the crowd thinned as people peeled off, walking down smaller paths to what Kenders assumed were nearby homesteads.

At one point, when she spotted two men in gray approaching from the opposite direction, she nearly leapt from the road. Their uniforms clearly marked the pair as Constables. Broedi had remained calm, acting as if there was nothing to worry about, even greeting the men as they passed.

The road rose in places and dipped in others. Atop the crests, she could see the Great White River to the east, flowing in the same direction in which they walked. A couple miles south of the city, the eastern ridge curled away, its long dark line meandering southeast. Sprawling, green grasslands broken up by small clumps of oaks ran clear to the horizon. The rock cliff to their right remained, looming over them and providing shade from the afternoon sun.

Neither of them had said a word since leaving the outskirts of Fallsbottom and the silence was making Kenders restless. For days now, she had wanted time alone with Broedi in order to discuss magic, yet now that she had it, she found herself reticent to broach the subject. Her hesitance baffled her. Usually, she leapt ahead without thought of the potential consequences. The past week had so jumbled her that she was actually exhibiting some caution.

The road ahead was empty save for a tiny dot of a wagon at least a mile away. Kenders looked over her shoulder, her gaze tracing the road's brown ribbon to where it disappeared into the trees. It, too, was bare of traffic.

"Do not worry, uora," rumbled Broedi. "We are alone."

Kenders glanced up to the hillman. "How can you be sure?"

Broedi drew in a deep breath, paused a moment, and then exhaled. "You can trust me. We are alone." He spoke with confidence. "You may ask your questions if you would like."

She stared at him through narrowed eyes. "What questions?"

"The questions you have been wishing to ask for days but have been afraid to voice in front of your kaveli."

The hillman's assumption irritated her, even if was accurate. A bit of her typical stubbornness flared. "I don't have any questions."

"My mistake, then. I apologize."

Realizing that she was wasting valuable time, Kenders swallowed her pride and readied to ask something. Still anxious about openly discussing the Strands, she chose to start with something innocuous, something she had been wondering since meeting the Shapechanger. "Broedi? How old are you?"

The hillman peered down at her. "That is not the question I was expecting."

"And what question were you expecting?"

He was quiet for a moment before answering. "To be honest, I am not sure. But that was not it. Why do you ask my age?"

"That first night, the way you talked about your kind, I got the feeling you're old."

Broedi looked over, a single eyebrow raised.

"Not that you look it. It's just that—" She stopped short and shook her head. This was not off to a good start. "Look, Father told us that ijuli could live for a thousand years, tombles a couple hundred. I suppose I'm just curious if hillmen are like ijuli or tombles? Or like us?"

"We are not 'like' any other race. Aki-mahet are aki-mahet."

A hawk cried out, its screech echoing off the cliff wall. Broedi tilted his head back, staring up to where the bird of prey soared overhead. A slight smile spread over his face.

"Fine, then," said Kenders. "Can I ask how long hillmen live?'"

Broedi answered without looking away from the hawk. "Nearly two hundred years pass from when we are gifted to our kaiti—mother—until we pass on to meet Maeana."

"Then you are more like us than ijuli?"

He dropped his gaze from the sky and stared at her. "Again, we are not 'like' anyone."

"You know what I mean."

"Yes, I do," rumbled the hillman. He glanced at the hawk again before facing forward.

Kenders waited for him to say something else, but Broedi remained quiet. Getting the hillman to say more than ten words at once was like trying to get Nikalys to share the last slice of a grape tart.

"You never answered my first question."

"Did I not?"

Kenders' eyes narrowed. "No, you didn't. So, I'll ask it again: how old are *you*, Broedi?"

"Ask a new question, uora."

"Answer this one, and I'll ask a new one."

He looked down at her, a slight smile on his face. "You are suddenly determined." He peered at her, his brown-eyed gaze oddly intense. "That is good." He stared at her a moment longer before facing forward again. "Now, ask a new question."

Unable to fathom why he would not answer what seemed to be an innocuous inquiry, Kenders moved on anyway. She hesitated, trying to think of something that might loosen Broedi's tongue, something other than "Can you teach me to not be a mage?" That would come later.

Staring up at him, she said, "So hillmen believe they go to Maeana's hall when they die." To Kenders, it was a statement, yet Broedi seemed to take it as a question.

"Another odd query."

"Why? You just mentioned her."

Broedi looked down at her. "So I did…" Staring down the road again, he nodded once. "Yes. Many aki-mahet believe that the Final Friend awaits us when we pass."

"Do you?"

The slight smile returned. "Do *you* believe the sky is blue?"

Kenders stared at the hillman for a moment before tilting her head back to look up. There were a few puffy, white clouds, but the sky was mostly clear. And very blue. Confused, she looked back to Broedi. "I don't understand."

"I do not *believe* the sky is blue, uora, for it is blue. I do not *believe* we see Maeana when we die, for it is so."

"You sound awfully certain about that."

"I sound certain because I am certain."

"How can you be?" pressed Kenders. "I mean, I believe in the gods. At least I think I do." She frowned. "Actually, I'm not sure."

"You should believe, uora. You insult the Celystiela when you question their existence. And they do *not* like to be insulted."

Thinking he was making a jest, she smiled wide and waited for him to join her. When his expression remained serious, her own grin faded. "What do you mean they don't 'like' to be insulted?"

"Simply that. They hold a high opinion of themselves. Their pride is soft."

She continued to stare, still waiting for something to indicate that he was jesting. "I'm sorry, but how would—could you know that?"

"Because I have met a number of them."

Kenders stumbled, tripping over a deeper than normal rut in the road. Recovering her balance, she stared up at hillman. "You've *met* a number of them? The gods? How?"

Broedi hesitated a moment before answering. "I have been to the Celestial Empire."

Doubt permeated her voice as she asked, "It's real?"

The hillman swept an arm outward, indicating the terrain around them. "As real as the land you see around us. In fact, this looks a bit like the area near the Seat of Nelnora. Fewer flowers here, though."

A deep furrow split Kenders' brow. "Are you mocking me?"

Broedi turned his gaze upon her. "I do *not* mock, uora." His tone was firm.

Kenders shook her head in disbelief. She was still getting used to the idea that Shapechangers were real. Now, she needed to add the gods and goddesses to the list.

"So...the Locking? The gods walking Terrene? It's all true?"

"I do not know to what 'all' you are referring, uora. Yes, the Celystiela walk the world. And the Locking certainly occurred, although few know the full story as it happened." He looked down at her. "Tell me your understanding of it."

"Well," sighed Kenders. "To be honest, I never paid much attention to the story. I thought it foolish. I know there was some sort of battle between the gods and that they became trapped here."

"That is all?"

Kenders shrugged her shoulders and nodded. "Sorry."

Broedi faced forward, took a deep breath, and after holding it for a moment, slowly exhaled. He began to speak, his deep baritone filling the quiet forest road.

"Ages past, the world was empty. The Celystiela—good, evil, and those that were neither—shaped Terrene, creating the lands and the animals, most of which would be strange to your eyes. Mine, as well, I would imagine. The nine evil Celystiela—you know them as the Cabal—directly opposed the nine good Celystiela, the High Host. War raged between them, both in the divine realm and on Terrene, claiming more mortal lives than I care to imagine. The remainder, the Neither, abstained from their conflicts and simply…were. That is how it was for a very, very long time."

He paused and looked over, perhaps to see if she was paying attention. She most definitely was. Facing forward, he continued.

"Nearly five thousand years ago, the god of Deception cloaked itself in disguise and visited each Celystiela, proposing a meeting, the purpose of which was to reach a truce between the Cabal and High Host. The disparate Celystiela agreed to meet on the condition it occurred on the mortal plane."

"Why?"

Looking over at Kenders, Broedi rumbled, "Because while on Terrene, the powers of the Celystiela are muted."

Kenders was curious how a god's power could be diminished, but held her question. "Go on."

"The Cabal, the High Host, and those that were Neither met on a mountaintop in the Red Peaks—although the summits had a different name then, a name that has been long forgotten. After all had arrived, treachery reigned. The Cabal surprised their brethren, unleashing all their powers at once and nearly overwhelming the High Host and the others. Naturally, they retaliated and a great cataclysm ensued. Fire poured from the ground. Lightning split the sky. Lakes boiled. Seas froze. Thankfully, the mortal realm gentled their power, else Terrene would no longer be."

"So they aren't all powerful? Because most people in Yellow Mud thought they were."

"Oh, they are powerful," rumbled Broedi. "*Very* powerful. Yet, they are not above seeking the aid of mortals." He gazed down at her, a strange look in his eye. "Would an all-powerful being need a mortal's help?"

She pondered the question but before she could arrive at an answer, Broedi resumed his story. "When the battle was over, the High Host and the Neither stood alone upon the ruined mountaintop. The Cabal were gone. Those who remained believed they had destroyed them."

"So they killed them?" asked Kenders. "Can you kill a god?"

Broedi shook his head, a deeper than normal frown spreading over his face. "No, uora. You cannot."

"Then where were the Cabal?"

"The cataclysm had been so great, so terrible that it had obliterated the Cabal's true forms and burned their names from existence. Yet their essence, their…souls, I suppose, survived by taking root in a mortal's body, pushing aside the person's soul and destroying it."

"You're saying they could look like—could *be* anyone? Any man? Any woman?"

Broedi nodded. "Or aki-mahet. Or ijul, tomble, dirgmour, atarkas, oligurt, kur-surus, nascepel. Any race, truly."

"Is there any way you can tell?"

"None that I know."

Kenders eyed Broedi for a long moment, suddenly concerned. With some hesitation, she asked, "You aren't one of the Cabal, are you?"

Rather than a quiet chuckle or quick dismissal she hoped he might give her, Broedi turned his gaze on her and rumbled, "What do you think?"

Kenders studied him. His kind eyes. The hint of a serene, calming smile on his lips. If he was of the Cabal, she was a fish. She shook her head. "That it was a silly question to ask."

His smile grew a fraction wider and he faced forward. She remained quiet for a few moments, thinking. The idea that anyone, anyone at all, could be one of the Cabal was unsettling.

Looking back to Broedi, she asked, "The other gods? What did they do?"

"Do, uora?"

"You haven't said how the gods came to be locked on Terrene." She swatted at a beetle buzzing around her head and missed.

"I was trying, but you interrupted me."

"Sorry." She swatted at the insect again and hit it, sending it tumbling to the dirt. "Will you continue you story?"

After taking a deep breath, Broedi complied. "The Celystiela who remained on the mountaintop attempted to return to their divine realm, but discovered that none could remember their home's name. Like the names of the Cabal, the battle had ripped it from existence. Without it, they were barred from returning home. Trapped on Terrene, the High Host and the Neither formed a new nation and shaped a new race—the divina—to serve them. Each built a great city celebrating his or her own self and that over which they hold dominion. To this day, that is how things remain." He looked back down at her. "Now, uora, do you still find the story foolish?"

It was an incredible tale, one she would have discounted as a playman's saga had she heard it from anyone else. Yet, coming from Broedi, it rang true.

She shook her head. "No…no, I don't."

Broedi nodded. "Good." Tilting his head back, he eyed the sun and rumbled, "We should find a suitable place to wait for your kaveli."

Kenders supposed the history lesson was over.

Turning toward the ridge, Broedi studied the cliff face. With a grunt and a nod, he headed off the road toward the rocks. "This way, please."

Kenders followed him into the forest, traipsing through ground cover that was much thicker than what they had experienced the last few days. The going was slow but they eventually broke through the trees and brush to emerge at the base of the cliff. Fallen rocks and boulders littered the area. One in particular was the size of her house in Yellow Mud.

"Is it safe to be this close?"

Broedi followed her worried gaze to the boulder. "Those only fall every few years. Most likely none will come down today."

"Most likely?"

Broedi smiled and moved off, walking along the base until he found a path to climb. Kenders followed Broedi without question, noting that she and her brothers had been doing a lot of that lately.

Upon reaching a spot with a clear vantage over the treetops, Broedi turned and scanned the horizons, starting south, sweeping east, and ending north, towards Fallsbottom. After a satisfied nod, he took off his leather satchel, sat on a wide rock, and pulled out his engraved bone pipe and smoking-leaf pouch.

Standing atop a rock a few feet below Broedi's stone, Kenders surveyed the valley, her gaze tracing the road they had traveled north and south. From here, they could clearly see anyone headed in either direction. She nodded her approval. "Good spot."

When Broedi did not say anything, she turned and looked up at him. His slight smile was back. "Thank you, uora. I thought so as well."

She stared up at the cliff behind him, eyeing the layers of tan and gray running through the exposed rock, some thick, some thin. "I wonder how something like that happens?"

"The river."

Kenders turned to regard the river before realizing Broedi had actually been answering her question. As she looked back to Broedi, she felt the crackling of magic and spotted a single orange Strand pop into view. It twisted, curling in on itself a few times, and headed straight for the bowl of Broedi's pipe. The smoking leaf flared orange, sizzled, and sent up a wisp of smoke. The sweet, cloying smell hit her a moment later, mingling with the smell of green things growing.

Broedi puffed twice, his eyes locked on her, watching. He pulled the bit free of his mouth and asked, "You saw that, yes?"

Kenders nodded slowly. "Isn't that dangerous? With the Constables so near?"

"The most capable Fire mage in all of Terrene could be standing on the road down there and would not have felt that. Much too small."

Kenders nearly asked him right then to help her mute what she was. Still, she hesitated. Saying the words aloud somehow made her fate as a mage final. Pretending as if the incident with the Strand of Fire had not occurred, she tilted her head back to stare at the cliff again. "When you said 'river,' did you mean to say the river did this?"

"I did. It carved this entire valley."

Gazing back at the expansiveness below, she asked, "How exactly does water carve rock?"

"Slowly."

She gave him a look she normally reserved for her brothers when they were teasing her. "I thought you said you don't mock."

"I do not."

"You're being truthful then?"

Pipe in his teeth, smoke curling out from his mouth, he gave a gentle nod of his head.

Her attitude changed from disbelief to amazement. Gawking at the cliff face, she asked, "How?"

He pulled his pipe free of his lips. "You witnessed what a lot of water can do in a short amount of time. Imagine what a river can do over ages."

The image of the wave rushing through Yellow Mud, tearing up houses, trees, and people flashed through her head. She lowered her gaze to the boulder as a sorrow-filled echo of helplessness rippled through her. The sense of loss she fought so hard to keep away suddenly swelled inside her. "I...I can't believe they're gone..."

Broedi sighed before responding, his voice soft and gentle, his tone sincere. "I am sorry for your loss, uora. Truly, I am."

She nodded, grateful, but did not say anything in response. She remained quiet, staring blankly at the ground, when the back of her neck tingled the way it does when someone is staring. Lifting her eyes, she found Broedi peering intently at her, studying, evaluating. She felt like a bunch of grapes on the vine as the farmer is deciding if they are ready to harvest or should be left to ripen a little while longer.

"You are strong. You will overcome this."

She offered him a tiny, half-hearted smile. "Thank you for the kind words." Looking away, she sighed, "I only wish they were true."

"There is no need to wish something true that already is. You *are* strong, uora. Stronger than you know."

She huffed and stared back at him, her eyes narrowed. "I'm *not* strong, Broedi. Mostly, I'm afraid."

He had yet to move, his gaze still boring into her. "Of what, exactly?"

Throwing up her hands, she exclaimed, "Well, let's see. For one, I'm afraid to fall asleep, afraid the dream will come again, that I'll have to watch my parents die yet again. *Every blasted night*, the wave comes, I stand there, and they die! I used to wake up terrified! And angry! Gods, I was so angry! But now? *Now*?!" She looked up and stared at the cliff without truly seeing it. Shutting her eyes, she exhaled, her twisted mix of emotions draining away and leaving only sorrow behind. "Now, I wake up crying..." So far, she had managed to conceal the nighttime tears from her brothers. She did not want them to worry about her.

"And *that*, uora, that is why you are strong."

She opened her eyes and peered up at the hillman. "That makes no sense."

Broedi leaned forward, a stream of smoke drifting from his lips. "Uora, you have faced more heartbreak, fear, and worry in a week than most do in a lifetime. A weaker soul—most souls—would lie down and let the misery consume them. *You* did not. *You* have pressed on." He sat tall and, using his pipe to punctuate each word, said, "You are *strong*."

She stared at him, a bit taken aback. She had never thought of it that way.

Broedi placed the stem of the bone pipe between his lips, drew upon it, and let the smoke curl from his mouth as he asked, "What else are you are afraid of?"

"Well, you might be used to being a mage and an outlaw, but I am not. If the Constables find me, they'll...Hells, I don't know what they'll do. But I know I'd never see my brothers again."

"Then we must ensure they do not find you."

"And then I'll teach a stone to swim," said Kenders with more derision than she meant. If the Constables wanted to find a mage, they would.

Broedi smiled, shrugged his shoulders, and then motioned to the rock upon which she was standing. "You should sit. Your kaveli will be a while."

Sighing, she turned around and sat with her back to the hillman. She wanted to be alone for a time and in this vast valley, she could almost pretend she was as long as she was not staring at a seven-foot-tall hillman.

As she cleared her mind, attempting to relax, the image of the crimson-robed ijul slinking over Lake Hawthorne's surface bubbled to the forefront of her mind. She squeezed her eyes tight and ground her teeth.

She and Nikalys had yet to share the full tale of what happened with anyone. Although she supposed that by now, Jak knew everything. She wondered how he would handle that.

Last night, Nikalys had asked her to promise that she would not share anything with Broedi and she had given it. Opening her eyes, she sighed. She was about to break her word.

"Broedi?"

"Yes, uora?"

"How much do you know about what happened to our home?"

He replied after a moment's pause. "More than you might think, but less than I would like."

"Do you know who was responsible?"

Another pause, longer this time, before he rumbled, "No."

Twisting around, she stared up at the hillman. "We do. Sort of..."

For a long moment, the hillman did not move. His eyes were excited and alert, but his face remained blank, absent any expression. "Will you tell me?"

Kenders plunged ahead, sharing everything that had happened, from the moment she felt the blue crackling to when she and Nikalys had picked through the rubble. She told Broedi about the ijul and the nine mages in gray, how she had almost been spotted, and how the ijul had killed his accomplices.

Broedi stayed silent throughout the story, puffing on his pipe, his eyes never leaving hers. When her tale was complete, he pulled the bone pipe from his lips and sighed, sending a long plume of smoke into the air. "You are sure the ones you saw on the lake wore gray?"

"Quite sure."

"And that there were nine?"

"Yes. Nine mages dressed in gray."

Broedi's gaze drifted to the ground. "That is unexpected."

Sitting a little taller, Kenders said, "Hold a moment. Do you know who they were?"

He remained quiet for a few heartbeats, his eyes vacant. Looking back to her, he asked, "Have you ever heard of the Strand Academies? In the Arcane Republic?"

Kenders stared at him, her expression blank. "What's an arcane republic?"

His slight smile returned. "*The* Arcane Republic is a nation of mages south of here, far across the sea."

"A nation of mages?" She grimaced. "That sounds...awful."

"It is, but for reasons other than what I suspect fuels your sentiment. Did you know the Oaken Duchies is the lone place in all of Terrene where magic is outlawed?"

Kenders shook her head, unsure she believed him. "Truly?"

"Most of the world gets along perfectly fine with magic, uora." He leaned forward again, resting an elbow on his knee. "You judge magic to be wrong because everyone around you says it is so. Of all the reasons to believe anything, *that* is the poorest."

Kenders looked away from him, her brow furrowed. She had not considered that. "Not everyone around us said so. Our parents used to tell us magic was but a tool."

Nodding his approval, Broedi said, "Now, *there* is spoken wisdom."

Kenders frowned. Magic might be a tool, but it was a dangerous tool. She stared back at Broedi. "These academies?" The word felt odd on her tongue. "What are they?"

"Places of learning," replied Broedi. Concern flashed in his eyes. "Can you read? Write?"

She nodded. "Mother and Father insisted we learn. Four times a week, we went to Mrs. Bodsworth—" She cut off as the image of her teacher lying against the pot-stove flashed through her mind. She mumbled, "Her body was the first we found." She expected some sort of response, but none came. Looking up, she found Broedi staring at the horizon, his eyes vacant and a little sad. "Broedi?"

His gaze shifted back to her and he gave a quick, apologetic smile. "I failed to answer your question, did I not? The Strand Academies are great centers of learning, dedicated to the study and instruction of magic."

"Have you been there?"

"It was a long time ago, but, yes."

He told her about enormous libraries filled with books and manuscripts, of formal classes focused on controlling and shaping the Strands, of the fantastic settings in which the schools were built, even claiming that one sat upon the slopes of a mountain that spewed fire from its summit.

When he was done, she asked, "And what do they have to do with what happened to Yellow Mud?"

A shadow fell over his face. "The classes at the academies each have nine acolytes. Acolytes who wear gray robes."

Kenders' eyes widened. "So, the academies are responsible? Why would they do that? Can someone be held accountable?"

The hillman stared at her for a long moment, his brow furrowed, then lifted his head, turning his stare northward. "We will wait for your kaveli now."

"What? No! If you know something, tell me!"

Broedi stared at her, a pensive expression upon his face. He seemed poised to say something, but instead shifted his gaze to peer over her head at the forest below. Bringing his pipe to his mouth, he said, "We will wait."

"Why do *you* get to decide when we're done talking?"

He did not respond. He did not even acknowledge her question. After a few heartbeats, she turned her back on him, seething.

Neither of them spoke for a long time.

After some of her frustration with Broedi drained away—some, not all—she realized her time alone with the hillman was slipping past. When Nikalys and Jak returned, the opportunity to talk freely about magic would be gone. Setting aside her anger, she turned around. "Teach me about the Strands."

He looked down at her and pulled the pipe from his mouth. "Why would you wish to learn how to use something which you believe to be wrong?"

"I *don't* want to use them. I want to learn how *not* to use them."

A slight frown crept over his face and he let out a long sigh. "I suppose that must do for now."

Kenders' eyes narrowed. "What does that mean?"

"It means I will help you, uora."

She blinked, perplexed. The rest of her anger faded in an instant, replaced by outright surprise. "You will?"

"I will."

"Just like that?"

"Yes," rumbled Broedi, tapping his pipe against his boulder. A soft breeze whipped away the ashes that fell from the bowl..

"Why?"

"Because you asked." He set his pipe on his leather satchel and looked to her. "Are you ready?"

Kenders sat a little taller. "Wait…now?"

"Is there something else you must do?"

She glanced around without knowing why. "I…suppose not." She stared up at the hillman and with more certainty than she felt, she said, "Yes. I'm ready."

Indicating a spot beside him, he rumbled, "Sit, please."

Tamping down the apprehension that was threatening to overwhelm her, she rose from her rock, moved to his, and sat. He began speaking at once.

"There are nine types of Strands, uora…"

CHAPTER 24: BRIGANDS

Jak hurried out of the dirty, rank stable, grateful to be back out in the mist of Fallsbottom. It took a few deep breaths to clear the stench of weeks-old manure from his nose. He looked over at Nikalys who was likewise sucking in fresh air. "When's the last time you think they cleaned those stalls?"

Looking a little ill, Nikalys asked, "What year were you born?"

Surprisingly, the three horses they had bought looked healthy and strong. Two were geldings, tan in color and identical in every manner except that one had a white ring around its right eye. According to the stable owner, the one with the white ring was called Goshen while its ring-less twin was Hal. The third horse, a mare, had black legs that faded to a light gray at her shoulder. Her name was Smoke.

Jak shook the small leather drawstring pouch that held the sum of their wealth and frowned at the distinct lack of clinking he heard. He hoped Broedi's plan did not require much coin.

Earlier this afternoon, they had left Hilltop using the same route by which they had entered. Ketus had favored them as two new guards were checking incoming traffic, saving Nikalys from a potential follow-up performance explaining how their non-existent run-in with Lord Haynes had gone.

As they made their way into Fallsbottom, they passed The Brown Horse and Cart where they had stayed with their father. They both stared at the inn as they walked by, but neither said a word.

The pair set to circulating through the soggy city, purchasing supplies with their dwindling coin from the Isaac family beltpurse as well as the few ducats Nikalys had scavenged in Yellow Mud. First, they stopped by a leatherworker and bought an extra sling, waterskin, and three saddlebags. At a provisioner's shop, they purchased a wide variety of items: a hunting knife for Jak, extra string for the lone bow they had, a pouch of salt, and a canvas-wrapped stack of dried rockeye strips. The salted fish tasted awful, but when the alternative was an empty stomach, Jak expected he would eat it. Nikalys took one sniff and swore he would starve first.

After packing their purchases in the saddlebags, they headed to the tailor's where they had each bought a new set of traveling clothes and cloaks, as well as a split riding skirt and top for Kenders. Jak managed to draw smile or two from Nikalys by holding the various dresses up and mimicking Kenders' common expressions and faces.

Loaded down with their purchases, they had made their way to the stable at the southern edge of the city. While trudging through the muddy streets, they passed two gray-clad Constables walking north, prompting the brothers to exchange a worried look with one another. The Constables were coming from the south, where Kenders and Broedi were. Nothing seemed amiss, but the brothers still hurried their pace.

As neither of them was accustomed to riding, they walked their new horses through the streets and out of Fallsbottom. Not long after the road turned dusty again—about a mile south of the city—they crested a small rise in the road and spotted a man lying, face down, a few hundred paces from them.

Nikalys made to rush to the man's aid, but Jak grabbed his arm and squeezed tight. "Wait."

Nikalys stared at him as if he were mad. "Why?"

Jak ran his gaze along the sides of the road, the trees, the broken rocks and boulders strewn about the area. "He could be bait."

"Bait? Bait for what?"

"An ambush."

Nikalys glanced north, asking, "This close to the city? They'd have to be mad."

"This isn't Yellow Mud, Nik. We are farther from home than ever. You have no idea what could happen out here."

Nikalys lifted an eyebrow. "And you do?"

Jak wanted to say, "Yes, I do," but he had promised Broedi three days of silence. Holding his tongue, he instead said, "What does it hurt to be careful?"

Nikalys pressed his lips together and sighed. "Fine. We'll be careful. Now, let's go help the 'bait.'"

They jogged down the dip in the road, Jak on the left leading Goshen and Hal, while Nikalys held Smoke's reins. Jak noted that it was impossible to see out of the gully, meaning other travelers—had there been any—could not see into it.

When they were two dozen paces from the man, Nikalys handed Smoke's lead to Jak and approached on his own. "Hey! Do you need help?"

The man, dressed in dark brown canvas pants and a ragged, torn shirt, lay motionless, entirely unresponsive.

Goshen nickered softly. Hal answered.

As Nikalys knelt beside man, a light rustling of leaves behind Jak caused him to spin around just in time to see a huge, black-haired man swinging a club at his head. As Jak released the horses' reins and lifted his left arm to block the blow, Nikalys cried out in surprise. Goshen, spooked by the sudden sound and movement, danced into Jak's attacker, throwing the bandit's aim off and robbing the intended blow of its full force. Nonetheless, when the wooden club slammed into Jak, pain shot up and down his arm, into his hand and shoulder. His eyes went round. He prayed his arm was not broken.

Off-balance from the horse bumping into him, the brigand stumbled forward, his follow-through sailing downward, ending with the club thumping into the dirt. Reaching out with his good arm, Jak grabbed the man's wrist and twisted hard. Something, be it elbow or shoulder, audibly popped. The man screamed in pain, dropped the club, and dropped to a knee in an attempt to relieve the pressure on his bent arm. A whiff of stale ale, weeks-old sweat, and filth washed over Jak.

The bandit was quick to recover, reaching out with his free arm to grab Jak around the waist. Already bent over, the man pushed upward with his legs, lifting Jak in the air a few inches, tipping him backwards, and driving him into the ground. Air exploded from Jak's lungs as the man's full weight landed on his chest. Gasping for breath and unable to move as the man straddled him, Jak watched helplessly as the brigand lifted a melon-sized rock into the air.

With a feral snarl, the man started to bring the rock down, aiming for Jak's face, when his arm stopped, frozen in mid-blow. Someone else's hand was holding the man's wrist in place. A fist flew forward, slamming into the black-haired man's nose with an audible crunch. The bandit dropped the rock—Jak had to twist quickly to avoid the stone—and slumped over, collapsing onto the dirt road.

Still gasping, Jak rolled over, readying himself for another attacker should one come. Squinting against pain and kicked-up dust, he had a difficult time understanding the scene before him. The man who had been lying in the road was still there, but was now on his back, bright red blood pouring from his nose. A second man lay on the ground next to the first, doubled over and groaning.

"Jak!" Nikalys kneeled at his side. "Are you hurt?!"

Twisting his head around, Jak peered up at a wide-eyed, anxious Nikalys. In between gulping breaths, he asked, "How in…the Nine Hells…did you do that?"

A relieved smile split Nikalys' face. "Come on, let's get you up."

Once Nikalys helped him to his feet, Jak stood in the road, his hands on his knees, sucking air as he tried to breathe normally again.

Nikalys patted him on the back. "Keep an eye on that one over there, he's still conscious. I'm going to go get the horses."

Looking up, Jak saw that their recent purchases had trotted a bit down the road, back toward Fallsbottom. As Nikalys chased after them, Jak turned his attention to the fallen men. He toddled over to the one groaning on the ground and kneeled beside him. Using the arm that was not throbbing, he pulled the bandit's head up by his long, grimy hair, and demanded, "How did the Cabal find us?"

The man, his face twisted in pain, responded with a confused, "What?"

Jak tugged the man's hair hard, eliciting a shout of pain. "Are you as deaf as you are ugly? I said, how did the Cabal know where to find us?"

The man stared at him as if Jak were mad. "What in the Nine Hells are you talking about?"

Jak paused. The man was genuinely befuddled.

The bandit tried to pull away, pleading, "I'm sorry, my Lord, truly. Please, show mercy on us."

"My Lord?" muttered Jak, baffled. "Who do you think we are?"

The bandit nodded at the man with the bloody nose. "Saul said you were buying the town and figured you heavy with coin. Said you were some rich noble's brats."

Jak stared down at the unconscious man lying on his back. These men were nothing but simple, brainless highwaymen. Scowling, he let go of the man's hair and shoved him to the ground. "When Saul wakes up, tell him he has as much sense as a blasted rock."

Hearing nervous nickering, Jak turned to find Nikalys walking up with the three horses. Gesturing to the men on the ground, Jak was about to ask Nikalys what had happened when his brother made a sign to keep quiet and then pointed south, down the road. Then he handed Jak the reins to Goshen and Hal, and started walking. Jak fell in beside him, silent.

Atop the next crest in the road, he took one last look behind them. The lone conscious brigand was crawling about the dirt, trying to rouse his friends. The moment they dropped below the rise, Jak turned to Nikalys. "Mind telling me what happened back there?"

Nikalys glanced over at Jak, his brow furrowed, his eyes filled with uncertainty. "What do you mean?"

"Well, let's see. In a couple of heartbeats, I get hit with a club, thrown to the ground, and was a moment away from having eveningmeal with Maeana. Meanwhile, you knock out one guy, cripple another, *and* have enough time to save my head from getting crushed like a grape? How in the Nine Hells did you do that?"

Nikalys shrugged his shoulders, appearing even more baffled than Jak felt. "Things just sort of...happened. The man on the ground flipped over and grabbed me, so I punched him. I heard something behind me, so I turned and saw the other guy and I...I...I don't know. Somehow, I kicked him. Then I looked up, saw the other guy about to slam that rock in your face and..." His eyebrows drew together and he shook his head. Bewilderment did not begin to describe his expression. "Jak, I have no idea how I got to you in time. One moment, I'm squatting on the ground, and the next, I'm holding that man's arm."

Jak studied his brother's worried expression, all the while struggling to mute his own reaction. Hearing Broedi's tale last night had ripped apart Jak's world. Realizing it was true hurt ten times worse. Nevertheless, he forced a smile, reached over, and grabbed Nikalys by the shoulder. "Hey, however you did whatever you did, I'm grateful. Thank you."

Nikalys gave him a tiny smile. "You're welcome. You can owe me one."

"One? Hells, Nik, I owe you five. Perhaps ten."

Looking over his shoulder, Nikalys asked, "Do you think they'll come after us?"

"Not if they're smart. But if they do…" He gave his brother a wink. "I'll let you handle them. All by yourself. I'll cheer you on."

With mock admonishment, Nikalys said, "That is a proper way to treat your champion."

As he had done a thousand times before, Jak gave Nikalys a brotherly smack to the head. "Come on, *champion*, we need to hurry if we're going to reach Broedi and Kenders before nightfall."

As the pair headed down the road, a determined smile spread over Jak's lips. As far as he was concerned, nothing had changed.

CHAPTER 25: MAGISTRATE

For two long days and two dark, seemingly never-ending nights, Nundle had kept a constant eye on the sea's horizon, afraid he might spot another sail on the blue. He never did.

Upon docking in the City of the Strands' harbor yesterday, Nundle had given the ten longleg sailors three gold arcans each instead of the promised two, a fortune for simple seamen. Out of the view of the men, he gave Abiv an extra five for the captain, hoping the sum might stave off the wrath the longlegs were sure to face when explaining why they had taken the *Morning's Mist* on a weeklong joy ride.

After leaving the docks, he had headed straight to one of the city's great libraries and asked he be shown the map room. An old, gray-haired longleg slowly—very slowly—led him to a large room lined with wooden shelves stacked with dusty parchment. When he asked if Nundle required any assistance, Nundle requested every map of the Oaken Duchies that the library had.

The old attendant made a face—apparently his offer to help had been mere formality—and shuffled off to a set of shelves grumbling about "ignorant mainlanders." Nundle had wondered if the insult was directed at him or the Oaken Duchies themselves and their outlawing of magic.

Back home in the Five Boroughs, magic users were shunned, but by no means were they named lawbreakers. In fact, nearly every culture Nundle had encountered in his travels treated magic with awe or reverence. The idea of it being banned seemed ludicrous and crude. Until his semester at the Academy at Veduin, he had never understood what could lead a nation to do such a thing. When it had become apparent Nundle was deaf to Fire, his preceptor banished him to the library where he stumbled upon Kemir, an atarkas from Mourlok. The pair struck up a friendly conversation and at some point, the topic somehow turned to the ban on magic in the Oaken Duchies.

Nundle's natural curiosity took over and questions soon poured forth. Kemir answered what he could, but pointed Nundle to a particular volume, *The Complete History of the Oaken Nation*. Over the course of the next few days, Nundle read the entire book.

Ages ago, the lands that now made up the eastern half of the Oaken Duchies was part of the L'antico Impero, a massive empire spread over four continents. Nearly nine centuries ago, an Imperial army general known only as

Nolbis led a revolt and, backed by his army, broke away from the empire. Inspired by the great oak forests that filled the land, Nolbis called his new nation "The Oaken Kingdom" and proclaimed himself sovereign, changing his name to King Alagar Rathburn.

For five mostly peaceful centuries the Rathburns ruled the Oaken Kingdom, expanding the western border further than it had ever been under Imperium rule. However, fortune, prosperity, and providence would not last indefinitely.

After three generations of war with the monstrous races of Sudash, the dukes decided the Rathburns were not fit to rule, deposed the king, and withdrew the tired and withered army. Hostilities with Sudash ceased.

Upon returning to the capital, Port Royal, the dukes debated what path their war-torn country must take. Ultimately, they chose to keep the country intact and rule it by a council of sovereigns, one from each of the ten duchies. The Oaken Kingdom became the Oaken Duchies and Port Royal was renamed Freehaven.

Through the next fifty years, power struggles among the ruling dukes and duchesses were constant. It was simply a matter of time before war broke out.

An advisor to Duke Alistair of the Red Peaks, a divina named Norasim, persuaded the noble that it was his destiny to unite the land again under the single banner of King Alistair. Swayed by sweet words and promises, the duke launched an invasion of his neighbors. His armies won battle after battle, slaughtering their enemies with ease. As time passed, the reason for their repeated victories became clear: the Red Peaks soldiers were no longer men.

In Nundle's opinion, it was at that point the factual history turned to playman's saga.

Duke Alistair's army had slowly morphed into twisted, demonic beasts with claws, horns, and black, cracked skin. Battles grew ever more one-sided until— in only three short years—the Red Peaks army had conquered the Northlands and the Foothills. The Oaken Duchies was on the precipice of collapse.

At some point during the campaign, the duke disappeared and Norasim proclaimed himself king. When the book's author claimed that Norasim was not mortal, but rather the incarnation of the god of Chaos, Nundle almost stopped reading, finding the notion to be ridiculous. Yet he had read on, too interested to quit.

Nelnora, the goddess of Civilization and Balance, concerned by what she saw, reached out to the other gods and goddesses and argued for intervention. She met resistance, though, as the official policy of the gods was to abstain from the affairs of mortal nations. Nelnora contended that this was different, that an army of demons led by the god of Chaos warranted their involvement. Eight agreed with her and offered aid, forming the Assembly of Nine.

Eight of the Assembly sent forth envoys to select individuals living in the Oaken Duchies. Each of the chosen, if they agreed, would be given a great gift of power from the god or goddess who had selected them. The ninth member of the Assembly, Sarphia, the Eternal Queen, would bestow near immortality upon them all.

Eight mortals came to the Seat of Nelnora and eight champions left, charged with driving back the demonic armies.

As the champions began their quest to defeat Norasim, Indrida, the Enlightened Oracle and sister of Nelnora, had a vision. Alarmed by what she had foreseen, the goddess sent a single scribing of the prophecy to her sister. Indrida's predictions so disturbed Nelnora that she ordered the parchment destroyed immediately, an order that was not carried out in its entirety.

A portion of the prophecy survived which the author of the history included in the book. The words remained etched in Nundle's mind to this day.

> *The roar of the Lions will drive back the spawn,*
> *And the lines of men, strong once again, will be redrawn.*
> *Yet that which drives man's soul will fray at the seams,*
> *While the strength of the Lions will fade as do last night's dreams.*

> *Torn apart by deceit and distrust,*
> *One will perish and One will be lost.*
> *One will leave, while Another will stay.*
> *And Two shall find each Other one day.*
> *Against his will, one must fight,*
> *While it falls upon the Half-man to unite.*

> *Chaos will rise again, unraveling what has been made,*
> *With Strife, Pain, and Deception in tow, lending aid.*
> *Hidden, then found,*
> *Willingly come around,*
> *The Progeny must rise to lead the fight,*
> *Along with new and old, seek to make it right.*

The author believed the first portion of the prophecy had come to pass when the eight champions—who came to be known as the White Lions—rallied the armies of the duchies, drove back the demon spawn, and ultimately destroyed them. Norasim was captured and executed.

The people of the Northlands and Foothills duchies began their long march on the road to recovery, rebuilding cities and lives. Nobles and citizenry alike blamed the tortuous events of the Demonic War on all magic and not merely Norasim's use of it.

A hundred years passed.

Most of those who remembered the Demonic War traveled to Maeana's realm, taking with them the memory of the White Lions' contributions. An anti-magic movement sprouted in the Red Peaks and grew outward like creeping, poisonous ivy. Mages—once respected and trusted—were now attacked as they walked down the street. The nation was primed for an uprising. Events near the port city of Carinius were the spark that lit the inferno.

Before the year 4748 after the Locking, Carinius was known for the abundance of fish and crab in its chilly waters. Afterwards, it became renowned for the thousands of people found along its rocky beaches, burned or drowned. Those who had survived the tragedy claimed to have witnessed several White Lions in the area at the time.

Accusations flew. The populace called for action.

The First Council convened in Freehaven and debated a radical proposal to outlaw the use of the Strands. Anti-magic fervor had not permeated the entire nation, and the leaders of the Southlands, Marshlands, and the Colonial duchies all argued vociferously against the proposal. Nonetheless, fear and distrust ruled the day and the measure eventually passed.

Magic, in any form, was forbidden in the Oaken Duchies.

The newly enacted law created a national organization, the Constables, tasked with tracking any use of magic and arresting the offenders. Schools and colleges of magical study were torn down, texts were burned, teachers and students detained. Initially, mages peacefully submitted to the authority of the Constables, believing that reason and sanity would eventually return and the law would be reversed.

They were wrong.

Rumors spread that those taken into custody were being executed. Remaining mages went into hiding or fled the duchies' shores altogether, scattering across the whole of Terrene. Some even came to the Arcane Republic.

The previously venerated White Lions were not immune to the new law. The council stripped them of their titles, named them outlaws, and sent the Constables after them. Eventually, the mage-hunters reported they had captured all eight. As time passed, mindless hatred of magic faded, but fear and ignorance easily replaced the void.

Nundle had found the entire tale both troubling and fascinating. Which is why, when he had found the letter in Preceptor Myrr's office three days ago, he knew he had to do something. He had to get to the duchies as quickly as possible.

After familiarizing himself with various maps of the Oaken Duchies, Nundle left the library and headed to the Bank of the Strands to retrieve his sizable wealth, having deposited it there when he had first arrived in the Arcane Republic. To him, such a concept was novel—an entire organization that existed only to hold people's coin, keep it safe for a small fee, and then give it back when they asked for it. It seemed a rather lazy and dishonorable way to make coin.

Afterwards, he spent the day wandering the various taverns of the Candlelight District, trying to ferret out some very specific information: the name of any Oaken Duchies refugee able to weave a port. Late yesterday evening, he had succeeded.

The informant had not known from which region the refugee mage hailed, but Nundle did not care. The Oaken Duchies was a large country, ten times the size of his own, but porting to anywhere in the duchies was a better option than taking a ship. Nundle's excitement was tempered when the rumormonger revealed that the refugee was now a magistrate of the republic. Gaining access to the longleg would be a challenge.

This morning, Nundle had risen with the sun, come to the House of Magistrates, and had requested to see Magistrate Ulius on a fabricated issue regarding an out-of-date permit for his non-existent pottery shop. The weasel-faced attendant had cursorily noted his presence and pointed to the bench on which Nundle had been sitting ever since.

Wincing, Nundle shifted—yet again—in an attempt to get comfortable. His bottom hurt.

The long wooden bench with a curved back would comfortably seat five or six longlegs, making it ridiculously huge for a single tomble. His legs hung over the side, swinging freely, a solid foot from the ground. After four years living in the Arcane Republic, Nundle was weary of climbing atop things upon which everyone else could simply sit.

He glared at the weasel-faced attendant. The longleg's ornate, cherry desk, while large and impressive, still seemed small in the cavernous hall. Towering, curved walls swept upwards to meet in a precise point high above the polished, black stone floor. Hanging from the peak was a large bronze chandelier ablaze with hundreds of candles.

The circular chamber was a lobby of sorts, with five identical desks sitting next to five identical doors arranged equidistant from each other. A single, tall entryway to the hall rested where the sixth door would be. The gentle, sweeping point atop the wooden doors mimicked the shape of the room's peak.

Three of the five desks were occupied, meaning that the magistrate was still inside his or her office. Nundle sighed. He would need to work fast.

Throughout the day, a half-dozen other officials had gone in the magistrate's office and came out again, yet still Nundle sat. He wished the magistrate would hurry and admit him. Every moment wasted was a moment Preceptor Myrr might walk through the chamber's entryway.

Suddenly, Nundle's stomach growled. Loudly.

The weasel-faced attendant behind the cherry desk looked up and gave him a disapproving stare.

Glaring at the man, Nundle said, "Pardon me, but sitting around and waiting *all* day has made me hungry."

A smirk spread over the attendant's face. "I would think one meal a day would suffice for someone of your stature."

Nundle returned the smirk but refrained from any additional sarcasm. If he had any hope of seeing the magistrate, he had to keep the gatekeeper happy.

A loud creak echoed through the room as Magistrate Ulius' door opened. An older longleg with thick bushy gray hair encircling his bald pate stuck out his head and stared at the attendant. Flabby jowls hung from the side of his neck and an additional chin suggested that the rest of the longleg was large and quite overweight.

"Are we finished, Marcus?"

"Yes, Magistrate, there are no—"

Nundle cleared his throat. In the quiet of the giant room where the loudest sound was the gentle scratching of quill on parchment, the sound reverberated, bouncing off granite. Magistrate Ulius jumped and turned his head all around, staring about the room and trying to discover from where the sound had come.

Nundle coughed again and the magistrate's eyes settled on the little tomble. As Nundle hopped off the bench and moved over to the door, the magistrate looked toward his assistant. "Ah…Marcus?"

The weasel-faced man's smirk returned. Even though Nundle now had a name for the longleg, he would remain "Weasel Face" to Nundle in perpetuity. "I am sorry, sir. But this tomble—" the smirk deepened "—requested a few moments of your time."

Nundle felt it necessary to add, "Which I did *very* early this morning."

The magistrate bristled. It was apparent he wished to be done for the day.

"Please, sir," pled Nundle. "I do not need much of your time."

Frowning, the magistrate mumbled, "I wish I could, but I have an appointment I must—"

"It's very important, sir," interrupted Nundle. He shook his traveling pack, filling the chamber with the sounds of coins clinking.

Magistrate Ulius' face changed in an instant. With a wide smile, he opened the door and said, "Please come in. I'm terribly sorry to have kept you waiting." He turned and disappeared back inside his office.

Nundle gave a smug smile to Weasel Face as strode into the magistrate's office. Two steps in, he stopped and stared about, his eyes opening wide. "Oh, my..."

Colorful cloth hangings covered the walls. Carved statues made of jade, obsidian, marble, polished granite, or ivory littered the desk and shelves. Oversized books sat open on ornate metal stands. Dozens of gaudy, expensive-looking items filled every nook and cranny of the room. Through the clear glass windows that overlooked the city, Nundle spotted three of the monuments to the Strands—Air, Fire, and Soul. The grand spires sparkled bright, white, orange, and silver in the late afternoon sun.

Nundle eyed the magistrate as the longleg moved behind his desk and sat in a throne of a chair. The longleg's love for food clearly matched his appetite for expensive objects.

Magistrate Ulius gestured behind Nundle. "Close the door behind you if you don't mind."

Nundle was happy to comply, eyeing the lock as he did so. He was relieved to see it set by simply dropping a latch into a slot.

Magistrate Ulius asked, "Now, how can I help you, Mister...?"

"Tweetlewood," replied Nundle, turning around. "Harlon Tweetlewood."

Nundle had used a series of false names since leaving Immylla, hoping they might gain him some time if anyone were tracking him. Namely, the preceptor.

"What a fun name to say!" laughed the magistrate. "Harlon Tweetlewood! It's a pleasure to make your acquaintance, Mister Tweetlewood." He eyed Nundle's traveling satchel. "You mentioned you have something important you wish to discuss?" The greed in his eyes shone nearly as bright as the spires outside.

"Ah, yes. Of course." Striding across the office, Nundle reached into his travel pack, pulled out a handful of coins, and dumped them on the desk.

The magistrate's eyes opened wide. "Mister Tweetlewood, you have my full attention." He pulled the pile of coin close and started to count.

Nundle decided to open the conversation with flattery. Most people enjoyed hearing how impressive they were. Looking around the room, he said, "You have a striking collection, sir. When growing up in Pyth, did you ever imagine rising to such heights?"

While Nundle knew the longleg was from the Oaken Duchies, he did not want to make the magistrate suspicious by heading straight into the subject. As Pyth was the region of the Arcane Republic where most longlegs lived, his fake assumption was both logical and understandable.

Magistrate Ulius shook his head. "I'm not from Pyth. I came to the republic as a young man." He glanced up. "I'm originally from the Oaken Duchies."

"Truly?" gasped Nundle, feigning shock. "I heard mages are hunted for sport there."

Still paying more attention to the gold than Nundle, the magistrate nodded. "Absolutely true. I myself was hunted for two turns. Barely escaped with my life."

"My, oh my, sir," replied Nundle, ladling on a healthy helping of awe. "That must have been terrifying. How did you escape?"

The magistrate cocked a bushy eyebrow. "Because I am smarter than those blasted Constables, that's how! From the moment they showed up in Huntersfield, I outsmarted them."

Nundle's ears perked up. Huntersfield was relatively close to where he needed to go. "Huntersfield, sir?"

"My home. At least it was."

Nundle wanted to smile, but he kept his joy buried. "They chased you from your home? How awful. What did you do?"

Seeming happy to have an eager listener to his tale, the magistrate leaned forward, resting his meaty arms on the desk. "I fled south to the outskirts of Silver Falls, living off the land and my wits."

Nundle could not believe his luck. Silver Falls was even closer.

"From there, I headed to the coast, to find a ship that could take me away from the madmen that hunted me like I was a beast."

With that easterly change in direction, Nundle's spectacular luck had run out. Nevertheless, Silver Falls was better than he could have hoped.

"When I reached Freehaven, I—"

"Excuse me, sir," interjected Nundle. He did not care about the rest of the story. "Silver Falls? That name sounds familiar to me. Now, why would that be?" He stared at the floor, pretending to retrieve some memory he most certainly did not possess. "Could you describe the place to me, sir?"

Visibly perturbed that the story of his daring escape had been halted, the magistrate quickly found something else about which to brag. "I should think so. I have the memory of a twenty-year-old! I hid in a grove of oaks atop a hill overlooking the town. Silver Falls seemed benign from afar—but I dared not go near it." The magistrate's eyes narrowed. "You see, the Constables had laid a trap for me."

Nundle somehow doubted that. "Then it was wise of you to stay in the wilderness, sir."

Magistrate Ulius dropped his voice to just above a hushed whisper. "Dozens of Trackers were after me. I saw them coming across the bridge over the river. But I outsmarted them, I did."

Pretending to be enthralled, Nundle said, "It sounds very exciting."

"Oh, it was, Mister Tweetlewood. Very exciting. And dangerous. Very dangerous, I tell you."

"You had to have been very brave, sir."

The magistrate shrugged, reminding Nundle of a shuddering pile of bread pudding. "I did what I had to do."

Nundle struggled to keep from rolling his eyes. "You said there were dozens of Trackers, sir?"

"At least. Perhaps a hundred."

"A hundred? Oh, my. How could you escape so many?"

"Skill, Mister Tweetlewood. Skill and cunning."

A chuckle threatened to burst from Nundle, but he swallowed it. "Excuse me, sir, but...I'm having a difficult time envisioning how you could escape so many. Perhaps you could take me there now and show me the hill? Rumor has it you know the Weave to create ports. Then you can tell me the whole exciting escape right where it all happened!"

The magistrate leaned back in his chair. "You must be jesting."

"Not at all, sir."

The longleg stared at Nundle for a few heartbeats, his two bushy eyebrows slowly drawing together. "Then you're mad."

Nundle had hoped simply asking would work. He sighed, steadying himself, and reached for the honey-gold Strands, watching the magistrate and praying the longleg was deaf to Will. Ketus was with Nundle. The magistrate ignored the Strands as Nundle knit a small pattern and directed it toward the longleg. After it vanished into Magistrate Ulius' sizable girth, Nundle said, "I think you should take us there now, sir."

While waiting for a response, he grabbed a few Air Strands, knitted another quick Weave, and looked back to the door. A small puff of air flipped the door's latch shut. Magistrate Ulius might not be able to feel Will, but odds were at least one of the attendants or other magistrates outside could.

Magistrate Ulius raised an eyebrow at the small display of Air magic, but seemed more focused on Nundle's suggestion. Upon seeing the longleg struggling with the decision, Nundle reached for more golden strings, wove a larger pattern, and directed it over the magistrate. "I would like to see that hillside, sir. *Now*, if you can manage it."

The magistrate stood, slammed the desk with an open palm, and exclaimed, "By the gods, I'll do it! Let's go, Mister Tweetlewood!" He walked around the desk and began to head toward the door. Shouts were echoing in the chamber outside now.

"Uh, sir? Where are you going?"

Magistrate Ulius answered without stopping. "I must tell Marcus where I am going, of course."

"I don't think that's necessary."

"Of course it is. I always tell him when I'm leaving."

Nundle groaned and reached for a large number of Strands this time, knowing he had just lit a beacon to any Will mage within a half of a mile. Upon completing the Weave, he directed it to the longleg and said, "Take me to the hill overlooking Silver Falls now. *Without* telling anyone."

The magistrate halted in the middle of his office and stared into the empty air where black and white Strands popped into view, quickly arranging themselves into an intricate pattern. Nundle tried to pay attention to the design, but the longleg wove much too rapidly. With the sound of shredding parchment, a jagged tear appeared two paces from the magistrate.

Nundle had read descriptions of ports, but this was the first he had ever seen. He found it rather disconcerting, watching the room flutter on either side of the ink-black slit as though it were a painting on a sliced canvas.

Without uttering a word, the longleg, a glazed expression on his face, took two steps forward, lifted back a flap of reality, and stepped through. Nundle suspected he had been a little too heavy-handed with the number of Strands he had used.

The shouting in the hall was louder now. Scurrying around the desk, Nundle scraped the gold coins he had given to the magistrate back into his bag. There was no point in leaving them behind.

Someone began to pound on the door, screaming for the magistrate.

Nundle rushed to the port but stopped before it, hesitant to jump into the utter blackness. He reached out a tentative hand and touched one of the flaps. A cool, tingling sensation ran up his arm.

With a boom and burst of flame, the office door flew across the room and crashed into a pair of bronze stands. The books they held went flying as the stands themselves clanged and bounced on the stone floor. Thick gray smoke poured through the doorway, providing a moment's cover for Nundle. Taking a deep breath, he peeled open one of the port's flaps and stepped through, expecting the initial tingling feeling to run through his entire body. Instead, there was nothing. Stepping from the stone floor of the magistrate's office, he put his foot down on rocky soil and emerged from the port beside the trunk of an oak tree. The longleg stood a few paces away, glassy-eyed.

Nundle scurried over, grabbed the magistrate's arm, and shook it. "Magistrate! The Constables are coming for you through that port! Close it!"

Panic flooded the longleg's eyes. He spun around, stared at the tear, and the flap disappeared with a slight 'pop.'

Nundle stared at the empty air, relief coursing through him. His knees felt weak enough that he gripped a nearby tree trunk so he would not collapse. "I cannot believe that worked…"

After a few steadying breaths, he turned in place, surveying the area. They stood atop a small hill among a grove of oak trees. Below him, to the north, a long ribbon of dirt road led to a gray stone bridge spanning a muddy brown river. Nestled on the opposite bank was a small city of flat-topped, wooden buildings. Nundle hoped that was Silver Falls.

He turned to examine the dazed magistrate, wondering what he was going to do with him. Nundle felt bad having tricked the longleg, but it had been necessary.

"Magistrate, I think you deserve a very long break from the rigors imposed on you by the duties of your office. Don't you?"

Nodding, the longleg said, "That would be nice."

"Tell me, of all the places you have been, which has been your favorite? The farther from the Arcane Republic, the better."

The magistrate was quiet for a moment before answering, his tone subdued. "I suppose the enclave would be—" His eyes lit up. "No! I know! There is this village in the mountains of Halawala. It was so peaceful there. No one ever asking me for anything." An expression of pure tranquility filled his face. "They made the most amazing root stew."

"That sounds wondrous, sir," said Nundle. "Why don't you open a port there right now, and visit? Take some time to rest—a few weeks, perhaps? That sounds nice, doesn't it?"

A happy, faraway smile slid over the longleg's face. "It certainly does."

Strands of Void and Air began swirling about the trees. Again, Nundle eyed the pattern, trying to mark its intricacies, but it was much too complicated to memorize. He shook his head, frowning. When he had time, he would need to find someone to teach him how to do this.

When the port opened, Magistrate Ulius immediately began walking toward it but stopped when Nundle said, "Hold a moment, sir." Nundle reached into his travel pack, pulled out a handful of gold—larger than the original bribe—and dumped it in the magistrate's meaty hands. If Nundle was sending the longleg on an extended trip, he should at least have some coin with him. "Thank you, sir. You've been a great help. You can go, now."

The longleg walked to the tear, lifted the flap, and stepped through. A few moments later, the rip disappeared, again with a soft pop. Nundle hoped the longleg would stay away for a few weeks, but chances were he would return to the City of the Strands within days, a week or so at the most. Nundle needed to move quickly.

As he turned to survey the town again, his foot scraped against something. Looking down, he saw the parchment he had swiped from Preceptor Myrr's office. It must have fallen out when he pulled out the gold.

He bent over, picked it up, and read it one more time.

Jhaell—

A merchant arrived in Redstone this morning and reported to the Office of the Constables some type of disaster in Yellow Mud. He claimed a giant flood had destroyed the town, killing everyone except a man he had met on the road to Smithshill. Before it was brought to my attention, the merchant had gone on to blab the story to three taverns worth of people.

Considering the timing of your visit here, I would venture to guess this was your doing. I pray you truly found the Progeny before causing such an obvious commotion. I have sent word to our friend in Smithshill to be vigilant for the man who apparently escaped.

—Everett

Nundle folded the letter, placed it back into his bag, and headed down the hill to the road below. He needed directions to Smithshill.

CHAPTER 26: REVELATION

Nikalys halted in the middle of the road, pulled his mother's necklace from his shirt, and looked at his brother who had halted beside him. "What do you think?"

Jak turned in a slow circle, staring in all directions, paying particular attention to the northern and southern paths of the road. Taking advantage of the break in travel, one of the horses Jak led, Hal, drifted to the roadside and started munching on grass.

After a few moments, Jak looked back to Nikalys and shrugged his shoulders. "Looks clear. Try it."

With the teardrop pendant tightly clasped in his right hand, Nikalys closed his eyes and visualized Kenders' face. A feeling of calm settled over him. "She's unharmed."

"Good," muttered Jak. There was relief in his voice, but less than Nikalys had expected.

Keeping his eyes shut, Nikalys rotated in place, trying to find in which direction the echoing bell was the loudest. After a few moments, Jak teased, "You know, you look rather silly doing that." Nikalys could hear the smile on Jak's face.

Grinning himself, he asked, "Perhaps you'd like to use the unlawful, magic necklace?"

"Oh, no. You're doing wondrous, Nik."

"Quiet. I can't concentrate."

"Anything for my champion."

Chuckling, Nikalys said, "Seriously, Jak. Be quiet." Jak seemed to have left his sullenness back in Smithshill.

When he thought he was facing where the ringing was loudest, Nikalys opened his eyes and found that he was staring at the rocky cliff to the west. After marking a boulder that reminded him of a fish standing on its fin, he turned to Jak. "They're up that way. At least Kenders is."

"That way it is," said Jak, pulling Hal's head up from the grass patch. The horse resisted, not done with his meal. Jak tugged harder and the horse came away after ripping up one last mouthful of grass.

Moving through the forest's undergrowth was hard going. The cooler temperature of the river valley, along with the shade provided by the cliff, allowed plants that would have withered near Yellow Mud to thrive here.

Brambles, thorns, and branches constantly scratching his arms and face put Nikalys into an increasingly foul mood. Based on Jak's mutterings behind him, his brother was not enjoying himself, either.

Feeling a sharp pinch on his arm, Nikalys slapped one of the many red iridescent beetles plaguing man and horse. He pulled away his hand to look at the mushy red mess and grimaced, wondering what was blood and what was beetle.

Nikalys spotted a break in the trees and headed for it, intending to find the fish rock and get his bearings. He resisted using the necklace again, unsure if he trusted Broedi's information on its traceability. Pulling Smoke along behind him, he stepped from the forest and found himself standing at the base of the cliff. He tilted his head back to look for his fish-rock marker, when he stopped short, surprised. "Huh."

Kenders and Broedi sat on a rock straight ahead. Amazingly, he and Jak had kept the right line. Hearing Jak exit the woods behind him, he turned and stared at his brother, smiling wide. He gestured up at their sister and the hillman. "How about that?"

Jak looked up and grinned, although the smile faded a moment later. "What's going on up there?"

Nikalys turned and looked back up to the boulder. Broedi and Kenders sat close to one another, face to face, eyes closed. From where he stood, it seemed as if the two were holding hands. A protective anger swelling inside his chest, he shoved Smoke's reins toward Jak and began to march closer to the boulder.

"Nik? What are you doing?"

Nikalys ignored Jak, striding forward, looking for a way to climb up to where his sister sat with the hillman. Unable to spot a clear path, he planted his feet and stared upward. "Hey!"

Kenders—sitting with her back to Nikalys—swiveled around and peered down to where he stood. A nervous smile spread over her face. "Oh! I—we didn't hear you coming."

"Obviously. What do you think you're doing?"

Her smile dwindling, she stammered, "We were...well..." She glanced at Jak, uneasy. "I asked Broedi to—"

Interrupting her, Nikalys called, "Broedi! Get down here!"

The hillman rose from his seated position, moved to stand beside Kenders, and stared down at Nikalys. "Are you upset, uori?"

"What do you think?"

From behind, Jak called, "Nik!" Glancing back, Nikalys saw Jak tying off the horses to a nearby tree branch while staring at him. Jak's eyes were anxious. "I think you should calm down."

Nikalys had no interest in calming down. Turning around, he glared up at Broedi. "Get down here, Shapechanger! I will not let you move on my little sister!"

Kenders gasped, an expression of embarrassed horror bursting over her face. "No! That's not what—"

Broedi shocked her—and everyone else—silent as he stepped past her and leapt from the boulder. He soared sixty feet through the air, nearly straight down, and with a resounding thud, landed spryly on his feet a dozen paces away. Pebbles rattled.

Eyes wide, Nikalys looked from the hillman, up to where Kenders sat atop the boulder, and back again. Broedi should have broken both legs trying that, yet he landed as a cat would when tossed from a barn loft.

Broedi walked toward Nikalys, his strides long and purposeful He stopped a few paces from Nikalys and glared. "Are you challenging my honor, uori?"

Forced to tilt his head back to meet the hillman's gaze, Nikalys summoned some courage to go along with his anger and said, "You promised you would keep our sister safe! Yet, here we find you...you..." He trailed off, not truly knowing what they had been doing. Whatever it was, it had looked inappropriate.

"Nikalys!" called Kenders. "You are being a fool!"

Ignoring her cries, Nikalys took a step closer to Broedi. "You can go now, Shapechanger. We're done with you."

Broedi shook his head. "I think not."

His blood pumping, Nikalys growled, "Leave!"

Broedi crossed his arms over his massive chest. "No."

Reaching up, he shoved Broedi hard, shouting, "Go!" He might as well have tried to shove the cliff. Broedi did not move.

"Nikalys!" cried Kenders. "Stop it!" She was hurrying down some hidden path Nikalys had failed to see. "He was only trying to help!"

"We don't need anyone's help! Not his! Not the Constables'! No one's!"

Having reaching the bottom or the path, Kenders skidded to a stop. "What do you mean 'not the Constables'?'"

Shifting his glare to her, he snapped, "They thought we were telling a tale. They're not going to do anything."

While Kenders' face fell, awash with disappointment, Broedi rumbled, "What did you expect? A massive water fibríaal? Mages walking on water?" His eyebrows lifted. "One of them an *ijul*? Your story is outlandish."

Nikalys' gaze whipped back to Kenders. "You told him!?" He was not sure with whom to be angrier, Broedi for calling their tragedy a lie or Kenders for sharing the truth after promising her silence.

Kenders nodded and, with a touch of defiance, said, "Yes, Nik. I did. He's done nothing but help us. I figured that he—"

"I don't *want* his help!" growled Nikalys. He glared up at the hillman. "We can take care of ourselves!"

"Can you?" rumbled Broedi. "Were it not for me, you and your sister would be dead."

"We have Jak now. We don't need you. We'll protect each other." He glanced over to Jak, looking for support, but Jak was still standing with the horses, staring at them, a worried look on his face.

In a low, sneering growl, Broedi asked, "Will you protect each other like you protected your parents?"

Nikalys' head whipped around, his eyes narrowing in an instant. "*What* did you say?" Despite his rising anger, he was shocked. To date, Broedi had been nothing but calm, stoic, and polite.

Kenders exclaimed, "Broedi! That's a horrible—"

With a deep, lupine-like snarl, Broedi barked, "Quiet!"

Kenders' eyes grew wide as an invisible force lifted her into the air, suspending her a foot off the ground and pinning her arms to her sides. She opened her mouth to scream, but no sound came forth.

"Go ahead," snapped Broedi. "Protect her."

The assault on Kenders finally spurred Jak to action. "That's enough! Put her down! I never agreed—"

Broedi roared, "Stay out of this!"

As if kicked by an unseen horse, Jak suddenly flew backwards and slammed into the tree with an audible thump. He slid down the trunk and slumped to the ground, his head lolling to the side. Blood dripped from his mouth.

Nikalys' heart stopped. He took two steps toward Jak's body, but halted as Broedi's baritone reverberated along the cliff base. "Where are you going?"

Nikalys whirled around and stared at the hillman, his eyes burning with hot, unbridled animosity. Broedi was as still as a granite statue, returning Nikalys' venomous gaze with his own hard glare. Nikalys hesitated, still unsure what to do, what he could do against a giant, shapechanging mage. He glanced at Kenders struggling in the air and then back at Jak's unmoving body.

"You are doing the same thing you did in Yellow Mud," rumbled the hillman.

Nikalys' brow furrowed. "What's that supposed to mean?"

"You stood there," growled Broedi, "*watching* as those mages made the fibríaal. You stood there, *watching* when they sent it toward your home. You stood there, *watching* as it destroyed everything." His eyes and voice turned cold. "You stood. You watched. And you did *nothing*."

A week's worth of churning, pent-up anger and emotion erupted in Nikalys. Letting out a primal, rage-filled scream, he charged Broedi.

"Aaaaaarrrgh!"

He had no plan. He simply wanted to pummel the Shapechanger.

When he was a few paces from the hillman, he launched himself at Broedi, his fist cocked. Broedi easily sidestepped his flailing attack and whacked his backside as he stumbled past. Off balance and unable to regain his footing, Nikalys tumbled forward, falling to the rough, rocky ground. Gravel dug into the palms of his hands. Rolling over, he glared at a scowling Broedi.

"You will need to move faster than that, uori."

Nikalys had no chance taking Broedi straight on. He needed to distract him somehow, perhaps get behind him. With his heart thudding in his chest, Nikalys stared to a spot just past the hillman. He needed to get—

Shift.

He was staring at Broedi's back.

One moment he had been on the ground, the next, he was standing here, just like the fight with the brigands. Too stunned by his sudden displacement, he simply stood in place and stared, wondering what had happened. His hesitation allowed Broedi to spin around, lay a giant hand on his chest, and shove hard. Nikalys stumbled backwards, tripped over a rock, and fell. His teeth rattled as his rear struck rock.

Broedi glared at him, eyes narrowed. "Too slow."

Thinking he might have a chance against the Shapechanger, some of Nikalys' anger and desperation dissipated. He knew what he needed to do now, even if he did not know how he was doing it.

Adjusting his approach and readying himself to strike, Nikalys looked up at Broedi and decided he want to be behind him again, but a little to his right. Nikalys stared at the spot, wanting nothing more than to be there instead of here.

Nothing happened.

Broedi asked, "You want to know what your iskoa and I were discussing? Visiting Greya's temple in Lakeborough."

Nikalys shifted his gaze to the hillman. "What? Why?"

A sneering grin filled Broedi's face. "So we can be joined in union. She said she feels safer with me."

Nikalys looked at his sister, stunned. She was an impulsive soul and prone to rashness, but this was selfish, thoughtless, and the epitome of brainlessness. "Are you mad?!"

Rather than meet his gaze, she was staring at Broedi, a horrified expression emblazoned on her face.

"If you would like," rumbled Broedi, "you and your kaveli may be witnesses to the event."

Nikalys' rage reignited like a handful of dry grass dropped in a bonfire. That union would never happen. He stared to the right of the hillman—

Shift.

—and began swinging his clenched fist upward, timing it perfectly as Broedi spun to face him. The strike was vicious, Nikalys' knuckles connecting with Broedi's jaw. He felt and heard the solid crack of bone on bone, his hand erupting with pain. The hillman's chin felt every bit the granite it looked.

Broedi backpedaled and crashed to a patch of hard-packed dirt, sliding over loose rocks and stones. Rubbing his jaw, he sat up, eyed Nikalys, and immediately began to shift, his nose and mouth fusing together and lengthening as though it were bread dough being pulled from two ends. Thick, golden brown and black fur sprouted from his skin, quickly growing into a heavy coat. Arms and legs thickened, his massive hands melted into heavy paws. Sharp, brown claws poked out from what used to be fingers.

The resulting beast rose from the ground, stood on its hind leg, and loosed a mighty roar that rattled Nikalys to his soul. The horses whinnied, their fearful nickering echoing along the cliff wall.

Nikalys knew it was Broedi, but his mind screamed bear. This was the first he had ever seen, but he had heard enough stories to put a name to the beast.

The bear lowered itself to all fours began loping toward Nikalys, a mass of fur and claws barreling down on him. Nikalys' anger evaporated, instantly replaced by abject fear. The bear had been nearly twice his height when standing, and even on all fours was taller than him.

Nikalys stood, rigid and unmoving, unable to rip his gaze away from Broedi's open, snarling maw. When the bear was only a dozen paces from him, instinct took over. His gaze flicked to a cracked slab of rock immediately behind Broedi—

Shift.

—and he drove his balled fist into Broedi's haunches, striking with more force than he thought himself able to muster. The bear roared in pain and turned its head, searching for him. Looking to the beast's other side—

Shift.

—Nikalys' fist connected with the bear's snout with a jarring crunch.

Shift.

He jammed his right knee into its ribs. Something inside the bear cracked.

Shift.

He lashed out with his fist, aiming for the bear's giant brown orb of an eye. "Stop!"

His blow halted in mid-strike. Surprised, he tried to pull back and punch again, but he could not move his arm. In fact, he could not move at all.

The shout had belonged to Kenders. He tried to turn his head to look at her, but he could not. All he could do was shift his eyes side to side.

In front of him, the bear staggered about for several moments before plopping down on its haunches. The whimpers of pain trickling from the beast were infinitely less fierce than the thunderous roar from only moments ago.

Steady, strident steps approached from the right. Kenders stepped between Broedi and Nikalys, an expression of sisterly rage on her face. "You, oafish, fish-brained, brutish lummox of a man—no, not a man! A boy! A silly, brainless boy!"

Nikalys glanced at the bear, worried it might attack Kenders, but Broedi seemed content to sit there in a slight daze.

With heat radiating from her eyes, Kenders continued to berate him. "Blast it, Nik! Why didn't you listen to me?!"

He looked back to her, confused why his sister was so angry with him. Broedi had antagonized him, restrained her, and assaulted Jak. The hillman was the aggressor. As though she could hear his thoughts, Kenders spun around and glared at the bear. "And you! What got into you? How dare you hang me up in the air like...like laundry! Why were you goading him on like that?! And that nonsense about our *union at Greya's temple*? Are you blasted mad?!"

If a bear could appear apologetic, Broedi did now.

An instant later, he began to shift, quickly reverting to hillman. The fur disappeared, the massive paws shifted back to giant hands and feet, and his head returned to its original shape. Once the transformation was complete, he remained sitting on the ground, rubbing his jaw and the side of his face. "I apologize, uora." His voice was calm, his tone contrite. "Truly, I do. I did not enjoy a moment of that." His normal demeanor was back: quiet, stoic, and polite. The crazed-eye Shapechanger was gone.

While Nikalys was trying to make sense of things and failing miserably doing so, Jak walked up and stood next to Kenders, shaking his head and smiling.

Nikalys' eyes went round.

Jak was fine. He looked the same as he had before the fight had begun. There was no blood, not even a scratch.

Sounding equal parts amused and amazed, Jak said, "You are a brave—and terribly gullible—idiot."

Nikalys was beyond confused.

Broedi stood gingerly, holding his left side. Once upright, he stepped closer to the three, wincing as he moved. Peering at Kenders, he asked, "How are you free? I did not undo the Weave."

"I don't know," answered Kenders, clearly still angry. "I saw the white Strands—Air, right?—in the pattern holding me and I...I...I don't know...I just unraveled them."

Broedi's eyebrows raised a fraction. He nodded at Jak, who was now staring at Kenders, studying her carefully. "And you did the same with his?"

Kenders nodded. Her anger seemed to be quickly fading. "Once I knew how to unravel mine, his was simple. The other one was harder, but—" She stopped and peered up at Broedi. "The white, silver, and gold. What was that?"

"A pattern used to make people see things that are not there," answered Broedi. "Very difficult to get right. It took me years of practice."

It dawned upon Nikalys that Broedi had only made it appear that Jak had been thrown into a tree, although he could not imagine why the hillman would do that. He tried to voice that exact question, but all that came out was a restrained grunt. He could not even move to talk.

Broedi glanced at Nikalys, still frozen in mid-punch. "And that, uora? How did you manage that?"

Kenders stared at Nikalys, wearing a pensive, bewildered expression. Stifling a tiny yawn, she shifted her gaze from Nikalys to the air around him. "I don't know."

Nikalys was shocked. Kenders was the one holding him in place. He had thought Broedi responsible.

"Think, uora," urged Broedi, his voice soft and encouraging. "What happened?"

Keeping her gaze on Nikalys, Kenders shook her head slowly and said, "He was beating on you—" she raised an eyebrow "—and after what you said, part of me did not mind. But, mostly, I just wanted him to stop."

"Did you use the pattern I used on you?" asked Broedi.

Kenders shook her head, yawning again. "I just wanted him to hold still and stop punching you. A bunch of the white Strands appeared, already in a pattern." She sounded and looked very confused. "Then I...threw it at him, I guess? And he stopped."

Nodding, Broedi rumbled, "Good, uora." He looked pleased. "Very good. Yet under no circumstance are you to ever do it that way again, do you understand? You must learn the correct way to Weave."

Kenders nodded, still staring at Nikalys as if in a trance. Now that her anger had worn off, she looked exhausted, like she had not slept in days.

Jak, who had been oddly silent throughout all of this, let loose a long sigh. Considering everything, he was handling all of this extremely well.

Broedi rumbled, "You can release him now, uora."

"How?"

"Feel the hold you have on them?"

Nodding, Kenders muttered, "Yes."

"Focus on that, imagine those Strands are you holding your breath, and then relax and exhale."

Kenders stared at Nikalys and, a moment later, whatever was holding him in place vanished. Stumbling forward, he managed to catch himself before he hit the ground. Righting himself, he stood tall and demanded, "What in the Nine Hells is going on?"

Oddly enough, Jak started to chuckle. Nikalys and Kenders both looked at him as if he were mad.

"Are you sure you didn't get tossed into the tree and hit your head?" asked Nikalys.

"So that's what you saw? Gods, the look on your face was awful. I kept calling out for you to stop and calm down, but you ignored me."

"That is part of the Weave, uori," explained Broedi.

Jak seemed to consider what Broedi said, shrugged with surprising nonchalance, and looked back to Nikalys. "Once I realized I was helpless, I just hung in the air and watched you beat on the bear. Impressive, Nik, in a 'what in the Nine Hells is happening here' sort of way, but definitely impressive."

"Why are you so calm?" asked Kenders.

It was a more than valid inquiry. Jak should be upset. Or shocked. Anything but utterly composed.

Despite asking the question, Kenders did not wait for Jak's answer, spinning to face Nikalys. "And how *did* you do that?"

Nikalys was about to say that he had no idea, when Jak spoke. "Ask Broedi. He expected something like this might happen."

A stunned moment of silence passed.

Shifting his gaze to Broedi, a suddenly suspicious Nikalys muttered, "You…expected this?"

Broedi dipped his head in apology. "In a manner of speaking. I had planned on waiting a little longer, but you presented me with an opportunity I had to seize. I needed to be sure."

"Be sure of what?" asked Nikalys.

"Unlike your iskoa, your abilities—if you had any—had not yet presented. As she only seems to be able to use her gifts when distressed, I provoked you in hopes of drawing yours out."

"Gifts?" mumbled Nikalys, thoroughly befuddled. "What in the Nine Hells are you talking about?"

Broedi's expression turned serious, his voice solemn. "As your kaveli said last evening, you are important, uori." He shifted to look at Kenders, adding, "Both of you."

Nikalys glanced at Kenders—her face was a mask of confusion—before looking to Jak. His brother held his stare, quiet and calm. Turning back to Broedi, he asked, "What does that mean?"

With a slight frown on his face, the hillman glanced northward and sighed. A moment later, he looked back to Nikalys and Kenders. "I have been hesitant to burden you with this so soon after your loss, but I do not think I can continue to wait. We are wasting time."

"Burden us with what?" asked Kenders. "What are you talking about?"

Broedi took a deep breath and exhaled. "You two are the—"

Jak took a sudden step forward, hand up. "Broedi, can you hold one moment? Please?" His gaze shifted between Nikalys and Kenders. "I won't be long, I promise."

Broedi glanced north again and pressed his lips together. Nodding, he said, "Quickly, please." He ran his gaze over Nikalys and Kenders once more before taking a few steps down the slope, giving the three siblings a modicum of privacy.

Jak took Nikalys by the shoulder, grabbed Kenders' hand, and led them even farther away from Broedi. He stopped and faced them, his expression a strange mix of affection and sorrow.

Visibly worried, Kenders asked, "Jak, what's going on?"

Looking between them both, Jak smiled and said, "I want you both to know that I love you very much. And no matter what, that will never change."

After exchanging bewildered looks with Kenders, Nikalys peered at Jak. "You obviously know something. What?"

"It's best Broedi tell you. Just know that I will do whatever I can to help. I will *never* leave your side. *Never.*" He stepped forward, wrapped his arms around them, and held them both. Nikalys did not know what to do but return the embrace.

From down the hill, Broedi cleared throat. "I am sorry, but we must be going." Jak gave them one final squeeze and released them. At once, Broedi rumbled, "Please get the horses, uori. And hurry."

Nodding, Jak turned and headed for the tree with the three horses tied to it. Nikalys watched him for a moment and then looked to Broedi. "Hurry? Hurry why? What is going on?"

Rather than answer him, Broedi peered at Kenders. "Recall the manner in which I lit my pipe, uora? That was the flickering light of a torchbug at dusk. What you just did was a bolt of lightning on the blackest of nights." He stared north again. "I would assume Trackers are on their way already."

Nikalys demanded, "*What* is happening?"

Broedi looked to him. "We will speak once we are moving."

Kenders stepped forward, and with a small stomp of her foot, exclaimed, "No, blast it! Tell us what is happening! Or I'll stand right here, wait for the Trackers to come, and point them straight to wherever you run off!"

For once, Nikalys welcomed for his sister's stubbornness.

Broedi was quiet for a moment, the corners of his mouth curling up into a wistful, almost wishful smile. "You remind me so much of your mother."

"You never met my mother," snapped Kenders.

"But I have, uora. She and I were close friends. Your father was my closest."

"That's impossible," muttered Nikalys. "We would have heard of you." He eyed all seven feet of the hillman. "*Especially* you."

Broedi stared north toward Smithshill, tilted his head back to eye the sky, and while letting out a tiny sigh, finally gazed back at them. "I will tell you some of what you need to know now. But when I say we must move, the questions stop, agreed?"

Nikalys and Kenders both nodded.

In a calm, kind, and yet somewhat pointed manner, Broedi rumbled, "In one sense, you are correct. I never met Thaddeus and Marie Isaac. From what you have told me, and from what I have observed in you and your kaveli, they were good, honest, and wise people. I wish I had known them. They raised you, guided you, and kept you safe. All things good parents do for their children." He paused for half a heartbeat before adding, "Only...you are not their children."

"What are you talking about?" asked Nikalys, baffled.

"You are not their blood, uori," rumbled Broedi. "They fostered you. Without a doubt, they loved you. But they did not bring you into this world."

Nikalys felt like the ground beneath him had fallen away. Shaking his head, he murmured, "You're mad."

"For this moment only, for your sake, I wish I were."

Silent and shaken, Nikalys stared at Broedi, pleading with eyes alone that he stop. He did not.

"Your true parents are Aryn Atticus, the Strong Arm of Horum, and Eliza Kap, the Masterweaver of Gaena, two of the White Lions who helped fight Norasim in the Demonic War. They were my friends. And you are their Progeny."

* * *

Jak stood several dozen feet from Nikalys and Kenders, gripping the horses' reins while listening to Broedi tell them some of what he had told Jak the night before. It was infinitely worse hearing everything a second time. Now, he had to watch Nikalys' and Kenders' hearts break.

Broedi had been thin with details last night, saying simply the pair were children of heroes from the duchies' past and that forces had been searching for them since their birth—before even—wishing them dead. Jak had fought the hillman's claims, but Broedi quickly silenced his protests by listing things that, while not conclusive support of the wild tale, made Jak concede there might be some truth to it.

The necklace that only led to Nikalys and Kenders.

The strange exchange Jak had with his parents in Yellow Mud.

The fact that his brother and sister looked nothing like him or his parents.

Eventually, logic overcame emotion. He was not sure he believed Broedi, but neither could he call the hillman a liar with any sort of confidence.

He had spent last night and this morning digesting Broedi's incredible story. It had taken him some time, but he eventually decided that he did not care if Nikalys and Kenders were blood or not. He had grown up with them. Every memory he possessed included them. They had loved Jak's parents as their own. They were his family even if they were not.

Nikalys and Kenders remained silent as Broedi spoke to them. Thinking back to his initial reaction last night, Jak supposed he had been quiet for a while, too. A person needed time to adjust to something like this.

After a short time, Broedi motioned for Jak to join the group. Jak sighed, knowing the next few moments would be the most awkward of his life. Steadying himself, he stepped forward, pulling the horses behind him. Nikalys and Kenders did not look up as he reached them.

Eyeing the trio, Broedi said, "I know you all have questions and I promise I will answer them later. For now, we must move to keep you safe. We will lead the horses through the woods, to the road, and then you will ride."

Without waiting for agreement, he turned and headed down the hill, evidently expecting them to follow. After a moment, Kenders walked after the hillman, glancing at Jak as she passed, the hurt in her eyes hitting him as if one of the nearby boulders had fallen on his head. Jak felt like he should say something, but did not know what. Kenders was likewise silent, as was Nikalys as he moved after Kenders. He did not even look at Jak.

Jak let out a long, mournful sigh, tugged the horses' reins, and followed.

CHAPTER 27: TRACKERS

Evening's gloam enshrouded the cliff's base, making it difficult to see much of anything in significant detail. Yet that did not stop the lone man standing there from trying. Six feet tall with olive skin, he peered downward, studying the ground, his thick, black hair hanging in his eyes.

Reaching a hand up, Cero brushed back his hair and rubbed his eyes. "This makes no sense."

Hearing footsteps, he pulled his attention from the dirt and scrabble at his feet and looked to the forest's edge just as Latius emerged from the trees, limping along while swatting at beetles.

Latius was an odd-looking fellow: shaggy blond hair, eyes that were too close together, an upturned nose, and reed-thin lips. Like Cero, he was dressed in gray, tough-spun traveling clothes suited for the wilderness more so than the expensive city tunics most Constables wore.

Catching Latius' eye, Cero asked, "Find anything?"

Latius shook his head. "Twenty paces in, the trail just stops. I'm sure it picks up again, but I can't find where. Too dark."

"We should have grabbed a torch before we left."

"Yeah, well," grumbled Latius. "I didn't think of it, and neither did you." He bent over and rubbed his knee. "Gods, this still hurts." He seemed more concerned about his hurt knee than why they were here.

They had been sitting in a Fallsbottom tavern when the incident had occurred. The surge of magic startled them both, with Latius jumping from his chair as though someone had stabbed his rear with a dagger, smacking his right knee against the table and knocking over their drinks. They had rushed from the tavern and hurried south, toward the disturbance. Arriving at sunset, they spread out to investigate the area. It did not take long before both Trackers were thoroughly perplexed.

Still rubbing his knee, Latius asked, "So what do you think happened?"

"I'm at a loss," sighed Cero, crouching to study the same stretch of ground he had already looked at a half-dozen times. He nodded at a series of markings in the dirt. "There was a struggle. Two or three men and either an older child or woman. That much is clear." Turning a bit, he pointed to the oddest thing he had seen in the wilderness since coming to Smithshill. "But that?" He shook his head. "They shouldn't be here."

"And you are sure those are from a bear's paws?"

"I am from the Northlands, Latius. I am quite familiar with the markings of bears."

"As am I," said Latius. He pointed to the massive set of prints. "Yet I have never seen any that size, have you?"

Cero gave a slow, wondering shake of his head. "No, I have not." He could have stood on one foot in the center footpad and not disturbed the print at all.

"So, then," sighed Latius. "What do we do?"

Cero glanced up to his fellow Tracker, curious. "What do you mean?"

Latius nodded at the bear tracks. "Do we report this?"

Standing tall, Cero glared at Latius and said, "Of course we report this."

"No one will believe us, Cero. A bear? Here?"

Indicating the tracks, Cero asked, "Do you see something different?"

"Oh, no, those are bear tracks. Giant, massive bear tracks. The problem is they are the only ones. Did the beast fall from the sky and then grow wings and fly away? We will be mocked."

Cero pressed his lips together, disappointed in his partner. "Do you deny the strength of the disturbance?

Latius frowned and dropped his head. "No."

"Then you know we can't let this go unreported."

Looking up, Latius asked, "Do you think Oliver will request a Gray Cloak?"

"Perhaps, but the nearest one I know of is in Redstone. This is up to us."

Latius murmured, "I suppose you're right." He was staring at the tracks again, a worried frown on his face.

Cero began to head back to the tree line, careful to avoid scuffing the tracks. "Let's go, Latius. We have a mage to hunt."

CHAPTER 28: COUNCIL

17ᵗʰ of the Turn of Sutri

Alpert swept into the council chamber and breathed a sigh of relief, the cool air within was a welcome change from the blistering heat outside. Channels running under certain rooms of the Regent's House carried water siphoned from Lake Hawthorne on its way over the falls. The constant flow kept the white granite floor cool and, in turn, the air refreshing compared to the summer heat.

When Duke Everett had granted him the regency here, he had been grateful at first. Years of keeping the man's awful secrets had finally been rewarded. He had arrived in the middle of a mild winter and, for five turns, had enjoyed his assignment. Then summer had come and nearly cooked him. The son of a baron, Alpert had grown up in the far western region of the duchy, in mountains where temperatures never approached the broiling heat outside.

He glanced down to ensure his outfit was clean and presentable, and gave a satisfied nod. There was no need to check his hair. He kept it cut so short that it was not possible for it to be mussed.

Six seats encircled the round table in the room's center, three of which were occupied by council members already here and waiting.

Cato Wadham—here representing the interests of the Smithshill Merchants Guild—was a fat, pig-faced man with a hand in every trading interest within the city. Any new business venture required his approval, something he was not above granting for the right sum of coin. A bright green shirt with puffed sleeves covered Cato's substantial girth, littered with crumbs from the pastry he was stuffing into his voluminous mouth. The fat merchant nodded a silent greeting to the regent, sending more crumbs tumbling down the man's two chins.

Fighting a grimace, Alpert nodded back and took his seat.

An empty chair rested on Cato's right, awaiting a yet-to-arrive council member. Next to the vacant seat and directly across from Alpert sat a man wearing what was clearly last season's fashion: a cobalt blue shirt with long sleeves that flared at the end. Councilman Jalano Maison, a slender man with a carefully trimmed black beard and bald head, was the sole Fallsbottom representative on the council as well as its most ineffective member. Easily swayed on most any issue, he sided with whoever was the last person to speak.

When Jalano offered a quiet, "Good morning, my Lord," Alpert wordlessly grunted back.

Next to Jalano sat Curate Lynea Whyte, here to speak for the interests of the holy orders. Lynea was a beautiful, shapely woman with long, auburn hair flowing over her low-cut, hunter-green robes—the garb of the Order of Chalchalu. Alpert had been pursuing her since his arrival in Smithshill, but she had turned aside every one of his advances. He offered her a smile, but Lynea did not return the favor, apparently believing that her even stare sufficed as a greeting.

Sighing, Alpert eyed the doorway, silently urging the other two council members to show soon. The wooden chair in which he sat was slightly larger than the others and the only indication of Alpert's rank over the rest of the council. Tradition dictated that only the duke could sit at the head of a table during the conduction of official duchy business. As a result, there were few non-round tables in any government building outside of Redstone, the duchy capital. There was one here, used only when Duke Everett was in Smithshill, a rare occurrence.

Not long after, the two remaining members of the council arrived. Alpert was relieved; watching Cato eat was making him ill.

Head Constable Oliver Goodwell swept into the room, bringing a rush of the accursed warm air with him. The man's long, thick black hair was combed perfectly in place and a neatly trimmed, symmetrical beard lined his cheeks and chin. As he sat, he raised a hand to check his coif.

Captain Edmund deCobb marched in next, dressed in full Red Sentinel regalia. Three diamonds embroidered in white thread adorned both shoulders of his black tabard.

As soon as the captain had taken his seat, Alpert ordered the clerk to shut the chamber door and started the meeting by blandly reciting the traditional opening phrase. "On today, Thirday the seventeenth of the Turn of Sutri in the year 4999 after the Locking, the Council of Smithshill convenes on behalf of our Lord Duke Everett to apply his law, dispense his justice, and see to the prosperity of his lands."

The words came out without emotion or thought, spoken more for the sake of the clerk in the corner tasked with recording the proceedings and not because he felt that it was important to say.

"First order of council is to address any of the open issues left unresolved from last week's meeting. Does anyone have something he or she wishes to address?"

Jalano sat forward as if he meant to speak but stopped when Alpert glared at him. Alpert had no interest in rehashing last week's mendacities. Jalano frowned and reclined in his chair.

Nodding, Alpert said, "Nothing then? Excellent. On to this week's items."

For the better part of the early afternoon, the council discussed routine issues. Disputes between business owners. Reports on minor criminal activity. Preparations for the Leisure Time festivals. Alpert paid attention when he had to, and let his mind wander when he did not.

As the meeting went on, Alpert noticed the Head Constable appeared on edge. He frowned inwardly, guessing the man's unease meant there was something significant to report. He prayed whatever it was would not ruin the rest of his day.

Once civic business was complete, Alpert turned to the Head Constable. "You seem anxious, Oliver. What's wrong?"

The Constable hesitated a moment before answering. "We had an event, my Lord. Two evenings ago."

Alpert's ears perked up. An actual report of magic use was rare. "Go on."

"Close to sunset, two of my Trackers were in Fallsbottom when they sensed a large—very large—amount of magic south of the city. They traced the disturbance to a clearing near the cliff where they found signs of a struggle as well as tracks leading into the forest." Oliver stopped talking and shifted in his chair, reaching up to run a hand over his beard.

After a few moments of silence, Alpert prompted, "And did they follow the tracks?"

"Yes, my Lord. At least as far as they could."

"What does that mean?"

Oliver dropped his gaze to the tabletop. "They, ah…ahem. They…lost the trail, my Lord."

A great, booming laugh burst from Cato. "Hah! The great Trackers finally have something to track and they lose the trail! Wondrous!"

The regent ignored Cato's outburst, never taking his eyes from the Constable. "*Both* Trackers lost the trail?"

"Yes, my Lord."

"That's disappointing, Oliver."

"Agreed, my Lord. I do apologize."

"Keep your apologies and bring me the mage."

"Mages, my Lord," corrected the Constable. "We believe there may be more than one. The tracks belonged to three or four people, one of them quite large." He paused again, rubbed his chin again, and added with some reluctance, "Along with a bear. Larger than a horse, they insist."

Cato guffawed louder, shaking like a bowl of Year's End pudding. After silencing the merchant with a sharp look, Alpert turned back to Oliver. "That's impossible. The nearest breed of bear is in the eastern Southlands."

"And those are rather smallish," said Lynea. "No bigger than a cow."

Still quietly chuckling—and jiggling—Cato said, "It seems your Trackers are out of practice, Oliver."

The Constable glared at the merchant and snapped, "If they say there was a bear, there was a blasted bear. If anything, the fact that a giant bear appeared in the valley only to disappear into thin air lends credence to the fact that magic was used."

"I agree with Oliver," said Lynea.

"As do I," muttered Alpert. Glaring at the Constable, he asked, "Why did it take you two days to bring this to my attention?"

"My Trackers insisted they could find the trail if given time. I gave them yesterday to search the valley but they came back with nothing. My deepest apologies, my Lord."

Captain deCobb cleared his throat, drawing everyone's attention. "My Lord? Something I was going to bring to your attention today might be pertinent to this topic. One of the western patrols returned this morning and related something rather disturbing. With your leave, I would like to bring my master sergeant in to report. He saw these things firsthand."

Nodding impatiently, Alpert said, "Of course."

Captain deCobb stood and moved to the oaken door. Opening it, he stepped aside and admitted a tall man with a Southlander-style beard and dark brown hair pulled back into a single bunch. The captain returned to his chair while the sergeant moved to stand beside Jalano. The contrast between the soldier and the Fallsbottom representative was stark. An aura of capability radiated from the soldier while the weak-willed Jalano slouched in his seat. It was like putting the sun next to a new moon. No one would look at the moon. No one could even see it.

"My Lord, this is Master Sergeant Trell," said Captain deCobb. He stared up at the soldier. "Sergeant, please tell the regent what you told me."

"Yes, sir," said the sergeant. He faced Alpert, took a deep breath, visibly composed himself, and began speaking. "My Lord, ten days ago, my men and I left to patrol the road and run through some training. As is routine, we talk to travelers along the way in order to assess the safety of the area. On the evening of the fourth day, one of my corporals stopped a young man heading east and brought him to my attention. Nothing seemed out of the ordinary with him. I, in fact, judged him an upright citizen. After talking with him briefly, I sent him on his way."

"The following afternoon, our patrol passed a turn off with a sign pointing the way to Yellow Mud. It reminded me of the young man from the previous night as he had given his name as Jak Isaac of Yellow Mud. Continuing down the Southern Road, we came across an eastbound train of porters claiming the road ahead was washed out as though a large flood had swept through the area."

"How is that possible?" asked Alpert. "There's been no rain for over three weeks."

The sergeant nodded. "I had the same thought, my Lord, which is why I urged the patrol ahead. We soon found the stretch of road the porters were talking about. It appeared as if there had indeed been a flood. So my men and I tracked the path north, through the hills. After a time, we began to…well…" He paused a moment, a dark shadow passing over his face, and gave a tiny sigh. "We began to find bodies, my Lord, bloated and decomposing. The smell was awful. They had been dead for a few days, just sitting out in the sun."

Albert noticed that both Cato and Jalano had turned a sickly shade of gray.

The sergeant pressed on. "Eventually, we came across what I assumed had been a small village, only none of the buildings was left standing. There were, however, more bodies. After a while, I stopped counting, but I estimate there to have been over two hundred dead."

Alpert exclaimed, "Two hundred!?"

"Yes, my Lord. Perhaps more."

"Bless the gods," muttered Lynea.

"The path of downed trees continued north into the hills," continued the sergeant. "The men I sent to follow it reported the gash went all the way to Lake Hawthorne. I pulled out my field map to determine where we were. There was no doubt, my Lord. We stood in the ruins of Yellow Mud."

Alpert was about to point out something when Cato beat him to it.

"That's where the young man from the road said he was from," said the fat merchantman. "He didn't mention what had happened to his home?"

"No, sir. He did not."

Alpert noticed the Head Constable with his head down, staring at the table, looking even more uncomfortable than before. "Oliver? You look ill."

Looking up, the Constable said, "My Lord, two days past, a pair of young men reported their village had been destroyed. According to them, a blond ijul in crimson robes sent a massive water creature from the lake into their village, killing everyone. They claimed they were the only survivors."

An icy shiv of fear stabbed Alpert's chest. Staring long and hard at the man, he asked, "And what was done in response?"

"Nothing," muttered Oliver. "It was recorded and sent to me, as all reports of magic are. I deemed the tale too fantastic to waste time on."

Alpert glared at the man, wondering if it would be appropriate to stand up and punch the Constable in the face. "You are proving to be a very ineffective Head Constable."

Oliver dropped his stare back to the table. "So it would seem, my Lord."

Looking back to the sergeant, Alpert asked, "I'm assuming you dispatched men to try to find the man you saw on the road?"

"Yes, my Lord. Two groups. One back the path we came, another along the road out of the village, but they never did find him. The rest of us buried the bodies, my Lord. The vultures and wolves were—" He stopped, paused a moment, then continued. "Well, my Lord, it simply did not seem right to leave them unburied. The moment we finished, we returned straight to the city to report."

Nodding, Alpert said, "Good man, Sergeant." Patting his forehead, he found he was sweating. The air in the room no longer felt cool.

The large oaken door to the chambers opened. A servant entered and bowed. "I apologize for interrupting, my Lord, but a rider from Redstone just arrived with a letter from Duke Everett. The man says he was instructed to deliver it the moment he reached Smithshill."

His anxiety growing, Alpert waved his hand, indicating that the messenger should enter. Emergency missives from the duke never carried good tidings. The servant stepped aside and a man in travelling clothes hurried in, still covered in road dirt. He approached and, with a bow, held out a rolled and sealed parchment.

Alpert took the offered parchment and immediately dismissed the man. Looking around the table, he muttered, "Pardon me." He stood, scraping his chair against the floor, and moved a dozen paces from the table. He broke the wax seal, unrolled the parchment, and began to read, his unease growing by the moment. By the time he reached the end, he was in near panic.

Keeping his back to the table, in as even a tone as he could manage, he said, "Captain, Sergeant, and Oliver—stay. Everyone else, leave."

Cato huffed, "My Lord, I believe we should—"

Spinning around, Alpert shouted, "Get out! Now!"

Cato hesitated a moment before standing and waddling out of the chambers, followed by Jalano, Lynea, and the clerk. The moment the door was shut, Alpert walked back to the table, careful to keep the parchment from Duke Everett rolled up.

"Captain, organize a quiet search of the city. Take whichever clerk took the report about Yellow Mud and have him describe those two men down to the number of hairs on their heads. If they are in this city, you are to find them, do you understand?"

"Yes, my Lord."

Turning to what seemed to be one of the few competent people in Smithshill, Alpert said, "Sergeant Trell, you have a new assignment. Take a detail of men and head south. Oliver, I want those two Trackers to accompany him."

"My Lord, the Constables do not report to the army or—"

"Shut up, Oliver," retorted Alpert. "Do it or I will be sure that your superiors in Freehaven know of your failings."

Grimacing, the Constable mumbled, "Yes, my Lord."

"Now, no one is to speak of my instructions here, understand? *No one.* I do not want rumors that mages are on the loose. Sergeant, move your men out south in small groups so they do not draw too much attention. Tell them it's for more training."

"Understood, my Lord."

"Oliver, Captain, you may go, now. Sergeant? You stay."

Captain deCobb stood and left. Oliver scampered out right behind him, clearly relieved to be leaving. Alpert waited until the Constable closed the door before turning his full attention to the sergeant. "What I am about to tell you cannot be shared with anyone. Not even your captain. Do you understand?"

Alpert could see the request made the soldier uncomfortable. That only reinforced the regent's belief that this man would follow the orders given to him. Sergeant Trell respected authority.

"Yes, my Lord."

"Once you have assembled your patrol south of Fallsbottom, I want you to wait for someone by the name of…Fenidar. He will help you in your search and has the authority to do whatever is necessary to apprehend those mages. They are dangerous and need to be treated as such, do you understand?""

A confused flicker darted over the sergeant's face. Questions danced in the man's eyes, but that is where they stayed. "Absolutely, my Lord."

"Good. You can go."

As the sergeant turned to leave, Alpert unrolled the parchment and read the message again. It left him cold inside.

After exiting the chamber, he strode down the hall, through the front atrium, and into the northern wing where his living quarters were. Although servants lined the halls, he barely noticed them. His mind was focused on the duke's letter.

Upon reaching his bedroom chambers, he opened the door and strode straight to his desk. He lifted the chain from around his neck, bent over, and inserted the attached key into the lock on the bottommost drawer. With a soft click, he unlocked the drawer and slid it open. He withdrew the single sheet of parchment resting within, placed it on his desk, and retrieved a quill from the inkpot across from him. He paused a moment, gathering his thoughts, and then began to write in a hurried hand.

Jhaell—

I just received a note from Duke Everett saying he sent you a message days ago and had not heard back. I can only hope that has been rectified in the time it took for his dispatch to reach me.

Word has spread of what we assume was your doing in Yellow Mud. The duke seems to think only one man survived. It now appears there were actually two, two young men who described you perfectly—crimson robes and all—to the Constables in Smithshill. Unfortunately, the incompetent fools didn't believe the tale and sent them on their way. That very evening, there was a magical event south of Fallsbottom. The timing is telling, don't you think?

I have dispatched Red Sentinels along with two Trackers to the south of the city. They are waiting for you; give the name Fenidar. Their sergeant is a capable man and should follow orders. No one knows about you besides him. Use him and the soldiers as you see fit.

—Alpert

CHAPTER 29: PURSUIT

Jhaell stepped from the black polished stone of the cavernous magistrates' chamber to the slate gray flagstone of the hall. From behind, the missing man's attendant called out, "You said you could help find the magistrate!" The plea rebounded through the chamber.

Jhaell ignored the man. He had lied in order to discover what the attendant knew. He had no way of finding the magistrate. The man had ported somewhere. The trail ended here.

"*Beelvra!*"

He hurried down the long hall, the slap of his hard-soled sandals resounding off the granite walls. Cloth tapestries representing the nine colors of the Strands lined the left side of the passageway, lit bright by the sunlight streaming through the arched windows on his right.

The magistrate's assistant continued to yell after him to come back, the cries echoing down the hall, almost mocking Jhaell. He increased his pace despite having no idea where he was headed, his long strides quickly taking him down the hallway.

There was no point in going back. Not here. Not anywhere. Not now. Not ever.

Five days ago, he had returned from his impromptu trip to Greycliffe to discover that he had left his parchments on his desk. Cursing his carelessness, he had quickly scooped up the parchments, put them away, and headed to bed.

The next morning, when he had gone to teach his class, the redheaded mainlander had been absent. Jhaell had thought little of it at the time. It was common for his students to sometimes not show. However, after three days had passed—each without the tomble in class—Jhaell had begun to wonder if he had quit.

Today, he had asked his class if any of them had seen the mainlander. All reported they had not since Jhaell had left him standing in the middle of the sea. After class, Jhaell had gone to the registry, hoping to learn that the tomble had withdrawn from the academy, leaving only eight acolytes in the class and Jhaell with more time to spend in the libraries. The book from Quan was looking promising.

However, according to the registry, the tomble was still enrolled. Jhaell's curiosity was piqued.

During the midday meal, he had made a rare appearance in the great hall, looking for the tomble, and had heard an interesting rumor. It seemed the tiny mainlander had commandeered a ship and sailed to the City of the Strands a few days ago. The cutter had only returned this morning with a boatload of apologetic sailors, claiming that they had been forced to sail against their will.

The story confused Jhaell. The tomble had never struck him as the foolish type. If he were caught, he would be severely disciplined. The Arcane Republic had very strict laws about using Strands of Will on citizens.

Jhaell had left the hall, smiling. It seemed that his class was on the verge of being cancelled after all.

Upon returning to his office, he had pulled out his parchments for the first time since Greycliffe to see if anyone had contacted him. However, when he spread them on his desk, he counted only nine. He tore apart his office, looking for the tenth sheet, but could not find it. Baffled, he had collapsed in his chair and tried to remember if he had done something with it.

After a few quiet moments, a sickening possibility washed over Jhaell like the wave he had sent into Yellow Mud. The last time he had all ten parchments was the night he went to Greycliffe, the same night the tomble had fled the academy.

Jhaell tried to convince himself he was leaping to conclusions, that he was being paranoid. Yet he could come up with no other explanation. After checking the nine parchments on his desk, he realized the missing one's match was in possession of Duke Everett, the sovereign of the Great Lakes Duchy. Where Yellow Mud had been.

Jhaell had sat in his chair, repeatedly cursing both his indiscretion and his carelessness. Centuries of faithful work for Tandyr might be in jeopardy. Along with his chance of ever seeing Syra again.

Jhaell could not fathom why the tomble had been here—if he had been—or why he had taken the parchment—if he had. The only conclusion at which Jhaell could arrive was something had been written on the parchment, something the tomble felt worthy stealing. Considering the timing of the events, Jhaell assumed it must have had something to do with Yellow Mud, although why the mainlander would care baffled him.

As little sense as it made, as implausible as it seemed, Jhaell could not shake the feeling that was exactly what had happened. He had immediately gathered his remaining nine parchments and some other items of importance from his office. If he found the tomble quickly and retrieved the parchment, he could retain his position at the academy, the duke would not be implicated, and most importantly, Tandyr would not learn of his mistakes.

After talking with the sailors of the *Morning's Mist* to ensure the rumor of the tomble's flight was true, he ported to the City of the Strands and began tracing the mainlander's steps. After a few distasteful hours of searching the city's dregs, he found a man who had directed the tomble toward the office of a magistrate. According to the man, the mainlander was interested in finding someone who could port to the Oaken Duchies.

Jhaell's irrational fear suddenly seemed quite sound.

He had rushed to the House of Magistrates and interrogated the man's attendant, discovering that the mainlander had succeeded in getting the magistrate to open a port. No one had seen the official in days.

Now, Jhaell slowed to a stop in the middle of the sun-strewn hall, closed his eyes, and muttered, "I am a fool…"

He wondered if he should go speak with the duke to inquire what had been written, but immediately discounted the idea. Doing so would admit he had lost one of the parchments, a parchment that may or may not have evidence of Tandyr's plans. Should Tandyr learn of Jhaell's folly, he would never fulfill his promise and, more than likely, would end Jhaell's life.

The sensation of dark crackling startled him from his reverie. Glancing down to the satchel on his hip, he spotted a few wispy Strands of Void fluttering around the bag. After looking up and down the hallway and finding it empty, he carefully pulled the set of nine parchments from his bag. He flipped through the sheets until he saw one with writing slowly appearing on it. The parchment belonged to Alpert, the regent of Smithshill. He moved it to the top and read from the beginning. By the time he was finished, his heart was thudding in his chest.

"This is bad."

He closed his eyes.

"This is very bad…"

When he and the students had ported to Redstone before the attack, they had arrived in one of Duke Everett's hidden courtyards. Plenty of people had seen him exit the Duke's Hall in his crimson robes. Rumors were bound to spread.

Things were falling apart.

Jhaell opened his eyes and read the parchment again. As he did, a hopeful, excited optimism filled him. Perhaps Yellow Mud had been the right place after all. Perhaps he truly had found the Progeny. His eyes went wide as he realized what that meant, his optimism morphing into horror.

"*Beelvra!* I set them loose!"

Thankfully, Alpert had shown some initiative and arranged things for Jhaell to pursue them. He stared at the parchment without seeing the words, thinking.

Were he to find the Progeny and eliminate them, his indiscretion in Yellow Mud would not matter. Nothing would. Without the Progeny, Tandyr could act with near impunity. Secrecy would no longer be necessary. And, ultimately, victory would be assured.

A smile crept over Jhaell's face. Then he would be with Syra again.

After shoving the parchments back into his satchel, he went to find a records room. He rushed through the maze of halls, ignoring the strange stares he received from officials going about their business.

Upon reaching the room, he threw open the door—letting it bang against the inside wall—and stepped into a stuffy, dark space. Wooden shelves packed with old, yellowed parchments and capped scrolls lined the walls. A lone young man in dark robes stood behind a tall counter, wearing a bored expression.

Jhaell ran to the counter and demanded, "Give me a quill and ink." In his hurry to leave the academy, he had forgotten his own. "And I'll need a private place to write."

Instead of complying with the request, the man glared at him. "No."

"No?" repeated Jhaell, equal parts incredulous and perturbed. "Why not?"

Lifting an eyebrow, the man said, "First, you burst in here and nearly break my door. Then you *order* me to give you ink and quill?" He shook his head. "*No.*"

Jhaell's destructive impatience flared. He reached to his belt, pulled out his thin-bladed dagger, and stabbed the man straight in the neck, releasing a crimson plume of blood that squirted onto the counter and splattered all over Jhaell's robes. After Jhaell pulled the longknife free, the man grasped his neck and tried to scream for help, but was unable to with his windpipe nearly severed.

Jhaell prayed the man was not a Life Mage and, for a change, fate was on his side. The man did nothing with the Strands, Life or any other kind, stumbling about before slumping over on the counter, bleeding and choking. As the light drained from the young man's eyes, Jhaell walked back to the door, closing and locking it. Returning to the counter, he peered over the ledge, and stared at the corpse. "You should have just given me the ink and quill."

Finding both lying next to the dead man, he reached out and grabbed the writing utensils.

He stood at the counter for a time, writing the same message on eight of the nine parchments. The ninth, the one to Alpert, he simply wrote that he was on his way. Once he was done, he rolled them up and placed them in his travelling bag.

Weaving Void and Air together, he ripped open a tear in the dusty records room, stepped through, and arrived in total blackness. A warm, unpleasant, musty odor filled his nose, smelling of old boots and dead rats.

Cursing, he fumbled about the enclosed space, knocking various unseen items over, searching with his hands. Ijuli had excellent vision in the dark, but required at least a modicum of light. After finding the handle for which he was searching, he wrapped his long fingers around it and lifted.

He opened the door to the closet and stepped into a cramped and dusty room. A simple straw-mat bed was pressed up against one wooden wall underneath a tiny, square window through which the warm light of evening sun streamed.

Jhaell had been paying rent on this room for years, ensuring it would always be empty for his use. Dozens of places like this existed for him in cities throughout the world, but he rarely used any of them in the duchies. The threat of exposing himself to the Constables was too great.

Glancing down, he realized that his robes presented a dual problem. First, they were now covered in dark bloodstains, and second, they could easily identify him as the person responsible for what happened in Yellow Mud. Ijul were rare here. Ijul wearing crimson robes even more so.

Reaching into the closet, he retrieved a set of spare traveling clothes: tan jute-cloth breeches, a brown shirt made of a light but durable material, leather boots, and a heavy, black, unadorned cloak. After changing, he buckled his belt around his waist with his wiped-clean dagger in its sheath. He moved to the door, unlocked it, and stepped into a dingy, dark hallway.

Lined with a half-dozen doors like the one he had exited, the hall was empty of people, but full of the sounds of talking and singing downstairs. Hurrying to the end of the hall and down the steps, he entered a tavern room brimming with a crowd of unclean, drunk men. A few of the less inebriated patrons in the room noticed his entrance, but most ignored him.

He moved across the room, dodging the patrons in the room, and approached the innkeeper. When he reached the counter, a smell of unwashed filth wafted over Jhaell.

The overweight, sweaty man glanced at Jhaell, looked away, and stared back an instant later, his eyes going round. Giving a Jhaell a nervous smile, the man stuttered, "Wel...welcome b-back, sir."

Jhaell placed a handful of gold arcans on the top of the bar. They were not the currency of the region, but gold was still gold. The innkeeper's eyes somehow opened even wider, his gaze fixed on the small fortune sitting before him.

"I am severing our arrangement," said Jhaell. "This is for you to go up to the room—*this very instant*—and burn everything you find there."

The man's head bobbed up and down. "Yes, sir."

"And if any of your blasted Constables show up, you play dumb."

The man nodded again, this time without saying anything.

Despite the man's odor, Jhaell leaned closer to the innkeeper and whispered, "If I learn that you speak a word of this situation to anyone, I will come back for you. Do you understand?"

This time the man did not move his head, but the fear in his eyes was answer enough.

Jhaell stepped from the bar and hurried to the front of the inn. After pushing open the door, he stepped outside, into the cool, mist-filled air doing its best to mask an otherwise warm day. Striding into the muddy street, he hurried away from The Brown Horse and Cart, heading south down the road and out of Fallsbottom. He had to find the encampment of soldiers as quickly as possible.

CHAPTER 30: SERGEANT

Nathan walked through camp, carefully studying his men. A moonless twilight had plunged the valley into a gloomy darkness, the tents and soldiers lit only by the flickering of campfires. The light, while meager, was enough to reveal the obvious.

The men were nervous.

He could see it in their faces and hear it in their voices. He swore he could feel their worry as he walked past. He had followed the regent's instructions, keeping his men without torch until they were all here, at which point he shared their orders. They had listened, their faces solemn yet determined. Most of these soldiers were from the original detachment that had discovered Yellow Mud with him. They had helped bury the bodies.

Captain deCobb had assigned an extra twenty men to his normal detachment, bringing those under Nathan's command to an even one hundred soldiers. Before leaving, Nathan had asked the captain to remove Footman Haynes from his command. He did not have time to watch after the nobleman's son playing soldier. This assignment was legitimate.

He walked among the tents, pretending to check on the security of the camp, but the truth was he was simply trying to calm his men with his presence.

His meandering eventually took him past where the two Trackers had set up their tent, off to one side of the camp and a noticeable distance away from the nearest soldier. The pair in gray sat before a small fire, facing the Sentinels, clearly as uncomfortable with the situation as were his own men.

Nathan ambled over to the pair, intent to learn what they knew. He was operating with much less information than he would have liked.

Stopping before the two men, Nathan offered them a smile and a nod. "Good days ahead to you."

Both looked up at his greeting but remained stone-faced and silent. After giving their name earlier, the pair had spoken nary a word.

Nathan's smile disappeared. "Have it your way then." He sat on a rock opposite them, entirely aware that members of his detachment were watching him. "Hope you don't mind if I sit down for a while."

The Trackers stared at him in silence.

Folding his hands before him, Nathan spoke in a low, even tone. "Gentlemen, I understand this is an unusual situation for you. It is for us, as well. However, those we are seeking apparently require a hundred swords pursuing them as well as the two of you. Speaking as a man who saw what happened at Yellow Mud, I wish we had thrice as many."

He paused as the two men exchanged a quick glance before looking back to him. Still, they remained silent. Whispers about Trackers filled every tavern and meeting room in the duchies. As a rule, the mage-hunters were withdrawn, quiet, and a suspicious lot. Nathan had to counteract that somehow.

"So, then," sighed Nathan. "This is what is going to happen: this odd expedition of ours will go smoothly. Why is that? Because I refuse to let it go otherwise. Now, for that to happen, I need my men to be alert, their eyes on the road and *not* on the two silent, mysterious Trackers in our midst. Is that clear?"

Cero eyed him for a long moment before nodding, his answer spoken in a confident, raspy voice. "I believe we understand, Sergeant."

"Good, then. Now, when I say, 'go', I would like the two of you to laugh as though I told the prize jest at the festival. Go."

Nathan began to chuckle, waiting for the pair to join him. At first, neither man responded, then Cero started to laugh along with him, albeit half-heartedly. Eventually, Latius smiled awkwardly. It would have to do.

As their phony jest concluded, Nathan looked between the pair. "Now, if you don't mind, I would like to see if we can work on an exchange of information. I am here with precious little to go on."

The two men again exchanged a look and then turned as one toward Nathan. A small muscle twitched in Latius' cheek. Nathan tried to figure if it was irritation or fear.

"I'll go first, then," he said magnanimously. "Let's see...well, to start, I can tell you why we're still sitting here and not already down the road. Interested?"

Nathan noted Latius' gaze shift to Cero. Whether officially or not, it seemed Cero was in charge of the pair.

After a heartbeat or two, Cero answered. "We had pondered on what the delay was."

"We're waiting for someone," said Nathan. "Does the name 'Fenidar' mean anything to either of you?" When neither Tracker showed any recognition of the name whatsoever, Nathan let out a disappointed sigh. "I suppose we will learn of him together, then."

"Why are we waiting for him?" asked Cero.

Nathan shrugged his shoulders. "Regent Alpert put him in charge. That's all I know." Nodding across the fire, he said, "Your turn to share something. Tell me what you found along the base of the cliff."

Cero launched into a short narrative describing how they had traced the magical activity to a location five miles south of Fallsbottom. Nathan purposely did not ask how exactly they had done that because he knew there would be no answer. The sky was blue, grass was green, Trackers tracked magic.

Cero described the giant bear marks that appeared from nowhere and just as mysteriously vanished. Four people had been there, one of them a giant of a man and one of them a girl or an older child, judging by the size of the footprints. Three horses accompanied them, led from the cliff and not ridden. After only a few steps into the forest, all traces of the group vanished. The Trackers believed the mage—or mages—used a minor bit of magic to erase their physical tracks. When Nathan pressed them about why they could not track that magic, both men grew tight-lipped, merely saying that they could not.

When they finished, Nathan said, "To be clear, we are looking for three men, a girl or child, and three horses." Incredulous, he added, "And a very big bear?"

Wearing an expression of mild embarrassment and chagrin, Cero shrugged. "I did not say it made sense, Sergeant."

Nathan sat back, confused. He had hoped the Trackers' report might clear things up. Instead, he had new questions to add to his already long list.

Hearing the sound of footsteps approaching from behind, he twisted around to see Footman Bedwin striding quickly to the Tracker's fire. Nathan motioned for the soldier to wait for him to come to him. Excusing himself, he stood and moved to meet the young footman.

When Nathan was a few paces away, the young man said, "Sergeant? Fenidar just arrived. He's waiting for you at your tent."

Bedwin's nervous expression gave Nathan pause. "What is it, footman?"

The man frowned, glanced around, and said quietly, "He's an ijul, Sergeant. A *saeljul*, by the looks of him."

Every so often, a group of tijul would move through Smithshill, but saeljul were rare in the region. In fact, Nathan needed only one hand to count how many he had seen in his life.

Withholding his surprise, he thanked Bedwin for fetching him and strode past the soldier, toward where he had staked his tent. As he strode amongst the camp, he shook his head in worried wonderment. Things were getting stranger by the moment.

A tall figure stood alone before Nathan's tent, shrouded in evening's shadow. Like all ijul, his facial features were elongated and his arms seemed too long for his body. The flickering light of the campfires made his white hair appear to glow an unnatural yellow-orange color. Nathan knew the tricks that low levels of light played on the eyes but the effect was eerie, nonetheless.

Dressed in brown traveling clothes and black cloak with a single, leather satchel slung over his shoulder, the saeljul looked every bit prepared for a journey through the wilderness. Still, Nathan easily marked him city bred. He suspected the ijul had never slept a night without the comfort of a feathered bed.

As the pair's eyes met, a small chill ran up Nathan's back. There was no logical reason for the sensation, yet something about this ijul gave him an uneasy feeling.

Nathan was still a few steps away from the tent when the ijul addressed him.

"You are the sergeant in charge here?"

"I am," replied Nathan, stopping before the stranger. "You are Fenidar?"

With a nod, the ijul said, "I am." He tugged at his shirt collar, confirming Nathan's suspicion that he was uncomfortable in his clothing. "I want the camp ready to move as soon as possible. I will not accept delay. We pursue some very dangerous people."

He spoke as though he expected immediate obedience. His voice exuded command.

"Do you mean for us to march through the night?"

"Is that a problem?"

Shaking his head, Nathan said, "Not necessarily. It will take a little while to strike camp. Do you have any objections to torches or advance scouts?" Traveling in complete darkness was dangerous.

"None. I leave that to your discretion."

Nathan stepped away, called Amiles over and told him to tear down the camp, make torches, and send out scouts. They were marching the night. The corporal nodded and moved off, his shouted orders cutting through the evening. Men leapt to their feet to comply. They were anxious to move.

Turning back to the ijul, Nathan said, "As we have some time, I was hoping I might ask you a few questions."

Fenidar regarded Nathan for a long moment, reminding Nathan of a cat's unblinking, unending stare. "First, tell me what you know."

Nathan did so, briefing the saeljul as quickly as he could, stopping for Fenidar's many interruptions. The saeljul asked numerous questions, most of which Nathan could not answer. When Nathan shared the tragedy of Yellow Mud, Fenidar had waved him on, uninterested in the details. He was much more attentive during Nathan's recounting of the meeting with the young man on the Southern Road. When Nathan relayed what he had just learned from the Trackers about the scuffle at the cliff, Fenidar halted him.

"These Trackers? They are here?"

When Nathan answered that they were, Fenidar asked that he send for them immediately. Nathan called to a footman, ordered him to bring Latius and Cero here, and then continued with his report while waiting for the Trackers to show. The moment they arrived, the saeljul asked to speak with them alone, turned, and stepped inside Nathan's tent without bothering to ask if he might use it.

The two Trackers glanced at Nathan with inquisitive eyes and followed Fenidar into the tent. Sighing, Nathan turned and watched his men tear down camp, impressed with their efficiency. They would be underway sooner than he had thought. His two best scouts, Blainwood and Hunsfin, rode past, torches blazing.

Hearing the tent flaps open behind him, Nathan looked back as the Trackers emerged from inside and hastened past without looking at him.

Curious, Nathan called, "Cero?"

The man did not look back as he hurried across the camp.

"Cero!"

The Tracker kept going.

Nathan frowned and peered at the entrance to his tent, waiting for the ijul to come out. When he did not, Nathan moved to the flaps and stuck his head back inside. Fenidar was sitting on Nathan's field stool, reading a parchment by candlelight. Without glancing up, Fenidar lifted a hand, indicating he wished for Nathan to wait silently.

Nathan's frown deepened, but he complied. Whatever the reason, the regent had placed Fenidar in charge, so Nathan would follow the ijul's orders. That was what good soldiers did.

After a few moments, Fenidar rolled up the parchment and placed it in his lap. He reached inside his bag, and pulled out a quill and sealed inkbottle. "I'm sorry, Sergeant, we will need to speak later. I have things I need to attend to."

Swallowing his irritation, Nathan asked, "Will you need a dispatch sent somewhere? I can have a man run something up to Hilltop before we get underway."

The hint of an amused smile touched the corners of Fenidar's wide lips. "Ah...no, that's quite all right. I have to make a few notes about things; that is all. Now, I'm sure you have plenty to do, don't you? Please, don't let me keep you."

Nathan understood he was being dismissed. "Should you need anything, send for me."

Fenidar did not respond.

After a few moments, Nathan withdrew his head and took a few steps back. Staring at his tent, he shook his head. He did not feel good about this at all.

Letting out a sigh, he turned his attention to the camp. Half of the tents were already down, fires were being extinguished with handfuls of dirt, the horses un-picketed and saddled. Leaving his soldiers to take care of themselves, Nathan strode back to where the Trackers had set up camp. Like the Red Sentinels, the pair was in the midst of packing their belongings.

"Cero!"

The black-haired man spun to meet his eye, but then quickly turned away. Nathan strode closer, stopped a few paces from the men, and watched them strap their gear to their horses. "What exactly happened back there?"

Cero glanced at Nathan and shook his head. "Nothing, Sergeant. Nothing at all. Fenidar just wanted to meet us and hear what we knew."

"You were hardly in there long enough to tell him much of anything."

Cero shrugged. "I talk fast."

Nathan shifted his gaze to the other Tracker. "Latius? What happened?"

Latius shot a furtive glance at his partner and continued his packing without ever meeting Nathan's eyes. "Nothing. Just like Cero says." He moved to the other side of his horse and busied himself with checking his saddlebags, ducking behind the roan.

Nathan glared at the pair a moment longer, let out a sound of disgust, and walked away. All in all, this expedition was off to an unsettling start.

CHAPTER 31: TRUTH

18th of the Turn of Sutri

Warmed by the late afternoon sun, Kenders sat snug in the saddle of her new horse, riding down the road and eyeing Nikalys' back. For days on end, her brother had been withdrawn, answering any question posed to him in as few words as possible. Sometimes he did not answer at all. He was making Broedi look talkative.

To say that the revelation about their parents had been a shock would be like saying the summers of Yellow Mud were slightly warm. She understood this was hard for him, but she was tiring of his mood. He was not the only one having to deal with a new reality.

When Broedi had told them that Thaddeus and Marie were not their blood parents, a swirling jumble of emotions had rolled over her: disbelief, denial, anger, wonder, fear. As they had hurried away from the cliff, rushing to the Southern Road, countless questions raced through her head, questions that were destined to remain there, echoing in the quiet cavern of her mind. Broedi had demanded complete silence that first evening, his head snapping around at every sound. Even the harmless chirp of a redbird had startled him.

Nikalys had seemed perfectly content to remain quiet, falling into a brooding silence that had made Jak's earlier mood seem festive. Throughout the remainder of the afternoon and evening, no one had said a word.

They had all begun riding their new horses once they reached the road. Broedi had no trouble in keeping up with the horses, despite the brisk pace they all kept. In fact, Kenders had the impression Broedi would have liked to move faster had he been sure the three siblings would not tumble from their mounts.

When Mu's orb had set and the moons rose, Broedi had not stopped, ushering them off the road to avoid the nighttime camps of other travelers. It was clear to Kenders that the hillman did not want anyone to mark their passage.

At dawn's first light, Broedi led the party deep into the forest in order to make camp, after which he finally permitted them to talk, albeit in whispers. The hillman refused to answer any questions, however, keeping his full attention on the quiet forest around them.

Kenders, physically and mentally exhausted, had tried to talk with Nikalys, but he refused. He had lain down and closed his eyes without saying a word to anyone. Kenders wondered if he slept.

Jak, however, had been eager to talk. Their conversation had been awkward at first, almost as if they were strangers. After a few uncomfortable exchanges, the uneasiness had passed and they were soon smiling and quietly chatting.

After too short a time, Broedi more or less ordered them to sleep; they were going to be on the move again shortly. The two exchanged a long hug and laid down on their bedrolls. For a long time, she laid there, thinking, qualifying everything she thought about her family life, categorizing everything and everyone. Blood parents. Foster parents. What it meant to be a brother or a sister, a father or a mother.

She eventually fell asleep, only to be awakened what felt like a moment later by a gentle shake from Jak. Groggy, she sat up and found that he had already saddled Smoke for her, letting her sleep a little longer. The gesture meant a lot to her.

Broedi relaxed his restriction on talking that second day, yet still would not answer any questions, which irritated Kenders. Nikalys remained uncommunicative throughout the evening and night yet again. Jak tried reaching out to him, but Nikalys rebuffed every effort. Jak took it in stride, but Kenders was disappointed in Nikalys. This situation was difficult for all of them, not just him. He was being incredibly selfish.

When Broedi awakened them this afternoon, he said they were only going to travel until dark. Tonight they would have a real camp. When Kenders pressed him to answer some questions, he agreed to do so tonight. She planned to hold him to that promise.

When the sun set, they moved into the forest, made camp, and settled in. Broedi left to hunt—with a sling this time—and returned with five small rock pheasants. Jak prepared the birds for roasting, and Kenders seasoned them with salt and the last of the hillsage before setting them over the fire. Throughout the meal's preparation, Nikalys sat at the edge of their camp and sulked.

Kenders glanced at Jak and found her eldest brother glaring at Nikalys. After three days of Nikalys' moping, he was getting irritated, too.

The land changed a little each day. Here, a mixture of dry, thin pine needles and dead leaves covered the ground of the camp. Broedi sat on a mossy ash log with his back to the fire, smoking his engraved bone pipe, little wisps of smoke curling up from the bowl. With a start, Kenders realized it was the first time since the cliff that she had even seen Broedi sitting down. He had remained vigilant on end for three days. She wondered if he had slept.

Other than the logs crackling in the fire and the soft hum of insects in the trees, the clearing was deadly quiet. Determined to finally get some answers,

Kenders stood, brushed some needles and leaves from her new green riding dress, and strode around Broedi's log to stop before the hillman. Even sitting down on a log, Broedi was nearly as tall as she was standing. He lifted his eyes as she arrived and stared at her. The sweet, heady aroma of the pipe smoke filled the air.

Folding her hands in front of her, she said, "I would like answers. Now." She supposed her tone was overly formal, perhaps a bit rude, almost as if she had given him an order.

Broedi considered her for a long moment, his deep brown eyes, studying her, evaluating. Finally, he nodded once, motioning for her to sit down in front of him.

Her eyebrows shot up. She had half-expected Broedi to put her off again. "Truly?"

Broedi's typical, slight smile crept over his lips. "Truly, uora."

Glancing past the hillman, she waved to an anxious Jak, beckoning him over. He flashed a relieved grin, stood from the ground, and strode to Broedi's log, kicking up leaves and pine needles as he hurried.

When he arrived, he murmured, "I wasn't sure if you wanted me to listen to this."

Kenders reached up and placed her hand on his arm. "This involves us all, Jak."

Jak nodded, a small, appreciative smile on his face. "Thanks, sis." She liked that he still called her that.

She peered over Broedi's head to where Nikalys stood, leaning against a tree trunk and pretending that he did not know what was happening. Raising her voice, she called, "Nikalys! If you are done pouting, could you come over, please? I don't want Broedi to have to repeat himself. You know how much he loves to talk."

As Broedi chuckled softly—surprising her a little—Nikalys turned and gave her an absolutely awful look, one of hurt swirling with a bitter, determined anger. Seeing him like that tempered some of her irritation with him. After Yellow Mud, he had been nothing but protective and supportive, especially regarding her being a mage. Perhaps she was being callous. Letting out a short sigh, she moved around the end of the log and approached him. He turned his back to her.

Kenders strolled up behind him and put a hand on his shoulder. He flinched. At once, every bit of annoyance she felt toward him melted away.

Without saying a word, she wrapped her arms around his waist and hugged him from behind, laying her head on his back. He tried to pull away initially, but when she held tight, he stood still and relaxed. After a few moments, he placed his hand on hers and squeezed.

The remained that way for a time, still and silent. Broedi and Jak left them alone.

Eventually, he patted her hand twice, which she took to mean that he was done being consoled. She released her embrace and he turned around to face her. Firelight gleamed in his tear-moistened eyes. "I don't know what I'm supposed to feel."

Kenders nodded slowly and murmured, "You know what? Me either. But that's no reason to be such a lout to Jak and me."

He pressed his lips together and sighed. "I know. I'm sorry." He shook his head, reaching up to rub his eyes. "It's just...I don't understand what's happening to me—or to you. None of this makes sense...I mean...we're not even...and Jak? Gods, sis, Jak's not our brother...?" He dipped his head and trailed off, sounding utterly lost.

Reaching out, she took his hands in hers. "Hey! Now, I don't have any idea what's going on either. But I do know that—blood or not—Jak *is* our brother."

Nikalys looked up, his gaze flicking over her shoulder to where Jak waited with Broedi. "You're right."

Pressing ahead, Kenders said, "Something else I know is this: that giant hillman back there has done nothing but keep us safe since he's met us. He says he was a friend of our...blood parents—" she was having difficulty deciding what to call them "—and I believe him."

Nikalys' expression turned hard. "I don't know if I do. There are too many questions."

"Yes, there are," agreed Kenders. She motioned across the clearing behind her. "And Broedi says he's ready to answer them now. So let's go see what he has to say."

Nikalys took a deep breath, held it a moment, and exhaled. "Right again. Let's go." Wearing a determined expression, he strode past her.

She followed him to the other side of the log where Jak was sitting on the ground, waiting. Nikalys moved to Jak, offered his hand, and when Jak accepted it, Nikalys pulled him off the ground, straight into a brotherly embrace. Soon, they were both smacking each other on the back. Neither of them had spoken a single word.

She huffed and shook her head. She had seen it a hundred times growing up and still never understood how the pair could make up like this. No words. Nothing. Just some backslapping.

When her brothers stopped pounding each other, Nikalys turned to Broedi. The hillman sat still, studying Nikalys, pipe smoke drifting from his nose and lips. Nikalys crossed his arms and spoke, his tone firm. "I want to be clear. I don't trust you, Broedi. Especially after whatever happened at the cliff."

Kenders winced. She had been hoping Nikalys might offer an apology for his sullenness.

The hillman pulled the pipe from his teeth. "One day, you will trust me, uori."

The muscles in Nikalys' neck and jaw rippled. "I doubt that."

"Nik?" muttered Kenders. "Be civil."

He glanced at her, pressed his lips together, and turned back to Broedi. "Regardless, I am willing to listen to whatever it is you have to say."

The hillman nodded once. "Then ask any question you like, uori, and I will answer what I can." Indicating the area before the log, he added, "Please, sit."

The three settled before Broedi; Jak with his back against the trunk of a young oak, Kenders next to him, and Nikalys beside her. Once seated on the soft bed of leaves and pine needles, Kenders stared up at Broedi. For a brief moment, she felt like they were children again at a Leisure Time festival, gathered by a bonfire to wait for a playman or their father to tell a story.

Moments of silence passed. A pair of squirrels chattered back and forth in the trees above.

Eventually, Broedi pulled his pipe from his lips. "For me to answer a question, one must be asked."

Kenders was startled when Jak spoke at once.

"Are you sure I'm not their brother?"

Broedi stared at Jak, a kindly look in his eyes. "I am, uori. Quite sure."

"Why?" pressed Jak.

"Because when Aryn and Eliza left, they only had two children." He looked at Nikalys. "A young boy with brown hair and brown eyes,"—he shifted his gaze to Kenders —"and a girl with hair the color of straw and eyes that changed colors with the sun and shade." He stared at Jak and gave a slight, reassuring smile. "They did not have an elder son with black hair. You may assume that your parents were truly your parents."

"You said 'when Aryn and Eliza left,'" noted Kenders "Left from where?"

With an apologetic tilt of his head, Broedi said, "That, I will not tell you tonight, uora."

Kenders' eyes narrowed. "You said you would answer our questions."

"Much like strange berries in the wilderness, some of my answers are safe, some are not. The answer to that question is not yet ripe. I am sorry."

Kenders frowned, disappointed that her first inquiry was going unanswered.

Silence returned to their little glade. The crackle and pop of the fire and the sizzling of the roasting birds filled the quiet. Nikalys ended it.

"So our blood parents were White Lions?"

Kenders stared glanced at her brother. He was certainly getting straight to the kernel.

"Yes," rumbled Broedi. "They were."

Incredulous, Nikalys said, "You will excuse me when I say that's utter madness."

Broedi tilted his head. "What makes you say that?"

Kenders answered for Nikalys, stating the obvious. "Because the White Lions are a myth, a playman's tale people tell at festivals or around a Seventhday eveningmeal."

A smile—larger than normal—spread over Broedi's lips. "Have I not cautioned you about dismissing that which you believe to be myth?"

Nikalys muttered, "This is different."

"Why, uori?"

Glowering at the hillman, Nikalys snapped, "This isn't a nice story about where hillmen came from. You are asking us to believe that we are the children of White Lions!"

Broedi held Nikalys' gaze for a long moment before sighing, twisting around, and staring back to the fire. "Perhaps one of you could grab the pheasants?" He faced them again, his gaze running over all three of their faces. "I am hungry, and I have a feeling this will take some time."

"I got it," said Jak, hopping up. He ran over to the fire, grabbed the five spits, and brought them back, handing one to each of them, keeping one for himself, and sticking the fifth upright in the soft dirt underneath the needle and leaf covering.

Broedi placed his pipe on the log beside him with care and took a large bite of the roasted bird. Kenders went to eat hers, but had to halt before biting down. The bird was sizzling and steaming. She wondered how Broedi had not burned his mouth.

After swallowing, Broedi nodded at Jak. "When I spoke with your kaveli, he shared with me the 'myth' of the White Lions as you know it. And I must say, whichever playman shared the saga in Yellow Mud should return every last ducat he took for telling the tale."

Looking from face to face, he said in a purposeful, deliberate tone, "The White Lions are real. And unlike what you have heard, none 'went mad' and killed those poor souls at Carinius. The god of Deception crafted that entire situation. Unfortunately, none of us knew that, or even who he or she was until it was much too late." A bitter, pensive frown spread over his face. "Which is more or less the entire problem with the Cabal..."

Kenders' eyebrows drew together at something Broedi had just said. In an instant, her mind dashed over every moment spent with the hillman since the giant lynx had leapt over the fingerprick thicket.

His stories.

His knowledge of all things magic.

His reticence to talk of the past, or to talk at all for that matter.

Eyes wide, her gaze locked onto the necklace hanging from his neck: a white stone carved in the shape of a lion's head.

"Bless the gods…"

Broedi's brown eyes turned to her.

With pure, unfiltered awe, she muttered, "You're one of them, aren't you? You're a White Lion…"

The hillman gazed at her for a long moment, unmoving. After letting out a deep sigh, he spoke with resignation in his voice. "I had not meant for that to be known yet."

Stunned silence swallowed the camp. After a few thudding heartbeats, she glanced over at her brothers. Both were gaping at Broedi, holding their spits and roasted pheasants before them, untouched. Off in the distance, a lone wolf howled, shocking them all back into the moment.

Lowering his spit and bird, Nikalys mumbled, "Well, that explains quite a bit."

Kenders turned her head to glare at Jak. "Why in the Nine Hells didn't you tell us that?"

Jak answered without ever taking his eyes from Broedi. "Because he never shared with me that rather important detail."

"I told you only what was necessary to get you to cooperate, uori," said Broedi. "Nothing more. It was for the best."

Jak scowled. He did not look satisfied with the answer. Kenders did not blame him.

Broedi put down his pheasant, jabbing the stick into the ground and leaving the roasted bird perched beside him. Kenders almost tossed hers in the leaves and needles. She no longer had an appetite. Nevertheless, she jammed her stick in the dirt, too.

Broedi rested his elbows on his knees and peered down at the three of them. "I will tell you the true story of the White Lions, not something that has been retold a thousand times by a thousand playmen who make their coin by embellishing the truth or leaving it out altogether. Knowing the true history will make the rest of what I must tell you easier to accept."

He reached behind the log, grabbed his waterskin, and after uncapping it, took a long drink. Once done, he closed the skin, dropped it to the ground—it sloshed as it landed—and picked up his pipe. After checking that it was still alight, he drew a long puff and let the smoke seep from his mouth as he spoke.

"When I was younger, I lived in the northern Red Peaks, near a river lowlanders called Clearwater, for its water was clean and pure, snowmelt from the mountains. While aki-mahet were part of the duchy, we kept to ourselves. For much of my life there, things were good. Game was plentiful, our farms were bountiful, and life was peaceful." A wistful smile touched his lips and spread into his eyes. When it disappeared, he continued.

"An adventurous few of our tribe chose to live among the men in the plains. They would occasionally come and visit those of us who remained in the hills, bringing with them stories of the world below. Their tales were how we first heard about the warmongering of Duke Alistair and his invasion of the Northlands and Foothills. But as the war had not yet touched us in the mountains, we did not care much what happened. That all changed in one night."

He paused and the thick muscles along his neck twitched. His pipe hung in his hand, already forgotten. When he resumed, his voice was hard and cold.

"They came with torches ablaze and took the husbands and elder sons, demanding they fight for the duke's army. Had I not been away on a nighttime hunt, I would have been taken as well. The children and women they left behind told unbelievable stories of twisted, monstrous men covered with horns, snouts, hooves, and other hideous deformities. Not believing them, I followed the tracks to see for myself and to try to help free those who were taken. When I came upon their camp in the woods, I saw that they were indeed demon-men, and they were doing something to my people. They were—" he grimaced "—forcing them to drink their blood. Black, thick blood that smelled of rotting things and burning flesh."

He twisted up his nose as though he could still smell it. "Fury gripped me." His voice burned. "Even though it would mean certain death for me, I made ready to help my people. I prepared myself to meet Maeana, was but a moment from charging when I felt a softness graze the back of my leg. Fearful that I had been discovered, I spun around and found a kisa standing behind me."

Kenders did not want to interrupt, but had to. "Pardon me? Kisa?"

"Forgive me, uora. You call them lynx."

As Kenders nodded her understanding, Broedi drew another puff on his pipe and continued. "Kisa are important to aki-mahet, revered as a…guardian of sorts. This kisa sat very still, his eyes fixed on me. After a few moments, he turned and walked away from me, away from the demons and my people. He stopped after a few steps and looked back to me. I sensed that he was my guide, calling me to follow, and so I did. I left my people behind." He paused a moment, closed his eyes, and then muttered, "I still hear their cries in my dreams."

Beneath the sympathy Kenders felt for Broedi bubbled the troubling thought that her nightmares might continue for the rest of her life, too.

Broedi reopened his eyes and gave a quick shake of his head before continuing. "For weeks, the kisa led me west over the mountains, farther than I had ever been from home. We traveled through country with green grasses, brilliant flowers, sweet fruits, and more game than I had ever seen. It was a blessed land. He shared his kills with me and I came to think of my companion as a friend. Eventually, he led me to a great city."

He shook his head in wonderment. "I had never seen so many buildings before. And none so tall and richly made. White marble. Sparkling glass." He smiled and looked at Kenders. "I suppose I must have looked as you did when you saw Smithshill, uora."

Kenders smiled back as Broedi resumed his tale. "The kisa led me into the city and through streets filled with a people unlike I had ever seen. Their skin was pale and their eyes all white. They were taller and thinner than the men I had known of the plains, yet still shorter than I was."

"Hold a moment," said Jak. "You're talking about divina, aren't you?"

"I am."

Nikalys lifted a hand and spoke. "So now you're claiming divina are not myth, either?"

"I am claiming nothing. I am telling you they are not."

"Truly?" asked Kenders.

"Truly," rumbled Broedi. "At the time, I was as surprised as you all are now. More so, actually. I was the one staring at them."

"Where were you?" asked Kenders. "Where had the kisa led you?"

"One moment, uora. I am almost to that point in my tale." He paused, puffing on his pipe. "My friend led me through the city, across a white plaza, and to a great stone building topped with a crystal dome. A single divina stood on the steps, waiting for me. In a voice echoing with the power of its master, he said, 'Welcome to the Seat of Nelnora. You have been chosen, Broedikurja Kynsipitka.'"

"Wait," interjected Jak. "Your name isn't 'Broedi?'"

"It is a part of my given name. Many of my friends would later call me Broedi as they had difficulty with my full name. I continue to use it as it reminds me of happier times."

Kenders tried to run his full name over her lips and found she had already forgotten how he had pronounced it.

After another quick puff on his pipe, the hillman continued. "I, along with seven others from the Oaken Duchies, had been brought to this city, to Nelnora's temple. Each of us had been chosen by one of eight Celystiela. Thonda, for reasons I still do not know, had chosen me."

With his gaze shifting between Nikalys and Kenders, he said, "Horum chose your father, a captain in the Northlands' army. Gaena chose your mother, a servant from the Colonial Duchy across the Sea of Kings. The eight of us were brought before the Assembly of Nine. They shared with us that the individual behind the invasion, the one responsible for the Red Peaks' demonic army, was the god of Chaos who, at the time, was a divina known as Norasim."

"We were given a choice. We could return to our lives as they had been, or we could accept their charge and oppose the evil being wrought against countless innocents." He lifted a single eyebrow. "Given such a choice, how do you say 'no?'"

In the past whenever Kenders had heard this story—never with so many details as now—it had seemed a nice tale, something a playman would recite for the evening saga after some juggling and singing. To learn that it was not myth, but rather history, chilled her to the bone. She pulled her dress closer around her, wishing they were on the other side of the log and closer to the fire.

"We were each touched by the Celystiela who had chosen us and given our individual gifts. I found myself with the ability not only to weave some of the Strands, but also to take the shape of nearly any beast I saw. The first I took was that of the kisa, to honor my feline friend who had led me to the Assembly. It remains my favorite to this day."

Kenders asked quietly, "What exactly did Horum and Gaena do to our parents?"

Nikalys shot her a dark look. She did not understand why until she thought about her choice of words. She quickly amended her question. "I mean our blood parents."

Broedi glanced between them for a moment before answering. "Horum granted Aryn incredible athletic ability. His strength and speed was astonishing. He could move short distances at will, faster than the eye could see." Shifting his gaze to rest on Nikalys only, he rumbled, "It seems that at least part of that, in its raw form, has passed through his blood and into yours, uori."

Nikalys dropped his eyes to the forest floor but said nothing.

After a moment, Broedi turned to regard Kenders. "Your mother was given a great gift by Gaena, perhaps the greatest granted to any of us. While Eliza already had the natural talent to touch some of the Strands on her own, Gaena's gift allowed her to do things that no mortal could."

The hillman leaned forward, his eyes alive. "Understand this. Those rare few who can weave are able to touch only a few types of Strands and their ability to wield each kind varies. A mage might be a master with Water, yet barely sense Life or Stone. Most mages can touch two or three kinds." Pointing to his chest, he said, "I can sense and use six. But, Eliza…" He shook his head and a proud smile spread over his lips. "Eliza could touch *all* of the Strands."

Kenders supposed it was as impressive as he made it sound, yet her knowledge of magic was so basic that it was like telling a deaf person how skilled a prize flutist was. She forced a look of solemn awe on her face anyway since Broedi seemed to be waiting for a reaction before sitting tall and continuing.

"Once we had our gifts from the Celystiela who chose us, Sarphia touched us all, granting us long life. Save for a quick and mortal wound, we were to live far beyond our normal years."

Kenders was surprised to find herself suddenly filled with a sense of hope. "Does that mean our blood parents are still alive?" She was careful to qualify them this time. She did not want Nikalys glaring at her again.

Broedi drew himself up, sitting tall on the log, sucked in a long breath, and released it slowly. His eyebrows drew together as he answered, his voice soft and deep. "I do not know, uora. I have not seen them since they left with you fifteen years ago. I can only hope they are."

"Why did they give us up?" asked Nikalys abruptly. "Did they not want us?"

Kenders glanced at him, wondering if this meant that he accepted Broedi's tale as truth.

Broedi's gaze snapped to Nikalys. "*Never* think that, uori. *Never!* Your parents loved you *very* much. They only gave you up in order to protect you."

"From what exactly?" demanded Nikalys.

Broedi lifted a hand. "Let me continue and I will explain. Stories must be told in proper order. You do not bake bread when it is still a bowl of flour and cup of water."

Nikalys scowled, but remained quiet.

As the White Lion took a puff of his pipe, Kenders glanced at Jak. He smiled at her and reached over to pat her arm in silent support.

Blowing out a stream of smoke, Broedi fixed his gaze on the three of them. "Now, after the Assembly had finished with us, we were taken to where the remnants of the Northlands' army were gathered. Your father told his superiors in the army what had happened, who we were, and that the Celystiela had offered to help."

An amused smile spread over his lips. "As you might imagine, they did not believe our tale. So, the eight of us offered to confront a nearby force of Norasim's army. Some brave men and women from the Milvia barony aided us that day, and we quickly dispatched a small group of demons. It was from that skirmish we earned our name, the 'White Lions,' for the black and white crest of Milvia under which we marched."

"Word of our deeds quickly spread throughout the remaining Northlands' army, and they followed us into battle against a larger force of demon-men. For the first time in years, the duchies won a sizable victory against Norasim's forces. We eight helped the resistance in any way we could. Some of us were great leaders, some of us brought raw power—magic or brawn—while others were exceptionally clever and devious. Together, we were a force."

"Norasim slowly began to lose ground. The Freelands, Great Lakes, and Long Coast duchies left their fortified borders and rushed ahead, pushing back against the horde. Finally, on the plains south of Brassburgh, the eight White Lions converged, along with the combined armies of five duchies, on Norasim and his demons. We defeated him and slaughtered his army. The Demonic War was over."

Broedi smiled grimly at the memory. "Tens of thousands had died. Homes, towns, villages, and even entire cities had been burned and destroyed. It was a great relief to see the god of Chaos defeated, even though we knew it was only temporary. He would manifest again in the future—all of the Cabal do eventually—and rise to challenge order and good. Time and generations passed. Many cities were rebuilt. Some were not. Through it all, the White Lions remained vigilant."

Broedi paused and tilted his head upward, staring through the leaves overhead and at the stars in the sky above. He stayed that way for a moment before letting out a long and weary sigh.

"As is the nature of most races, people remembered the bad and forgot the good. They remembered the evil wrought by Norasim's magic, forgetting how our gifts and magic had helped defeat him. People began to fear magic itself, forgetting it is the character of the mage that matters. It was troubling to watch happen."

"Nearly a century after the end of the war, eight villages and towns along the Carinius coast were destroyed. Burned first, then flooded. The evidence that magic was used was indisputable. Word spread that some of the White Lions were seen in the area before the attacks. Only none of us were."

"Then why the rumors?" asked Jak.

"Excellent question," rumbled Broedi. "And the one we asked ourselves as the eight of us stood on Carinius' beaches. Aryn and I suspected the god of Deception and the god of Fear had a hand in what had occurred, but we could not prove any of it. So the rumors grew unchecked, spreading like a wildfire on a Borderlands' prairie. In stunningly short order, the First Council decreed all magic to be outlawed and named us criminals."

Broedi stared hard at the three of them. Biting off each word, he asked, "After everything we had done for the people, we were now *lawbreakers*?"

The three Isaac children stared back in silence. Kenders almost felt like apologizing.

Broedi glared at them for a moment longer before taking a deep breath and exhaling. When he resumed speaking, he was calm again. "Some of us wanted to fight the council's misguided law, but others felt we should accept their rule and serve in a hidden role. The dissent caused a rift in our group. Your parents and I were of like mind and traveled to the Celystiela to ask for their assistance. To avoid the new Constables, we moved overland like everyone else—I on foot and they by horse." He looked at Nikalys and Kenders. "It was actually then, during our journey west, your mother and father became close and fell in love."

"When we reached the Seat of Nelnora, the Celystiela would not see us. According to Nelnora's servants, she 'did not deem the current actions of mortals to be a sufficient threat to the balance of the world.' So we traveled to the Seats of Thonda, Horum, and Gaena, and were rebuffed in each. The Celystiela were done with us. They had used us and then tossed us aside."

"For our own safety, your father, mother, and I remained far from the duchies for a time. We lost contact with the others as they went their separate ways. To this day, I have not seen the other five since the First Council's decree."

Seeming to notice that he had only taken a few bites of his roast pheasant, Broedi reached down, plucked the stick from the ground, and took another mouthful now. Kenders glanced at hers. She was sure it was cool enough to eat now, but her appetite had yet to return.

After Broedi had swallowed, he continued, saying, "Years later, your parents and I returned to the Southlands and lived in secret. While spending some time near the Sea of Kings' coast, we learned of a prophecy issued back when the White Lions were formed. It seemed that after the Assembly of Nine charged us with our task, Indrida, the Enlightened Oracle, had a vision. A written copy of it found its way into our hands."

A frown creased his face and he shook his head. "It was disturbing to read, even more so when we realized that but a portion of Indrida's prophecy had been fulfilled. Much was yet to come."

Her voice quiet in the still of the night, Kenders asked, "What did it say?"

Broedi took a deep breath and began speaking.

"The roar of the Lions will drive back the spawn,
And the lines of men, strong once again, will be redrawn.
Yet that which drives man's soul will fray at the seams,
While the strength of the Lions will fade as do last night's dreams."

"Torn apart by deceit and distrust,
One will perish and One will be lost.
One will leave, while Another will stay.
And Two shall find each Other one day.
Against his will, one must fight,
While it falls upon the Half-man to unite."

> *"Chaos will rise again, unraveling what has been made,*
> *With Strife, Pain, and Deception in tow, lending aid.*
> *Hidden, then found,*
> *Willingly come around,*
> *The Progeny must rise to lead the fight,*
> *Along with new and old, seek to make it right."*

When done, he waited a short time, letting them absorb what he had said. While Kenders did not know what most of it meant, the end had made the hair on the back of her arms stand on end.

"Time passed," rumbled Broedi, "and eventually your mother found herself with child." He looked to Nikalys. "You were born on a cool harvest day eight turns later, uori." The corners of his mouth curled up a bit. "You came out screaming like a banshee."

Nikalys' eyes narrowed. "You were there?"

Broedi nodded. "I was. I stood with your father outside the room as Eliza gave life to you."

"Name the day," demanded Nikalys.

Broedi answered without hesitation. "The twelfth of the Turn of Rintira."

Kenders eyes widened a bit. The date was indeed Nikalys' yearday. She stared at her brother, wondering if he was willing to accept Broedi's incredible tale yet. He continued to glare at Broedi, unmoving, as the hillman continued.

"For the first few turns of your life, your parents argued often about what they should do with you. Indrida's prophecy worried them. Your mother thought you should be hidden and kept safe, away from us. Your father wanted to defend you with his life. He did not want to give up his son." A wistful smile spread over his lips. "You were obviously too young to remember, but your father was so proud of you. Aryn carried you everywhere he went."

Kenders glanced back to Nikalys and found her brother staring at the dirt, his chin pressed to his chest.

"Before they decided on a course of action, Eliza was with child again." He turned and looked at Kenders. "A turn before you were due, uora, we were discovered by agents of the Nine Hells. We repelled their assassination attempt and learned that the Cabal also knew of the prophecy. They were hunting the White Lions, having concluded as we did, that the 'Progeny' would be children of the Lions. No White Lions, no Progeny. Prophecy goes unfulfilled."

"After the attack and your birth, uora, your father conceded the pair of you were not safe with them. When they told me they were leaving, I believed they were going to hide *with* you, not give you over to be fostered. It would seem they had other plans, ones they did not see fit to share with me." He sighed and muttered, "They left and I have not seen them since."

The hurt and longing in his voice was plain. He truly missed them.

"For ten years, I waited, leaving them to be. For the past five, however, I have been looking for Aryn, Eliza, and the two of you. I was in the Great Lakes Duchy when the Weave your mother placed on the case was triggered, alerting me that you were in danger. The rest, you know."

He took a bite of his pheasant and chewed slowly. It seemed he was done with his story.

Kenders' gaze drifted about the clearing, eventually settling on an oak branch hanging low into their camp, its leaves fluttering in a gentle nighttime breeze. She was still looking at the branch, without truly seeing it, when Nikalys spoke, minutes later.

"So, our parents...our *blood* parents. They loved us?"

Broedi's brown eyes softened. "Very much. More than most, it seems. Their love drove them to do the hardest thing a parent could: leave you in the care of others and walk away."

Nikalys nodded ever so slightly and dropped his head again.

"Why my parents?" asked Jak. "What about them made two White Lions think that they could watch over them?"

Broedi looked at Jak and shrugged. "I do not know how they found your parents or their reasons for choosing them. Yet it would seem they made an inspired decision. Your parents kept them safe for fifteen years and loved them as their own. They are heroes in my eyes."

The beginnings of tears teased Kenders' eyes. She ached and mourned for the parents who had raised her, yet the yearning to see her blood parents was almost equally strong. The dual feelings were confusing. She wondered how she could miss people whom she had never truly known.

Broedi stood from the log and stretched, his long arms reaching almost to the branches of the oak above them. Dropping his arms, he smiled at Jak and rumbled, "And whether Aryn and Eliza meant to or not, they found a very good kaveli for them as well."

Jak smiled as a bit of color came to his cheeks. With a friendly, mocking tone, he said, "Ah, Broedi, you're such a flatterer."

Kenders laughed a little through the tears, grateful for the moment of levity. Even Broedi chuckled, a deep, rumbling, yet somehow quiet, laugh.

Suddenly, Nikalys jumped up, startling them all. "Are you all mad?! How can you just laugh like that?! Did the two of you even listen to what he said?" His face a mask of anger and denial, he darted around to the other side of the log. "Kenders! If our blood parents are White Lions, they are outlaws! Just like you!" He glared at Broedi. "Him, too!"

With an edge in his voice, Jak muttered, "*Nik*. Calm down."

"No!" shouted Nikalys, turning his hot gaze on Jak. "How can you both just sit there and take everything he says as complete, utter truth?! White Lions?! Prophecies?! Meeting the blasted gods?! It's madness! Blasted madness!"

Kenders raised a hand, pleading, "Please, Nik. Yelling helps nothing."

Nikalys stopped in his tracks and glared at her. It took him a few deep breaths before he appeared to relax. Sighing, he ran both hands through his hair. "I'm sorry." He looked askance at the hillman. "It's too much for me to believe, Broedi. Any of it. It's all...too fantastic."

"He knew your yearday," said Kenders.

"He's a mage! Perhaps it was a trick!"

"The necklace," rumbled Broedi. "How do you explain it away?"

Nikalys' hand flew to his neck. Tugging at the leather cord, he pulled the silver pendant free of his shirt. "What about it?"

"It belonged to Eliza," said Broedi. "She bought it in a market in Cartu at least a century before you were born. She placed a Weave on it—bound to you and your iskoa alone—so that she would know where you were at all times and if you were safe. I assume she gave it to Marie Isaac to do the same."

Nikalys stared at Broedi for a moment dropping his gaze back to the necklace. "There has to be another explanation."

Kenders stared at her brother and shook her head, wondering what it was going to take to convince him.

Jak muttered, "Now would be a good time for the case, Broedi."

"Excellent idea, uori," rumbled the hillman. "Will you please get it for me?"

Kenders shot her brother a perplexed look as he stood and went to retrieve where Broedi had put the leather case. The hillman had been carrying it since Smithshill. Upon returning to Broedi, Jak handed it over to the White Lion and then came to stand by Kenders' side.

Glancing at her brother, she whispered, "What's in the case?"

Jak shrugged his shoulders and murmured, "Broedi only told me it was something that belonged to your father. Something meant for Nikalys."

Kenders' eyes narrowed as she stared back to the hillman.

Broedi approached Nikalys, stopping a few paces away. He lifted the case, holding it at arm's length and in Nikalys' direction. "Perhaps this will help you accept what I have shared."

Nikalys stared at the bundle, clearly skeptical.

Remembering that there was not a single seam or cord along the bundle's length, Kenders asked, "Shall I get a knife?"

"Thank you," rumbled Broedi. "But that will not be necessary." Holding Nikalys' gaze, he urged, "Take it."

As Nikalys reached out with both hands, Kenders found herself leaning forward in anticipation. The moment Nikalys touched the leather, Kenders felt a tiny crackling inside of her. For a brief moment, she spotted a Weave of silver and gold Strands around the case before they quickly unraveled and faded.

A slit appeared down the length of the package and the leather fell to the sides, exposing a richly made, reddish-brown scabbard emblazoned with a golden emblem of some sort of bird. Sticking out from the top of the scabbard was the silver and gold hilt of a sword. The grip and guard sparkled brilliantly in the light of the fire, but it was the pommel that drew her eyes. A silver ring encircled an impossibly white stone carved into the face of a roaring lion. A belt made of the same rich brown leather was folded beneath the scabbard.

So focused on the scabbard and sword, she almost did not see the rolled-up parchment stuck between the folds of the belt. Nikalys did, though, and with his eyes drawn tight, pulled the scroll out and turned it over in his hands. He moved to the fire and opened it.

"What is it?" asked Kenders.

Nikalys glanced up with rounded eyes. "It's a letter." He stared back the parchment in wonder. "From…Aryn."

With a rush of nervous excitement, Kenders hurried to her brother's side and stared down at the black words scrawled on the yellow parchment in a neat, practiced hand.

Nikalys —

I have spent countless days thinking what words I would write in this letter. Even now, as I put ink to parchment, I still do not know what to say. Yet I must write something now as your mother and I are leaving shortly.

If you are reading this, I will assume you know the truth. Or at least some of it. Thaddeus has promised to tell you and Kenders when you are old enough to understand.

No doubt you have questions about why your mother and I have done this, but realize that it is our deep love for you and your sister that have driven us to leave you both behind. Thaddeus and Marie are good people. Steadfast, strong, and admirable parents. I pray this letter finds them and little Jak well.

I have lived longer than any man should, son. Many of my days have been wondrous. Many I am still trying to forget. Let me take this opportunity to share with you what I learned through the years.

Stay strong. Be resolute. Live well. Love fully.

Follow this bit of advice, and the rest of life is almost simple.

I am sorry that all I can offer you is my sword and some words on a parchment, but it is the fate Greya has given me and I must do with it what I can.

I pray you never face the horrors your mother and I have, but considering your heritage and Indrida's blasted words, I suspect that is a foolish hope. Nevertheless, it is one to which your mother and I cling. It is why we are leaving you. We are going to try to make it so you never read this letter.

As I write this, it has occurred to me that I do have one more sliver of advice for you, something that took me a very long time to understand and accept: Do what you must, when you must. Move on as best you can, as soon as you can. Else, the shadows of the past will darken your present and douse the light of future's promise.

Watch over your sister, please. If she grows up to be anything like she is now, I'm certain she can be a handful. In fact, that dribble of ink in the corner is her doing. She is sitting on my lap and cannot seem to sit still.

I must go now. Your mother is telling me to hurry.

We both love you very much.

Be safe.

—Your father, Aryn

One last thing: should a tall fellow by the name of Broedi ever track you down—and your mother insists he will—trust him with your very life, son. I have done so countless times and that overgrown tuft of fur has always come through.

Kenders reached up and wiped away the tears that were rolling down her cheek. Sniffling, she glanced over at Nikalys and saw he was struggling to remain stone-faced. She slipped an arm around his waist and gave him a small squeeze. "See, Nik? They did love us."

Nikalys nodded silently, his lips quivering.

Kenders looked back to the letter and stared at the black blob in the corner. The corners of her mouth turned up slightly as a wistful, sad smile found its way on her face. Pointing at the ink stain, she muttered, "See? I've always been trouble."

The comment had the desired effect as a tiny chuckle slipped from Nikalys.

Kenders glanced over at Broedi and Jak. Both were impossibly still.

The moment she met Jak's eyes, he asked quietly, "What does it say?"

Kenders looked to Nikalys. "Can they see it?"

With a silent nod, Nikalys handed the parchment to Kenders and stared into the flames. Jak and Broedi moved to the fire, kicking up leaves as they approached. She handed the letter to Broedi and waited as he and Jak read it, side-by-side.

Tears welled in Jak's eyes and Kenders assumed it was because of the mention of his parents. Broedi showed no reaction at all until the very end when a slight smile touched his lips.

Looking up, the hillman said softly, "It is a good letter." The smile grew a fraction. "Which is odd. Aryn never was very good with words."

Jak glanced up at Broedi, lifted a single eyebrow, and said, "Overgrown tuft of fur?"

Broedi's smile grew a bit more. "Aryn favored the term."

Nikalys asked, "Can I see that?"

Looking over, Kenders found her brother pointing to the opened leather package still clenched in Broedi's left hand.

The hillman lifted his arm and extended it. "Take it, uori. The Blade of Horum is yours now."

Nikalys' face was blank. He reached up haltingly, took hold of the scabbard and sword, and gently lifted it from Broedi's hand. He studied the hilt of the sword, lightly tracing a finger over the stone carving of the white lion's head. Placing one hand on the hilt of the sword and the other around the scabbard, he drew the blade, the quiet whisper of steel scraping leather filling the clearing.

Kenders gasped.

The blade of the sword was made of some sort of white metal that seemed to glow in the light of the fire. All along its length, the metal shimmered bright, much brighter than it should have given the meager light from their small campfire. Kenders blinked and tilted her head, thinking she had merely caught the sword at an odd angle.

Nikalys took a few steps back from the fire and held the sword upright. Even as he moved farther from the light of the fire, the white blade held its gleaming glow.

Kenders said encouragingly, "It suits you." In one aspect, it did. In another, he looked exactly what he was: an olive farmer holding a glowing sword.

Jak voiced his support. "She's right, Nik."

Nikalys glanced at Jak with uncertain eyes. He stared back to the blade, tilting his head up as he studied its length. With a confused expression, he muttered, "Is it just me, or is it...glowing?"

Broedi rumbled softly, "It is the Weave inside the blade, uori. When the dirgmour forged it for Aryn, Eliza added a Weave so it would never dirty nor dull. Even after cutting stone."

Nikalys stared at Broedi with incredulous eyes. "It cuts stone? That's impossible."

Broedi rumbled, "I assure you it is not."

Grinning, Jak said, "Try not to cut off any fingers, Nik."

A small smile graced Nikalys' lips as he peered back to the sword. A moment later, the smile slipped away, replaced by a bewildered frown. "What in the Nine Hells am I supposed to do with it?"

"Learn to use it," answered Broedi.

Kenders stared up at the hillman. "Are you going to teach him?"

Broedi shook his head. "Unfortunately, I do not know the art. I have never seen a need to learn."

Kenders supposed the fact Broedi could change into a lynx or bear negated the need to know how to use a sword.

"Just think," muttered Jak. "For fifteen years, that's been hidden in our home."

Kenders sighed. The sword had not been the only thing hiding in the Isaac home. Looking to Nikalys, she said, "Please tell me you believe Broedi now."

Nikalys nodded at the sword. "This is difficult to deny." Pointing to the letter still clasped in Jak's hand, he added, "And that even more so." Sighing, he turned his gaze to the hillman. "I'm sorry for my behavior, Broedi. What you shared was…not easy to hear."

Broedi inclined his head, accepting the apology with grace. "Aryn had a difficult time accepting things he did not want to hear as well, uori." He paused and, with a hint of wonderment in his voice, said, "Seeing you stand there with his sword is strange for me. Yet good."

Kenders was relieved that everyone was in a decent mood once again. Considering what they had been through, it was rather remarkable. However, nothing said tonight had addressed a very important question that was yet unanswered. "So now what?"

Broedi, Nikalys, and Jak all turned to stare at her.

Jak said, "Good question."

As one, the trio of siblings shifted their gaze to the White Lion.

After a short sigh, Broedi rumbled, "We head south, to a safe haven. I will try to help you both with the gifts you have inherited, although I fear I will only be able to aid you, uora. Aryn and I talked about his capabilities at times, but even he did not understand how he did what he did." He eyed Nikalys and said apologetically, "I will share with you whatever I can remember."

Nikalys gave an appreciative nod of his head. "Thank you, Broedi. Anything would be helpful."

Turning to Kenders, Broedi said, "And when it is safe, we will resume your lessons on the Strands, uora."

Kenders remained quiet, unsure how she felt about that. Knowing she was the daughter of a White Lion mage could not chase away her unease about being a mage herself.

"Where exactly is this safe haven?" asked Jak.

"South," rumbled the hillman.

"'South' is a big place," noted Jak. "Feel like narrowing that down some?"

"I do not. It is best this way, uori. Please trust me."

Jak frowned, obviously unhappy with the lack of a clear answer, but he did not press further. None of them did, although Kenders wondered why Broedi was reluctant to share their destination.

Nodding south, Broedi said, "Sometime tomorrow we will reach the outskirts of Lakeborough. There, we will move along the river for a while, until we are past the city. Too many eyes in Lakeborough."

Nikalys said, "Sounds like a decent enough plan." He carefully sheathed the sword, having to try several times to get the point of the blade into the scabbard, and fit the belt around his waist.

"Do not wear that while we are on the road, uori. A blade and scabbard as fine as those will draw unwanted attention."

"I know. I was just trying it on."

Kenders was not sure if Nikalys had known or whether he was just saying he did.

"I suggest we all get some rest," said Broedi. "We have a few weeks of travel ahead of us."

Suddenly hungry, Kenders asked, "May we eat first?"

Broedi smiled. "Of course."

She, Nikalys, and Jak retrieved their untouched birds and began to walk back to the fire. As they moved away, she noted that Broedi sat on the log again. Stopping, she returned to the hillman. "Are you going to get some sleep as well?"

"I will stay up a bit longer, uora. I am not tired."

He was lying. Kenders could see the weariness in his eyes and the bags under them.

"Broedi…"

He nodded to where Nikalys and Jak sat across the clearing. "Sit, eat, and then sleep. Do not worry about me. I will be fine."

She nodded, said her good nights, and moved to her brothers. They talked while they ate, trying to make sense of everything. Long after they had finished eating and had laid down to rest, Broedi continued to sit on the log, staring northward. He was still there when Kenders fell asleep.

CHAPTER 32: LONGLEGS

19ᵗʰ of the Turn of Sutri

"Please don't get sick on the skins, little one."

Nundle glanced up as Pelter strode past pushing the long wooden pole along the side of the raft, urging it along the shallow and slow-moving river. Summoning a weak smile, he mumbled, "I'll do my best." The stack of reedcord-bound lion pelts upon which he sat reeked, the smell catching in the back of his throat with each breath.

Pelter offered a kind smile and continued along the rickety raft. Nundle watched the longleg, praying he could keep his word. His stomach was twirling about like a seed falling from a whirlerwhip tree.

When Nundle had accepted the riverman's offer for passage, he had pictured the craft he would be taking to be a smaller version of the ships he had taken to or around the Arcane Republic. Instead, Pelter's "ship" was a square of tarred logs strapped together with frayed rope.

Besides Pelter, three other longlegs manned the raft. All four were equipped with long wooden poles that they used to push themselves from small sandy islands or rounded rocks that frequented the river. They all wore breeches cut off at the knee and thin, sleeveless shirts, attire to help them keep cool as they labored in the hot afternoon. Just watching them from atop his perch of lion pelts made Nundle tired.

They had been underway since dawn, and Nundle had hoped he would have grown numb to the smelly animal skins by now. It had yet to happen. He tried breathing through his mouth to avoid the odor, but that only resulted in his tasting the stench.

Despite the stink and rickety watercraft, Nundle was glad to be on the move again. When he had walked into Silver Falls, intent on finding directions to Smithshill, he hardly expected he would be there three days.

Silver Falls was either a large town or a small city; Nundle could not decide which. The buildings had been strange to his eye, wooden log walls held together with mortar of river mud, and topped with thatched, grass roofs. A few stone structures stood taller than two-stories, but they were rare.

The people of Silver Falls had been nice enough and the streets safe to walk alone. The souls he met took him to be a child until he insisted—repeatedly—

that he was well over seventy years old. After that, he became a novelty of sorts, with people coming from around the city to see the "bizarre, red-haired, wee person."

Nundle had originally hoped to make his way unobtrusively through the duchies, yet his mere existence seemed as if it might cause a fuss among longlegs. It was then he began working on a story to explain who he was and why he was here.

He had asked the locals exactly how he might make his way to Smithshill. Everyone agreed the shortest route was to head north over the Dunnerstone Bridge, follow the Plainsmen Road to Huntersfield, and then turn due west and head overland through savannah flatlands. After a few days, he should run into Lake Hawthorne and would be able to find Smithshill to the south, at the mouth of the Great White River.

Unfortunately, it seemed the trip overland was quite treacherous. Ferocious, wildmane lions dominated the eastern savannah, while spirits of ancient battles waged by empires long forgotten supposedly haunted great swaths of the western grasslands. Nundle had little desire to be eaten by lions, or to meet the ghosts of obsolete kingdoms, so he asked if there was a safer, decidedly less lethal way to get to Smithshill.

Pelter, an enterprising young trader, offered to take Nundle with him on his next run down the Sterling River. The riverman was due to take a shipment of wildmane pelts to a ferry landing on the Great White River, transfer them to carts, and bring them to market in Lakeborough. When Nundle learned said journey would only take two and a half days, he leapt at the offer, but was forced to wait three days for the trappers to show with the pelts. The past three nights had been long ones. Nundle spent more time staring at his inn room door, waiting for a Constable's knock, than he had sleeping.

Finally, the trappers had arrived last night, allowing Pelter and his crew to cast off at sunrise today.

Not long into the trip, Nundle had asked Pelter if he were the captain of the vessel. The question prompted outbursts of laughter and endless, good-natured teasing from the crew of three amiable longlegs. Every time the laughter died down, one of the longlegs would salute Pelter and say, "Aye, Captain Pelter, sir!" and another round of chortling would begin. Pelter took the jesting in stride.

For most of the day, the Sterling River was still except for little ripples where rocks broke the glassy surface, disturbing the gentle current. Mature trees stood on shore, their graceful branches drooping far over the river, shading the shoreline yet leaving the middle open to the mercy of the scorching sun. Yellow birds with dark blue heads darted from tree to tree, chirping away while hefty white birds with brown beaks paddled alongside the raft as if escorting it.

Nundle passed the day by asking the longlegs all sorts of questions about the area. He needed information as he had arrived in a country knowing only what he had read in a history book written well over a hundred years ago. The rivermen answered his inquiries with smiles and questions of their own, curious how he had come to be in their land and where he was headed.

For the most part, he lied. He claimed he was an explorer from the Five Boroughs who had set off looking for adventure years ago, taking a ship west around Mourlok, the great dirgmour nation, on his way to the remnants of L'antico Impero. After a year there, he had traveled west again, landing on the shores of the duchies. Most of the details he used in his tale came from a journal he had once read of a true explorer who had followed a similar path.

Pelter and the other longlegs seemed to enjoy his tale. Nundle suspected they did not believe most of what he shared, but they still accepted far more of it as truth than was.

When they asked where he was headed, he lied and said he was heading to the Borderlands as he had always wanted to catch a glimpse of an oligurt or mongrel. Almost as soon as he said it, he wondered why he had. He would be terrified to be within a hundred miles of such monsters.

At the mention of the Borderlands, the rivermen shared some uneasy glances. Their reaction piqued his interest and he began asking questions about the westernmost duchy. It seemed the last time the rivermen had made a trip to Lakeborough, stories filled the city, stories about roving bands of oligurts, mongrels, and razorfiends marauding through the Borderlands.

Their story puzzled Nundle. He knew from his studies that the races of Sudash were tribal in nature, groups that typically warred amongst themselves. Rarely did they organize together in large enough groups to pose much of a threat to neighboring countries.

Nundle pried for more information but quickly realized they had told him everything they themselves knew. Such was the way of rumors. Heavy on hearsay and gossip, light on details and corroboration.

The night and the following day were uneventful, with the most excitement being the constant slapping of some small biting insect the longlegs on the raft called bodflies. Nundle cursed the winged pests. By the following morning, he was covered from head to toe with little, red, itchy bumps. Pelter and the longlegs found his unending scratching quite humorous. He did not.

Near the end of the second day of their trip, the Sterling River dumped the raft into the Great White River, where it picked up speed with the faster current of the larger river. The rivermen had to be much more diligent as the number of rocks increased and the water churned. Nundle held on for dear life.

Just before midday on the third day of their journey, Nundle spotted a small settlement along the western shore. He watched with admiration as the four longlegs expertly guided the raft to the docks and tied it off. Nundle offered to help unload the lion pelts, but much like when he had offered to help with the poling earlier in the trip, they refused. Either they were being polite or they were afraid he would drop some of the pelts into the river. Regardless, Nundle moved onto the sandy shore, waiting while the longlegs moved the pelts from the raft, up the dock, and onto a wagon Pelter had rented from a man he called a "wheelhawker." Nundle was unsure if it was the title of a profession or an insult. With the way Pelter grumbled about the price he was forced to pay, perhaps it was both.

Once the wagon was loaded, Pelter climbed aboard the driver's seat and offered Nundle the seat beside him. The other three longlegs climbed on the back of the wagon and sat with the smelly pelts. Within minutes of leaving the ferry landing on the river, Nundle heard snoring, looked back, and saw the three longlegs were asleep. How they could sleep on the reeking skins with all the jostling and jerking was beyond Nundle.

They had been traveling for some time when, as the wagon rounded a bend, Nundle spotted a very large oak tree lying before them, stretching across the road.

"Hells," muttered Pelter as he pulled the horses' reins, stopping the cart. "The landing master is supposed to make sure this road is cleared." He tossed the reins on the driver's seat in disgust and sat back, glaring at the fallen tree.

"What do we do?" asked Nundle.

"I don't suppose you have an axe with you? That tree is too large for the four of us to move."

"I'll help if you'd like," piped up Nundle.

Pelter looked over at him and smiled. "I don't doubt you would, little friend, but I'm afraid it would take at least ten men…to move…" He trailed off, his gaze shifting away from the tomble and into the thicket alongside the road. Any bit of friendliness drained from his eyes.

Nundle turned around to find a number of longlegs stepping from the undergrowth, each with an unkempt beard on their dirt-streaked face. Their ripped and disheveled clothes might have had a color to them at one point, but were now just various shades of grimy brown. Most carried some type of crude, makeshift weapons like tree branches or wooden clubs. One longleg carried a shovel, another, an axe.

The only unarmed longleg strode before the wagon's front and stood in the middle of the road, flanked by two larger longlegs carrying thick clubs. He smiled up at Pelter and spoke with surprising politeness. "Good days ahead, travelers! Greetings to you on this fine afternoon!"

Pelter eyed the man and said nothing.

Nundle looked around and counted eight longlegs in total surrounding the wagon. Pelter's crew was awake now, sitting up and staring about the wagon cart.

The tone of the longleg standing in the road turned a mite sharper as he called out a second time. "I said, 'Good days ahead, travelers!'"

Sitting very still, Pelter responded, his voice remarkably calm. "End the show. What will it cost for you to let us by?"

The longleg's eyebrows lifted a fraction. "Cost? Why would it cost you anything to move along the duchess' road? I have no claim on it." He turned around and looked at the tree in the middle of the road. "But you do seem to have a problem as there's a very large tree in your way. Unfortunate for you." The longleg faced the cart and, for the first time, seemed to spot Nundle. "Oh ho! That's no boy. Bless the gods, what is a tomble doing with a bunch of river rats?"

Figuring it best not to answer the question, Nundle held his tongue.

The longleg eyed Nundle a moment longer before shrugging and returning his gaze to Pelter. "It would seem Ketus is with you today, river rat."

"I would have said he abandoned us," said Pelter, his eyes narrowing.

Smiling wide, the longleg said, "Come now. Don't say that. The way I see it, you are quite lucky."

"How do you figure?" asked Pelter.

"Well, you are in dire need of a few woodaxes, yes? My friends and I could stay here and guard your wagon while you, your men, and your little friend walk on to Lakeborough to find a couple. You come back, chop things up, and then off you go, on your wondrous way."

"Hah!" snorted Pelter. "We'll be lucky if there's a wheel spoke left when we get back. I'd be out my shipment and I'd owe the wheelhawker for the wagon and the horses."

The longleg shrugged his shoulders. "I can't help it if bandits come along while you're gone, now can I? It's not as if we could stop them. We're simple folk armed only with sticks and clubs." His eyes narrowed a fraction. "Which I've noticed is more than you have. Don't you know it's dangerous to travel unarmed in the forest? Brigands are about." A few of the longlegs surrounding the wagon chuckled.

Nundle peered around him again, eyeing the dirty longlegs. Pelter and his crew did not deserve this. They were good, honest souls who had treated him with respect and friendship, some of the first longlegs to do so in a long time. What was happening here was not right.

In a clear, high voice, Nundle called out, "Can you give us a moment, good sir? I would like to confer with my associate."

"Associate?" repeated the bandit, clearly amused. "How fancy." He gave a sweeping, mocking wave of his arm. "Please, by all means, little one, confer."

Leaning over, Nundle tapped Pelter on the shoulder. The trader bent down, a concerned look on his face, surely wondering what Nundle could possibly want to talk about now. Lowering his voice so only Pelter could hear, Nundle asked, "How far away is Lakeborough?"

"We'd make it by dark if we were still moving. Later if we walk. But trust me, their offer is not serious. They're here to rob us." Pelter had misunderstood why Nundle was asking the question, but that was fine.

Staring up at the longleg, Nundle whispered, "Whatever happens, just go along." Sitting tall, he eyed the longleg waiting in the road.

The brigand grinned wide. "So, after conferring, little one, do you agree to our proposal?"

"Actually, I have a counteroffer."

The longleg's eyes narrowed, his amusement melting away in an instant. "Are you jesting?"

Nundle began to reach out for the golden Strands of Will, hurriedly plucking and weaving them into his favorite pattern. He quickly crafted eight small Weaves, one after another and directed them at the longlegs from the forest. Once the golden patterns faded into the bandits, Nundle smiled and spoke.

"This is *my* proposal: you help my friends here drag that oak tree off the road. Then, as it is such a hot day, I suggest you head to the river for a swim and cool off." He glanced at a few of the grime-encrusted longlegs. "It seems you all could use a bath, anyway. Then, after a nice swim, rent a raft and head down river for a few days. Do some fishing, perhaps?"

Pelter leaned over, hissing, "Are you mad?"

Nundle lifted a finger. "Hold a moment..."

Almost immediately, most of the longlegs around the wagon began to talk quietly amongst themselves that perhaps the "runt was right." Nundle frowned. His Weave could push them to do what he wanted, but it could not make them mind their manners.

The leader, however, did not seem as agreeable. He stared at Nundle, a deep frown on his face.

"I think it is a fair offer, don't you?" prompted Nundle.

The longleg's eyes narrowed. "I don't know..." He was wavering. Strong-willed people needed a bit more encouragement than others.

Nundle reluctantly pulled together a few more Strands of Will, crafted a larger Weave, and directed it at the leader. Glaring at the longleg, he abandoned being polite about things. "Move the tree, go to the river, and then go fishing."

Pelter leaned over, whispering, "Keep up that nonsense, and they'll beat us senseless!"

Nundle did not respond. Rather, he kept his eyes on the longleg in the road and waited. A few moments later, the bandit leader spoke. "I think you're right, runt." Pelter gaped at the brigand as the longleg swiveled, turning to gaze at the fallen oak. "As soon as we help you with this tree, I *do* think we'll go swimming. Then perhaps a little trip downriver." The other seven longlegs all murmured their agreement.

Pelter and the three rivermen sat absolutely still in the wagon, shocked, staring at the bandits as if they were pigs standing on hind legs and offering to do a little dance for them.

The leader began walking to the tree. "Come on! I don't have all day to waste!"

The other bandits followed after a few moments of stunned inaction, so did Pelter and his men. The rivermen hopped off the wagon, hurried over, and helped the bandits pull, push, and drag the oak to one side of the road. Nundle sat in the cart and watched, praying he had not just done something terribly foolish.

As soon as the longlegs were done, the bandits headed east down the road, offering quick farewells of "Good memories, runt" as they passed Nundle.

The rivermen slowly drifted back to the wagon, stopping in front of the horses. All four stared up at Nundle, a knowing look in their eyes. Nundle stayed silent, unsure of what they might say or do. Finally, Pelter spoke.

"How long will that last?"

Nundle shrugged. "On them? A day, perhaps two. It will wear off on some sooner than others, which I suspect will lead to few disagreements amongst their little band. Let's hope it falls apart."

One of the other longlegs asked, "Have you done anything like that to us?"

Nundle gave a firm shake of his head. "Never."

"Would we know it if you had?" asked Pelter.

"Honestly, no, but I promise I have not. You're good people. Besides, I know it is dangerous to…ah…'suggest' things in this country."

The four rivermen glanced at one another, never speaking a word yet saying quite a bit. After a few moments, Pelter looked back up to Nundle. "You just saved me quite a bit of coin. Perhaps our lives, even. For that, I am grateful."

The others nodded, grudgingly agreeing with Pelter.

"But when we near Lakeborough, Nundle, we will stop, let you out, and you will walk into the city on your own accord. I promise—" he glanced at his crew "—*we* promise to keep your secret safe as thanks for your help, but will not roll into town with you sitting beside me."

Nodding, Nundle murmured, "I understand."

With that, the rivermen climbed aboard the wagon again. Pelter sat as far as he could from Nundle on the driver's seat while the three men in the back sat straight and remained awake for the rest of the extremely quiet journey.

By evening, plumes of smoke rising into sky and the not overly pleasant aroma of crowded city indicated they were near Lakeborough. When Pelter slowed to a halt, Nundle knew why. He climbed down, taking his increasingly ragged canvas bag with him. Pelter said his goodbye, but the three men in the back remained silent.

Nundle considered using the Strands to make sure they would not talk for a few days, but resisted the urge. These men had helped him and were kind, Nundle would not do that to them. Moreover, he was too close to a city now. There might be Constables near.

Nundle pulled out a gold arcan and looked up to Pelter. "Thank you for everything." He tossed the coin up to the longleg.

Pelter caught the gold piece, studied Nundle for a long moment, and then tilted his head. "I'm starting to think that perhaps—just *perhaps*—all mages aren't bad."

Nundle offered Pelter a slight smile. "Some are quite nice, I assure you."

Pelter nodded slowly, a pensive frown on his face. With a sigh, he slipped the coin in his pocket. "Think again about traveling to the Borderlands, little friend. It'd be a shame if you got eaten by a mongrel."

Nundle's grin faded.

Pelter snapped the reins and the horses and cart began rattling up the hill. Nundle eyed the three longlegs in the back with the lion pelts and smiled at them. All three gave a small grin in return. One waved.

After waiting for the wagon to roll over the hill, Nundle slung his traveling sack over his shoulder and started up the dirt road.

CHAPTER 33: LAKEBOROUGH

Nundle felt like an ant amongst a herd of stampeding cattle. Countless people rushed about, bumping into one another, hurrying through the streets in one direction or another. He dodged them as best he could while looking around, trying to get his bearings.

Tall wood and stone buildings lined the streets, every one of them topped with a flat roof upon which vendors hawked their wares. Hanging from the colorful awning-covered stalls were long poles with painted signs announcing whatever wares the peddlers sold. On the ground level, most shops had their doors open with proprietors standing outside, shouting for patrons to come closer. Sets of stairs laden with people snaked up the buildings' sides.

It would seem that he had wandered straight into Lakeborough's market district.

The sweet, spicy aroma of some sort of baked good caught Nundle's attention, and he spent a short while following his nose to the source: a cream-colored bun layered with honey, spice, and a thick slab of some kind of gooey sugar. Nundle ordered one, gulped it down in no time, and asked for a second. It survived as long as the first. He ordered a third—prompting the fat baker to grin wide and give a wondering shake of his head—but stopped in the middle of it when he started to feel queasy.

Leaving the bakery, he waddled around the city for a while, trying to decide his next course of action. With the day nearly over, he would be foolish to travel overnight on the open road in a strange country without having a better idea of what the region was like. He needed to find a place to rest for the night.

He ducked into a shop that sold wooden platters and cups and asked the owner for an inn recommendation. The longleg gave him a short list of directions ending with "look for the blue sign with the bald, mustached man holding a cleaver over his head and yelling." Nundle gave the man an odd look at the description, thanked him anyway, and then headed back out into the streets as twilight arrived.

In no time at all, Nundle found himself standing before a tall, slate blue river-rock building, the few square windows glowing yellow from the light within. Reaching up on his tiptoes to lift the handle, he opened the door, stepped inside, and closed it behind him with a soft thud.

The mouth-watering aroma of something roasting washed over him, savory and good, a welcome contrast to the sweets on which he had gorged himself earlier. Round wooden tables filled the room, half of which were occupied by longlegs. A lone, dark-skinned tijul sat alone in the corner, draped in a green cloak. The quiet hum of conversation filled the room.

Nestled in the far wall was a stone hearth, the fire within—along with a few dozen beeswax candles—filling the room with a warm glow. Some sort of black metal venting system ran from the hearth and through the wall, most likely to carry the heat outside as the room was not overly warm. A long, simple, wooden counter ran the length of the room on the right, with two doorways leading elsewhere in the building. At the end of the bar, a flight of stairs climbed upwards.

Nundle moved to the bar and, with some difficulty, climbed atop one of the tall wooden chairs. A stout female longleg with a wide face stood behind the bar, looking out over the room with a confused expression. With a start, she noticed Nundle standing on the stool at the end of the bar by the door and rushed over.

"Pardon me, sir. I heard the door open, but when I came out, I didn't see anyone. Welcome to The Screaming Butcher. My name is Heriot. How may I be of service?"

Nundle smiled. He was so used to being looked down at—in more ways than one—by longlegs, it was going to take some getting used to being treated with kindness.

"I was hoping I could rent a room for the night."

"Of course. The price is ten copper ducats. Fifteen if you would like eveningmeal tonight and morningmeal tomorrow. Twenty if you would like to stable your horse for the night."

Still unfamiliar with the monetary system here, Nundle reached into his traveling pouch, retrieved a silver arcan, and handed it over to Heriot "Will this suffice for the room, eveningmeal, and something to drink? I have no horse, so stabling isn't necessary."

Heriot took the coin, one side of which had the Nine Towers of the Strands etched on it while the other had an image of the sun rising—or perhaps setting—over a mountain range. The innkeeper stared at the silver coin for a moment, placed it between her teeth, and bit it. After pulling it out, she shrugged. "Silver is silver. Welcome, sir." She leaned forward, resting her elbows on the bar. "You know, we don't see too many tombles in Lakeborough. What brings you to the area?"

"Well, you see, I'm an explorer—"

With a start, Heriot stood straight. "Where are my manners? You pay for a meal, it's mealtime, and there I go, asking questions. I am a terrible host! Would you like a plate of lamb now?"

The roast did smell delicious, but Nundle's stomach was still full from the pastries. "I'm fine for now, thank you. And there is no need to apologize for asking questions." He was actually grateful. The innkeeper had given him a wonderful opportunity to practice his tale explaining his presence in the duchies. "I would be happy to tell you."

The story he shared was similar to the one he told the rivermen with some additional details he had learned from the Pelter and his men. When he mentioned his intention to visit the Borderlands, Heriot's eyes darkened.

"Oh, no…" The innkeeper shook her head. "Do *not* go there. Much too dangerous. Oligurts and mongrels roam freely now. And razorfiends! With their sharp blade quills and beady black eyes…" Heriot shuddered. "They are fearsome looking, they are."

Nundle seriously doubted she had ever seen a razorfiend. Smiling, he said, "In my journeys, Heriot, I've found that the farther a story travels, the further it strays from the truth."

"Perhaps," conceded Heriot. "But do not take my word for it." She pointed over his shoulder and into the room. "Those two men are from the Borderlands and claim to have seen the horde firsthand."

Twisting around on the stool, Nundle spotted a table with two dark-skinned longlegs dressed unlike anyone else in the room. Both wore light tan, draping shirts and soiled white headbands wrapped around their foreheads. The thinner longleg on the left wore a thoughtful expression, nodding along as his companion talked, yet seeming not to be listening. The larger longleg on the right did not appear to notice his friend's lack of interest, continuing to gesture wildly as he spoke. Both had close-cropped black hair and beards.

Nundle was not sure how he had not noticed the pair before. They stood out in the room like a blazing torch in the dead of night.

Heriot said, "They say they're on their way to Freehaven to plead with the First Council. To hear them tell it, Duke Vanson can't protect his own lands. Or is uninterested in doing so, if you believe the man on the right there."

The story of the raids in the Borderlands had piqued Nundle's interest earlier. Now, presented with the opportunity to learn more from longlegs who were actually from there, Nundle intended to take it. He turned back to Heriot. "Whatever they are drinking, bring them another. And something for me as well. Nothing strong, though."

Heriot nodded and moved through a doorway behind the counter. Nundle hopped off the stool and walked to the table with the two Borderlanders, receiving a few drawn-out looks as he crossed the room. Wondering if he might have some sweet bun stuck to his face, Nundle ran his hand over his face to check and found it clean. Apparently, he himself was the novelty.

He moved to the far side of the table and stepped between the pair of longlegs. With him standing and them sitting, he was able to look them right in the eye. Nundle opened his mouth to introduce himself when the larger, more rambunctious man locked eyes with him.

"Bless the gods...what in the Nine Hells are you?"

"Boah!" admonished the thinner man on Nundle's right. "That is rude, even for you."

Boah tore his eyes from Nundle and looked at the other Borderlander. "You're right." He stared at Nundle again and spoke in slightly more polite tone. "Pardon me. What in the Nine Hells are you, *sir*?"

Nundle wondered if he should have stayed on the stool at the bar.

"Please excuse my friend, little one," said the thin longleg. "He was born without manners and never took the time to learn any." Inclining his head, he said, "My name is Joshmuel Alsher, and he is Boah Rasus. We are of the village of Drysa. My pleasure—and his, I assure you—is to meet you in peace today." He gave Nundle a small, seated bow.

Unsure how to respond to what sounded like a ritual greeting, Nundle performed an awkward bow of his own. "I am Nundle Babblebrook, um...of the village Deepwell. My pleasure is to meet you in peace today, too." He paused and gave them a hopeful smile. "Did I say that right?"

As both longlegs chuckled, insisting he had done fine, Heriot arrived and, with one hand, placed three mugs on the table. She slid two in front of the Borderlanders—eliciting profuse thanks from them both—and the other one she placed opposite to where Nundle stood. In her other hand, Heriot held a small wooden crate that she placed on a chair by the mug.

Thanking her for her foresight, Nundle stepped around to the other side of the table and climbed the chair as Heriot stood by, making halting movements as if she intended to try to help Nundle up. He made it on his own, more than a little relieved that the innkeeper did not try to lift him up and place him on the crate like a sack of potatoes.

Once situated, and after Heriot had moved away, Nundle smiled at the two longlegs across from him. "Heriot mentioned the two of you are from the Borderlands. I was hoping in exchange for the drink, you might tell me more about your home. I was hoping to visit the region soon and—"

"No!" interjected Boah, throwing up his hands and waving them back and forth. "Gods, no! A visit to the Nine Hells would be more enjoyable!"

The outburst earned him a few sidelong glances from the other patrons as well as a sharp look and murmured warning from Joshmuel. "Boah...please lower your voice."

After a quick glance around the room, Boah pressed his lips together.

Looking back to Nundle, Joshmuel explained, "Talk of home upsets him." He glared at Boah again. "Sometimes I wonder if it is wise for him to go to Freehaven. One outburst like that before the First Council and we will be thrown from the chambers."

Boah nodded, grunted, grimaced, and sipped from his mug all at once. Nundle supposed there was an admittance of guilt in there somewhere.

"What he says is true, though," said Joshmuel. "The Borderlands are not safe for visitors." He lifted an eyebrow. "For anyone, truly."

"Why not?" asked Nundle.

The two Borderlanders turned to look at one another. Boah nodded at Joshmuel. "I told the last man who asked. It's your turn. Besides, you seem to like the practice."

Joshmuel took a long sip from his ale, set the mug down, and leaned forward, placing both arms on the table. "For generations upon generations, those of us in the western Borderlands have lived under constant threat of oligurts, mongrels, and razorfiends raiding our lands and homes. Years might pass, generations even, without any sign of the Sudashians, but eventually some glory-hungry chieftain or pack leader would raid us. Villages burned, people died, and the duke would respond, sending the Dust Men forth to repel the invaders."

"Pardon me," interrupted Nundle "Dust Men?"

"The Borderlands' army," said Boah.

Joshmuel nodded, adding, "The Southlands have the Southern Arms, the Great Lakes have the Red Sentinels, and the Marshlands, Reed Men. I have had no dealings with any of the others so I do not know what they are called. Perhaps they have no name. Who is to say?"

"You have had 'dealings' with them?" said Nundle, eyebrow raised. "That sounds ominous."

Joshmuel smiled and shook his head. "You misunderstand. I mean only that I have seen them, said good day in passing. That is all."

As Joshmuel seemed a respectable sort, Nundle did not press the issue. "So these...Dust Men fought the invaders?"

"They would," said Joshmuel, nodding. "They would fight and they would win, driving the raiders back. Our ancestors would rebuild, refusing to give up our lands, refusing to give in to fear." He sighed and continued, his tone somewhat weary. "Of course, the raiders would come again. And the Dust Men would drive them back. And we would rebuild."

Wearing a sympathetic frown, Nundle asked, "And the raiders would come again?"

"Such is life in the Borderlands," said Boah.

Nundle did not think that sounded like much of a life.

Joshmuel leaned forward. "A year ago the cycle changed. Men, women, and families who lived closer to the border than we—" he indicated himself and Boah "—began to come east. Raiders had come again. Only instead of a few hundred, now there were thousands, tens of thousands. Oligurts, mongrels, and razorfiends all banded together, fighting as one."

"But they don't do that," said Nundle. "They hate one another."

Both Borderlanders studied him closely, their eyes narrowing. Joshmuel asked, "And how did you know that?"

Nundle smiled and shrugged. "I like to read."

"Joshmuel sat back a little, his eyebrows climbing a fraction. "A wondrous and worthy luxury. And informative, it would seem, for you are correct. Such cooperation amongst the Sudashians is unheard of. Their constant warring amongst each other was the one thing keeping the Borderlands truly safe."

"What about your Dust Men?" asked Nundle. "Have they not fought back?"

A mirthless, derisive chuckle slipped from Boah. "They are blasted worthless."

"Why do you say that?"

Joshmuel gave a sad shake of his head. "They do not seem up to the task."

Boah eyed his countryman, a bitter smirk on his face, and muttered, "That, or Duke Vanson chooses not to fight back."

"Why would a duke do nothing while his lands are invaded?" asked Nundle.

Staring at Boah yet answering Nundle, Joshmuel said, "That, my little friend, is the same question I ask Boah every time he makes such an outlandish statement."

"Then explain the actions he has taken," rejoined Boah. "Or better yet, hasn't taken!"

Joshmuel held his friend's gaze for a moment before dropping his head to stare at the table. "I cannot." He picked at the carved wooden handle of his mug. "As much as I wish I could."

Nundle glanced between the pair. "I don't understand. What has—or hasn't—the duke done?"

Boah peered over at Joshmuel and raised his eyebrows expectantly, seemingly daring his companion to answer. Nundle sensed that he had stepped into the middle of a long-running debate.

Joshmuel reluctantly looked up from the mug in front of him. "Every Sudashian attack, *every* single one, the Dust Men arrive far too late to drive them back."

"If they arrive at all," grumbled Boah.

Joshmuel shook his head, a frown on his face. "It seems rather improbable that their scouts could be so wrong so often, or the army so slow to respond, but I can think of no other logical explanation."

"No other explanation?" asked Boah, his eyebrows arching high. "Why do you continue to willfully ignore what is happening? Or—again—*not* happening?"

Joshmuel shot a sidelong look at Boah and sighed.

"What's that mean?" asked Nundle.

Joshmuel stared across the table. "The duchies typically aid one another against bandits, raids, and the like. Just today in fact, I saw a band of Red Sentinels moving through town, although I am not sure what they are doing here. We could use them in the west."

Boah growled, "Perhaps they would be there if Vanson would blasting ask."

"So the duke has not asked for aid?" asked Nundle.

With a shrug of his shoulders, Joshmuel said, "If he has, none has been sent. No Reed Men. No Red Sentinels. And without their help—" he let out a quick, heavy sigh "—the Borderlands will fall."

"What do you hope to gain by going to Freehaven?"

Boah set his now-empty mug on the table and scratched his bearded chin. "Any duchy citizen may petition the First Council on the first day of each turn. We go there to ask that *someone* do something since Vanson seems content to sit on his rear in Gobas and wait for an oligurt knock down the door to the Duke's Hall."

Joshmuel said, "We had hoped to make it there by the Turn of Thonda, but as that is but twelve days away, and we are here..." He shrugged. "We will have to wait until Rintira's turn."

"Surely the First Council knows about this by now, don't they?" asked Nundle. "People in the east have already heard rumors." He told them about the stories shared by Pelter and his crew. When he was done, Boah shook his head, frowning.

"It's nice to know word has reached this far east, but...if they hear much more, they'll stop believing and start laughing."

Confused, Nundle asked, "What does that mean?"

Both men were quiet, staring at one another for a few moments. Eventually, Boah mumbled, "People are going to find out eventually."

Joshmuel looked like he had swallowed something that did not agree with him. He studied Nundle for a few heartbeats, judging. With a definitive nod of his head, he spoke. "What I tell you now I have seen with my own eyes, so do not doubt my words." He paused to look around them, leaned closer, and spoke in a hushed murmur.

"My eldest son, Zecus, and I were riding patrol around the lands near our village. There had been rumors of a group of oligurts nearby and we went to see if they were true. Understand, little one, that the land where we live is harsh and dry. Rain comes only during the winter turns, briefly coloring the land green. When the rains stop, everything browns again, leaving dead, dry grasses everywhere as tall as a man. It is difficult to see much of anything unless you are on a hill or a horse."

Nundle was beginning to wonder why anyone would want to live in the Borderlands.

"Zecus and I rode to a hill that overlooked where the Sudashians had been seen. Spread below us in a wide valley was a sight I still see in my sleep. Thousands of oligurts, mongrels, and razorfiends camped together. Each race stayed with its own, and there was no fighting between them."

"As unnatural as water flowing uphill," muttered Boah.

Nodding, Joshmuel said, "What stabbed at my soul, however, was seeing men, both light and dark skinned, spread throughout the camp. At least I thought they were men." He hesitated a moment, frowning. "Then I saw one with horns like a bull. Great wide horns, poking right out of the side of his head. Other men had horns as well, or the snouts of boars and legs like a goat. Or a horse!" Joshmuel's brown eyes bore into Nundle. "Demon-men, little one. I am not afraid to say it. I saw men of the Nine Hells."

Nundle suddenly felt quite ill.

Demon-men in the duchies. Just like the last time the god of Chaos marched.

The letter in his pocket suddenly seemed to weigh as much as a cartful of rocks.

Joshmuel sat back in his chair and sighed. "Zecus and I rode back to Drysa as fast as we could and packed our household. We tried to convince others we needed to run, but only a few listened. Boah here was one. We took our families east to Gobas."

Crossing his arms, Boah took over the story. "We tried to gain an audience with Duke Vanson, but we were turned away at the gates. No surprise, there. We tried warning everyone we saw, but we were hailed as false prophets. Mocked. Spit upon. So, we continued east into the Marshlands. We left our families in Demetus and started our journey east."

Their tale chilled Nundle to his soul. Any doubt that he had done the right thing by coming to the Oaken Duchies was gone.

He asked the Borderlanders a dozen questions, but neither man could give him more information than they had already shared.

Heriot came over and asked if they would like to eat anything. Nundle declined and excused himself, blaming road weariness, but offered to pay for the

Borderlanders' meal. They refused, claiming the drink was more charity than they should have taken. Not wanting to insult the men, Nundle wished them luck on their journey east and headed to his room. As he passed the bar, he handed Heriot another silver arcan and asked the innkeeper to give Joshmuel and Boah a platter of lamb and squash and claim it was on her.

He made his way upstairs, found his room, and settled on the straw mattress inside. He tried to fall asleep, but ended up lying in the dark for a long time before finally drifting off. His night was full of unpleasant dreams.

CHAPTER 34: INVADERS

20th *of the Turn of Sutri*

Sand and grit pelted the back of Zecus' hand as he lifted it to pull back the scarf covering his face. The wind whistling in his ears, he peeked out only for a moment, ensuring that his horse was still on course and following the rest of the group. The howl of the sandstorm was so loud that it masked the sound of the horsemen around him.

Squinting against the dust buffeting his face, he spotted the hunched forms of two horsemen in front of him through the storm's gloom. Morning's sun might have broken the horizon to the east, but its light had no hope of reaching the valley. The dust and bits of parched grass whipping through the air saw to that.

He was part of a double column snaking through a gully between two hills. The men with whom he rode were dressed in drab tans and ivory. Long, multi-colored scarves of reds, yellows, and oranges hung from their brow, held in place by the white cloth bands wrapped tight around their crowns. Glancing to his right, he saw his column mate—Zecus had yet to learn his name—also had his scarf drawn up.

Effectively alone due to the storm, Zecus raised the scarf over his face and contemplated the strange series of events that had placed him in this particular procession through this valley.

After leaving his mother, sisters, and younger brother in Demetus—a decision he regretted more as the days passed—Zecus had ridden west, back toward his home. His father might have chosen to run from the Sudashian horde, to beg some distant eastern nobles for aid, but Zecus wanted to stand and fight.

Demetus had been a disaster. He had worked as a simple day laborer for a time, yet as more and more refugees poured into the city, work grew scarce. The little he could find paid almost nothing while, at the same time, prices for everything steadily increased. In short order, the Alsher family was scrounging for food. Zecus, his mother, two sisters, and brother had become beggars. The dishonor had stung deep. It still did.

Ultimately, Zecus resolved that the only way he could better his family's plight was to go home to defend the Borderlands. Or die trying.

Leaving had been difficult. His mother begged him to stay but he would not listen. Neither her tears nor those of his youngest sister could persuade him. He left them with the remainder of the family's meager coin and set out, doing his best to push their sorrowful faces from his mind.

As he went west, he passed countless families migrating east, forced from their homes by the Sudashian invaders. When he asked what the Dust Men were doing about the invasion, he received blank, defeated looks or bitter grumbles of "Nothing."

Zecus rode through Gobas, the Borderlands' capital, on his return home, and found it to be in even worse shape than Demetus. The city, bursting with people, was bare of supplies. He supposed his mother, sisters, and brother were actually slightly better off in Demetus.

He arrived in Drysa a few days ago and found the Alsher's former home nearly deserted. Most of the squat, tan sandstone and earth buildings were empty, shops and homes deserted with their stretched-hide doors hanging open. Of the few hundred who had lived in Drysa, only a handful remained, most of them too old or feeble to travel.

Besides the elderly and infirm, there had been one young man left with whom Zecus had grown up. Emiah had become a scavenger, collecting anything of value his former neighbors had left behind and claiming it as his own. Stepping into Emiah's home, Zecus had spotted the hardwood table from the Alsher home and bristled at the man's boldness. Hardwood was precious in the Borderlands. Weak bulboa wood was readily available and used for small tools or utensils, but the porous wood easily broke. That table had been a point of pride for Zecus' father.

That first night back in Drysa, Zecus had shared his frustrations with Emiah, his desire to fight back against the invaders. Emiah said men were gathering in the north, men who were doing whatever they could to slow the invasion. Zecus immediately offered to ride with Emiah, to seek out these men and join them. Only after some goading by Zecus did Emiah reluctantly agree to go. The pair had left the next morning on two of Emiah's "newly acquired" horses, heading north through the sweeping brown grasslands.

As they had ridden, Emiah asked dozens of questions about what Zecus and his father had seen from the hilltop. Zecus answered Emiah's queries plainly, sharing everything about the horde. With each offered answer, Emiah grew quieter. When Zecus awoke the next morning, he found himself alone. Emiah was gone. None too surprised, Zecus was simply grateful the coward had left him a horse.

Continuing north alone, ignoring the danger of being a sole traveler in a land at war, he plodded along for several more sweltering days, keeping a careful eye out for any sign of a resistance group, the Sudashians, or the water holes that spotted the region. The wells were the only year-round source of water in the Borderlands. Most villages were built around such water holes, and as he moved north, he had come across one abandoned settlement after another. There was plenty of water for himself and his horse.

For days, he searched for the resistance, but his efforts were futile. He was beginning to think no such group existed. In the end, they found him.

Yesterday evening, he had gone to sleep on a bare spot of dirt beneath the branches of a bulboa tree and awoke in the middle of the night, surrounded by a half-dozen men, a spear point pressed against his throat. They were a patrol for the elusive resistance.

After a few tense moments, Zecus persuaded them of his intention to join them. Grim-faced, the men welcomed him to their ranks and rode northeast, eventually meeting up with two larger groups that brought their number near thirty. He tried to ask questions, but was repeatedly shushed. The men traveled in complete silence, keeping careful watch on the hilltops. Zecus found himself staring up the rises, unable to see a thing in the dark, but staring nonetheless. Just before dawn, the windstorm arrived, thrashing the group with sand and straw.

An insistent gurgling from his stomach reminded Zecus that he had not eaten today. Reaching into the leather pouch hanging from his belt, he searched for the strip of canvas in which he had wrapped the remainder of last night's eveningmeal, charred boa lizard tail. Just as his fingers grazed the rough cloth, a strange, screeching shriek swirled amongst the wind's howl.

Zecus sat straight in his saddle, gripping his knees tight as his horse danced sideways. The screech reminded him of a child's terrified squeal, a possibility he dismissed out of hand. The whipping wind twisted sounds, making them seem like things they were not.

He pulled his scarf from his face to peek out—the dust stung his eyes—but could not see anything beyond a dozen paces. His horse began moving forward again, prancing more than walking, apparently anxious to stay with the other horses of the double column.

He was starting to wonder if he had imagined the sound when another wailing cry cut through the wind. He turned his head in all directions, searching for the source. Other men had also dropped their face scarves, braving the dust storm and scanning the hillsides. Zecus' heart quickened when he realized that he was not imagining the cries.

A moment later, the muffled, alarmed shouts of men filtered through the sandstorm, only bits and pieces decipherable through the wind.

"—cut off from the—"

"—on the hill—"

"—trapped in and—"

The shrieks grew louder, closer, more frequent. New sounds, deep grunts and growls, joined in. Men drew swords, whipping their heads around in all directions, their colorful scarves flapping freely in the wind. Horses pranced and danced, tossing their heads. The man beside Zecus spun his mount in a stationary circle, peering up the hillside.

They were under attack, something for which Zecus was not prepared in the slightest. He had no sword and even if he did, he would have no idea how to use it. He was a goat-herder. His hope had been that when he arrived at the main camp, the men there would give him a sword or staff and teach him how to fight. All he had was his throwing knife, a bow, and a dozen arrows rattling around in a quiver.

Shaking off his nerves, Zecus swiveled in his saddle and pulled his bow from its case. He bent the limbs together, stringing the weapon faster than he ever had. In this wind, a fired arrow would be useless against anything more than a dozen paces away, but he was not going to just to sit here on his horse like a sack of grain. Something was coming, and he would be as ready as he could be.

His column mate sat in his saddle, a longsword upraised in his right hand, his left shielding his eyes from the wind and sand. Zecus was about to call out and ask for guidance when the rider abruptly turned to look in Zecus' direction. His eyes widened. Loosing a sharp curse, the man drew a dagger from his belt with his free hand and flung it at Zecus.

Zecus bent down, over his horse's neck, as the heavy dagger whizzed through the air. To his left, there was a wet thunk followed by a deep, bellowing roar.

Twisting his head, Zecus spotted a giant, gray-skinned figure but ten paces away. The monster was well over six and a half feet tall with a shorn head, deep set pitch-black eyes, an oversized flat nose, and two yellowed tusk-like teeth jutting up from between thick, gray-green lips. A shaggy-furred animal skin tunic draped over its massive chest and hung to its knees. A massive wooden club with spiked, metal cleats on one end lay on the ground, next to the creature, dropped as the beast clawed at the dagger jutting from its throat. Black blood squirted from the wound in the neck.

Zecus realized he was staring at an oligurt, one who would have crushed him with the discarded club had it not been for the man beside him. As he gaped, the oligurt stumbled away, swallowed by the dust storm.

Zecus twisted to face his savior. "Thank you!"

"You're lucky! She almost got you!"

Zecus nodded his head in hasty agreement. It took a moment for the man's words to register fully. "She?"

He stared back into the storm, wondering what the males looked like. Swiveling around to face his column mate, he spotted a small figure rushing through the blowing dust toward the man. "Behind you!"

As the man spun around, Zecus drew an arrow from his quiver, nocked it, pulled the string back, and shot at the sand-shrouded figure. The wind grabbed hold of the shaft and carried it away into the storm.

Before the man could raise his sword, the figure leaped from the ground and landed on the man and his horse. A half dozen small, dark blades burst through the man's back. Blood squirted out, much of it whipped away by the wind. The man screamed, joining the cries of other men up and down the column.

He struggled with the creature, twisting and turning in his saddle, but it was pointless. In a few short moments, the man stopped thrashing and the blades retreated, sliding back into his body. Limp and lifeless, his corpse slid from the horse, falling to the ground in a heap.

Zecus stared at the man's body, stunned. He had saved Zecus' life just moments ago and now he was dead. Zecus did not even know his name.

A bone-rattling roar startled Zecus from his shock. Looking over his shoulder, he spotted another oligurt swinging a wooden club toward his head. Instinct took over and he rolled out of the saddle—to his right and away from the oligurt—trying to avoid the impending blow.

He was too slow, however. His left temple exploded in pain.

The world went black.

CHAPTER 35: FATE

21ˢᵗ of the Turn of Sutri

The sound of voices in the streets below greeted Nundle as he awoke. Cracking open his eyes, he stared at the sky out his window. Based on the dim, nameless gray he saw, he guessed dawn had yet to arrive. After rising from the straw mattress and stretching, he moved to the window, stood on the tips of his toes, and looked outside.

Even at this early hour, people filled the streets, carrying large canvas bags slung on their back or balancing baskets full of all sorts of goods—fruit, vegetables, clothes, rugs, trinkets—atop their heads. As the general flow of traffic was towards the merchant district through which he had walked yesterday, Nundle assumed they were vendors on their way to set up their stalls.

He headed downstairs and was surprised to see Heriot behind the counter considering the early hour. When he made such a remark, the longleg smiled and said it was her job to be last to bed and first to rise.

Nundle accepted a loaf of soft bread and a few slices of a hard white cheese for his morningmeal, along with a cup of a sweet, weak wine. When he inquired about Joshmuel and Boah, Heriot informed him the pair had already left. Disappointed that he would not be able to say goodbye to the two Borderlanders, Nundle finished his meal and headed out of The Screaming Butcher with a word of thanks. Heriot tried to give Nundle back some coins saying that the food and the room had not cost nearly what he had paid, but Nundle refused. Heriot was an honest person, hard worker, and kind soul. Nundle was happy to have overpaid.

Deciding that he could use one last sweet bun before he left the city, he retraced his steps to the bakery. While people openly stared at him as he passed, they were always polite, offering smiles and wishes of "Good days ahead." Other than the "all magic is outlawed" nonsense, he decided the Oaken Duchies was a pleasant enough place.

After finding his way back to the baker, he bought a single pastry—only one, having learned his limit—and asked the man for directions to where he could buy traveling supplies. The simple canvas bag he had brought from the academy was beginning to fall apart.

The kindly baker gave him directions to a building around the corner, telling him to look for a forest green awning with bright, white stripes situated on a rooftop.

With a word of thanks, Nundle left, ducking and dodging his way through the increasingly crowded streets, trying to avoid being stepped on. Upon rounding a corner, he spotted the building the baker had described. Three stories tall, the first floor was made of smooth, light gray river rock while the upper two stories were a darkly stained oak. The building was one of the few he had seen that was so tall; most Lakeborough structures were only one or two floors.

After walking to the northern side of the building, he climbed the stairs to the rooftop. Custom seemed to dictate that people went up the northern steps and down the southern stairwell.

Once on the rooftop, he moved straight to the green awning with white stripes and greeted the vendor. The longleg was still setting up his goods but seemed happy to have a customer so early in the day. He was helpful, giving Nundle his full attention while the tomble looked over a vast assortment of leather travel packs, waterskins, bedrolls, firesticks, skinning knives, slings, snares, walking sticks, and more. Realizing how vastly underprepared he was for his trip, Nundle bought one of nearly everything. The vendor could not stop smiling.

Remarking that it seemed the tomble was going on a long trip, the peddler noted that the sandals and ragged gray robe that Nundle wore would not last long on the open road. Nundle had to agree. His acolyte garb was made for the paved halls and walkways of the Strand Academies, not for extended travel over dirt and rock roads.

The longleg directed him to another vendor with a bright blue awning on the same rooftop, one who sold children's boots and clothes. Pushing aside his initial reticence to wearing clothing meant for longleg children, Nundle bought some proper breeches and a shirt, along with a new set of boots. After thanking both vendors, he moved to the southern side of the building in order to walk down the stairs.

When he reached the edge, he stopped for a moment and looked down at the city around him. The hundreds of colorful awnings made it look as if someone had chopped up a rainbow and sprinkled it over the rooftops. Three sprawling stone structures rose high above the rest of the buildings; Nundle figured they were temples. The streets below were as busy as they had been when he had arrived yesterday, perhaps more so.

Nundle was about to head to the south side of the building to climb down when something in the crowd below caught his eye. Two columns of longlegs in red and black uniforms were riding on horses down the center of the street. Behind them were more longlegs with dark blue uniforms trimmed with gold.

He ran his gaze along the procession, back to front, curious about the matching uniforms. Upon reaching the head of the column, Nundle froze. "Impossible…"

Preceptor Myrr, situated atop a black horse with a white mane, was leading the column. The saeljul wore tan traveling clothes rather than his normal crimson robes, but Nundle did not doubt the ijul's identity. The white-gold hair and elongated features were unmistakable.

Panicking, his heart racing, Nundle leapt back from building's edge and slipped behind the nearest vendor stall. If the preceptor happened to look up, Nundle's size and bright red hair would have given him away in a heartbeat. He reached into his pack and pulled out the wide-brimmed hat he had just bought and jammed it on his head, tucking his hair under the cap.

The vendor of the stand behind which he was hiding spoke, his tone conversational. "Red Sentinels."

Nundle glanced up at the vendor and found the longleg peering down at the procession. "Pardon?"

Motioning below, the longleg said, "They're Red Sentinels. From the Great Lakes."

Remembering his conversation with the Borderlanders from last night, Nundle said, "They're soldiers, right?"

The vendor nodded. "That they are." A frown creased his face. "It's surprising, though. Can't imagine why the duchess granted permission to let them ride here. Word is she and Duke Everett never were on the best of terms."

Nundle's head snapped up at the name. "*Duke* Everett? The duke of the Great Lakes is named *Everett*?"

The vendor peered at him, his brow furrowed and eyes curious. "Um…yes?"

Nundle's heart pumped as though he was in the middle of a Leisure Time post race. "Where does he live?"

The longleg's eyes narrowed. "Redstone."

Nundle's eyes widened a fraction. The letter he held was from an "Everett" and spoke of a city named "Redstone." While it was possible that both names were a coincidence, Preceptor Myrr's presence said it was not.

He stared back to the street, wondering how the preceptor had found him. Even if Magistrate Ulius had returned and shared what had happened, the preceptor should never have been able to track Nundle to Lakeborough. His gaze settled on two men riding beside his former teacher, flanking the ijul. "The pair in gray. Who are they?"

The question drew another curious look from the longleg. "Constables. Trackers from the look of them." He paused before asking, "You are new to the area, I take it?"

Nundle ignored the man's question. His heart was beating so fast that he thought it might burst. "Constables? Here? How?"

The mutterings were simply Nundle musing aloud, but the vendor answered him anyway.

"Word is they're hunting some outlaw mages. Something about a whole village being destroyed in the north. Not sure about the ijul up front, though. I've never heard of a saeljul in any duchy army. And he's not wearing gray, so he's no Constable."

Nundle's heart slowed a bit. They were not here for him. Which meant, most likely, the preceptor was after the Progeny.

"You said mages?" He glanced up at the vendor. "More than one?"

The longleg shrugged. "One is enough, isn't it? Terrifying thought, thinking they might be wandering the city."

"Ah...yes," mumbled Nundle, suddenly uneasy. "Terrifying."

"To answer your question, though, yes. More than one mage. A friend sold a smoking pipe to a Sentinel yesterday who said they were hunting four lawbreakers." His eyes went wide. "Four! Can you believe it?"

Nundle stared at the man blankly. He could not believe it. The letter he carried mentioned only one survivor from the preceptor's attack. Peering back down to the column of soldiers, he muttered, "Four?"

He stayed like that for a few moments, his mind racing. With a decisive nod, Nundle turned back to the longleg peddler. "Do you know where I can buy a horse?" He paused then added, "A very small horse?"

CHAPTER 36: LESSONS

24ᵗʰ of the Turn of Sutri

Jak sat alone in the grass, an anticipatory grimace on his face, and muttered, "Please get it right this time."

Fifty paces away, a small, indistinct tongue of flame appeared several feet over tonight's campfire. It wavered in place for a moment before dissipating in a disappointing puff of smoke. Sitting beside the fire, Kenders slapped her open palms against her knees and shouted, her voice ringing out over the prairie. "Hells!"

Jak sighed and shook his head. If she kept that up, she would have bruises.

Sitting in the grass across the campfire from Kenders, Broedi said something to her, his demeanor indicating that he was not pleased. Kenders nodded, an expression of frustration mixed with determination on her face. Broedi spoke again, pointed toward the fire, and then sat back. Kenders' gaze shifted back to the flames.

"Oh, good," sighed Jak. "We're trying again."

Tonight's lessons were going poorly. As he had previous nights, Broedi would demonstrate what he wanted her to do, Kenders would insist she saw "the pattern," and try to replicate it. Then, more often than not, something would explode.

Earlier, Jak had been sitting closer to the fire than he was now, but after one of Kenders' accidents singed his shirt and set patches of the tall Southlands' grass on fire, he had moved back to where he sat now. While he was finding Kenders' lessons interesting to watch, these with fire were dangerous.

When the hillman did the magic, the campfire would flare and bend into different shapes. So far, Jak had seen a sphere, a cube, and once—to his surprise—a small bird. Mouth agape, he had watched the bird of fire fly a graceful circle about the camp, soaring overhead, before disappearing into a puff of white smoke.

"How's she doing?"

Glancing over his shoulder, Jak found Nikalys approaching through the waist-high grass, the ever-present swishing sound of the tall blades masking his footsteps. They had moved into the grasslands a few days ago and Jak was already tiring of the constant rustling.

Days after skirting Lakeborough, they had come to a fork in the road. Rather than take either, Broedi had instead led them straight, off the road and into the forest. For a day, they had moved through thinning clusters of trees before the land finally gave way to endless fields of green grass spotted with white and violet wildflowers. The land was beautiful, yet alien. Jak had spent his entire life where the wilderness' palette had been restricted to dirty yellows, dusty greens, and every imaginable shade of brown.

As he watched his brother draw closer, the sunset-soaked sky behind Nikalys forced Jak to squint. Streaks of orange and purple clouds filled the western horizon, a bright and colorful backdrop to Nikalys' dark silhouette. Despite the glare, Jak could see that Nikalys was returning from his evening hunt empty-handed. Jak frowned. That meant a choice between salted rockeye or an empty belly tonight.

Jak's gaze slipped to the scabbard hanging from Nikalys' hip. Nikalys had taken to wearing the sword once they left the road, although Jak wished he would not. He was a danger to himself and everyone else with the blade. One night, he had drawn the weapon as if to practice with it and had nearly skewered his horse.

Lifting a hand to shade his eyes from the setting sun, Jak repeated Nikalys' original question with a dry chuckle, saying, "How's she doing? Well, let's see. She nearly set the grasslands afire twice already, she almost burned off my shirt, and I've had to chase down Hal twice and Goshen once after a few small explosions. Other than that, she's doing great."

Wearing a slight grin, Nikalys asked, "So, better than normal?"

Jak smiled back. "Much."

Letting out a heavy sigh, Nikalys plopped down beside him.

"Soooo, then," said Jak, drawing the words out. "Salted rockeye tonight?"

"Unless you can convince Broedi to turn into the lynx and catch something."

Jak sighed. That had not happened in quite some time. The hillman had explained that the magic necessary to shift into an animal was more than he felt comfortable using right now.

Arranging the scabbard on his hip and settling in the grass, Nikalys asked, "Did she fight him tonight?"

"Not too much," said Jak with a small shake of his head. He glanced at Nikalys. "Truthfully, I think she was a little anxious to start this time."

When Broedi had first started the nightly lessons, Kenders had refused to work with him, saying she was too worried she might accidently do something wrong. Broedi had been patient and, for the first two evenings, simply had Kenders sit across from him and watch while he did small feats with Water and Air. On the third night, Kenders had finally tried herself.

At the moment, Broedi was speaking softly to her across the fire, quiet enough that neither brother could hear his words. Kenders was nodding quickly, a frustrated scowl on her face, as though he was telling her something that she had already heard from him multiple times.

Jak shook his head and frowned. He had seen that look a hundred times while growing up in Yellow Mud. No longer a reluctant pupil, Kenders' natural stubbornness was beginning to assert itself.

Broedi sat back and, a moment later, the fire flared and rose up. Flames shot up from the logs and molded into the shape of the bird again. Spreading its wings of fire, the bird circled the heads of the two mages once before melting away in midair.

"Impressive," mumbled Nikalys. "Him or her?"

"Based on how things have been going? Him. The last time he did the bird, she tried and—" A burst of fire flew out a few paces in all directions, interrupting Jak and causing Kenders and Broedi to both scamper back. Jak finished his original thought, sighing, "That happened."

Nikalys chuckled as Kenders cursed—none too quietly—to herself. Broedi was up and walking around the campsite, stamping out patches of smoking grass.

Turning to Nikalys, Jak asked, "What about you? Getting any better with your...whatever it is?"

Nikalys' expression darkened, his eyes narrowing. "Not at all."

The look on his face reminded Jak of when their father had tried to teach a young Nikalys how to pick grapes from the vine without bursting any. For a week, Nikalys had ended each day with sticky hands and a scowl. On the day he finally managed to pluck bunches without squishing a single grape, he wore a giant smile all evening.

Nikalys shook his head, clearly frustrated. "Blast it, Jak! Nothing I try is working. *Nothing.* Sometimes I think I can feel something, but when I reach for it—poof! It's like trying to grab smoke."

Broedi also had been trying to help Nikalys, although that amounted to little more than telling him stories about Nikalys' blood father. According to the hillman, Aryn had been a master swordsman, using Horum's gift of speed and strength to move about a battlefield like a frenzied firefly on a dark night. Broedi claimed Aryn once single-handedly cut down a hundred enemies before they had any idea what was happening to them. Those stories, while enjoyable to hear, were not helping Nikalys learn how control the gift.

Nikalys began gesturing with his hands, trying to illustrate something that made sense only to him. "When I get it to work, it's so easy...I want to be over there and like that—" he snapped his fingers "—I'm there. I almost can feel myself moving, but then again, I can't." He glanced at Jak. "Does that make any sense?"

Jak gave him a look as though Nikalys had just asked if he knew what it felt like to fly through the sky like a bird. As much as he would have liked to help, he was not really qualified to do so. Instead, he offered a weak, "Keep trying, I guess?"

Nikalys sighed and nodded. "Yeah. That's about all I can do."

By now, Broedi had extinguished the small fires, returned to his spot across from Kenders, and was urging her to try again. Even from where they sat, Jak could see the angry, determined look on her face as she stared into the empty air above the fire.

Nikalys muttered, "I have a bad feeling about this..."

The campfire's flames flared and a small bird of fire appeared above it. The bird took a few beats of its wings as Kenders happily exclaimed, "I did it!"

The moment she shouted, the firebird rapidly expanded into a ball of flame and exploded, causing both Jak and Nikalys to jump even though they were at a safe distance. The staked horses threw up their heads, whinnying. Both Hal's and Goshen's eyes rolled up, going white. Smoke merely danced sideways a few steps before stopping; the mare was made of stronger stuff.

The gentle breeze blowing east across the plains quickly carried away the smoke, revealing a stern Broedi speaking to an abashed Kenders.

"You know," muttered Nikalys. "I much prefer the Air lessons."

Chuckling aloud, Jak said, "Me, too."

"Uori!"

Broedi was waving them over. They stood, brushed themselves off, and strolled to where Kenders and the hillman waited. As they approached, Nikalys held his hands up in front of his face, palms outward. "Is it safe to come close?"

Kenders glared at him, grumbling, "If you aren't careful, I'll burn your eyebrows off."

Nikalys raised said eyebrows. "With your aim, you might roast Jak instead. I heard you tried once already."

Kenders shifted her angry gaze to Jak. "What have you been telling him?"

Jak held up his hands and shook his head. "Hey. Keep me out of this."

Frowning, Kenders stared back to Nikalys. With sarcasm coating her words like ants on a squished grape, she asked, "So, great hunter, what did you find for us tonight?"

Nikalys' mood changed in an instant, his tone turning terse. "Grass, Kenders. Lots of grass. The horses like it so I thought you might, too." He enjoyed teasing their sister, but rarely handled it well when she did it back.

"Wondrous!" shot back Kenders. "Perhaps I can stuff some in your mouth to keep it occupied!"

Jak rolled his eyes. He had witnessed—and participated in—enough of these minor arguments to know this would not end well.

Sitting in the grass beside his leather bag, packing his pipe full of smoking-leaf, Broedi rumbled, "Uori. Uora. That is enough." The admonishment was gentle yet firm.

While Nikalys and Kenders both shut their mouths, they continued to glare at one another. Their sharp moods were simply born of frustration. Given a few moments of quiet, Jak figured they would both realize it and relax.

Eyebrows raised, Broedi peered at Jak and asked, "Have they always been like this?"

"That was mild."

Broedi's familiar, albeit miniscule smile returned and he lit his pipe with a quick, magic flame.

Nikalys sat down, reached into his traveling pack, and pulled out the well-worn package of salted fish they had purchased in Fallsbottom. He took a long, hard, wrinkly piece from it and tossed the package to Jak. After catching the package, Jak sniffed it, wrinkled his nose, and tossed it back. "I'll pass, thank you."

Staring at his piece of fish, but not taking a bite, Nikalys said, "Broedi, I have a question."

"Does the rooster announce his plans to crow when he sees the day's first sunbeam?"

Nikalys looked over at the hillman, his brow furrowed. "Pardon?"

"Do not announce you have a question, uori. Simply ask it."

A slight, perturbed frown creased Nikalys' face. "Fine, then. Why can't I control my 'gift?' Or Aryn's 'gift,' I suppose? And how in the Nine Hells can I learn?" He took a bite of the salty fish and began chewing.

With smoke curling from his nose and lips, Broedi sighed, "I do not know. Perhaps because you are young? Or that Horum's gift was passed to you through blood and not given directly? I have no certain answer. I will say that your father had some trouble at first, as well. We all did, truthfully."

"What about our blood mother?" asked Kenders, "Did she have trouble?"

"Yes and no. Eliza had worked with some of the Strands before Gaena called her. But her talents required much practice afterwards."

"I thought you said she was a servant," said Nikalys, swallowing his bite of fish and making a face. Remembering the taste, Jak's curled his upper lip, joining his brother in a sympathetic grimace. The rockeye was truly awful.

Broedi nodded, puffing on his pipe. "She was. To a baron who had the wisdom to keep a court mage on hand." The hillman turned his head and stared north while continuing to speak. "He found her at a small school for mages in the Colonial Duchy."

Jak exchanged a quick look with Nikalys. Broedi had done it again. Despite the hillman's reassurances that they were free of pursuit, the brief glances to the north had not ceased. If anything, they had increased in recent days. Kenders marked the look, too, softly voicing the question they were all thinking.

"We're still not safe, are we, Broedi?"

He looked back to her, remained quiet for a moment, and then asked, "What do you mean?"

"You keep looking north," said Kenders. "That's the ninth time today."

Nikalys said, "I've noticed them, too."

"We all have," added Jak.

Broedi glanced from face to face. "Have I been that obvious?"

"Yes, you have," said Jak with a smile.

"That is disappointing…" He let out a quiet sigh and nodded slowly. "To answer your question, I do not know if we are safe. I would think we should be after so many days. Yet…I cannot help but feel we are being followed."

"Perhaps you just need more sleep?" suggested Kenders.

Jak agreed. Every night, Broedi was still up when they went to sleep and he was the one to shake them from their slumber in the morning.

"A week of sleep would not shake this, uora. It is a part of Thonda's gift, a sense that animals possess that men and most other races do not. It is what makes a cat's fur rise for no apparent reason. Or why a dog growls while staring at empty air." He stared at her. "My worry does not come from lack of sleep. It is *why* I cannot sleep."

"The Trackers, then?" asked Kenders. "Are they still following us?"

Broedi shook his head. "I do not know."

"What about the saeljul?" muttered Nikalys. "Perhaps he's still after us?"

A pensive frown marred Broedi's stoic expression. "Perhaps, uori. I do not know."

"Who is he, anyway?" asked Jak.

Broedi sighed again, heavier this time, and closed his eyes. "I do not know."

Kenders leaned forward. "Do you think he might be one of the Cabal?"

Broedi's endless tolerance cracked. Opening his eyes, he glared at Kenders, his eyes wild and intense. "I do not know! I wish I did, but I do not. *Every* question you are asking, I have asked myself a thousand times. Understand that I am as blind to much of this as the three of you."

The edge in Broedi's voice shocked all three siblings quiet. The only other time Jak had seen Broedi this animated was by the cliff, and that had been a ruse. This was honest emotion and therefore was much more concerning.

After a few moments filled only with the quiet rustle of the breeze tickling the prairie grass, Broedi closed his eyes and took a deep breath. He let it back out slowly then rumbled, "I am sorry, uora." He reopened his eyes and looked to Jak and Nikalys. "You as well, uori. My words were sharp."

"Actually," began Kenders, "I appreciate you being candid for once."

The hillman's slight smile returned to its rightful place. "I can understand that."

Staring north, Nikalys crossed his arms. "You know, if something or someone is following us, I say we just face them and fight. Now." He waved at the grass. "Here."

Both Jak and Kenders gaped at him. Kenders beat Jak to the obvious, asking, "Are you mad?"

Pointing to Broedi, Nikalys said, "According to him, we are supposed to stop something bad, right? Let's just face what's coming and get it over with."

Jak shook his head. "Nik, don't be a fool."

"How am I being a fool? I just want—"

"Stop," rumbled Broedi, his tone firm and unyielding. "The only thing you will be facing is south while you sit on the back of your horse."

Nikalys glared the hillman. "Why? Why not fight now?"

"Because you are *not* ready! If it is the Cabal on our heels, they will kill you, your kaveli, and your iskoa, all before you could draw breath to beg for your life. At the moment, you are a sapling! To face the Cabal, you must be a thousand strong oaks."

Nikalys held Broedi's ardent gaze for a moment before dropping his head to stare at the trampled grass. "I just..." He trailed off, sighed, and looked back up. "If it is the ijul following us, I just want him to answer for what he did. That's all."

"Hells, Nik," said Jak. "Don't you think we *all* feel that way? Broedi's right, though. The other night, you nearly sliced open Goshen and—" he pointed at Kenders "—she's doing her best to set the prairie on fire! You're not ready!"

Muscles rippled along Nikalys' jaw. He looked like he wanted to argue but all he did was mutter, "I know."

After a quiet, tense moment skipped past, Kenders turned to Broedi. "If it is the Cabal following us, could they truly find us out here? In the middle of nowhere?"

Chewing on the bit of his pipe and staring into the campfire, Broedi sighed and shook his head. "Yet another question I cannot answer."

Nikalys asked, "Could they know where we're headed?"

"We must hope they do not."

"Care sharing that information with *us*?" asked Nikalys.

"There's no point in asking that," said Jak. "He's not going to tell us."

Broedi pulled his gaze from the fire and peered up at Nikalys and Jak through a cloud of pipe smoke, but did not respond. Their destination was still a mystery. Each time they asked, Broedi shrugged off the question.

"That's what I figured," said Nikalys, his gaze still on the hillman. "Even though I don't understand why not."

When Broedi continued to remain silent on the subject, Jak announced what seemed obvious to him. "It's simple, Nik. If we don't know where we're going, we can't tell anyone if we get caught."

The hillman's intense gaze shifted to Jak alone, a glint of admiration in his brown eyes.

"He's right," mused Kenders, looking to Broedi. "Isn't he?"

Broedi looked from face to face, sighed, and rose from the grass. Standing, he turned his back to them and stared out over the prairie. Waves of grass lit by the setting sun rippled in the light breeze, reminding Jak of a reddish-gold blanket. They waited for Broedi to answer. When he did finally speak, it was only to relay instructions.

"Tonight, we keep watch throughout the night. I will go first while the three of you sleep. In order of birth, you three will each take a turn. Go to sleep, please. We move at dawn."

Still quite hungry, Jak nonetheless prepared to sleep for the evening. They all did.

As he lay in the grass, eyes closed, listening to the rustling of the prairie, he wondered how long it would be before Broedi shook him awake for his turn. As sleep began to claim him, his wonder shifted to if the hillman would wake him at all.

CHAPTER 37: SHADOW

25ᵗʰ of the Turn of Sutri

Nundle lay on his belly, staring at the soldier's camp splayed out below him, praying the brush and fading twilight were enough to hide him. The forest had begun to thin out today, leaving few precious trunks for him to hide behind. He wondered what he was going to do once all the trees were gone.

Some type of large, wiggling thing squirmed beneath his shirt where his chest pressed to the dirt. Resisting the urge to jump up and shake the crawly critter from his person, Nundle instead pressed his body down hard until he heard a crunching sound. The moving stopped and Nundle grimaced.

The road the soldiers—and therefore, he—had been following split below. From Nundle's perch, he could make out two branches going in opposite directions in the moonlight, both lined with the same thinning forest in which Nundle now hid. He had been lying here since sunset, hoping to glean some idea which direction the group was heading. By the time Nundle reached this fork tomorrow on his horse, the preceptor and soldiers would be long gone in one direction or the other.

Tents with red and black pennants flapping over them were on the eastern side of the road, outnumbering the tents with the blue and gold flags on the western side by two to one. The two groups of soldiers were working together, yet there did not seem to be much camaraderie between them. Nundle would have made a large bet that even during the day, red and black rarely rode beside blue and gold.

Cookpots hung suspended over a dozen flickering fires, the light of the flames responsible for the shadows dancing against the canvas tents. Staked horses stood in double rows away from the road, already fed and rubbed down from the day's ride. Soldiers milled throughout the camp, doing all sorts of things with which Nundle was unfamiliar—soldier tasks, he supposed—following the same routine they had every other night.

Nundle had developed a low opinion of soldiering life. Tear down camp, ride all day, set up camp, then do it all over the next day. Nundle had experienced only a few days of the routine, and he was already tired of it.

Despite his nightly observations, Nundle still had no clear understanding of what was happening, what the preceptor was doing exactly, or why he was doing it. He had learned a few important things, however. For one, it seemed that the tall, bearded head soldier of the Red Sentinels did not much care for the preceptor, instantly raising the longleg's stature in Nundle's eyes. Witnessed exchanges between Preceptor Myrr and the soldier had grown increasingly testy in recent days.

As Nundle stared below, the savory smell of some type of meat and root stew wafted from below, taunting the hidden tomble. His stomach grumbled even as he silently pleaded with it to remain quiet. After foolishly eating his entire supply of salted Southlands boar on the first day, his meals on this excursion had been cold and sparse: handfuls of foraged blueberries.

He shifted to relieve his cramped muscles and checked that his new hat was still pulled tight to cover his hair. With a tiny, worried sigh, he whispered to himself, "Which way are you going?"

He supposed he could just try to follow tracks tomorrow, but that made him nervous. He was a merchant and a mage, not a woodsman.

Suddenly, Preceptor Myrr stepped from his tent and called to the two Trackers sitting at a nearby fire. The pair jumped up, ran over to him, and listened as the ijul spoke. Moments later, they were hurrying off to opposite sides of the camp.

Nundle frowned. Preceptor Myrr showed no fear of the Trackers. On more than one occasion, Nundle had sensed the use of the Strands, yet the longlegs in gray did nothing. He was beginning to question the effectiveness of the feared Constables.

The Tracker with the black hair headed into the Red Sentinels' section of the camp, which was closer to Nundle's hiding spot. After seeking out the bearded Red Sentinels' leader, the two spoke briefly. Even from a distance, Nundle could see the soldier's agitation in his responses as the Tracker appeared to beg with him. Finally, the Sentinel leader stepped past the gray-clad longleg and, with long, determined strides, marched to the fork in the road with the Tracker in tow.

The pair arrived at the branch where the preceptor stood waiting, his back toward the approaching men. The Sentinel leader might have said something to the ijul, but if so, the preceptor ignored him. Nundle wished he could hear what they were saying. He knew of a small Weave of Air that would help with that, but he did not dare use the Strands so close to Preceptor Myrr.

The three men stood in the fork of the road with the bearded soldier pacing back and forth and the Tracker shifting uneasily from one foot to the other. The preceptor paid no attention to either of them.

When the blond Tracker marched up with the Southern Arms' leader, Preceptor Myrr turned and addressed the group. He pointed down one branch of the road, then the other, and finally directly to the south, into the forest.

Whatever the preceptor said, the Red Sentinel soldier appeared not to agree, motioning back to his camp with crisp, sharp gestures while speaking.

"You would be wise to calm down," whispered Nundle to himself. Preceptor Myrr's patience was as thin as the ice on a pond after the first freeze.

The exchange went on for a few moments longer when Nundle suddenly felt the crackling of magic. As Preceptor Myrr wove a quick Weave of Will, the black-haired Tracker took a step back, staring directly at the large, golden pattern hovering in the air.

Nundle muttered, "So that's how you track…"

Preceptor Myrr directed the completed Weave at the bearded soldier and spoke again. The soldier stopped arguing at once and stood perfectly still. After one last, brief exchange with the Red Sentinel, the preceptor gave an impatient nod and waved the soldiers away. The Trackers remained.

Both soldiers returned to their respective camps and began to shout orders, motioning to the resting soldiers. Within moments, all of the Southern Arms soldiers and half of the Red Sentinels began to tear down camp and pack.

Nundle started to worry. "Uh-oh…"

Feeling the familiar crackling again, Nundle's gaze snapped back to where the preceptor still stood with the two Trackers. He watched, fascinated, as the saeljul wove two copies of an intricate, extremely complex pattern. Gleaming gold Strands twisted with the inky black of Void that Nundle felt more than saw in the gloom of night. Bright white Air joined the design later, looping through the Weave in a circular swirl. It was a masterful Weave, but to Nundle's eye, one that was incomplete. Gaping holes dotted the design, most likely filled with Strands Nundle could not touch.

The Weaves settled over the two Trackers, wrapping around them and drawing tighter until the patterns disappeared inside the longlegs' bodies. Both Trackers held unnaturally still throughout the process. When the Weave was gone, the two longlegs walked away, leaving the saeljul standing alone in the road. After a time, Preceptor Myrr moved back to his tent and retrieved his personal items from inside, allowing the soldiers to dismantle the tent and pack it up.

Nundle's worry deepened. "Oh, this is not good…"

Soon, those soldiers who were leaving were packed and ready. Nundle watched helplessly as two groups left and one remained. The preceptor headed down the southwest fork branch, accompanied by the Southern Arms soldiers while half of the Red Sentinels headed southeast with the blond, shaggy-haired Tracker. The Red Sentinels' leader stood at the fork, watching both groups ride away, the second half of his command still encamped.

By now, Nundle was panicking.

He wanted to follow the preceptor, but there was no way he could get back to his horse, ride here, and navigate around the remaining soldiers without the Sentinels capturing him and asking questions. Perhaps he could lie his way past them and pursue the preceptor, but he could not count on that. Nor could he use a Weave of Will to get past the soldiers, with the one Tracker still below able to sense it.

"What do I do...?"

While eyeing the Red Sentinel leader standing in the road, Nundle had a thought. It was apparent the soldier did not much like the preceptor. Perhaps Nundle could speak with him and figure out what was happening once the preceptor was far away. Very far away.

With the beginning of an idea forming in his head, Nundle scooted back from his perch. Once clear, he stood and hurried through the woods, back to his horse, silently planning exactly what he was going to say.

CHAPTER 38: FORK

Nathan stood in the middle of the moonlit road, his arms crossed over his chest, a bitter frown stretched across his lips as he watched his men march away. A frustrated, quiet curse slipped from his lips.

"Hells."

He glanced over his shoulder, staring to the southwest where Fenidar and the Southern Arms were riding in the opposite direction. Nathan had argued effusively with Fenidar over the utter lack of wisdom behind the saeljul's "plan," yet for some reason, he had ultimately agreed to it. He still could not understand why he had done so. He briefly considered recalling his men, but immediately felt compelled to dismiss his concern.

Splitting his men up in the Southlands was one of the worst things to do. They should have never even crossed the border into the duchy without formal permission, but Fenidar had insisted.

The ijul had driven a hard pace to date, repeatedly making the men march through the night. Upon reaching Lakeborough, Fenidar had met with the regent and somehow convinced him to allow the Red Sentinels to search the streets, inns, taverns—every corner of the city—for the lawbreakers they were pursuing. He had even persuaded the man to contribute Southern Arms soldiers to aid in the city's search. Nathan had been beyond surprised when the same group of soldiers had then ridden south with them.

After Lakeborough, Fenidar tried to resume the overly brisk pace but Nathan had successfully argued against riding through the night again, insisting men and horses needed rest to remain effective. Fenidar had initially listened to reason, but the saeljul grew increasing agitated as each day passed with no sign of the mages.

This evening, Fenidar's patience had ended.

After Cero had retrieved Nathan, the Red Sentinels' sergeant strode up to Fenidar and demanded to know what was so important that it could not wait until morning. Fenidar had ignored him. Nathan had looked over at Cero to see if he knew what this was about, but the man would not meet his eyes. Since the ijul had shown up, the Trackers had become Fenidar's lackeys.

Once the Southern Arms' sergeant arrived at the fork with Latius, Fenidar shared with them his "intense disappointment" that they had not caught up to the outlaws. As a result, the ijul was splitting their force into three groups: two were to head down the branches of the road, and the remaining one would head straight south into the forest.

Nathan had vehemently refused to split his men. Nevertheless, that was exactly what he had done, only managing to successfully argue that his contingent—the one heading south—not leave until morning. While traveling on the road at night was possible, heading through the forest was much too dangerous. An unexpected, unseen rabbit hole would cripple horses, forcing men to walk or double up and slowing everyone down.

Fenidar had been irritated, but nonetheless agreed to let Nathan and his group leave at first light and then push on as hard as they could. Fenidar had taken the Southern Arms with him, and sent Latius with the other half of the Sentinels led by Corporal Holb.

When Nathan had asked what they should do should they catch up to the outlaws, the ijul had assured him that Cero and Latius would know what to do.

Nathan kept an eye on his men's backs as they headed down the road, melting into the night. Occasionally, he would spot a stray flash of silver where the moons' light reflected off a helmet. When he had not seen a glint of moonlight for a while, he turned and headed back to camp to get some sleep. At dawn, he was heading into a forest about which he knew nothing to chase an enemy about which he knew little. All under the orders of an ijul he did not trust.

With a disgusted grunt, he shook his head, and muttered, "This is a poor use of good soldiers."

CHAPTER 39: BULLOCKBOAR

Zecus' world was completely, utterly black. The only breaks to the darkness were the rhythmic white flashes paired with thudding bursts of pain in his head. Upon realizing his eyes were drawn tight, he cracked them open and was rewarded with bright torrent of sunlight searing his eyes. He blinked against the brilliance, trying to focus on his surroundings.

In front of him was a mass of bulging, undulating, dirty pink and mud-brown hide splotched with patches of black fur. He stared, watching as it heaved repeatedly in a constant pattern. It took him a moment to fight through the thick cobwebs coating his thoughts before reasoning that he was lying across the back of some sort of animal as it walked. With the realization came a flood of smells—a mixture of animal waste, slop, and musty sweat. He grimaced, wondering how he had not smelled the malodorous concoction sooner. He could almost taste it.

He tried to lift his head a bit to get a better idea of his surroundings, but was unable to summon the strength. His nose and ears might be starting to work, but his muscles remained a step behind.

Rather than lifting his head, he tried to roll it to the right to alleviate the pain on his left temple. Using an extreme amount of effort relative to such a simple task, he swiveled his head successfully so that he was staring forward. A thick, gray, tree trunk filled his field of vision.

When the tree trunk moved, flexing like a muscle, recent events began to bubble from the depths of his memory, slowly allowing him to piece things together. The tree trunk was not a tree trunk. It was an oligurt's leg. And if that were the case, it meant Zecus was draped over the back of one of their mounts.

Besides the Sudashians he and his father had seen that day on the hill, there had been large, beastly creatures grazing the dry grasslands that resembled a cross between a plains boar, a bear, and a wild dog. Zecus' father had named them bullockboars.

For reasons unknown, Zecus' assailants had not killed him. Rather, they had apparently strapped him to a bullockboar's back and were taking him with them. Although, wherever that might be, Zecus doubted he wanted to go.

He tried to move his hands and feet, but found both bound tight, his arms wrapped behind his back and tied at the wrist. Rope dug into his legs, just above his boot tops. As he struggled with his bonds, a deep, guttural sound came from behind his bullockboar.

"Rorrargh! Udok rauthil!"

The sound of leather creaking beside him sent a rush of panic through Zecus' chest, providing him a shot of energy that allowed him to lift his head. He stared up, straight into the black eyes of the oligurt riding the bullockboar.

Its grayish green lips with the yellowed fangs grinned at him as a massive fist hurtled toward his head. Again, Zecus reacted too late, but still managed to turn his head, softening the blow a bit. A brilliant flash of lights exploded, rivaling the bright evening sun.

His world went black. Again.

CHAPTER 40: NUDGE

26th of the Turn of Sutri

Nundle sat on the back of his small chestnut horse, repeatedly glancing between the two branches of road and wondering if he was making the right decision. The dirt-covered campfires of the soldiers' camp were cold, yet the smell of wood smoke still hung in the air. The morning sun hung low in the eastern sky, already threatening to turn the day hot and uncomfortable yet again.

He released a long, drawn-out sigh and, pushing aside any last bit of doubt, urged his horse straight south with a determined "Get on!" Nundle and horse moved off the road and down a small, rocky decline spotted with shrubs and grass.

Once engulfed by the thinning forest, Nundle set to following the tracks of the soldiers' horses. As it turned out, his worry over being able to follow them through the wilderness was unfounded. The markings of fifty horses tromping through virgin forest would be difficult for anyone but a blind person to miss. He kept a careful ear out for sounds that did not belong in a forest, listening for anything beyond birds singing, animals scurrying, and trees creaking with each gust of wind.

The day passed without event but as evening approached, he began to grow uneasy. He had no idea what the terrain ahead was like. Should the soldiers move into an area where tracking became too difficult for his meager skills, he was afraid he might lose them. Yet if he rode too long, he might accidentally overtake them and ride straight into their camp.

Looking west, he stared through the drooping branches. Dusk was near. He pulled his horse to a stop and considered his options while eyeing the sky, debating himself if he should stop or continue. Suddenly, a loud voice shot through the clearing.

"Hold right there!"

Nundle jumped and nearly fell from his saddle. Twisting his head in all directions, searching for the source of what most definitely was an order, he threw his arms up in the air and shouted, "I'm unarmed!"

As soon as the words left his lips, he realized what a profoundly brainless thing it was to say. He had assumed the cry belonged to a soldier, and his instinct was to convey that he was not a threat. Yet it was possible the yell came from some random bandit who would now see Nundle as an easy mark.

He continued to hold his hands over his head, thinking that if he dropped them now, the bandit or soldier might assume he was reaching for a weapon. Peering through trees and brush, he spotted a red and black figure skulking toward him, sword drawn, and sighed with relief. Not a bandit.

His relief was brief, however, as he realized that the very soldiers he had hoped to avoid had just captured him. He wondered if he should turn his horse and crash off through the forest.

"If you bolt, I'll order my man to shoot!" called the soldier.

Nundle quickly scanned the trees and bushes around the longleg and saw nothing.

"I assure you he is there," said the soldier. "With an arrow drawn and orders to shoot if you run."

Nundle eyed the longleg, wondering if he was bluffing.

The doubt on Nundle's face must have been clear for the soldier twisted his head around and shouted, "Hollins! A warning, please!"

The faint twang of bowstring—somewhere to Nundle's right—was followed an instant later by a soft, whistling whoosh rushing past him, an arm's length from his nose. Hearing a loud thunk to his left, Nundle turned to spot an arrow embedded in a tree a dozen paces away, the shaft and black feather fletching quivering. Looking back to where he thought the shot had originated, he scanned the trees and bushes, but could not see anything.

Sagging in the saddle, Nundle sighed and swiveled to face the Sentinel with the sword. The longleg stood less than a dozen paces away, staring at Nundle with an equal mixture of curiosity and caution.

Giving the soldier the friendliest smile he could manage, Nundle asked, "Why are you firing upon a simple traveler, good man?" He tried to sound jovial, but his nerves added a tremor to his voice.

"Simple traveler, eh?" The longleg's gaze danced over Nundle, taking in his clothes, small horse, and traveling bags. "Rather far from home, aren't you?"

Nundle remained quiet. The longleg had no idea how right he was.

A moment later, the soldier asked, "Why you are following us?"

Nundle decided to play ignorant. "Following who?" Turning his head in all directions, he made a show of scanning the forest. "How could I be following you if I did not know you were there?"

"You, little sir, are a liar."

"I swear I did not know I was following anyone. Truly."

The soldier sheathed his sword, apparently deciding that Nundle was not much of a threat. He did not give an order for the mysterious, hidden bowman to stand down, though. "Say I do not believe you, little traveler. Instead, let us say that you know all about the soldiers traveling ahead of you."

"Soldiers? What soldiers? There are soldiers—"

Raising his voice, the longleg interrupted, saying, "*And* we know that you have been trailing us for the better part of the day."

Nundle felt a flicker of pride. They thought he had only been following them for today. He thought the title, "Nundle Babblebrook, Master Woodsman" had a nice sound to it.

He shook his head. "Truly, I know nothing about any soldiers."

"Then why are you in these woods? Why stray from the roads? Seems an odd choice."

Nundle stared at the longleg in silence, his mind racing for a logical answer. After a moment, he offered, "Perhaps I enjoy the wilderness?" It was a weak reason and the soldier knew it.

"End the show, little playman. Hollins and I have been watching you since midday. And you, despite your claims, have been following our path straight away."

Eyebrows arching, Nundle asked, "Since midday?" He rescinded his self-granted title of "Master Woodsman."

The longleg nodded once. "Since midday. Now, care to answer my question?"

"That depends. Which one?"

"Why are you following us?"

Nundle remained quiet, biting his lip, trying to think of any way out of this that did not involve using magic. Coming up with nothing, he let out a long sigh and stared at the soldier. "Let's say I am simply curious why soldiers of the Great Lakes are traipsing about the Southlands?"

"Ah…now we're getting somewhere," said the soldier.

"Care to answer *my* question?"

"I think it's best I let the Master Sergeant address that. Lucky for you, you'll have a chance to ask him soon enough."

Without thought, Nundle asked, "Might he be the tall one with the long dark hair and beard?" At once, he regretted his bumble.

The soldier's eyes narrowed sharply. "Just how long have you been following us?"

Nundle stared at the longleg, gave a weak grin, and shrugged. "Ah…well…" Deciding that it was a good idea to keep his mouth shut, he said, "Take me to this 'Master Sergeant' of yours and I can explain."

"You most definitely will." The Red Sentinel stepped close and grasped the bridle of Nundle's hors. "Now, hop down. I don't want you trying to ride off on us."

Nundle began the arduous task of dismounting, first swinging his right leg back over the horse's rear, then, while holding one side of the saddle, his slid his belly along the horse's flank, letting his legs dangle in the air.

"Do you need help?" asked the soldier, concern in his voice.

"No, thank you," grunted Nundle. He let go and landed on the ground, managing not to fall over as he had the first few times he had dismounted. Turning around to peer up at the soldier, Nundle smiled. "You should see me try to get on the beast." He stared at the chestnut. "Or saddle him. I bought the smallest one I could find but…" He shrugged and stared at the longleg again. "There's a reason tombles don't ride horses."

A grin crept over the soldier's face. "I suppose so." Swiveling to the west, he shouted, "Hollins! Let's go!"

Curious as to where the bowman was hiding, Nundle peeked under his horse' neck and was shocked when a solider stepped from behind a tree nearly two hundred paces away.

"That was quite a shot from that distance," muttered Nundle.

The soldier standing with him said, "It was. Which surprises me. Hollins isn't very good with a bow. In fact—" He stopped and turned to the approaching soldier. "Hey, Hollins! What were you aiming for?"

"His hat!"

Nundle's stomach dropped. Looking up at the soldier holding his horse, he asked, "Good thing he missed wide and not low, eh?"

The soldier set off to the south, leading Nundle's chestnut horse by the reins. Nundle followed while Hollins brought up the rear. They moved through the forest until the sun was a giant glob of red peeking through trunks and branches.

Nundle smelled the soldiers' camp first, smoky campfires and charred wood mixing with something scrumptious cooking. His stomach growled. Shortly after, the sounds of soldiers talking and laughing, pots banging, and metal clanking metal filtered through the trees.

Nundle and the two soldiers emerged from the trees and into a large clearing. As they walked through the camp, the Red Sentinels stopped whatever they were doing to stare at him as he strolled past. Figuring it was best to be polite, Nundle smiled and nodded. Most nodded back, a few even returned his smile.

Hurrying to draw even with the longleg leading his horse, he said, "I take it most of them have never seen a tomble?"

The soldier shook his head. "Some have. Although I bet they could count how many on a clumsy woodcutter's hand. For some, I suspect you're their first."

"You didn't stare at me like they are."

With a quiet chuckle, the soldier said, "Because you aren't a novelty to me." He glanced down, adding, "I'm originally from the Foothills." The way in which he spoke indicated he believed that explained everything.

Not grasping the implication, Nundle said, "I don't understand." His response drew an odd look from the soldier.

Furrows split the longleg's forehead. "I'm from Rodrics Field." Again, it was as if that should be sufficient to clarify things.

Nundle shook his head. "I'm sorry, but I am unfamiliar with the area."

The longleg looked as confused as Nundle felt. "Rodrics Field. You know— the city within a day's ride of the Four Towns?" He might be trying to make things clearer, yet was failing miserably.

Baffled, Nundle asked, "And what might the Four Towns be?"

The soldier slowed his step and peered down at Nundle, his eyes narrowed. "The Four Towns. The tomble villages?"

Nundle nearly tripped over his feet. "Tomble villages? Where?"

"I just told you. In the Foothills, just west—" He cut off and stared at Nundle for a moment before asking, "Where exactly are you from, little one?"

"Deepwell," said Nundle. "In the Thimbletoe Province. You know, the Five Boroughs?"

Understanding washed over the soldier's face. "Oh! I had just assumed you were from one of the Four Towns. Poor assumption on my part. My apologies."

"To be clear, you're saying there are tombles living in the Foothills Duchy?"

The soldier nodded. "I am. In four separate towns. Hence the rather unoriginal name."

"Why?"

"Why the name?" asked the soldier. He shrugged his shoulders. "I couldn't—"

"No! Why are there tombles living in the Oaken Duchies?" Besides a few places towns scattered just inside the borders of Cartu, he had never heard of a tomble settlement outside the Five Boroughs.

"Ah," mused the man. "I misunderstood. Well, let's see...I once knew this tomble from Tinfiddle. I recall him saying they all left a while back because of..." He trailed off, his face scrunching up in thought. After a moment, he shrugged his shoulders. "Hells, I don't know. Bumbar talked too much. I rarely paid attention."

Nundle stared at the man in quiet awe. "Bumbar" was certainly a tomble name. "You don't know which province they came from, do you?"

The soldier peered down at him. "You're asking questions I couldn't hope to answer."

Nundle asked a few more anyway, and all remained unanswered. Falling back a few steps, he tried to make sense of what he had just learned. On top of everything else, Nundle now had a new set of questions about something else entirely.

The soldiers led Nundle and horse to a small group of longlegs sitting between two tents. The tall, bearded Red Sentinel sat at their center, talking with the others. The moment he noticed Nundle, he stood and scrutinized the tomble. Nundle stared back as the soldiers who had captured him gave their "Master Sergeant" a quick, concise report.

Once they were finished, the bearded soldier turned his full attention on to Nundle. "So, little tomble, mind telling me why you are following us?"

Nundle had wanted this meeting to occur later—perhaps a day or two from now—but fate had nudged him along a little earlier than he would have liked.

"Happily," said Nundle. "But in private, please. If you don't mind, sir." The use of the word "sir" prompted a few soft chuckles from nearby soldiers, their mirth cut short by a sharp glare from the sergeant.

"First off, I am not a 'sir.' You may call me 'Master Sergeant,' 'Sergeant Trell,' or just 'Sergeant.'"

Not entirely understanding why it mattered, Nundle agreed to the request. "Yes, Master Sergeant."

"Better. Now, should you like to speak in private, we will still have to do it out here in the open somewhere. I am without my normal command tent."

"I know," said Nundle with purpose. Wanting to draw the longleg's full interest, he added, "It headed southwest last night with the Southern Arms." It appeared he succeeded. The sergeant's brow furrowed as the soldiers sitting on the ground nearby glanced at one another, mirroring their leader's expression.

The sergeant frowned. "Follow me, please." He ordered Nundle's horse be tended to and began walking away from the campfire. Nundle followed.

They headed up a small hill upon which stood a massive oak tree, its sprawling, mature branches spreading far over the grass like a top-heavy mushroom. As they walked, the sergeant slowed, allowing Nundle to catch up with him, and then looked down. "I must say, your horse is the smallest I've ever seen, Mister...?" He trailed off, expecting Nundle to give his name.

"I will share my name when I feel I can trust you."

The sergeant nodded, accepting his answer. "Fair enough. Please understand if I am equally cautious about you."

"Of course, Sergeant." Tilting his head back, he stared up at the longleg. "How did you know I was following you?"

The soldier shrugged. "Something told me to keep an eye behind me today. Although—" he glanced down and gave Nundle a friendly smile "—you are *not* what I expected."

Nundle grinned back.

Stopping by the large oak's trunk, the sergeant motioned around them. "This is as private as it gets, little one."

Nundle looked around him. The previous days' forest was mostly gone now, the area dominated mostly by tall grass and shrubs. Content that they were alone, the tomble stared up at the soldier. "Before I begin, I feel it necessary to say two things. First, despite what I plan to share with you, please understand that I have only the best interest of you, your men, and all of the Oaken Duchies in mind."

The longleg's eyes narrowed. "That sounds rather ominous."

"Probably because it is."

Frowning, the sergeant asked, "And the second?"

"I want your word that you will listen to my entire tale before you take any action or make any decision."

"You are not in the position to make such a demand."

"Then consider it a polite request rather than a demand."

The soldier remained quiet for a long moment, his gaze locked on Nundle's face. "As you ask something I would mostly likely do anyway, I see no reason not to give my word." He gave a single, firm nod. "I will hear you out."

Nundle released a breath he had not recalled holding and peered up to the soldier. "Do you trust your men, Master Sergeant?"

The sergeant answered without hesitation. "With my life."

"And what about the Tracker with you?"

The longleg crossed his arms over his chest and frowned. "Exactly how long have you been following us?"

"Truthfully? Since Lakeborough."

Sergeant Trell's gaze bored into him. Nundle forced himself to stare back, meeting the soldier's eyes for what seemed like an eternity. Finally, the longleg sighed and motioned to the grass. "Let's sit. I feel rude talking down to you." Nundle found a gnarled oak root jutting from the soil upon which he sat. The sergeant settled across from him, flat on the grass so they were near eye-level with each other.

Once seated, the sergeant said, "To answer your question: no, I do not trust the Tracker. He seemed a decent man when we met. But now?" He glanced back to the camp, a perplexed expression on his face, and gave a tiny shake of his head. "Not so much." Looking back to Nundle, he added, "His name is Cero. But perhaps you already knew that as well?"

"I did not. Although I did know the name of another in your company. One who left last evening."

"Who?"

Watching the sergeant's face carefully, Nundle said with emphasis, "Jhaell Myrr." He expected anything from simple acknowledgement to a passionate curse regarding the ijul. Instead, he received a blank expression.

"I'm sorry. Who?"

"Jhaell Myrr," repeated Nundle, confused.

Sergeant Trell shook his head. "I know of no man by that name. Was he in the Arms?"

Nundle was dumbfounded. Upon finding his tongue, he said, "I've watched you travel with him for days now. I've seen your disagreements with him. Hells—I saw you arguing with him at the fork last night. I thought he was going—"

"Hold a moment," interrupted Sergeant Trell. "Are you speaking of Fenidar?"

"Fenidar?" Now it was Nundle's turn to be confused. "Who's Fenidar? I'm talking about the saeljul, Jhaell Myrr."

Sergeant Trell's eyebrows drew together. "I know him as Fenidar."

"Fenidar?" repeated Nundle again. Bewildered, he stared at the ground, mumbling, "Why the false name? I mean, perhaps he's afraid of being marked a mage, but nobody here would know that on name—"

The sergeant held up a quick hand. "Hold. He's a *mage*? Regent Alpert said nothing about that."

Mystified, Nundle asked, "Who is Regent Alpert?"

Nundle had been hoping that his conversation with the Red Sentinels' leader would provide some clarity to recent events. Instead, his list of questions was getting longer while his list of answers remained blank.

Waving his hands in front of him, Nundle said, "Let's start with something simple. The saeljul you've been traveling with I know as Preceptor Jhaell Myrr. He's a teacher of magic at the Academy at Immylla in the Arcane Republic. I was a student of his." He grimaced. "Briefly."

Sergeant Trell's eyebrows rose. "*You're* a mage?"

"I am," said Nundle. Considering his location, he felt it necessary to add, "A nice one, though. As most of us are."

The sergeant looked back to the camp, concern rippling over his face. "How is it the Tracker did not know?"

"From what I've observed, they are no different than any mage when it comes to detecting magic. If I don't reach for the Strands near him, he'll never know what I am."

"The Strands?" muttered Sergeant Trell. "What are—" He cut off, lifted a hand, and paused a moment. "It would seem we both hold different clues to the same riddle. Why don't you start at the beginning and tell me what you know about Fenidar, or whatever his name is."

Nundle smiled. That was his plan all along.

He told Sergeant Trell everything that had happened since he had taken the parchment in the preceptor's office, save for the contents of the letter. He was holding that for later. The sergeant listened to his story, interrupting only to ask the occasional intelligent question. By the time he reached the end of his tale, Sergeant Trell had dropped his head to his chest and was staring at the ground. Even after Nundle stopped talking, the soldier did not move.

Nundle waited, silent.

He was beginning to think he should say something when the soldier finally looked up. "I tend to be a good judge of a man—or tomble, I suppose—and I do not think you are playing me for a fool. You say this ijul was a teacher of magic from the Arcane Republic and I believe you. It explains much."

Nundle was relieved that the soldier believed him.

"But I have one question for you, tomble."

"Ask away."

Sergeant Trell leaned forward, draping his arms over his legs and clasping his hands in front of him. "You took rather drastic action based on a single letter. A letter about which I've noticed you've been deliberately vague. What did the message say?"

Nodding, Nundle said, "Granted, I have been vague. But only because its words might be hard for you to accept."

The soldier gave him a grim smile. "I've accepted this much, haven't I?"

Sighing, Nundle reached into his leather travel pack, retrieved the parchment, and handed the letter over to the longleg. The sergeant unfolded it and held it up to catch the last bit of twilight, his face going through a series of expressions as he read: curiosity, sadness, anger, confusion, betrayal, and finally shock and disbelief.

When he was done, the sergeant waved the parchment in his hand and asked in a quiet, yet harsh, voice, "Do you realize who this is from?"

"I do now," said Nundle, his tone grave. "When I first saw the letter, I was focused on what it said rather than whom it was from. When I discovered your duke's name, I thought perhaps it might be a coincidence, but…I don't think so anymore."

The sergeant did not reply. He was reading the letter a second time. "Too much of this rings true for me to discount it. This, for instance: '*claimed a giant flood had destroyed the town.*'" He stared at Nundle, his eyes intense. "Tomble, *I stood in the ruins of Yellow Mud. I saw the destruction with my own eyes.*"

Nundle found that to be a rather surprising coincidence.

Sergeant Trell looked back to the letter. "And this? '*Killing everyone except a man he had met on the road to Smithshill.*'" He held up the parchment. "I met that same man. I *spoke* with him."

Nundle's eyebrows drew together. That definitely crossed the line dividing happenstance from destiny.

The sergeant continued, shaking his head in dismay. "But if I accept all that as truth, I must believe the rest as well. Which is madness."

"I can sympathize," said Nundle. "When I discovered my teacher was involved with something as sinister as what that letter describes, I was shocked. I knew I needed to do something to warn them."

"Warn who?" Tilting the parchment to catch the last rays of sunlight, the sergeant asked, "These... 'Progeny?'" He looked to Nundle. "Who are they?"

Lifting his eyebrows, Nundle murmured, "That, Sergeant, is the most important part of the story." The wind shifted, bringing with it a waft of whatever the soldiers were cooking. Nundle's stomach grumbled. "Ah...might we get something to eat, perhaps? I've had nothing but blueberries for days."

Sergeant Trell immediately called over to the camp for two bowls of stew. The soldier who brought them apologized to Nundle for the size of the wooden bowl and spoon, saying that they did not have anything smaller. Nundle insisted that the giant bowl was just fine and set to devouring the stew.

The sergeant did not pester him with questions as they ate, instead making idle conversation about how they were running out of vegetables and roots and would soon need to hunt for food or find a place to purchase supplies.

Nundle's stomach filled before the bowl emptied. He set the remainder of the stew aside and let his food settle for a moment. Blue Moon had risen over the trees to the north, a pale oblong oval against a backdrop of stars, only the brightest of which were visible in the late dusk sky.

A quick examination of the camp revealed most of the soldiers sitting around their campfires, staring at Nundle and the sergeant. The Tracker stood off to the side by himself, his gaze locked on Nundle alone, the rather unsettling expression he wore lit by the campfires' flickering. For reasons unknown, Nundle shuddered and looked back to Sergeant Trell.

"Thank you for the meal. Much better than a handful of blueberries."

"You are quite welcome," answered the soldier as he put down his own bowl. Picking up the preceptor's letter, he asked, "Do you suppose we can continue?"

"Of course," said Nundle. He paused, gathering his thoughts while wondering how the longleg might take this next bit of information. "Have you ever heard of the White Lions?"

A deep furrow split the soldier's brow. "I've heard the legends."

In a somewhat cryptic tone, Nundle asked, "What if I said that their epic was not legend?"

Sergeant Trell paused a moment before replying with newfound skepticism. "I would say you have a great deal of talking ahead of you to convince me you're not mad."

As succinctly as he could, Nundle covered the history of the Oaken Duchies up to the inception of the White Lions. He explained what had happened with the Assembly of Nine in the Celestial Empire, and how the White Lions had repelled the demon army of Norasim. The sergeant nodded at the parts that sounded familiar to him, and listened with patient interest at the new. When Nundle reached the tale of the scourging of the Carinius coast, the sergeant interrupted.

"That part always bothered me."

"Why?"

"They were heroes, honored servants of the duchies. Then suddenly they kill thousands of people?" He shook his head. "It never made sense."

"I would agree. And once you hear Indrida's prophecy, I expect you might draw a different conclusion as to what happened at Carinius."

A frown creased Sergeant Trell's face. "What prophecy?"

Nundle recited the three stanzas, word for word. Sergeant Trell listened, the frown on his face deepening into a full scowl by the time Nundle was finished. "That's a nice verse, but what does it mean?"

Shrugging his shoulders, Nundle said, "I'm not entirely sure. But when I saw that letter, when I saw 'the Progeny,' I had to act." With a start, he realized that the sergeant still held the parchment. "Speaking of which—I don't suppose I could have that back now?" It was the only proof Nundle had that some sort of conspiracy was taking place.

The sergeant paused a moment, worrying Nundle that he might not give it back, but then reached over and handed the letter over. "You have given me much to consider, tomble."

"Please, call me Nundle, Nundle Babblebrook." There was little point in hiding his name now that he had told the sergeant everything else.

Sergeant Trell gave him a polite nod and smile. "Good days ahead to you, Nundle Babblebrook."

"You, as well, Sergeant."

The sergeant's smile widened. "You're in the duchies now, Nundle. You'll need to act as such if you want people to stop staring. The expected response is 'And good memories behind.'"

"Well, then. My apologies." Reciprocating the nod and smile, Nundle said, "And good memories behind, Master Sergeant."

"And as long as I'm correcting you, feel free to call me Nathan. You aren't in the army. But please, only in private. In front of the men, I remain Sergeant Trell. Is that understood?"

"Completely, Sergeant—ah, Nathan."

With a satisfied nod, Nathan said, "Now, any other unbelievable tales you are going to ask me to accept as truth?"

Nundle smiled and shook his head. "Not tonight."

"Good. Then let me tell you what I know of our riddle, and we'll try to figure out what to do about it all."

Nundle leaned forward, anxious. "Please do."

Sitting beneath the grand oak, the pair talked deep into the night.

CHAPTER 41: FARM

27ᵗʰ of the Turn of Sutri

Nikalys was miserable.

Day after day of sitting in Goshen's saddle, the horse's jagged backbone digging into his rear, was enough to drive him mad. His muscles were sore, his skin raw, and his bones weary. He tried not to focus on his suffering, but as he spent his entire day staring at endless, uninterrupted fields of grass, he could not help it.

Growing up, he had never been a stranger to backbreaking work. Mornings after long, dawn-to-dusk days in the groves or vineyards would certainly find him sore. Yet his body had never ached like this. He twisted in his saddle—yet again—trying to stretch out his back but there was no relief to be had.

Before this journey, he had only sat on a horse to satisfy a dare from friends. If you wanted to travel somewhere, you hitched the horse to a cart and rode to your destination while sitting on a nice, comfortable, wooden seat. Nikalys missed that seat. Perched atop the back of a bony horse, being jarred, jumbled, and jostled all day long was a horrible way to travel.

"That's it," he muttered to himself. "I've had enough."

He pulled on Goshen's reins, drawing the horse to a standstill. Slowly, painfully, he lifted his right leg over the horse's rear. Bending his left leg—foot in stirrup—he stretched his right to the ground as every muscle in his legs screamed at him. Once both boots were on the ground, he sighed, relishing the wondrous sensation of not being on the horse. A tiny, relieved smile touched his lips.

Taking advantage of the pause in travel, Goshen bent his head to the ground, ripped a mouthful of Southlands grass, and looked back at him. If a horse could smile, Nikalys thought Goshen would be doing so right now. The horses certainly enjoyed the unending prairie.

A little ahead of him, Jak spoke. "Something wrong?"

Looking up, Nikalys found his brother—still astride Hal—stopped a few horse-lengths ahead and staring back. Beyond Jak, Kenders and Broedi continued moving through the grass, her atop Smoke and the hillman striding beside her.

"I've had it, Jak. My rear—Hells, all of me—hurts. I'm going to walk for a bit."

Grabbing Goshen's reins, he took a few halting steps, his face contorting into a twisted bundle of scowls and winces. Thighs, knees, calves, and ankles complained with each movement.

"You look like an old man," teased Jak, grinning. "Shall I ride off and find you a walking stick?"

Nikalys glared at his brother. "Please do. I need something to knock that smile off your face." Parts of him started to loosen, but he still moved slowly. Upon reaching where Jak waited, he nodded to where Broedi and Kenders were quickly outpacing them and said, "You know, for someone with six senses, you'd think his hearing would be better. They don't even seem to realize we've stopped."

At that exact moment, Broedi halted and, putting a hand on Smoke's neck, stopped Kenders as well. The hillman turned halfway and stared back at the brothers.

Nikalys' eyes narrowed. "Show-off."

With his own moans and grunts, Jak dismounted and the brothers walked side-by-side. Glancing over, Nikalys found Jak walking as gingerly as he was. Throwing a friendly elbow at his brother's side, he said, "Looks like you need to find two walking sticks."

"Hey, I'm every bit as sore as you are. The only difference is *you* are the one complaining like a girl."

From up ahead, Kenders shouted, "I don't appreciate that!"

Both brothers turned and looked toward their sister. She and Broedi were still a hundred paces away.

Jak leaned over and whispered, "How did she hear that?"

Nikalys lifted an eyebrow and murmured, "I think she's been holding out on us."

They continued their approach, silent now, walking through the ever-present, waist-high grass. Kenders glared at them both, a stern expression upon her face. As they drew near, Jak smiled wide and asked, "Have I told you how beautiful you look today, sis?"

The compliment did nothing to chase away Kenders' frown. "Truly, Jak? 'Complaining like a girl?'"

Jak's grin slipped a bit. "So you heard that?"

"I did."

Looking between Broedi and Kenders, Nikalys asked, "Magic, I suppose?"

Broedi rumbled, "A simple Weave of Air and Soul." He shifted his gaze to Kenders. "We have been working on it all morning. Only now did she get the pattern correct."

Jak said, "What wondrous timing for us."

Nikalys smiled, happy not to be the target of Kenders ire. Taking a moment, he turned his head, staring out at the endless prairie around them. "Broedi, is the entire Southlands one giant field of grass?"

"No, uori, it is not," rumbled the hillman. "And had you not stopped, you would have never asked the question." Broedi faced south and resumed walking, leaving the three siblings behind.

Jak called after the hillman, "What does that mean?"

Broedi did not stop nor look back.

Nikalys peered up at Kenders, thinking she might have an explanation.

With a shrug of her shoulders, she said, "Don't look at me. I haven't the slightest idea what he's talking about."

The three of them set off after the hillman, Kenders urging Smoke into a quick trot, while Nikalys and Jak hurried on with their horses in tow. Up ahead, Broedi had stopped again and was still facing south. The line of grass appeared to fall away right past where he stood.

When Kenders halted beside Broedi, she turned back and waved her hand to Nikalys and Jak, urging them to hurry. Gritting his teeth, Nikalys broke into a slow jog, wincing as new muscles revealed their aching presence. Jak shuffled alongside, his quiet groans mimicking Nikalys' grunts.

Upon arriving beside Kenders and Broedi, they stopped. Apparently, the Southlands were not one, endless prairie.

They stood atop a gradual slope leading into a shallow valley, at the bottom of which flowed a wide, muddy river less than a quarter mile away. Halfway between them and the riverbank sat a river-rock cottage—no bigger than the Isaac home in Yellow Mud—topped with a pitched roof of bundled prairie grass, dried and bound with cords.

On the side of the building that faced them was a single, closed door along with two uneven holes no bigger than a water bucket. Well-tended fields flanked the cottage, each filled with a variety of vegetable crops. A half-dozen chickens strutted around the four-wheeled wagon sitting before the home. Seven horses—all under saddle—stood beside the wagon, their reins leading to the cart and tied off.

Jak said good-naturedly, "Look at that. Someone went and ruined the prairie by putting a river—"

A woman's raw, knifelike scream cut Jak short, shattering the stillness of the prairie and turning Nikalys' insides cold.

"Noooooooooo!"

The door to the house burst open and a small girl—no older than four or five—with long black hair ran out. Dressed in a common tan field-dress, she scurried away from the house, crying and screaming. Her terrified shouts, while awful, did not match the soul-rending shriek from a moment ago. A burly, bearded man emerged from the house, following the girl. The toddler looked back at him and screamed even louder, her eyes wide open.

Before he knew what he was doing, Nikalys let go Goshen's reins and was running down the slope, vaguely aware that Broedi was rushing along beside him.

From inside the building, through the open door, a woman screamed, "Run, Helene!" The voice matched the first, ear-splitting scream.

Nikalys watched in horror as the man trailing the toddler drew a longknife from a sheath on his belt.

From atop the hill, Kenders shouted, "No!"

Both the man and little girl looked up the slope. The toddler screamed louder and shifted directions, aiming for the tall grass east of the farm. The man paused a moment, his wide-eyed gaze darting between Nikalys and Broedi, before looking back to the fleeing girl. With a flick of his wrist, he flipped the knife in the air and caught it, switching his hold from handle to blade. He drew his arm back, preparing to throw it at the little girl.

Still two hundred paces away, Nikalys muttered, "Please work," stared at a spot right before the brigand—

Shift.

—and grabbed the man's wrist. Twisting hard, he felt and heard bones shatter.

The brigand dropped the knife, screaming in agony. The shocked look on his face lasted only a moment as Nikalys drove a fist into his nose with a loud, sickeningly wet crack. The bandit crumpled to the ground, landing in a heap beside his knife.

Expecting retaliation, Nikalys pulled his throbbing fist back and stared down at the man. He did not move. Nikalys' stomach soured as he wondered if he might have just killed the man.

"Nik!" Jak's shout pulled his attention from the bandit and back up the hill. Goshen and Hal stood alone at the hilltop, their reins dangling in the air. Kenders was thundering down on Smoke while Jak was running, arm outstretched and pointing to the house. "Turn around!"

Broedi, who was much closer, was also pointing. "Uori!"

Turning his head, Nikalys spotted four men rushing from the stone building, directly at him. They were dressed in dark, tattered clothes just as was the man he had just knocked out. Or killed.

"Oh, Hells..."

Three of them had swords drawn while the fourth held a thick wooden club. Nikalys considered drawing his own blade, but stayed his hand. He was more of a danger to himself with the sword out than a threat to the bandits.

Suddenly, a deafening, feral roar ripped through the air. The brigands rushing him skidded to a stop, staring beyond Nikalys with wide, fearful eyes. The cry startled Nikalys as well, yet he did not turn around. He knew what was behind him.

The enormous, golden-furred lynx sidled up to stand beside him, a low growl rumbling deep in its throat. The fowl around the wagon scattered, clucking and screeching as they flapped their wings and half-ran, half-flew away. The seven tethered horses—their eyes rolled up in their heads—whinnied in terror, repeatedly yanking their heads back in a futile attempt to free themselves.

Hearing hooves pounding behind him, he assumed Kenders was drawing ever closer. Jak would not be far behind.

The nearest brigand—a lean man with wild black hair and a shaggy beard—stared at Nikalys, his sword gripped tightly in his right hand, his gaze flicking to the still-sheathed Blade of Horum on Nikalys' hip. The man was probably wondering why Nikalys had yet to draw, a decision Nikalys was reconsidering, out of the corner of his eye, Kenders moved into view on the other side of Broedi.

Speaking in an anxious whisper, she asked, "What do we do!?"

As he had no idea, Nikalys kept quiet, his gaze darting between the bandits, the horse, and the house. Seven saddled horses meant seven men. With one unconscious—or dead—and four in front of them, Nikalys reasoned two men must still be inside the stone cottage.

Jak finally reached them and stopped beside Nikalys, his breathing heavy. "What now?"

The second person in mere moments asking for direction prompted Nikalys to hiss, "How should I know?"

"Hells, Nik! I thought you knew what you were doing—" He cut off, letting out a quiet, surprised "oomph."

Nikalys looked over and found Jak, chin on chest, staring at his stomach. Looking down, Nikalys spotted a white-fletched arrow shaft protruding from Jak's gut, just below the ribs. Jak took a step forward, stumbled, and began to fall to the ground. Nikalys reached out, caught his brother by the arm, and gently eased him to the grass. Jak's eyes were wide, seemingly more in shock than pain.

An anger hotter than a thousand bonfires burned inside Nikalys' chest. Staring into his brother's eyes, he said, "Lie still."

Nikalys stood and faced the brigands. None had a bow, meaning the arrow had come from within the house. He eyed the darkened doorway, expecting to see another shaft fly out at any moment, when a great whoosh of wind blew past him, shoving him in the back as it rushed toward the house. The roof launched high into the air, the bundles of grass ripped apart by the gust. Clumps still bound by cord dropped to the ground while individual blades floated down like harvest leaves from an oak.

A moment later, the wall with the door appeared to shimmer and shift. The river rocks lost their shape, crumbling and collapsing into a piled heap of sand. The door remained upright for a moment before tipping over, falling outward, and making a solid thud as it struck the ground.

Through falling grass and a cloud of dust rising from the sand, Nikalys spotted two men—one of whom held a bow—standing inside the ruined cottage, near where the door had been. A young woman stood in the back corner. All three were looking between the sky and the sand pile, most likely trying to figure out what had happened to the house. Nikalys certainly was.

The bowman recovered from his shock first. While yelling at the others to fight back, he pulled an arrow from a hip quiver, nocked it on the string, and raised the bow, preparing to fire.

Eyeing the dirt ground just beyond the former threshold of the home—
Shift.

—Nikalys grabbed the man's shirt with one arm and, somehow, lifted the man clear off the ground. The startled bandit dropped his weapon and clasped Nikalys' arm, smacking it. Bow and shaft struck an overturned table, clattering as they tumbled to the ground.

A vicious roar split the air behind him. A moment later, the men outside began to scream.

Holding the man suspended before him, Nikalys hesitated, unsure what to do next. His indecision cost him.

Pain exploded behind his right ear.

He dropped the man he held, stumbled forward a step or two, and collapsed to the house's dirt floor, falling to his hands and knees. He shook his head, blinking repeatedly, trying to chase away the tiny balls of lights flashing before him. Through the haze, he saw a pair of eyes staring up at him, blank and lifeless.

The body of a bearded man dressed in the simple tan clothes of a farmer lay next to him. A precise, clean cut spread from one side of the man's neck to the other. Crimson blood still oozed from the wound. The man appeared to be the right age to be the little girl's father.

The hot fury that surged through Nikalys again cleared his head in an instant. Pushing himself up so that he was kneeling, he whirled, expecting that the man who had hit him would come and finish him off. He was right.

An unclean man, both shorter and stockier than Nikalys, was advancing on him, a thick, wooden stick with a dark metal cylinder at the end, raised and ready to strike. Nikalys looked to a spot on the man's right—
Shift.

—wrenched the weapon free, and slammed it into the bandit's chest, eliciting a sickening crunch as metal smashed bone. Nikalys' gifted strength sent the man flying back to crash into one of the remaining walls. The brigand bounced as he hit the stone, slid down the wall, and slumped on the ground.

Nikalys was staring at the crumpled body, wondering if he had killed again when a rage-filled battle cry exploded to his right.

Spinning around, he found the other man charging him. Lifting the weapon he had just used, he found that he was holding nothing but a short handle of wood. The blow to the bandit's chest had snapped off the metal end. He was weaponless again.

A whistle of air kissed his ear. The man charging him stopped, threw his hands up to his face, and began screaming. A white-fletched arrow shaft protruded though his clasped fingers. From its placement, Nikalys guessed the other end was in the man's left eye.

A flood of crimson poured from the man's hands and down his face as he stumbled about the interior of the cottage, bumping into overturned chairs and tripping over the farmer's body. Screaming the entire time, he managed to make it to the small opening in the sand pile where the door used to be. Catching the edge of the pile, he tripped and fell atop the heap of pulverized wall. His movements turned wild and random for a few heartbeats before ceasing completely. His shrieking stopped.

Looking behind him, Nikalys found the young woman standing against the far wall of the cottage, holding the bandit's bow and staring at the body on the sand. She had killed the murderous bandit with his own bow and arrow; justice colored with irony.

She appeared to be near Nikalys' age—or perhaps Jak's—and wore a simple dress similar in color and style to that of the dead farmer. Her hair—long, glossy, and as black as a moonless night—framed a face with high cheekbones, dark eyes, and full lips. Nikalys thought she might be pretty were her face not a twisted mask of hatred and sorrow.

Nikalys took a step toward her. "Are you alright?"

She looked up at him and raised the bow up, holding it like a club. Her eyes, brown and large, burned with a cold fury.

Nikalys held his hands up. "Don't worry, I'm not going to—"

"Nik!" cried Kenders, her voice filled with panic. "*Nik!*"

Glancing to the front of the house, he saw Broedi—as a hillman again— kneeling on the ground beside Jak. Kenders was sitting with Jak's head resting in her lap, but staring at him in the house.

Forgetting the girl, Nikalys ran to the sand pile, leaped over it and dashed toward his brother. He passed the bodies of the four other brigands from outside, all of whom were most definitely dead, the chunks of flesh missing from their necks rather indicative of their condition.

Skidding to a halt, he dropped to a knee beside his brother. "Oh, gods…"

Jak had clasped his blood soaked hands over his stomach where the arrow stuck out. He was coughing, each hack sending more frothy blood dribbling down his cheeks to drip on Kenders' green dress. A frustrated Broedi was trying desperately to get Jak to let go of the arrow shaft.

"Uori! Please! I must take a look."

Nikalys felt helpless. He placed his hands on his head, fingers interlocked.

Jak's wide-open eyes repeatedly shifted between the arrow and the faces peering down at him. Kenders joined with Broedi, pleading for Jak to release the arrow and let the hillman look at the wound. Nikalys remained quiet, unable to find his tongue to speak.

Finally, when Jak moved his hands aside, Broedi ripped open his shirt, wiped away the excess blood, and began probing the area around where the arrow was lodged. With each poke and prod, Jak let out a small, pain-filled gasp. After a few moments, the hillman relaxed. "You will be fine. It looks worse than it is."

Nikalys stared at the hillman. "Are you sure?" He wanted to be relieved, but was wary.

"Quite," rumbled Broedi. He looked to Kenders. "Uora?"

She did not respond, her gaze remaining fixed on the bloody arrow wound. "Uora!"

Startled, Kenders looked up, her eyes full of worry and—this surprised Nikalys—utter exhaustion. She appeared as if she was going to pass out at any moment.

"Your kaveli will be fine," rumbled Broedi. "I can help him heal this. Please, go find the little one that ran. Be gentle. She will be scared."

Nikalys glanced to the grasslands southeast of the farm, having forgotten all about the toddler. Not seeing her anywhere, he figured she must be hiding in grass.

A woman's voice called, "Hold a moment!"

Turning back to the house, he found the raven-haired young woman approaching them. Her gaze danced over each of them several times, cautious and judging. In a firm tone, she said, "You all stay where you are."

"We mean you no harm," rumbled Broedi, his tone gentle.

"Sweet words can hide sour intentions. You stay here. I'll find my sister on my own." With that, the woman began to march toward the eastern grasslands.

Staring after her, Kenders muttered in disbelief, "Sour intentions? We risked our lives for them."

"Imagine you are her, uora," cautioned Broedi. "She does not know us from the bandits who assaulted them. Trust is earned, not given."

"We saved them," insisted Kenders.

"And I saved you from three wolves, yet none of you trusted me for a week."

Kenders' mouth was already open, some sort of protest ready, but Broedi's rather salient point squashed it.

"Hey!" said Jak through hissing breaths. "Can we please get the arrow out?"

"Of course, uori."

Nikalys glanced back to the woman and noticed she was heading in the wrong direction. The little girl had ended up running more to the south.

Kenders must have marked the same thing. "She's going to need help whether she likes it or not. That's the wrong way." Letting out a sigh, she bent over and gave Jak a small kiss on his forehead. "Don't you die on me."

Through gritted teeth, Jak grunted, "Wouldn't consider it."

Kenders placed Jak's head on the grass, rose, and hurried away after the young woman, calling out and pointing in the direction that the toddler had run. The black-haired woman stopped and eyed Kenders for a moment, her stare wary. Soon, however, the pair was walking together through the waist-high grass. Gentle calls of "Helene" filled the air.

A gasp of pain pulled Nikalys' his attention back to Jak. Reaching down, he patted his brother's shoulder. "You're going to be fine."

"I certainly hope so."

Broedi was prodding around the wound again. Stopping, he looked up and stared into Jak's eyes. "Are you ready?"

"Is it going to hurt?"

"Very much so."

Nikalys grabbed Jak's right hand and held it. Jak squeezed back, shut his eyes, and clenched his teeth. "Go."

Rather than pull it out, Broedi placed his hands on both sides of the arrow. Moments later, the shaft began to wiggle and withdraw from Jak's stomach seemingly on its own. Nikalys winced, gritting his own teeth as Jak's grip grew so tight that he was afraid bones might break. In short order, the barbed triangular head of the arrow popped out and the shaft fell to the grass.

Jak let out a wheezing huff and exclaimed, "Blast the gods! That hurt more than getting shot!"

Staring at the hillman, Nikalys said, "It didn't hurt me when you took the thorns out."

"The thorns were not as deep," replied Broedi as he probed around the wound again. "Nor did they have large, barbed arrowheads on them."

Nikalys peered down at Jak's face. His brother looked pale. "He'll be okay, won't he?"

"He will be fine once I help him heal." A frown creased the hillman's face. "Unfortunately, we will need to stay here while he sleeps."

"I can sleep on a horse," muttered Jak.

"No," rumbled the hillman with a gentle shake of his head. "For the Weave to work, you must sleep soundly. We will rest for a day." He glanced northward. "We should be safe that long." The confidence with which he spoke did not reach his eyes.

Looking back to Jak, Broedi placed his hands over the wound and glanced at Nikalys. "What did you find in the house, uori?"

Nikalys stared out to the woman walking with Kenders. "Her and two more men." The dead farmer's vacant stare flashed before him. "Actually, three. He was dead, his throat slit." His voice dropped to an angry whisper. "I think he was the girls' father." As he watched the young woman striding through the swishing grass, searching for her little sister, a massive wave of guilt flooded over him. "If I hadn't got off my blasted horse, we could have made it here in time to save him."

"Life is one long series of 'ifs,'" rumbled Broedi. "What is done is done."

Nikalys glared at Broedi, disappointed in the hillman's callousness. "What's done is done? If I hadn't complained about a sore rear, their father might still be alive!"

Nodding, Broedi said, "Yes, and had I decided to let you sleep a moment longer this morning, the little girl would be dead, and the other would be in worse shape."

"Worse than dead?" asked Nikalys incredulously. "How is that exactly?"

"Think, Nik," answered Jak, grunting through his pain. "Seven brigands kill the father and try to kill the little girl. But the pretty young woman is alive and untouched?"

Disgust, pure and cold, welled up in Nikalys as he realized what Jak was inferring.

"You saved her from an awful ordeal, uori," rumbled Broedi. "And saved the life of her iskoa. Take solace in the sweet and do not dwell on the sour."

Nikalys went quiet as Broedi worked on Jak's wound. The girls' cries for the toddler drifted on the air, mixing with Jak's muted grunts of pain. After a few moments, Nikalys muttered, "Broedi, I think I killed a man."

"A fate well deserved."

Knowing their deaths were justified did nothing to cure the sick feeling inside Nikalys. Killing another man was a horrible experience, even if the man was a murderer. His gaze drifted over the four men who lay dead in the front of the remnants of the house. Blades of grass from the blown-off roof dusted their corpses.

"Broedi, how many men have you killed?"

The question had been more of a thought than actual inquiry, but the words slipped out, taking Nikalys by surprise.

Broedi removed his hands from Jak's stomach and stared at the ground. A long, weary sigh slipped from his lips. "I do not know." He lifted his gaze up to Nikalys and said, "Know this, though. Taking a life never gets easier, uori. And *that* is a good thing. Should it ever become something you do without thought or conscience—" his gaze shifted to the corpses of the four mutilated men "—then you are no better than them."

Nodding, Nikalys glanced down at his brother and found Jak's eyes shut. Panic rushed through him. "Broedi?"

"He is only sleeping," rumbled the hillman as he rose from the ground. He patted Nikalys on the shoulder. "Come, we must clean this mess." He moved off toward the ruined home.

Nikalys eyed Jak, ensuring that his brother was indeed merely asleep. Jak wore a peaceful expression, his chest rising and falling at a slow, relaxed pace. New skin covered the arrow wound, pink and clean of blood. By no means was it fully healed, but the injury was weeks beyond where it should be.

Letting out a sigh of relief, Nikalys looked up and noticed Kenders and the woman were walking back toward the house now, side-by-side, the pretty, black-haired woman holding her sister in her arms. They were still a good distance off, but the little girl's sobs were audible.

Nikalys looked over at the dead bandits and frowned. The little girl should not see any of this. In all honesty, he would have preferred if he did not need to see any of it as well.

Catching Kenders' eye, he motioned for them to stay where they were, pointing to the clearing and then at the little girl in her sister's arms while shaking his head. Kenders nodded and reached out to stop the woman. Once he was sure they were not coming back right away, Nikalys turned toward the house.

Broedi was standing by the pile of sand that had once been the front wall, staring into the ruined cottage. As Nikalys approached from behind, the hillman flipped the man on the sand over with his boot. The bandit toppled over to his back to reveal the arrow sticking from his eye.

Glancing back to Nikalys, Broedi rumbled, "I did not realize you were so accurate with a bow."

"That wasn't me," said Nikalys, stopping beside Broedi. He pointed to the man slumped against the wall. "That was."

Broedi glanced at the man Nikalys indicated and then back at the arrow-pierced man at their feet. "If not you?"

"The woman," replied Nikalys. "She shot him as he charged me. Nearly took my ear off."

Broedi raised an eyebrow, turned, and stared across to where Kenders and the two sisters stood. "It would seem you owe her thanks as much as she owes you."

Nikalys studied the raven-haired girl from afar and muttered, "I suppose I do." Pulling his attention from the woman, he gestured around at the ruined home. "That was a neat trick you did with the roof. And the wall."

"It was not me."

Nikalys turned his head to stare at the hillman, his eyes full of doubt. "*Kenders* did this?"

Staring at the sand pile, Broedi nodded once. "She did."

Nikalys had yet to see her do anything so grand with magic since the first night with the lightning. "Did *you* teach her how?"

"Yes and no. Mostly no, though. The Weave of Air she used was a variation of something we have worked on, although she used many more Strands today. Many, *many* more." He bent over, scooped up a handful of sand, and, letting it fall through his fingers, rumbled, "But this?" He shook his head. "I cannot touch Strands of Stone, uori. Her gift allowed her to do this." Tossing the remainder of the sand to the ground, he peered at Nikalys. "Speaking of gifts, I saw—rather did not see—the way you moved. You looked like Aryn. Do you know how?"

"Not at all. I didn't know what I was doing. Or thinking, I guess, running down here like I did."

"Instinct is sometimes more valuable than days of thoughtful deliberation." He stared at Nikalys and added purposefully, "*Sometimes.*"

Nikalys frowned, reached behind his right ear, and gingerly touched the large welt quickly forming there. "Well, my instincts got me a nasty bump on the back of my head."

A thoughtful expression came over Broedi's face, accompanied by a quiet sigh. "We must find you a teacher to help you master your father's sword."

As far as Nikalys was concerned, Aryn Atticus was his father in blood only. He did not bother correcting the hillman, though, simply saying, "That would certainly be helpful."

Broedi climbed the sand pile and moved to stand over the dead farmer. Crouching beside the body, he gently closed the man's eyelids. "We must bury him. For his daughters' sake."

Nikalys agreed wholeheartedly. Staring down at the two dead brigands in the home, he asked, "And them?"

"We bury them, too. Face down."

Nikalys gave a silent, firm nod of approval. Within the Oaken Duchies, burying a person face down indicated that Maeana should not give the soul another chance to walk the world again. Nikalys did not know the reasoning behind the tradition, only that it was used for the worst of the worst, the unredeemable.

Staring out to where Kenders stood with the two sisters, he let out a long sigh. "And what about them?"

"I do not know, uori."

"They can't stay here," advised Nikalys. "These bandits might have friends."

"*That* much I know," said the hillman. Standing tall, he exited the home, patting Nikalys on the back as he passed. "Check on the first man you attacked. If he is alive, secure him and bring him to the back. And stuff a rag in his mouth. I do not want him shouting when he wakes up." He peered out to the three girls. "They have been through enough."

Nikalys turned and strode across the clearing, aiming for the man who had chased the toddler from the house. With trepidation trickling through him, he bent over and placed a hand on the man's filthy neck, searching for the throb of a heartbeat. Upon feeling a steady thumping, Nikalys let out a small, relieved sigh. He had only killed one man today.

Looking up, he spotted Smoke nearby, calmly munching on grass. As he shuffled over to the horse, he glanced up the hill and saw Goshen and Hal standing atop the slope, also eating. He pulled a length of rope and the salted rockeye wrapping from Smoke's saddlebags and returned to the unconscious man.

As he knelt beside the bandit, he glanced up to see Broedi carrying two bodies, one on each shoulder, around to the back of the house. Binding the man's wrists, he wondered what Broedi planned to do with the bandit after the man awoke.

When the man was secure, he stuffed the salty fish rag in the bandit's mouth and stood. After picking the man up, he hefted the brigand over one shoulder and strode past Jak. Staring down at his softly snoring brother, Nikalys smiled and murmured, "Don't worry, I've got this."

Nikalys stopped at one of the dead men, bent over, and lifted the bandit onto his other shoulder. As he headed toward the rear of the house, Broedi rounded the corner and came to an immediate standstill. He stared at Nikalys, a curious expression on his face.

Nikalys slowed his gait. "What?"

Broedi smiled his typical, slight grin. "While I can carry two men without problem, uori, I am surprised you can."

Without thought, Nikalys had lifted the second man with ease. There was no way he should be able to carry two full-grown men. Let alone without feeling even a bit of strain. His eyebrows drew together. "Me too…"

"Horum's gift is growing in you," said Broedi, moving to pick up two more corpses. "Come. I saw shovels in the back. We should begin digging."

Together, they walked to the rear of the house where Broedi grabbed two shovels and headed down the slope that led to the river. Broedi dropped the dead men he carried next to the others already there. Nikalys did the same with the men he held, setting the one who was still alive to the side. As Broedi started to dig, Nikalys moved around to the front of the house and picked up the last dead bandit, bringing him around to where Broedi had the beginnings of a hole.

"Where should we bury the father?" asked Nikalys. "He deserves better than being buried here." He eyed the dead bandits. "With them."

Pausing his digging for a moment, Broedi scanned the area. "Perhaps ask the eldest what her wishes are."

Asking a daughter where she would like them to bury her father was not a conversation Nikalys wished to have. Nevertheless, he nodded and turned, walking up the rise and to the front of the house.

As he rounded the corner, he was surprised to see Kenders sitting on the ground beside Jak, the little girl curled up in her lap. Even at this distance, Nikalys could see that his sister was crying.

He scanned the area for the older sister, but did not see her. Curious, he glanced back to Kenders and she jutted her chin in the direction of the house. Nikalys turned, looked into the ruined home, and saw the young woman sitting beside the dead farmer. Nikalys heart dropped into his stomach.

Taking a deep breath, he slowly strode toward the sand pile and stopped just beyond the former threshold, beside the flat-paneled door on the ground. Keeping his voice quiet and respectful, he murmured, "Pardon me?"

The woman glanced up at him. Tiny trails of tears lined her face, yet her expression was not one of grief. In fact, if not for the wetness on her cheeks, Nikalys would not have known she was upset. Her icy stoicism made Broedi look jovial.

She eyed him for half a heartbeat and then went back to staring at her father without every saying a word.

Sighing, Nikalys stepped over the fallen door and moved to an overturned chair. Righting it, he sat down and waited. Neither one of them said a word for a long time.

The faint sounds of Broedi's shovel entering earth and the muffled sobs from the clearing outside mixed with breeze swishing through vegetable fields and prairie grass. As long as she did not yell at him to go away, Nikalys would sit here quietly, lending a bit of life to this house of death.

Eventually, the woman broke the quiet, her voice quiet and subdued yet with an edge to it. "Father told them they could have our entire harvest if they would just leave. But they...wouldn't..." She trailed off, biting her lip.

Nikalys stared at her profile and remained silent.

She shook her head slowly. "They cut his throat without a second thought. *Right* in front of Helene." Her voice caught. "She watched him die." Her head snapped up and she glared at Nikalys. "She's only four!" She looked and sounded like she wanted to kill the men all over again.

"I'm sorry," he said quietly.

He wanted to help her somehow, to offer some consolation, but knew nothing could counter the anguish she was feeling. Yellow Mud had happened less than three weeks ago. He remembered. Words were powerless right now.

She stared back to her father and with a venomous twist in her tone, she muttered, "I'm glad they're all dead."

"All but one," corrected Nikalys quietly. "He's tied up out back."

The woman's gaze shot to him. "One's alive?"

Nikalys could only nod in response. The sudden mix of fire and ice in the woman's eyes startled him.

She jumped to her feet and hurried past him, clambering over the sand pile and rushing around the corner of the house. Suddenly uneasy, Nikalys quickly stood and followed.

When he reached the rear of the cottage, she was already two dozen paces ahead of him, heading down the hill, striding with purpose, almost jogging. Broedi had stopped digging and was watching the woman approach, silent. She ignored him entirely, staring instead at the men on the ground. Stopping in front of the bound and gagged man, she reached down and drew a beltknife from the body next to him.

Nikalys' eyes went wide as he began to rush down the slope. "Wait!"

Without a moment's pause, the young woman slit the unconscious man's throat, drawing the blade across the bandit's neck in one, swift—and very deep—stroke. Blood gushed and bubbled from his wound.

Nikalys skidded to a halt and stared.

The woman dropped the knife and stood over the man, watching the life drain from the brigand. He died without ever waking up.

Hurrying farther down the slope, Nikalys glared at Broedi and demanded, "Why didn't you stop her?"

Broedi looked over at him, his expression calm and serene. "He helped kill her father. He deserved death."

"He was defenseless!" exclaimed Nikalys. "Tied up! Hells, he was *unconscious!*"

With a slight tilt of his head, Broedi asked, "Would such a man have shown you the mercy you are willing to confer upon him?"

Nikalys glared at the hillman, wanting to argue but unable to do so. Logically, Broedi was right. These men would have not given a second thought to killing him or anyone else. Yet it still felt wrong.

The woman turned, looked at Broedi, and said, "I was rude and ungrateful to you earlier. Thank you for saving my sister and me." She peered over at Nikalys. "Both of you."

Nikalys stared in wonderment at the woman. She had just murdered a helpless man and—two breaths later—she was apologizing for being impolite.

"You are welcome," rumbled Broedi, inclining his head. "I am sorry for your loss."

The beautiful young woman nodded once, moved to the free shovel, and picked it up. "If you will excuse me, I would like to go bury my father." Glaring at them both, she added firmly, "A task I wish to do alone." She immediately turned and walked up the slope, heading toward one of the vegetable fields. Marching to the center of a plot of purplish-red longpeppers, she began to dig.

Nikalys was still staring up the hill at her when the sounds of digging resumed behind him. He turned and looked at Broedi, already standing in a shallow depression. The hillman dug fast. "Does what she did not bother you?"

Broedi answered without pausing. "Some lives are not worth mourning, uori." Tossing a shovelful of dirt aside, he glanced at Nikalys. "There is another shovel by the house."

Nikalys shook his head in disgust and muttered, "Dig the blasted hole yourself."

Spinning around, he climbed the slope and strode toward the front of the house, walking past the woman in the field without glancing at her. In a daze, he wandered back to where Kenders sat with Jak, holding the toddler. He collapsed to the grass and stared at nothing.

"Nik?" murmured Kenders. "What's wrong?"

With disbelief filling his voice, he said, "She just walked up to the man, took a knife and—" He stopped, realizing that the little girl was staring at him with big, brown eyes, listening to every word he said. She was a miniature version of her older sister but with shorter hair. He shook his head. "No matter."

The girl kept staring at him. After a few moments, she spoke, her voice tiny. "Did you stop the bad men? They hurt my Papa."

Kenders started a little and looked down at the girl. Eyeing Nikalys, Kenders said, "That's the first thing she's said since we found her. Sabine tried to get her to talk, but..." She trailed off and gave Helene a small squeeze.

Nikalys looked to the longpepper field. Sabine, then.

He sighed and looked back to Helene, a potent, swirling mixture of sorrow and sympathy filling him. What he and Kenders had been through had been difficult, but to be four years old and watch your father have his throat slit was unthinkable.

He summoned as comforting a smile as he could and said softly, "Yes, Helene. We stopped the bad men. They won't hurt anyone ever again. I promise."

Helene remained still for a few heartbeats, appearing as if she were considering his words. Then, she climbed from Kenders' lap, scurried across the grass, and climbed into his, wrapping her arms around his neck and burying her head underneath his chin. In a petite, sad voice, she mumbled, "Thank you."

Unsure how else to respond, he enveloped the little girl in his arms. "You're welcome."

He looked over to Kenders and found her wiping away tears with the back of both hands. Feeling wetness rolling down his own cheek, he squeezed the little girl in his arms, wanting nothing more than to shield her from any more hurt the world would throw at her.

CHAPTER 42: SISTERS

Kenders eyed the cookpot hanging over the fire in the midst of considering a third helping of soup. It was surprisingly good, despite its odd combination of ingredients.

Earlier, she had stared on as Sabine tossed sliced longpeppers, chopped bits of some sort of red and fleshy fruit, and chunks of a white tuber into the pot, wary at what eveningmeal was becoming yet happy they would not be eating rockeye tonight. After expressing her relief regarding the variation from the salted fish, Sabine had asked if she could have some.

Nikalys had handed the dried strips over, frowning as Sabine added them to the pot with the vegetables. Amazingly, when they tried the soup, it was delicious, the saltiness of the fish mixed well with the odd vegetables. Even Nikalys had admitted so.

Deciding that she had already eaten too much, Kenders set her bowl down and stared west. The sun hovered above the horizon, half-hidden by voluminous clouds that looked heavy with rain. Mu's orb shone bright, lining the dark gray clouds with a bright orange-tinted silver thread. The stiff breeze blowing over the grasslands carried the hint of wet metal in the air, confirming Kenders suspicions that rain was coming.

The campsite was quiet, as it had been for some time now.

She sighed and looked across the fire to Nikalys. Helene was sitting in his lap again. Apparently, the little girl had formed an attachment to him. To Nikalys' credit, he was handling the situation wonderfully. He had not complained once.

Beyond some mundane chatter about stew, there had been little conversation since making camp several dozen paces away from the house. Kenders did not know what to say, and apparently neither did Nikalys. Jak was softly snoring still, blissfully unaware of what was going on, and Sabine seemed about as talkative a person as Broedi. The hillman sat a half-dozen paces from the fire, smoking his pipe and staring into the fire. Occasionally, he would look up and either glance at Sabine or stare over his shoulder, up the hill, and to the north.

Earlier, not long after Helene climbed into Nikalys' lap for the first time, Kenders had retrieved their horses and tied them to the wagon beside the dead bandits' mounts. Seeing Sabine digging in the vegetable field, Kenders approached and asked if she would like help. In a manner that was neither polite nor particularly rude, Sabine declined the offer, never ceasing her digging.

Leaving the woman alone, Kenders walked down to where Broedi labored and again offered her help. He declined as well, instead asking her to look through the dead men's belongings and see if there was anything of use.

She had made a small pile of coin purses, knives, swords, and arrow quivers before tucking them in her riding dress and carrying them up the slope. Moving past Sabine, she saw the young woman nearly done digging her father's grave. After dumping the collected items on the back of the wagon—it seemed as good as place as any—she moved over to Nikalys and gently pried Helene from his arms. Then, with a silent nod, she indicated that he should help carry the father's body to the field. Nikalys frowned, but stood nonetheless, and went to retrieve the girls' father.

Kenders had done whatever she could to occupy Helene's mind with anything other than the day's events. She learned that the girl's favorite flower was something called a "purple dancer" and her favorite song was "Happy Times at the Fair." Kenders had asked Helene to teach it to her and was just getting the melody when Nikalys rounded the house's corner. When he waved her over, she stood and looked toward Helene with a questioning expression. Nikalys nodded and waved again.

She carried Helene to the field where she found a sweaty, stoic Sabine standing next to a hole and mound of fresh earth. Their father was inside, arms folded over his chest. Sabine took Helene from Kenders with a quiet word of thanks and moved to stand next to the grave.

Nikalys and Kenders left the sisters alone and returned to where Jak slept. Broedi finished burying the bandits and came to sit with them. No one spoke a word.

After a time, Sabine and Helene exited the field and moved to the house. Helene sat on the pile of sand while Sabine began to gather things from their home, seemingly intent on leaving with her sister at once. Broedi insisted the pair stay, pointing out there might be more bandits in the region. She agreed to stay the night—reluctantly—and then surprised them all by offering to make soup.

Now, with eveningmeal past and having no one with whom to talk, Kenders sat alone with her thoughts. She shifted her gaze to the ruined farmhouse and frowned, trying to make sense of what she had done earlier with the Strands.

It bothered her that she had reached for them without a moment's hesitation. While it seemed natural at the time, her open embrace of magic made her uncomfortable in retrospect. With each day that passed, fate seemed to be nudging her further along a path that she was not sure she wanted to tread. She sighed, reached up, and ran her fingers through her hair. Life had been simpler before she knew she could touch the Strands.

"Did you know I like sweetberries?"

Startled from her reverie, Kenders turned to look at Helene. The little girl was staring up at Nikalys from his lap.

Nikalys glanced down, his eyes remaining unfocused for a moment before locking on to Helene's face. It seemed his mind had been elsewhere, too. "Pardon?"

"I like sweetberries," said Helene. "Do you?"

A small, amused grin spread over Nikalys' face. "You know, Helene, I've never had any. Are they good?"

Helene nodded her head vigorously. "Of course. They're *sweet*berries."

Nikalys' smile grew a fraction even as Kenders felt one grace her face, as well. Glancing over at Sabine, she caught the slightest upward curl of lips. Only Broedi showed no reaction. He did, however, look north again. As he turned back around, Kenders caught his eye and asked a question she had been wanting to for a while now.

"Should we be worried?"

Broedi held her gaze for a moment before glancing at Sabine. The young woman sat, legs crossed, staring at the darkening eastern horizon. Looking back to Kenders, Broedi rumbled, "There is a chance, a very good chance, they might have seen the...signal from earlier." He paused and nodded at her. "It would have been quite bright."

Kenders frowned. She had guessed that was the case. Both Weaves—the Air for the roof and Stone for the walls—had been accidents, borne of pure wish rather than skill. She had nearly passed out after the second one.

Sabine, her gaze still eastward, spoke for the first time in a while. "If you are afraid of Constables, the nearest office is over a week's journey west. Actually, Fernsford to the east might be closer. Not sure, actually. Never been to either. Regardless, I don't think they can track magic *that* far."

Broedi, Nikalys, and Kenders all stared at Sabine in perfect, complete silence. The hillman recovered first, saying, "Magic?"

Sabine turned to look at Broedi, her eyes overflowing with incredulity. "A roof flies into the air, walls crumble to dust, and a giant man turns into a giant lynx?" She shook her head and huffed, "I'm no fool."

Broedi was quiet for a moment then rumbled, "Most in the duchies fear magic."

Sabine cocked her head to the side and sighed. "Well, I'm not one of them."

"Why?" asked Broedi.

Sabine held his inquisitive stare for a moment, frowned, and then shifted her gaze to the fire. A moment later, Kenders felt a faint, orange crackling. The campfire's flames flared, climbing a foot higher to envelop the cookpot, and then quickly returned to normal.

Kenders shot a look at Broedi, thinking he had been the source of the magic and wondering what had been the purpose of the display. The hillman, however, was still staring at Sabine, his eyes wide and alert. Realizing what had happened, Kenders turned her gaze to Sabine and gawked.

Sabine was a mage.

The revelation stunned Kenders. Yet it was nothing compared to the shock experienced a moment later when Helene sat tall in Nikalys' lap and clapped her hands together excitedly.

"Again, Sabine! Do it again!"

Broedi's intense gaze shifted to Helene, as did Kenders'. Nikalys alone kept his eyes on Sabine.

"Hold a moment...you're a mage?"

Sabine shook her head. "Not much of one. I can do that little trick with the fire and I can make a bucket of water cold. That's all. Nothing like you three did earlier."

Helene squirmed around in Nikalys' lap to peer over at her big sister. "Make the blue ribbons, Sabine! They're prettier than the orange ones."

Kenders stared at the little girl, unsure if she should be confused or surprised.

During her lessons with Broedi, she had learned that it was unusual for anyone to be able to see the Strands vividly unless they were extremely attuned to that particular type. Many mages—most according to Broedi—who could touch a certain type of Strand might only catch a small glimpse of color. They wove the magical strings on feel alone. It was why most mages required years of study to before they could be effective.

Yet, here was a four-year-old girl who could see both the flickering oranges of Fire and the rippling blues of Water.

Everyone was silent, except Helene who repeatedly asked for the "pretty blue ribbons." Her pleas became more and more insistent until Sabine snapped, "Hush, Helene! Not now!"

The little girl shut her mouth and, with a hurt, pouting look, turned to hug Nikalys tight.

Instant regret filled Sabine's face. "I'm sorry, Helene." Her little sister did not turn around. "Helene?"

Broedi abruptly asked, "Can you see the Strands when you weave?"

"What?" asked Sabine, shooting the hillman and annoyed look. "Weave? Weave what?" She turned back to peer at Helene, a remorseful frown on her face.

"When you do magic," began Broedi, "how do you do it?"

Sabine shrugged. "By feel, mostly. Mother tried to teach me when Father was not around. She showed me the two little tricks with the fire and the water. She stopped after that, though. Said I did not have the talent to do more."

Nikalys asked, "And where is your mother?"

"Passed," replied Sabine. Turning to face the longpepper field, she added, "In fact, she's buried a few feet next to where I just—" She stopped, shooting a quick glance Helene. "She's with our father."

Broedi inclined is head and with honest sympathy, rumbled, "I am sorry for you loss, uora."

While Sabine's brow wrinkled at the hillman's strange word, she nodded nonetheless. "Thank you." She stared at her sister's back, a sad frown spreading over her face. "She passed the day Helene was born."

Kenders winced, inside and out. Deaths during childbirth were all too common. Kenders almost needed two hands to mark the number of mothers who had died in Yellow Mud over the last five or six years.

A moment of quiet passed, after which Broedi, Nikalys, and Kenders all murmured belated condolences. Sabine nodded throughout their nice words. For a moment—just a moment—she looked soft and vulnerable. She was quiet pretty when her hard edges softened.

Once the kind words fell away, silence filled the camp, a silence eventually broken by Sabine herself.

"You know," mused Sabine, staring at the prairie, a melancholy smile on her lips. "I've lived here my *entire* life. I've never been much more than a day in any direction…" She shook her head and sighed. "When I was little, Mother and Father would talk about when they lived near the city." Her eyes lit up. "Gods, but it sounded wondrous! So many people in one place! So much going on!"

She motioned to the landscape. "Out here it was us, the river, the crops, and the grass. *So much* blasted grass. I wanted to see the city, but my parents said it was better here. We were *safer* here. It wasn't until I was ten years old that I finally understood what they meant by that…"

Sabine paused and stared back toward her house. Kenders had noticed that when Sabine sat down earlier this evening, she had made sure that her back was toward the stone cottage.

After a long moment, she turned back to face them and, with a strange expression on her face, asked, "If you grew up never having seen a horse, what would you say the first time you saw one?"

The question struck Kenders as more than odd.

Sabine gave a dismissive wave of her hand. "No matter, it's a strange question, I know. When you see something new, something…unique for the very first time, you are surprised, yes? Shocked? Scared, perhaps?" Her eyebrows drew together. "Now, imagine the opposite. Pretend you have lived your whole life with something that seems entirely normal to you, but one day, you discover it is not only unnatural, but against the law." Her tone was decidedly bitter. "In fact, it's the entire reason your family has to live in the middle of nowhere!"

Helene lifted her head from Nikalys' shoulder and peeked over at her sister. "Sabine? Are you mad?"

The elder sister took a deep breath and exhaled. "No, dear. Not at all. Please, close your eyes."

Helene laid her head back down as Nikalys patted her back.

Sabine waited a moment before continuing, her tone noticeably more restrained. "When I was a girl, if there was a bad dry spell, Mother would make water run uphill from the river to the fields. On hot days, we always had cool, clear water to drink even though the river is most definitely not clear or cool in the summer. What she did was as natural to me as the wind blowing across the plains. I didn't know how she did it, just that she did…"

She paused, her eyes going unfocused.

"It was spring, I had just turned ten, and Mother started a fire in the hearth like she always did and I…felt it…a sort of soft buzzing in my head…"

Kenders understood what she meant. Although for Kenders, there was nothing soft about it.

"I said something to Mother about it and she…ah…well, she got upset. She insisted I never speak of it to anyone, ever—even Father, *especially* Father. I didn't understand, but she was so insistent that I agreed. Unfortunately, Father still found out." She sighed and shook her head. "Gods, did he ever blame Mother something fierce. When he calmed down—eventually—he said we'd make do. After all—" she waved to the grasslands "—out here, no one would ever know what I was. Father got past his anger at my meager 'talent' and we continued to live as we always had."

"A few years later, Mother said she was pregnant." A sad smile touched her lips. "We were all so happy. Especially me. I was finally going to have someone to talk to besides Mother or Father. Granted, my brother or sister would be years younger than me, but I was excited nonetheless." Her gaze shifted to where Nikalys held Helene. "Seven turns later, Helene was born. Mother did not—" Her voice caught, her eyes twitched. She lifted a hand to wipe a lone tear that was sneaking down her cheek. "Mother did not survive the birth."

Kenders looked over at Helene. The poor girl had never known her mother and had watched bandits murder her father. Greya, goddess of Fate, had been unusually cruel to her.

After a few moments of heavy quiet, Sabine resumed speaking, her voice steady once again. "It was hard on Father. *Very* hard. He was alone, had a farm to run, and two daughters to rear. I did what I could, raising Helene more as if she was my daughter than my sister. We managed."

She took in a deep breath and exhaled slowly. "Last summer, when I did one of my two 'tricks'—cooling water—Helene starts clapping, laughing, and calling out for the 'pretty blue ribbons.' Father was outside in the fields, so he had no idea what was going on. Curious, I made the fire in the hearth flare and, again, Helene started to clap, demanding more of the orange ribbons."

"I'm sorry," muttered Nikalys. "Ribbons?"

Sabine glanced at him and smiled slightly. "Father would go to Stooert—" she waved a hand in a general northwest direction "—for flour and supplies. Things we could not make ourselves. Every time—*every* time—he would come back with a small gift for each of us. One spring, he brought Helene and me silk ribbons for our hair. Helene says the magic looks like shiny ribbons."

Broedi rumbled, "As apt of a description as any."

Kenders agreed. The Strands did look a bit like ribbons.

Sabine let out a quiet sigh, her gaze on Helene. "I didn't want Father to be angry with Helene the way he had been about me, so…we kept it a secret. Somehow, we kept it a secret…" She stared in the direction of her father's grave amongst the longpeppers. "He never did learn the truth."

After a few moments of quiet, she turned back to the fire. "A few turns ago, a dozen men came by the farm. They demanded a 'shield tax' from Father, saying they were keeping the region free of troublemakers and deserved to be compensated for it." The disgust in her voice was unmistakable.

"Father paid them what little coin we had and they went away. Last turn, ten of them came back asking for more. We did not have it, but father promised he could pay after selling our leftover crop in Fernsford. They left, but seven came back today and demanded early payment. We did not have it, so they…" She hesitated and wrapped her arms around herself. "They said that I could pay them instead. Father struck the man who said that, and…" Pressing her lips together, she stood quickly, and moved a short distance away from the fire.

Kenders made to stand, intending to go and comfort her, but a small headshake and murmured "uora" from Broedi stopped her. His eyes, brown and wise, conveyed a simple message: leave Sabine alone. She complied and instead simply eyed Sabine. Beyond the farm girl, early evening stars were visible in the east.

After few quiet moments, Kenders peered back to the hillman and, in a low, whispered tone, asked, "What do we do? We can't leave them here by themselves. And they can't go into any of the cities where there are Constables."

Still cradling Helene, Nikalys muttered, "She's right."

Broedi nodded. "I know." A pensive scowl filled his face. He was clearly struggling with something. "Give me a moment, please. I am thinking."

Kenders, sat back, shut her mouth, and waited. She wanted more than that, but pressing Broedi when he did not want to talk was a waste of time.

Eventually, Sabine returned to the fire and sat without saying a word. Nobody did for a time. Even Helene remained quiet, resting snug in Nikalys' arms. Kenders thought the girl had fallen asleep until she shifted and looked up at Nikalys' face. She gave him a tiny smile, reached up to graze his cheek, and then laid her head back down. It was as if she were simply checking to see if he was still there.

Broedi eventually broke the silence with a long, weary sigh. He looked at Sabine and rumbled softly, "I wish to try something, uora."

Suspicion flooded Sabine's eyes. "What?"

Broedi shook his head. "I assure you, nothing that would be harmful to you or the little one."

Kenders suspected she knew what the hillman was planning. Catching Sabine's eyes, she offered a friendly smile. "Don't worry. Broedi's harmless." After a brief pause, she added, "Mostly."

The hillman glanced at her, his eyebrows raised slightly. Kenders shrugged. Harmless was a relative term.

Sabine remained motionless, the expression on her face wary. "What do you want to try?"

Broedi picked up the waterskin beside him, uncorked the top, and poured a puddle of water on the ground. A moment later, Kenders felt the now-familiar crackling of magic and watched as a few brilliant, blue Strands of Water danced around the spilled water. Turning her attention to Sabine, she watched the young woman tilt her head and squint, evidently straining to see what Kenders could spot as plainly as the midday sun in a cloudless sky.

Helene sat tall in Nikalys' lap and twisted around to stare at the Water Strands, her eyes bright and a wide smile on her face. "Those ribbons are much prettier than yours, Sabine." She spoke without fear.

Kenders admired the little girl's courage, yet it struck her that a four-year-old was exhibiting more bravery than she was. She did not know what to do with that realization.

Using the Strands of Water, Broedi wove a simple pattern and the puddle of water drew up, off the ground, and flowed back into the skin. Once inside,

Broedi replaced the stopper and stared at Helene. "Can you see the blue or orange ribbons better?"

As Helene stared at the large hillman, her expression darkened. With worried eyes, she looked to her sister. After Sabine nodded her head—somewhat reluctantly—Helene peered up at Nikalys. He gave a reassuring smile and patted her back gently. "It's fine, Helene. Broedi's a nice man."

Looking back to Broedi, Helene whispered, "Both are shiny." She paused. "Blue is prettier, though."

With a nod, Broedi placed the waterskin on the grass. A moment later, Kenders felt a small surge of gold and orange. Strands of Will combined with the flickering orange of Fire in a pattern Kenders was still trying to master. She noted a subtle difference in the Weave this time, however.

A tiny man of flickering fire, no bigger than Kenders' hand, appeared above the flames of the campfire. The orange man pranced about, doing a funny little dance in midair. Helene laughed gleefully at the display.

"What colors do you see now?" asked Broedi.

"Orange!" giggled Helene. "I like the him! He's funny!" She looked at her sister. "Sabine? Why can't you do that?"

Sabine did not answer. She was staring at the figure over the fire, an anxious frown affixed on her face when the dancing man disappeared with a soft poof, prompting a disappointed "Oh…" from Helene.

Again, Broedi picked up the waterskin and uncorked it. The crackling returned and Kenders saw the rippling, cobalt blue strings joining with sparkling silver as Broedi poured the water onto the ground. Instead of the water splashing onto the ground, though, it took the amorphous shape of another small man.

Helene shouted in delight, "Those look like your necklace, Sabine!"

Everyone looked to Sabine as the farm girl reached to her neck, pulled out a simple silver chain necklace, and stared at it.

Lowering the waterskin near the ground, Broedi said, "Climb back in, please." The figure of water stepped over and climbed into the hole, disappearing. The hillman looked at Sabine and asked, "Have you sensed anything besides the blue Strands?"

Sabine shook her head slowly, all the while staring at Helene nervously.

Broedi tried two other small weaves of Air and Life, but neither sister responded. As Broedi released the green Weave of Life, halting the rapid growth of a patch of grass, Helene spoke up.

"Can you make the brown ribbons again?"

Kenders exchanged a quick look with Broedi. She knew Helene was speaking of the Strands of Stone she had inadvertently used to pulverize the house wall. Kenders prayed Broedi would not ask her to do something with them now.

"Not now, little uora," replied Broedi gently. "It is late and you should get some sleep."

Kenders breathed a sigh of relief.

Shaking her head, Helene said, "But I'm not tired." She immediately yawned.

Managing to sweep aside the worry resting on her face, Sabine outstretched her arms, smiled, and said, "Come here, Helene. Let's lie down. And *no* arguments, please."

While a pouty look crossed Helene's face, she nonetheless climbed from Nikalys' lap and began walking to her sister. Halfway to Sabine, she halted, turned around, and ran back to Nikalys. She wrapped her arms around him and gave him a kiss on his cheek. "Good night, Nik-lys."

Kenders smiled. She had yet to get Nikalys' name right.

Clearly surprised by the display of affection, Nikalys nonetheless smiled at the little girl. "Good night, Helene. Get some sleep. I'll see you in the morning."

After he gave her a quick hug, Helene scampered back to Sabine. Launching herself into her sister's arms, she demanded, "Sing me my song."

Sabine glanced at the group around the fire with a touch of embarrassment. "Not tonight, dear."

A bit more emphatically, Helene said, "Sing me my song, *please.*"

Kenders raised a hand to cover the amused, uninvited smile that spread over her face.

Shaking her head, Sabine smiled—a true smile—and began to sing in a soft, soothing tone. Five notes into the song, and Kenders was in awe. Sabine's singing was stunning.

Beautiful. Melodious. Soothing.

Her voice put every playman Kenders had ever heard to shame. She, Nikalys, and even Broedi stared, enthralled by the private performance.

After a few repetitions of "Happy Times at the Fair," Helene was sound asleep. Sabine moved her sister to one blanket and covered her with another, both of which she had taken from their ruined home. For a short while, she sat there, stroking her younger sister's hair, softly humming. Once Helene was in a deep sleep, Sabine let the song fade away and turned back to the rest of them. The creased lines on her face betrayed her true anxiety.

Without preamble, she asked, "What does all of…*that* mean?" It was obvious she was referring to Broedi's displays with the Strands. "Is Helene alright? Will she be safe?"

Kenders glanced at Broedi, curious to hear his answer.

After letting out a long sigh, the hillman asked, "What did your mother tell you of the Strands?"

Sabine stared at him, her expression cold and blank. "The Strands?"

Kenders sighed. This sounded familiar.

Thus began Broedi's explanation of magic to Sabine. He spoke of weaving, the nine types of Strands, how different people could be strong with some and weak with others, how some people were born with the ability and others did not discover it until later in life. Sabine never spoke a word, listening with a healthy amount of respect. When he was finished, Sabine sat still for a moment then peered at Broedi.

"So…you are saying that because Helene is able to see these 'Strands' so clearly, she will be able to 'weave' them?"

"Perhaps," rumbled Broedi. "With training, she can."

"Is there any way to make it go away?" asked Sabine, the worry in her voice clear.

A moment passed before Broedi turned his gaze on Kenders. "Perhaps you should answer her question."

With raised eyebrows, Kenders asked, "Me?"

Broedi nodded, silent, and held her gaze. Sabine turned to stare at her, too.

Staring at Sabine, Kenders saw a young woman worried about the same things over which she had agonized. Magic was as much a burden as it was a gift. Kenders was about to offer what little words of comfort she could when Nikalys surprised her by speaking first.

"Sabine, I know you are afraid for your sister." He turned his gaze to Kenders. "Trust me, I know what that's like." He paused a moment before looking back to Sabine. "When Kenders and I were growing up, our parents would tell us that magic is like a spade. You can use it to grow food or smash in a man's head. The spade, however, remains a spade. It is a tool. A tool that relies on its wielder to choose its purpose."

"But a farmer can drop a spade if they wish," said Sabine. "I don't have that choice. Helene doesn't have that choice."

"True," acknowledged Nikalys. "Magic *is* a part of you, Sabine. It *is* a part of Helene. But that's all it is: a part. You're more than just that one part, aren't you?"

More than a little surprised at the wisdom he was displaying, Kenders stared at her brother, knowing that he was speaking to her as much as he was to Sabine. It seemed that even if she doubted her destiny as a mage, Nikalys was embracing it for her.

When Sabine did not answer Nikalys right away, he nodded to where Helene was softly snoring. "She seems like a wondrous, sweet soul. And I think as long as she has you—" he shifted his gaze to Sabine "—to keep an eye over her, she will be fine. You both will."

Sabine shook her head. "None of that changes the fact that magic is outlawed."

"And are all laws just?" rumbled Broedi.

"Just or not, it *is* the law," stressed Sabine. "And I doubt the Constables will give me the opportunity to argue the merits of it as they drag us away." She looked over to her sister and sighed. "We can't stay here, but I can't risk taking her around other people. If she starts trying to use these Strands…" She trailed off, shaking her head.

A few moments of silence passed before Broedi spoke, his deep baritone soft and gentle. "Then come with us."

Kenders turned her head and gaped at the hillman, stunned that he would suggest such a thing.

"He's right," muttered Nikalys a moment later. "You should come with us."

Wondering if both her brother and the White Lion had gone mad, Kenders asked, "Pardon me, but is that wise?" She would have liked to provide the long list of reasons why it was not, but held her tongue in front of Sabine.

"Perhaps not," said Broedi as he gazed at Kenders. "Yet of the sour choices before us, this is the sweetest."

"How do you figure?" demanded Kenders.

Nikalys sat forward, again answering a question not directed to him. "As I see it, Sabine has three choices." Lifting his hand, he extended a lone finger. "One: she can stay here, at this ruined house and farm, waiting for bandits to return." A second finger joined the first. "Two: she can take Helene to a city and have no coin, no family, and a constant threat hanging over them that the Constables will discover them as mages." He extended a third finger. "Three: they can come along with someone who might be able to offer a safer place to live their lives." His eyes glinted in the firelight. "Sound familiar?"

Kenders felt as if she should still protest, but did not. Nikalys had made his point well. Very well.

Sabine asked carefully, "Safer place?" Her eyes held a glimmer of hope. "What do you mean? Where is it?"

Nikalys nodded at Broedi. "Ask him. But don't expect an answer."

Turning a cautious eye toward Broedi, Sabine asked, "Where is this safer place?"

The hillman sat very still, his gaze fixed on Sabine's face. After a few quiet breaths, he asked, "You do not trust me, do you?"

Sabine answered without hesitation. "Not at all."

Broedi sighed and placed his now-extinguished pipe in his mouth. "We head south, through the Blackbark Forest, to a hold on Storm Island."

Shocked, Kenders glared at Broedi. "Hold a moment! We've been asking you that for over a week and nothing! She asks *once* and you tell her?"

"I said I would tell you when you the time was right. Now is that time. We do not have time to earn her trust as I did yours." Peering at Sabine, he asked, "Had I not told you where we are going, would you have considered coming with us?"

Sabine shook her head. "Absolutely not."

Broedi looked back to Kenders, wearing an expression as though that settled the matter. Kenders pressed her lips together and sighed. Broedi could be maddening at times.

Nikalys asked, "Does that mean you *are* coming, then?"

"I haven't decided yet," muttered Sabine.

Nikalys was quiet for a moment, his gaze drifting over to where Helene lay sleeping, her tiny snores drowned out by Jak's louder ones. "The two of you are not safe here."

Sabine closed her eyes. "I know."

"Or in any city where—"

Eyes shooting open, Sabine snapped, "I know!"

Nikalys froze for several heartbeats, then dropped his gaze to the fire and wisely remained silent, as did everyone as they awaited Sabine's decision.

Broedi reached into his satchel and withdrew his pouch of smoking-leaf. With nothing else to do, Kenders watched him pack the pipe again and light it with a tiny Weave of Fire concentrated over the bowl. The leaf's sweet smoke drifted through the air.

She studied the hillman, wondering about the Blackbark Forest and Storm Island he had mentioned. She had never heard of either. Then again, she had never heard much of anything beyond Yellow Mud or Smithshill. Broedi could have said they were heading to White Moon and she would have had a better idea of what to expect.

After what seemed a longer time than it probably was, Sabine sighed and looked at Broedi. "You're right." Shifting her gaze to Nikalys, she added, "Both of you. It is the sweetest among the sour. If you will have us, we will go with you." She glanced down at the sleeping form of Helene. "I'll do whatever I can to keep her safe."

"A wise choice, uora," rumbled Broedi. "Your dedication to your iskoa is admirable."

Ignoring the compliment entirely, Sabine asked, "Why Storm Island? What makes it safer than any other place?"

Kenders turned to stare at Broedi and said with purpose, "What an *excellent* question. Why, Broedi?"

"I'd like to know, too," said Nikalys.

Broedi puffed on his pipe while staring at each one of them in turn. Ending on Sabine, a slight smile touched his lips. "You should have asked that *before* you said you were coming."

A soft chuckle slipped from Nikalys and, despite her irritation, Kenders smiled. Sabine, however, remained stone-faced.

Broedi rose from the ground, stood tall, and stretched. "I wish to walk the area to ensure our safety. The rest of you should sleep." He motioned toward Jak. "We ride as soon as he wakes."

As he turned north, heading up the hill, Sabine looked between Nikalys and Kenders. "He didn't answer my question."

Eyeing their new traveling companion, Kenders said, "It's best you get used to it."

Sabine frowned and stared after the retreating hillman. Kenders would have bet good coin she was rethinking her decision.

CHAPTER 43: WEST

28th *of the Turn of Sutri*

Jhaell lifted his gaze from his horse's mane and sighed.

Before him, verdant fields undulated in a light breeze, waves of grass rippling across the sun-soaked land through which the dirt road upon which Jhaell's horse trod cut a meandering, russet ribbon. Near a rogue clump of oaks, the tan roofline of a rustic house stood against the vast wilderness. Overhead, white clouds climbed upon one another, tumbling and rolling across the sky.

Jhaell stared at the scene without truly seeing it. The same frown that had rested upon his face for days on end curled downward a fraction further. He felt defeated, desperate, and—despite the fifty blue and gold-clad soldiers trailing him—very alone.

For days now, he had been heading west simply because he had no idea what else to do. He forced the soldiers to march day and night, driving them to the point of exhaustion. Should he care to look over his shoulder, he would have seen a dozen men slumped over, asleep on their horse. It was a wonder they did not slide from their saddles.

He had been in this backward country for over a week now, yet there had been no sign of the Progeny. None. A tiny ember of hope smoldered deep within him that all of this was a massive misunderstanding. That he was chasing phantoms. That these events were some sort of terrible, cruel coincidence. That the real Progeny were elsewhere in the world. That Tandyr would not hold him responsible.

Letting out a long and deep sigh, Jhaell shut his eyes. He knew he was fooling himself.

The thudding of a horse's hooves yanked him from his piteous reverie. The beast drew beside Jhaell and its rider—most likely the Southern Arm' sergeant—cleared his throat.

Jhaell ignored him.

The man cleared his throat again.

Still, Jhaell did not react. He did not want to talk.

In a quiet, hesitant tone, the man murmured, "Sir?"

Simmering inside, Jhaell opened his eyes, turned his head, and glared at the man. It was the sergeant indeed. "What?!"

Shrinking under Jhaell's withering stare, Sergeant Rowe was quiet for a moment before he managed to say, "Ah...Fenidar, sir, I would respectfully remind you—again, sir—that some of the horses are nearly lame. Soon, half of my men will be walking on foot."

Twisting in his saddle, Jhaell examined the soldiers behind him. The beasts did look ragged, even more so than the men. If horses started falling, they would never catch their prey. Assuming the Progeny even came this way.

When he had split the soldiers, Jhaell had chosen the westerly route based on what was happening in the Borderlands. At the time, it seemed logical the Progeny might head there. With each plodding step of his horse, he regretted his choice.

"Sir?" prompted the sergeant. "May we rest or not?"

Jhaell faced forward, barely glancing at the man as he did. He tilted his head back and eyed the sky. Mu's orb hung low. Early dusk was not far away. "Can they not hold out until sunset, sergeant?"

"They are exhausted, sir. They need rest."

Jhaell squeezed his eyes shut, drew in a deep breath, and mumbled, "I should have never gone to Yellow Mud..."

The sergeant leaned over. "Pardon, sir?"

Jhaell ignored him, too busy blaming himself for everything that had led him here.

Had he not tried to impress Tandyr, had he not reacted rashly while standing on that bluff, had he not done a half-dozen other things without prior thought, then he would not be here. Most likely, he would be sitting in the library at Immylla, reading, searching, and seeking some mention of what Tandyr sought.

That was Jhaell's purpose.

That was what he was good at doing.

That was what would reunite him with Syra again.

Suddenly, he felt the dark crinkling of Void. Opening his eyes, he stared down at his bag. Someone was writing to him, the first time in three days. Without looking at the soldier, he said, "Tell the men to make camp. We will stay the night but leave before the sun rises, understand?"

In a voice filled with relief, the sergeant said, "Thank you, sir." He rode away at once, shouting orders to halt and set up the tents. The soldiers gave a weary, almost-mocking cheer that Jhaell did not much appreciate.

Pulling on his mount's reins, he stopped his horse, dismounted, and walked away, leaving the beast in the road. Someone would come and see to it.

He moved to the roadside and sat while waiting for the soldiers to stake his tent. Reaching into his bag, he pulled out the parchments and shuffled through them. Upon finding the one with writing, he placed it on top and read. It was from Baron Morus, a duchy nobleman loyal to Tandyr. The man was an advisor in the court of Duke Rholeb, the sovereign of the Marshlands, who had proven adept at providing useful information.

Jhaell—

We have a growing problem here. Refugees are coming every day now. The city can no longer hold them. The stories about the invasion are too numerous to discount any longer. Duke Rholeb sent yet another rider to Gobas today, asking Duke Vanson for an explanation or if he requires aid.

Jhaell paused a moment, affording himself a slight smile knowing that Duke Rholeb would never hear a reply.

As you requested, I have sent a patrol of Reed Men east, toward you. Remain on the Phinon Road, and they will reach you in a couple weeks. Might I inquire as to why you need them? I must admit, I was surprised to hear you were even in the duchies.

—Morus

Jhaell dismissed the message with a simple Weave of Air, watched the black words fade, and then slipped the parchments back in his bag without writing back. There was no good answer to the baron's question. A message that included, "I tried to kill the Progeny, but instead, I think I let them loose, and now I cannot find them" would not help his situation.

He glanced up to see if the soldiers had his tent ready. They did not. The men were slogging about, truly exhausted. Sighing, he dropped his head and stared at the ground.

While at a loss as to what he should do, he knew with certainty what he could not. His time at Immylla was finished, his prolonged absence at the Academy long past the point where he could explain it away. Distinguished One Hovathil had probably already set in motion the requisite process to terminate his position.

He still wondered what had become of the tomble and the stolen letter. He—again—considered porting to Redstone and speaking with Duke Everett, but—again—dismissed the idea. The duke would turn Jhaell straight over to Tandyr to further his own position.

Jhaell ran his fingers through his hair and sighed.

Perhaps he should simply tell Tandyr what he had done. The god might allow him to serve in some other way. He could certainly help with the advance in the Borderlands; Sudashian mages were crude with the Strands. While the thought of being surrounded by oligurts, mongrels, and razorfiends was more than unpleasant, he would do what was necessary.

Jhaell lifted his head and stared at the tired soldiers. If he somehow managed to stumble across the Progeny, these soldiers would be of little use to him. Perhaps he should visit Tandyr's army and attempt to arrange something with one of the demon captains. Sudashians, while vile creatures, were much more resilient than men.

After thinking it through, he realized it was his best option. As soon as he could, he would port west and find the nearest Sudashian camp. They should litter the Borderlands now. It would not be hard to find one.

After that, he would visit Tandyr's agent in the Southlands. If the Progeny had headed that way, perhaps there would be some sort of rumor about mages making its way through the land. Jhaell silently chastised himself for not giving the woman there one of the parchments.

"Sir, your tent is ready."

Glancing up, Jhaell found a soldier standing a few paces away. "Good."

If he was going to open a port, he needed the privacy of the tent. He did not dare weave openly in the presence of these men. They would stab him in the back the moment they realized he was a mage.

He stood and scanned the area for the lone tent with the red and black pennant on it. Upon spotting it, he took a single step then stopped. The tent was a dozen paces from where the soldiers had staked the horses. Jhaell had to sit upon one of the reeking beasts all day long. He had little interest in resting next to them.

"Soldier, who thought it a good idea to put my tent next to the horses?"

The man glanced to where the tent stood before turning back to face Jhaell, his eyes wide. "I'm terribly sorry, sir. We will move the horses immediately."

Jhaell looked toward the staked horses and saw that a few of them already had relieved themselves on the ground. Restraining himself as best he could, he muttered, "I do *not* want to sleep next to their filth. Move the tent, not the horses. Do you understand?"

The blue and gold clad solider nodded once, apologized again, and scampered away toward Jhaell's tent while shouting for the men to take it down.

As he watched the men scurry about, Jhaell congratulated himself on keeping his patience. Bad things happened when he did not.

CHAPTER 44: DEMON

Zecus awoke and slowly opened his eyes.

At first, he thought it was late dusk or early dawn, but the light was wrong. Seeing some type of cloth or canvas wall facing him, he reasoned he was in a tent of sorts. He was on his left side, lying in grass and dirt, his ankles and wrists still bound.

The air was warm, stuffy, and filled with an unpleasant odor he could not place. Outside, he heard metal clanging, the thudding of wood on wood, and voices shouting, voices that reminded him of the guttural grunting of an angry boar. As he lay there, unmoving, he noticed the sound of slow, steady breathing inside the tent. He was not alone.

Zecus rolled onto his right side and peered through the dimly lit tent. A man lay on his back, arms folded across his chest, staring at the peaked ceiling. A thick rope ran from his legs to a large metal stake driven into the ground, pressing the rope into the dirt. Zecus followed another length of rope running from the stake to his own legs.

Looking back to the man, he asked, "Who are—" His voice cracked, failing him. He tried to cough, but his throat was impossibly dry.

The man pointed to the side of the tent and spoke, his voice raspy. "You may want some water from the bucket." A short cackle followed his suggestion. "Then again, you might not."

Zecus tried to sit upright but what should have been a simple task was a struggle. He was weak and dizzy, his arms and feet bound. It took him a few tries, but he eventually succeeded. The old man made no effort to help.

Once in a sitting position, he scanned the tent and noticed a single, vertical line of light on the tent wall to his right. A skinny ray of sunlight slipped through the flaps and stretched across the trampled grass to illuminate a wooden bucket to his left. Zecus scooted on his rear to the bucket and peered inside. Ambient light reflecting off the liquid's surface revealed the water a few inches below the lip of the bucket. Maneuvering himself onto his knees, he attempted to bend over to drink but without his hands to brace himself, he fell to the ground, only just avoiding knocking over the bucket.

The old man laughed. "Well, that was foolish. There's a ladle right there."

Zecus twisted his head and spotted a wooden spoon behind the bucket. He had not seen it, but even if he had, he could not have used it. Moving his arms behind his back, he croaked, "My hands…"

"Ah, yes. Forgot about that," muttered the old man. "They'll stop doing that eventually. Here, let me help you."

Zecus lay on the ground for a moment, listening as the man scuffled closer. Water sloshed, wood slid against wood.

"Sit up," ordered the man.

With great effort, Zecus complied. The man was kneeling before him, holding out a ladle filled with water, a wicked smile on his face. "Drink up."

Zecus leaned forward, took a large mouthful from the ladle, and immediately turned his head to spit the foul tasting muck out, splattering it all over the side of the tent. It tasted like a dozen filthy men had taken a bath in it two weeks ago.

The man holding the ladle began to laugh hysterically.

The disgusting water had at least moistened Zecus' mouth, allowing him to ask, "Gods…what is that?"

"They say it's water. Not sure I believe them, though. It's best to drink it only when you have to. And right now, stranger, you look like you have to. So, close your eyes and take a big swallow."

Zecus eyed the man doubtfully and, for the first time, noticed the man's condition. He was light-skinned with wild, stringy white hair and ripped rags for clothes. While Zecus could not make out the color of the man's eyes, he was uneasy with the way they shifted about, never settling on anything for more than a brief moment.

"Go on," urged the man. "Drink."

Steeling himself, Zecus gulped down two large mouthfuls of the water and sat back, gagging. The man sniffed the water, made a disgusted face, and tossed the ladle back in the bucket. "Just wait until it's time to eat."

Zecus coughed out, "Where am I?"

"You, young man, have the unfortunate luck to find yourself in one of the Nine Hells." The man began laughing as though he had just said something terribly funny, clapping his hands together as if he were applauding.

Peering at the man with narrowed eyes, Zecus muttered, "Pardon?"

The man's cackling abruptly cut off. He tilted his head side-to-side, his eyes darting about. "Did you hear that?"

The sounds from outside had remained unchanged since Zecus had awoken. He shook his head. "I heard nothing."

The odd man scuttled over to one side of the tent, sat with his legs pulled to his chest, and began stroking his hair while mumbling to himself.

Zecus shook his head. The man was clearly mad.

Unnerved, Zecus turned his attention from the man and tried to puzzle out what he was going to do. His first thought was of escape so he scooted over to the stake in the ground and kicked it a few times, trying to knock it loose.

When the metal stake held fast, he shifted around until he could grip the handle with his hands and pulled. Still, the stake would not budge. After a few tugs, he quit trying. He was too weak.

Heavy footsteps approached the side of the tent with the slit of light splitting the canvas. Zecus stared at the flaps, listening to an exchange of gruff, guttural grunts outside.

In the darkness, the madman's voice scratched, "Talk, stranger. And don't stop."

Looking over at the man, Zecus said, "Pardon?"

"If you don't talk, it will kill you. If you stop talking, it will kill you. If you look at it wrong, it will kill you. Tell it what it wants to hear, and you'll live." He cackled again, quieter now. "That's why I'm still here."

Zecus was about to ask what "it" was when the tent's entrance split open, flooding the dark interior with sunlight. Squinting against the sudden brightness, Zecus spotted the silhouette of a very tall, very wide figure stride toward where he lay on the ground. Without a doubt, it was an oligurt.

Wary, Zecus stared at the beast, thinking it was going to knock him out again. Instead, when the monster reached him, it reached down, grasped the handle of the stake, and yanked upwards, freeing the pinned ropes underneath. After pulling Zecus' rope out, the oligurt slammed the stake back in the ground, pressing the madman's length back into the ground.

Turning to Zecus, the oligurt growled, "You stay quiet."

Zecus was more than a little taken aback. He had no idea oligurts could speak Argot.

The beast grabbed Zecus' legs and lifted, slinging him over its shoulder. Zecus' head slammed into the oligurt's back, setting his head throbbing anew.

The gray-skinned monster wound up the rope attached to Zecus' legs and lurched back toward the tent entrance. As they exited, Zecus spotted the madman in the corner smiling a wide, toothless grin while waving his hand in silent farewell.

Once outside, bright light of day temporarily blinded Zecus. New smells— a rotten-sweet stench, acrid smoke, the aroma of roasting meat—assaulted his nose. It was unpleasant.

He cracked open his eyes and, after letting them adjust to the brightness, lifted his head to look around. Not far from the tent he had just left—a tall brown canvas structure with two points atop it—a large bonfire roared. Two wooden crosses rose from the grass, just far enough from the fire that they would not catch. A naked man was on each, their arms strung out to the sides, heads hanging limp.

Gagging, Zecus shut his eyes tight and breathed through his mouth. After a time—and a few tentative breaths to check that the air was free of roasting-man smell—he re-opened his eyes.

Everywhere he looked, canvas tents covered the plain. Faded red and yellow pennants painted with strange symbols flew above most, flapping in the breeze. Bonfires roared everywhere, their smoke responsible for the thick haze drifting through the camp. While he did not see any more men roasting, he did spot a few goats sizzling on spits.

Oligurts lounged about the tents and fires, every one huge, bald, and draped in animal hide tunics. Each one that met Zecus' eye sneered. The camp's din was loud, but he was sure that they were growling at him.

As Zecus and his captor wound their way through the camp, they passed a makeshift wooden pen filled with hundreds of bullockboars, giving him his first decent look at the animals other than when he was lying over the back of one.

The creatures were a time and a half larger than a horse and astoundingly ugly. Foot-long white tusks jutted forth from a long snout that looked more bear than boar. Thick, dark brown fur covered their heads but stopped halfway down their necks. Pink skin splotched with black patches covered the rest of their bodies. It almost looked as if the head belonged to a different animal. The legs were shaped like a wolf's, only thicker and more muscular. Instead of paws, they had cloven hooves.

Zecus was still eyeing the pen when the oligurt carrying him let loose a low, angry growl that Zecus felt as much as heard. After a few more paces, the oligurt stopped.

Something—most definitely not an oligurt—hissed, "What do you want, gray-szzkin?"

The voice made Zecus' skin crawl, reminding him of the nerve-stinging squeaks of rock grinding against rock.

"Move aside," grunted the oligurt. "The ohraeg wants to speak to this fleshling."

"You are aszz much a fleszzling as he iszz."

"If I am late bringing the prisoner, I shall tell Urazûd you were the reason why."

The chittering voice snapped, "Stazsla mirtinz!"

In response, the oligurt loosed a deep, threatening snarl. The other voice clicked and hissed a few times, turning shrill enough that Zecus could not help but wince. When the oligurt growled even louder, the hissing halted. A moment later, the oligurt went quiet, too.

"Passzz then. And szztay away from our burrowszz."

Letting out a grunt of disgust, the oligurt resumed walking. After a few steps, Zecus was able to get a clear look at the soul with whom the oligurt had been speaking.

Had Zecus been standing, the top of the creature's head would have only come up to the middle of his chest. Thick, shiny quills ranging from black to a dark, iridescent blue covered the figure, as though dozens of knife blades had been bundled together and draped from its body. It even had quills on its long, pinched face, although they were shorter and softer-looking than the ones hanging from its thick forearms and wiry legs. The creature wore brown leather breeches around its upper legs while its chest was uncovered.

Beady, black-as-a-moonless-night eyes remained fixed on Zecus' face as he moved away on the oligurt's shoulder. The creature raised its right arm as if to wave when, with startling suddenness, every quill on its hand and forearm sprang to attention, flaring out to create a thicket of sharp blades.

Zecus' mouth fell open. He was staring at a razorfiend.

Turning his head in all directions, he found dozens upon dozens of the creatures surrounding him. Some were a mix of black and dark blue like the first, but there were other colors as well: dark grays, crimsons, and greens. Most were shirtless, although some wore a crisscrossing, leather harness. They all wore the same style of short breeches that stopped above what must be their knees.

The camp's composition changed. Here, there were no tents, no fires, and no oligurts. There were still pennants though, hanging from sticks that jutted out from the large earthen mounds that filled the area. They reminded Zecus of colossal anthills.

The oligurt did not walk very long before stopping again. "I have brought the fleshling for the ohraeg."

"Paszz, grayszzkin."

With a flapping of canvas, Zecus was plunged back into darkness. He was in another tent, one much larger than his last. His eyes adjusted quickly and after glancing around, he saw why: a ring of torches illuminated the interior.

The oligurt took a few steps in before hefting Zecus off its shoulder and placing him on the ground. Bending over, the monster growled, "Behave, fleshling." Damp and dank breath came with the warning, a palpable mixture of rotted meat and filth that Zecus tasted as much as smelled. Trying not to grimace in disgust, he nodded his understanding of the instructions.

With a grunt of satisfaction, the oligurt turned him around, helping steady him as his feet were still bound together. "As you commanded, Urazûd."

Zecus' eyes went round.

A dozen paces away, a bald man sat in a stout, wooden chair. Thick, black, ridged horns jutted from the sides of his head, spiraling upward and coming to a point nearly a foot above his forehead. His eyes were blood red and fixed on

Zecus, boring into him. He wore some sort of black metal armor on his chest and legs.

The demon-man, this spawn of the Nine Hells, spoke, his voice trembling with a strange, throbbing power. "Retreat to the entrance, Rorrargh."

"The rope will not reach," rumbled the oligurt, still holding the length leading to Zecus' feet.

"Where exactly do you think he will go? Leave the rope and step back."

As the oligurt dropped the rope beside Zecus and backed up to the tent's entrance, Urazûd shifted his gaze back to Zecus and studied him. The diabolical glint in his eyes turned Zecus winter-rain cold, even in the hot tent. After a long stretch of quiet, he spoke

"What is your name?"

Having no desire whatsoever to converse with a demon-man, Zecus pressed his lips together and remained silent.

"Reticent, I see," said the demon. "Then allow me to go first. I am Urazûd, servant of Chaos." He paused a moment, reached up, and scratched his face. It sounded like his nails were scraping the bark of a tree. Large flakes of skin fell away as he scratched, reminding Zecus of a molting snake. "Now. As you know my name, it is only proper I should know yours."

Zecus remained silent.

After a few moments, Urazûd leaned forward. "Your name is all I ask. What harm is there in sharing that?"

Still, Zecus did not respond.

The demon's blood-red eyes narrowed. Anger flashed across his face, his lips curled into a vicious snarl, and, in what might have been Zecus' imagination, the torches appeared to flare for a brief moment. "I have asked you your name twice, now. *Nicely.* I will not do so a third."

The man in the tent had said that to stay alive, he needed to talk. So, Zecus squared his shoulders, stared into the creature's eyes, and said with twice as much courage as he felt, "My name is Zecus Alsher of the village Drysa, demon, and I do not fear you."

The anger faded in an instant as an expression of calm claimed Urazûd's face. "Zecus…Zecus…" He repeated the name as if tasting the first bite of a foreign food. "You know, Zecus, there are two types of souls who claim they do not fear my kind. Courageous ones, of which there are few, and foolish ones, of which there are a vast many." His chair creaked as he leaned even further forward. "The odds do not favor you."

Determined to be in the former group, Zecus asked, "Where are the men I rode with?"

"Dead," replied Urazûd without hesitation. "Three survived the attack. One died on his way to me, the other refused to speak. So, here I am left with you.

Tell me, Zecus, exactly how many of you are there? And where I can find your camp?"

Zecus' eyes narrowed. "Pardon?"

"You and your fellow resistance fighters are like a cloud of gnats: an annoying, mostly harmless nuisance that is nonetheless slowing our advance. I am tired of the delays. More importantly, my master is growing impatient."

It seemed the demon-man thought Zecus knew significantly more about the Borderlands resistance than he truly did. Should he tell Urazûd that he had only just met the men, he was sure he would be roasting on a wooden cross in short order.

His mind raced and, within moments, he had a plan. By no means was it a good one as it mostly involved lying until he thought of something better. Drawing on every bit of inner strength he could summon, he said, "I will tell you what you want to know, demon." Urazûd's eyes shone with anticipation. "But I ask for something in return."

A slight, almost amused grin spread over the demon-man's lips. "Ask your favor. However, do not assume I am a gracious host."

"After I give you what you want, you set me free."

The demon-man's face was an unreadable mask, the blood red eyes quietly simmering like a pot of water over a meager fire. "First, I want to hear what you have to say. Then you will have my answer."

As it was probably the best Zecus was going to get, he said, "If you have a map, I can show you where we hide."

Keeping his gaze on Zecus, Urazûd called, "Rorrargh! A map!" Softening his tone, he added, "And a chair for our guest."

Rorrargh stuck his head through the tent entrance to relay the order, prompting a terse exchange with the razorfiend guards outside. Shortly thereafter, a razorfiend entered the tent with a rolled-up parchment in one hand while dragging a chair in the other. Torchlight danced along the fiend's iridescent crimson and black quills.

Glancing over his shoulder, Zecus watched the figure approach, resisting the urge to hop from the creature's path. As the razorfiend passed him, it released the chair and continued past, stopping to stand in front of the demon-man. Bowing, the razorfiend handed the parchment over.

Taking a gamble, Zecus said, "I would have a much easier time pointing things out if my hands were not tied."

Urazûd glared at him for a moment before looking at the razorfiend. "Cut the rope from his hands." The razorfiend bowed and began to turn toward Zecus wearing an expression he interpreted as a grin when Urazûd added, "Only the rope."

The bladed creature hesitated a moment, a disappointed frown replacing its grin, before slinking behind him. Zecus shuddered as the fiend's cool, hard quill brushed against his wrists. They felt like metal. With one slice, the bonds fell away.

Stretching his arms before him, Zecus rubbed his wrists as he watched the razorfiend creep from the tent. As it passed the oligurt, the razorfiend flared its quills, a metallic rattle filling the tent. Rorrargh jumped back and lifted its thick fists, growling. The fiend chittered softly—laughing, Zecus supposed—as it slipped through tent's entrance.

After turning back to Urazûd, Zecus asked, "How do you keep them from killing each other?" The question was an honest one. He did not understand what kept the two races from tearing each other apart. They obviously hated one another.

"I have my ways," replied the demon-man as he unrolled the parchment. "Most of the time, they behave. Although, there is still the occasional…disagreement. I deal with those as I must." There was an odd, almost lustful glint in Urazûd's eyes. His nostrils flared.

"I've only seen oligurts and razorfiends here," said Zecus. "Where are the mongrels?"

Urazûd looked up sharply, his eyes narrowing. "This camp does not have any of their kind here. I would expect you to know that."

Panic surged through Zecus. He had already stumbled in his bluff. Trying to cover his folly, he said, "I don't know what camp this is. How long was I unconscious? A day? Two? More? I could be miles from where we were attacked."

Urazûd rose from his chair, stalked toward Zecus, and stopped as few paces away. Zecus was surprised to see that the demon-man was no taller than he was, discounting the horns. He had expected the demon-man to be taller. Even more remarkable was the odor emanating from Urazûd. The seductive, almost syrupy sweet smell stirred memories of the bluebells that would cover the Borderlands after the winter rains.

"Sit down, Zecus. We have much to discuss."

Zecus complied and sat on the rickety wooden chair beside him while trying to ignore the impossible, intoxicating bouquet of flowers.

Urazûd held the parchment up before him. "This is where we are it now." He pointed to a dot with the name Midiah written in flowing script beside it. "Where are you hiding?"

"Where outside of Midiah?" asked Zecus.

"Not outside. We are in it."

Zecus stared into the demon's red eyes, confused. He knew Midiah to be a small town of several thousand tough, frontier people. "I did not see any buildings."

"That is because they are gone. Now, show me the locations of your camps and—" He stopped, the corners of his eyes tightening, and looked back to the tent's entrance.

Hearing the flaps open, Zecus risked a look back. Two razorfiends, hanging in midair, floated into the tent, clearly startling Rorrargh as they passed. A man with brilliant, bright blond hair—almost white—dressed in unusually cut, tan clothes stepped into the tent. He was oddly proportioned, his arms too long for his body, his fingers too skinny. His features were strange, too, with eyes and lips wider than looked right.

Halfway to Urazûd, the razorfiends stopped moving, yet remained suspended in air. The stranger continued past them and toward Zecus and Urazûd. As he drew near, Zecus realized it was no man at whom he was staring. This was something straight from a playman's tale. This was an ijul.

The stranger stopped beside the chair, glanced at Zecus, gave him a dismissive frown, and then stared at the demon-man. "Your guards told me that I would have to wait until you were done with your prisoner. I do not like to wait."

Urazûd eyed the ijul for a long moment before responding. "Why are you here, Jhaell?" His tone was a mix of annoyance and begrudging respect. "Should you not be safe in your school, reading books? Looking for Tandyr's prizes?"

A muscle twitched in Jhaell's cheek. He looked back down at Zecus. "Do you plan to kill him soon?"

"That is to be decided."

"Then let us talk in private. There is something I wish to discuss with you."

Urazûd nodded and the pair strode to the back of the tent and spoke in hushed tones, leaving Zecus unable to hear anything they said. At first, Urazûd appeared surprised by what the Jhaell had to say, then angry, and finally pleased, nodding along enthusiastically as the ijul spoke.

Suddenly a number of shrieks and roars filled the air, drifting in from the camp. Urazûd's head snapped up as he stared at the tent's entrance. Looking back to the ijul, he barked, "Release my guards." The two razorfiends still hanging in the air fell to the ground, landing spryly on their feet. Urazûd glared at them and shouted, "Find out what's happening!"

The pair rushed from the tent. Moments later, one reentered and exclaimed, "The grayskinszz attacked our burrowszz!" It eyed the oligurt not more than a few paces from it, hissing, "Steclimizz stavilz!"

Rorrargh took a step forward, glowering at the fiend. "Kerairg othar nergh!"

"Stop it!" bellowed Urazûd as he strode across the tent. "If *either* of you touch one another, I will kill you where you stand!"

The oligurt and fiend continued to stare at one another, but they remained quiet.

"You seem busy," said Jhaell. "I will leave you to things."

Urazûd whirled around to face the ijul. "Come back when you are sure you have found them, Jhaell. I will be ready." Pointing to the razorfiend, he shouted, "You! Show me where they fight. Rorrargh, stay here and watch him." He glared at Zecus for the briefest of moments then strode from the tent, following the razorfiend guard.

The oligurt moved to the tent entrance and stared outside, watching whatever was happening as the sounds of fighting drew ever closer to the tent. Zecus tried to stare past the oligurt to see what was happening, but the beast's bulk blocked any view he had.

A few moments later, Zecus heard the unexpected sound of ripping parchment. Turning back to where the ijul stood, Zecus spotted what he thought was a second slit in the tent wall, one that had not been there a moment ago. Only when the ijul reached up and drew back a flap, blackness waited within rather than expected sunlight. Without pause, the ijul stepped through and disappeared in the void.

Zecus stared, baffled, wondering where the ijul had gone. A half a heartbeat later, he realized it did not matter. Wherever the ijul was now, it was not here.

He glanced back to the oligurt to find the monster still staring outside. Bending over, he gathered the rope still tied to his feet and then slowly rose from his chair, careful to keep his balance. Once upright, he took one last look at the distracted oligurt and then began to hop toward the new flap. He made it a few jumps when an alarmed snort arose from behind him.

"Orag huthrang!"

Zecus ignored the oligurt, focusing solely on the flap as he bounded around Urazûd's chair. Behind him, the oligurt thudded after him. Stumbling, Zecus dropped the rope he carried yet managed to avoid falling himself. With one final hop, he leapt headfirst into the blackness, crashed face first into a sturdy wooden beam, and fell into a pile of dry straw. He lay there a moment, dazed, before sitting up, the scent of hay and horse thick in his nose.

He was in a long, dimly lit building. Tall double doors were at both ends and a few open-air windows were high above him. Small rooms lined the walls, each with a five-foot tall wooden door topped with two feet of open space. As he stared, the yellowish-tan head of a horse—a white stripe on its nose—emerged from one of the openings and stared straight at Zecus.

He scanned the entire building again, searching for the ijul but the room was empty. Looking behind him, he saw a black slit hanging in midair through which the rope tied to his feet led. On either side of the tear, the world appeared to flutter, shimmering like summer heat rising from sun-cooked earth.

His eyes widened as the rope began to retreat through the split. He threw his arms around the beam into which he had crashed and held tight as the rope drew taut, pulling his legs back toward the hole. Zecus looked for something to cut the rope, but there was nothing but straw nearby. Hanging on the wall across the room were a dozen sorts of strange metal tools, but they were most definitely out of reach.

Inevitably, his grip on the beam began to slip. Zecus was weak from not eating, and his arms sore from being clasped behind his back. Nevertheless, he closed his eyes and squeezed the wooden beam as hard as he could, determined to take the post with him.

A soft pop filled the building, the tension on his legs released, and he crumpled to the ground. Breathing heavily, he glanced back to his feet, and saw the slit and flaps were gone. The world was solid again. Pulling his legs closer, Zecus grasped the rope and held it up. The end was severed clean.

With relief washing over him, he collapsed back into the pile of straw.

"Bless the gods."

A moment later, he sat right back up. The hole—undoubtedly magical— might open again at any moment. And there was the issue of the missing ijul.

Crawling to the wall with the tools, Zecus found a strange, double-bladed metal apparatus. Whatever its true purpose was, Zecus was happy to use its sharp edge to cut through the rope binding his feet.

Once free, he stood and, as quietly as possible, approached the tall double doors closest to him, keeping an eye up the long passage to the other set. Another horse, this one a solid reddish-brown color, stuck his head out from another of the small rooms. It stared at him and let out a low, inquisitive nicker.

Zecus glared at the horse and shushed it. The horse whinnied in response.

Turning from horses, he examined the set doors in front of him. Whoever had been here last had not shut the sliding doors all the way, leaving a small space through which Zecus peered.

He gasped.

The world outside was impossibly green. Thick bunches of verdant, flowering bushes sprouted up from waist-high grass. Swaying, emerald-leafed trees towered high into the sky, thrice as tall as the bulboa trees of the Borderlands. A small dirt path strayed from the doors, lined with bushes covered in bunches of tiny, purple flowers.

The ijul was hurriedly striding down the road, away from the building, his bright blond hair taking on the warm colors of an evening sun. Confused, Zecus glanced at the sky and saw the reds and oranges of early twilight. When he had entered Urazûd's tent, it had been late afternoon.

An unexpectedly cool breeze whistled through the crack and tickled his face. The air was somehow thicker and heavier, full of life and the sweet scent of flowers.

Zecus watched the ijul walk away, ready to run should he turn back. When the ijul disappeared around a bend in the path, Zecus counted twenty heartbeats and then stepped back from the doors.

Turning around, he sprinted to the other end of the building—past the two staring horses—and found the set of doors there shut tight. He grasped of the door's wooden handle and pulled it open a few inches, wincing as a loud clank echoed through the building. He peered through the crack between the doors and was again struck by how alive the land was. Like the other side, a dirt path led away from the building, meandering down a gentle slope before twisting around a bend and disappearing into the trees. A slight breeze blew from the west, carrying with it wispy, white puffs with tiny seeds attached.

He held his breath and did not move, listening carefully, praying the loud clang had not alerted anyone to his presence. Other than the soft chirping of birds outside and another inquisitive nicker from a horse behind him, the world was quiet.

Looking over his shoulder, he found a few more horses had poked their heads out of their rooms and were staring at him. He counted seven in total, spread among eight rooms. Hurrying to the eighth, horseless room, he found it packed with oddly designed saddles, bridles, ropes, and tack. For some reason, every saddle had looped leather straps hanging from the sides. Dismissing the oddity, he grabbed the nearest one and rushed from the room, taking a bridle and a pair of saddlebags on his way out.

Hurrying down the walkway, Zecus headed toward the first horse he had seen after arriving through the magical flap, the yellow-tan one with the white striped nose. The beast had been both alert and quiet, qualities he valued in a mount. Unlatching the door, he slid it open, went inside, and saddled the horse once he figured out the unfamiliar straps and buckles. The horse remained motionless, patiently waiting, sometimes even looking back at him as if inquiring what was taking so long.

After leading the horse from the straw-filled room, he moved to the wall with the hanging tools. He examined the array of odd implements, trying to decide if any of them were suitable to use as a weapon. He had no idea where he was or what dangers he might face. He selected the double bladed metal tool he had used to cut his ropes and slid it into a loop on the saddle. He also chose a long wooden staff with a flat metal head on one end. Resting it on his shoulder, he led his horse to the second set of doors. He was not proud that he was stealing, but he had no choice.

He slid one door open just wide enough to get the horse out, moved into the open air, and stepped back to stare up at the building. A dark blue coating covered the wooden structure with some panels colored a bright white. Why someone would waste so much precious wood on a home for horses was beyond Zecus. A quick glance at the trees towering over him and he realized Borderlanders might do the same thing with this much wood.

He pulled himself up into the saddle, laid the staff across his lap, and directed his mount down the path. He kept the pace slow and quiet until he was some distance away from the building, and then urged the horse to a canter. As the leather straps on the saddle banged into his feet, Zecus realized their purpose and slipped his boots into them both.

The dirt path led to a larger roadway that ran north and south, judging by the evening sun shining straight into his eyes. The northern stretch of road ran arrow-straight up a gentle slope through trees and brush. A handful of horses with riders was on the way, heading in his direction so Zecus turned left and headed south. Until he knew more about where he was, he did not want to talk to anyone.

He kept his horse at a steady trot while trying to puzzle out what had happened. The ijul was a mage, of that there was no doubt. And while he was more than grateful to be free of the demon-man, he now had to figure a way to get back home. Perhaps some of what he had seen could be useful in repelling the invaders.

Catching a flash of movement ahead of him, Zecus looked up to see a pair of light-skinned men on horseback riding around a bend, straight toward him. He could hardly leap off the road without drawing undue attention to himself, so he kept a steady pace, hoping to ride casually past the men. The two men approached, staring at him with quizzical expressions yet offering a pleasant "Good evening" as they passed. He hastily returned the nicety while wondering at their odd accent.

After the bend, the countryside opened up. The road sloped down a hill, leading to a gray stone bridge that spanned a wide, sparkling surface that reflected the light of the setting sun. With a start, Zecus realized that the shining surface was water. He tugged his horse's reins and stopped in the middle of the road.

"Bless the gods…"

He gawked at the sight below, shaking his head in disbelief. Much like ijuli, "rivers" existed only in playmen's tales. During his time in Demetus and the Marshlands, he had seen plenty of water—more than ever before—but it was all dank and stagnant.

It took him a moment before he noticed the two men standing at the bridge's edge, staring up at him. He marked the pair as soldiers by their matching blue and gold uniforms and wondered if they could help him. They would certainly be able to tell him where he was. Then again, asking questions such as "where am I?" might lead down paths he did not want to travel.

Zecus turned his horse around and rode back around the bend. As soon as the soldiers were out of sight, he veered west, off the road and into the thick grass and tall trees. After a time, he aimed south a bit, intending to make his way to the river while ensuring he would be far enough west to remain out of sight of the soldiers.

By the time he made it to the riverbank, Mu's orb had dipped below the horizon, the sky a layered mix of pinks and oranges. After slipping off his horse, he collapsed on the muddy shore and gulped from the river, drinking as much as he could. The water was not clear—in fact, it was rather gritty—but it soothed his parched throat. His stolen horse came and drank beside him, finishing long before he did.

Once his thirst was slaked, he scooped water and splashed it in his face. He winced as he brushed a giant lump sticking out from his forehead. The bump was incredibly tender to the touch and scabbed over with dried blood and bits of grass. Scratches and scrapes covered the rest of his face. It suddenly occurred to him why the two strangers in the road had gaped at him. He thought what he must have looked like to them and laughed aloud.

He inspected his clothes and found them covered with dirt, grime, and his blood. He stripped off everything and stepped into the water to clean himself, gingerly washing the open wounds on his temple and face. He cleaned his clothes as best he could, rubbing out most of the dirt but giving up on the blood stains.

When he was done, he put on just his underclothes and boots, mounted his horse, and hung his shirt and breeches on his stolen staff to dry. By now, the sun had disappeared below the western horizon and the sky's colors had deepened to a dark violet. Tall cliffs of clouds lined the southern horizon where jagged lightning bolts danced between sky and ground.

Zecus shook his head in wonderment. "Trees, rivers, *and* rain?" This was a blessed land.

He decided to continue heading west, staying along the river for no other reason than the clean water it provided. Perhaps he would come across a village or town where he could bargain for food. Although, with nothing to trade, he would likely have to beg instead

He put heel to horse and rode west. Off in the distance, thunder rumbled.

Chapter 45: Trail

Sutri's Leisure Day

Nathan stared at the glistening plain, beads of water from last evening's rain clinging to the grass and sparkling in the morning sun. The vista was almost beautiful enough to make him forget what he was doing: riding uninvited through the Southlands, a tomble mage by his side, tracking people whose prophesized destiny was to thwart the gods of the Cabal.

He shook his head and sighed. It was all a bit overwhelming.

Following his late-night discussion with Nundle, Nathan had decided to continue southward for no other reason than his gut pointed him in that direction. A couple days ago, his instinct seemed vindicated when a scout picked up a trail in the grasslands. Nathan had immediately sent three scouts ahead to follow the path with instructions to return should they find something important. The rest of the Sentinels had been following the path since.

Nathan looked to his right, glancing at the tomble that had both solved some mysteries yet foisted new ones upon him. Nundle rode atop his small chestnut horse, a bittersweet smile fixed on his face as he gazed at the glittering, sun-soaked plain. The Sentinels, their number currently at forty-four, rode fanned out behind them.

"You look melancholy, little one."

Nundle glanced over, arched an eyebrow, and said, "I've been meaning to talk to you about that."

"About what?"

"I'm not permitted to call you by your name in front of your soldiers, but you can call me 'little one?'" His tone was one of gentle teasing.

Nathan chuckled, dipped his head in apology, and said, "Pardon me, *Nundle.*"

Nundle bowed his head graciously. "You are pardoned."

"Nevertheless, you are a touch somber this morning, are you not?"

Nundle waved an arm, gesturing toward the grassy plains. "Only because this reminds me of home. Granted, there is no place in the Boroughs where grass grows this high—if there were, we'd lose one another in it—but the way the sun shines on it..." He trailed off, the wistful smile returning. "It looks a bit like the winter wheat fields outside of Deepwell."

"How long have you been away from home?"

Looking over, Nundle asked, "What day is it?"

"Sutri's Leisure Day," answered Nathan. He had been keeping a record of their trip and knew the exact day without doubt.

"Let's see, then," sighed Nundle, his face twisting up in thought. "It's been five years, three turns, and...twelve days."

Nathan's eyes narrowed. He had expected an estimation of time, not an exact count.

Nundle smiled and explained, "I left home the day after my sixty-seventh yearday. Rather easy for me to remember."

"Ah," said Nathan, nodding his understanding. "Did you leave someone behind? A wife? Children?"

"Goodness, no," said Nundle shaking his head vigorously. "I've never married. I was rather close once, but..." A somewhat guilty frown spread over his face and his eyes went unfocussed. A moment later, he shook his head and muttered, "Let's leave it at that. I was close once."

Nathan could sense a story there, a story Nundle wished to keep private. Respecting the tomble's wishes, he moved on. "Family, then? Any brothers or sisters?"

That question brought a smile back to Nundle's face. "You could say that. Three older brothers: Mather, Coblin, Filmar. And two younger sisters: Jolsi and Rillo. My mother, father, twelve aunts and uncles, fifty-seven first-cousins, and only the gods know how many seconds and thirds."

Nathan smiled wide. "With a family that big, do you think they've noticed you're gone?"

"Without a doubt. I sort of made a deal about things when I left." He shook his head, frowning. "That last evening was truly unpleasant, telling my family I was leaving, but not telling them why or where."

"Why couldn't you tell them?"

"Because they didn't know what I was. In the Boroughs, mages might not be outlaws like they are here, but they—we, I suppose—are looked down upon. Shunned by 'proper' society." His frown grew into a full scowl. "Something I was guilty of doing myself before I learned I was a mage, too." His voice dropped to just above a whisper. "It's *not* a time of my life I am particularly proud of. I hurt people I cared about."

Hoping to raise tomble's spirits, Nathan said, "You know, you should visit the tomble villages in the Foothills Duchy. Perhaps it will ease a bit of the homesickness."

Nundle looked up at him, the frown falling away and replaced by open curiosity. "What can you tell me about those?"

"Very little, truthfully. Legend says that the tombles who fought in the Demonic War founded them."

Nundle's eyes opened wide. "Say that again?"

"What? That the tombles who fought in the Demonic War founded them?"

Nundle remained quiet for a moment, an astonished look on his face, before saying, "That's what I thought you said. You're saying tombles, *tombles* fought in the Demonic War?"

"Why is that so shocking?"

"For a number of reasons, I suppose. To start, in all the histories I read, there never any mention of tombles fighting in that war."

"Books often leave details out," noted Nathan. "They're but one person's view of events."

"True, but even if that were the case here, there's the rather important fact that tombles do not war. *Ever.*"

Nathan looked over, confused. "What do you mean?"

"Just that. Tombles do not war. We never have."

It was Nathan's turn to be surprised. "Never?"

"Never," said Nundle with a firm shake of his head. "Aggression of any sort is dealt with severely in the Boroughs. War is simply *not* done."

"Are your neighbors equally as peaceful?"

"Thankfully, yes. Jularrn has always had a good relationship with the Boroughs. And Cartu—well, if you know anything about Cartu, you know they are too busy with themselves to bother much with us."

"Let us say I know nothing about Cartu."

Nundle looked over at Nathan, eyebrows arched. "Truly?"

"Truly. I know the Great Lakes well, a bit about the surrounding duchies, but beyond that?" He shook his head.

"Are you not curious about the rest of Terrene?"

"I am as curious as anyone, Nundle. But in this particular matter, my duty does not require me, nor does it leave me any time, to satisfy it."

Nundle was quiet for a heartbeat or two before a smile slowly spread over his face. "Well…as we have nothing *but* time as we ride…?"

Nathan chuckled, shrugged his shoulders, and accepted the implied offer. "Why not? It will fill the day. Tell me, Nundle, what have I been missing?"

Over the remainder of the morning, Nathan's understanding of the world expanded. Quickly.

Nundle began with Cartu, telling him how over eight hundred years ago, a mountain exploded in fire and ash on the western coast of Mantioch, wiping out most of the region. The countryside remained desolate for a century before a myriad of races—men, saeljul, tijul, erijul, dirgmour, atarkas, and even divina—settled the deserted lands. They formed a new nation—the Commonwealth of

Cartu—that, today, rivaled the Oaken Duchies in size. Its system of rule was much different from the duchies, with decisions made by large body of individuals from the various races and cultures. With so many differences between them, however, achieving agreement on anything was nigh impossible.

Nathan interrupted him at that point. "Seems an odd way rule a country."

Nundle peered up at the taller man, squinting against sun and pulling down his wide-brimmed cloth hat to shade his eyes. "May I speak freely? I do not wish to offend you with my opinions."

"If I have not proven that I can be open-minded, I am not sure what else I can do."

Nundle smiled and offered a nod of concession. "Quite true."

Nathan had accepted everything the tomble had told him, despite some of Nundle's outlandish claims. The same instinctual sense that had made Nathan uneasy the moment he had met the saeljul—be his name Fenidar or Jhaell—told him Nundle was an honest soul telling the truth. In fact, his immediate trust of Nundle ran so deep that the morning after their long talk by the oak tree, he ordered three men to ride as fast as they could to catch Corporal Holb with a distinct change in orders. He was done following Fenidar-Jhaell's orders

One thing Nathan had not done, however, was share Nundle's story with the men. He was still trying to work out how to inform the soldiers the truth about Fenidar, the duke, and the fact that their sergeant was making decisions based on a centuries' old prophecy and the word of a mage. He had yet to come up with anything even remotely acceptable. Until then, Nundle was to remain silent on the subject of magic, something to which the tomble had readily agreed.

Nundle hesitated a moment, looked away briefly, and then stared back. "Well, to be honest, I find the idea of lords and ladies absurd. Nobles ruling simply because they are nobles? It's…silly." He shook his head, scoffing, "It takes *no* skill to be born to the right parents."

Nathan's opinion of Nundle continued to increase. "Nundle, your observation does not offend me in the least. In fact, I happen to believe the same. Although, I would not give voice to such an opinion in most company. Some nobles might not be fit to rule, but rule they do. And questioning their authority is…unwise."

"I shall keep that in mind," said Nundle.

After a moment passed—filled by the quiet rustle of prairie grass, the steady clop of horse hooves, and the murmured conversations of the men behind them—Nathan looked back to the tomble. "So how is ruling done in your home, then?"

"Well," sighed Nundle. "Similar to Cartu, but with few people and less time-wasting. Our towns have councils chosen by those who live there. I served on Deepwell's for two years, actually. It was dreadful."

Smiling, Nathan said, "Villages and towns do the same here."

"Ah, but in the Boroughs, you see, we use councils for everything. Towns, villages, cities, provinces. Even the country."

"The country is run by council?"

"It is."

"Chosen by whom?"

"Everyone," said Nundle. "Well, *almost* everyone. You must be past your fifteenth yearday."

"What happens if people choose poorly?"

"Then we are ruled by poor leaders," conceded Nundle. "But at least it is our own fault and not because fate gave some noble a lout of a son or daughter. Admittedly, it happens more often than one would hope—poor leaders elected, that is. And many are in it just for power and prestige. I've always sort of felt sorry for them in a way…"

Nathan sat in his saddle, thinking through what Nundle had explained and comparing it against with which he was familiar. After a few moments, he stared back down to the tomble. "Honestly, your system does not sound better than ours. Just different."

A wry smile spread over Nundle's face. "I was just thinking the same thing."

Out of the corner of his eye, Nathan spotted a flicker of movement far ahead on the southern horizon. He instinctively leaned forward to get a better look but all he could make out was a tiny dark dot moving through the grass.

"It's one of the scouts," said Nundle.

Nathan glanced over. The tomble was also staring south. "How can you tell?"

"We—tombles, that is—have better eyesight than longlegs—ah, men. Sorry."

As the scout drew closer, Nathan recognized him as Wil Eadding, a young footman with short, light-brown hair and a face that had yet to produce a man's whisker. Wil was a natural with the sword—by far the best in the company—but his other skills were lacking, which was why Nathan had sent him with the two best scouts in the Sentinels. He had hoped Wil would learn something.

When Wil arrived, he wheeled his reddish-brown horse around and fell in beside Nathan. The horse was breathing hard, spit flying past the bit clenched in the back of its jaw.

Looking over, Nathan said, "Morning, Wil. Does your horse need water?" He might need to say something to Wil about not riding his mount so hard.

"No, Sergeant. I found some rainwater in a hole not too far back." He reached down and patted his Hawthorne Red on the neck. "He should be fine."

"Then report. What did you find?" When the footman glanced past the sergeant to eye Nundle, Nathan said, "It's fine, son. Speak freely."

For the most part, the men had taken a liking to the tomble. He was sure they had a long list of questions as to who Nundle was and why Nathan had so readily accepted the tomble into their ranks, but they held their tongues as good soldiers were trained to do.

"Of course, Sergeant." Wil nodded southward. "In a couple of miles, we'll come across the remains of a camp. Hunsfin, Blainwood, and I searched the area a couple days back, but didn't find much besides the remnants of a campfire, some burnt grass, and the signs of three horses."

"Three, you say?" asked Nathan. The Trackers had found evidence of three horses by the cliff south of Smithshill. It most likely was a coincidence, but he hoped it was not.

"Yes, Sergeant. Three."

Nundle leaned forward to peer around Nathan. "Pardon me, but could you describe the burnt grass for me?"

A tiny furrow appeared in Wil's brow. Shrugging his shoulders, he said, "Not much to describe. There were patches of burnt grass all over. Mostly near the campfire."

"Huh," mumbled Nundle. He turned away and stared south, a pensive expression etched on his face.

Seeing that meant something to him, Nathan prompted, "Nundle?"

Nundle spared a brief glance at Wil, then looked to Nathan and gave a quick shake of his head. "Not now."

Guessing that whatever the tomble was thinking had to do with magic—which meant it would have to wait—Nathan looked back to Wil. "So, then. Burnt grass. Well, as it rained all of yesterday, the burning had to have occurred sometime before two evenings ago."

Wil nodded along in agreement. "That's what Blainwood said."

"I hope that is not the only reason you came back, Wil. If it's not too far ahead, we would have come across it on our own."

Arching his eyebrows, Wil said, "Oh, no, Sergeant, there's more. Much more. The trail ultimately leads to a farm on a river where—" the young man paused and rubbed his hand over his face, grimacing "—well, where something happened."

"Start from the beginning, Wil. And be clear with the details."

Wil then recounted everything the three scouts had found at the farm. Signs of a bloody fight. A ruined house missing its roof and a wall. A large pile of sand where the missing wall had once stood. Two fresh graves, a small one in a longpepper field a much larger one further down the hill.

When Wil was done, Nundle asked a number of very unusual, very specific questions about the sand: what it looked like, the color of it, if the grains were all the same size or varied with chucks of rock. Nathan again supposed the queries had something to do with magic, and wondered what it all meant. Once the tomble was done, Nathan eyed Wil and asked a question of his own.

"What could you gather about the graves?"

Grimacing as if he had swallowed something rotten, Wil said, "Hunsfin wanted to dig them both up, but Blainwood and I refused. He left the single grave alone, but said he had a feeling about the larger one, so he found a shovel, and dug into one side, just deep enough to find that whoever was buried there was facedown."

"Were they now?" asked Nathan, surprised by that detail.

"What?" asked Nundle, glancing between Nathan and Wil. "What does that mean?"

"That they were lawbreakers," answered Nathan. "Murderers or the like." He looked back to Wil. "How many bodies were in the grave?"

"Don't know for sure," said Wil. "Blainwood didn't want to waste the time to dig it all up. But we figured six or seven."

"And you said the house was small, yes?"

Wil nodded. "Single room, big enough to hold three or four people. There were three sleeping pallets, so I'd say three people lived there."

Quickly developing a theory as to what happened, Nathan asked, "And a single grave in the field nearby?"

"Yes," replied Wil. "Although why it was in the same field they grow crops is odd."

"Different customs for different people, Wil," said Nathan. "Could Blainwood tell how many horses had been there? I'm guessing around ten?"

Wil paused for a moment before answering. "He said nine or ten." His eyes narrowed. "How did you know?"

"Think it through, Wil. One of two things happened. Either the people we are following attacked the farm, killed seven or eight people—at a house that holds three—buried one in a field and the rest together like criminals, or…" He trailed off, wanting Wil to come up with the more likely alternative on his own. It would make the footman's story more convincing when he shared it with the rest of the men, which was something Nathan was counting on him doing.

It only took the young soldier a moment before he answered. "Or, they *stopped* an attack, killed the brigands, and buried them face down. The lone grave probably belonged to someone who lived at the farm."

"Exactly," praised Nathan. "Excellent job."

Wil began to nod his head slowly. "That would certainly explain everything else we found."

Nathan's eyebrows drew together. "Everything else?"

"Yes. Away from the house, we found the remnants of a campfire, not much more than a day old. And a trail that led east, along the river with at least four, perhaps five horses."

A disappointed frown spread over Nathan's face. "You forgot to mention that in your report."

Wil's face fell. "I did, didn't I?"

Nathan rewarded his men with praise when they performed well, but remained firm with them when they did not. With a hard edge to his voice, he said, "You had plenty of time to think through what you needed to say on your ride back."

Wil sat straight in his saddle, his lips pressed tight. "Yes, Master Sergeant." The young man was clearly upset, but Nathan could tell it was with himself and not his sergeant.

Still, what Wil had left out did not jeopardize the scenario Nathan envisioned. However, it did change what happened after the attack at the farm. Those whom they were following had ridden away with two more horses—and probably people—than when they had arrived. "I assume that Hunsfin and Blainwood followed the trail east, then?"

Nodding, Wil, said, "They did. We camped last night at the farmhouse, but once the clouds cleared and there was enough moonlight, Hunsfin and Blainwood left to follow the trail and I started my ride back here."

"It's dangerous to ride at night, Wil."

"I was careful, Sergeant. I went slow."

Nathan did not have too much room to chastise the young man. Since meeting Nundle, he had kept his men marching past twilight every day, stopping only when all the stars were out. He did not like doing it, but he was hoping to close the distance on their prey.

"How far to the first campsite?" asked Nathan.

Wil stared south. "A mile now, perhaps two."

"Thank you, Wil. Now fall back into the column."

The young footman nodded and pulled his reins back, halting his horse to wait for the body of Sentinels to catch up to him while Nathan and Nundle rode ahead. A glance at Nundle revealed the tomble slouched in his saddle, his eyes forward without looking at anything in particular. There was an introspective air about him.

Twisting to the side, pretending to stretch his back, Nathan chanced a look back at the company behind him. A handful of men were riding near Wil's horse, listening to the footman speak.

"You know," began Nundle, his voice quiet enough that it would not carry, "I had a high opinion of you before we met, Nathan, but you continue to impress."

Swinging back around in his saddle, Nathan looked at Nundle. "Pardon?"

"At first, I didn't understand why you were leading him on that way, but now?" Nundle paused, turned, and gave Nathan a sly grin. "In no time at all, the story about how these 'outlaws' helped save the innocent farmers from dastardly bandits will make its way through the ranks. I would not be surprised if, by this time tomorrow, there had been thirty murderers in the grave they found. All stopped by those we follow." He lifted a single eyebrow. "I'd bet a gold round—or ducat, if you prefer—that the word 'heroes' will have been whispered a dozen times by nightfall."

Nathan returned Nundle's slight smile with one of his own. "I keep forgetting you're much older than you appear." He had been shocked when Nundle said he was over seventy years old. Even baby-faced Wil looked older than Nundle. "Thankfully, young Wil did not catch on to what I was doing. Wisdom comes with time, does it not?"

Nundle's grin widened. "My father used to say, 'If age is all it takes to be sage, why are there so many old fools?'"

Nathan chuckled while nodding his head. "True. *Very* true." After sparing a glance back at the soldiers, he looked back to Nundle and lowered his voice to ask, "Think you can tell me why the burn marks interested you? And the sand at the house?"

"Do you mind if I wait until we reach the campsite first? I want to be sure before I say anything." He glanced over. "Oh, and when we get there, keep the men back."

"Is it dangerous?"

"I doubt it. I merely wish to speak in private."

Nathan nodded, turned to his detachment, and ordered a quick trot. He wanted to get to this campsite as quickly as possible.

Soon, an area of trampled grass broke the constant blanket of green ahead of them. Nathan halted the column and ordered the soldiers to hold back while he and Nundle inspected the camp. As he dismounted, he noted Cero off to the side, away from the rest of the men, staring at him—and Nundle—with a strange intensity.

Nundle had already slid off his horse and was walking toward the campsite. Nathan followed, leaving his horse with Nundle's. As he approached the campsite, he found the tomble strolling about the edges, stopping to inspect haphazard patches of charred ground. It looked as if a drunken man with a lit torch had stumbled all over the camp, constantly falling down.

When Nundle dropped to his hands and knees and pressed his face near the ground to sniff one of the burnt areas, Nathan's curiosity got the best of him. "Nundle?"

"Hmm?"

"I take it these patches mean something to you?"

"They do." Nundle hopped up and brushed himself off. "You remember what I've shared with you about magic—how it is a weaving of one or more types of Strands?"

Nodding, Nathan muttered, "And?"

"Well, during my time at the Academy of Veduin, when I was trying my hand with Fire—and failing miserably at it—the first thing the preceptor had us try were simple exercises meant to teach us how to control the Fire Strands. They are the most volatile of the nine, bouncing all over the place, dancing, flickering." He shrugged. "At least that's what the other acolytes said. I never felt even the smallest flash of orange. I was so disappointed! You see, I had found this book that taught how to combine Will, Soul, and Fire to make these wondrous creatures called 'fibríaals.' Soul and Will I can do, but Fire? No matter what—"

"Nundle?" said Nathan, cutting the tomble off. When it came to the topic of magic, his new friend had a tendency to ramble. He nodded at the burnt grass. "What are these?"

"Yes, well, even for those who *could* touch Fire, learning to control the Strands was a struggle. For the first few weeks, there would be...accidents when a Weave would go awry. The acolytes' courtyard was covered with charred, black marks." He looked around the trampled grass. "Similar to these."

Nathan looked about the days-old camp, his eyes narrowing. "You're saying we're following someone who is just learning how to control their abilities?"

Lines split Nundle's brow, his eyes narrowed and he pursed his lips together. "Nathan, if this—" he gestured around him "—was the only thing we knew about them, I would have said that we are dealing with novices. Untrained mages, even."

"If they're only learning, how did they defeat the bandits at the farm so easily? We're following three people here, and they stopped seven or eight marauders?"

"I was wondering the same thing, but then your scout spoke about the missing wall and sand pile. Remember what he said? The sand was *identical* in color to the remaining walls! The grains uniform in size!"

"You'll forgive me if I don't understand the significance."

"The sand *used to be* the missing wall, Nathan. Pulverized into dust! How?"

Again, Nathan had no logical answer. Of course, with magic, logic no longer applied. "You said there was a type of Strand...earth or stone, right?

Could some of those have been used to do it?" He felt uncomfortable even suggesting the possibility. Not thinking of magic as a tool of lawbreakers was going to take some getting used to.

Nodding enthusiastically, Nundle said, "*Exactly*. Strands of Stone. Ah, but here's the problem with that. To rip apart a single wall while leaving the other three untouched, all without uprooting the earth itself takes a great deal of power *and* skill. Only a master of Stone could do something like that."

Nathan frowned, imagining what would happen if an army had a mage capable of that. Stone fortresses would be useless. The tactical advantage could be tremendous. The idea excited him until he thought about being on the other side of such a maneuver.

"So, then," said Nathan. "Are they novices or masters?"

Nundle peered up at him, his expression blank. With a shrug of his shoulders, he said, "I don't know."

Crossing his arms over his chest, Nathan dropped his head, stared at his boots, and sighed. "Wondrous. Yet another unknown." After a moment, he lifted his head and peered at the little tomble. "Is there anything you think you will gain from visiting the farm?"

Nundle considered the question before replying. "If you trust your scout's report, no. Why? What are you thinking?"

"That we don't waste any more time than is necessary." Nathan turned to walk back to his mount.

His horse looked up at him as he approached, staring at him while methodically chewing a mouthful of grass. Placing a boot in the stirrup, he swung his other leg over and settled in the saddle. Shielding his eyes from the sun with his hand, he looked to the southeast, away from the trail that headed almost due south.

Nundle scampered over to his own horse and started to pull himself up in the saddle. Nathan had not asked if Nundle needed help after the first time had earned him a scathing look and terse "No, thank you."

Nathan looked over his shoulder and called, "Footman Eadding!"

The young soldier directed his horse forward, coming to stand alongside Nathan. "Sergeant?"

"You are certain their path headed east, along the river?"

"Yes, Sergeant."

Nathan pointed to a single tree fortuitously placed among the grassy plains on the southeastern horizon. "We head that way. Wil, take a few men and ride ahead. Stay in view, though."

The young footman nodded and moved back to the company of men, calling out a few names. Wil and three others began to trot ahead, over the plains and toward the lone tree, their horses' hooves thudding on the rain-softened ground.

By now, Nundle had made it up on his horse and was breathing hard from the struggle. "We're going to leave the trail?"

"Yes, Nundle, we are."

A moment passed. Nundle frowned. "Is that wise?"

"I don't know, honestly." Turning so he was facing Nundle, he said, "I might not have read many books about distant lands, but do know a bit about our neighbors. The river ahead of us is the Erona. It is a very wide, very deep river. They will not be able to ford it."

"You forget they may have *other* means at their disposal, Nathan."

Nathan pressed his lips together and said firmly, "I have not forgotten. I'm merely hoping that after what they had to do at the farm, they're going to try to remain quiet and unobtrusive."

Nundle said softly, "It's a gamble."

"It is," admitted Nathan. "But it's a small one compared to what you have proposed we do should we catch them."

Nundle lifted an eyebrow and conceded, "That's true." Staring closely at Nathan, he asked, "Have you thought any more about my suggestion?"

"I have."

"And?"

A few moments passed before Nathan replied, "I believe I am coming around."

With a satisfied nod of his head, Nundle said, "Good." The tomble turned his head to watch the retreating backs of the men riding across the prairie. "And have you decided how you are going to tell your men?"

"Still working that part out." Before Nundle could press him further, he looked behind him and called, "Quick march, trot!"

The Red Sentinels were soon thundering over the plains.

CHAPTER 46: EAST

1st of the Turn of Thonda

A turn ago, Jak found the idea of riding a horse unsettling. Now, however, despite the persistent soreness, the rhythmic shifting of Hal's stride was actually relaxing, lulling him into a lazy, restful daze. He might have even fallen asleep in the saddle were it not for his uncomfortably damp clothes.

The weather was changing. A rainstorm had moved through a few days ago, bringing with it a fresh, cool breeze that had remained constant ever since. Another short squall blew through this morning, dropping fat, chilled raindrops that had soaked the entire group to the skin. Everyone was still drying out.

Jak rode at the rear of their unusual procession. When the left the Moiléne farm, they had taken two of the bandit's horses with them while turning the other five loose. The plan had been for Sabine and Helene each to have her own horse. More often than not, however, Helene insisted on riding with someone. If given the choice, she always chose Nikalys.

All day today, Helene had sat in Nikalys' lap, pestering him with one question after another about the Isaacs' life in Yellow Mud. Her innocent inquiries were unintentionally clever, and the arbitrary manner in which she asked them managed to keep most everyone smiling.

Why do grapes grow on vines but olives grow on trees?

Why do you need a barn to store your wagons in when Papa just left his outside?

What is an ash tree and why is it called an ash tree? Did somebody burn it?

Nikalys bore the unending barrage with more grace and patience than Jak would have guessed he possessed, responding to each question as best as he was able. When he did not have the answer—or the question itself was unanswerable—he would make one up. Earlier, when Helene had asked why a hoe was called a hoe, Nikalys had explained—with a straight face—that whenever you struck the ground with it, you must yell "Hoe!" else the tool would not bite into the earth. Helene seemed dubious at first, but when Nikalys insisted it was true, the girl giggled and seemed to accept it as fact.

Jak marveled at Helene's resilience. He supposed she might be too young to understand fully what had happened at the farm. Truthfully, Jak was not entirely sure he understood everything about that day. He remembered very little after being shot by the arrow.

When Jak had awoken the morning following the attack, a pounding headache and very sore stomach had greeted him. He had peered down and—to his amazement—found only a bright red scar where the arrow had pierced his gut.

With a groan, he sat up and found the stunning, raven-haired woman from the farmhouse resting in the grass a few paces away, staring at him with cool yet curious eyes. Kenders introduced her as Sabine and Jak stumbled over himself while trying to offer a proper greeting. He started and stopped three times, before finally murmuring a simple, "I'm Jak."

While Broedi saddled the horses and prepared to leave, Nikalys and Kenders shared everything that had happened while Jak had slept. He was surprised to learn that both Helene and Sabine—the Moiléne sisters—were also mages.

Before leaving the farm, Broedi called everyone to the cart before the house and handed out some of the dead bandits' equipment. For Jak's part, he received a veritable duke's arsenal: a beltknife, a steel longsword with a leather scabbard, and a quiver of hawk-feather arrows. He strapped everything on, wondering all the while how soldiers maneuvered with so much stuff hanging from their bodies.

Broedi had tried to hand over one of the bandit's bow and quiver to Sabine but she refused, wanting nothing to do with the brigands' belongings. She acquiesced when he said she might need it to keep Helene safe and strapped them to her saddle. Over the past three days, however, Jak had noticed she went out of her way to avoid touching the weapon.

When Broedi finally announced they were ready to go, Helene threw a small fit, upset that she had not received anything. While the hillman seemed at a loss as to what to do, Kenders came to the rescue by giving Helene one of their remaining firesticks and telling her it was a "secret stick of fire." Elated, the little girl proceeded to skip about the camp with the firestick, waving it in the air and singing.

Even now, three days later, Helene grasped the firestick in her small hand while bedeviling Nikalys with her questions. Jak smiled. Helene was a more than welcome addition to their group. His gaze then shifted to the elder Moiléne sister and his smile slipped away. As was often the case, the corners of Sabine's mouth were curled downward. He thought it a shame that a girl as striking as Sabine spent so much time with some variation of a scowl on her face. The few times she flashed a smile—mostly in the evenings when she was sitting with Helene—it had been radiant. He wished she would do it more often.

"Oh, gods…"

Turning to his right, Jak was surprised to find Kenders riding beside him. "When did you get here?" Kenders typically rode beside Sabine. In fact, he would have sworn that was where she had been a short time ago.

"You might have noticed me coming if you weren't gaping at Sabine."

Jak's neck and cheeks grew warm. "I wasn't gaping at her."

Arching a single eyebrow, Kenders said, "Oh, come now…"

He could continue to protest, but knew that Kenders would see through it. Frowning, he leaned toward his sister and muttered, "Please don't say anything?"

Kenders rolled her eyes, drove her heels into Smoke's side, and rode ahead. She trotted past Nikalys and Helene, saying hello to both, fell in next to Sabine, and immediately leaned over and said something to the young woman.

His heart thudding in his chest, Jak mumbled, "You wouldn't dare…"

After a moment, Sabine glanced back at him—her face expressionless— then turned back to Kenders and said something in response.

Jak squeezed his eyes tight. "Oh…wondrous." His stomach hurt now and it had nothing to do with the arrow wound.

Kenders and Sabine had been getting along well since leaving the farm. Most nights, after Helene was sleeping, the pair would sit together and talk in hushed tones. Whenever Jak asked Kenders what they discussed, she told him it did not concern him. Once, he had reminded her to be careful she did not mention the prophecy or the White Lions to Sabine. Kenders, in turn, glared at him and reminded him that in order to walk, he must put one foot in front of the other. Jak supposed he deserved that.

As they had for days, they hugged the slow-moving river as they traveled east. Broedi named it the Erona and said that should they follow it to its end, they would find themselves near a town named Masons Bay on the Sea of Kings' coast.

Jak had listened, somewhat incredulous, as Broedi described the vast, cold sea, insisting it was tens of thousands of times larger than Lake Hawthorne. When Kenders asked if the plan was to follow the river to the coast, Broedi had offered a curt "No," and gone quiet again. Even though the hillman had shared their ultimate destination, he had yet to reveal any additional details. Getting information from Broedi was like trying to squeeze water from a rock.

For the hundredth time today, Jak reached around to his backside and scratched. The moist cloth chafing his skin had long ago passed being an irritant. Modesty alone kept him from taking his clothes off and letting them air dry as they traveled. He wished there was some way to squeeze every drop of water possible from shirt and breeches.

"Hold a moment…"

He looked up to where Broedi walked, leading the spare horse, twenty paces ahead of Kenders and Sabine. A slight smile spread over his lips as he kicked Hal in the sides, urging the horse into a trot. As he approached Nikalys and Helene, he said, "Hey, Nik? Are your clothes still wet?"

Nikalys looked over as Jak drew alongside. "Gods, yes. Quite uncomfortable."

The miniature version of Sabine leaned forward and gave Jak a wide grin. Her black hair whipped freely in the breeze, straight into Nikalys' face, forcing him to spit out the strands that made their way into his mouth.

"Hi, Jak!"

Jak smiled back. "Good days ahead, Helene. Are you having fun with Nikalys?"

She nodded her head up and down, sending more hair into Nikalys' face. "Uh-huh. He's very smart."

Nikalys looked at Jak, gave a sheepish smile, and shrugged his shoulders.

"Is he?" said Jak. "He certainly had me fooled."

Nikalys' expression soured.

"Nik-lys answers everything I ask him," said Helene. A pouty frown spread over face. "Sabine always tells me to stop asking silly questions."

As one, Jak and Nikalys swiveled their heads to look forward and found Sabine staring back at them, the ever-present frown on her face. "Perhaps I should just let the boys answer all of your questions from now on?"

Jak and Nikalys responded at the same time, talking over one another.

"Hey—he's the one making up—"

"Boy? I'll have you know I'm—"

They both stopped at the same time and glanced at each other. A moment later, they turned back toward Sabine and resumed talking, again at the same time.

"It's not Jak's fault that—"

"Nik is just having some—"

The brothers halted again and turned to one another. Jak stared at Nikalys, waiting for him to resume speaking while Nikalys was apparently doing the same for Jak. After a few heartbeats, a distinctive, familiar chortling drifted through the air. Facing forward, Jak found Kenders twisted around in her saddle, peering back at them, and laughing. Sabine's frown faded, her expression shifting into one of minor amusement before she faced east.

"You two are funny," said Helene. She was also laughing at them, her smile wide.

Shaking his head, Nikalys murmured, "Girls are odd."

"I agree," muttered Jak.

Helene insisted, "No we aren't!" Her grin was gone, replaced by a wounded frown.

Looking down at her, Nikalys smiled and said softly, "I don't mean you, Helene. You are perfect. Not odd at all." He gave her a little squeeze.

Jak leaned over and whispered conspiratorially, "We're only talking about *older* girls."

"Oh," said Helene, the hurt washing away quicker than a bucket of water would rinse away a day's worth of field dust. She tilted her head and, after a moment's consideration, said loudly, "You're right. Sabine *is* odd."

Jak and Nikalys both began to chuckle. As small children are wont to do, Helene joined them, laughing without knowing why and only because they were. Jak was peering at the little girl's happy face when Nikalys' mirth suddenly ceased. Glancing at his brother, he followed Nikalys' gaze forward. Kenders and Sabine were looking back, glowering at them both. Jak stopped snickering at once, swallowing his final chuckle.

After a long moment, Kenders and Sabine both faced forward. At once, the brothers looked at one another and restrained, silent grins returned to their faces.

Remembering why he rode up here in the first place, Jak said, "I'm going to go ask Broedi something before we get in more trouble."

Nikalys nodded ahead to Kenders and Sabine. "Good luck riding past them."

Jak smiled. "I'll manage." Looking to Helene, he added, "I'll see you later."

"Good mem-ries, Jak!" sang the little girl.

He was about to ride away when he stopped and looked back to the toddler. "Helene? Why don't you ask Nikalys about the time we went swimming and a fish swam into his breeches?"

The siblings had been swimming with friends at Lake Hawthorne when Nikalys had run from the water, screaming. He danced about the lakeshore for a few moments, kicking his legs before stripping naked and pulling a halock from his pants. Nikalys loathed it whenever Jak or Kenders brought up the story.

Clapping her hands excitedly, Helene tilted her head back to stare up at Nikalys. "Tell me the fish story, Nik-lys!"

As Jak rode away, chuckling, he could feel Nikalys' gaze boring into his back. His lightheartedness quickly faded as he realized the friends who had been swimming with them that day were all dead now. He shoved the memory away, wishing he had never brought it up.

After taking a wide berth around the girls, keeping his eyes straight ahead to avoid their gaze, he approached Broedi. He was still a half-dozen paces behind the hillman when—without turning around—Broedi rumbled, "Hello, uori."

Slowing Hal to a walk beside Broedi, Jak looked over. "How did you know it was me?"

"Perhaps I guessed?"

"Did you?"

A slight smile touched the corners of Broedi's mouth. "No. Part of Thonda's gift is excellent hearing."

"I see," muttered Jak. He eyed the hillman closely. "And how much did you hear?"

Broedi's smile grew a fraction wider than normal. "You will rarely make a good impression on a young woman by calling her 'odd.'"

"Nik said that, not me."

"Yet you agreed."

Frowning, Jak admitted, "True."

Looking over, Broedi rumbled, "What question did you wish to ask?"

"Well, I was hoping you could perhaps use the Strands to wring the rest of the water from my clothes? They're still damp, uncomfortable, and incredibly itchy. I figure you could...just..." He trailed off and stopped. Broedi did not look like he much cared for the suggestion.

"Uori, the Strands are *not* for doing laundry."

Jak let out a tiny sigh. "No, I suppose not."

Facing forward, he spotted a break in the eastern horizon where a large, dark shape jutted up from the soft green. Squinting, he tried to make sense of what he was seeing, but he was still too far away. Forgetting about his wet clothes for the moment, he pointed in the direction of the dark lump. "What is that?"

Broedi answered without even looking. "The ancient ruins of an Imperial fort. Castrum Viridis Ager." Anticipating Jak's next question, he added, "Fort of the Greenfields."

Jak stared east again. It had to be massive for him to be able to make it out from this distance. "How old is 'ancient?'"

"A good question," rumbled Broedi. "And one I cannot answer. Perhaps a thousand years?"

Intrigued, Jak asked, "Are we going to pass it?"

"Yes. It sits near the river."

"Can we stop and look at it?"

Broedi twisted around, glanced at the sky, and then faced forward. "Perhaps. But not tonight."

Jak also looked west to eye the late-afternoon sun. They had plenty of time in which to reach the fort before nightfall. "Why not? We'll get—"

Broedi but him off, saying in a firm tone, "We wait until morning."

"Why?"

"It will be safer, then."

Curious, Jak asked, "Safer?"

"That is what I said."

Jak's eyes narrowed a fraction. "And exactly *why* is it safer, Broedi?"

Peering over at him, the hillman rumbled, "Because it is."

Jak sighed. It truly was like squeezing water from a rock. "But we can look tomorrow?"

"In the morning, yes."

Satisfied with that, Jak asked, "Can I tell the others?"

"If you desire."

"Then I shall," said Jak, already turning Hal back around, a smile spreading over his face. He was excited to visit the ruins.

CHAPTER 47: HUNGER

Each growl of Zecus' stomach was more insistent than the last. He had tried to satisfy his hunger by drinking as much water as he could, but it had not helped. He needed food.

Yesterday, he had come across a field of waist-high, thorny bushes covered with oval, orange fruits the size of his thumb. Breaking them open revealed a mushy red pulp that carried the faint, unappealing scent of a freshly sharpened knife. Yet when he placed a bit of the pulp on his tongue, he was pleasantly surprised the fruit both sweet and tart. His hunger drove him to pick and eat a large number of fruits in a short period. That had turned out to be a poor decision.

Not long after, he became violently ill. Until he rid his stomach of the fruits, he alternated between heaving while on his hands and knees and lying on the ground, curled up in a ball. His stolen horse—which he had named Simiah—stood next to him, watching, seemingly admonishing him for being so foolish as to eat strange berries.

As Zecus had moved northwest with the river, the trees thinned, leaving more and more open space filled with tall grass. It almost reminded him of home, save for the fact that everything was green here.

He still had no idea where he was. He had expected to come across a settlement or farm by now, but the soldiers on the bridge were the last souls he had seen. While absent of people, the land was full of life. Small, furry animals with long ears hopped through the grass, bounding away anytime he tried to approach one. Yesterday, he spotted a tusk-less wild pig running through the prairie, twice as large as the ones in the Borderlands. All Zecus could do was sit on his horse and watch helplessly as weeks of food charged away.

He knew that as long as he had water, he would be fine for a time. Granted, he was sluggish from the lack of food, but it did not take much energy to sit in a saddle all day. He reached down and patted Simiah on the neck. "It is a good thing I found you."

As the horse blew a puff of air through his lips, Zecus reminded himself that he had not actually found Simiah. He promised himself to atone for his thievery later. Somehow.

He had alternated between traveling along the riverbank with periods where he rode atop the sloped hill that accompanied the river. Currently, he was in what he thought of as the "valley," even though it was more of a gentle depression. He directed Simiah to the river's edge, dismounted, and tried to trick his stomach again by gulping mouthful after mouthful of water. Simiah did not drink. He simply stared at Zecus.

Sitting up, Zecus wiped his mouth and eyed the horse. "I know. More water."

Simiah lowered his head, sniffed at the grass, and ripped a mouthful from the ground. Zecus watched the horse chew, wondering if perhaps he should try a few blades. Simiah certainly seemed to enjoy it.

After drinking his fill, Zecus looked upriver, and was surprised to find that it took a sharp bend to the north, cutting off his view a half mile ahead. He blinked. "Where'd that come from?" Besides the physical weakness due to lack of food, it would seem his mental alertness was suffering.

Curious to see what was around the bend, Zecus said, "Time to head back up the hill, Simiah. Are you sure you don't want some water?"

Simiah ignored him, intent on eating grass.

Shrugging his shoulders, Zecus said, "You had your chance."

He remounted using the leather loops hanging from the saddle and, with his staff set across his lap in the saddle, urged Simiah up the hill. Halfway up, one of the long-eared furry animals burst from a short bush and dashed away, disappearing into the tall grass. Zecus frowned, listening to the animal scamper away. It was as if they were taunting him.

As man and horse crested the top of the slope, Zecus pulled Simiah's reins tight, stopping the horse. He stared with wide eyes, shocked by what stood in front of him. "Bless the gods."

A thousand paces away, the remnants of towering, gray stone walls—wide at the base and thinner at the top—rose from the plain, thrice as high as the surrounding trees. Some sections had gaping holes where stone had crumbled away and lay in massive piles among the grass. Towers stood at the edifice's corners, the pinnacles of which bulged outward like angular mushroom heads.

Zecus remained quiet, staring through the gaps in the walls, watching and listening for any sign of life within the ruins. Other than the grass waving in the prairie breeze, the gentle swishing pairing with the quiet rustle of the trees' leaves, he saw—and heard—nothing.

"What do you think, Simiah? Shall we take a closer look?" A moment later, Zecus shook his head and sighed. "Why am I asking you?"

The gray stone fortification loomed ahead, beckoning.

Perhaps some of the furry animals made a home in the ruins. If he could corner one, catch it, and somehow light a fire, he could finally satisfy his gnawing hunger. Glancing at the afternoon sky, he figured sundown was still some time away. He could spend the rest of the day hunting then sleep here for the night.

As Zecus kicked Simiah's sides and rode toward the ruins, he smiled. Perhaps the goddess Greya had taken pity on him. His fate seemed to be taking a turn for the better.

CHAPTER 48: DECISION

Nundle decided that, most of the time, riding a horse was not awful. He certainly appreciated the distance one could cover compared to what his short legs could. Presently, however, he loathed it. Instead of the gentle back-and-forth rocking of a leisurely walk, he was in the midst of a jarring trot, bouncing up and down, his teeth clattering. He felt like a dusty rug being beaten clean with a stick.

For two days straight, they had been moving in alternating bursts of trotting and walking in order to keep the horses fresh. Yesterday afternoon, the group finally reached the Erona River. After the horses drank their fill and the soldiers topped off their waterskins, the bulk of the group returned to the top of the slope. To Nundle's great relief, scouts picked up a trail by the river's shore whose markers matched those they were following. Nathan's gamble had worked.

Most of the Sentinels traveled on the plains, parallel to the river, while a few scouts stayed with the trail below to ensure it did not lead to the river's edge and disappear. Nundle prayed that would not happen; his inability to touch Strands of Water would leave them with no way to follow.

The pace set by Nathan provided little opportunity for talking but plenty of time to think. And that was exactly what Nundle had done, puzzling through everything they knew about the "outlaws" and how it might apply to the prophecy.

It was said the goddess Indrida withheld most of what she foresaw from mortals in order to prevent people from trying to alter events to either fit or thwart her words. The few known prophecies of hers were notorious for their ambiguity, often only making sense after the events had occurred. Even so, that never stopped people from trying to guess what the future held. Nundle was no exception.

He had originally assumed that when the Progeny would "rise and lead the fight," they would be as powerful as the White Lions had been, but the inept display with the Strands of Fire had given him doubts. He realized he had been making assumptions all along and chastised himself for doing so. Just last evening, Nathan had asked a brilliant, insightful question: how many Progeny were there? Nundle had stared at the soldier, his expression blank. He had no idea.

A quiet, subdued discussion had followed where the sergeant and Nundle took turns in pointing out how little they truly knew. Afterwards, Nundle had not slept well, tossing about in his bedroll as his mind raced. The two nearly full moons had not helped his attempt at slumber.

"To a walk!"

Nathan's shout startled Nundle. He glanced up, surprised. They had only started trotting a short while ago. As the company slowed, he turned to Nathan. "Is something wrong?"

"We'll find out soon enough," said Nathan as he pointed south.

Swiveling his head, Nundle spotted two horsemen riding toward them, having just crested the slope that led to the river below. Feeling a flash of panic, he muttered, "Oh, gods. They must have crossed the river."

"Look closer."

Nundle peered across the plain noted the pair riding toward them wore mismatched tan tunics and breeches, not the red and black of the Red Sentinels. Nundle cautioned himself again to stop making assumptions. "Those aren't the scouts from the river."

"No, they're not," said Nathan, his voice betraying a hint of nervous excitement. "That's Hunsfin and Blainwood. And if they are returning, they'll have something important to report."

Nundle watched the pair approach, his heart thudding in anticipation. "Important and 'good?' Or important and 'bad'?"

Nathan never did answer him.

When scouts were a hundred paces away, Nathan ordered the company of Sentinels to halt. The two longlegs pulled up their horses, stopping but paces from Nathan and Nundle. The soldier on the left was short for a longleg with shaggy, dark brown hair that hung to his shoulders. His partner was years older with short black hair and a face that reminded Nundle of a crag of rocks sticking from a cliff, complete with a scar that started at his right ear, drew across his cheek, and ended at the corner of his mouth.

Nodding to his soldiers, Nathan said, "I'm glad you were able to find us. I was afraid my change in direction would cause problems."

The longleg on the left said, "We were a little surprised when we stumbled upon Bedwin and Erdswick down by the river. Hadn't expected to see you for another day or so."

"After Wil's report, I decided to take a chance," said Nathan.

"And it's a good thing you did, Sergeant," replied the longleg. He paused and gave a confident, triumphant smile. "Hunsfin and I caught up to them."

Excitement washed over Nundle like a burst of hot air from a just-opened baker's oven.

Keeping his tone even, Nathan ordered, "Details, Blainwood. Keep it concise."

Blainwood nodded and shifted in his saddle. Nundle could almost see the longleg gathering his thoughts.

"After leaving the farm, we pushed hard. The further east, the fresher their signs. Based on the ground we made up, I'm guessing they only travel during daylight. Not too long ago, we spotted a group on the horizon moving along the river. Four horses with riders—two women and two men—and a fifth led by a…uh…well…" He trailed off as his eyebrows drew together. He almost looked embarrassed.

"A what, Blainwood?" prompted Nathan.

The footman glanced at Hunsfin before saying, "Well, Sergeant. Let's just say it was a *very* large man."

Nundle sat straight in his saddle, his excitement tripling in an instant. Unable to restrain himself, he asked, "How large?"

Blainwood glanced toward his sergeant. After Nathan nodded, the footman said, "Blast the gods if he wasn't seven feet tall."

The cragged-face Hunsfin spoke, his voice like gravel grinding under a boot heel. "Taller."

Blainwood looked at his fellow scout and said, "Right, well, Hunsfin keeps insisting he was taller, but…honestly—have you ever heard of a seven foot tall man?"

With a slight, knowing smile, Nundle murmured, "Not a man, no." This meeting was going to be even more thrilling than he had thought.

His response drew an inquisitive look from Nathan. Nundle shook his head once. He could not share what he was thinking in front of the two scouts. None of the Red Sentinels knew what was truly going on.

Moreover, Nundle wanted to be careful that he was not making another assumption. He supposed it was possible that another hillman had just happened to stumble upon a handful of mages at the same time his ex-preceptor seemed intent on destroying the Progeny mentioned in Indrida's prophecy. On second thought, that seemed rather unlikely.

Looking back to his soldiers, Nathan asked, "What else? Anything?"

Blainwood swatted at some sort of insect buzzing around his horse's head before answering. "It looked like the two men were armed, although the giant was not. We watched them for only a moment and then decided to return and find you."

"How far ahead are they?" asked Nathan,

"I'd say if we ride hard, we could catch them by sunset," answered Blainwood. He looked over at Hunsfin. "What do you think?"

"Before the moons shine at least," grated Hunsfin.

Nathan sat tall in his saddle and stared east. "Good job, men. Very good." He nodded at the other Sentinels. "Fall in. And say nothing to anyone."

As the two longlegs directed their horses back to the main column, Nathan remained motionless, his gaze fixed eastward although he did not appear to be looking at anything in particular.

"Nathan? Are you all right?"

The sergeant drew in a long, deep breath, held it a moment, then exhaled slowly. In a quiet, cryptic tone, he asked, "These are strange times, Nundle, are they not?"

The odd response caught Nundle off guard. Before he could ask what Nathan meant, the sergeant called over his shoulder for Wil. Once the young longleg rode up, Nathan ordered him to gather up the scouts along the river. As Wil galloped away, Nathan called out for a quick trot and headed east. The Red Sentinels followed.

Nundle expected a question or two from the sergeant about why the giant had interested him. Instead, Nathan rode in silence, apparently wrapped in his own thoughts.

When Wil and the scouts returned, Nathan motioned for them to fall in without saying a word. Nundle was beginning to wonder if they were going to ride in quiet the rest of the day.

"Nathan?"

The sergeant looked over, his face drawn tight. "Not now, Nundle." He used a tone normally reserved for when he gave orders to the soldiers. Nundle shut his mouth.

With hooves thudding on prairie ground, Nathan led the group toward a pair of old oaks rising from the grassy plains. One was mature and vibrant with thick, expansive branches coated with countless summer-green leaves. The other was obviously diseased with spotty foliage covering only a quarter of its branches. It was more a mass of jumbled sticks than a tree.

When they were a hundred paces from the oaks, Nathan halted the Sentinels with a raised hand. The sounds of forty-nine longlegs commanding their horses to stop rang out over the plains.

Nundle stared at the bearded longleg, intensely curious. "Nathan? What are we doing?"

The sergeant looked over to Nundle, a shrewd, sly smile on his face. Saying nothing, he spun his horse around and faced the assembled Sentinels. Nundle did the same, anxiously staring at Nathan the entire time.

"Draw up!" commanded Nathan. "I have something to say, and I don't want to shout!"

The Sentinels nudged their horses closer, edging between one another until there was a two-row semicircle of horses and soldiers. Nundle spotted Cero, the

Tracker, by himself behind both rows. Suspicion hung heavy in the longleg's eyes.

Once the soldiers had settled, Nathan sat tall in his saddle and addressed the Red Sentinels, his tone confident and firm. "You are good soldiers." He paused a moment, letting the lone sentence hang in the air before continuing. "You are tough. You do your duty. You follow orders without question."

Scanning the two rows, seemingly staring every soldier in the eyes, he said, "For weeks now, we have been trailing a group of individuals because we were ordered to do so. We were told these people were mages, outlaws. That they had to be captured. That they were a threat."

Nundle now understood why Nathan had been so quiet earlier. Without a doubt, this had the markings of a carefully considered speech.

"Men!" said Nathan, his voice clear and crisp. "Like you, I grew up listening to the stories about magic. How it hurts people, tricks them. That those who use it cannot be trusted, that they should be feared."

Nundle eyed his new friend carefully, wondering at the direction Nathan was going with his talk.

"When we were given this assignment, we accepted it with dignity and resolve, despite any personal fears we might have about magic and mages. To date, we have been executing our orders to the best of our ability, pressing on with little evidence that we were on the right trail. *Now*, however, based on what Blainwood and Hunsfin have seen, we not only have solid evidence that we are on the right track, but that we have nearly caught up to our prey."

The announcement prompted an excited murmuring from the longlegs. Cero seemed especially tense, fidgeting in his saddle.

Nathan held up his hand, quieting the longlegs. "Now, beyond being good soldiers, I judge you all to be good men. Honest. Thoughtful. Intelligent. I respect you as men as much as I value you as soldiers. Which is why I feel comfortable asking you do something that goes against everything I've ever taught you, against every instinct you have as a soldier." He paused, took a deep breath, and spoke clearly, without reservation. "Men, I want you to ignore our orders."

Again, the soldiers began talking amongst themselves, although louder this time whilst wearing confused expressions. Pressing on, Nathan yelled over the soldiers, "I expect you to hear me out!"

It took a few moments, but the Sentinels quieted and stared at their sergeant, more than a few with something between mistrust and disbelief. Nundle eyed the soldiers, swallowing a lump that suddenly appeared in his throat. He prayed Nathan knew what he was doing.

"Thank you," said Nathan. "Now, since we began our pursuit, a number of things have bothered me about our task. Why were we—the duke's soldiers—sent to hunt mages? Is that not why we have the Constables?"

Most of the soldiers nodded agreement. A few glanced back at a stone-faced Cero.

Rushing ahead, Nathan offered a one question after another to his soldiers. "And Fenidar? Who is he? Where did he come from? Why did the regent hand command to the saeljul?" The longlegs shook their heads, agreeing with Nathan.

"And what of Lakeborough? Not only did we march *straight through* a Southlands' city, but a contingent of Southern Arms joined us!? Arms and Sentinels, side-by-side, traipsing about the countryside, looking for mages? When have any of you heard of something like that happening?" All but a handful of the soldiers were shaking their heads.

"Now. When I asked Fenidar these questions, he refused to answer me. And despite my growing reservations about him, I did my duty. I followed his lead because the regent had *ordered* me to do so. But then Fenidar forced us to split our forces." He paused and shook his head. "I should have said no. That it was foolish and brainless! But I did not. For some reason, I agreed."

That was actually a falsehood. Nathan knew exactly why he had agreed because Nundle had shared with the sergeant what had happened that night by the fork in the road. While Nathan had been disturbed and angry to learn that he had been the target of a Weave, he had also seemed relieved to discover that the poor decision had not been his.

Twisting his saddle, Nathan eyed Nundle. "Now, I know you have you all been wondering about our little friend here."

Nundle's heart nearly leapt through his chest as every soldier—and one irate-looking Tracker—turned to stare at him. He felt himself shrink a few inches under the weight of their collective gaze.

"The night Nundle arrived, he brought with him information that answered some of these question even while creating more. What he told me was difficult to accept. Yet that is what I did. I believed him. I trust him." Nathan paused and let out a heavy sigh. "Men, there is more to this story than you've been told. *Much* more."

To a longleg, the soldiers looked uneasy.

"We are going to share with you everything we know. I ask you to hold your questions until we are done."

Nundle looked askance at Nathan and whispered nervously, "We?"

Turning his gaze to Nundle, Nathan said, "Tell them why you were following us. Tell them what you told me."

Wary, Nundle glanced at the soldiers before glaring at Nathan, yelling at the sergeant with his eyes alone. A warning would have been nice. "Ah...which parts?"

"All of it, Nundle.

"*All* of it?"

Nodding, Nathan said, "Exactly as you told it to me."

Nundle faced the soldier and offered a nervous smile. He hesitated for only a moment before launching into same story he had shared with Nathan that first night, telling them the truth about whom they had been following, about the preceptor. They appeared skeptical, even more so when he revealed he was a mage, too.

"Show them, Nundle," muttered Nathan.

He shot a worried look at the sergeant. "Are you sure?"

"Quite," said Nathan with a nod. "Something small will suffice."

Taking a deep breath, Nundle wondered what might be an appropriate display. Settling on something he had learned in his first weeks of studying Air, he reached for a number of the white Strands, knit them together quickly, and released the Weave.

A blast of wind rushed over the plains, pressing the grass flat to the ground and buffeting the soldiers, forcing them to lift their hands and shade their eyes from bits of grass and dust. After a few heartbeats, the breeze faded.

The soldiers lowered their hands and stared at Nundle with a mixture of fear and awe. They certainly accepted his story now.

A moment later, Cero called out, "Under the authority of the Constables, I order you to surrender yourself into custody!" Looking to the soldiers before him, he said, "An outlaw stands before you! Take him!"

Whether or not they considered doing so, Nundle would never know as Nathan exclaimed, "You will do nothing of the sort! Hold your positions!" His voice shot across the still plain like a peel of thunder. When none of the soldiers moved, he shifted his gaze to the Tracker. "Constable, you have no authority—none!—over my men. You cannot—you *will* not order them to do anything, understood?!"

Showing an incredible amount of resolve, the Tracker held Nathan's intense stare. "Then *you* give the order to arrest him."

Nathan shook his head. "Not yet."

Nundle stared in open astonishment at Nathan. "What do you mean, 'not yet?'"

Without taking his gaze from Cero, the sergeant said, "Continue with your story, Nundle. And quickly, please."

Nundle wondered if he should instead take off on his horse and ride away as fast as his little chestnut could carry him. If Nathan intended to arrest him, then Nundle had severely misjudged the longleg. Praying he had not, he steadied himself, turned back to the soldiers, and resumed his story.

He shared the true history of the White Lions, a story few of them appeared to know based on the interested, thoughtful expressions the soldiers wore. Then he recited Indrida's prophecy, line for line. The longlegs—even Cero—sat, enthralled.

When he was finished, Nathan looked over and asked, "May I have the letter?"

Nundle reached into his pocket, pulled out the folded parchment, and, leaning over, placed it in Nathan's outstretched hand.

Nodding his thanks, the sergeant turned to the Sentinels. "This is the message that brought our little friend to us. Please, try to restrain yourself as I read it."

The soldiers stared at each other, clearly uneasy, as Nathan unfolded the parchment and began to read. Despite his request, he had to pause a few times as the longlegs reacted. When he revealed that Preceptor Myrr had been responsible for the destruction of Yellow Mud, many of the soldiers cursed, turning visibly angry.

Once Nathan was able to calm them, he resumed reading. As he neared the final lines aloud, Nundle braced himself. He doubted this would go over well.

"'I have sent word to our friend in Smithshill,'" read Nathan, "'to be vigilant for the man who apparently escaped.'" Nathan paused, looked up to his men, and said solemnly, "It is signed, 'Everett.'"

A moment of stunned silence passed before shouts of disbelief pierced the air. For as many soldiers who cried out, there was an equal number who sat silent, nodding their heads slowly, seemingly unsurprised by the revelation.

One of the Sentinels shouted, "Perhaps it's from someone else named Everett!"

"Oh, come on, Bedwin!" called Hollins, the soldier who had nearly speared Nundle with an arrow. "You've heard what people say about the duke. How he took the Sovereign's Chair? Why would this surprise you?"

During that first night, Nathan had shared with Nundle some of the rumors that swirled around Duke Everett. The duke's father, the well-respected and well-liked Gill Redlord, had died in a fall from his horse two winters ago during a hunting excursion with his son. There were more than a few whispered questions as to how accidental the tumble had been.

Bedwin stared at Nathan and asked, "What do you think, Sergeant?" Most of the soldiers turned to eye Nathan as well, waiting for his assessment. Despite everything, these longlegs still looked to him for guidance.

Nathan let out a heavy sigh before answering. "I believe that this missive is in fact from the duke."

Nundle eyed the soldiers, wondering if anyone else would protest the point. He was only mildly surprised when no one did.

One of the scouts, Blainwood, called out, "Who's the friend in Smithshill?"

Nathan answered without hesitation. "For my coin, I believe it to be the same man who put Fenidar—or Jhaell as he is truly named—at the head of our column."

Wil asked, "Are you suggesting the regent is involved, Sergeant?"

"I am not suggesting it, Wil," said Nathan. "I am *saying* it. Regent Alpert and Duke Everett are entangled in all of this."

Some of the longlegs grumbled, visibly uncomfortable.

Nundle pressed his lips together. Admittedly, he knew little about the social order of the Oaken Duchies, but he suspected that accusing a duchy's sovereign of conspiring with the Cabal was not a common, happy occurrence.

Raising his voice over the increased muttering, Nathan called, "So! This is where we are!" The murmuring quieted. "I will not order you to disobey the regent. I refuse to put you in that position. What I *am* going to do is something that I doubt has ever happened in the history of the Sentinels. You get to make the decision *yourself.*"

While Nundle glanced over at the sergeant, surprised, the nearly fifty soldiers stared at him, their faces expressionless.

His voice unwavering, Nathan continued, saying, "You have two choices. The first, come with me and when we find these supposed outlaws—*and* the farmers I believe they rescued—stand with me as we try to learn their piece."

The men remained silent, waiting for the other option. Nundle thought it a good sign they had not immediately shouted Nathan down.

"Your second choice is that you may arrest me for treason and resume carrying out your original orders. I promise to submit quietly and not interfere with your task."

The men sat in their saddles, clearly stunned.

While Nundle had asked Nathan to talk to the Sentinels, to explain things to them before approaching the Progeny, he had never expected this. Never.

Nathan looked beyond the soldiers, to the Tracker, and said, "Cero, should the men choose to arrest me, you are welcome to take Nundle to the Constables. I will not stop you."

Nundle turned to gape at Nathan. "Pardon?!"

Nathan ignored him, his gaze reserved for his men alone.

Wil was the first to speak, his voice full of disbelief. "Sergeant? Are you asking us to vote?"

"I am."

Clearly dubious, Blainwood asked, "Like...for village council?"

"Exactly," replied the sergeant. "I have terms, though. Simple ones. Whichever choice gets the most votes wins. Those who voted the other way *must* abide by the decision. With or without me at the head, we proceed as a unit. Can you all agree on that?"

The soldiers looked at one another and, after a few moments, they were nodding their heads.

"How is this going to work?" asked Wil.

Nathan looked to the Tracker. "Cero? Come here, please."

Cero's suspicious gaze remained fixed on Nathan as he directed his horse through the lines.

As the Tracker halted before them, Nathan said, "Behind me stand two trees that Greya and Lamoth have conspired to place before us," he said, invoking the names of the goddesses responsible for fate and nature. "Does everyone have their flint and steel?"

Each soldier reached to wherever he stored his small, oiled leather pouch that contained a flint and steel striker, char cloth, shredded fibers, and oak bark tinder used for basic spark-based fire-starting.

"Good," said Nathan. "Cero and Nundle will each sit behind one of the trees, blindfolded."

Peering at Nathan, Nundle asked, "We will?"

"Yes, Nundle. You will." Turning to Cero, he said, "As will you. You both have an interest in seeing how this plays out, do you not?"

Cero nodded. "I will go along with this for now."

Nathan looked back to Nundle. "And you?"

Nundle stared at the sergeant, a large frown on his face. This gamble by Nathan was either a brilliant tactical move or a terrible, foolhardy mistake. Nundle could not tell which. Supposing that he could always use the Strands to free himself should he come out on the losing end, Nundle put his faith in Nathan and nodded once.

Facing the soldiers, Nathan called, "One at a time, you will walk behind each tree and drop your pouch into the helmet of the person you side with. Cero, to arrest me and pursue the outlaws. Nundle, to speak with the lawbreakers and see if there is more to this tale. I will not vote. Nundle and Cero are not soldiers; they get no vote. With the three men I sent after Corporal Holb, that leaves forty-seven. Therefore, the side with at least twenty-four votes wins. I will *not* reveal the final count—only the ultimate decision. Is everything acceptable?"

The men nodded slowly. They were clearly nervous.

Glancing between Nundle and Cero, Nathan said, "After each vote, you will take out your pouch and place it in a bag. This way, no one will know another's choice." He studied his men. "You can vote your conscience without fear of repercussion. Are there any questions?"

The soldiers remained quiet. A few shook their heads.

Nathan dismounted his horse and handed the reins to the nearest soldier. "Eadding, Blainwood. Your helmets, please." After the two soldiers unhooked the headpieces from their saddles and handed them to the sergeant, Nathan looked at Cero and Nundle. "Let's get to it."

After Nundle and Cero dismounted, the trio walked in silence to the two trees. Nearly fifty paces of open grassland separated the healthy and diseased oaks. Cero and Nathan went left, toward the sickly tree while Nundle headed for the vibrant, strong oak. Both sat down with his back to his respective tree trunk.

Nundle watched Nathan bend down to tie a length of cloth around Cero's eyes. The sergeant placed one of the Sentinels' silver, domed helmets on the ground in front of the Tracker and gave him a leather bag for the flint and steel pouches. Neither longleg said a word. When he was done, Nathan walked to Nundle, kneeled down, and handed him a helmet and a bag.

Nundle stared at the sergeant and said pointedly. "I would have appreciated you discussing this with me in advance."

"If I had, you would have tried to talk me out of it, I think."

"Perhaps I would have. Regardless, I would have liked the opportunity to at least think this through." Cocking an eye, he asked, "Are you sure *you've* thought this through?"

"A man should choose his own fate, Nundle, not have someone else choose it for him."

Nundle regarded his friend for a moment before sighing and taking off his wide-brimmed hat. "Blindfold me, then."

The sergeant took a piece of rough burlap and wrapped it around Nundle's head and eyes, tying it off in the back. When he was done, he patted Nundle's shoulder. "Ketus be with you."

"Save some luck for yourself. You might need it."

A smile entered Nathan's voice. "Oh, I think not."

Nundle was left wondering what Nathan meant by that as the sergeant walked away, his boots scraping the ground. Looking around him, Nundle tested the cloth's effectiveness at blocking his sight. He realized if he strained, he could still make out basic shapes through the blindfold, but no details. As he reached up to scratch his nose—the burlap itched quite a bit—Cero called out to him.

"Once this nonsense is over, mage, I intend to place you under arrest!"

Nundle faced the direction of Cero's voice and called, "I'm not even a citizen of the duchies! I fail to see how your misguided laws apply to me."

"Any magic in the duchies is forbidden!"

"Is it, now? Tell me something, Cero! How old were you when you first discovered *you* could do magic? It's how you track, isn't it? You feel the Strands, don't you?"

Silence greeted Nundle's shouted question, silence filled only by the rustling whisper of prairie grass and oak leaves.

Cero never did answer by the time Nathan shouted, "Both of you be quiet! I'm sending the first soldier now!"

Nundle held his tongue and waited, nervous with anticipation.

He heard a faint rustling in Cero's direction, followed by a clink as a soldier dropped his pouch into Cero's helmet. The soldier then moved past Nundle, around the tree, and back toward the Sentinels. Disappointed by the start, Nundle rationalized it was but one vote.

The next soldier approached Nundle first. After rounding the tree, the longleg stopped for a moment and then moved to Cero. Nundle's heart sank like a rock in a pond when he heard a second clink for Cero.

The next three longlegs also chose Cero's side, each muffled clink dashing Nundle's hopes even further. Finally, the sixth soldier dropped his pouch into Nundle's helmet. After the longleg passed, Nundle reached in to the metal helm, removed the pouch, and placed it in the leather satchel next to him.

The soldiers passed quicker now, one arriving almost immediately after the previous had left.

It did not take long before Nundle stopped worrying about the outcome of the vote. While the first five sided with Cero, the next forty-two soldiers all dropped their pouch into Nundle's helm. Once the majority was secured, Nundle sat back, relaxed, and marveled at what was happening.

Once the forty-seventh and final soldier left, Nathan called out. "Hold while I come to tally!"

Moments later, Nundle heard the steady stride of boots in the grass. As the footsteps drew near, Nundle reached up and pulled the blindfold off his head. Nathan approached and dropped to a knee, a slight smile on his face. "Forty-one or forty-two?"

With open surprise, Nundle answered, "Forty-two. But...how did you..." He trailed off, eyes narrowing. "You *knew* how they were going to vote?"

Nathan's smile turned sly. "Not all of them. Hunsfin is a tough man to read at times." He picked up the bag with the pouches of flint and steel and gave Nundle a hand up.

As Nundle brushed bits of grass and dirt off his clothes, he asked, "If you knew how this would turn out, why did you do it?"

"Because they have a stake in things now. Infinitely more so than had I ordered them to follow my lead." With that, he turned and began to walk toward where Cero sat.

Nundle stared at Nathan's back a moment, thinking over the soldier's words, before following. As he passed between the two trees, he looked over at the soldiers waiting patiently beside their horses. After hurrying to catch up, Nundle reached Cero the same time as Nathan. The Tracker sat, slumped over, the burlap strip still tied around his eyes.

Stopping a few paces away, Nathan said, "You can take off the blindfold yourself, Cero."

The Tracker reached up, yanked the brown cloth off, and glared up at the sergeant. "This charade does not absolve you of your crime, Sergeant. This vote has *no* standing in duchy law!"

"I wonder," mused Nathan. "Would you have said the same thing if you had won?"

Cero remained silent but continued to glower.

Nathan squatted down to look the Tracker square in the eye. "This is my offer, Cero. You and the five men who voted with you can leave. Now. Ride away to the regent or Fenidar—or whatever the blasted ijul's name is—and tell them you haven't the slightest idea where the people you were sent to find are. Other than 'in the eastern Southlands.'" I doubt they'll be happy."

Cero's face twisted with frustration. He did not seem to like that option much.

"Or," began Nathan, "You can come along quietly and see for yourself what is truly going on. If you still feel the need to run and report after we catch up with these 'outlaws,' I will let you—and anyone else who wants to—ride away, untouched. You have my word."

Eyeing the sergeant, Nundle said, "Are you sure that's a wise idea? I mean—"

Nathan held a hand, interrupting him. "I'm sure, Nundle."

The Tracker and the soldier eyed each other for a number of heartbeats. Eventually, Cero said through gritted teeth, "I will come."

"A wise choice," muttered Nathan, rising from his crouch. "Now, we will go over and tell the men the results. You will both agree the vote was fair and never mention the total. *Never.* Is that clear?"

When both Cero and Nundle nodded their agreement, Nathan took Cero's bag of flint and steel, emptied it into Nundle's nearly full bag, and said, "Let's go hand these out and get moving."

Cero stood and began walking back to the soldiers, leaving Nundle and Nathan behind.

As Nundle watched the Tracker scurry away, he felt it necessary to say, "I don't trust him, Nathan."

"I know," said the sergeant. He slung the bag over his shoulder and began to walk away from the tree, back to the soldiers. Nundle followed. After a few steps, Nathan looked over. "Have you ever heard the phrase, 'Fools surround themselves with their friends, wise men surround themselves with their enemies'?"

"No," said Nundle. "Doesn't seem to make much sense."

"If Cero is here, then he's not causing problems elsewhere."

"Then why did you tell he could go?" asked Nundle.

"Because I knew he wouldn't."

"I see," sighed Nundle. "Well, have you ever heard the saying, 'Be wary of the tame snake; he bites when you least expect?'"

"No, I have not." A pensive frown crossed his Nathan's face. "I see your point, though. Is that a bit of Boroughs' wisdom?"

A slight smile spread over Nundle's face. "Actually, I just made it up."

Even as the pair chuckled over the jest, Nundle could not shake the feeling that keeping Cero around was a sour idea.

CHAPTER 49: RUINS

Kenders sat astride Smoke, staring at the ancient fort that was still a quarter-mile away while slowly shaking her head in awe. She could not fathom why something this massive stood isolated in the middle of the plains. All of Yellow Mud would have fit inside, twice over. Nobody had spoken a word since Broedi had called for a halt.

Nikalys finally broke the quiet, echoing her own thoughts. "Why in the Nine Hells would someone build this monstrous thing here?"

While Kenders did not expect an answer, Broedi provided one nonetheless.

"Ages ago, fragmented city-states covered much of this region. Much of the duchies, truthfully. Then L'antico Impero arrived on the eastern shores and marched west, warring as they went, building fortresses to ensure their dominance of areas once they were conquered." He nodded at the towering walls. "This is one of them."

"How long ago was this built?" asked Kenders.

"I am not sure, uora. Before the birth of the Oaken Kingdom and that was eight centuries ago."

Kenders shook her head in quiet wonderment. Last year seemed a long time ago to her. Eight hundred years was an impossible span of time to consider.

Jak asked, "Are you sure we can't go take a closer look now?"

"We wait," rumbled the hillman. "It will be safer in the morning."

Jak turned to Broedi. A slight, almost teasing grin was on his face. "Safer how, Broedi?" He seemed to be daring the hillman to answer.

Broedi remained quiet for a moment before saying, "We must make camp." Tugging the reins of the spare horse, he strode forward, away from the group.

As the hillman walked away, Jak mumbled, "Like water from a rock..."

Kenders looked over at him, wondering what he meant by that. She, too, was curious why they must wait until morning to visit the fort, but had chosen not ask the question. If Broedi wanted to share something, he would. If he did not, no amount of begging would get him to divulge his secrets. The exercise was pointless.

Suddenly, she realized what Jak's mumbled phrase meant. "Clever..."

Jak was in the midst of sliding from his saddle. Upon landing on the ground, he looked up at her. "Pardon?"

She jutted her chin at Broedi and lifted an eyebrow. "Water from a rock?"

Jak flashed a wide smile. "Am I wrong?"

Kenders shook her head as a grin matching Jak's spread over her face.

The group settled into the evening routine of making camp: pulling the saddles from the horses, retrieving supplies from the saddlebags, clearing the sleeping area of sticks and rocks. Feeling the need to wash up, Kenders volunteered to head to the river to replenish their waters. After moving all of the waterskins to Smoke, she peered at Sabine. The raven-haired beauty stood with her back to the men, facing Kenders. "Sabine, would you like to come to the river with me?"

"Gods, yes," sighed Sabine. "I could use a swim to wash off."

Both Nikalys and Jak looked up, stared at Sabine for a brief moment, and then simultaneously broke off their gazes an instant later. Kenders expected their suddenly rosy cheeks had little to do with the evening sky.

Looking to Helene, Kenders asked, "Would you like to come, dear? Just us girls?" The toddler was following Nikalys about the camp, stomping down grass to clear an area for tonight's fire.

Helene shook her head. "I don't want to wash."

Kenders looked to Sabine who gave a small shrug of her shoulders.

"Perhaps tomorrow, then," said Kenders. "Promise to stay close to Nikalys."

"I will!"

Kenders and Sabine wandered down the slope leading to the river, the sunset-filled sky on their right and the fort on their left. As they ambled down the hill, shooing away the iridescent green beetles that hummed over the prairie grass, Kenders found her gaze continuously returning to the fort's crumbling battlements and towers. She tried to imagine what the fortress had looked like when it had been in use.

"It is impressive, isn't it?" asked Sabine.

Nodding, Kenders muttered, "Yes, it is." She paused, picturing soldiers walking along on the walls, staring out at the lands below them, keeping watch for enemies. "To think, this was built before the duchies even existed."

"Must have been a wondrous time. No duchies means no ridiculous laws outlawing magic."

"Did you know it wasn't always that way? In the duchies, I mean. Magic used to be accepted. Celebrated, even."

Sabine peered at her, a dubious expression filling her face. "Truly?"

Kenders nodded. "Truly."

Lifting her eyebrows, Sabine mumbled, "No, I didn't know that." Her eyes narrowed. "How is it you do?"

Pushing a stray lock of hair behind her ear, Kenders replied, "Broedi told us all about it when he told us the story of our—" She stopped, catching herself before mentioning her blood parents. "When he told us some history of the duchies."

"I see," said Sabine, her tone rightly skeptical. "The history of the duchies."

For a few moments, they walked in an uneasy silence filled by Smoke's clopping hooves clopping beetles buzzing past. Kenders prayed Sabine would let the topic slide. Her prayer went unanswered.

"Kenders, do you think I am brainless?"

"Of course not."

"Then stop treating me like I am."

Shaking her head, Kenders protested, "I don't know what—"

"Don't," interjected Sabine firmly. "Don't pretend you're brainless either. Just be quiet for a moment and listen."

Worried where this was going, Kenders nonetheless nodded. "Go on."

"I know you four have a secret. One bigger than you being a mage. Now, I understand secrets, I've lived with them my whole life. You are more than welcome to keep yours."

Kenders was surprised. "Truly?"

Nodding, Sabine said, "Not only did you save me and Helene from the brigands, but you offered me something I cannot give her on my own. The promise of safety. So, yes. Keep your secrets. I don't need to know."

Kenders eyed Sabine, unsure what to say in response.

Sabine held her gaze for a few moments before staring down to the river, a slight smile on her face. "Considering my limited options at the moment, I would follow you even if you were one of the Cabal." It was clearly a sarcastic comment, one meant to lighten the mood, yet it failed miserably. Kenders shot a sharp look at her, one Sabine did not see as she continued talking. "Let's see, Broedi would be the god of Deception because there is *so* much more to him then he lets on. Nikalys could be—"

"Stop it!" hissed Kenders, the words slipping out hard and quick. "The Cabal are *not* something you jest about! My parents are dead because of them!"

Sabine halted in place, reached out, and grabbed hold of Kenders' shoulder. "*What* did you say?"

Kenders dropped her head, angry with herself for letting such an important detail slip. Broedi was not going to be happy. Or her brothers. Both had been reminding her daily to say nothing with Sabine. "Nothing. Forget I said anything" She tried to pull free of Sabine's grip. "Let's go get the water."

Sabine's fingers tightened on Kenders' shoulder, her eyes wide and intense. "Forget that you said the Cabal killed your parents? Sorry, but I can't do that. Tell me what that means."

Kenders sighed, lifted her head, and stared at her friend. "I can't, Sabine. Truly, I can't."

Sabine took a step back and stared at her for a long, quiet moment. Her stare grew chilly. "Are Helene and I in danger by being with you?"

Kenders winced before muttering, "Perhaps." Seeing a shadow pass over Sabine's face, she quickly added, "But Nik and Broedi are right. You're safer with us than without."

"I don't know if I believe that anymore."

Kenders dropped her head to stare at the dusk-lit grass. "I don't suppose I would, either, if I were you...." She wavered for a moment, poised to tell Sabine everything, but managed to hold firm. Hoping to cause a drastic change in subject, she forced herself to smile and looked up. "You know, there's one thing I can tell you."

"What?"

Leaning closer to Sabine, she murmured, "I think my brothers are taken with you. Both of them."

For a moment, Sabine gave no indication she had even heard what Kenders said, her face remaining blank. Kenders had successfully knocked the young woman entirely off balance. Finally, Sabine sighed and gave a dismissive shake of her head. "I have enough to worry about. I will not add men to the list."

"I'm simply warning you. I've lost count the number of times I've caught them staring at you when they think no one is looking."

"Were I interested—and to be clear, I am *not*—I would not know where to begin."

"Well, I just thought you should know. That and that they're both good souls. And I'm not just saying—" She stopped short as she caught a flicker of a movement amongst the ruins.

Sabine turned at once, following Kenders' gaze. "What? Did you see something?"

"I'm...not sure." Her eyebrows drew together. Lifting a hand to point up, she asked, "See that opening up there? In the tower?"

"Yes."

"I swore something moved past it."

They both stood motionless on the hill, watching the gap in the tower. Bathed in dusk's light, the old fort seemed almost sinister now whereas before it had been majestic.

As the moments passed and neither of them saw anything unusual, Kenders began to doubt herself. With her eyes still fixed on the ancient stronghold, she mumbled, "Let's go get the water. I want to be back before it gets dark."

"No wash?"

"I'll wait until tomorrow."

Sabine shrugged her shoulders. "Fine. Let's go." She turned and resumed walking down the slope.

Kenders remained in place a moment longer, staring at the fort. Something about the ruins made her uneasy, something she could not name. Letting out a tiny sigh, she turned to follow Sabine when she felt the distinct, white crackling of Strands of Air. A moment later, she heard Broedi's voice, urgent and firm, right beside her.

"Uora. I need you to return. Now, please."

Kenders spun to her left, expecting to see hillman there while wondering how he had managed to sneak up on her. However, only Smoke was there. The horse stared at her and nickered.

"I am up the hill, uora."

Looking up the slope, she saw Broedi staring down at her. Jak was at his side, waving his arms anxiously. Answering her unasked question, the hilllman said, "It is a Weave of Air. One to send one's words. Now, hurry back. Quietly." He sounded almost as worried as Jak looked. And if Broedi was upset, his reason was good.

Turning around, she called in a hushed shout, "Sabine!" Two dozen paces down the hill, Sabine stopped and looked back. Keeping her voice low, Kenders said, "We need to go back."

"Why?"

"I don't know. Broedi told us to come back—now."

Sabine's gaze drifted up the hill. "How did he—?"

"Magic Let's go. It sounded important."

Understanding lit up Sabine's face like a flash of lightning at night and she started scrambling up the hill. Kenders waited for her then hurried up the slope, tugging Smoke's reins behind her.

Halfway up, Kenders felt the crackling of magic again, pure green this time. Strands of Life. As she looked up, wondering what Broedi was doing, the bright white sensation of Air filled her a second time. A Weave quickly came together before the hillman and faded away the moment it seemed complete. A stiff wind blew past the girls, staggering them as it rushed to the river below, flattening a swath of prairie grass as it went.

Kenders and Sabine were both out of breath by the time they reached the hill's crest. Kenders stared around, surprised at the area's condition. When they had left, Broedi and her brothers had been preparing camp, but now the area looked pristine. Not a single blade of grass was bent. In fact, the moment someone lifted their foot, the grass below would stand straight, any creases straightening in an instant.

Jak, Nikalys, and Broedi were all facing northwest, staring at the grassy horizon. Helene had both arms wrapped tightly around Nikalys' leg.

Hurrying to stand with them, Kenders asked between ragged breaths, "What's happening?"

Broedi looked over at once. "We must go. Quickly and quietly. Lead the horses—no one rides." Pulling the reins of the spare horse and Sabine's mare, he began walking toward the fort.

Staring at Broedi's back, Kenders asked, "Go where? Better yet, go why?" When the hillman did not respond, she looked to her brothers. "What's going on?"

Nikalys scooped up Helene, held her in the crook of his arm, and hurried after Broedi, his expression grim. He glanced at the girls as he passed but said nothing as he was busy murmuring words of comfort to a visibly afraid Helene.

Kenders looked to her older brother who was still staring at the horizon, holding the leads to Hal and Goshen. "Jak?"

Looking over, he held out Hal's reins to Sabine. "Here. We can talk while we walk." After Sabine took the leather straps, the three of them began hurrying after Broedi and Nikalys. Keeping his voice low, Jak said, "We were making camp when Broedi suddenly stands up, straight as a wagon pole, and looks back that direction." He motioned with his head behind them to the northeast. "Then he looks at Nik and me and says in that bizarrely calm way of his, 'Horses are coming.'"

Panic rushed through Kenders, shocking her like a leap into cold water. "Bandits? Or…something else?" She was vague on purpose.

After shooting a wary glance at Sabine, Jak said, "Broedi's not sure. But he wants to avoid whoever it is. As soon as we picked up camp, he did something that made the grass grow again. Then there was that big gust of wind that blew all the way down to the river."

"Did he say why he did that?" asked Kenders.

Jak shook his head. "He was too busy telling us to stay quiet."

Sabine spoke, her tone cool and poised. "It's a false trail."

Kenders looked over at Sabine. They young woman seemed infinitely less rattled than she was or Jak sounded.

"You're probably right," said Jak. "Didn't think of that."

"I don't understand, though," said Sabine. "I thought he wanted to avoid using magic."

Kenders was in the midst of wondering the same thing. If agents of the Cabal were pursuing them, the chances were good that they had mages with them, perhaps even the saeljul from Lake Hawthorne. If any of them could touch Air or Life, Broedi had just set off a small burst of light in a very dark room. Worried, Kenders looked over her shoulder. The horizon was still clear.

"I guess he hopes they're bandits?" suggested Jak. "If they are, they might just follow the false trail and think we crossed the river."

Kenders glanced down at the wide, swift-moving Erona River. She doubted even the most brainless brigand would believe they had forded the water here. Looking back to Jak, she asked, "And if they're not bandits?"

Jak shrugged his shoulders. "I don't know."

Kenders stared ahead. Broedi seemed to heading straight for the ruins. "Are we going into the fort?"

"I don't know."

"But he said it wasn't safe. Why is he taking us inside if it's not safe?"

"I don't know!" hissed Jak, clearly exasperated. "Broedi didn't exactly share his plan. As always, he tells us what to do, we nod our heads, and then off we go."

She stopped pestering Jak. He had no better idea what was happening than she did. Staring ahead, she found Broedi and Nikalys far ahead of them, the pair moving much faster than the rest of them could manage.

Feeling Sabine's eyes on her, Kenders looked over. The young woman seemed to be on the verge of asking something, but instead pressed her lips together and faced forward, her expression calm and determined. Kenders breathed a tiny sigh of relief.

As they rushed through the grass, Kenders repeatedly glanced over her shoulder, looking for any movement on the horizon, but fading daylight thwarted her. Mu's orb was gone for the day, and the reds and purples of dusk were already turning into warm grays. Night was near.

The stronghold soon loomed over them. A greenish-black moss covered parts of the stone walls giving the fort a strange, mottled look. The wall facing them was hundreds of paces wide and mostly intact except for a single, wide opening where the blocks had crumbled completely to the ground. It looked as if a giant axe had slammed down, almost cutting the fort in two.

Nikalys and Broedi had stopped near the gash to wait for them and were staring past Kenders' group to the northwest horizon. Once everyone was together, they resumed walking, scuttling along the wall's base, heading toward the northern tower. After they rounded the corner, the old fort blocked any remaining daylight, draping them in shadows.

As they ran, Kenders glanced at Broedi. "Are you sure you heard someone coming?" Other than her own heavy breathing and the sounds of the group hurrying along, she had heard nothing.

"Yes, uora," replied Broedi. "I am sure." While he sounded calm, there was a definite undertone of urgency in his voice. "And they are getting closer. Keep moving."

Kenders frowned and continued running along the wall. A couple dozen steps later, for just a moment, she felt a soft, muted burst of silver as if someone were weaving. Looking at Broedi and seeing nothing, she dismissed the flicker as her imagination gone awry. A moment later, she felt the tiny surge again. This time, she sensed the source was within the fort. "Broedi? I'm not sure we should go in here."

Without breaking stride, Broedi looked at her. "Why is that, uora?"

She eyed the stronghold's walls, her gaze traveling upwards as she ran. The towering walls were close enough for her to reach out and touch, but she did not want to. Frowning, she looked back to the hillman. "Something does not feel right in there."

Broedi stared at her as though he were having a difficult time understanding what he saw. He had yet to respond when, moments later, they came across an opening. Then he rumbled, "Stop, please."

Their group came to a halt, standing before a great archway nearly twenty feet tall that led into a dimly lit, grass-filled courtyard. Shadows swarmed the fort's interior, uneven and misshapen. Crumbled stone structures littered the yard, once buildings but now nothing more than piles of rubble.

Kenders' unease grew as she stared inside the fort. Others apparently shared her disquiet.

Jak mumbled, "Now I wish we could wait for morning."

"As do I, uori," rumbled Broedi.

The horses stomped their feet. Hal and Goshen tossed their heads, Smoke let out a low nicker.

The hillman took a few steps forward, peering into the yard. His nostrils flared, and he took two quick sniffs of evening air. A slight frown crossed his face. Glancing at Nikalys, he said, "Give the little one to her iskoa."

Without questioning why, Nikalys moved over and handed a frightened Helene to Sabine. The toddler was sniffling, barely holding back tears. As she buried her face into Sabine's neck, Nikalys moved back to Broedi's side. The moment he did, the hillman whispered an unexpected order. "Draw your sword, uori."

Nikalys stared at Broedi, eyebrows arched. "Are you sure?"

"I am."

Nikalys reached for the Blade of Horum's hilt and drew the shimmering sword from its scabbard. The combination of White Moon's reflected light paired with the Weave within the metal gave the blade a soft, white glow. Sabine let out a short gasp as she stared at the sword. Nikalys had wisely kept the blade sheathed since meeting the Moiléne sisters. Glowing swords prompted questions.

With Nikalys holding the blade before him, Broedi took a single step forward and called—softly—through the archway. "We mean you no harm if you mean us none."

Kenders tensed. Perhaps her eyes had not been playing tricks on her earlier.

The White Lion took another step forward. "This place can be quite dangerous at night. I can offer you protection if you would like." He tilted his head back and glanced at the sky. "Decide quickly, though. You do not have much time."

Nothing stirred inside.

A moment later, Kenders heard a low rumbling, almost like distant thunder. Spinning around, she spotted a mass of tiny lights on the northeast horizon. "Broedi...?"

"I know, uora," murmured the hillman. Raising his voice, he called back into the courtyard. "If you do not come forward by the time I count to three, I will send my master swordsman in to force you out."

Nikalys' head whipped around to face Broedi, his eyes opened a fraction wider than normal.

"One. Two. Thr—"

A man stepped from behind a stone pile and into a puddle of moonlight, a long wooden staff slung over his shoulder. Kenders stared, surprised. She had never seen a man with such dark skin.

"Come closer, please," ordered Broedi.

The man stood in place for a moment before approaching the entranceway, leading a pale horse behind him. Stopping a few dozen paces away, he asked, "Who are you? And who are those men following you?" His speech was odd, his words flowing together, each one connected to the other without a break in between.

"I will explain later," rumbled Broedi. He paused a moment, studying the man. "You are from the Borderlands, yes?"

The stranger's gaze danced over each of them while he nodded slowly. "I am."

Kenders was stunned. She could not imagine what a Borderlander would be doing this far east.

Broedi looked back at them and motioned for everyone to head inside. "Quickly, please. Before night falls completely."

Despite everyone's clear hesitation, they all strode through the arch. The moment Kenders set foot inside the walls, the strange sensation of muted silver Strands bubbled again, only this time it was thrice as strong and accompanied by a surge of black. "Broedi, what is—?"

"Later, uora. Keep going."

Putting her trust in the hillman, Kenders approached the dark-skinned man standing in the overgrown courtyard. As she neared, she realized the staff he held was actually a farmer's hoe. Glancing at his horse, she spotted sheep shears for cutting wool strapped to his saddle. This man's presence made less sense by the moment.

As they reached the stranger, Broedi looked at Nikalys—who still held his sword at his side—and said, "Please put that away. And keep it sheathed no matter what happens. I do not want you accidently hurting anyone."

It took Nikalys three tries, but he managed to slip the shimmering blade back into its scabbard. Throughout the effort, the Borderlander stared at Nikalys with narrowed eyes. "You said he was a master swordsman."

"I lied," rumbled Broedi. Looking around, he stepped into a deep shadow beside the ruins of some sort of building, stared at them, and said, "Gather close, please."

Sounding bitter, the dark-skinned man demanded, "What's going on?"

Jak shrugged his shoulders, muttering, "Your guess is as good as mine."

Broedi, for once, offered an answer. He spoke in a rushed yet quiet voice, all the while staring up at the walls. "When the Imperials built these forts, they had mages fold great Weaves into the stones." He looked to the dark-skinned Borderlander. "As dusk fell, you began to see things, yes?"

The man's gaze danced around the courtyard, eventually resting on the battlements above. He answered with some hesitation. "I thought it was just the shadows playing tricks."

"We should be so lucky," rumbled Broedi. "The souls of the soldiers who died defending this fort still patrol at night." He shifted his gaze to Kenders. "*That*, uora, is what you are feeling, although I am astounded you can. Those Weaves have been stretched thin by the centuries." He stared at walls again, muttering, "When it is truly night, when no light of day remains, the souls of the soldiers come forth and repel any intruders."

"They'll attack us?" asked Nikalys. "Why?"

"Because that is what they do."

"But we mean them no harm," said the Borderlander. He glanced around at Kenders' group, adding, "At least I do not."

"Our intentions are meaningless," rumbled Broedi. "They fight. They do not think. There is no reasoning with them."

Helene began to whimper, which prompted Sabine to start rocking her.

Shaking his head, Nikalys asked, "So our only options are to stay out there—" he motioned to the entrance "—and face whoever is following us, or stay in here and fight off what? Spirits? Souls?"

"Hopefully, neither," said Broedi. "I can knit a small Weave of protection that should keep us hidden from the spirits. Pray that our pursuers follow the trail to the river."

Kenders could feel the silver and black Strands strengthening, thickening. Worried, she muttered, "Broedi? It's getting stronger."

"I know. Even I can feel the Strands of Soul now." He glanced up at the sky again. "Everyone, please stand close and *remain quiet*, I will begin the Weave."

The Borderlander asked, "What is a weave?"

"Magic," muttered Jak.

The man's eyes widened as he took a step back from Broedi. "Magic? But that's—"

"Hush, outlander!" hissed Sabine. "Either get close or get out."

The man stared out the archway, frowned, and then moved closer to their group, pulling his horse with him. Everyone else stood close, shoulder-to-shoulder.

Kenders both felt and saw bright, shining silver Strands seemingly emerge from thin air. Broedi quickly and skillfully arranged them in a netlike pattern. Helene stopped her soft sobbing for a moment, pulled her head from Sabine's chest, and stared up at the Weave, her eyes full of wonderment. When Broedi was finished, the net expanded and began to drift over the group.

The Borderlander stood perfectly still, looking around expectantly. Turning to Jak, he murmured, "Will it hurt?"

"Only at first," whispered Jak. "Then it tickles."

Kenders reached over, smacked Jak's arm, and hissed, "Not now!" She looked to the Borderlander. "No, it won't hurt." The Weave, now settled over the group, slowly faded from Kenders' sight. "In fact, he's done."

Helene whispered, "That was pretty."

Looking around the courtyard, the Borderlands man asked, "What was?"

"Quiet!" ordered Broedi, his deep voice hushed. "The Weave will keep us hidden from the spirits' view, but it will not mask our sound. And any noise you make—*any*—will awaken them."

Nobody said another word. Kenders remained motionless, repeatedly scanning the courtyard as they stood there, waiting.

White Moon asserted its dominance of the night sky while Blue Moon crested the northwestern wall, adding its pale blue rays to the courtyard. Together, they cast odd, mismatched shadows. Flickers in the dark would catch her attention, but after staring into the murky shadows, she would realize it was simply the grass rippling in the breeze as it whistled through cracks in the walls.

So focused was she on what was happening in the interior of the fort that she did not notice the rumbling of galloping horses until it was so loud that it could no longer be ignored. A shout from outside drifted into the fort and the host of horses ceased their thudding. Everyone remained silent and impossibly still. Even Helene managed to stay quiet, her eyes shut tight, her head buried in Sabine's neck.

After a time, a few distant, unintelligible shouts filled the night. Kenders was not sure, but they seemed to be coming from the direction of river. She offered a prayer to Ketus, hoping whoever it was would take the bait.

She glanced at the others and saw they appeared as anxious as she was. Even Broedi appeared worried, his gaze darting around the courtyard as much as staring out into the nighttime prairie. Her brothers flanked Sabine and Helene, Nikalys his hand on his sword hilt, Jak with a bow he had somehow managed to string without Kenders noticing. As she eyed the arrow he already nocked on the string, she wondered if you could even shoot a spirit.

Looking to her left, she stared at the Borderlander and noticed for the first time that his face was badly injured as if he had been beaten. His eyes were wide and alert, with only a hint of panic, and he held his hoe as one would a weapon, prepared to fight. She was impressed. Most people in this situation would have run from the fort, screaming.

The thudding of horses' hooves resumed and approached the fort, albeit at a less frantic pace than earlier. Kenders stared through the tall, arched entranceway and watched as several dozen flickering torches appeared on the flat plains. A couple hundred paces from the fort, they all stopped. Kenders prayed that night's shadow was sufficiently obscuring her group so the horsemen could not see them.

The men and their torches began to creep toward the fort. Kenders tried to get Broedi's attention, wondering what he wanted them to do, but the hillman was peering out the archway. The anxiousness from before was still there, but so was a small amount of surprise.

Nikalys whispered, "What do we—"

A quick, hard look from Broedi cut him off as Kenders felt the Strands about the fort swirl, spinning in a frenzy. She flashed Nikalys a wide-eyed glare and put a finger up to her lips, urging him to be quiet. He held up his hands in apology and after a few moments, the silver and black Stands calmed, returning to their normal pattern of drifting about the fort.

The men on horseback drew close enough that she could see they wore uniforms, which she reasoned meant they were not bandits. Moments later, she was astonished when she recognized the livery as belonging to the soldiers of the Great Lakes Duchy. She could not imagine what Red Sentinels were doing this far south.

So stunned was she by the realization, Kenders nearly missed the small figure riding at the head of the column beside a tall, bearded man. Based on stature alone, she would have sworn it was a child. The tiny individual lifted up an arm, pointed straight at the group standing in the shadows, and leaned over to say something to a bearded man.

Kenders stomach dropped. They had been spotted.

She flashed Broedi a desperate look. The hillman was still staring out the archway, frowning. Glancing around the group, she found nearly everyone staring at him, waiting for guidance. Nikalys, with his hand on the hilt of the sword he was not to draw. Sabine, with her arms wrapped around her sister. The Borderlander, gripping his hoe.

Jak was the lone exception. He was staring out the entranceway while wearing an expression of complete and total surprise.

After a few moments, Broedi motioned for them to move forward and out of the shadows. At first, no one moved. The hillman glared at them all, waved his hand forward again, and stepped forward, clearly expecting they comply with his order. They did and everyone scooted into the moonlight.

The reaction of the soldiers varied, but most exhibited some combination of surprise, fear, and determined resolve. The little man—Kenders had decided it was most definitely not a child—wore a smile on his face, almost as if he was happy to see them. The bearded soldier appeared a bit more wary, but he also seemed pleased.

Sensing movement to her right, she turned to find Jak gesturing wildly with his hands, trying to communicate something to Broedi without speaking. He was repeatedly pointing out the entranceway, stroking his cheeks, and then jabbing a finger into his own chest. Confused, Kenders looked out the archway.

The bearded man kicked his horse and rode closer, stopping only a dozen paces on the other side of the entryway. In a clear, deep voice, he called out, "I recognize you, as well, Jak Isaac of Yellow Mud!"

Kenders gasped and spun to look at Jak.

Nikalys did the same, uttering, "Hells, Jak!"

Exasperated, Jak exclaimed, "That's what I was trying to tell you!"

Kenders felt the swirling silver and black Strands surge. The intensity of the crackling was staggering.

From outside, a high-pitched voice called out, "Nathan! Something's happening!"

No longer able to hold her fear in, Helene began to cry and Sabine began to sing, trying to calm her.

All around the courtyard, clumps of white mist began to form, swirling in the air. On the tops of walls. In the shadows. From the piles of rubble. One moment there was nothing, a blink of an eye later, a white fog had coalesced. Silver and black Strands popped into view and rushed into the mists, knitting themselves together into shapes that resembled men.

A large, strong hand grabbed her shoulder. Whirling around, she looked up into Broedi's dark eyes. They were wide and wild. "Unweave them if you can, uora!"

He released her and jumped back. Gold, silver, and green Strands popped into existence, twisted together into a quick, complex pattern, and sank into Broedi. A moment later, his body began to change, morphing into that of an animal.

To her left, an unearthly, hollow voice screamed, "Vallo per vestri ago!" The cry echoed as though it was in a small room and not here in the open courtyard.

Whirling, she saw the figure of a man several dozen paces away, composed of what could only be described as mist and moonlight, softly glowing in the night's gloom. He held a stubby sword in one hand and a round shield in the other, his armor reminding her of a tortoise shell. The transparent, insubstantial man began to move toward her, quickly breaking into a run, his eyes wide and fixed directly on her.

As he rushed through the mixed light of the two moons, he appeared to soak up the illumination around him, drawing it into his shape and turning opaque. By the time the ancient soldier was a dozen paces from her, he looked as solid as any of them, even if he was still the color of the combined moons: a soft bluish-white light.

Kenders surprised herself by reaching for the bright white Strands of Air and weaving them faster than she ever had before. One finished, she directed the completed pattern at the man, expecting it to lift the charging soldier off the ground. She watched in silent horror as the pale figure passed right through the web of white Strands. He lifted his sword, readying to strike at her.

Backing away, she threw her arms up to protect herself, tripped over a chunk of stone, and fell. As she tumbled to the ground, she glimpsed a long wooden staff swing over her and catch the charging spirit square in the forehead with a decidedly solid thud. The soldier collapsed like any normal man would, but before he hit the ground, the bonds holding him together came apart and the pale, shining figure melted back into the moonlight.

Looking up, she found the Borderlander standing over her, holding his hoe in two hands, staring at where the soldier had been only a moment before. Shaking his head, he released one hand from the hoe, reached down, grabbed Kenders' forearm, and lifted her up to her feet.

Staring into his dark eyes, she said, "Thank you for—"

His eyes went wide. Shoving her back to the ground, he gripped the hoe and spun around in a quick circle to strike another moonlight soldier that had come at her from behind. She landed on her back just as the end of the hoe connected with the soldier's gut. Unlike the first spirit, this one did not disappear when struck. Rather, the ghostly soldier grabbed the pole and pulled the Borderlander to him. The dark-skinned man stumbled over Kenders, on his way to impaling himself on the spirit's outstretched sword.

Kenders focused on the ghostly figure, frantically searching for the pattern inside the man. Her first lesson on unraveling a Weave had only been yesterday and it had been on a simple, single-Strand Weave of Air.

Taking a chance, she plucked a single Strand of silver and another of the black and pulled. Just as the Borderlander was about to fall on the stubby sword, the spirit winked from existence. Light poured from it like water rushing from an overturned bucket, splashing back into the courtyard.

The Borderlander tumbled to the ground with his hoe. He had barely touched the ground before he leapt up to stand ready. Kenders pushed herself off the ground and turned in a circle, surveying the situation.

All across the courtyard, dozens of ghostly, bluish-white soldiers moved toward the group. Broedi—as the massive golden bear—roared about, smacking back any spirit that got too close. Nikalys was popping about Sabine and Helene, holding a rock, appearing next to a soldier long enough to bash it in the head before moving to the next closest figure. Jak stood off to the side of the Moiléne sisters, drawing arrows from the quiver on his hip and firing them.

With horror, she watched a soldier materialize behind Jak and quickly draw in enough of the surrounding moonlight to turn solid. The spirits were forming quicker.

She was focusing on the white figure, trying to remember exactly how she had pulled the other apart when, suddenly, the figure dissipated. Confused, she looked about the courtyard and saw that the little man from outside was charging into the fortress atop his horse, his gaze locked on Jak. Her eyes widened as the Red Sentinels followed him through the archway, screaming their own battle cries to match the spirits'. Some carried torches, some carried shields with the Great Lakes' crest, but every one of them held long, gleaming metal swords.

Panic gripped her for an instant before she realized that the Red Sentinels were attacking the moonlight army. Whatever the reason, they were helping. Two sets of soldiers, one from the present and one from centuries past, were soon locked in mortal combat. Over the din of the fighting and screaming, a voice of absolute authority bellowed, "Get to the plains!"

Spinning around, she saw the bearded man screaming and motioning for to them to move. The mounted duchy soldiers were forming two lines running from the entryway, creating a hollow column leading to the door.

Jak's voice joined in with the Red Sentinel leader. "You heard him! Get out of here!"

He grabbed Sabine's shoulder and began dragging her toward the doorway. Sabine held Helene tight in both arms, shielding her screaming sister as she ran. Nikalys followed behind, slowly backing his way toward the door, smashing any soldier that got too close in the head with his rock. Kenders scampered past him and Broedi, rushing for the doorway.

Upon reaching the arch, she spun around and began shifting her attention from one moonlight soldier to the next, unraveling as many as she could, as quickly as she could. Yet it seemed for every glowing soldier she made disappear, another formed elsewhere in the courtyard.

The Borderlander broke through the line of Smithshill soldiers, carrying a bleeding Red Sentinel on his shoulders, and sprinted for the entryway. He rushed past her to join Jak and Sabine already standing in the open plains.

The bearded soldier called, "To the grasslands!"

The two columns of Red Sentinels began to collapse back to the archway. Kenders stood beneath the arch's peak, unraveling spirits as the duchy soldiers streamed past her on both sides. Soon, only Nikalys and Broedi remained inside the courtyard, fighting nearly a dozen glowing, bluish-white men at the same time. Dark gashes covered Broedi's fur. Nikalys had a large wound on his right shoulder, blood dripping to the ground, glistening in the moonlight.

Kenders eyes went wide. "Nikalys!"

To her left, a high-pitched voice shouted over the sounds of battle, "I'll get the boy, you get the White Lion."

Turning quickly, she found the small red-haired man standing beside her, no longer on his horse. She was about to ask how he could possibly know who Broedi was when the white crinkling of Air mixed with the golden of Will filled her. She stood in awe, watching the little man craft a pattern she had never seen. Hoping that he was truly helping, she tried to mimic the Weave, but had an impossibly difficult time following along. She had yet to work on combining different types of Strands.

By the time the little man flung his completed Weave at Nikalys, Kenders' feeble attempt had fallen apart. She started again, but had no idea of what she was doing. She screamed in frustration, cursing her inexperience.

A great rush of air whooshed from above the fort as a twisting mass of dust and debris swept into the courtyard. It lifted Nikalys from the ground and, spinning him around, sped toward the door, leaving Broedi alone in the moonlit courtyard, surrounded by over two dozen spirit soldiers.

She stared at the twister, wanting the exact same thing for Broedi.

She needed it.

Now.

A second, fully complete Weave of white and gold popped into existence as a wave of exhaustion rushed over her. Her knees buckled and she stumbled forward, almost collapsing to the grass yet somehow managing to remain upright.

Another spiral of dust coiled around the bear, picked him up, and rushed to the archway. The little man grabbed her and pulled her to the side as Nikalys and Broedi flew from the fort and into the plain. Pulling her arm free from the small mage, she turned and stumbled after them. Nikalys fell to the ground as the Weave around him dissipated. Staring at her own Weave, she willed it to stop. Broedi the bear thudded to the ground and skidded through the grass.

Seeing the Red Sentinels in a long line, facing the fort with swords at the ready, she glanced back over her shoulder. The moonlight soldiers stood at the archway's threshold, staring out at them. Turning around, she sprinted to where Nikalys lay in the grass. Dropping to her knees, she flipped him over and gasped. The wound on his shoulder was deep. She saw white and assumed it was bone.

"Oh, gods…Nikalys…"

She wished she had practiced more with Life. In fact, she wished she had practiced more, period. Perhaps she could have prevented this. She was starting to wonder if she could do with Nikalys' wound what she had just done with the twister of air when Broedi's voice thundered over the plains.

"Uora!"

Glancing over, she found the hillman—no longer the bear—sitting on the ground, glaring at her. His legs, arms, and chest were wet with blood.

"Do *not* try to help him!" ordered Broedi. "Do you understand? It is too dangerous!"

Kenders was about to ignore him when, standing a few paces away, the little mage from the fort said, "I can help."

Broedi shifted his gaze him. "You are a Life mage?"

With wide eyes, the man nodded. "Yes." Red hair poked out from under his wide-brimmed hat.

Pointing to Nikalys' wound, Broedi asked, "Can you tend that?"

Nodding again, the stranger said, "I can."

"Then do so," rumbled Broedi. "I will see to the injured soldiers."

"What about you?" asked Kenders. "You're hurt, too!"

"I will be fine, uora." His brown eyes bored into her as he rose from the ground. "Let the tomble help your kaveli."

Staring at the small man as he approached, she blinked twice. "Tomble?"

Upon reaching her, the little man—no, tomble—tried to gently push her to the side. "If you could scoot over just a bit?" His gaze was on Nikalys, his eyes full of worry.

Looking down, she saw that Nikalys looked a shade or two paler than only a moment ago.

In a kind, calm voice, the tomble said, "I promise I will only help him."

Reluctantly, she moved back, letting the little mage crouch down and examine Nikalys' shoulder. Feeling a hand on her shoulder, she looked up to find Jak standing beside her, staring down at Nikalys, his eyes brimming with concern. She reached up to grab his hand and squeezed. Sabine stood distance away, holding Helene, rocking her and singing quietly while staring in their direction.

A lustrous, green crackling filled her. She watched the tomble weave dozens of Strands of Life together, knitting them into her brother's injured shoulder. She marveled at the complexity of the design and the skill with which the tomble wove it.

She shook her head, muttering, "Gods, I have so much to learn..."

Since that moment on the shores of Lake Hawthorne, when she stared out at the water creature rising from the lake's surface, to now, she had been terrified of what she was. Ashamed. Embarrassed. Fearful.

Despite knowing her true heritage, despite knowing her supposed destiny, despite it all, she had been unable to shake the feeling that every time she reached for even a single Strand she was doing something wrong.

In that instant, as she watched her brother bleed, every bit of reservation, worry, and fear fled. Magic was a tool, a tool that—at this moment—was helping save Nikalys' life. And it killed her that she was not the one wielding it.

Moments later, the tomble stood, faced her and Jak, and smiled. "He will sleep the night while he heals, but he'll be fine. Cheer up." He eyed them both a heartbeat longer before hurrying past, heading back to the soldiers.

Nikalys indeed looked slightly less pale than moments ago, his breathing steady and regular. Jak squeezed her hand tight as she slumped down into the grass, closed her eyes, and sighed. Kneeling there with eyes closed, she noticed she could still feel the constant crackling of magic. Upon reopening her eyes, she turned to look at the soldiers. Most were standing while still staring at the fort, but a group of injured men was lying on the ground. Broedi was crouched over one while the tomble was rushing to another.

One man had a long gash across his face, directly over his right eye. Kenders cringed, guessing that his eye was gone, but could not tell for sure as he had his hands clasped over the wound while screaming. Blood oozed from his fingers. Another soldier was rocking back and forth, cradling his left arm. It appeared his hand was gone. In all, she counted nine men with grievous wounds.

Kneeling amongst the infirm was the bearded man, consoling the men as best he could. Other soldiers scrambled about, using traditional, non-magic means to aid the injured that the tomble and Broedi were not treating.

Kenders mumbled, "This is our fault."

Jak bent over. "Pardon?"

She did not repeat herself. Rising from the grass, she pulled her hand free of Jak's grip and began to walk to the soldiers. Behind her, she heard Jak call after her. "Kenders?"

She moved to where the injured men lay. While each man's face bore the torment of his wounds, most looked up at her approach. Instead of resentment or anger, she saw satisfaction and pride on their faces. She did not know why these men had helped her, her family, her new friends, but that did not matter. All she knew was that she could help these men in return.

Positioning herself at the center of the line of injured men, she took a deep, steadying breath, stared at them, and willed them to be better.

She wanted these men to be whole again.

Now.

An incredible, impossible surge of Life filled the air around her. The world glowed a bright, luminescent green.

"Uora, no!"

Weaves began to pop into existence all around her, one right after another. With each one, a hammer-stroke of exhaustion slammed into her like a horse's kick to the gut. Broedi continued to yell for her to stop, but she did not listen. The tomble stood nearby, staring wide-eyed into the air with open wonderment. Struggling to stay on her feet, Kenders directed the Weaves over the wounds of the men on the ground.

Those tending the injured gasped, watching as lacerations sealed in front of their eyes. The man with the sword cut across his right eye pulled his hands away, wiped the blood from his face, and began to blink both eyes in amazement. The soldier with the severed hand pulled his arm from the rag wrapped around it and wiggled fingers on a hand that had not been there moments before.

Within moments, all nine men were healed. Fully. None had even a scratch.

Smiling, Kenders collapsed to the ground, bone tired, and shut her eyes. Someone rushed to her side. Unable to fight the exhaustion, she gave herself over to sleep.

CHAPTER 50: CHANCE

Jak held Kenders in his arms, staring at her with a strange mix of awe and worry, when he heard footsteps approaching. Looking up, he saw a clearly disappointed Broedi marching toward them, his steps long and quick. The little man who had helped Nikalys—a tomble if Broedi was to be believed—scurried after the White Lion, his eyes round as ducats as he stared at Kenders. The tomble's hat was gone now, revealing a mass of red hair atop his head.

Peering up at Broedi, Jak asked, "Will she be all right?"

The hillman knelt beside Kenders, placed his hand on her head then slid it down to her neck. Speaking in a tone a frustrated parent uses with a misbehaving child, he rumbled, "I expect she will sleep for a long while. Which is good. As long as she is out, she cannot do anything as foolish as this!"

"Will she be all right or not?!" snapped Jak. That was all he cared about right now.

Broedi shifted his gaze to Jak and the harsh expression softened at once. "Yes, uori, she will be fine."

Relieved, Jak muttered, "Good." Then he slid his arms under his sister, picked her up, and left Broedi behind, moving to where Nikalys already lay in the grass. Sabine was sitting at his side, holding Helene in her lap.

"Hi, Jak," whispered Helene. "Be quiet. Nik-lys is sleeping." She looked at Kenders with worry in her eyes. "Is Kenders sleeping, too?"

Giving the best smile he was able to muster, he said, "Yes, dear. She's very tired."

Sabine peered at him over Helene's head, her expression one of deep concern.

"Truly," said Jak. "Broedi said she'll be fine."

A tiny, relieved smile spread over Sabine's lips.

Kneeling down, he laid his sister beside Nikalys, resting her head on the grass and brushing her hair from her eyes. He remained kneeling, staring at the pair, wondering at what point his life might start making sense again.

"Jak?" muttered Sabine. When he looked up, she nodded at the now-whole soldiers. "Did Kenders do that?"

He remained quiet for a moment before nodding slowly. "Yes. Yes, she did."

"How?"

If he shared the truth—that his sister's blood mother was a White Lion and champion of Gaena, the goddess of magic—the chance was high Sabine would name him mad. At times, he still had a difficult time believing it. Strangely enough, he felt relieved as he looked her square in the eye and lied. "I don't know."

He stood before she could press him, turned, and looked around the moonlit prairie. Broedi was staring down at the tomble, stone-faced, as the little mage, head tilted back, likewise peered up at the hillman. Put one tomble on top of another's shoulders, and Broedi might still be taller. Looking past the odd pair, he saw the man he recognized as Master Sergeant Trell checking on the previously injured men.

Jak was beyond baffled at how the soldier had come to be here. Jak could have drawn the man a map to this fort and the sergeant would have not been able to find this place. Frowning, he shook his head slowly and mumbled to himself, "Well, this ought to be an interesting conversation."

"Jak?"

Glancing down, he found Sabine still staring up at him, her expression calm and steady.

"Mind telling me who all those men are?"

"Soldiers of the Great Lakes. Red Sentinels."

"Why are they here?" She nodded at the sergeant. "How does he know your name?"

Jak held Sabine's gaze and remained silent. He had no idea how to answer that.

Sabine sat back, a frown spreading over her face. "Did you and your family do something wrong, Jak?"

A dry, somewhat derisive chuckle slipped from him. "We were born. Does that count?"

Now it was Sabine's turn to remain quiet for a moment or two, a chilly look of determination resting on her face. "Jak, *what* is going on here?"

Reaching up, he rubbed his eyes and sighed. "How about I go find out?"

"You do that," snapped Sabine. "And then, I want you to come back here and start talking. I want to know what I've gotten myself and my sister into!"

Helene tilted her head back to look at her sister. "I'm scared, Sabine."

Sabine looked down, somehow managed a smile, and gently stroked Helene's hair. "Don't be, dear. Everything is fine." When she peered back to Jak, her eyes were icy again. "*Isn't* it?"

Jak sighed and crouched beside the pair. Trying to ignore Sabine's glare, he peered into Helene's big brown eyes and smiled. "You're sister's right. Everything is fine." When the toddler did not respond, he changed tack. "You know, Helene, I could use your help. Do you think you can you do something for me?"

The little girl nodded, silent.

"Good." Pointing to Nikalys and Kenders, he said, "Your job is to make sure they sleep well? Can you do that?"

Helene looked over at his brother and sister and nodded again.

Reaching over, he tousled her hair. "Thank you very much." He shifted his gaze to Sabine. "I'll be right back."

As he stood and faced the chaos around him, Sabine said, "I want answers, Jak."

Striding away, he muttered to himself, "I'm not sure you do." He headed toward Broedi and the tomble first, walking up as the little redheaded man was speaking excitedly.

"—she heal them all at once? And so quickly?"

Broedi was eyeing the tomble with caution. "She is gifted, that is all." As Jak approached, he looked up. "Are they—"

The tomble interrupted. "Gifted?" He was incredulous. "Gifted?! What she just did should be impossible!"

Broedi replied, "Yes, well—"

"She didn't even let them heal themselves! She just did it—" He cut off, his eyes widening as though he had suddenly arrived at the answer to a playman's riddle. "Eliza Kap! *That's* who her mother is, isn't it? The Masterweaver!"

Jak stepped between the tomble and his siblings' unconscious bodies, his hand shooting to the hilt of the sword he did not know how to use. "Broedi?" The name carried with it a clear question: what do we do?

The tomble stared up at Broedi, his eyes even wider, and whispered in awe, "So you *are* Thonda's champion..." As a low, lupine growl emanated from Broedi's throat, the tomble threw up his small hands and took a few steps backwards. "Ah...I should explain."

"Yes, you should," growled Broedi. "And quickly." His voice carried a clear warning.

While keeping his gaze locked on the hillman, the tomble called over his shoulder, "Nathan? A moment, please?"

Sergeant Trell—kneeling beside one of the previously injured men— glanced up, peered at the trio, and frowned. After patting the soldier's shoulder, he stood and strode toward the group, his gaze darting from person to person.

Jak.

Broedi.

Sabine and Helene.

Nikalys and Kenders.

Jak and Broedi for a second time. His stare remained on them, darting back and forth, as he stopped beside the tomble. "Nundle, what did you say to make the rather large Shapechanger look so upset?"

"I may have gotten a bit ahead of myself."

"We spoke of this, Nundle."

"I know, I know. But I did not expect all of…this." He waved around at the fort and the injured soldiers. "I got a little excited."

"Who are you?" rumbled Broedi. "And why are you here? *With* a Tracker?"

Alarmed, Jak glanced around the camp, searching. "There's a Tracker here?"

"Yes," growled Broedi. "There is."

Holding up a hand, Sergeant Trell said, "First off, the Tracker will not touch any of you. Should he try, I'll tie him to a horse and send him back into that fort. I understand our appearance might be worrisome, but we mean you no harm. In fact, we—" he glanced down at the tomble "—simply want an opportunity to speak with you."

Nodding quickly, Nundle said, "Very much so, please."

Jak exchanged a quick look with Broedi. For once, the hillman appeared as surprised as any normal soul might be.

After a moment, when neither of them responded, Sergeant Trell spoke again. "Jak, I once gave you a chance to explain yourself. All I ask is that you return the favor."

Jak looked back to the soldier. "It's not up to me, Sergeant."

Broedi rumbled, "How is it you know each other?"

"You know the soldiers I met on the road before I found you in the woods?" said Jak. He nodded at the Red Sentinel. "This is the sergeant I spoke with. It's what I was trying to tell you in the fort. I recognized him."

Broedi lifted his eyebrows. "That seems quite the coincidence."

Jak agreed wholeheartedly. "An impossible one, I'd say."

Sergeant Trell turned his head to stare at the looming ruins. "Speaking of the fort, do we need to worry about those…whatever they were?"

Nundle shook his head vigorously. "Not at all. They're confined within the walls. They only guard. They will not sally forth."

"You are sure of that?" asked the sergeant.

"The tomble is correct," rumbled Broedi, his intense and somewhat curious gaze resting on Nundle. "The Imperial soldiers will not trouble us out here."

Sergeant Trell met Broedi's eyes and, after a moment, nodded. "Good to know. Now, if you don't mind, I need to see to my men." He stared about the grasslands. "We'll set camp here and, after that—" he glanced between Broedi and Jak "—I'd like to trade tales. What say you?"

Jak looked to Broedi. The hillman was still glaring at the soldier. He was clearly unhappy with the situation. "Broedi?"

Without taking his eyes from the sergeant, Broedi rumbled, "Yes, uori?"

"He's right. He treated me fairly on the road." Looking to the soldiers, he added, "And they helped us in the fort. I say we listen. Besides, Nik and Kenders are passed out. We're not going anywhere for a while."

Broedi was quiet for at least a half-dozen heartbeats, his gaze never leaving Sergeant Trell's face. Finally, he rumbled, "We will listen."

Sergeant Trell nodded once. "Good." Glancing at Jak, he gave a wondering shake of his head, a tiny smile on his face. "Nice to see you again, Jak."

"You as well, Sergeant."

With that, the soldier turned and strode back to his men, calling out orders for camp to be set up. The soldiers leapt to obey. Even those who had been injured joined in, seemingly unaffected by their ordeal.

After a few moments, Broedi looked at Jak. "I'm going to check on your kaveli and iskoa." He glanced at the tomble before looking back to Jak. "Say *nothing*, uori."

Jak nodded as Broedi moved off then turned to study the soldiers, looking for the corporal and the nobleman's son but spotting neither. He soon realized the group before him was about half the size of the detachment he had visited along the Southern Road. As the Sentinels hurried about, they were continuously glancing over at Jak's group, expressions of wonder affixed to their faces.

"I think they're trying to make sense of what just happened."

Jak looked down to find the tomble still standing beside him. "You can add me to that list."

Nundle peered at Jak, straining as though he were trying to see something that was invisible. After a few increasingly uncomfortable moments, Jak pointed to his brother and sister. "Well, then...I'm going to go check on them."

Nundle nodded. "Of course. Go, go." He smiled wide.

Jak gave the tomble one last curious look before spinning around and walking back to where his siblings lay. He felt Nundle's gaze following him the entire way.

Broedi was standing over Nikalys and Kenders, his arms crossed across his chest as he watched the soldiers. Besides Sabine and Helene sitting on the ground, they were alone.

As Jak approached, he looked to Broedi. "What now?" He caught a glimpse of Sabine glaring at him, but ignored it.

"We will listen to what they have to say."

After stopping beside the hillman, Jak faced the soldiers, too. "What do you suppose the tomble's story is?"

"I hope to find out."

Hesitant to say too much in front of Sabine and Helene, Jak paused before saying, "He seems to know quite a lot about…things."

"That's it," said Sabine, her tone firm. "Look at me. Both of you." While Jak peered down at her, Broedi did not take his gaze from the soldiers. Focusing solely on Jak, she said, "I said I wanted answers, Jak."

Jak simply stared at her, at a loss how to respond.

When neither of them replied, her gaze, cold and steady, darted between them both. "Are you running from the Cabal?"

Now Broedi looked away from the Red Sentinels, his gaze shooting to her. "What did you say?"

Sabine nodded as though he had just confirmed something for her. "Kenders slipped up and almost told me, but said she couldn't unless you—" she pointed at Broedi "—said it was fine. I was content to let you have your little secret—" she glanced at the soldiers and the fort "—only it seems that it's not so little." Glaring at Jak alone, she said, "I said it before, Jak, I deserve to know what I've gotten myself and my sister into!"

When she finished, she sat motionless, her steady-eyed gaze boring into Jak and Broedi. Now that she was quiet, Jak heard a couple of quiet sobs. Helene had begun to cry again. Sabine noticed as well. Her eyes softened as she dropped her head and pulled her sister tighter.

"Hey, it's all right. Shhh. Everything is fine. There's nothing to be afraid of." After a few moments of consolation, Sabine's glare returned to Jak and Broedi. In a softer tone than before, yet no less intense, she said, "Tell me. *Now.*"

Jak admired Sabine's tenacity. She simply wanted to protect her sister, her only remaining family. The same thing Jak wanted. He respected that. Looking to Broedi, he said, "I think we should tell her. She has a right to know."

Sabine shot him a grateful look, while the hillman remained quiet and pensive. After a long moment, Broedi sighed and nodded once. "On one condition."

"And what is that?" asked Sabine.

"Once you know the truth, you must stay with us. I will not allow you to leave."

Jak was not sure he liked the sound of that. "What are you saying? They're captives?"

"Name it what you will," rumbled Broedi, staring at him. "If they know the truth, they remain with us. Too much is at stake."

Jak wanted to argue with Broedi, but a glance down at his unconscious brother and sister shoved away his reservations.

Sabine peered up at Broedi, a frown on her face. "The offer of safe haven remains?"

"It does," answered the hillman.

Without a moment's hesitation, Sabine nodded. "Agreed, then. Even with the madness that follows you, you remain the sweetest of the sour."

Helene shifted in Sabine's lap to stare up at her sister's face. "Are we staying, Sabine?" Her tear-stained cheeks glistened in the light of the soldier's torches.

Sabine offered a tiny, reassuring smile while patting her sister's back. "Yes, dear, we are."

"Good." Helene rested her head back on Sabine's shoulder, snuggled closer to her sister, and yawned.

Letting out a short sigh, Sabine stood from the grass and eyed Broedi and Jak. "I'm going to put Helene to sleep. When I come back, we will talk, yes?"

Broedi inclined his head. "If you so desire."

With a satisfied nod, Sabine strode off, away from the chaos of the camp.

Jak caught the first few hummed notes of *Happy Times at the Fair* before the soldiers' commotion swallowed the song. Sighing, he looked over to Broedi. "I guess our secret isn't much of a secret anymore, is it?"

With his gaze on Sabine and a slight frown on his face, Broedi rumbled quietly, "Do not worry, uori. I have others."

CHAPTER 51: STORY

Broedi watched the soldiers closely as they moved about the prairie, staking horses and erecting tents, their actions efficient and focused. Considering what they had just been through, he thought they were handling themselves well.

Tuning his full attention to the bearded sergeant, he watched the man walk about the camp, seeking out each of the previously injured men. Upon finding one, the sergeant would stand with the soldier and talk with them for a moment. Then, with a firm pat on the back, he would send the Sentinel on his way. By simply looking at them now, one would never know they had been grievously hurt.

With a slow, frustrated shake of his head, Broedi peered down at Kenders. What she had done was beyond astounding. The tomble had been correct in his assessment: it should have been impossible.

The energy it took to summon and control Strands of Life was much greater than other types of Strands. No one knew why. When a Life mage aided someone, the accepted approach was to craft a Weave that helped the person's body heal itself. A small Life Weave and a full day's rest could do the same thing that an enormous pattern could do all at once.

Broedi doubted that even Eliza could have accomplished what her daughter had. Kenders was strong with the Strands. Stronger than he could have imagined. Yet, despite her prodigious capabilities, her understanding of the Strands was in its infancy. He hoped there would be sufficient time to let her grow and learn. As of this moment, she was unprepared for what was surely coming. They all were.

He reached up to scratch his chin as he stared at her, wondering how to handle what seemed to be the next challenge with the young girl. Nikalys and Jak had alluded to Kenders' impetuous nature—and Broedi had seen flashes of it—but impulsiveness paired with her gift made for a sour and potentially lethal mixture. A weary sigh slipped from his lips. Dropping his chin to his chest, he rubbed his eyes. He was tired. Very tired.

Eliza and Aryn's children would be sleeping for a while—Kenders perhaps more than a day after her foolishness—leaving him plenty of time to deal with the new problem facing him.

After lowering his hand, Broedi blinked a few times. Looking back to the soldiers, his gaze happened to fall upon the Borderlander whom they had discovered inside the ancient fort. The young man was standing off to the side by himself and wearing a perplexed expression. He had a ragged and weary look to him; the old injuries on his face spoke to confrontations prior to the one in the fort. He was staring at the soldiers, seemingly caught between trying to decide if he should stay in place or run off into the night.

Tilting his head in Jak's direction, Broedi rumbled, "Uori?"

Jak still stood beside him, quiet, apparently lost in his own thoughts. He looked up at Broedi. "Yes?"

Nodding to where the stranger stood by himself, Broedi said, "I would like you to speak with the Borderlander. Find out who he is and why he was in the fort, please. His presence here is unusual."

"More unusual than fifty Red Sentinels, a tomble, and a Tracker?"

A slight smile crossed Broedi's face. "Perhaps not, but it is close."

"Sure," said Jak. "I need to thank him, anyway. He saved Kenders. Twice." He strode away, aiming for where the Borderlander stood looking lost and very alone.

Turning his gaze onto the other mismatched man in the camp, the gray-clad Tracker, Broedi found the Constable already staring at him. He held Broedi's gaze for a long moment, glaring without flinching, before shifting to peer at Nikalys and Kenders. With a tiny shudder, the man turned and hurried away quickly, into the hubbub of the soldier's camp. Broedi's stare followed him until he disappeared among the picketed horses. Thonda's Strand twitched. Something about the Tracker made Broedi very uneasy.

Looking for the tomble, Broedi spotted him now conferring with the sergeant some distance away. He tried listening to what the pair was saying, but the din of the camp drowned out their conversation. Instead, he simply watched the pair, observing. The tomble repeatedly glanced over at him with nervous eyes, clearly aware that Broedi was scrutinizing them. After the fifth time looking over, the tomble nodded to Broedi while saying something to the sergeant. The man looked over as well, said something in response, and the two began to walk in his direction.

Broedi waited. When they reached where he stood guard over the Progeny, the sergeant spoke without preamble.

"Are you ready, Shapechanger?"

"I am."

The sergeant nodded. "Should we speak here or...?" He trailed off and glanced at Sabine. The moment Helene had fallen asleep, the young woman had returned to sit beside Nikalys and Kenders. Helene was softly snoring in her lap.

"Here," rumbled Broedi. As he lowered himself to the grass, he caught a quick, grateful look from Sabine but did not acknowledge it. He kept his gaze fixed firmly on the tomble and the soldier.

The sergeant sat opposite Broedi while Nundle settled on the soldier's right, across from Sabine. Laid out between them were Nikalys and Kenders, asleep and oblivious. Broedi considered retrieving his pipe, but his bag was where the injured soldiers had been and he did not want to leave the children alone.

Once settled, the sergeant cleared his throat and asked, "Are we waiting for Jak and your other companion?"

Broedi supposed that, from their point of view, the Borderlander was a part of their group.

Sabine shook her head. "The Border—"

Interrupting her, Broedi said, "They will join us shortly." The tomble and sergeant already seemed to know quite a bit, there was no need to clarify what they did not. At least not until Broedi got more from them. Sabine stared at him with questions in her eyes, but he ignored her again.

With a resolute nod, the soldier said, "Fine, then. First, proper introductions. My name is Nathan Trell, Master Sergeant with the Red Sentinels out of Smithshill." With a knowing glint in his eyes, he asked, "I believe you recently passed though there, yes?"

Broedi remained quiet while keeping his face clear of reaction, determined not to give anything away. After a few moments, Sergeant Trell pressed his lips together and turned to his companion. The tomble sat, gawking at Broedi. Upon realizing that everyone was waiting for him to introduce himself, his eyes went wide

"Oh! I...ah...I'm sorry...I...I am Nundle Babblebrook of the Thimbletoe Province in the Five Boroughs. A former merchant out of Deepwell, a former student of the Strand Academies, and now...well, I don't have much of a position with anyone anywhere."

Considering what they knew about the attack on Yellow Mud, the mention of the Strand Academies made Broedi instantly suspicious. Managing to keep his tone even, he rumbled, "A former student of the Academies, you say?"

"Ah, yes. You see, I was studying there when I found this letter in Preceptor Myrr's office. After that, I went to the docks to find a boat—"

Sergeant Trell cut in, saying, "Nundle? We talked about this. Make the dough, then bake the bread. Else we'll all be very confused."

Nundle shot the sergeant an apologetic look. "You're right, Nathan. Sorry."

Sergeant Trell turned back to Broedi. "You have our names now. Would you care to share yours?" When Broedi did not answer, he shifted his gaze to Sabine. "What about you, miss?"

Sabine looked over at Broedi, apparently awaiting guidance from him. Seeing no harm in sharing the farm girls' names, he nodded, at which point she eyed the sergeant. "Sabine Moiléne." Nodding to her sister, she added, "And this is Helene."

"Your names betray you as Southlanders," said Sergeant Trell. "Might I assume you two are from the farm by the river?"

Broedi's eyes narrowed. He was starting to wonder what they did not know.

After a long, quiet moment, Sabine nodded. "We are."

The sergeant hesitated a moment before asking in a gentle tone, "Was it your husband you buried?" He glanced at Helene. "Her father?"

Apparently, there was a limit to their knowledge.

Sabine gave a quick shake of her head. "No, no. It was…" She paused to take a deep breath and then said, "It was our father. Helene is my sister."

Compassion filled both strangers' faces. Nundle leaned forward to murmur, "Oh, my. I'm…I'm so sorry for your loss."

"As am I," added the soldier.

"Thank you," replied Sabine.

Broedi eyed tomble and soldier. Their sympathy was honest, a good mark for them.

With his gaze still on Sabine, Sergeant Trell nodded to Broedi and the sleeping children. "Am I right in assuming that they interrupted an attack there?"

Sabine nodded, saying, "They saved us."

A look of quiet relief flashed over the sergeant's face as he shifted his gaze to Broedi. "And you? What is your name? Or will you suffer me calling you 'Shapechanger?'"

Mildly surprised, Broedi looked to Nundle. "How is it that you know of me, but he does not?"

"Ah…" Nundle shot a sheepish look at the soldier. "Because I have not told him who you are yet." As the sergeant twisted to stare at the tomble, Nundle said, "I am sorry, Nathan. Truly, I am. When your scouts mentioned a seven-foot tall man, I hoped it was him…but we had just finished talking about too many assumptions…so—" He stopped and stared at Broedi. "The scorch marks by the campsite—that was you, wasn't it? Teaching them about the Strands? But how is it they—"

"Nundle!" The sergeant's interruption was firm. "Mind answering his question? For him and me? How do you know him?"

Nundle turned to stare at the soldier, a tightly wrapped bundle of energy ready to split open. "Do you truly not know who this is?"

Sergeant Trell eyed Broedi. In a slow, hesitant voice, he muttered, "Should I?"

"His necklace, Nathan!" exclaimed the tomble, pointing to Broedi's neck. "Look at his necklace!"

Sergeant Trell gaze dropped to the carved ivory lion's head attached to the leather cord. His eyes widened as recognition flooded his face. "Bless the gods…" He looked back to Broedi's face. "You're one of the White Lions, aren't you?"

Broedi had watched the entire exchange with growing unease. He considered trying to deny the fact, but doubted they would accept his claim. He could only hope for everyone's sake that their intentions were good.

After letting out a long and solemn sigh, Broedi answered. "I am."

An excited squeal burst forth from Nundle as he clapped his hands, prompting Sabine to stare at him as though he had three heads. Smiling wide, Nundle recited, "'While it falls to the Half-man to unite?' That has to be what the line means! Am I correct?"

Broedi's nervousness swelled. The words were from Indrida's prophecy.

In a reverence-laden tone that made Broedi feel uncomfortable, Nundle said, "It is truly an honor to meet you."

Broedi nodded, quietly acknowledging the comment, unsure what else to do. On the outside, he maintained a façade of calm, while inside he continued to reel from the fact that this strange tomble knew so much about him, the Progeny, and the prophecy.

Taking advantage of the quiet moment, Sabine leaned forward and asked, "Pardon me? But what is a 'white lion?'"

Broedi, Nundle, and Sergeant Trell turned in unison to stare at her. Almost everyone in the duchies had at least heard the legend of the White Lions, even if most had the details wrong. Broedi thought it odd Sabine knew nothing.

With three pairs of eyes staring at her, Sabine shrugged her shoulders and said, "What? It's an honest question. What's a 'white lion?'"

Broedi opened his mouth to explain, but shut it a moment later as Nundle leapt into the tale, starting with the Assembly of Nine, explaining the Demonic War, the scourging of the Carinius coast, and ending with the outlawing of magic. The tomble's telling of the story was impossibly, disturbingly accurate. An improbable fluke of fate might explain away the soldiers' presence. Yet to find a tomble—a former Academy acolyte at that—who knew as much as this one did was unfeasible.

A new kind of worry wormed into Broedi's consciousness, one that had nothing to do with the soldiers, the tomble, or even the Tracker. Impossible occurrences such as this had happened frequently during the Demonic War. His eyes narrowed. Someone or something was twisting fate.

Throughout Nundle's telling, Sabine stared between the tomble and Broedi, her mouth parted. Once he finished, she focused all of her attention on Broedi. "That's quite a tale." Her dubious expression betrayed an evident reluctance to accept it as real.

"Surprisingly, most of what he said is true," rumbled Broedi. He looked back to the tomble. "While I am curious how it is you know so much, I care more about *why* you are following us." His eyes narrowed. "And how you found us."

Nundle opened his mouth to answer when the sergeant put his hand up. "My turn, Nundle." As the tomble nodded and bowed his head, Sergeant Trell turned his gaze to Broedi. "I will tell you what I know, starting with when I was ordered to find you, up until I met Nundle. Stop me when I get something wrong."

Broedi nodded. "Go on."

The sergeant went on to relate a strange and disturbing tale involving the regent of Smithshill, Constables, and a saeljul. Broedi was glad Nikalys and Kenders were asleep. Had they heard of a saeljul's involvement, they would have reacted inappropriately.

When Sergeant Trell reached the point where he had found Nundle following him, he gave a wave his hand, indicating Nundle should pick up the telling. Sitting forward with legs crossed, Nundle proceeded to share his own incredible story. A deeper than usual scowl spread over Broedi's face upon hearing that the sergeant's Fenidar and the tomble's Jhaell Myrr was the same person.

At his story's conclusion, Nundle reached into his hip-sack, withdrew the letter that had prompted the tomble to take some rather incredible risks, and handed it to Broedi. What he read turned him colder than a swim in the Sea of Kings in the middle of winter. He needed to get this letter to Storm Island. Quickly.

Sabine asked to see the letter and he handed it to her. She had wanted the truth. She would have it.

After reading it, she asked what the Progeny were. To Broedi's surprise, Nundle recited the prophecy word-for-word, explaining afterwards that he had read it in a history he had found in a library. Broedi was disturbed to learn Indrida's words had become so readily available.

Broedi sighed. Everything had suddenly become much more complicated.

He studied the pair before him. Sergeant Trell seemed earnest and honest, as did Nundle. He had no doubt that they were meant to be his allies, that whoever was bending destiny had brought them to him. The question was why. Knowing the pair would never be able to answer it, he instead asked a different question altogether, one that was no less important.

"What do you want from us?"

Sergeant Tell took a deep breath, exhaled, and said, "Well, we want to know your side of the story. I am disobeying direct orders by sitting here with you. I should be trying to subdue you—not that I'd have much chance of that—in order to bring you to justice. The gods know the Tracker wishes that was what I was doing." He paused, reaching up to scratch his beard, then said,

"But here's the thing. You might be mages, you might lawbreakers, but I don't think you're dangerous. Or wicked, or any of the things the regent or Fenidar said. In fact, I now believe you're all pretty much the opposite of that. What I want from you, Broedi, is to know if I'm right."

Tilting his head back, Broedi stared up into sky and the dual moons shining down on them. He wished Aryn and Eliza were here. They were always better at making decisions than he ever was, especially Aryn. After letting out a heavy sigh, he dropped his head, stared at the pair, and then proceeded to tell them— and in effect, Sabine—everything he had already told the children. .

He told them about how Eliza and Aryn had hidden away Nikalys and Kenders for their protection, entrusting their care to a husband and wife in Yellow Mud. How Jak was not blood to the pair, but was as good a sibling as one could hope. When he told them how the saeljul had used his nine acolytes to help destroy the village before he murdered them, Nundle's face turned ashen. Broedi doubted it had anything to do with the moonlight.

He shared how he had found the Progeny, how Jak had survived the flood and tracked his siblings to the forest clearing. He told them everything, quickly, succinctly, and without exaggeration. When he was done, he stared at the soldier sitting across from him and asked, "Does that answer your question, Sergeant?"

With as solemn a face as a person could wear, the man nodded, and muttered, "Yes…yes, it does." He took a deep breath, exhaled slowly, and ran his hands through his hair, tugging at his cord-bound ponytail.

Sabine leaned over to Broedi and whispered, "Is all of this true?"

"It is." He looked at her closely and the little girl she held. "And now that you know, you are bound to us. I cannot let you leave with that knowledge."

"No," murmured Sabine. "I suppose you can't…"

Her maturity regarding the matter impressed him. He gave her sympathetic, kind smile. "I promise we will do whatever we can to keep you and your iskoa safe."

Sabine looked down at Helene. "Our mother used to say, 'Only fools make promises they cannot keep.'" She stared back at Broedi, a hard and cold glint in her eyes. "You aren't a fool, are you?"

Broedi held her gaze, curious at her choice of words. He had not heard that particular turn of phrase in a long time.

Hearing footsteps, he looked over to and found Jak and the Borderlander approaching the group. While Jak carried with him a troubled expression, the Borderlander's hopeful countenance was out of place for the night.

"Broedi?" mumbled Sabine.

He looked back to Sabine and found her staring at Nikalys and Kenders. "Yes?"

"So, they're going to save us from some great evil? Something the Cabal is responsible for?"

"If Indrida's words are to be believed, yes."

Staring up to him, she asked the most pertinent question of the night, a question those at Storm Island had been asking for centuries. "And what sort of great evil would that be, exactly?" Nundle and Sergeant Trell joined her in peering at him, waiting for his response.

Often when Broedi did not answer a question, it was by choice. This time, however, his silence was not voluntary. He had no answer for her for there was none to give. Pressing his lips together, he spoke the truth. "I cannot."

"But you said you'd tell me—"

Interrupting her, Broedi said, "I cannot tell you, uora, because I do not know the answer. I do not know what the Cabal is planning. No one does."

Jak arrived with the Borderlander as Broedi delivered his answer. Standing at his siblings' feet, he said, "Actually, that might not be true." Worry coated his words. He nodded to the Borderlander. "Everyone, this is Zecus." As one, they turned to stare up at the tall, dark-skinned man. "Please tell them *exactly* what you told me."

CHAPTER 52: WATCHER

As the Borderlander began his tale, Nelnora released the Weave, letting the shimmering window that allowed her to observe the group fade away. There was no need to watch any longer. They were together now and on the proper path. The number of gentle nudges necessary to facilitate this had been many, a good deal more than she felt comfortable doing, but events had forced her hand.

With a content smile resting upon her lips, she strolled from the center of the dais and down the white marble steps, her gait elegant and graceful. She gripped the sides of her silver silk robes as she stepped from the bottom stair, lifting them enough so as not to step on the hem. Late afternoon sunlight shone through the faceted crystal dome high overhead, cut into countless tiny rainbows that littered the chamber's walls and floor and danced through her golden hair.

As she strode to the room's arched entrance, the echoes of her bare feet lightly slapping against the cool marble rebounded through the cavernous hall. For the moment, the observation chamber was empty.

Upon reaching the two towering, dark-stained hardwood doors, she created a short Weave to remove the wards she had placed earlier. Touching the silver-levered handles, she gave a slight push. Both doors swung outward, making no sound whatsoever, to reveal a large antechamber, its floor covered by a rug patterned with alternating black, gray, and white diamond shapes. Nelnora knew for certain that there were an equal number of all three shades, properly balanced as all things should be.

The servants she had sent out a short while ago were standing and waiting in three orderly rows, staring at her with white, iris-less eyes. Each wore a white tunic, maroon breeches, and a short, cylindrical black hat. The figure at the forefront, tall with white hair that had a faint bluish tint to it, stepped forward and offered a deep, gracious bow.

"Eminence, how may we serve?"

Tenerva's voice, deep and full, echoed as he spoke. It was a quality shared by every divina who still served the gods and goddesses, the resonance of their deity's power coursing through them. When a divina left the service of their god or goddess, that power evaporated like a bead of water dripped on a hot stone pulled from a fire.

Fixing her gaze on her high priest, Nelnora said in a crisp, clear voice, "Send a message to Ashana. Tell her that I thank her for her help and will let her know if I need her assistance again in the future."

"Yes, Eminence," replied Tenerva. "Is that the entirety of the message?"

"Were there more, I would have told you."

"Of course, Eminence," replied the divina. "Is there anything else you require?"

"No, that is all. You may resume your duties."

"Thank you, Eminence," said Tenerva. He faced the rest of the divina assembled and spoke, his voice throbbing with power. "Resume your watching."

The host of priests filed past their goddess, bowing as they went, and entered the round chamber. As they took up positions around the circular room, she sensed them reaching for the Strands. Within moments, dozens of shimmering windows to the world encircled the room. A priest stood beside each, watching, observing, and—if necessary—recording any pertinent information in the books resting on pedestals beside them.

Nelnora, the Watcher of the World, the goddess of Civilization and Balance, ambled around room, staring from window to window while musing over what she had just accomplished. Despite what was happening in the Borderlands, her brethren dallied. Most were content to wait for things to sort themselves out, believing the Cabal would fail before they achieved anything of significance. Nelnora knew better.

Pushing aside her worries for the time being, she focused on the windows, watching and searching.

One view overlooked a great, sprawling city filled with intricate, winding waterways rather than streets. Towering pyramids and sandstone structures rose up into the sky, majestic beside the interweaving canals. Wide, flat boats full of people choked the channels, slowly drifting beneath great, hanging gardens that spanned the water.

Another window revealed an expansive underground city carved out of midnight-black rock. The buildings were circular, absent sharp angles, and dotted with dozens of windows through which dim, yellow light spilled forth. Torches lined the streets along with tall, skinny lamps topped with glass spheres glowing with a soft green light. Citizens strode about, an even mix of squat dirgmour—their skin the color of soot—and the even shorter, colorfully dressed atarkas.

Yet another glowing portal showed a city built amongst the boughs of thick-trunked trees, the curved structures connected by sweeping wood and rope bridges. Buhanik traversed the walkways, methodically shuffling along, their skin resembling tree bark, their hair like prairie grass. Groups congregated wherever a pool of early morning sunshine lit up a section of the city.

Nelnora stopped when something in the tree city caught her eye, a lone figure who was wholly out of place. On a great wooden platform nestled near the pinnacle of the treetops, a tijul sat in a chair while conferring with four elder buhanik standing nearby. He lounged lazily, running his fingers through his dark brown hair. A spear rested against his chair.

Nelnora tried to temper the rush of excitement she felt as she murmured to the priest, "Where is that?"

The divina referred to the book on her pedestal before answering. "The city is named Buhaylunsod, Eminence. In the Primal Provinces."

"Do not close this window." Pointing to the figure in the chair, Nelnora said, "Do *not* stop watching him."

"Yes, Eminence."

A slight smile touched Nelnora's face. Things were coming together.

CHAPTER 53: DECEPTION

Duke Everett Redlord sat slumped in his chair, staring at his empty plate, a frown on his face. Tonight's dishes had not interested him in the slightest, bland and uninspired. Nevertheless, he had eaten merely to distract himself from the tedium laid out before him.

The low hum of dozens of discreet conversations filled the dining hall, mixing with the constant clatter of pottery plates and the soft clinking of silver goblets. The banquet table that ran down the middle of the room was so wide that polite conversation was only possible with one's immediate neighbor.

The hall itself was vast, twice as long as it was wide and tall. Monumental, bleached white stone columns with ornate designs carved into them lined the sides of the hall, stretching from the flagstone floor to the arched ceiling. A column stood every twenty paces, breaking up the red sandstone block walls.

Everett's gaze fell upon an attractive young woman standing beside one of the columns and holding a flagon of wine, awaiting a guest to lift his or her cup overhead. He assumed she was new, as he would have remembered such a pretty face. Perhaps feeling his gaze, the servant glanced up and met his stare at which point he offered her a smile. Even from across the room, he saw her blush.

"...would sell more casks, and treasury revenue would increase. Perhaps it is something that his lordship would take under advisement?"

Pulled from his admiration of the girl, Everett looked at the foppish fellow who had just finished talking. He wore one of those new caps that were the current fashion, crimson with a white ball of fuzz propped on top. Everett thought they looked ridiculous.

The man, a hopeful grin affixed on his face, asked, "What say you, my Lord?"

Everett did not respond immediately. He could not stop staring at the inane-looking hat, tilted to cover one ear, but raised up off the other.

The petitioner's grin slipped a bit. "My Lord...?"

Giving the man a thin yet diplomatic smile, Everett said, "You make some excellent points. Thank you for bringing this to my attention." He had no idea about what the man had been prattling.

The man's smile returned in force. "Thank you, my Lord. The Brewers Guild thanks you, as well. You honor me with your time and consideration."

Everett muttered under his breath, "Yes, I do."

The man leaned forward. "Pardon, my Lord?"

"Nothing," said Everett. He gave a dismissive wave of his hand, shooing the man like the pest he was. "Good evening."

The man stood, gave a deep bow, and tuned to scurry back to his assigned seat for the evening. Everett watched him go, honestly trying to recall the petitioner's name. He could not.

A skinny, wrinkled man with wispy white hair stepped forward, stopping on Everett's left. Referring to the parchment he clasped, the man leaned over to whisper, "The next petitioner is Baron Brampton. He wishes to discuss a disagreement he has with Baroness Yarrow about a grove of trees that sits between their lands. Both lay claim to it and—"

Everett silenced the man with a raised hand. "Can this not wait for some other time, Grandy?"

In a polite, yet firm tone, the steward replied, "My Lord, you have canceled formal court too often as of late. Tonight's feast is required to clear up some of the duchy's business. You cannot postpone duty indefinitely."

Frowning, Everett grumbled, "Fine." He eyed the long table and the guests on both sides. "How many more of them must I speak with?"

"All of tonight's guests have something they wish to address with you."

Everett's eyes widened. There had to be close to one hundred and fifty people here. "I have to talk with *all* of them?"

"Yes, my Lord," mumbled Grandy. "And these are just those who are of suitable class with which to dine. I have close to nine hundred outstanding petitions for you to attend to."

Duke Everett turned his head to glare at his steward. "*Nine hundred?!*"

The shout echoed through the immense dining hall. His guests quieted for a moment before quickly resuming their conversations, pretending to ignore the duke's outburst.

Lowering his voice, Everett asked, "Is there no other way to handle these petitions, Grandy? Cannot one administrator or another talk with them?"

Wearing a stiff smile that did not reach his eyes, Grandy muttered, "No, my Lord. I respectfully remind you—again—the *law* dictates that *you* resolve them." He paused before adding, "As your father did, my Lord. Admirably so, might I add."

Everett's glowered at his steward. "Tread carefully, old man. I will do things as I see fit. I am *not* my father."

The wrinkled skin around Grandy's eyes crinkled further. "No, my Lord. You are most definitely not."

Everett pressed his lips together. Were this any other soul, Grandy would not live to see Mu's orb crest the eastern horizon. However, without the steward, the operation of the castle—perhaps of the entire duchy—would come crashing down. Even so, that did not mean Everett had to put up with the man's insolence.

With a loud scrape of wood against stone, Everett shoved his heavy chair back and stood. While the collective gaze of the room on him, his was reserved for Grandy alone. "I am not feeling well, Steward. Please apologize to my guests that I will be unable to attend the remainder of the evening."

Without waiting for—or caring about—Grandy's response, he walked away from the table, a spiteful grin spreading over his face as he went. The thought of Grandy having to deal with a roomful of angry guests amused him.

As he reached the double doors at rear of the room, two members of his personal guard fell in behind him. Once a servant opened the doors for him, Everett strode through and marched down the passageway, admiring his castle as he went. His smile spread wider. He liked that he could call it that now. The Duke's Hall was his.

Everett's father had passed on to see Maeana two winters ago after a nasty fall from a horse during a hunt along Lake Hawthorne's western shores. Duke Gill had taken Everett with him on the excursion in a misguided attempt to strengthen a weak-at-best bond between father and son. At the behest of his father, Everett had spent his formative years traveling from one duchy city to the next, familiarizing himself with the land he would someday rule. While he never made any real friends in his stops—Everett did not quite grasp the concept of friends—he did make valuable contacts and powerful allies. Some were very powerful.

He stepped through a door leading to an open-air walkway, leaving the torch-lit hall behind. The sandstone beneath his feet radiated heat, having cooked all day in the summer sun. By the time he reached his bedchambers, his feet were moist with sweat.

Before heading inside, he moved to the waist-high stone railing while his guards stood off to the side. Everett smiled at the cityscape laid out below him, lit by the combined illumination of the two, nearly full moons. Redstone, the capital of the Great Lakes Duchy, rested at the bottom of the elevated hill upon which the duke's castle perched. Wooden poles with torch lamps lined the cobblestone streets crisscrossing the expansive city. Tens of thousands lived below him.

This city was his, as was the entirety of the Great Lakes. Yet his ambitions reached beyond these borders, ambitions that would soon be fulfilled.

With a smile and a sigh, he turned and sauntered toward the entrance to his bedchambers. The double doors were open wide—as most in the castle were—to allow air to flow freely. Summer lasted a long time here in Redstone, and the heat was stifling, even at night. As he crossed the threshold, he recalled the servant girl from the dining hall. Stopping, he turned back to the two guards who had accompanied him.

"You two, return to the hall and fetch for me the blonde girl with the red ribbon in her hair. She was serving wine. Tell her I wish to see her."

The guards exchanged an uneasy glance before the one on the left said, "My Lord, the captain's orders are to keep your lordship guarded for the remainder of the evening."

Everett smiled at the soldier. "Well, now, I would never ask you to disobey an order from your captain."

The man visibly relaxed. "Thank you, my Lord."

Everett's grin fell away. His eyes and voice turned cold as he snapped, "Then again, as I am the blasted duke, I will gladly *order* you to disobey!" He pointed down the walkway and shouted, "Now, go!"

Both men bowed and quickly retreated, mumbling their apologies.

Everett watched them scamper down the passageway before turning to enter his spacious bedchamber. Soft, bluish-white moonlight streamed through the open doors and windows, illuminating half of the room. A massive, canopied bed covered with red satin sheets and a dozen silken pillows rested in the center of the chamber. Richly made furniture—dressers, desks, and chairs—lined the walls.

He slipped off his sandals, placed his feet on the polished black marble floor, and let out a contented sigh. As he stood there, savoring the relief, he glanced around the room and frowned. Every torch in his room was unlit. Nor were his chamber servants here waiting for him, as they should be. His frown blossomed into a full scowl. "This is unacceptable."

A woman's voice wafted from a darkened corner of the room. "Try not to be angry, Everett. I sent them away."

Everett whirled about, a moment away from calling for the guards, when he recognized to whom the voice belonged. "Blast it, Raela! Must you do that?"

"I'm sorry, my Lord, did I startle you?" Raela's tone was laden with false innocence.

He peered into the unlit part of the room, trying to spot her. However, the moonlight streaming through the open windows cast stark shadows in his bedchambers, providing any number of places in which she could hide. "You know you did."

With a light rustling of cloth, she stepped forth from a black shadow and into a pool of moonlight. Everett's breath caught at the sight of her.

Raela was stunningly beautiful. Diminutive, with light, pale skin, she looked almost fragile, but Everett knew better. Although she could pass as a woman, she was erijul, her features carrying a hint of the ijulan race, which was by no means an unpleasant thing. Everett thought it gave her an exotic, sensual look. Light brown hair, straight and glistening in the moonlight, fell unbound to her shoulders, swishing as she stepped barefoot across the marble floor toward him. Her piercing, ice blue eyes never left his face as she crept closer. Not for the first time, he was reminded of a cat stalking its prey.

She wore a sleeveless gown of white gauze that grazed the floor as she walked. The flimsy material reflected some of the light from the moons, but was translucent enough that Everett could see her pleasing shape beneath the dress.

With a sly, knowing smile, she murmured, "It is good to see you as well, Everett."

She drifted past him, as close as she could without touching him, and continued to the canopied bed. An intoxicating perfume of soft rose petals and honeybells washed over him, filling his nostrils and tickling his mind. She moved around to the far side of his bed and slowly lay down on her stomach. The gauzy gown she wore draped open in front of her, allowing Everett an even better view of what already was barely covered.

He quickly looked away from his bed to stare at the floor, trying to clear his mind. "How is it that you got past all of my guards?"

With a touch of playful reproach, she said, "Truly, Everett?"

He pressed his lips together and shook his head. "No matter." It had been a foolish question to ask. Simple guards were no match for her talents. Compelling his voice to remain steady, he asked, "What do you want, then?" Unable to keep his eyes from her, his gaze returned to the bed. "Are plans shifting?"

"No, sweet, dear Everett." She played with her hair, twisting it around her fingers before letting it fall. "Our plans remain the same." She rolled over on her back and stretched, writhing about on his bed, tightening and relaxing her muscles. Letting her head fall back over the edge of the bed she stared at him upside down, her silky brown hair hanging. "Would you like to lie here next to me? I'm sure you had a long day of doing whatever it is you do."

Shutting his eyes, he shook his head, trying to clear away both the image of Raela and the scent of her intoxicating perfume. Before he reopened them, he turned around to face the double doors and the night outside. He loathed not being in control, and Raela not only stripped that from him, she relished doing it.

Taking care to control his breathing, he whispered, "Why are you here, then?"

"Straight to the kernel, then?" asked Raela. She gave a short, pouting sigh. "You are so predictable."

He heard a rustling behind him followed by padded footsteps approaching. Raela appeared at his side and stood next to him. The scent of flowers was overpowering.

"Tandyr is curious if you have heard from Jhaell." Most—but not all—of the coy sensuality was gone, snuffed out as easily as a candle flame. "He has proven difficult to reach as of late. I inquired about him at his little school, but it seems he has not been there for two weeks."

Pushing aside the erijul's allure, Everett turned to face her. "Difficult to reach is an understatement."

She raised a questioning eyebrow. "What do you mean by that?"

Everett strode through the dark room to a colossal, ornate oaken desk. Sitting in the desk's chair, he reached to a bottom drawer, opened it, and pulled out the parchment Jhaell had given him when Raela had first put the pair in contact. He stood and walked back to where Raela waited.

"I sent this message to him nearly three weeks ago. Only this time, the writing never disappeared, which—according to how he said this works—means he never cleared it after he read it." He was about to hand the parchment to Raela when he stopped. Studying her, he asked, "I'm curious, have there been any recent, any *important* developments you would like to share with me? Anything regarding the prophecy?"

Raela's thin eyebrows drew together, creating a tiny furrow in her otherwise smooth brow. "What do you mean?"

Everett pressed his lips together. So she did not know. He had feared this was the case. Sighing, he handed the parchment to her.

Raela accepted the letter and lifted it to the moonlight to read. Her expression quickly shifted from one of concerned curiosity to that of shocked fury. The moment she was done, she tossed the message back to him and spat with a rank bitterness, "Beelvra!"

Everett was not expecting the magical parchment. It glanced off his hands and floated to the floor.

Raela whirled around in place, simmering with rage. "That blasted fool!" All alluring softness was gone from her, replaced with an intense, harsh anger. "He was supposed to *tell* us if he found them! Not try to eliminate them himself!"

Nodding along, Everett said, "After I did not hear back from him, I sent a note to Alpert via messenger. I eventually received a missive back saying that two men had appeared in the Constables office to report the destruction of Yellow Mud." He stared intently at the erijul. "*Two*, Raela." He pointed to the sheet of parchment on the floor. "Not just the one that the merchant in that letter mentioned." He paused before adding quietly, "And there's more."

The erijul's eyes widened as she hissed, "What?"

The duke had not seen Raela this angry in some time. She scared him a bit. "Alpert reported a large magical disturbance south of Smithshill the same day these visitors showed up at the Constables. A bit of a coincidence, don't you think?"

"Tell me that Alpert did something about it."

"He did," replied Everett. "He sent some Sentinels to find the outlaws. Along with two Trackers and…." He stopped, not wanting to tell her the worst part.

Raela demanded, "What is it, Everett?"

Everett sighed and muttered, "He put Jhaell in charge of the expedition."

Raela's ice-blue eyes burned with the intensity of a fully stoked blacksmith's forge. He could almost feel the rage radiating from her, much like the heat from the sandstone on the veranda. There was nothing beautiful about the erijul now. Then again, she was not truly an erijul. She was the god of Deception incarnate.

Her eyes bored into him. "Why did you not contact us?"

His eyes opened a fraction, surprised at the question. "And how would I do that exactly?" He jabbed a finger at the parchment on the floor again. "The one person I *can* contact has ignored me for two weeks!"

Raela took a step forward, her eyes glinting in the moonlight. "Are you claiming innocence in the matter?"

"Of course I am! Jhaell is the one who did not follow instructions! Jhaell is the one who flooded a village in my duchy. *My* duchy! Jhaell lost the Progeny, not me! This is not my fault!"

"Alpert is *your* man. *You* made him the regent of Smithshill. *You* brought him to Tandyr's service. And as he was the one to give Jhaell the opportunity to continue his mistake, this—all of this—is *your* fault."

Everett glared at Raela. "You can't possibly think that!"

"I can think whatever I want! And I can guarantee that Tandyr will think as I do once I'm done explaining your and Alpert's foul-ups to him."

A burst of panic exploded in Everett's chest. "Raela, please!"

The manner in which she glowered at him, he expected to be slapped, punched, or something worse. "You have *no* idea what you have done." She gave a disgusted shake of her head, turned, and strode away, her bare feet slapping against the polished marble as she walked.

"Raela, please…Raela!"

She ignored his repeated pleas until she reached the entranceway where she stopped and looked back. Waving a hand around, gesturing at his room, his castle, she said, "You think this, all of this, is yours? That you are impervious? I helped put you here, Everett, and I can just as easily help it collapse on your head." Lifting one of her long arms, she pointed out to Redstone. "In case you are oblivious, your people? They don't like you very much. A few whispers in dark corners, a lie or two fed to the sheep is all it would take. Tell me, Everett, do you have enough soldiers to stop every peasant out there?"

He glared at her, silent, knowing that her threat was not an idle one. He had benefited too often from her talents in the past to doubt her effectiveness.

Raela turned and retreated, heading through open double doors. "Start praying, Everett. And not to me, please. I've had all the whining I can take."

He watched her moonlit figure sweep past his windows and down the passageway. Dropping his chin to his chest, he stared at the marble floor.

This was bad.

If Tandyr were to blame Everett for Jhaell's mistake, the god would no doubt rescind his promises. Nor would that not be the end of Tandyr's retribution. In a daze, he bent over, picked up the parchment, and began to return to his desk.

"You sent for me, my Lord?"

Turning around, he found the blonde serving girl from the dining hall standing in the doorway, a coy smile on her face.

As she took a tentative step onto the marble, he glared at her and muttered, "Get out."

She stopped short and stared at him, her brow knitted up in confusion. "But, my Lord. I thought—"

Fury welled up inside him and a feral sneer raced over his lips. Pointing to the doorway, he screamed, "Get out!"

The girl hesitated briefly before turning and running into the night, fleeing down the open-air passageway, her sandals beating on the sandstone as she fled.

Returning to his desk, Everett collapsed in his chair, and rested his chin in his hand. "Blast it Jhaell. You had better fix this."

CHAPTER 54: SWORDSMAN

2ⁿᵈ of the Turn of Thonda

Nikalys lay on his back, staring up at the billowy clouds marching across the sky and assigning familiar shapes to them in his head. After marking one as a slightly disfigured wolf's head, he sighed and let his head fall to the side. Kenders was still sleeping peacefully beside him, oblivious to the goings on around her.

Earlier, when he had first awakened, he had been alarmed to find Kenders unconscious. Thankfully, Jak was there also and, after assuring him she would be all right, had filled him in on what she had done for the soldiers.

Broedi came to check his shoulder wound and, after finding it nearly healed, pronounced him fit with a reserved frown. According to the hillman, he should have slept longer and his wound should not be as whole as it was. Broedi wondered aloud if the gift given to the White Lions by Sarphia, the goddess of Immortality, had slipped into Nikalys as well. Whatever the reason, Nikalys was grateful for his quick recovery.

As the hillman was attending to him, a joyful, high-pitched scream rang out over the prairie just before Helene tackled him, leaping into his arms. Sabine had walked up after her sister, and while her greeting was decidedly less enthusiastic than Helene's was, the genuine warmth she displayed was unexpected yet welcome.

After a short reunion, Broedi ushered everyone away, insisting Nikalys lie down again to ensure a full recovery. Nikalys protested that he felt fine, but the hillman would have none of it.

Sabine pulled a reluctant Helene with her, announcing they were both going to take a short swim in the river, followed by a long nap. Jak left as well, promising to fill Nikalys in later, after he rested more. Ever since, he had been lying in the grass beside Kenders.

Watching one last cloud drift past—it looked like a three-legged horse pulling a wagon—he decided he had enough. He was anxious to discover what was going on.

Sitting up, Nikalys reached his arms high overhead and stretched, amazed that his shoulder did not hurt. He could remember the pain—and shock—

when the moonlight soldier's blade had cut him. Looking toward the camp of Red Sentinels, he shook his head with wonder. "So, what…we're friends now?"

Near the main grouping of tents, Jak stood with the Borderlander from the fort as well as the bearded man who Nikalys guessed to be the Sentinels' leader. The trio had their backs to him, watching a dozen soldiers practicing their sword work. The persistent clang of metal striking metal had been one of the reasons Nikalys had been unable to fall back asleep.

As the soldiers seemed friendly, Nikalys wondered if he could get a quick lesson before Kenders awoke. The Blade of Horum might be strapped to his hip, but he had no more idea what to do with it now than when he first pulled it from the scabbard.

With one last look at his sister, he stood and began walking to where Jak was. As he sauntered over, a puff of wind carried with it a now-familiar sweet and smoky aroma. Looking up, he spotted Broedi with his bone pipe in hand, deep in conversation with the little redheaded tomble.

Broedi eyed him and nodded, which Nikalys took to mean the hillman was granting approval that he be up and about. The tomble turned and looked at him, staring with wide eyes. After a few uncomfortable moments, Nikalys looked away and continued to where his brother stood. As he drew near, Jak turned and smiled wide.

"I see Broedi give you permission to get up."

"In a manner of speaking," replied Nikalys with a grin. "I stood up and he didn't tell me to lie back down."

The bearded soldier and Borderland both faced him while the rest of the soldiers continued their sword practice. Nikalys caught more than a few furtive glances in his direction.

Pointing to the soldier, Jak said, "Nikalys, this is Sergeant Trell."

The sergeant scrutinized Nikalys so closely that he felt like a crate of olives being evaluated by the Smithshill inspectors.

Nikalys shot a quick, inquisitive glance at his brother and received a nod back indicating everything was fine. Shrugging, he looked at the soldier. "Good days ahead, Sergeant Trell."

"And good memories behind, young man."

Jak nodded to the dark-skinned Borderlander. "And you remember the man we met in the fort, don't you? This is Zecus, from the village Drysa." He looked at the Borderlander. "I got that right, didn't I?"

The man inclined his head. "You did." He faced Nikalys, bent at the waist slightly, and said respectfully, "My pleasure is to meet you in peace today, great warrior."

The Borderlander's words sounded like a ritualistic greeting. Not knowing what the correct response was, Nikalys simply repeated the phrase back. "It is my pleasure to meet you in peace today, as well, Zecus."

The Borderlander's face was cut and bruised as though he had been in a tavern fight, something Nikalys had not noticed last night. It had been dark and he preoccupied. As he was studying the man, the entirety of the Borderlander's salutation registered. "Hold a moment. Great warrior?"

"He's been doing it all night," said Jak with a grin. "'The great warrior this, the great warrior that.' It's a bit much, in my opinion. So you bashed in the heads of a dozen spirit soldiers? They were made of moonlight." He winked at Nikalys. "A thick cloud could have wiped them out just as easily."

The jest prompted a quiet chuckle from Sergeant Trell and a polite smile from the Borderlander. Nikalys stared at the three men, bewildered. Everyone here seemed completely at ease with one another. "I'm very confused right now."

"That is to be expected, uori."

Nikalys turned to his left and was surprised to find Broedi standing beside him. For a man of his size and stature, the hillman could move with surprising stealth. Coming around Broedi's left, the tomble stood in front of the hillman and stared up at Nikalys, eyes still wide.

Looking from face to face, Nikalys asked, "Would someone please tell me what is going on?"

Broedi, at first alone, and later, with the help of the others, revealed what they had discussed last evening after Nikalys had passed out. The shared stories combined to form one of the most incredible sagas he had ever heard, better than anything any playman had ever recited at a Leisure Day festival. Once they were finished, Nikalys stared at Broedi, wholly incredulous.

"All of this is true?"

"I believe so," rumbled Broedi. "Too much of what they say aligns with what we already knew."

Unable to help himself, Nikalys asked, "Truly? A massive army of oligurts and razorfiends—"

"And perhaps mongrels," interjected Nundle.

"Fine. And mongrels. They're invading the Borderlands? Right now?"

"I can assure you, great warrior, they are," said Zecus. "Most villages in the west have been destroyed or abandoned. When the demon showed me the map, he said we stood on the remains of Midiah. I believe he was truthful." Zecus' eyebrows drew together. "I am grateful Drysa was nearly empty when I returned. I pray my neighbors are safe."

The tomble looked up at Zecus in surprise. "You are from Drysa?"

Zecus nodded. "I am."

A perplexed expression affixed itself to Nundle's face. "I must have missed that last night."

"Things were confused last evening," rumbled Broedi. He peered down at the tomble. "Does that mean something to you?"

"It does…" muttered Nundle. Looking up to Broedi, he said, "I met two men from Drysa when I was in Lakeborough." His gaze shifted to Zecus. "They were on their way to Freehaven to petition the First Council about the Sudashians. Joshmuel and Boah. Nice fellows. I spent the—"

Zecus interrupted, saying, "Joshmuel Alsher and Boah Rasus?"

Nundle stared at the Borderlander. "Yes, how did—" The tomble's eyes grew round. "You're Joshmuel's son, aren't you?"

As the Borderlander nodded slowly and silently, the group glanced at one another, clearly surprised by the chance occurrence. Everyone except Broedi, that is. Nikalys noticed the hillman staring between Nundle and Zecus, a pensive, almost concerned frown affixed to his lips.

Nikalys almost asked him what he was thinking, but the fact there was an army marching on the duchies demanded his attention for the moment. "So the Borderlands' duke—"

"Duke Vanson," offered Zecus quietly.

"Fine," said Nikalys. "So, Duke Vanson's not fighting back? Why?"

Nundle pointed to Zecus. "That's the same question I asked his father."

"We have evidence of one duke already involved in a conspiracy," rumbled Broedi. He wore a deeper frown than typically graced his face. "Why not another?"

"But to what end?" asked the sergeant.

Broedi shook his head. "Again, I do not know. Yet it would seem the Cabal has begun their quest, whatever it may be." He looked to Zecus. "Are you sure there is nothing more you can tell us? Names mentioned? Places? Anything?"

"I am sorry, great lion," said Zecus with a slow shake of his head. "The demon's name was Urazûd, the ijul's was Jhaell. He was supposed to be searching for something." He bowed his head. "I am remorseful I cannot offer more."

"Do not apologize," said Broedi. "You have been more than helpful." After a brief pause, he added quietly, "And please stop calling me 'great lion.' Broedi will do."

Zecus lifted his head but did not respond.

"So, then," began Jak. "The god of Chaos is 'searching for something?' How wondrously ambiguous."

"Believe it or not, uori, it is more than we knew during the last war. Norasim's intentions were never clear. Some believed his nature drove him to sow chaos for chaos' sake, but I was not one. I felt there was an ultimate goal behind his actions, a goal that may remain today."

"What sort of goal?" asked Sergeant Trell.

"Again, Sergeant, I do not know." Broedi's gaze drifted westward. "I will say this: I expect things will go worse for us than last time."

"Worse?" scoffed Nikalys. "What could be worse than a demon army led by one of the Cabal running over the land?"

Broedi shifted his gaze to Nikalys. "An army led by four of the Cabal running over the land."

"Pardon?" asked Jak.

Peering up from under his wide-brimmed hat, Nundle said, "According to Indrida's prophecy, when Chaos returns, he—or she—will have the help of Strife, Pain, *and* Deception. Four of the Cabal, working together."

"Nundle is right," said Broedi. "Their goal, whatever it is, must be important to bring them together. Cooperation among the Cabal is rare, even more so than trust." He dropped chin to chest and stared at the grass by his feet. "I had hoped we would have more time…"

The four men, tomble, and hillman all went silent, each of them trapped within their thoughts. Letting out a heavy sigh, Nikalys reached up and rubbed his eyes. The gentle plains breeze had dried them out as he had watched the soldiers' sword practice throughout the long conversation

Dropping his hands, he returned his attention to a particular pair of Sentinels. One—not much older than Nikalys—was clearly the most talented of the bunch, even to Nikalys' untrained eye. Every move the young man made appeared effortless, crisp, and half a breath faster than his opponent's.

Breaking the group's silence, Nikalys muttered, "Sergeant?"

The bearded soldier glanced up. "Yes?"

Nikalys pointed to the young swordsman. "Who's that?"

Sergeant Trell turned to see whom Nikalys meant. "His name's Wil. Wil Eadding. Why?"

"Do you think I could get a lesson from him?"

The sergeant faced Nikalys, his eyes slightly narrowed. "You have a good eye. Wil is by far my best swordsman."

"Is that a yes, then?"

Sergeant Trell nodded slowly, his gaze never leaving Nikalys' face. "I believe that can be arranged."

"Thank you," replied Nikalys, turning back to watch the pair spar. "I'd appreciate it."

Wil advanced on his opponent, thrusting his blade. The other Sentinel tried to parry, but his footing was all wrong. Wil easily got past the man's guard, halting before hurting his fellow soldier, but eliciting a disappointed curse from the other man nonetheless. Nikalys gave a disappointed shake of his head. Had Wil's opponent set his feet correctly, he would have had no trouble turning the blow aside.

A heartbeat later, Nikalys froze and blinked once in surprise. He was more than confident in his assessment even though there was no possible way he could have known that.

"You said you wanted more time, Broedi," said Jak. "Time for what?"

The question was a good one, good enough to pull Nikalys' attention away from his confusion over his unexpected knowledge of swordplay. When he looked over to Broedi, he found the hillman staring at him and wearing a thoughtful frown.

"Neither your kaveli or iskoa is ready to face a challenge like the one that approaches." He motioned toward where Kenders lay asleep. "She is incredibly powerful, yet inconsistent, untrained, and rash. A dangerous mix." Gesturing at Nikalys, he added, "And you, uori, you may carry Aryn's blade, but when threatened, you pick up a rock and fight like a common farmer."

"Hells, Broedi, I am a farmer."

Displaying an unusual amount of agitation, Broedi said, "No, uori. You are *not* a farmer. Circumstances merely permitted you to pretend you were for the last fifteen years."

"And who created those circumstances?" shot back Nikalys. "My blood parents—your friends!—put me there and ran off!"

"They did what they thought was best. They were following the fate Greya laid out for them."

"Fate had nothing to do with this! They *chose* to leave me, to leave us!" The passion with which he spoke surprised him. He had thought he had come to terms with all of this.

The hillman folded his arms over his massive chest. "Fate has everything to do with this, uori. And this—" he motioned to the soldiers, Kenders, Jak, the tomble, and the sergeant "—*this* is *your* fate. The sooner you accept it, the better."

Nikalys shook his head. He no longer recognized his life. And each day that passed only warped it further. Lowering his voice, he mumbled, "I just want everything back the way it used to be."

Broedi's eyes burned. Muscles rippled along his jawline. "What you *want* does not matter."

Nikalys scowled at the hillman. "And neither does what *you* want, apparently. Because you're right, Broedi. You. Are. Right. I'm *not* ready. For any of this." He took a few steps forward and turned his full attention to the practicing soldiers. He felt the gaze of the others fixed on his back but he ignored them. Let them stare.

For a few moments, the prairie was quiet, other than the clanging of the Sentinel swords. As Nikalys watched, he noticed Wil's opponent turn his wrist too late on a parry. A moment sooner and he would have been in the perfect position to strike back.

Jak finally broke the uneasy quiet. "What exactly is at Storm Island, Broedi?"

Without looking back, Nikalys mumbled, "Don't waste your time, Jak."

His brother did not listen. "You aren't just looking to keep them safe and hidden, are you?"

There was a noticeable pause before Broedi responded. "No. We are not."

Curious, Nikalys turned to look at the hillman. "We? Who is 'we'?"

Broedi remained silent, his gaze shifting from face to face. "What I am about to tell you must not leave this circle. Is that understood?"

Nikalys glanced around him. The practicing soldiers were a couple dozen paces away. Other than the six people here, no one would be able to hear Broedi's words unless he shouted.

After securing quiet agreement from them all, Broedi eyed Nikalys. "After the magic was outlawed, your parents and I spent some fifty years away from the Oaken Duchies. When we returned, we lived along the Southlands eastern coast for a time. Aryn and I were somewhat concerned about being discovered for who and what we were, but Eliza was brazen. She would have walked into Old Royal Square in Freehaven had we let her. She was still quite upset with the First Council."

While Nikalys listened, his gaze kept returning to the soldiers' sword practice. Wil was now sparring two men at once, his tactics and form much different than they were before.

"We moved as the whim struck us," rumbled Broedi. "Other than the odd looks I received for being aki-mahet, we were treated as nothing more than traveling strangers passing through. At one point, we came across the road that leads to Storm Island. After some…discussion, we headed out to the isle. There was the hope we might find an old friend."

Nundle interrupted, the excitement in his voice clear. "You were looking for another of the White Lions, weren't you? The Shadow of Ketus?"

Broedi peered down at the tomble, admiration in his eyes. "For one so small, you hold a great wealth of knowledge."

The tomble gave a slight smile and shrugged. A touch of pink bloomed in his cheeks. "Thank you."

Broedi rumbled, "May I ask how you know that?"

"The history I read had some details on a handful of the White Lions. It said Ketus' champion was from the 'isle of whipping wind and thrashing seas.' A bit flowery, if you ask me. The author could have just said, 'Miriel Syncent hailed from Storm Island.'"

"Regardless," began Broedi, "you are correct. Eliza and Miriel had been close friends at one time, but the two had a falling out years before the First Council's decree. Eliza desired to put the past behind them. She missed their friendship." He shook his head and let out a long sigh. "Aryn and I argued it was a waste of time. Even if Miriel had returned to her homeland—which seemed unlikely—we doubted we would find her."

"And why is that?" asked Sergeant Trell.

"Because of Ketus' gift to Miriel," rumbled Broedi. "If she so desired, she could hide in an open field on a sunny day. During the war, she would walk straight into the thick of battle unnoticed and always emerge unscathed. She was a tremendous scout, and the luckiest soul Terrene has ever seen save Ketus himself, I would imagine."

"I bet she was a lot of fun to play knuckles with," said Jak with a smile.

The jest brought a grimace to Broedi's face. "She was not. Many a merchant and noble lost tidy sums to her over the years."

Nikalys pulled his attention from the practicing soldiers long enough to say, "That doesn't seem like a very honorable thing for a White Lion to do. Use your gift from a god to win at gambling?"

Broedi turned a steady eye to him. "Have you lived your life without fault, uori?"

Confused by the question, Nikalys nonetheless answered honestly. "No..."

"Neither have I," rumbled the hillman. "We all have flaws. Even the White Lions." He paused before quietly adding, "Especially the White Lions. Putting us on a pedestal will only set you up for disappointment when we fall from it."

Nikalys considered Broedi's point, but it was not long before the insistent ringing of sword meeting sword pulled his attention back to the soldiers. As he looked back over, he caught Sergeant Trell staring at him while wearing a thoughtful expression. The sergeant held his stare for half a heartbeat before looking to Broedi and asking a question.

"So, did you find her? The other White Lion?"

"We did not," rumbled Broedi, "much to Eliza's disappointment. We did, however, find something else, something rather unexpected." A slight smile spread over his lips. "Although, I suppose it was the unexpected that found us. We were spending an evening in small village when a man approached us, then quietly—and accurately—named us for who we were. He said he was with an organization that both needed our help and was willing to offer theirs. They called themselves the Shadow Manes."

Nikalys muttered, "The Shadow Manes?" He started to turn toward Broedi and stopped, noticing that Sergeant Trell was staring at him again. The man's gaze was unnerving, as though he was taking Nikalys apart piece-by-piece, examining how he worked. Shaking off the sergeant's stare, Nikalys peered at Broedi. "What are the Shadow Manes?"

"At that time, they were a small group of mostly men and women dedicated to keeping the true memory of the White Lions alive. Imagine our surprise when we learned their founder was Miriel, some thirty year prior."

"I thought you said you didn't find her," noted Jak.

Broedi shook his head. "We did not. Shortly after the creation of the organization, Miriel disappeared and has never returned. It has been over two hundred years."

Nundle asked, "What sort of help did they need?"

"And offer?" added Sergeant Trell.

"Good questions," rumbled Broedi. "Both of them." Looking to Jak and Nikalys, he asked, "You recall when I told you how we first came to be aware of Indrida's prophecy? It was the Manes who shared it with us. Shortly after Miriel disappeared, they stumbled upon it and recognized that the fight against Chaos had not ended with the Demonic War. They sought mages as ardently as the Constables did, except their intent was to bring them to Storm Island to teach them the Strands to be prepared for when Chaos would rise again."

With evident skepticism, Sergeant Trell muttered, "I cannot believe that I have never heard of such a group."

Wearing a wry smile, Nundle said, "It would not be much of a secret organization if you had, Nathan."

"That's true, I suppose," conceded the soldier.

"Aryn, Eliza, and I had a purpose again," continued Broedi. "We helped the Manes in any manner we could, scouring Terrene, looking for evidence that Chaos had resumed his or her plans, whatever they might be. Each time we returned, we would find the society larger than when we had left. A town sprouted around the enclave, filled with supporters of the Manes. To this day, they go about their lives as anyone else, remaining ever vigilant for signs of the prophecy, waiting for when they must rise and fight. A little over eighteen years ago, preparations were begun in earnest. A child was on the way. The time of the Progeny had come."

Nikalys stared at Broedi, realizing what the hillman was saying. "Is that where I was born, then?"

"Yes, uori. Eliza gave birth to both you and your iskoa in the keep."

Nikalys supposed he should be was grateful to have a bit more of his true history. "I thought you said when I was a baby, you were discovered and attacked."

"We were," said Broedi with a nod. "Shortly before your iskoa was born, agents of the Cabal somehow broke through the protective Weave that keeps the enclave hidden. Many good people passed on to Maeana defending you that day, uori."

Nikalys did not know what to say to that. The number of people who had died because of him was not limited to friends and neighbors of Yellow Mud. People he had never met had given their lives for him based on nothing more than the ancient words of a goddess. He was still dwelling on that when Broedi resumed his story.

"Shortly thereafter, your parents decided to leave the enclave. They did not want to put the Manes in any additional danger. While I did not agree with them, I understood their need to go." Broedi frowned. "Many were upset with me when they discovered I knew of their intent to leave but did not stop them. Many, to this day, remain so."

Jak spoke up, asking, "I don't suppose you have an army there?" A crooked smile spread over his lips. "Because that would be nice considering what Zecus has told us."

"No, uori, there is no army," rumbled Broedi. "We have but two hundred fighting men at the most." He shifted his gaze back to Nikalys. "But there are people waiting to teach you what I cannot. As time passed and Aryn and Eliza did not return with you, preparations shifted. The Manes believed you would eventually return as Indrida's prophecy said you must. They strove to find master mages, experts in the martial arts, teachers of history, literature, philosophy, military tactics, logic, and strategy. Truly, if it were not a secret, it would be one of the greatest centers of learning in the world."

"But it's not a secret anymore, is it?" asked Nikalys. "The Cabal found it already."

"They did," acknowledged Broedi. "And we expected further assaults, but none have come. As I said before, trust among the Cabal is rare. We concluded that those who attacked us had not shared the enclave's location with others."

Nikalys shifted his gaze back to the swordsmen. "So, now what?" He felt even more overwhelmed than before. "I'm supposed to go there and what? Study?"

Broedi drew in a deep breath and let it back out, slow and heavy. "That was the hope, yes. However, now we know what is occurring in the Borderlands, I expect we will not have the time. Nevertheless, we will head to the enclave and try. You should at least be safe there while we discover Chaos' true plan."

With frustration creeping into his voice, Nikalys asked, "And what then? What in the Nine Hells are we supposed to do then?"

Broedi delivered his answer with complete confidence. "You and your iskoa will become the champions Terrene needs you to be."

A derisive huff slipped from Nikalys and he turned to stare at the hillman. "Will I now?" He did not care what Indrida's prophecy said. "I'm no champion. This? This is blasted madness." Apparently, he was not the only one to think so.

"He's right," grumbled Sergeant Trell, his voice carrying an acerbic edge. The soldier was standing rigid, glaring at Nikalys with critical, disbelieving eyes. "He is a child. They both are."

"Nathan…" admonished Nundle quietly. "Try to understand. This must be a lot for a boy to—"

"Exactly," snapped Sergeant Trell. "A *boy*. I don't care if his parents were White Lions. If *this* is who we must rely on now, then Maeana's hall will soon be brimming with souls."

"Now, hold a moment!" shot back Jak, leaping to Nikalys' defense. "You don't know anything about him!"

"I know enough," barked the soldier. "I know that a turn ago, he was tending olive trees and taking afternoon swims. I know that last night, he needed *our* help to get out of that fort. If not for us, you would be dead. All of you."

Nikalys glared at the sergeant. While the man's statements were true, his tone was unnecessarily malicious.

Nundle muttered, "What's gotten into you, Nathan?" The tomble appeared baffled.

"What's gotten into me?!" exclaimed Sergeant Trell, his eyebrows arched high. "For *weeks*, I've been following these people, putting my men in danger simply by being in the Southlands." Pointing at Nundle, he growled, "Then *you* put these ideas into my head about a blasted prophecy and how I should forsake everything to help them. And then when we catch these 'almighty' Progeny, *we* end up saving *them*!" He turned back to Nikalys and shook his head with disgust. "By the gods, does Greya ever have a cruel sense of humor! The fate of the blasted world rests on the shoulders of children!"

The sergeant's loud outburst had brought sword practice to a halt. The soldiers stood still, staring at their leader, weapons hanging at their sides. To a man, they appeared shocked.

Nundle said angrily, "Remember what one of those *children* did for your men last night, Nathan!"

"A fine trick, for sure, but look what happened to her." He pointed to Kenders, still lying prone in the grass. "She helps a few men and then passes out. I wonder if the god of Chaos will let us schedule naps for her during battle? She's even more useless than he is!" He jabbed a finger at Nikalys.

Sergeant Trell's harsh, ungrateful words directed at Kenders were too much for Nikalys to take. Glaring at the man, he growled, "Watch your tongue!"

The sergeant ignored him, shook his head, and said, "I'm done with this! All of it!" Twisting around, he called over his shoulder, "Eadding! Hunsfin!"

The gifted swordsman Nikalys had been watching stepped forward, accompanied by one of the men with whom he had been sparring. The pair hurried over and stood in front of Sergeant Trell with swords in hand, sweating from practice.

"Come with me," ordered Sergeant Trell With that, he turned and began to stride toward Kenders. Hunsfin followed instantly, while Wil hesitated a moment before hurrying after the sergeant.

"Nathan!" called Nundle. "What are you doing?"

"What I should have done all along!" shouted Sergeant Trell over his shoulder. "Arrest the outlaws and take them back home. I'll let the Constables sort this out."

Incensed, Nikalys glared at spot just beyond the sergeant and his men— *Shift.*

—and stood before the three soldiers, blocking their path to Kenders. "You will *not* touch her."

While the two footmen appeared shocked by his sudden appearance, the sergeant did not. Sergeant Trell took another step forward and, lowering his voice, threatened, "Get out of our way."

Nikalys placed his right hand on the silver and gold hilt of the Blade of Horum, his fingers brushing the white stone carving of the lion's head on the pommel. He set his feet into a ready position and prepared to draw the sword. "How about you—all of you—get on your horses and ride away instead? *Now.*"

Sergeant Trell gave a loud bark of a laugh and exclaimed, "Or what? Are you going to fight me?"

"I will if I have to."

The sergeant laughed again and pointed at Nikalys' sword. "I *know* you haven't a clue how to use that." Glancing about the ground, he added, "And I don't see any rocks nearby." With a stunningly quick flourish, he unsheathed his own sword and leveled the tip at Nikalys chest. "Move aside, *Progeny.*" He twisted the name into an insult.

Nikalys was furious, yes, but beneath his anger, he was baffled. When Jak had shared the tale of his meeting with the sergeant on the Southern Road, he had sworn the man to be kind and respectful. The man before him now was the complete opposite. He glanced at the rest of the group and found Broedi restraining the tomble, while Zecus was struggling to hold back Jak. He could not understand why no one was helping him.

Looking back to the sergeant and his two men, Nikalys said through gritted teeth, "You will *not* take my sister from me." The absolute conviction in his voice, as hard as the white steel of his blade, surprised him.

"Yes," said Sergeant Trell, his voice equally firm. "We will." The soldiers on either side of the sergeant began to slide away to the side, giving each of them room to work.

Nikalys drew the Blade of Horum from the ornate leather scabbard. The white blade flashed in the sunlight, the metal appearing to twist and shimmer while still keeping its eternally sharp edges. All three soldiers—even the self-assured Sergeant Trell—gaped at the sword.

"I will not let you," growled Nikalys.

The sergeant blinked once, pulled his gaze from the sword, and then glared at Nikalys. "Have it your way, then. Eadding? Hunsfin? Take him."

The older, jagged-faced man on Nikalys' right rushed immediately, his sword raised high over his head. Hunsfin bellowed as he swung his blade down, throwing his whole body into the attack. Nikalys calmly raised his own sword up in his right hand, blocking the blow and redirecting it to the side where it sailed downward to strike the grassy ground with a soft thunk.

Nikalys stared, shocked twice over. He had no idea how he had parried the blow or how he had done it with one arm. Hunsfin's vicious attack should have shattered his bones.

Hunsfin quickly recovered from the deflection and brought his blade back off the ground, quickly whipping it through the air, aiming at Nikalys' exposed side.

Somehow, Nikalys knew the attack was coming and easily dodged it with a quick hop backwards. After the blade passed him by, he stepped forward and reached out with his left hand to shove the man in the chest, intending to knock the soldier off-balance. To his surprise, Hunsfin flew back nearly a dozen paces to land in the prairie grass.

A slight whistling of air warned him of an attack from his left.

Ducking forward, bending at the waist, he sensed a blade fly over his head. Anticipating a reverse follow-up attack, he stuck his shining sword into the air, leading his rise from the impromptu bow, and was rewarded with a solid clang of metal on metal. The gifted swordsman's blade was right where Nikalys had expected it. Shoving the man's blade aside, Nikalys spun around to face his attacker.

Wil was already coming at him again, his sword upraised. Nikalys bent his knees, pulled his sword closer to his hip, and easily parried the man's driving assault. Wil withdrew and began to circle to his left. Nikalys remained in place while continuing to face him, entirely aware that he was being drawn into a position to allow the sergeant to flank his rear. He shifted his stance again, holding his blade vertical with the hilt low and centered to his body. It was a better defensive position, although he had no idea why.

Once Wil had Nikalys between him and Sergeant Trell, he advanced, attacking with a dizzying combination of thrusts, stabs, and cuts. Nikalys, in awe of himself, turned each aside with ease.

Seeing an opening in Wil's assault, Nikalys reached out, grabbed Wil's shirt, and spun around, easily dragging the man with him as if he were a half-empty sack of flour. As he turned, he spotted Sergeant Trell moving toward him, preparing to strike. He shoved Wil away, causing the man to stumble, backpedaling wildly before he fell to the ground.

With a yell, Sergeant Trell attacked.

Nikalys repelled the sergeant's persistent attacks, flipping the older man's sword aside effortlessly. Without intentional thought, Nikalys began to advance on Sergeant Trell, using short, swift probing strokes meant to keep the soldier occupied. Despite the sergeant wanting to take his sister, Nikalys did not want to injure anyone unless it was a last resort. He did not want to kill again.

Two separate shouts cut the air, and at the edge of his vision, he saw Hunsfin rushing him on his right and Wil charging on the left. Nikalys stepped back from the sergeant, set his feet properly, and waited.

All three men attacked at once, raining blows on him.

Stabbing and thrusting.

Slashing and bashing.

Nikalys repelled their combined onslaught with ease. Even when two blows seemed to come at him at the same time, he somehow turned both aside. While he felt light and fast, it seemed the men were moving incredibly slowly, as though their limbs were stuck in giant vats of cold fish oil.

At that moment, something inside Nikalys clicked, a force shifted deep in his soul. One moment, he had no idea how to control whatever was buried inside of him. The next, he understood with dazzling clarity.

A smile slowly spread over his lips as he stared at the grass behind Wil—

Shift.

—reached out, and grabbed the man's sword hand from behind. With a gentle twist, he disarmed the man, caught the sword as it slipped from Wil's hand, and flung it away. As the freed sword climbed into the air, he spotted Hunsfin's blade coming at his head and turned—

Shift.

—lashing out with the shimmering Blade of Horum. Nikalys sliced clean though Hunsfin's sword, leaving only a hilt with a hand's length of sheared metal sticking from the guard. He stared at a spot at the center of the three men—

Shift.

—gave a quick shove to Wil's chest, spun, and did the same to Hunsfin. Both soldiers flew backwards in opposite directions just as Wil's sword reached the apex of its arc, the metal blade glinting in the sunlight. Whirling around, he faced Sergeant Trell. The man was staring at him, mouth agape.

Shift.

Nikalys grabbed the sergeant around the neck with his left arm and spun the soldier around to face everyone. Holding very still, he gazed at his impromptu audience.

Jak and Nundle were no longer struggling to break free. In fact, Jak, Nundle, Zecus, and most of the Red Sentinels stood as still as statues, their collective expression one of pure wonderment. Broedi was the only one showing a unique emotion.

Pride.

As Nikalys stared at everyone, Wil's tossed sword made a muted ringing sound as it struck the grasslands two hundred paces from where he stood.

With his arm still around Sergeant Trell's neck, Nikalys whispered diffidently into the man's ears, "You are *not* taking my sister." Raising his voice, he shouted, "*No one* is touching her!"

Breathing hard from exertion, Sergeant Trell choked out a response. "I had no real intention of doing so, son…"

The man's tone gave Nikalys pause. The sergeant sounded calm and collected, the venom from before gone. Sergeant Trell dropped his sword to the ground with a soft metallic clatter and gripped Nikalys' forearm with both hands, trying to free himself. Nikalys held fast without much trouble.

Broedi began to stride toward Nikalys and his prisoner, calling out, "Let him go, uori! I believe the sergeant made his point!"

"Point?" muttered Nikalys. He stared at the hillman, a blank look on his face, and shouted, "What point?"

"Son?" gasped Sergeant Trell as he frantically clapped at Nikalys' arm. "Could you let go? I can't…breathe…"

Broedi reached them, placed a hand on Nikalys' shoulder, and said gently, "Release him, uori. He is not your enemy."

A sneaking suspicion that he had been duped—much like how Broedi had tricked him back by the cliff—crept over him. Nikalys freed the wheezing man and Sergeant Trell slumped to the ground.

"Blast it!" exclaimed Nikalys while Glaring at Broedi. "Did you put him up to this?!"

The White Lion shook his head. "The sergeant did this on his own."

Straddled on his hands and knees, breathing hard and rubbing his neck, Sergeant Trell said in a ragged voice, "And if I'd had any idea you were that fast and strong, I probably would have reconsidered my approach."

By now, a wary trio of Jak, Zecus, and Nundle had drawn closer. All three appeared as confused as Nikalys felt. Nikalys scanned the area and saw the two soldiers he had been fighting were both sitting up, slightly stunned, but otherwise fine. The rest of the Red Sentinels were staring at him with wide eyes.

Looking back to the sergeant, Nikalys asked, "You said all of that just to get me angry, didn't you?"

Sergeant Trell gave an apologetic shrug of his shoulders. "And I'm only a little sorry about it."

Nikalys gaped at the man. "*Why?*"

Sergeant Trell raised a hand from his half-prone position. "Help me up?"

It took Nikalys a moment to extend a hand and pull the man to his feet. "I don't understand."

The sergeant brushed some stray blades of grass from his uniform while studying Nikalys, the glint in his eyes reminding Nikalys a bit of the way Thaddeus would sometimes look at him. "One look at you, and I knew you had a good soul. You just proved your heart is stout, *and* that you possess certain talents that are literally god-given. But none of that matters because you also have a problem, son, one problem that sours all of the sweet. Do you know what that is?"

Nikalys blinked, caught between being surprise and confused. The tip of his sword drooped. "Pardon?"

"You doubt who you are," said Sergeant Trell. "You doubt your place in the world. You doubt that you can do what is expected of you, despite having no idea what that is." His eyebrows drew together. "You lack the *one thing* that will allow you to be who you need to be, young Nikalys. *Confidence.*"

Nikalys stared at the sergeant, a blank expression on his face. He did not know what to say.

After a moment, Sergeant Trell took a step closer and, lowering his voice, said gently, "I get that all of this is a lot to take in. You and your sister have been thrust into an unimaginable position. It must feel like the world is on your shoulders alone. Here's the thing, though. You aren't alone. Son, when I watched what your sister did last night for my men—" he shook his head "—it took all of a single heartbeat for me to know that I would do *whatever* I could to help you both." A tiny smile touched his lips. "Even if that means taking a beating to help you realize you're more than you think."

Nikalys continued to peer at the sergeant in silence. He felt like he should thank the man, but could not find his tongue.

Taking advantage of the quiet, Nundle spoke up, his voice quiet and reserved. "While I'm certainly glad you did not go mad, Nathan—and for a moment, there, I was worried—you knew he had never practiced with a sword before. How could you know that he would be able to do that?" Without giving the sergeant the opportunity to respond, the tomble turned to Nikalys. "How *did* you do that?!"

"Yeah, Nik," muttered Jak with quiet awe. "That was amazing. You were a blur."

Nikalys shrugged his shoulders and was honest. "I have no idea." He dropped his head to stare at his sword.

"It is because you are Aryn's son," rumbled Broedi. "Part of Horum's gift allowed him to observe a style of fighting, and with a trivial amount of practice, replicate every move perfectly." He paused to smile. "You are more like your father than we could have hoped."

"Hold a moment," said Jak, his tone incredulous. "Nik learned how to use a sword by just watching the Sentinels?"

"He did," replied Broedi, a watchful eye on Nikalys. "However, unlike Aryn, *he* did not need to practice first. That is…new." He stared at Nikalys a moment longer before turning his gaze on Sergeant Trell. "I, too, am curious how you could have known he would respond to your attack as he did."

Sergeant Trell bent over to retrieve his sword from the grass. Upon standing upright, he nodded at Nikalys. "He might have been a novice when he walked over, but he was soon studying them with the critical eye of a swordmaster. Granted, I could not be sure, but I had a hunch. And more often than not, my hunches turn out right." He lifted a lone eyebrow. "I'm just glad I had the men practicing defensive drills today."

Nikalys asked, "How could you be sure I wouldn't hurt someone?"

"I judge you to be a man who would not hurt another unless there was no sweeter choice. Am I wrong?"

Nikalys responded at once. "No."

"See?" said the sergeant with a nod. "Another correct hunch."

Broedi said, "It was a very dangerous gamble, Sergeant."

"Perhaps. But one I could take with you and Nundle here to help if any of us were injured."

"Unlike the girl, Nathan," said Nundle, "I cannot make limbs grow back. What she did is most unusual."

The sergeant shot a searching look to Broedi. The hillman in turn shook his head side-to-side. "Nor can I. Today could very easily have been the end of your command, Sergeant."

Sergeant Trell turned a shade paler than a moment ago. Offering a weak smile, he said, "Good thing that did not happen, then."

The man's tentative bravado brought a slight grin to Nikalys' face. Holding the Blade of Horum out, arm's length from his body, he twisted the sword in the air, staring at its brilliance. Using it in the manner for which it had been forged had been exhilarating. "Can you show me more, Sergeant?"

"I can and will," said the soldier. He took a step closer and crossed his arms over his chest. "But there's a small matter I need to discuss with you first."

Nikalys dropped his sword to his side. "Go on."

Sergeant Trell drew himself up to his full height. "My men and I are currently in violation of our oath as Sentinels. In the eyes of duchy law, we are every bit the criminal you are, especially me. I cannot return home. Which, knowing what I know now, I would not do anyway. Instead, I ask to accompany you."

Nikalys' eyebrows arched high. "You what?"

"As I said before, I want to help," said the soldier. He paused as Wil and Hunsfin approached, stopping to stand behind him. "And while I will not speak for my men, I have a feeling most will offer their services as well."

Nikalys did not know what to say. This was unexpected.

Without waiting for an answer, the sergeant turned to Broedi. "You will need all the help you can find for the coming war, and make no mistake, war is coming. From what Zecus described, an invasion force is headed this way. Why Duke Everett is in league with the Cabal remains a mystery to me, but I do not need to understand why the sun shines hot to feel its warmth."

Wil took a sudden step forward, his gaze on Nikalys. "My Lord? Sergeant Trell is right. I, too, would like to accompany you. I'd be honored to fight at your side." Sergeant Trell looked over at the young soldier and nodded his approval.

Nikalys was staring at Wil when Hunsfin stepped forward as well. "As would I, my Lord." His gravelly voice matched his rough face.

The odd process continued when Zecus approached, bowed at the waist, and said, "I will give my blood as well, great warrior. If you and your sister will lead my home to freedom, I would be at you side."

Nikalys stared from face to face, quietly stunned. These four men were offering to forsake everything they knew in order to follow and fight with him against the Cabal. The complete, unwavering determination in their eyes was as inspiring as it was astonishing.

Looking back to Sergeant Trell, Nikalys asked, "What about your families? Wives? Children? You'd leave them behind?"

The sergeant gave a small shake of his head. "The Sentinels do not accept family men into our ranks. Should a soldier join in union, he must leave the army. We have had the luxury of peace for so long that we have been afforded rules such as these."

"Do you not have mothers or fathers?" protested Nikalys. "Brothers and sisters?"

Sergeant Trell's eyes narrowed. "Son, if this evil is not stopped, they—our mothers, fathers, brothers, sisters, all of them—will perish. We either help you, or we go home and die with them."

"I also offer my help," piped up Nundle. "Perhaps I can aid in your sister's training? I'm quite skilled with Strands of Will—excellent, in fact, if you ask me. I can also touch Charge, Life, a bit of Air, and Void, as well—although I only recently discovered my talent with Void. Honestly, I could use some help with that myself." He stared up at Broedi. "Do you have any Void mages at the enclave? Perhaps one—"

"Nundle?" interrupted Sergeant Trell firmly. "You are not to mention that place, remember?"

Nundle glanced at the sergeant, then to Hunsfin and Will, and frowned "Ah...yes. Sorry." Looking back at Nikalys, he said, "What I mean to say is that I would like to help as well, my, uh...Lord Progeny?" He spoke as if he were testing the title. Nikalys thought it sounded absurd.

Nikalys looked to Broedi, wondering what he thought of their offers. He was more than surprised when the typically pensive and overly careful hillman nodded his agreement without hesitation. "We should accept, uori. We will need every good soul we can find."

Jak slid over to stand beside Nikalys, leaned close, and murmured, "I agree. And I think Kenders would, too."

Nikalys looked between Broedi and Jak for a moment. A few heartbeats later, he came to the same conclusion. They would need all the help they could get. Turning back to the men—and tomble—before him, he said, "I will accept on three conditions." He stared at Sergeant Trell. "The first is that you and Wil give me as many lessons as you can between here and Storm Island."

Jak leaned over again and muttered, "Me, too."

"Jak, too," added Nikalys. "And Zecus if he's coming with us." The Borderlander gave him a grateful nod. "And he'll need a proper sword to call his own. We can't have him fighting the Cabal with a hoe."

Sergeant Trell nodded. "Promise not to destroy any more of our blades and you can have your lessons."

"I'll do my best," said Nikalys, a slight smile on his face. "As for the second condition: each of your men must choose for himself if he wishes to join and help. If any want to leave, they must do so by sundown. Should they learn of our destination, however, they must remain."

"A fair offer," said Sergeant Trell. "And the final condition?"

Looking around the assembled group, Nikalys said, "No one is to call me 'my Lord,' 'great warrior,' or—" he glanced down at the tomble "—'Lord Progeny.' It sounds absurd. 'Nikalys' will do. Or simply 'Nik.'"

His request was mostly met with smiles and nods of agreement. Only Hunsfin did not grin. Nikalys wondered if he could.

"As long as we're naming conditions," said Sergeant Trell. "I have one of my own."

"What is it?" asked Nikalys.

"After meeting and speaking with Nundle, I sent three of my men to find the other half of my company, those who Fenidar—sorry, Jhaell sent east. I would like to meet up with them if possible and extend them the same options you have given us here."

"I am sorry, Sergeant," rumbled Broedi. "But we do not have time to search for your men."

"You won't have to," replied the soldier. "Their orders are to head to the Fernsford Bridge and wait for us there. Which, unless I'm mistaken, is the direction we are headed?"

A curious glint entered Broedi's eyes. "May I ask why you sent them there?" Nikalys thought the fortuitous order odd as well.

After letting out a quick sigh, Sergeant Trell said, "Honestly, I don't know. The idea came to me, it felt right, and so I went with it."

The hillman continued staring at the soldier, a pensive expression on his face. After a few heartbeats, he nodded. "We must cross there anyway. Besides, Duchess Aleece would not be amused at having a group of Red Sentinels camped out in the Southlands indefinitely."

With a nod of gratitude, Sergeant Trell said, "Then, if you'll excuse me, gentlemen, I must discuss this with the men. They have another choice to make." He glanced at the Borderlander. "Zecus, come with me. We'll see about finding you a sword."

A smile crept over Zecus' face and he strode off with Sergeant Trell, Wil, and Hunsfin back toward the field tents and soldiers. The bulk of the Sentinels were standing there, waiting, and began to gather in a circle as Sergeant Trell approached.

Nikalys eyed the group as the sergeant spoke, anxious for what their answers would be. Standing there, he realized with a start that he had made the decision to allow the soldiers to come more or less on his own. Broedi had not challenged him at all.

"How is it going?" asked Jak, his voice low.

Nikalys looked over at his brother, unsure what Jak was asking, and found him staring at Broedi.

"Quite well, uori," murmured the hillman. "Some have questions, but the sergeant is answering them satisfactorily."

Recalling Broedi's excellent hearing, Nikalys muttered, "I keep forgetting about that."

"Me, too," said Jak with a smile. "It only occurred to me now because I was wishing I could hear what they were saying—" he glanced at Broedi "—and I remembered I knew someone who could."

The tomble stared up at the trio, a confused expression on his face. "I don't understand." Looking around him, he said, "I'm not overly proficient with Air, but if you were using a Weave to listen, I'm sure I would have noticed."

"It is not a Weave, little one."

Jak said, "He has ears like a blasted barncat."

"Truly?" asked Nundle, eyebrows arched. "How interesting." He tilted his head back to stare up at the towering hillman. "That detail was not in the *Complete History of the Oaken Nation.*"

"Doesn't sound very complete, then," quipped Jak.

With nothing to do but wait for the soldiers' decision, Nikalys turned back around to check on Kenders and found her still lying down in the grass. "I wonder how much longer she'll sleep."

"A while, I'd think," said Nundle. "What she did last night surely took a lot out of her. To be honest, it should have killed her."

Alarmed, Nikalys—and Jak—swiveled to stare at the tomble and, in unison, exclaimed, "What?!"

Broedi let out a heavy sigh, shaking his head. "I had asked you not to share that with them."

Nundle scrunched up his face, obviously upset with himself for the mistake. "So you did. Sorry."

Pulling his attention from the soldiers, Broedi stared at the brothers. "Try not to worry. Give her time to sleep, and she will be fine."

With a strange note to his voice, Jak asked, "And how much time do you think she'll need?"

"I am hoping she will awake by morning," rumbled Broedi. "Hopefully no later than the afternoon."

Jak nodded to where Kenders lay. "Looks like you're off by a day or so." With that, he stepped past them and towards her.

Broedi, Nundle, and Nikalys all turned to find Kenders sitting up, her elbows resting on her knees, her head in her hands. Her hair, bright and blonde in the sunlight, hung in front of her face as she stared at the ground. She did not seem to be faring too well.

"Impossible," muttered Nundle.

Broedi remained silent, an expression of wonder hovering just beneath his typical stoicism. Looking to Nikalys, he said, "It would appear she has a very bad headache. Take my bag and give her some meadowsweet. Just a pinch."

Scanning the area for the hillman's bag, Nikalys spotted it on the ground where Broedi and Nundle had been sitting earlier. Curious, he stared at the bag across the field—

Shift.

—and with a smile, picked it up. Staring to where Kenders sat, hunched over—

Shift.

—he kneeled beside her and placed a gentle hand on her back. "Hey? How are you feeling?"

Without looking up, Kenders mumbled, "Like I got kicked in the head by a horse."

Hearing footsteps, Nikalys looked up to find Jak approaching, a smile on his face.

As Jak kneeled on the other side of Kenders, he winked at Nikalys. "Show-off." Nikalys chuckled and began rooting through Broedi's satchel for the meadowsweet.

Kenders, her gaze still fixated on the ground, asked, "Are the soldiers okay?"

"They're fine, sis," said Jak. "And in better shape than you."

"Good." She sounded relieved. "How long have I been sleeping?"

"Just the night and morning," answered Jak.

Looking up, she squinted against the brightness and quickly lifted a hand to shade her eyes. "Did I miss anything?"

Nikalys exchanged a wide grin with Jak. "Only a little."

CHAPTER 55: STRUGGLE

Cero lay on his stomach, staring at the tomble and the giant through the tall grass. The dirt and dry bits of prairie that had wormed their way into his shirt itched like mad, but he fought the urge to scratch. Once he heard what the boy had said about the Shapechanger's hearing, he was afraid to move. He was even afraid to breathe.

When the boy had first gotten up and gone to talk with the sergeant, Cero had circled around behind a tent and moved into the grass, slinking along the ground like a derolla snake. The strange compulsion to know what the boy said was too strong to resist.

Unfortunately, he had only caught a few spoken phrases as the wind whistling through the prairie had masked most of what was said. He would have liked to move closer, but had not dared. The need to learn about the boy and girl was tempered only by the urge to remain hidden.

The Southlands breeze stalled for a moment, allowing a few words from the tomble to reach Cero's ear.

"—do not trust the Tracker. I think he—"

A stab of panic pierced Cero's chest with the force of an arrow fired at five paces. Believing he had been discovered, he nearly leapt up and ran away. Yet something stopped him. Against all logic, the impulse to keep quiet and unnoticed pushed him down even further into the grass. After a few dozen thudding heartbeats, the pair rewarded his unnatural patience by moving away from him and toward the girl who had just awakened. Cero closed his eyes and allowed himself a tiny sigh of relief.

Once his heart and breathing slowed, Cero reopened his eyes and peered through the grass, studying the girl and her two brothers as they sat on the ground, talking. He wished he could hear what they said, but it was impossible to get close to them. Frowning, he began to scoot backwards. He was not going to learn anything more by lying here.

Once he had moved a safe distance back, he turned and, remaining on his stomach, crawled back to the tents. He stood slowly, ensuring that no one could see him, brushed himself off, and hurried behind the nearest tent. As he stood there, taking deep, steadying breaths, his gaze drifted to the ancient Imperial fort that loomed over the prairie. Eyeing the battlements atop the walls, an icy darkness abruptly swelled inside his soul.

Quiet, mumbled words fell from his lips. "Not high enough..."

Looking to the towers instead, he judged them sufficient. A fall from one of those should kill him, assuming he could find a complete set of stairs leading to the top. He had taken three steps toward the fort when he stopped and shook his head, trying to clear his mind. He shoved the cold, dark feeling inside him away, fighting against its black chill. It took a few moments, but it faded, leaving him standing in the grass, blinking, shivering.

"What in the Nine Hells was that…?"

He could not fathom why such a horrible thought had entered his mind. He was certainly in a difficult situation, but killing himself was not the answer.

Turning around, he gathered his nerves as best he could and strode into the main camp, heading straight for the grouped Sentinels. Sergeant Trell stood, his arms crossed over his chest, scanning the men in front of him while he spoke.

"—each of you has the choice. As soon as she is ready to move, we strike camp and head for the bridge. If you are not going with us, tell me before we march. You can go, free and clear. No one will stop you." The sergeant's gaze fell upon Cero. He paused a moment before continuing, his eyes never leaving the Tracker. "If what you've seen so far has not swayed you, then nothing will. You *all* have the opportunity contribute to a story that playmen will retell for centuries. Will you play a part? Or will you run?" He finally looked away from Cero and back to the gathered soldiers. "Go, men. Think. And decide."

The sergeant turned and motioned for the strange Borderlander to follow him. Cero still did not understand the dark-skinned man's role in any of this.

The assembled soldiers began to disperse. Some stayed in small groups, talking in hushed voices, while others went off to stand or sit alone. To a man, they all avoided Cero, leaving him isolated amidst the tents and smoldering embers of last night's fires.

As he idly watched a pair of butterflies flutter around a patch of purple wildflowers, Cero thought through the madness of the past weeks. Mages, Fenidar, prophecies of Indrida, the Cabal, the letter supposedly from Duke Everett. While he was still reluctant to believe the fantastic claims made by the tomble, the evidence was becoming increasingly hard to deny.

Something deep inside of him was screaming out that these "outlaws" were anything but, that they were good people preparing to do great things. Yet something more powerful was tamping that belief down, stomping on it like all the bent grass around him.

As he tried to reconcile his conflicting feelings, the icy, dark feeling swelled inside him again. His right hand drifted the beltknife strapped to his thigh. His thumb lightly traced the handle of the short blade, curling around it as he cradled the tacky leather of the grip in his palm. With unthinking slowness, he began to draw the blade from its sheath. A quick slice across his neck was all it would take. Then he would be free.

His eyes went round and he pushed the darkness away, shoving it back from wherever it had come. Slamming the knife back into the sheath, he grabbed his temples with both hands and screamed, "Blast the gods! Stop it!"

A group of Sentinels sitting nearby stared at him, their expressions a mix of shock and disdain. They rose from the ground and moved away as one, mumbling to one another as they went.

Cero had not felt like himself in weeks, although these urges to kill himself were new.

"What is *wrong* with me?"

Turning, he hurried to his tent and began to tear it down, hoping that by staying occupied he would keep the dark thoughts at bay. He had no idea what he was going to do once he was done packing.

CHAPTER 56: MEETING

6ᵗʰ of the Turn of Thonda

Sabine straddled the back of Goshen, sitting behind Nikalys, her arms wrapped around his midsection and her head resting on his back. The first time she had ridden with either of the boys—Jak, originally—she had tried to sit on the horse without touching him, keeping her arms to her sides. However, once the group had broken into a trot, she had been forced to throw her arms around Jak to keep from falling, surprising him as much as she had herself.

After a few days of alternating with the boys, most of the awkwardness of the odd arrangement had passed. Her ease with the brothers had even reached a point to where she felt comfortable enough even to try to nap as they rode.

Her current effort to sleep, however, had failed despite the fact that she was exhausted. For a while now, she had simply watched her sister who was sitting in Kenders' lap, waving the red-tipped firestick in little circles while laughing and giggling.

Sabine smiled—a rare event as of late—and sighed.

Nikalys mumbled, "Awake now?"

"Never fell asleep." Sitting tall, she added, "I've just been watching Helene."

He turned to stare at the little girl. After a few quiet moments, he murmured, "You know, I envy her."

"You do?" She leaned to the side a bit in order to see his profile. "Why?"

"Just look at her. She's free of worry. None of this bothers her." He frowned and muttered, "To her, this is some grand adventure."

That was not entirely true. While Helene might appear carefree to her new friends, Sabine knew otherwise. However, she did not know Nikalys well enough to share the girl's secrets. Not yet, at least.

She did know him well enough though that she recognized this mood. The young man carried his newfound responsibility with him nonstop. At times, it seemed he tried to carry everyone else's responsibility, too. Patting him on the back, she said, "Things will work out, Nik. Try not to worry too much."

He glanced at her, offered a tiny smile, and faced forward.

Sabine sighed again, only this time a tiny frown accompanied the exhalation. Moments like this, she wished she still had her own horse.

As Nikalys and Kenders had slept the morning away following the attack in the fort, Sergeant Trell had sent his men across the plains to look for their horses. During the confusion inside the ancient stronghold, Sabine and the others had lost track of the mounts. In the end, the soldiers recovered all but Sabine's horse and the spare Broedi had been leading.

As every Sentinel had chosen to accompany them, the combined group now had fifty-three horses for fifty-four riders. Over a dozen soldiers had endeavored to have her ride with them, but she turned down every offer, blushing some as she did so. When she asked Broedi what to do, he offered to take the form of a horse himself so she could ride. Horrified, she had insisted she would rather walk the rest of the way. Only after she refused did she see the slight smile he wore and realize the hillman had been jesting.

In the end, she ended up taking turns doubling up with Kenders, Nikalys, and Jak. While she was with one, Helene would ride with one of the others.

She rested her head on Nikalys' back again, determined to try to get some rest. Since discovering the truth about her companions, she had not been sleeping well. Neither had Helene, but there was nothing new about that. From the day she was born, bad dreams had plagued Helene's nights, dreams she rarely, if ever, shared with Sabine. Strangely enough, since leaving the Moiléne farm, the nightmares' intensity had lessened some, which had surprised Sabine. After what had happened, she would have expected the dreams to get worse, not better.

Nikalys took a deep breath, lifting Sabine's head up a little. A tiny smile spread over her lips as she listened to Nikalys' heartbeat. Despite all the madness, she found herself growing fond of him. He was a kind soul, if a bit moody at times. He was fiercely loyal to his siblings, Helene absolutely adored him, and without his heroics at the farm, Sabine and her sister would likely be dead. Nikalys was her hero in every sense of the word.

Yet he was not the only one.

Sabine lifted her head and looked to her left, where Jak sat astride his horse. The elder 'brother' had stood with her and Helene at the fort, refusing to leave their side until they were safe. In her eyes, Jak was as brave as his brother. Perhaps more so, considering he did not have any special gifts from the gods on which to rely. Plus, he was a very handsome looking man.

She shut her eyes and sighed. If she had to be swept up in some playman's saga, she could have done infinitely worse than the one she was in now.

Nikalys patted her hands gently. "Hey, wake up. The rest of the Sentinels are approaching."

Not bothering to tell him she was not sleeping, she lifted her head and peeked over his shoulder. A number of red-and-black clad horsemen rode toward them at a steady trot from the east, cantering through the sparse trees and grass.

Sometime yesterday, she realized that the grasslands of her youth were more or less gone, having melted away behind them. At one point, when there had been at least a dozen tress in sight, she asked Kenders if they were in a forest. Her friend stared at her, smiled kindly the way one does when a child asks a silly question, and said "Not quite."

As she eyed the approaching soldiers, she asked, "How do you think this will go?"

"Well, I hope," replied Nikalys. "Sergeant Trell seems to think that most will join with us once they've had a chance to think things over."

Sabine glanced about, looking at the soldiers already riding in a loose circle around them. "Good, then. The more protection, the better."

"What?" asked Nikalys, his tone filled with mock hurt. "You don't think I can keep you safe? I'm getting quite good with the sword, you know."

It was the truth. In the three days since leaving the fort, Nikalys had become increasingly proficient with his father's sword. Each evening, when the party would stop and make camp, Wil and the sergeant would spar, using different techniques and styles of swordplay. Nikalys would sit and watch in complete silence.

When the two Sentinels were done, Sergeant Trell would step aside and motion for Nikalys to try, and then move on to give lessons to Jak and Zecus. Nikalys would stand, draw his white sword, and execute every move against Wil without flaw. The exhibition had become the centerpiece of each evening with every soldier standing in a wide circle, watching Nikalys in awe.

Pulling her arms from around his waist, she patted him on the back and said, "You're good, Nikalys. But having fifty more soldiers around isn't going to hurt."

He nodded, still eyeing the new arrivals. "It will unless we can find a way to hide them in plain sight."

Sabine sighed heavily. "True."

It was a well-known, thoroughly discussed problem that faced the group. According to Broedi, the area of the Southlands through which they would soon be traveling was heavily populated. Villages and countless farms dotted the area between Fernsford Bridge and Fernsford itself. Even more waited south of the city. Expecting a hundred Red Sentinels to pass through unnoticed was a fool's hope.

Once the two groups of soldiers reached one another, everyone stopped. Soldiers on both sides dismounted and began to mill about, happily greeting one another. The new arrivals eyed Sabine's small group—along with Broedi and Nundle—with barely restrained curiosity. Sergeant Trell ordered the men to gather and began to talk, explaining the situation. At a certain point, he called Nundle forward, and the little tomble began to tell his story.

Sabine sighed. This was going to take a while.

Unable to do much more than sit on a horse and wait, she let her gaze wander. Near the back of the assembled Sentinels, she spied Cero, the black-haired Tracker, speaking to another man similarly dressed in gray. "Look," she whispered. "The other Tracker."

His voice solemn, Nikalys muttered, "Already saw him."

There had been more than a few discussions regarding Cero. Nundle did not trust the man and was not shy about sharing his opinion. Sergeant Trell argued for giving him a chance, insisting that he had a feeling about the Tracker. After Broedi weighed in and agreed with Sergeant Trell, the matter seemed mostly settled. Until the time someone would bring the subject up again.

Sabine had kept a close eye on Cero as they had ridden east and noted some very odd behavior. On more than one occasion, she caught him mumbling to himself while caressing the handle of his beltknife. Sometimes, he would hold the blade before his face and stare for moments on end. Then, with a vicious shake of his head, he would shove the knife back into its sheath while muttering to himself. Sabine believed the man to be mad.

After Nundle completed his tale, Broedi stepped forward and spoke next, explaining both who he was and the true story of the White Lions. As expected, most of the new arrivals stared at the giant with disbelieving eyes.

"This should be fun," whispered Nikalys. "Watch their faces." The darker mood from before was gone. In fact, he sounded like an eager, overly excited child.

"I know, Nikalys," said Sabine, grinning slightly. "I was there last night, if you remember."

She had sat with everyone last evening when the planning for this meeting was underway. Sergeant Trell would tell the men his tale, then Nundle. Broedi was to reveal himself as a White Lion, followed by Nikalys showing the soldiers what he had been able to learn with the sword. Kenders had wanted to put on a show as well, but Broedi forbade her from doing anything, insisting she had too much work she needed to do in order to control her power.

Suddenly, Broedi's form began to twist and flow, shifting from that of a tall and strong man into a towering, golden bear. A stunned whisper tumbled from Sabine's lips. "Bless the gods…" Even though she had seen the beast before, she had never seen the transformation. In the fort, she had been too busy consoling Helene.

Once the shift was complete, Broedi stood on his hind legs, his thick golden-brown fur hanging from him, and let out a tremendous roar. The soldiers, even the ones who had already seen the bear, took a few, wide-eyed steps back. Horses whinnied, pulling at their reins as soldiers held tight.

Nikalys muttered, "I thought we decided lynx last night." He sounded a bit put-off.

"You know," teased Sabine, "I think you should go tell him you're disappointed with his choice. Right now, in fact."

Nikalys glanced back and smiled. "I'm actually trying not to make a habit of arguing with giant bears."

She returned his grin with one of her own.

Last night, it was during the long and—in her opinion—pointless debate as to what animal form Broedi should take when Sabine had excused herself. Her experience with men was limited, but already she decided they liked to talk more than was necessary.

Broedi returned to his normal, giant self and stood before the soldiers, his arms crossed. While the new arrivals stared in shocked silence, the soldiers who had already seen the bear smiled wide at their friends' awe, poking elbows in the stunned soldiers' sides. Sergeant Trell turned and looked back to Nikalys and Sabine and motioned with his head.

"My turn," said Nikalys with a low chuckle.

Sabine scooted back, preparing to dismount from the back of Goshen. "Would you like me to hop—" She stopped upon realizing she was now alone atop the tan horse. Nikalys was standing next to Broedi with his shining, white sword in hand. Her heart racing, Sabine muttered to herself, "Blast it…"

From the reaction of Broedi, Nundle, and the sergeant, it was apparent they had not expected Nikalys to arrive like that either.

Sergeant Trell called out for four men from the new arrivals to step forward and challenge Nikalys. Urged on by the Sentinels who knew Nikalys' capabilities, four soldiers stepped forward, swords drawn, and arranged themselves in a line, preparing to face him one at a time. When Sergeant Trell ordered for them to all attack Nikalys at once, the new arrivals hesitated. The soldiers who had traveled with Nikalys for days grinned in anticipation.

The four men surrounded Nikalys and began to probe at his defenses. As Sabine expected, Nikalys had little trouble with them, moving from opponent to opponent in the blink of an eye. One moment he was facing one man, the next, he was parrying a blow from the soldier behind him. The sound of steel on steel rang throughout the area, pinging and clanging with frequency of a hard rain pelting the earth.

After Sergeant Trell called for a halt to the display, he gave an impassioned speech about the danger rising in the west. He told them about the evil gods of the Cabal and demons leading armies of Sudashian oligurts, mongrels, and razorfiends. By the time he was done, Sabine herself was ready to leap from the saddle and charge headlong into a line of ten-thousand oligurts. He then offered the same choice the soldiers already accompanying them had needed to make. Leave now and go home, or stay and help fight.

The men dispersed, talking among themselves, weighing their options. Sabine kept an eye on the new Tracker, most interested by what his reaction would be. The two gray-clad men stood alone with their heads together, whispering quietly. Cero repeatedly pointed downriver in the direction they had been traveling while the other man shook his head and pointed to the northwest.

"Nik overdid it a bit, don't you think?"

So engrossed in the Trackers' distant argument, Sabine had not noticed Kenders ride up beside her. Looking at her friend—still with Helene in her lap—she nodded. "Your brother can be a bit of show-off at times."

"Jak's worse," said Kenders. She was quiet for a moment before looking over, a sly grin spreading over her face. "You know, some girls like that in a man."

Without hesitation, Sabine said, "And some girls like exotic men from faraway lands." She eyed her friend. "What say you about that?"

Sabine had felt the stares of many of the younger Red Sentinels over recent days. From their evening chats, she knew Kenders had experienced the same. Yet while Kenders ignored every one of their appreciative gazes, Sabine had caught her eyeing the young Borderlander.

Kenders stared at Sabine through narrowed eyes and murmured good-naturedly, "Quiet, you." She winked and stuck her tongue out.

Smiling, Sabine returned the gesture.

From Kenders' lap, Helene piped up, saying, "Sabine! You said it's not polite to stick out our tongues!" Her tone contained a type of righteous admonishment that can only come from a child when catching an adult's mistake.

"You're right, dear. I'm sorry. I should not have done that. It was rude of me."

Clearly pleased with herself, Helene looked up at Kenders and smiled, just missing Kenders pulling her tongue back into her mouth again.

Looking down, Kenders said, "Well done, Helene. It's very nice of you to help your sister with her manners."

Sabine rolled her eyes and looked away, chuckling to herself. Off to the side of the Sentinels, she spotted Jak and Zecus together. The pair had dismounted and was practicing their sword work. While neither man had Nikalys' unnatural proclivity for the sword, both had been working hard at learning the more traditional way. Sabine found herself eyeing Jak as he swung the sword in slow, exaggerated movements, attempting to get the form right before speeding up to a respectable pace.

"So what now?" she asked without looking away from the pair. "Once the new Sentinels make up their mind, that is?"

"I don't think we have an answer yet," said Kenders. "We could always try to ford the river. Broedi says he knows a way to make the surface of the water hard—neat, huh?—but he's hesitant to do so. He says it takes more effort than he would like to exert. His control over Water is not very extensive."

"What about Nundle?"

"He can't touch Strands of Water at all." A disappointed frown spread over her face. "And I've been 'forbidden' to try."

Sabine sighed and said, "I could make the water clear and cool. But only a little at a time."

Kenders flashed a grin. "We'll keep that in mind if we get thirsty."

Sabine smiled back, but her mirth was forced. She found herself surrounded with people of tremendous talents and power while she was left being quite normal. Even Helene showed promise, according to Broedi.

After a short while, Broedi, Nikalys, and Nundle came walking through the grass toward them, grim expressions on all three of their faces.

Sabine muttered, "They don't look very happy, do they?"

"No, they don't," said Kenders. As the trio neared the girls' horses, she raised her voice and asked, "What's wrong?"

"We have another problem, uora," rumbled Broedi.

"Wondrous," said Sabine with a shake of her head. "What now?"

As the three of them stopped, Nundle stared up from under the wide brim of his hat. "The second bunch of Sentinels have brought some information that makes things difficult for us."

"More than they already are?" asked Kenders.

"Yes, uora," rumbled Broedi. "Quite a bit more."

Sabine asked, "What's the new problem?"

Nodding his head back in the direction of the soldiers, Nikalys said, "It seems that some Southern Arms did not take kindly to a large contingent of Red Sentinels in the Southlands. A 'Corporal Holb' from the new group said that the morning after they set up camp on the northern side of the river, they awoke to find the southern shore lined with blue and gold. Just over a hundred Southern Arms were waiting for them, watching."

"Why?" asked Kenders "Do they fear an invasion by fifty men?"

"Doubtful," replied Broedi. "I would assume they are merely curious. It is beyond unusual for the soldiers of one duchy cross into another. In fact, it is against agreed-upon law."

"Did they attack?" asked Sabine.

"Thankfully, no," rumbled the hillman. "They had the sense to simply watch. And wait."

"So, now what?" asked Kenders. "I'm thinking they won't let us cross when we show up with even more Sentinels."

Lifting a single eyebrow, Nundle said cryptically, "They might not, assuming they were still there."

"They're not there now?" asked Kenders.

Nundle shook his head. "Not anymore…"

Sabine was confused. "If they aren't there anymore…what exactly is the problem?"

Nikalys reached up and rubbed his chin. "They aren't there because they followed Corporal Holb's Sentinels here."

"Why?" asked Kenders, her voice full of worry. "Are they going to attack?"

"Nathan doesn't think so," said Nundle. It had taken Sabine a few times hearing the tomble call the sergeant by his first name before she realized Sergeant Trell and Nathan were the same person.

"Neither do I," rumbled Broedi.

Kenders, with frustration creeping into her voice, asked, "Well then, can we go around them?"

Nikalys shook his head. "They'll see us try."

"What if we go now?" suggested Sabine. "Head north first, then east? Go around them."

Broedi pointed to the southeastern horizon. "No, uora. *They* will see us try."

Sabine stared in the direction he indicated, but did not see much besides the natural greens and browns of grass and trees. A few patches of wild flowers—oranges, blues and yellows—broke up the earth tones.

Confused, she started to ask, "What are you—?" She stopped when some of the flowers on the horizon moved, and not gracefully as if teased by the wind. Looking closer, she realized that a few men on horses were waiting in one of the wildflower patches. "Oh."

Nikalys twisted around and stared southeast. "You have to wonder what they're thinking now, seeing the Sentinels double in size."

"They didn't ask why the Sentinels were here?" asked Sabine.

"They did," said Nikalys. "But Sergeant Trell had given Corporal Holb strict orders to say that they were here on 'official business for the duke' and nothing more." He frowned. "Apparently, that did not satisfy the Southern Arms."

Sabine shook her head and sighed. For a group trying to be inconspicuous, they seemed to be attracting an awful lot of attention.

The group fell silent, doing little more than frowning at one another. Sabine tried to think of a solution around the problem and was sure everyone else was doing the same. As the quiet dragged out, Helene twisted in Kenders' lap to stare at Sabine. "Are more soldiers coming, Sabine?"

"We hope not," muttered a preoccupied Sabine.

"Why not?"

"Because they're not like these soldiers." She waved a hand at the Red Sentinels still milling about and talking.

"Why not?"

Sabine hesitated, struggling with how to explain the situation to a four-year-old. "Well...because they're just different."

"Why?"

"Helene!" snapped Sabine. "Right now, I need you to be quiet. Can you *please* do that for me?" Her words and tone were both harsher than she had intended. A lack of sleep had her on edge.

Helene dropped her chin to her chest. "Sorry, Sabine."

Sabine eyed her little sister, sighed, and was a heartbeat away from apologizing when Helene looked back up. "Nik-lys said they wear blue and gold. I like gold." She smiled wide. "It's my new favorite color."

The innocently offhand comment chased away Sabine's ire. A tiny smile graced her lips. "Since when, dear?"

"Since this morning," giggled the little girl. There were times when it was impossible to keep Helene's spirits down for very long. "Sabine? Are the soldiers different because they have different colors?"

"Well...yes. Their uniforms are different." She shook her head. "But that's not what...makes..." She trailed off as the seed of an idea planted itself in her head, sprouted, and bloomed in an instant. Turning her gaze to Nikalys, she asked, "How many of them did you say there are?"

"A little over a hundred. Why?"

Sabine grinned wide at her little sister. "Helene, dear, you are the smartest little girl in the world." Her sister beamed at the compliment despite having no idea why she had received it. Facing Broedi and Nundle, Sabine said, "I have an idea."

CHAPTER 57: ARMS

Beads of sweat dripped from Nundle's brow, rolling down his cheek, neck, and into his shirt collar. Today was a tad warmer than recent days had been, but the heat was only partially responsible for his perspiring.

He looked to his right to eye the hillman walking beside him, easily keeping pace with Nundle's chestnut horse. "Again, just to be certain, exactly how far are we from Fernsford?"

The White Lion kept his gaze straight ahead while he answered. "The city is not quite a day's ride south of the bridge, a bridge we are still a half-day's ride from reaching."

"That's close if things go bad."

Broedi nodded once. "Agreed."

Kenders, riding her horse on the other side of the White Lion, said, "Don't worry. We'll be fine." The expression she wore was a brave and resolute one, but her tense shoulders and rigid posture betrayed her. She was nervous.

Nundle eyed Broedi again. "Cero couldn't tell you anything about the Constables office in Fernsford? How many Trackers they have? How far they patrol? Anything?"

Broedi shook his head. "He was…reticent to speak with me. The other Tracker was even less cooperative."

Nundle could not stop the frown that affixed itself on his face. "Even if Cero *had* told you something, I am not sure I would believe it. If he told me the sky was up, I'd ask for proof." He eyed Broedi and said with purpose. "I *still* think we should send him away."

"I would rather have the Trackers with us," rumbled the hillman. "Where I can see them."

"That's what Nathan says," replied Nundle. "It's just that…whenever Cero's nearby, I…" He paused, trying to think how to describe it. "You know what it feels like when you think a spider is crawling on the back of your neck? It's like that. And to be clear: I don't like spiders." He shuddered.

Broedi eyed him, a slight smile on his face. "You are letting your worries best you." Nodding at Kenders, he added, "I believe you are more nervous than she is."

Nundle and Kenders protested in near unison. "I am not nervous!"

Broedi turned his gaze straight ahead while softly chuckling. "I apologize, then. I was mistaken. Now, please, no more talking. I must listen."

Kenders and Nundle complied and the trio moved through the trees in silence. As he had been doing for three days now, Nundle stole more than a few sidelong glances at Kenders. He could not decide what astonished him more, that he was riding beside the most powerful mage in all of Terrene, or that she did not understand just how talented she was.

Broedi had shared with him that Kenders was capable of touching each type of Strand that the White Lion knew: Life, Soul, Will, Air, Water, and Fire. From the night in the fort, Nundle knew she was also capable of touching Void. Taking into account what she had done with Stone by the farmhouse, and her initial summoning of lighting using Charge, it reasoned that Kenders could touch all nine types of Strands. Aside from what he had read about Eliza Kap, he had never heard of such a thing.

Nundle's gaze drifted to Broedi and his wonderment deepened. A half-dozen years ago, he had had been sitting in his trading office with his partner Bom, going over ledgers and discussing shipping routes. Now, he was with Thonda's champion and the Progeny of Indrida's prophecy. This was madness.

"Do not panic," rumbled the hillman, his voice soft. "But we are about to be stopped."

Nundle's head snapped up. He scanned the trees and grass, but did not see anyone.

"Halt!"

The shout startled him, his mount, and Kenders' horse, apparently, as the mare tossed her head and nickered. Broedi reached out and grabbed the bridles of both beasts, and in a low, quiet voice, said, "Remember. Say *nothing*."

Nundle nodded in silence. He was happy to let Broedi do the talking.

Three longlegs dressed in blue and gold stepped from behind tree trunks, not more than a couple dozen paces ahead. Nundle was surprised at how similar their uniforms were to the Red Sentinels' livery. Where the Sentinels had black, the Arms had a deep blue, the same for red versus gold. The biggest differences were the duchy crest and the helmet. The Southern Arms' crest was a white embroidered arm grasping a sword on a golden shield. And instead of the silver, domed helm of the Sentinels, these men wore golden, cylindrical helmets with a flat top. It looked as if they wore metallic ale mugs upside down on their heads.

The middle longleg ambled closer, his right hand on the hilt of his still-sheathed sword. He had a bushy golden beard and deep blue eyes, absurdly matching his uniform. The two Southern Arms flanking him followed a few steps behind, one with his sword drawn while the other held a crossbow at the ready. They both sported beards as well; one was a solid black, the other brown that flashed red when he stepped into the sunlight.

Twenty dozen paces from Nundle's group, the soldiers stopped and stared. After a moment, the one with the golden beard cocked an eyebrow and spoke.

"Were I a betting man, I would have lost a tall stack of ducats just now. You three are most definitely *not* what I expected."

"And were I a betting man," rumbled Broedi. "I would be rich now as I was expecting to be stopped by Southlands' soldiers."

The longleg—Nundle dubbed him "Goldbeard"—removed his hand from his sword hilt and crossed his arms. "Did you now?" He ran his gaze over each of them again, slowly and with purpose. "We saw you with the Sentinels." He looked to Broedi alone. "Or rather, we saw *you* with the Sentinels. Mind telling me why there's an entire company of them this blasted deep into the Southlands?"

Broedi offered the longleg a friendly smile before rumbling, "Not at all."

The agreeable answer seemed to take Goldbeard by surprise. After a momentary pause, he nodded. "Go on, then."

"I will happily share the details with you—" Broedi glanced at the other two soldiers "—with all of you, but first, I must speak with your captain." His smile turned apologetic. "I am sorry, but those are my orders."

"Orders?" Goldenbeard's eyes narrowed. "Whose orders?"

Broedi shook his head. "I am not permitted to share that with anyone but the captain."

Goldbeard eyed Kenders, a frown on his face, then shifted his gaze to Nundle. Wilting a bit under the longleg's rather intense scrutiny, Nundle tried to hold back the nervous smile that crept over his face but failed.

Looking back to Broedi, Goldbeard asked, "So, to be clear, your orders are to speak with the captain?"

"That is correct," rumbled Broedi.

"Well, that will be rather difficult to do as we have none with us. *Lieutenant* Madric is in charge."

Nundle winced. The soldier had called their first bluff.

Broedi remained unfazed, though. "The captain is not here?" A pensive frown spread over his lips. "That is unexpected." As he went quiet for a moment, Goldbeard shot Nundle an even more suspicious stare than the last. Nundle managed to halt a worried grin this time, but only because he focused on trying to swallow the lump that had suddenly appeared in his throat.

After letting out a sigh of resignation, Broedi said, "I suppose the lieutenant will have to suffice then. Why your captain did not see fit to come himself is not my problem. I expect Duchess Aleece shall have words with his superiors." Waving a hand to the east, he said, "Lead on, please. We are wasting time."

Goldbeard lifted a hand. "Hold a moment. What's this about the duchess?"

Broedi pressed his lips together and sighed. "I did not mean for that to come out."

Goldbeard ran his gaze over the three of them again. "You're saying you're here on the duchess' orders? Duchess Aleece herself?"

Nundle could understand the man's disbelief. The claim that the Southlands' sovereign would associate with the three of them was tougher to chew and swallow than last week's bread.

After a brief pause, Broedi rumbled, "She did. Now, please, take us to the lieutenant."

Goldbeard seemed as if he was about to challenge them further, but instead shrugged his shoulders. "We'll just let Madric sort this all out. Follow me." He turned and began walking east. The two flanking soldiers stepped aside, letting Nundle's trio pass, and then fell in behind.

As they headed east through the wilderness, Nundle eyed Kenders a few times, praying that the lone, rushed lesson he had given her would be enough should things go poorly. Kenders caught him staring at one point and gave him what was clearly a forced smile. She was unmistakably and undeniably nervous. Nundle sighed and faced forward. So was he.

After an uncomfortably quiet journey, Goldbeard led them into a clearing filled with Southern Arms and their horses. The mounts were picketed but still had saddles on their backs, ready to ride at a moment's notice. On the far side of the group was a lone tent, standing beneath the sprawling boughs of a mature oak.

Upon noting that every longleg here sported a beard, Nundle gave a slow, wondering shake of his head. The thought of having one's face covered with fur was horrid. One evening, he had inquired about its apparent itchiness to Nathan, but the sergeant said it was not a bother. A few moments later, Nundle caught him scratching his face.

Goldbeard glanced back and held a hand up for them to halt. "Wait here." He strode toward the tent, leaving them alone in the middle of the camp, surrounded on all sides by ogling soldiers.

A look at Kenders revealed the girl glancing about, her gaze quickly shifting from one soldier's face to another. Broedi, on the other hand, was the picture of serenity, wearing a calm and relaxed expression. It was as if he stood alone in the clearing, enjoying the peaceful tranquility offered by the wilderness.

Goldbeard reached the tent and entered. A moment later, a skinny longleg pushed his way through the crowd with Goldbeard in tow. He wore the same uniform as the rest, but had a white cloth mantle draped over his right shoulder. His hawkish nose, thinning brown hair, and sharp, darting eyes all contributed to the man resembling a common river crane.

He stopped before them and stared, his face a mask of bewilderment. In a chirping voice that farcically matched his bird-like appearance, he demanded, "Who in the Nine Hells are you and why are you here?!"

Tactfully ignoring the soldier's rudeness, Broedi rumbled, "Good days ahead to you, sir. Lieutenant Madric, is it?"

"Forget the pleasantries," snapped the solider, his gaze dancing over Nundle and Kenders. "All I want is answers."

A frown spread over Broedi's face, accompanied by a quiet sigh. "As you desire, sir. I am here on behalf of Duchess Aleece and Duke Everett to oversee the commencement of the exercise. The Sentinels are ready to begin if you are."

"Exercise?" The lieutenant's face scrunched up in confusion. "What exercise? What are you talking about?"

Nundle felt the golden crackling of Will and watched Broedi weave the Strands together into a familiar pattern. Nundle spared a glance at Kenders to ensure she was paying close attention. This was only the second time she had seen it.

Once the Weave was complete, Broedi directed it over the lieutenant. Once it had melted into the soldier's body, Broedi spoke. "The exercise between the Arms and the Sentinels, Lieutenant. That is why you are here, is it not?"

Nundle could see the longleg struggling against Broedi's suggestion, but the soldier still nodded. "Of course. That is why we're here."

A low murmur started among nearby soldiers and rippled outward. Goldbeard, standing behind the lieutenant with a very surprised expression on his face, leaned toward his officer. "Sir? What is he—what are *you* talking about?"

Lieutenant Madric's eyes went blank and he began to stutter. "Well, the joint exercise that is to be…there is a…"

Nundle frowned; the lieutenant could not possibly answer Goldbeard's question without some guidance. Thankfully, Broedi provided it.

"Lieutenant Madric must be at a loss for words now that the time is at hand. It is certainly understandable. It is a great honor to have been chosen by the duchess."

By now, a steady thrum of confusion coursed through the assembled Arms. Nundle eyed the soldiers, the frown on his face deepening. These longlegs carried themselves differently than Nathan's soldiers. They looked to be of a rougher cut and not nearly as respectable.

A longleg on Nundle's left shouted, "What's he talking about, Lieutenant?"

Broedi took a step toward Lieutenant Madric. "Perhaps I should explain things? You should go to your command tent and begin preparations."

The officer's face was drawn taut, tiny muscles twitched along his eyes and jawline as he fought against the Weave. Nundle had seen this often enough to know the soldier was close to pushing aside the suggestion. Not wanting that to happen, Nundle quickly whipped together a second Weave of Will, directed it over the longleg, and spoke.

"It sounds like an excellent idea to me, Lieutenant. Head to your tent and we'll explain everything to your soldiers." His Weave and his words earned him a sharp glare from Broedi, one he pretended not to see it.

Any resistance within the lieutenant melted away. Nodding slowly and speaking in a hollow, distracted voice, he said, "Yes, please explain to the men about the exercise. I...will be in my tent." With that, he turned and strode across the clearing. His men parted to let him pass while staring at him with befuddled expressions. Nundle breathed a tiny sigh of relief.

Even before the lieutenant disappeared into his tent, Goldbeard turned back to the trio, took a step forward, and demanded, "What in the Nine Hells is going on? What exercise are you talking about? Nobody ever said anything about any blasted exercise!"

Using a calm and patient tone, Broedi explained, "Duchess Aleece gave explicit orders that nothing be said to the rank until your command was approached by a special envoy. We are that envoy. I will be happy to report to her that the lieutenant followed her orders so well. He seems an excellent officer."

A derisive snort burst from Goldbeard. "He's an idiot, a pompous fool who only got this command because he is some coastal nobleman's brat."

The open disdain displayed for the lieutenant surprised Nundle. He had become accustomed to the way the Sentinels venerated Nathan. From the grumbling emanating from the bulk of the soldiers, it was apparent the low opinion of the lieutenant was widely held. Nundle frowned, his nervousness increasing threefold in an instant.

The confident smirk on Goldbeard's face slipped some as Broedi drew himself up to his full height and squared his shoulders, seemingly growing a foot taller and wider. In his deep, thudding baritone, the hillman said, "It is unwise to speak about your superior officer in such a manner."

Goldbeard huffed and stood as tall as he could. "Madric knows how things work. We pretend to listen to what he says, but we run ourselves."

"This is disappointing," said Broedi. "I am sorry to say that I will need to include this in my report to the duchess. Regardless, we will proceed with the exercise."

The grumbling amongst the soldiers grew louder. They did not believe the show.

The hope had been to explain the false exercise to the Arms, have their leader endorse it, and everyone would be on their way by late afternoon. Nundle could see that was not going to happen now, which meant they would soon need to rely on their secondary plan.

He shot a quick glance at Kenders. Her eyes were round, her back straight as a wagon pole, and she repeatedly wound and unwound her horse's reins around her hands. Nundle shook his head. This had not been a good idea.

His best guess was that he could hold sway over twenty, perhaps as many as twenty-five of the soldiers at once. Broedi admitted that his limit was something similar. Unfortunately, over a hundred upset soldiers surrounded them now.

Goldbeard stepped forward, pointed an accusing finger up at Broedi, and shouted, "Who are you truly? You expect us to believe that Duchess Aleece sent you?" Spittle flew from his mouth, catching on his thick, gold beard as he sneered, "A hillman, a tomble, and a *girl?!*"

The longleg's very valid point was the same one Nundle had asked earlier, before they had left the safety of the Red Sentinels, as well as a half-dozen times more along the way.

Broedi stood still, his face a mask of calm. "Are you questioning our—?"

"I'll bet you're *mages!*" spat Goldbeard. "You did something to Madric, didn't you?!"

Nundle's eyes widened a fraction. This soldier was as insightful as he was belligerent.

As the Arms began to shout obscenities, crowding ever closer to the trio, Broedi hung his head and, with resignation in his voice, rumbled, "Nundle? Uora? Now, please."

As fast as he could, Nundle began to pull together Strands of Will, quickly stringing them together. Considering the soldiers' currently riled state, he erred on the side of caution and made each Weave a powerful one. He felt and, after glancing over, saw Broedi also working with the honey-gold Strands. Alarm flashed through him, however, when he noticed that Kenders had yet to begin.

He had ten completed, golden patterns ready to use before Kenders started her first. Her initial attempt fizzled and fell apart, the golden Strands fading away in an instant. She tried again and nearly had the design complete but, at the last moment, twisted two of the Strands in the wrong direction. While it was a valid Weave of Will, it was one that would trick the target into thinking he or she was covered with hundreds of tiny bugs. As it would not do to have half the Southern Arms lying on the ground and scratching themselves, Nundle reached out and pulled Kenders' incorrect pattern apart.

Glaring at a stunned Kenders, Nundle hissed through gritted teeth. "Focus! You can do this!"

Visibly frustrated, she shot back, "No, I can't!"

"Try!"

"I don't know what I'm doing!"

Broedi ignored them both, distracted by both his task and trying to look as intimidating as possible to stave off the angry Southern Arms.

Nundle heard the sounds of metal sliding against leather as swords were drawn. There was no time for Kenders to do this the correct way.

"Forget the weaving!" exclaimed Nundle. "Just do what you did at the fort!"

She shook her head, clearly reticent, and glanced at Broedi. "But I—"

"The result!" shouted Nundle. "Focus on the result!"

Shouts of alarm pierced the air. Some of the Arms had spotted the Sentinels approaching through the trees. Nundle spun around in their saddles and stared westward. If these soldiers were not subdued shortly, bad things would happen.

"Now, Kenders! We don't have time!"

The hesitation on her face fled, replaced by firm determination. With a quick nod, she turned around and took a deep breath. A moment later, an impossible surge of gold swelled around the clearing. Nundle nearly lost control of his own completed Weaves, gasping in wonder as thousands of dancing, gold strings popped into existence around him. Nundle had never seen so many Strands of Will in one place.

Close to eighty Weaves of Will had appeared in an instant, each of them perfect. Looking back to Kenders, he found that she was still sitting upright in the saddle, drawing breath and conscious. He sighed with relief, "Oh, thank the gods..."

Broedi tilted his head back, eyed the Weaves, and then glared at Kenders. Wearing a deep frown, he ordered, "Now." His voice was firm, calm, and entirely out of place in midst of the raucous crowd.

Broedi directed his Weaves of Will first, placing them on the soldiers nearest him. He then began crafting the second pattern needed for their secondary plan to work, a simple one of shining white Air.

Nundle waited to see where Broedi's Weaves went, then guided his to another set of longlegs. Once he had chosen his targets, he turned to Kenders. "Your turn."

Her face taut with concentration, Kenders sent sixty, perfect Weaves of Will descending on every remaining Southern Arms soldier in sight. She wisely held the extra in reserve—hovering over the unaware soldiers' head—should any of the Arms resist.

Once every soldier in the area had been wrapped with his personal Weave, Broedi spoke, his voice reverberating through the clearing thanks to his Weave of Air. "All of you need to calm down and be *quiet*." Anyone within a few hundred paces would hear Broedi as if he were standing beside them. Preceptors at the Strand Academies had often used the pattern when giving a lecture to a large body of acolytes.

At once, nearly every soldier went silent. The handful who continued to mutter and mumble were those under Nundle or Broedi's control. Every single

Southern Arm on whom Kenders had placed a Weave stood still as a statue, relaxed and at peace.

Calling over the thudding of the approaching Sentinels' horses, Broedi said, "Those of you with swords out, please sheath them." Without protest, the Arms slid their naked blades back into their scabbards. "In a few moments, Red Sentinels will be arriving. When they do, *you* will do nothing."

Left waiting for the Sentinels to show, Nundle turned his attention to Kenders. She appeared woozy, but at least she was awake. "Are you all right?"

She gave a lazy nod and muttered, "Tired..." She sounded exhausted.

"Try to hold on until he tells them everything they need to do."

She nodded again, silent this time. Her eyelids drooped low. It would not have surprised Nundle if she tumbled from the saddle and was asleep before she hit the ground.

Sentinels atop their horses began to emerge from the trees. Nundle swiveled in his saddle to watch, curious. He, Broedi, and Kenders had left before Nathan had received all of the new arrivals' decisions and he was eager to know how many had elected to stay. He tried to count the unfamiliar faces as the red and black clad soldiers filed into the clearing, but with everyone moving about, it was impossible to keep an accurate tally of new soldiers versus old. After realizing he had counted the same blonde longleg three times, he gave up.

Spotting Nikalys and Jak riding alongside Nathan—Nikalys with Helene in his lap, and Jak with Sabine behind him—Nundle lifted a hand and waved. The Isaac brothers rode straight for Kenders, one moving to either side of her. Nathan pulled up on Nundle's left, frowning as he surveyed the blank stares of the Southern Arms. "So I take it the first plan did not go well?"

Nundle huffed, "You could say that."

Nikalys eyed Kenders, his brow furrowed with worry. "You look a little ill, sis."

"I'm fine. Although, I'd like a nap."

Jak reached out and grabbed Kenders' hand. Sabine stretched over to pat her back, murmuring congratulations. She gave them both a weary smile.

Nikalys turned his concerned stare onto Nundle. "I'm getting tired of having to ask this, but is she going to be all right?"

"Give her that nap and, yes, she'll be fine." Nundle eyed the exhausted girl and sighed. They had been lucky. Knowing that the window for heavy suggestion was closing quickly, Nundle looked over to Nathan. "Are you ready? We should get this going."

The sergeant nodded and asked with a hint of unease, "How exactly will this work again?"

"Simple. Broedi tells them to listen to whatever you say, and you tell them exactly what they need to hear."

"And they'll do whatever I tell them?" The disbelief in his voice and eyes was clear. Even though he had once been subjected to the same Weave of Will, the sergeant remained dubious this would work.

"Within reason, yes," replied Nundle. "For instance, you cannot order them to cut off a hand. There has to be the rational possibility they might do what you ask on their own. Simply explain that what we want them to do is part of a soldier exercise, and they will most likely do it."

Nathan glanced over, his eyebrows raised. "Most likely?"

"There's always a chance some might resist." He tilted his head back and looked at the remaining twenty Weaves of Will overhead. "But Kenders can help if that happens."

Nathan, along with the others stared into the air.

"More…Weaves are up there?" asked Sabine.

Nundle nodded. "Quite a few." Dropping his stare, he said, "We should start, Nathan."

"Let's try this, then," sighed the soldier. "I'm ready whenever, Broedi."

The White Lion began to speak at once. "Master Sergeant Trell of the Red Sentinels is here to explain the details of the exercise. Listen to him carefully and trust that he speaks with the direct authority of your sovereign, Duchess Aleece."

Without consulting anyone, Nundle crafted a quick Weave to duplicate the sound projection effect Broedi was using and directed it to Nathan just as the soldier began to shout.

"Soldiers of the—" He quickly cut off as everyone in the clearing covered his or her ears, wincing. His raised voice plus Nundle's Weave meant he had effectively yelled straight into everybody's ears.

Looking over, Nundle said, "You needn't shout, Nathan. Just talking will…do…" He trailed off, wilting under Nathan's glare. "Sorry."

A quieter, no less firm voice of the sergeant filled the clearing a moment later.

"Soldiers of the Southlands, you are here today at the behest of your sovereign to participate in an exercise designed to help ascertain the effectiveness of our respective armies in rooting out spies. We Sentinels are to continue into the Southlands, while you gentlemen are to march into the Great Lakes. Consider it a competition of sorts. The group that remains undiscovered the longest can claim their fellow soldiers are the more vigilant ones."

One of the Southern Arms shouted, "And how exactly is that supposed to work, Sergeant?" The longleg pointed to his blue and gold uniform. "We'll stick out like an apple in a mushroom barrel."

"That's true, solider," agreed Nathan. "Very true, in fact." He paused and smiled. "Of course, that's only if you *look* like an apple…"

A few of the sharper longlegs in the crowd began to nod. One called, "You want us to switch uniforms?"

"Those are our orders," said Nathan with conviction.

After a few additional, innocuous questions, the Southern Arms soldiers seemed to accept the story. A pleasantly surprised Nathan ordered his Sentinels forward, instructing Corporal Holb to organize the uniform exchange. The corporal began matching Southern Arms with Red Sentinels, trying to get men of the same height and build paired together. Once a match was made, the two would strip off their tabards and breeches and trade them. Anything red and black was given to the Southern Arms while anything blue and gold was handed over to the Sentinel soldier.

Within minutes, the clearing was full of half-naked longlegs, chattering and exchanging clothes.

Nundle glanced over to find Kenders covering her eyes with her hand, her cheeks a deep, rosy red. Sabine was doing the same thing on the back of Jak's horse while simultaneously trying to get Nikalys' attention, pointing to Helene sitting in his lap. "Nikalys! Could you please?"

The little girl was watching all of the activity with a confused look on her face. "Nik-lys, why are all the soldiers taking their clothes off?"

Nikalys quickly covered her eyes. "Uh, it's a hot day, dear. They're going to go for a swim."

Nathan dismounted, found a man that looked like he would be about the right size, and began to disrobe. Nundle noted with amusement the lack of insignias on the Southern Arms' uniform.

After taking a moment to glance around the chaotic scene, Nundle asked, "How many of the second group came along?"

"All of them," answered Jak.

Nundle lifted an eyebrow. "Truly?"

Jak nodded. "Even the other Tracker came."

While Nundle frowned at that, he supposed it was a good thing that nobody was running off to report them.

Pointing at the crowd of soldiers, Nikalys asked, "How long before the suggestion wears off?"

"A few days for some," rumbled Broedi. "Which is all we need." He stared at Kenders with narrowed, curious eyes. "Although, those who are under your Weave, uora, might march all the way to Redstone and kneel at the Sovereign's Chair if we told them." Broedi's tone was an even mix of respect and reprimand. "You *must* learn how to control your power."

"I know," mumbled Kenders through a yawn.

"Do you?" replied Broedi. "Any capable Will mage within a day's ride would have felt what you did. Again, I remind you, and *others*—" Nundle received another sharp look from Broedi "—that using your gift as you did exposes us. Do *not* do that again! Am I clear?"

As Kenders nodded in silence, Nundle dropped his eyes, only a little bit sorry for his role in what had happened. Had Kenders not done what she had, blood would have been spilt today.

A few moments of quiet passed as the assembled group shifted in their saddles, suddenly uneasy. Thankfully, Sergeant Trell brought a halt to the awkwardness by walking up fully dressed in the blue and gold uniform of a Southern Arms footman.

Holding out his arms, he asked, "What do you think?"

Nundle was grateful for the change in topic. "The colors suit you."

"It feels unnatural," said the soldier. He pulled and tugged at his sleeves. "And a bit snug."

"I think you look fine," replied Nikalys with a lopsided grin. "Footman Trell."

Glancing at his new uniforms' shoulders, Nathan frowned. "Fitting, I suppose. With the recent decisions I've made, I've more or less forfeited my rank." Looking up, he gave the group a slight smile. "Good thing I'm doing the right thing or that might bother me more."

As Nundle had been eyeing the two groups of soldiers, he noticed a problem. "Nathan?"

"Yes?"

"Well, while you look every bit a Southlander, many of your soldiers don't. Their faces are too bare."

Nathan glanced around the crowd. "That's an excellent point."

"And the new 'Sentinels' look a little odd with their beards," added Jak. "Perhaps one last order for them before we send them on their way?"

Nathan smiled and said, "I wonder how many of my men can even grow a beard." He strode away and began talking with both sets of longlegs, having the original Sentinels hand over their straight razors to the Arms.

The entire exchange was drawing to conclusion when Nundle happened to look upon the lone tent in the clearing. Catching Broedi's attention, he pointed to the tent before sliding from his horse. The pair then walked to the tent to see what the Southern Arms lieutenant was doing.

Broedi reached the tent first, opened the flap, and stuck his head inside. A half a heartbeat later, he withdrew it, stood tall, and looked down to Nundle, an amused glint in his eyes. "I believe the lieutenant could use a little more guidance."

When Nundle arched an eyebrow, Broedi stepped aside. "See for yourself."

Nundle moved to the tent, grasped the canvas, and lifted back a flap. Sunlight poured into the darkened interior, fully illuminating the lanky form of a nearly naked Lieutenant Madric. The man stood in his underbreeches only, holding his uniform in outstretched arms. "I am ready for the exercise to begin."

Nundle blinked twice, stepped back, and let the flap fall shut. Peering up at Broedi, he said, "Sorry. Not my size." The hillman chuckled softly as Nundle strode away, heading back to his horse.

CHAPTER 58: MESSENGER

Horses' hooves clopped and cracked on the bridge's hard limestone, the irregular staccato impossible to ignore after weeks of muted thuds on dirt and grass. The children rode far ahead of Cero, near the front of the column with Sergeant Trell, the White Lion, and the tomble. He was at the rear and more than content to be here. It was easier to suppress the dangerous thoughts when the children were further away.

Cero lifted his chin from his chest and gazed ahead at the girl's harvest-straw locks. In an instant, the dark, confusing urges returned, surging through him. Quicker than ever, his hand shot to his hip where it found nothing but an empty sheathe. In an earlier moment of clarity, he had packed the knife itself at the bottom of his saddlebags.

Grabbing his thigh, he dug his fingers into the meat of his leg, and muttered, "Gods, I'm going mad."

He turned his head to his right and stared at the brilliant sunset, wishing Mu's orb would burn this terrible compulsion out of him. The sun had almost reached the horizon, a heavy globule of red and orange hovering above distant treetops. Long, ribbon-thin clouds lined the sky, their pink and red streaks marking the day's passing. The muddy Erona River snaked from the west, swelling to fill the nearby landscape.

As Cero eyed the river, the icy darkness inside him swelled again. If he leapt from the bridge right now, he could simply sink below the water's surface. Drowning, after all, was just as effective as a knife to his throat.

Shoving the coldness away, Cero shook his head and glared at the mane of his horse, hissing, "Hells!" The suicidal thoughts came with greater frequency now. Everywhere he looked, he saw ways to end his life.

Latius' voice pierced his study of the coarse hair draping from his horse's neck. "Are you all right?"

Afraid to look up and see something else that might prompt another intrusive thought. Cero kept his eyes down. "I'm fine." He could feel Latius peering at him. Staring hard. Watching him. Unable to take the scrutiny, he finally looked to his left and snapped, "What?!"

Latius held his gaze for a long moment before turning to stare straight ahead. "Nothing."

Cero dropped his chin to his chest and shut his eyes, focusing solely on the sound of the horses' hooves racking against the bridge, hoping Latius had the good sense to keep quiet. He did not. The Tracker spoke up only a few horse strides later.

"I've noticed you're a bit on edge, Cero. Did something happen with the—" he dropped his voice to a whisper "—lawbreakers before I showed up? Did they do something to you?"

Cero reopened his eyes but did not look up. "What do you mean, 'Did they do something to me?'"

"You remember what—" again with the lowered whisper "—Fenidar said, right? They are *not* to be trusted!"

Cero rolled his eyes and shook his head. "You know what, Latius? I don't much care what Fenidar said. He lied to us. And he's a blasted mage himself." He finally looked over to his fellow Tracker. "I don't know why you won't accept that."

"Because it's a lie, Cero. A lie spread by—"

"Stop," interrupted Cero with a firm shake of his head. "Just stop that. It's not and you know it."

Latius went quiet and, after a moment, stared straight ahead. "Whether he is or isn't does not change the fact that the regent put him in charge and ordered us to track down the lawbreakers. Now that we have, our responsibility is to see to it that these dangerous—"

Cero jabbed a finger in the direction of the group at the head of the column, quietly growling, "They are *not* dangerous!"

Latius' eyes narrowed and his scowl deepened. "Do *not* start with that again."

When the two Trackers had reunited, Cero had tried to convince his fellow Tracker that more was going on than they had been led to believe. Latius had refused to listen. He was of the opinion they should return and report on their findings at once.

In a firm, quiet voice, Cero insisted, "You know what? Believe whatever you want, Latius. And if you don't mind, I'll do the same."

"You're considering going with them, aren't you?" asked Latius. "All the way south?"

Word had spread of their ultimate destination, even if the reason for it being so had not.

Cero cast a sidelong glance at Latius. "I don't know. Perhaps. It's just..." He trailed off, conflicted. Instinct told him the children were worthy of his help, yet the darkness pulled at him. "How do you not see what this is, Latius? That's a blasted White Lion walking up there!"

"Even more reason to go back now and report," muttered Latius. "Imagine if we were to catch one of the White Lions, to *truly* catch one? We'd be heroes, Cero!"

Irked by the man's single-minded focus, Cero hissed, "Have you not heard a blasted word I've said since we met up? The story you know about the Lions is a lie! *They* were the heroes!"

Unrestrained rage flashed over Latius' face, his eyes flaring hot, his lips curling into a wicked sneer. "Our orders were simple and clear: find them, discover where they're going, and report! Well, we've found them, we know where they're going. Now I intend to go report!"

Cero was taken aback by the fury behind Latius' words. The Tracker had always been a meek soul.

Through clenched teeth, Latius growled, "And I am leaving *tonight*."

"Tonight? Why so soon?"

"Soon?" huffed Latius. "I've already wasted the entire day. And you've wasted four! What in the Nine Hells are you waiting for? You saw what they did to the Southern Arms! Think what these mages could do with an entire army in their thrall! So, yes, tonight I'm leaving and heading north. Either come with me or be an outlaw like the rest of them. It's your choice, *Tracker*."

The sound of horses' hooves abruptly softened. Cero looked up to see that they had reached the southern shore and were back on dirt road again.

The soldiers were already fanning out west along the banks of the Erona. A few near the head of the column were dismounting in preparation to make camp. The group was heading through Fernsford tomorrow, and Sergeant Trell had announced his intention to start before dawn in order to arrive while markets were still open. Supplies were running low, and the company needed to restock.

Latius leaned over and murmured, "I'm leaving after both moons are up. You had better be with me." With a snap of his reins, he directed his horse off the road and headed towards the camp.

Cero pulled his horse up, stopping at the end of the bridge, and looked over the company below. He sighed, looked back over his shoulder, and stared at the water rushing under the bridge. It was not too late to go back and toss himself into the river. Shutting his eyes, he willed the dark urge to go away.

Torn between wanting to help and wanting to end his life, Cero was a tortured soul.

* * *

The soldiers' nighttime campfires dotted the riverbank, peeking through the trunks and branches of the trees, spilling light onto the rippling river. Cero stood alone, leaning against the bridge's stone wall, watching the few Sentinels still awake move about the camp. He had been here for some time now and had yet to see any sign of Latius. He was beginning to worry that the man had sneaked away before Cero began his wait.

After the two Trackers had separated earlier, Cero spent a long time sitting on the outskirts of camp, thinking about what he wanted to do. He never even unpacked his tent. Soldiers stared at him oddly as he sat, head in hands, alone on the slope leading from the bridge to the bank. Cero ignored them all.

When he had come to the bridge, he still had not known what his plans were, so he staked his horse on the eastern side of the southern bank, out of sight of the soldiers' camp. If he did leave, he did not want the Sentinels to see him, although he was not sure how he would get across the bridge without the horse's hooves making a racket.

Perhaps they would let him leave. The tomble mage certainly would be happy to see him go. Cero would be equally glad to be away from Nundle. The tomble's words, shouted at him when he had sat beneath the diseased tree, had unnerved him, pulling back the cloth on a secret Cero had kept covered for years.

As a boy, he had lived a good and simple life in a small Northlands village. Cero had spent countless afternoons in his father's smithy, watching the man work. At age eleven, his father took him as his official apprentice, licensed through the local guild in Tymnasis.

No longer a son visiting his father in the workshop, Cero suddenly had duties and responsibilities. He tried hard, doing whatever his father asked, and enjoyed the work without complaint. Yet for reasons he could not name at the time, he found himself drawn to the forge's glowing fire and the sparks kicked up by grinding wheel as metal grated against stone. At times, he was derelict in his duties, standing motionless in the middle of the smoky shop, staring at the forge's pulsing orange embers or the wheel's dancing sparks. His father had taken his interest to mean that he was eager to try his hand with the tools and asked Cero if he would like to work the grinding wheel.

It had proven to be a disastrous mistake.

His father showed him how to press the edge of the metal to grind away the rough spots but Cero was unable to concentrate on the lesson, infinitely more interested in the sparks jumping from the sickle they were making. Frustrated by Cero's inattention, his father berated his son in stern yet fair manner. Cero's temper flared in response and, somehow, he willed the grinding-wheel sparks together, forming one giant bolt that lashed out at his father.

His father flew back, crashed into a table, and collapsed to the ground, smoke curling up from the charred wound in the center of his chest. For the rest of the afternoon, Cero sat next to his father's dead body, crying, not understanding what had happened.

Two Trackers came the next day and took him away. He never saw his mother or sisters again.

The Constables transported him to an isolated stone building just east of Ravensport in the Long Coast Duchy and threw him into a dark and dank cell. For days on end, he lay in the cell, crying, listening to the waves crashing on the rocky breakers outside his tiny window.

Time passed and Cero grew used to his prison. Most memories of those first few years were blurry and indistinct. It was not until later he learned why that was so.

One day, a man dressed as a Gray Cloak had visited him. He asked Cero questions about what he had done, how much he knew about magic, and how he felt about it. Cero apparently answered the questions satisfactorily as the Gray Cloak had him removed from his cell and began training him to be a Tracker.

The Institute of Constables had dozens of imprisoned mages, all sufficiently subdued with relaxing herbs as Cero himself had been. On demand, they would perform small feats of magic, and Cero and the other Trackers in training would watch and learn what the forbidden craft felt and looked like. Cero learned to sense whenever a mage used fire, sparks, air, or attempted to bend a person's will. In addition, he and the other Trackers were taught the ways of the woods and wilderness, molding them to become the perfect hunters of a very specific prey.

By the time Cero was assigned to the office in Smithshill, he had come to accept everything the Constables had told him: magic was wrong, mages were dangerous, and the Constables were necessary to keep order in the duchies.

Now, as he stood, slouching against the Fernsford Bridge, Cero shook his head in disgust, scoffing at everything he had swallowed. "Lies…all of it…" Mages could be great heroes. These young people proved it. They were not dangerous or wicked. They were the opposite, in fact, destined to stop a true evil from hurting the world.

Right then, at that very moment, Cero decided that he needed to help them no matter the consequences. A heartbeat later, the strongest surge of chilled darkness yet rushed through him.

He tried hard to fight it, but instead found himself slowly climbing the bridge's waist-high wall. Simply jump into the water, sink, and his struggle would be over. He could be free of everything and stop worrying about any of this. The part of him that felt "real" warred with the coldness, struggling for self-preservation, but it was overmatched.

Soon, he was standing atop the wall, illuminated by the bright light of the two moons. Nighttime's warm breeze blew past him, ruffling his black locks. He could feel the edge of the limestone wall through his boots as his toes slipped over the edge. The water rushing below called to him, beckoning him to jump.

Suddenly, an explosion of clear-headed resolve burst inside and beat down the darkness. He quickly scooted back from the edge and slid off the wall, collapsing onto the cobbled path of the bridge. He gripped the wall, digging his nails into the stone. He shut his eyes, blocking out everything, and took a few deep, ragged breaths. After a few moments, the sensation passed. He pressed his forehead on the cool stone. He felt like weeping.

"It's getting worse…"

Perhaps the White Lion could help him. Or the girl, Kenders. Or even Nundle, despite how rude Cero had been to him. First, though, he had to address the issue of Latius. If Cero was going to help the Progeny, the first thing he had to do was stop his fellow Tracker from leaving.

He lifted his head, turned to walk to the bridge's southern end, and stopped after taking a single step.

Latius stood several paces away, alone, staring at him with a grim smile that shined bright in the moonlight. His gray Constables' cloak draped from his shoulders to graze the bridge's limestone deck, the nighttime breeze playing with the cloth. They eyed one another quietly for a few moments before Latius spoke.

"You, too, then?"

Pretending nothing was amiss, Cero asked, "What do you mean?"

Visibly irritated, Latius shook his head. "You know what I mean, Cero. The urges? A longing to end it all?"

Cero glared at his partner, but said nothing.

Latius tilted his head, studying Cero with sharp, critical eyes. "I'm not afraid to admit it. Why are you?"

"I don't know what you're talking about." Cero suspected he did not sound very convincing.

"It's like a cold, icy fire burning inside of you, isn't it?"

Cero shook his head slowly. "I don't know—"

"End the show!" hissed Latius, his face twisting into a sneer. "It started the moment you found them, didn't it?"

Cero stared at the other Tracker but kept silent, afraid another surge would accompany an acknowledgement.

Latius took a single, measured step closer. "The only thing that eases it for me is the thought to return to Fenidar and share what I've found."

A rush of irritation burst inside Cero. "Hells, Latius! That's not even his blasted name!" He shook his head. "Besides, how could you report to him? We don't even know where he is."

A humorless chuckle burst from Latius. "Don't we?"

Cero's eyes narrowed. "It's been almost two weeks since we've seen him. How could we possibly know…where…?" He trailed off and turned his head to stare northwest. The saeljul was in that direction. Far away, but in that direction. Something was calling to Cero, begging him to return.

"Ah…so you *do* feel it, then?" The words seeped from Latius like Fallsbottom mud oozing from under a pressed boot heel. "Whatever *that* is, Cero, I plan on following it. I want the urges to—no, I *need* the urges to stop." Latius took another step closer. "Honestly, I don't know how you've resisted this long."

"Where's your horse?" asked Cero. "Are you planning to walk there?"

"I made the mistake of setting up camp with the soldiers." He tapped his left temple with his hand. "I was not thinking straight, you see." As he dropped his arm, Cero noted his other—the right—was hidden behind his back. "And once I set the tent, well, I couldn't just pack all of my gear right in front of them. Much too suspicious. They're keeping a close eye on me, Cero." He was only dozen paces away now. "*You*, however, never made camp." A strange, unsettling smile spread over his face. "Tell me, Cero. Where's *your* horse?"

Cero's gaze danced between Latius' twisted grin and the man's hidden right arm. "What's behind your back, Latius?"

Latius began to chuckle quietly. The soft laughter was strange, almost ghoulish, and absent any true mirth. "I'm going to do you a favor tonight, Cero. You might want to thank me."

The cold, dark urge returned and, for a moment, Cero was tempted to ask Latius to slice his neck or bash in his skull. He let out a feral growl and slapped the side of his head as though he could physically smack the thought out. Latius' maniacal laughter grew louder.

Successfully shoving the sensation away, Cero stared at Latius. It seemed obvious the man's intentions were not good. Unfortunately, Cero had no weapon with which to defend himself. His beltknife was still stowed away in his saddlebags on his horse. Wondering if he should call for help, his gaze shot to the soldier's camp.

"Think your new friends will help you?" jeered Latius. Moonlight and madness danced in his eyes. "You're a disgrace to the Constables, Cero. I used to look up to you, but now I see how weak you are." He continued his slow advance.

Cero held his hands up and began to back away. "Latius. Hold and think what you're doing. This isn't you."

"Keep your twisted tongue to yourself, mage-lover!" With a growling sneer, Latius lunged toward Cero, pulling his hand from behind his back to reveal a long beltknife that flashed in the moonlight. "I will not succumb to your lies!"

He charged, holding the blade low at his side, preparing to thrust it into Cero's gut. As he stabbed, Cero leaped backwards, barely avoiding the knife's tip. Latius immediately drew the weapon upwards and to his left, slashing at Cero's face. Again, Cero hopped out of the way, but he heard the breathy whistle of the blade as it cut the air before his nose. He scrambled backward as Latius came at him again, the long dagger held low and in the same position as the first attack.

Cero tensed, gambling that the man would repeat his assault. Combat training for Trackers was rudimentary. Latius and Cero most likely knew the same few basic attacks.

Latius stabbed again, missed, and raised the blade for a sweeping cut to the face. Before he could unleash the attack, Cero ducked low and charged Latius, barreling into the other Tracker.

Cero felt the man's knife slice across his back, catching on his shoulder blade and sinking deep into his flesh. A searing pain shot though him as he tackled Latius to the ground, driving his left shoulder into the man's stomach. A grunt of pain and whoosh of air exploded from Latius as they collapsed in a heap. Cero heard the beltknife rattling on the stones of the bridge, free of Latius' grip.

Cero pushed himself up and began to scramble away, looking around for the knife. The open wound across his right shoulder blade burned. A hot wetness flowed freely down his back. For a moment, the urge to lie there and bleed to death filled his soul.

Loosing a primal, furious scream, he shoved the thought from his head and scanned the bridge for the knife. The blade lay only a few feet away, wet with his blood. He clambered toward it on hands and knees, the handle of which was almost in reach when he felt Latius clamp down on his right ankle and pull him back. Lashing out with his left foot, Cero drove his boot heel into Latius' face. Something cracked and Latius screamed, releasing the hold on Cero's ankle.

Lying on his stomach, Cero crawled the final few paces to reach the knife. With a shout of triumph, he grasped the dagger's hilt with his right hand.

As he flipped over, his eyes went round. Latius had stood and was already leaping toward him. Cero held the dagger upright with two hands and Latius landed on him, the blade sinking deep into the Tracker's chest, bouncing off bone as it slipped into his body. The pommel nut dug into Cero's stomach.

Latius' eyes opened impossibly wide as a small gasp of air rushed from his lips. His breath smelled of onions. A moment later, wet, thick blood poured over Cero's hands and chest. Not knowing what else to do, he hung on tight to the handle.

Latius coughed, splattering blood onto Cero's face. For some reason, that bothered Cero more than the fact that he had just plunged a dagger into another man's body. Cero shoved hard, pushing Latius off and to his left. He slid back a few feet, gaping at what he had done. "Gods…"

Latius lay in the middle of the bridge with legs outstretched, coughing up plumes of dark blood. The man's own beltknife was buried to the hilt in his chest, the somehow-bloodless white stone at the end of the handle shining bright in the moonlight.

His head falling to the side, Latius gazed at Cero. The man's expression was even more grotesque now, a twisted, evil visage swirling with pain and anguish. He stared at Cero with mad, maniacal eyes and whispered through blood-frothed lips, "Thank you."

Cero suddenly had the feeling that he had been used. Latius had admitted to the same urges as Cero. Perhaps he had simply wanted Cero to do what he could not do himself.

As life slowly drained from Latius' eyes, his expression shifted. Fear replaced the crazed manic look in his eyes as they opened wide and locked on Cero's face. In a voice filled with pure terror, he whispered, "Oh, gods, Cero…I'm so sorry. I didn't…mean…to…" His lips stopped moving, his face went slack, and his head lolled to the side.

Cero stared at the dead man, wondering how he was going to explain this to the sergeant and the others. His gaze shifted to the beltknife sticking from Latius' chest.

The darkness swelled inside of him.

He started scooting toward Latius' body, intending to retrieve the knife and plunge it into his own chest, when an unearthly, bloodcurdling screech filled the night. Realizing the shriek was emanating from the corpse, Cero scrambled backwards, smacking into the bridge's wall. He cried out in pain as the collision sent a jolt of pain along his wounded back.

The nightmarish screech grew louder by the moment, until the howl grated against his soul, digging into his ears and scraping the inside of his head. He clasped his hands over his ears in a vain attempt to block out the cry. With rounded eyes, he watched an opaque, black smoke rise from the wound in the center of Latius' chest. Curling up into the air—slowly at first but increasingly faster—the murky mist gathered rather than dissipate, clumping together above Latius' body.

The screeching was unbearable. Cero thought his head was going to burst. He shut his eyes, praying to all the gods for the sound to stop.

Sensing the colors gold and white, his eyes popped open.

Magic. This had something to do with magic.

He watched the smoke coalesce into the vague shape of a tall, thin man, only with too-skinny legs and arms. After a few more excruciating moments, the screeching ceased and the black mist stopped streaming from Latius' body.

The dark figure hovered above the bridge and reached for the sky, stretching its unnatural limbs as though it had awakened from an eternal slumber. Cero's hands fell from his ears and he gaped. The entire creature was nothing more than shifting smoke yet solid enough that it blocked out the stars in the sky, a black silhouette against a night sky, soaking in moonlight, devouring it.

The pitch-black entity swiveled its head side-to-side as though it were searching for something. Little wisps of nothingness flared around its edges as it moved. At one point, its gaze turned toward him, and Cero gasped. Its face was devoid of features save for two, softly glowing silver eyes devoid of irises or pupils.

Suddenly, the creature's head turned sharply to the northwest. Letting out another piercing shriek, it took two loping steps and leapt over Cero and the side of the bridge.

Lightheaded and weak, Cero twisted around and started pulling himself up. It was an effort, however. The cut on his back was deep and he had lost—was losing—a lot of blood. Yet he managed to stand and look to the river below, expecting to see rippling waves where the thing had plummeted into the river.

There was nothing. The surface was smooth.

Another short screech shattered the quiet night, emanating from the Erona's northern bank. It took him a moment to spot it, but he did. The shadow was racing through the grasses on the other side at an incredible rate.

"Bless the gods…"

As the shade dashed into the woods, Cero's legs gave out. Slumping down to the ground, he fell to his stomach, grateful he was not on his throbbing back.

Screams and shouts ricocheted through the night. Lifting his head, he spotted a giant hill lynx running toward him, its yellow eyes bright with reflected moonlight. Others ran behind the massive cat, one of whom carried a glowing sword. Weary and exhausted, Cero dropped his head to cold limestone. The moment he did, he heard the voice of the boy, Nikalys, immediately to his left.

"Nine Hells…"

Summoning some strength, Cero rolled over a bit to find Nikalys standing between him and Latius' body. The young man's sword shimmered white in the moonlight.

Nikalys glared at Cero and demanded, "What happened here?"

"He attacked me," mumbled Cero. "We struggled, he cut me, I got the knife, and Latius fell on it. I was only defending myself—" He stopped as the enormous lynx reached the bloody scene. The cat paused only long enough to sniff Latius' body before sprinting away, a blur of golden brown fur running north.

The boy stepped closer to Cero. "What was that thing that jumped from the bridge?"

"I don't know," whispered Cero. "It came from inside Latius."

Nikalys kneeled beside Cero, his face twisted up in confusion. "It *what*?"

Too tired to keep his head up, Cero let it fall to the limestone. With the right side of his face pressed against the ground, he continued, "He died, and that...*thing* came from inside of him."

Nikalys glared at him, clearly dubious. Not having the strength to plead with the boy, Cero simply closed his eyes and listened to the sound of feet pounding on the bridge draw closer.

"What in the Nine Hells happened here?!"

Cero recognized the voice as belonging to Sergeant Trell.

Nikalys quickly conveyed what Cero had told him, ending it with a judgmental, "I'm not sure I believe him."

Someone else kneeled beside Cero. He felt a gentle pressure on his left shoulder, pulling aside his bloody cloak. A young woman gasped. "And I'm sure he just sliced open his back on his own, then?"

It was the boy's sister, Kenders—the mage.

Sergeant Trell ordered, "Cero, I need you to roll over."

"His wound is too bad for that," protested Kenders. "We should help him first."

"It's all right, dear. We only need a moment." Cero recognized Nundle's high-pitched voice. "I think I know what Nathan is looking for."

Kenders leaned down to him and asked gently, "Can you roll over? Please? Then we'll tend to your wound. I promise." The kindness in her voice was unexpected.

Cero grunted an acknowledgement and tried to turn over, but failed. He was getting weaker by the moment.

After a second, unsuccessful attempt, Kenders said, "Here, Nik, help me."

Together, the pair started to roll him over. As soon as he was fully on his right side, Sergeant Trell said, "That's good enough. I believe him. Lay him back down."

"You believe him?" asked Nikalys, still sounding suspicious. "Why?"

"His hands and shirt are soaked with blood, not splattered. The only way that happens is if Latius truly did bleed out while lying on top of him."

Nundle said, "He could have pulled him down on top of him after stabbing him."

"Does that sound likely to you?" asked the sergeant.

"I suppose not." Nundle paused a moment before adding. "Cero could have attacked him first."

Seeing a chance that he might be absolved of any wrongdoing, Cero forced out, "That's Latius' knife sticking in him. Mine's in my saddlebags. Go and check my horse—he's on the southeastern bank." He tried to nod toward the south end of the bridge, but the small motion set his back aflame.

Sergeant Trell said, "Let him lie back down, please."

As Kenders and Nikalys helped return him to his stomach, the sergeant called out for Cero's horse to be brought forward. Soon, Cero heard horse's hooves coming up the bridge. The horse stopped, and after sounds of someone rummaging through what he assumed were his saddlebags, he heard a grunt of satisfaction.

"Here's his knife," said Sergeant Trell. "He's telling the truth." Cero would have liked to look up to see everyone's reaction, but he was too tired. "Now, help him, Nundle. That cut is deep."

Quick and light footsteps approached and the tomble kneeled beside him.

"Perhaps I should try?" asked Kenders.

"No," said Nundle. "Broedi would toss me in the river if I let you."

"But this is only one man, not nine. I can do it the right way. I've watched you work on Zecus."

"No," replied Nundle firmly. "Getting a Weave of Life correct takes patience and an incredible amount of practice."

At this point, Cero did not much care much who attempted save his life.

Kenders muttered bitterly, "Fine."

In a professorial manner, Nundle said, "Now watch as I use only a bit of Life to first weave a small pattern that will staunch the bleeding. After that, I'll use another one where the goal is to aid him, but let...his..." The tomble trailed off, then asked in bewilderment, "What is that?"

Cero felt a flicker of gold and white dance within him.

"Ah!" exclaimed Nundle at same moment a loud gasp rushed from Kenders.

Sergeant Trell and Nikalys asked simultaneously, "What happened?"

Cero wondered the same thing, but did not have the energy to ask.

Nundle's voice was full of confusion as he answered. "I...I directed the Weave on the wound and...and ..."

Kenders took over, muttering, "I swear something inside of him reached out and unraveled it. The Weave was there one moment and falling apart the next. It was like—" She cut off suddenly.

Cero was wondering why when he caught what sounded like an animal breathing accompanied by the soft brush of fur on stone. Moments later, Broedi's voice rumbled, "That is because a very powerful Weave inside his soul does not want him to live. And if we do not remove it from him before he dies, another Soulwraith will be unleashed."

The White Lion's words shocked Cero, but all he could manage was a quiet moan. The thought that he would turn into same type of black fiend that had climbed from Latius terrified him.

"A what?" asked Nundle.

"Soulwraith," rumbled Broedi as he moved closer. "During the Demonic War, Norasim's army used them to gather information, sending his followers into our midst. Once the host learned whatever it was sent to discover, they would slit their own throat and release the wraith to rush back to its master." The White Lion knelt beside Cero. "Nundle, describe for me—exactly—the pattern you saw Jhaell use on the Trackers. What Strands were used?"

Cero tried to remember if the saeljul had subjected him to magic, but could not. He supposed that if one were under a magical compulsion to commit suicide, it would probably be best if the person were unaware.

"Will, Void, and Air," answered Nundle. "I think there was a fourth, though. There were large holes in the pattern I saw."

"Soul," rumbled Broedi. "It is a *very* twisted use of the Strands." His tone revealed obvious distaste. "I suspect the moment they found us, they wanted to end their life and return to Jhaell."

Kenders muttered, "That's awful…"

"How did Cero fight it?" asked Nundle.

"I do not know," answered Broedi. "Perhaps his own will is strong, perhaps—" He stopped short. "We can talk of this later. Right now, we must remove the Weave. Uora, I need your help."

Without a moment's hesitation, she asked, "What do I do?"

"Remember how I told you to not rely on your gift?" rumbled Broedi "To only Weave the correct way?"

"Yes?"

"For now, forget I ever said it. *Will* the Weave inside this man to come apart."

"Are you sure?"

"I am."

Unconsciousness was not far away for Cero. The edges of his vision were getting fuzzy, which he found odd considering his eyes were shut. He tried to plead for someone to do something, but all that came out was a weak croak.

"*Now*, uora. He is dying."

Moments later, it felt as if a thousand, tiny bubbles erupted inside his body, starting in his chest and radiating out to his arms, legs, fingers, and toes. The sensation reminded him of when he knew someone was doing magic, yet it somehow felt backwards. When the fizzing reached his head, it paused a moment, trying to hold on, refusing to let go. Cero pushed against it, forcing whatever it was out of him. He refused to become one of those wraiths.

Finally, like a stick bent too far, something cracked.

In an instant, Cero felt light and free. Smiling, he succumbed to the blackness that called him.

*   *   *

Dashing across the nighttime plain, What-Had-Been-Latius ran with impossible speed, its "feet" barely touching the ground. As the shade whisked along the prairie, the plains grass fell to the sides, crumbling and withering. Not a single ray of moonlight reflected off the figure. It swallowed every beam of light that touched it.

Thoughts flitted through what had once been a consciousness, a jumbled mixture of agonizing horror and fear, paired with a single-minded purpose to reach its creator. The soul of Latius would push up to the surface at times in a desperate attempt to escape. He wanted to begin his journey to Maeana's hall. However, the Weave suppressed the soul, feeding off it.

Every time he tried to burst free, the wraith unleashed a terror-filled screech that carried over the flat plains. Wildlife bolted, running in fear until collapsing from exhaustion.

What-Had-Been-Latius sprinted ever faster. It had a message it must deliver.

CHAPTER 59: FERNSFORD

7ᵗʰ of the Turn of Thonda

Kenders stared straight ahead, along the column of soldiers. At three-quarters of the way back in the line, she had a difficult time seeing the head of the column. Yet she judged it must have nearly reached the four city guards she had spotted when coming down the hill now behind them. Reaching up to brush a few loose strands of hair behind her ear, she sighed and prayed things would go smoothly.

A lack of basic supplies had forced the company to move into Fernsford rather than around it. Sergeant Trell had offered to take the soldiers through the city and meet the rest of them on the other side. Remarkably, Broedi had said no, they would all move through the city together. Kenders and her brothers had been surprised. Broedi had avoided Lakeborough. They expected the same here.

She turned to her left, eyed Nikalys, and murmured, "What if this doesn't work?"

Nikalys glanced over. "It will." He sounded less confident than she would have liked.

On the other side of Nikalys, Jak leaned forward, his saddle leather creaking, and said, "Be ready if it doesn't, though. We might need you to do to the whole city what you did to the Southern Arms."

"Are you mad? I can't do that to a whole…" She trailed off as a smile spread over both her brothers' faces. "You are a lout, Jak." As the pair exchanged a quick look and a quiet chuckle, she glared Jak and asked, "Perhaps you'd like to walk through the city naked? One Weave of Will should be safe enough, I'd think."

Jak looked back to her. Seeing the humorless expression on her face, his smile quickly faded. "You wouldn't."

"Wouldn't I?"

On her right, Broedi rumbled, "That would be unwise, uora." He strode beside her, holding Smoke's halter as he walked.

"Please, Broedi?"

The hillman turned to meet her gaze, the look in his eye one of disappointment and quiet bewilderment. Before leaving this morning, he ordered both her and Nundle to forget they knew anything about magic until he told them otherwise. Jak had been elsewhere at the time.

"Just one Weave?" she begged. "I promise to keep it small." She gave him a quick wink, not serious in the slightest. She knew better.

After a moment, Broedi faced forward and nodded. "Just the one."

Jak leaned forward in his saddle to peer around Kenders. "You must be jesting!"

The hillman shifted his gaze to Jak, a slight smile spreading over his lips. "Yes, uori. I am."

Jak let out a sigh of relief and sat back in his saddle. "Not funny."

Kenders took a moment to enjoy her brother's momentary unease then looked back to Broedi. "I would like to point out that you once told me you don't mock."

Broedi shook his head. "I do not."

"Then what was that?"

"*That* was jesting," said Broedi with a slight grin. "There is a difference."

Chuckling, Kenders gaze drifted forward. They had ridden up a slight rise and she could now see the head of the column drawing even with the guards. Her mirth fell away as her earlier worries came rushing back. "Broedi, is this safe?"

"No. Yet it is what we must do." He turned to eye her. "And as long as you look less guilty than you do now, we should be fine." He looked to Nikalys and Jak. "The same goes for you two." Twisting around, he stared to where Nundle and Sabine—with Helene in her lap—rode behind the trio of Isaacs. "You as well."

To a man, woman, child, and tomble, they all nodded.

Facing forward, Broedi rumbled, "Now, please remain quiet. I want to hear how it is going with the guards."

Kenders stared ahead and watched the exchange as well. Sergeant Trell was to the far left, still wearing the uniform of a footman. In the center, the soldier she knew only as Blainwood wore the uniform of a Southern Arms' sergeant, appearing to be in command of the company. No one had taken the uniform of the lieutenant, figuring it would draw too much scrutiny. The final member of the front trio was Cero, sitting stiffly in his saddle as his back was bound tight with rags beneath his Constable grays. He was well enough to travel, but would need a few more Weaves of Life. The knife wound had been deep.

The man had been quite surprised when they shook him awake this morning by the river. He believed he had perished on the Fernsford Bridge. She, her brothers, Broedi, Nundle, and Sergeant Trell all sat with him as he repeatedly apologized for his behavior, professing his desire to help and swearing he would do whatever he could to prove himself. Sergeant Trell announced his immediate belief in the man and Broedi liked the idea of having another person able to sense magic. Nundle and Nikalys had their reservations, but they lost the short debate as she and Jak cast their lot with Cero.

They struck camp and headed for Fernsford, their pace quick. Without knowing how far away Jhaell Myrr was, it was impossible to determine exactly when the Soulwraith would reach the saeljul. Everyone expected that once it did, Jhaell would follow, using the same manner to travel to the region that had brought Zecus to the Southlands.

Kenders shuddered and looked over her shoulder to the northern horizon. Only twenty of the soldiers were behind them, lining the dirt road that ran up the hill before disappearing into the forest. For all she knew, the saeljul could be just over that rise.

As she stared back, her gaze fell on Zecus. The Borderlander had volunteered to ride with the rear guard this morning, anxious to help in any manner he could. She thought it very brave of him. He caught her eye, nodded his head, and smiled. Her cheeks and neck feeling suddenly warm, she smiled back and started to turn around when her gaze met Sabine's. Something in her friend's eyes made her stop.

A coy smile on her lips, Sabine asked, "What were you looking at?"

The flush in Kenders' cheeks deepened. "The road."

Sabine lifted an eyebrow. "Anything else?"

"*No*," stressed Kenders, glaring at her friend. "Just the road."

Broedi rumbled, "The two of you must have a different understanding of 'quiet' than I do."

Kenders twisted around quickly. "Sorry, Broedi."

Broedi said nothing in response, his gaze on the guards. As Sabine muttered a quiet apology as well, Kenders shot one last terse look toward her friend. Sabine winked back. Nundle, riding on his small chestnut horse beside her, was grinning, too.

Feeling her brothers' smiling eyes on her, she turned to them and raised her eyebrows, daring them to say something. After a moment, the pair faced forward, amused grins affixed to their faces. With a huff, Kenders joined them in staring at Fernsford.

'Sergeant' Blainwood was speaking with the guards now. Using a story Broedi fed the man last night, he was to explain that they were a company of Arms from Prince's Port on their way to Fargrove, a city on the western coast of the Southlands. Kenders and the rest of the non-soldiers were travelers on their way to Fargrove as well, and were moving with the soldiers simply for safety's sake.

Assuming the guards accepted the story, the group would move into the city at which point the soldiers and Nundle would head to the marketplace while everyone else was to find a quiet tavern and wait—out of sight—until the soldiers had replenished their supplies. There had been a brief moment of consternation last night regarding how the company was to pay for their purchases when Nundle had jumped up and run to his saddlebags. He returned with a sack of gold, stunning everyone, and offered to pay for everything.

Thankfully, the city guards did not appear overly interested in the column and waved them past without much pause. As Kenders' group drew near the guards, Broedi glanced at them all and said, "Smile, please."

Kenders forced a tiny grin on her face as they passed the guards, and even managed a polite, "Good days ahead."

One of the men smiled wide at her and rejoined, "And good memories behind, miss." The wink accompanying the greeting earned the man a hard look from her brothers.

The guards eyed Nundle and Broedi a moment longer than the rest of them, but let the odd pair pass without a verbal challenge. Kenders thought that if this truly were part of a joint infiltration exercise between the two duchies, the Southlands would be failing miserably.

Once past the guards, Kenders relaxed and studied the city ahead, still a half-mile down the road. The buildings were much different from the tiny homes of Yellow Mud or the flat-topped structures in Smithshill. Houses and shops had sharp-angled roofs, some rising into peaks while others had but a single slope on one side. Every building was at least two stories tall—with some reaching as many as five floors—and seemed to be constructed almost entirely of wood. In most cases, the first floor was a few feet smaller all around than those above it, giving the appearance that the houses were carefully balanced, poised to fall over. The wood and plaster walls were a mix of creamy whites or tans, crisscrossed with wide beams of black wood.

The place was certainly foreign, but overall, Kenders liked it much better than Fallsbottom. The fact that she was not dripping wet had a lot to do with that.

Curious what the Moiléne sisters thought of their first city, Kenders swiveled in her saddle and looked back. Helene's grip on her sister's forearms was tight and her eyes wide. Sabine's lips were parted as she stared. Kenders wondered if that was how she had looked when she had first seen Smithshill.

Before they moved into the city proper, Nikalys and Jak fell back to ride on opposite sides of Sabine, leaving Kenders alone with Broedi. Nikalys would occasionally lean over and whisper to Helene, trying to get the little girl to smile and relax and, after a while, it began to work. Soon, both sisters had settled down and even seemed to be enjoying the strangeness of the city.

The people of Fernsford were friendly, nodding and wishing them all 'Good days ahead' as the column rode past. Besides the preponderance of bearded men and a slight difference in fashion, the Southlanders were refreshingly similar to Great Lakes citizens. Broedi and Nundle continued to draw more than a few long stares.

Heading for the market district, the company passed through a section of the city where the style of architecture was slightly different, the buildings taller, wider on average, and appeared to have less wear.

Upon noticing the differences, Kenders felt a flicker of excitement. Staring at Broedi, she asked, "There was a fire here, wasn't there?"

The hillman glanced at her and, with a hint of surprise in his voice, said, "Yes, there was. A couple decades ago. How did you know?"

Peering around her, she said, "Our parents said they met here, but left after a great fire." She quickly clarified, "And I do not mean Aryn and Eliza."

Broedi offered a kind smile. "I know, uora." He, too, studied the buildings. "It is interesting they were here during the fire. Gamin was here as well."

"Gamin?" asked Kenders, looking back to the hillman.

"The current head of the...ah, instructors at the enclave." Kenders knew he meant mages. "He and his brother, Sevan, grew up here. Sons of a baker, I believe."

"Will Gamin be one of my teachers?"

The hillman nodded. "He will. Although not your first." A smile touched his lips. "I have someone else in mind for that."

"Who?"

"I believe I will keep that secret, uora."

With a frown and a sigh, Kenders asked, "Why?"

His grin spread wider than normal. "Some surprises are worth the wait."

She shook her head, mildly frustrated, and turned her attention back to the city streets, trying to imagine a young Thaddeus and Marie walking them. After a few moments, she mused, "I wonder where the truth ends and the playman's tale begins..."

Broedi looked over. "What do you mean?"

"So much of my history, my family's history was a lie."

"Take comfort knowing that at least some of it is true."

Kenders sighed. "The lies outnumber the truths."

"So?" rumbled the hillman. "Lies themselves are not inherently wrong, uora. A lie told for the right reason is often better than the truth told for the wrong. Your parents loved you. *All* of them. *That* is what is important, not a marking of lies and truths."

Overcome by a sudden burst of melancholy, she looked back to her brothers, both of whom were looking around at the bustling city, pointing out things to one another and the Moiléne sisters. A few heartbeats passed before she faced forward. Neither she nor Broedi spoke another word until they reached the open-air market.

After everyone had tied their horses to one of the numerous hitching posts flanking the long rows of vendor stalls, the soldiers gathered in a group with Nundle. The former merchant and the soul with the coin was to go with the Sentinels through the market. As they were assembling, Kenders asked the tomble to purchase a new cord to bind her hair. Her last one had snapped weeks ago and she was tired of having hair in her face.

While Sergeant Trell talked with the soldiers, discussing what they were to look for and purchase, Broedi turned to the remaining group. "Come with me."

The Isaacs, Moilénes, and Zecus followed the hillman through a maze of several streets, passing all sorts of tradesmen and odd shops. Broedi turned from the congested ways, led them down a deserted side alley, and stopped beneath a wide sign hanging low over the street. Tilting her head back, Kenders saw the faded painting of a man dressed in green robes, sitting on a stool and resting his arm on the back of a deer.

"Go inside and order something to eat if you like," ordered Broedi. "Talk to no one but the tavernkeep. Do you understand?"

Kenders shared a worried look with her brothers as Sabine voiced the question they were all thinking. "You aren't coming in with us?"

"I am not."

"Why?" asked Nikalys.

"Because I am not."

"That's not an answer, Broedi," said Jak.

"It might not be the one you want, but it is an answer."

A frown rested on Nikalys face as he muttered, "Ever the secret-keeper, aren't you?"

"I will keep secrets as long as I have reasons to do so, uori."

"When will you be back?" asked Kenders worriedly.

"Soon," rumbled Broedi. "I promise."

Zecus stepped forward, offered a slight bow, and politely asked, "Do you require assistance, great lion?"

"Do not call me that," ordered Broedi. "Especially here." As he glanced up and down the empty alley, Kenders felt a flash of sympathy for the Borderlander. He had simply wanted to help. "And no," continued Broedi, "I do not need help. I *need* you to do as I say." He nodded at the tavern. "Go inside, sit down, and wait until I return."

If Kenders had learned anything in her time with the White Lion, it was that arguing with him was like climbing a tree covered with poison yergold. It was possible, but infinitely more trouble than it was worth.

Jak muttered something about finally getting a good meal, strode to the door, gripped the handle, and pulled. The door rattled but did not open. "Seems they're closed."

"Push, uori."

Jak shoved the door gently and it cracked open, setting off the tinny ring of a small bell. Looking back, he gave a sheepish grin. "My mistake."

Nikalys—carrying Helene in his arms—reached up and smacked Jak lightly on the back of the head. The brothers chuckled as they stepped into the building together with Zecus and Sabine following them through the entryway. Kenders paused at the door and looked back to find the hillman watching them. She did not want Broedi to go.

"You will be fine, uora. I will return shortly."

Nodding slowly, she turned and ducked into the dark interior of the tavern. As she closed the door, she looked out to see Broedi already striding down the alley, back in the direction from where they had come. Sighing, she shut the door and faced the dark room. She blinked a few times as her eyes adjusted to the dimness.

The only wall with windows was the one through which they had entered. A meager amount of sunlight streamed through the glass-covered openings combining with the light of a half-dozen torchlamps lining the back wall. She counted eight rickety tables in the dingy room, only one of which was occupied by a single man, his head resting on arms draped over the tabletop. Save for his loud snoring, the room was quiet until the sound of wood dragging against wood drew her attention to her right.

Everyone had gathered at one of the tables and were in the midst of pulling out chairs to sit down. She headed for one of the empty chairs and, as she arrived, Zecus reached for it and pulled it out for her. Surprised, she paused a moment, stared at the man, and gave him a smile. "Thank you."

He nodded and waited for her to sit before gently sliding the chair forward. Once she was seated, he moved around the table to sit beside Jak, who was to Kenders' immediate left. Nikalys was directly across from her, Sabine to her right. Helene had her own chair—a coup for the child as evidenced by the wide smile she wore—between Nikalys and Sabine.

As everyone settled, Sabine glanced at Kenders and winked, wordlessly commenting on Zecus' act of kindness. Kenders was relieved she had the decency to remain silent. Jak, however, was apparently absent of grace. He leaned close and spoke in a low—but not low enough—voice. "That was nice of Zecus."

She glared at him. "Quiet."

He gave her a teasing smile and whispered, "I would have pulled it out from under you."

Kenders hissed, "And then I would have picked it up and cracked it over your head."

Jak leaned back, chuckling to himself. Kenders stole a quick glance at Zecus, but he seemed unaware of the quick exchange. The Borderlander was running his hand over the tabletop, staring in wonder at the dark-stained wood.

Nikalys leaned forward, elbows on the table, and appeared to be ready to say something when a door that led to a back room creaked open. A bald man with a thick, black beard stuck his head into the room, looked around, and started when he saw them. After pushing the door open completely, he stepped into the room and strode straight to their table. He wore a simple tan tunic, dark cloth breeches, and a greasy stained burlap apron that hung from his neck.

Stopping before the table, he eyed them all—pausing an extra moment on Zecus—before giving them a wide smile. Kenders noted he was missing more teeth than he still had.

"Welcome to the Curate and Black Doe. My name is Manique. Good days ahead to you all."

The man's accent was odd. Kenders thought it sounded as if he had food stuffed in his cheeks.

After the table completed the traditional greeting, Manique asked, "How might I serve you today?"

Jak said, "We'd like something to drink and eat if possible."

"Thirst I can satisfy," said Manique with an agreeable nod. "As for hunger, I'm afraid all I have is morningbread, cheese, and last night's smoked fish. I've nothing fresh yet today. People normally don't come until midafternoon."

Nikalys nodded at the snoring man across the room. "What about him?"

Manique twisted around, glanced at the slumbering fellow, and then looked back to the table. "Vone doesn't count." He winked, adding, "He never leaves."

Helene stood on her chair to peer across the room. "Does he always sleep on the table like that?"

Manique chuckled. "Only when he's not sleeping on the floor, little miss."

Sabine reached over and placed a hand on Helene's back. "Sit down, please. You'll fall."

As the little girl complied with a pouty frown, Jak glanced around the table and said, "Unless anyone objects, I suppose just bring us whatever you have." He reached into the front pocket of his breeches, pulled out the last of the Isaac family's ducats, and placed them on the table. "And the weakest morningmeal wine you have, please."

When no one raised a voice of protest, Manique scooped up the coins and hurried away, disappearing back through the doorway.

The man had not been gone for a half a breath when Nikalys leaned forward and asked, "Now where do you think Broedi's off to?"

Kenders sighed and shook her head. "You might as well ask 'why does the sun shine?'"

"Think he'll tell us when he gets back?" asked Nikalys.

A dry chuckle slipped from Jak. "Does a barncat like the rain?"

Nikalys frowned, crossed his arms over his chest, and leaned back. "I'm getting a bit weary of the secrets."

Zecus' chair squeaked as he leaned forward. "Pardon, but may I speak?"

Nikalys glanced at the Borderlander, one eyebrow cocked. "Are you asking permission to talk?"

"I am."

A deep furrow split Nikalys' brow. "Why?"

Replying as if the answer were obvious, Zecus said, "Because honor requires it, great warrior."

"I told you," said Nikalys with a sigh. "It's 'Nikalys.' Nothing more."

Zecus eyed him for a moment, frowned for some reason, and then said, "You honor me. Thank you. Now, may I speak?"

Nikalys let out an exasperated sigh. "Gods, Zecus, you don't need—"

"It's a Borderlands thing, Nik," interjected Jak. "Just say 'yes.' It'll be easier."

Nikalys looked back to Zecus, sighed again, and nodded once. "Yes, Zecus, you may speak."

"Thank you, gre—" He stopped short as Nikalys eyes narrowed sharply. "Thank you." Looking around the table, he said, "There is something that mystifies me about the—" he lowered his voice "—great lion."

"Only one thing?" asked Jak

The Borderlander smiled. "No. There are many for sure, but one in particular. Why is it that he holds so tightly to his secrets?" Kenders chuckled at the question, which seemed to startle the Borderlander. His eyebrows drew together and he sat a little straighter in his chair. "I am sorry if my question was ignorant."

Kenders leaned forward, shaking her head. "No, you misunderstand. I am not laughing at you or your question. You simply asked something none of us can answer."

Zecus' expression softened. "I see." He gave her a tiny, sweet smile. "Then I apologize for my rush to judgment." Kenders held his gaze for heartbeat or two. His cuts and scrapes were mending nicely, revealing what a pleasant face he had.

"Tell me, Zecus," said Jak. "Have you ever tried squeezing water from a rock?"

Zecus shook his head. "I do not understand."

"It's a saying these three use," sighed Sabine, "to indicate just how difficult it is to get Broedi to share information."

"It is appropriate," said Zecus. He was quiet for a moment, staring at the tabletop, then glanced around the table again. "And no one knows why he is like that?"

Kenders was surprised when Jak actually answered.

"For certain? No. But I can guess." Once everyone's gaze was on him, he said quietly, "You can't be forced to share what you don't know."

"What's that mean?" asked Sabine.

Jak stared across the table. "It's pretty simple. As long as Broedi doesn't tell us certain, important, how-to-stop-the-Cabal things, we can't be forced to tell—"

"Jak," interjected Nikalys, firmly yet quietly. "Not now." He nodded his head in Helene's direction.

They did not speak about a number of things in front of Helene. The fact that someone determined to kill them was likely pursuing them was atop the list. Sabine had confided in Kenders the little girl already had difficulty sleeping. She did not need something else about which to be scared.

Jak looked to the toddler, frowned slightly, and nodded. "Later, then."

There was a moment of heavy quiet in the room, only a moment, before Helene spoke up, startling them all.

"I know someone is chasing us."

They turned as one to stare at the little girl. She was sitting perfectly still in her chair, staring at the tabletop. A heartbeat later, Sabine asked, "What was that, dear?" Her tone was nonchalant on its surface but worry clearly bubbled underneath.

"Someone is chasing us," murmured Helene.

Sabine offered a reassuring smile. "No one is chasing us, dear."

Helene turned suddenly to glare at Sabine, her eyes burning with an intensity that should be foreign to a child. "Yes, someone *is*." She looked around the table, an expression of absolute certitude on her face. "I know it!"

Everyone here had been extremely careful to keep the truth from Helene. Leaning forward, Kenders asked, "Who told you that, Helene?"

The odd intensity faded in an instant as Helene shook her head, mumbling, "No one."

Nikalys reached over and gave her a gentle pat on the back. "Then why do you think someone is following us?"

Helene's gaze returned to the center of the table. She sat in silence for a number of heartbeats, looking tiny in her large, wooden chair. Finally, she muttered, "I don't know." The evasive note in her voice prompted Sabine to press her.

"Truly, Helene. You can tell us."

Helene gave a feeble shrug of her shoulders. "I don't want to."

Jak tried next. "Why don't you—"

Helene's head snapped up. "I don't *want* to!"

Feeling a flicker of orange crackling, Kenders' head looked up just as three Strands of Fire popped into existence. The torchlamps along the back wall flared suddenly, sizzling and hissing. Zecus and Jak turned their heads at the sudden sound.

Eyes widening, Kenders stood from her chair, nearly knocking it over. "It's all right, Helene." Sweeping around Sabine's chair, she dropped to a knee beside the girl and wrapped her arms around the toddler. "You don't have to tell us anything if you don't want to…"

Helene flung her arms around Kenders and squeezed tight. The orange crackling winked from existence like a candle's flame extinguished by a sudden draft. Looking over, Kenders saw the Strands of Fire were gone.

As she consoled the little girl, everyone at the table stared at her, curiosity in their eyes. Looking to Nikalys, she mouthed a single word.

"Magic."

Nikalys stared at her for a moment, appearing confused, then glanced at the back of Helene's head. He arched his eyebrows, asking a silent question. After Kenders nodded, a deep, worried frown spread over his face. Looking around the table, he said quietly, "Let's talk about something else, yes?"

Recognizing Nikalys' cue, Jak leaned forward, resting his arms on the table. "You know, Helene, I saw a baker on the way here and was sure I smelled sweet cakes. I bet Broedi would let us stop on our way back and get one if we ask. What do you think?"

Helene pulled her head from Kenders' embrace and looked at Jak. "What's a sweet cake?"

Jak's eyes widened in mock astonishment. "What's a sweet cake? Oh, my, Helene. You are in for a treat."

As he explained the concept, successfully brightening the little girl's mood, Manique returned with the food and wine. They all picked at the meal and sipped the weak wine. Sabine's worried gaze never left her sister.

Kenders, on the other hand, never stopped watching the door, fervently praying that when it opened, Broedi would be on the other side and not the Constables.

CHAPTER 60: BETRAYAL

9ᵗʰ of the Turn of Thonda

Jhaell roasted in the midday sun, standing in the midst of a confused land. Grassy plains lay to the east, waving in the breeze while the thinning edges of an oak and ash forest stood to the north. Hulking foothills rose on the western horizon, the beginnings of the dry, rolling lands of dead grass and struggling bulboa trees. One day's ride south and the soupy mush that gave the Marshlands its name would hazard any traveler.

Yet all Jhaell could see now was the dirt road beneath his feet as he stared at his feet. His golden-white hair hung in his face, swaying in the easterly breeze. A soft, nearly silent curse slipped from his lips. "Zilrya eilamengil…"

There had been no sign of the Progeny. He had not sensed even a flicker of a Strand that was not his own. None of his contacts had seen or heard anything. Unfortunately, that was the good part of his miserable situation.

Yesterday afternoon he received a message on the parchment whose mate resided with Alpert in Smithshill. He grimaced after reading the first sentence, realizing the author was not the regent, but rather Raela, the god of Deception incarnate. Jhaell immediately shredded the parchment, severing any connection he had with Smithshill, and spent the rest of the day on his horse wondering what he should do.

Later in the evening, he received another note from Raela, this one using the parchment of his contact north of Fernsford. Raela's second message was effusive in its description of what would happen should he not provide an update. Again, he tore up the parchment without responding.

Once in his tent last night, he ported to every location he knew of in the southern duchies, seeking some mention of those he sought. There had been nothing. Nothing at all. Not even a rumor of a rumor.

He had returned before dawn and sat, staring at the canvas wall, trying to figure out what to do next. For two hundred fifty years, he had done everything Tandyr had asked all so that he could hold Syra in his arms again. One impetuous act had ruined everything.

The Southern Arms' sergeant had finally come to his tent mid-morning and asked if they were going to march today or not. Even though he believed it pointless, Jhaell had said yes. Not long after midday, they had stopped where they were now.

"Sir?"

The bubble of introspection around him burst. Jhaell turned to glare at the man who had spoken. "What?"

"We have been standing here for a while now," mumbled the sergeant. "My men are getting nervous." His gaze darted past Jhaell. "I don't think the Reed Men take too kindly to us being here, sir."

Jhaell turned around, looking to where a second set of soldiers and horse stood in the road. Over sixty men stared back, dressed in dark green uniforms trimmed in white. He realized he must have been standing here for some time. Half the men had dismounted and were standing beside their horses. The other half were still in their saddles, their posture stiff and uneasy. All wore anxious expressions on their faces.

Looking back to Sergeant Rowe, Jhaell asked, "Why the discomfort?"

"Unless prior permission is granted by a nobleman, soldiers of one duchy are not allowed to enter another."

"Why not?"

"A provision from centuries ago, sir," said the sergeant, glancing back to the Reed Men. He was clearly on edge. "When dukes did not trust one another."

Eyeing the green and white clad soldiers, Jhaell asked, "Are you saying they have every right to attack you?"

"Under the strictest interpretation of law, yes. But they most likely will not, sir. No blood has been shed between—"

A piercing shriek rang out over the plains, floating on the air for a heartbeat before quickly cutting off. The sergeant's head whipped around. Reed Men and Southern Arms alike swiveled in their saddles or spun on their heels, staring in all directions, searching for the source of the cry. Jhaell joined them, scanning the prairie as a tiny ember of hope flared in his chest.

The unearthly screech came again, piercing the air.

Sweet, wondrous relief burned hot in Jhaell. Fixing the direction of the eerie scream, he turned to the southeast and waited. A smile of joyous anticipation spread over his face.

The eerie screech was getting closer, advancing upon their position at a tremendous speed. Jhaell peered down a small grassy slope filled with brush, searching. Birds hiding in the tall grass fled, leaping into the air and flapping their wings furiously as they headed northeast, away from the shrieking.

Sergeant Rowe, his voice quivering, muttered, "Gods, what is that?"

So grateful that one of the Soulwraiths was returning, Jhaell had forgotten the soldier was standing beside him. Truthfully, he had forgotten about all of the soldiers.

Looking over his shoulder, he found Reed Men and Southern Arms alike pointing and talking, clearly alarmed by the unnatural shrieks. Horses absent riders were trying to run away, their eyes rolled back and white with terror. Those still mounted fought their steeds, trying to calm them.

"Beelvra…"

The situation was tenuous. In short order, a Soulwraith would be here and standing before him, waiting for instructions, at which point, these soldiers would undoubtedly name him mage. Jhaell scowled, angry with himself. As he had done with the acolytes in Yellow Mud, he had left himself but one choice.

Staring at Sergeant Rowe, he knitted a quick Weave of Air and ripped the breath from the man's lungs. The soldier's eyes bulged as he grabbed his throat with both hands and collapsed to his knees, choking in sweet silence. The other soldiers were too involved with the wraith's shrieking to notice what was happening to the sergeant.

Jhaell began to eliminate the men as quickly as he could. Soldiers watched as their fellows fell from saddles and collapsed to the ground. Horses newly free of riders bolted, galloping northwest through the grass and away from the screeching sounds of the Soulwraith.

Soon, men began to call out the obvious. "He's a mage!"

Some reached for their weapons and shouted to attack. Others cried out that they should flee. Jhaell could not let either happen.

Forgoing his attempt to suffocate them all, Jhaell strung together a single, massive Weave and directed it at as many of the men he could manage. The Weave yanked dozens of soldiers from their horses, drawing them together as if a giant rope had encircled them and pulled taut. Men flew from their saddles, screaming out as they slammed together. The weapons that some had drawn inadvertently pierced others.

He captured a fair number of the soldiers in this manner, but at least a dozen men of both groups escaped. He watched them ride west down the road, helpless to do anything about it. Rumors were going to spread. Although, if the shade was returning, that might not matter. Turning his back on the screaming soldiers, he rotated to face the onrushing Soulwraith.

Staring southeast, Jhaell spotted a tall, lithe form rushing through the grass. To Jhaell's eye, it looked like a living construct of Void Strands, meshed together to form a tar-black almost-man hastening toward him, three times as fast as the swiftest horse. Soldiers stopped screaming that he was a mage and began to shout in terror as they spotted the wraith.

When the creature reached him, it stopped with unnatural suddenness. One moment, the wraith had been tearing across the land. The next, it was standing motionless before him.

Jhaell stared, in awe of his creation. This was only the second Soulwraith he had ever seen, but the first he had ever crafted.

He circled the creature, wholly fascinated, marveling at its complexities and contradictions. It looked to be made of moonless-night black smoke, yet solid at the same time. He wanted to reach out and touch it, but the surrounding blades of grass that were curling up and turning black informed him that he should not. Strange, silver eyes shone brightly, the only recognizable features on the shades' black face. Truly, it was remarkable.

After returning to stand before the Soulwraith, he stared up into its silver-orbed eyes. "Who were you?"

A mournful voice screeched from the figure, echoing as if shouted from a deep cavern. "I wasss Latiusss!"

Jhaell frowned. He had been going in the wrong direction. "So they went east, then?"

"Nooo!" howled the voice. "Sssooouth!"

Uncertainty stabbed at Jhaell. He had sent Latius east. Cero had gone south. "Then how did you find them?"

The wraith's tortured voice screeched, "Theeey found uss!"

The last bit of elation Jhaell felt evaporated. "Tell me what you were sent to find."

With a voice that rose and fell, alternating between shrieks and screams, the Soulwraith cried out, "Theee Progeny live! Theee Championn of Thonda guiiides them to Storrrm Islannnd."

Jhaell took a step back, his eyes going round, his mouth falling open. If Thonda's champion was involved, it meant that things were even worse than he had thought. If Raela or Tandyr learned of the White Lion's involvement, Jhaell would never even get a chance to beg for mercy. He would be dead on the spot.

Jhaell needed to end this on his own. Quickly.

He questioned the Soulwraith, drawing forth even more disturbing details. The Progeny were two in number—brother and sister—growing in power and learning how to use their abilities. When the wraith revealed that soldiers of Smithshill had joined with the Progeny, rather than capture them, Jhaell let loose a string of curses in ijulan and Argot both.

"Why would they do that?!"

"Theee tombllle isss rresponssible," screeched the wraith.

Jhaell felt like he was going to get ill. Peering at the Soulwraith with rising dread, he asked, "The tomble's name. What is it?"

The shade replied in a twisted, eerie wheezing. "Nnunndlle."

Gripping his hands into tight fists, Jhaell let forth a powerful shout of anger that rolled across the land. As the yell faded, he dropped his gaze to the road and stared at the ground. The number of coincidences necessary for something like this to happen should be infinite. It was as if fate was conspiring against him. After a few moments, he shook his head.

"No matter…"

The important thing was that he knew where they were headed. Glaring at the wraith, he asked, "When did you die?"

The Soulwraith replied mournfully, "Threeee nightsss ago."

He had no time to waste.

Reaching for Void and Air, he quickly completed the Weave for a port, tearing the world in two. He moved the group of screaming men hanging in the air through dual curtains of reality. Urazûd's oligurts would appreciate the gift of fresh meat.

Turning to the Soulwraith, he said, "You next."

With a pleading cry, the creature howled, "Relleeeasse meee!"

"No," muttered Jhaell. The wraith might come in useful. "Through the port."

The Soulwraith let out one last mournful screech before taking two long strides and leaping through the black slit. Praying that Urazûd was prepared, Jhaell followed, feeling hopeful for the first time in weeks.

Chapter 61: Forest

12ᵗʰ of the Turn of Thonda

Nathan peered down the gently sloping hill and let out a low whistle of wonder.

"Bless the gods…"

A mile ahead, the northern edge of the Blackbark Forest awaited them. Trees two to three times taller than any Nathan had seen in all his years in the Great Lakes Duchy stretched east to west, horizon to horizon. A mottled green and mossy brown canopy topped the massive forest like a thick, heavy blanket. The narrow road upon which their horses stood twisted down the hill, leading into the woods below.

Nathan, Nikalys, Nundle, and Corporal Holb sat on their horses while Broedi stood beside them. The dirt way allowed only the five of them to stand side-by-side. Dense shrubs and thickets of brambles lining the path prevented anyone from stepping off the road.

Sitting on Nathan's right, Nikalys muttered, "It makes the forest by Lake Hawthorne look like…" He trailed off, seemingly searching for an analogy. After an extended pause that prompted his companions, one after another, to look over at him expectantly, he finally continued, "Hells. I don't know. Those trees are big."

Nathan smiled at the boy's honesty and turned his attention back to the scene below.

Standing on Nikalys' other side, Broedi rumbled, "The trees in the forests of the Primal Provinces are even taller, uori."

"I'm not sure I can imagine such a thing," said Nikalys.

"They are rather impressive to behold," replied the hillman. "Some even have great cities built among their branches."

Nikalys, Nathan, and Corporal Holb all leaned forward, saddle leather creaking, to gawk at Broedi.

Nathan let slip a disbelieving, "Truly?"

Nodding, Broedi rumbled, "I would not lie."

"Cities in trees?" asked Nikalys in disbelief. "Who builds cities in trees?"

"Buhanik," answered the hillman, looking over. "You might know them as 'thorn.'"

"Hold a moment," said Corporal Holb. "Thorn are real?"

"As real as you and I, Corporal."

Nathan said, "You're mocking us, aren't you?"

Broedi shook his head slowly, his familiar slight smile gracing his face. "I do not mock, Sergeant."

On the far side of Broedi, a light chortling drifted from Nundle. "I told you it's a big world, Nathan."

The three men sat in their saddles, staring at one another, unsure if they should believe the hillman's claim. Sighing, Nathan added thorn to his list of myths that were anything but.

After a few quiet moments filled only with Nundle's light laughter, Corporal Holb looked to Nathan. "Scouts, then?"

Nathan nodded. "Three. They are to stay within shouting distance."

"Yes, Sergeant."

Corporal Holb pulled on his horse's reins, directing his horse back a few steps in order to turn around and head back to where the company of soldiers waited. Nathan's gaze lingered on the soldier's face for a moment; Amiles looked odd with a beard. All of the men did.

As the soldier trotted away, Nathan faced forward. "I wish he would stop calling me that."

Peering around Broedi, Nundle said, "You'll always be their Master Sergeant, Nathan."

"I've no more rank than you do, Nundle."

"If you would like," said Nikalys, his gaze still fixed on Blackbark Forest, "I can name you a master sergeant in the new army of the White Lions. Or perhaps lieutenant? Captain?"

Nathan shook his head. "I'm no officer."

Nikalys turned to give the sergeant an appraising look. "You know what *your* problem is, Sergeant? You doubt who you are, your place in the world. You lack the *one thing* that will let you be who you need to be, Sergeant Trell. *Confidence.*" He gave Nathan a wink and, after digging his heels into the sides of his horse, began to ride down the hill toward the forest.

Nathan watched the young man ride away for a few moments before turning to eye Broedi and Nundle, both of whom wore an amused smile. "Well, now. *He's* certainly becoming comfortable with himself, isn't he?"

"He reminds me more of his father every day," rumbled Broedi.

Hearing the sound of horses' hooves draw near, Nathan looked over his shoulder and found Blainwood, Hunsfin, and Cero approaching. He nodded to the trio as they rode past, giving the Tracker an extra-long look and a smile. Cero smiled in return.

The man had made a remarkable recovery after that peculiar night on the bridge and had been a different person since, proving himself a worthy addition to their group. His scouting skills rivaled those of Blainwood.

Even Nundle had accepted the man's obvious transformation. He had even reached out to Cero, offering to teach the man some magic, but the former Constable had politely rebuffed the tomble. He said he was happy to lend his services as a Tracker but had no desire to use magic himself.

Once the scouts were past Nikalys, they broke into a canter to put some distance between them and the main group. Hearing another horse approaching from behind, Nathan glanced over just as Jak slid into the vacant slot in the trail. Upon getting his first clear look at the forest, a low whistle—much like Nathan's own from only moments ago—slipped from the young man.

"Bless the gods..."

The repeat performance set Nundle and Broedi to chuckling.

Jak looked over at the pair, his eyebrows drawn together. "What?"

Nundle and Broedi's only response was to smile wider as both began to move down the road.

Shifting his gaze to Nathan, Jak asked again, "What?"

"Don't worry about it, son," said Nathan with a grin. He nodded his head, indicating the slope. "Let's get going before your brother rides off for Storm Island all by himself."

Jak eyed Nathan a moment longer before shrugging his shoulders. He kicked his horse and trotted down the dirt road, giving Broedi and Nundle an odd stare as he passed them, on his way to catch up to Nikalys.

Turning to the group behind him, Nathan found his men patiently waiting, along with Kenders, Sabine, and little Helene perched before her sister on their new horse. He signaled that they were ready to begin again, and the company of blue-and-gold-clad Sentinels moved down the hill.

As they neared the forest, Nathan allowed himself a moment of relief. He was glad to reach the cover of the trees. The past five days had been anxious ones.

Once they had left Fernsford, fully restocked, everyone had kept a close eye on the northern horizon, none more so than Broedi. When Nathan would awake at night—a frequent occurrence since Yellow Mud—he usually found the hillman staring north, smoking his pipe. Sometimes, Nathan would join him and they would both stand there, silent, waiting. Jhaell was coming. Of that, he—and apparently Broedi—had no doubt.

It was not long before the Blackbark Forest fully engulfed their group. The air, already comfortable, cooled considerably once they were free of direct sunlight and marching in the canopy's shade. Tonight's campfires would no longer be just for cooking eveningmeal.

By Nathan's accounting, the calendar was reaching the middle of the Turn of Thonda, which, according to Broedi, was the beginning of harvest in the region. Back home in Smithshill, the season would not come for a few more weeks. Nathan was surprised at how different terrain and climate could be between two places that looked so close on a map.

Chuckling to himself, he mumbled, "It's a big world..."

"Pardon?"

Nathan looked over to find Jak beside him. The young man had taken to riding with him on and off during the day. Nathan welcomed the company. The boy was polite, pleasant, and had a quick wit about him. He possessed an inquisitive mind, as well, often pressing Nathan about Sentinel tactics and sword techniques. Nathan was happy to answer his questions, especially as Jak had shown some early skill with the blade. Both he and Zecus practiced diligently, although Jak was making quicker progress than the Borderlander.

Eyeing Jak, Nathan said, "I was just thinking about how much larger the world seems once you leave home." He paused, reconsidering his choice of words. "Although, I suppose it's not home any longer, is it?"

"No, it isn't," muttered Jak. He gave a sad shake of his head. "Home is gone, Sergeant."

Something in Jak's eye and tone told Nathan that riding in silence for a while would be a good thing. Turning away, he set to scanning the trees and thin underbrush around them.

It was clear how Blackbark Forest had earned its name. There were a handful of different types of trees, but the most prominent by far were the towering behemoths that climbed high overhead. Their trunks were as wide as Nathan's horse was long and wrapped with a dark brown, almost black bark. Ridged and rough, it was the only feature of the trees for the first seventy feet before branches jutted out. The boughs spread wide and far, mingling with its neighbors, the long, green pine needles coating the branches choking off sunlight.

The trail they were following had widened considerably once in the forest, allowing the company to spread out. Some of the men even rode off the road as there was nothing to hinder them other than the occasional lost sapling or fallen log. For the time being, he and Jak were alone.

After keeping quiet for what he deemed an appropriate amount of time, Nathan eyed the young man and decided to broach a subject he had been avoiding for over a week. With a careful, measured, and neutral tone, he said, "You know, Jak, the day after we first met on the Southern Road, my men and I marched west."

Jak's face grew taut but he did not look over. He knew where this was going. "Did you, now?"

"We did," replied Nathan. "And, eventually, we came across Yellow Mud." He waited for Jak to say something, but the young man remained silent, his eyes forward. "I cannot imagine what it was like for you, Jak. To go through what happened there. Or for you or your sister and brother to see it afterward." The trio might not be true siblings, but as they continued to treat and name each other as such, Nathan would do the same.

When Jak still did not respond, Nathan sighed and pressed on. "You know, eighty of these men—" he motioned to the soldiers spread out behind them "—stood with me that day, in Yellow Mud's ruins."

The young man finally looked over, a surprised expression on his face. Perhaps he had never considered that before.

"Greya was cruel to me and my men that day, Jak, forcing us to see what we did."

The bloated corpses strewn about the muddy ruins still haunted Nathan's dreams. More than a few times since Yellow Mud, he had awakened in a cold sweat. Even now, the gruesome visage filled his mind's eye. Forcing his attention back to the living, green forest around him, he looked to Jak and found the young man staring at him through narrowed eyes.

"Why are you bringing this up now?"

"Well," sighed Nathan. "While I cannot possibly understand what you went through, what you lost that day, I want you to know I carry the tragedy with me. I vowed that day to see justice done, and I intend to keep my oath."

Several moments passed before Jak responded. "I'll bet you thought I had something to do with it, didn't you?"

"I won't lie. It crossed my mind."

"I would have suspected me, too," sighed Jak. "It's why I left so blasted fast after meeting you. I needed road between you and me. I knew if you learned what happened, you'd hunt me down."

"You know I tried, don't you?"

The tiniest of smiles cracked Jak's face. "And you failed."

"A good thing, I'd say."

Another long pause dragged out between them. Sensing that Jak was not finished talking, Nathan remained quiet, listening to the birds while he waited. Jak proved him right, nodding in the direction of Nikalys and Kenders. "I'm nothing like them, you know."

"What do you mean by that?"

Jak shrugged. "I'm...ordinary."

Nathan could not hold back a quick burst of laughter, which predictably drew a sharp eye from Jak. Holding the young man's gaze, Nathan said, "Of all the words that describe you, 'ordinary' is not one of them."

"Look at what they can do," protested Jak. "Kenders with her magic and Nik with—"

"Hold a moment, Jak," interrupted Nathan, waving a hand. "How does what they can *do* define who you *are?*"

Lines split Jak's brow. It was obvious the young man had no idea how to answer the question.

Nathan leaned closer, making sure he had Jak's full attention. "Through all of this madness, despite *everything* that's happened, you have stayed by their side. You've been there for them to lean on, just like an eldest brother should be. You've been their one piece of sanity in a world that has gone mad. You're not ordinary, Jak. You're blasted exceptional. Remarkable. Wondrous. Pick whichever word you like."

Jak dropped his head, clearly embarrassed by what Nathan was saying, and muttered, "Sweet words, Sergeant. Sweet words…"

"No. They're *true* words. Look, you might not have a prophecy written about you, or any sort of powers from the gods, but you are *essential* to this endeavor. The fate of the world might rely on Nikalys and Kenders, but your brother and sister rely on *you.* Don't you *ever* forget that."

Jak looked up, stared at him for a long moment, and then turned away to peer into the forest, leaving Nathan to wonder—again—if he might get a response. After a few heartbeats, he faced forward and listened to the rustling murmur of horses kicking up leaves and pine needles. Snippets of quiet conversations amongst the group floated on the air.

After a time, Jak cleared his throat and spoke, his voice thick. "Sergeant?"

Looking over, Nathan found Jak staring at him. The young man's eyes were glistening. "Yes?"

"Broedi mentioned that you and your men buried the bodies."

Nathan said softly, "We did."

Jak gave an almost imperceptible nod and muttered, "Thank you."

"You're welcome, son."

Jak turned away again. This time, the silence between the pair lasted until it was time to make camp.

CHAPTER 62: OLIGURTS

15ᵗʰ of the Turn of Thonda

While the soldiers were finishing the teardown of last night's camp, extinguishing fires and burying waste in the soft, loamy soil, Zecus was already in Simiah's saddle and waiting for the order to begin moving. He had been ready for some time now, having been up since before dawn. Or whatever passed for dawn in this strange place.

Here, the sun did not peek over the eastern horizon in the morning. The overlapping, never-ending screen of tree trunks saw to that. Rather, the gloom-enshrouded woods slowly shifted from pitch-black night to dimly lit day, suggesting that light was sneaking through somewhere, somehow. A thick blanket of mist coated the forest floor at night and remained for a time after daybreak, meandering about the tree trunks and brush, obscuring anything beyond a couple dozen paces.

As he waited, he stared around him, still captivated by the grandness of this place. Three days ago, when they had first entered the forest, Zecus had ridden with his mouth agape long enough that a few soldiers had good-naturedly mocked his wide-eyed expression. The lush grasslands and the trees he had seen to that point were wondrous to him, but the towering monstrosities surrounding him now were alien. That first night, when no one was looking, he had moved to one of the trees and patted the rough bark to ensure it was real.

Travel through the untamed forest had been slow since they had left the road, but Broedi seemed pleased with the progress they were making. When the open road had turned due east, the White Lion had instead taken then group southeast, through the cover of the forest.

Spotting a dark shape moving through the cool morning haze, Zecus watched the hulking yet somehow lithe form of the hillman emerge from the mist and approach. As was proper, Zecus did not offer a greeting. The soul with higher honor should speak first.

Broedi stopped before Simiah and lifted his hand to the horse's nostrils. Simiah ran his nose along the hillman's palm and let out a warm puff of air, gently nuzzling Broedi's hand. Looking up to Zecus, Broedi nodded and rumbled softly, "A pleasurable morning to you, uori."

Giving a small bow from Simiah's saddle, Zecus said, "And to you."
Broedi's knowledge of Borderlands' customs was extensive, and Zecus was
grateful that he went out of his way to use it. It made the strangeness of the
surroundings slightly easier to endure.

"Did you sleep well last evening?" asked Broedi.

Shaking his head, Zecus said, "I did not." When Broedi raised an eyebrow,
he added a short explanation. "Bad dreams."

Sleep had arrived late last evening and teased him throughout the night,
coming and going as it pleased. Strange, fitful dreams about being back in the
Sudashians' camp had plagued him. He had awakened this morning with the
remembered scent of the oligurts' rankness in his nose.

"I am sorry to hear that," rumbled the hillman. Scratching Simiah's white
stripe, he looked up and asked, "Would you like some company, uori? I am
traveling with the rearguard today."

Zecus was surprised. Broedi had been leading their expedition ever since
entering the forest. "Of course. I would be honored to journey with you."

"Good," rumbled Broedi, patting Simiah's neck.

Curious, Zecus asked, "If you are walking with the rearguard, may I ask
who is to choose our path today?"

"I gave instructions to Cero. He will be able to keep us on the correct path."

Whatever strangeness had surrounded the Tracker—Zecus was still not sure
he understood what a Soulwraith was—was gone now. Cero was an accepted
member of the group, and one whom Zecus found to be an agreeable sort.

A soft, fleeting whistle floated through the fog and trees, the signal for the
group to begin moving. Soldiers fell into a loosely grouped column and began to
ride, heading southeast for yet another day. At least Zecus hoped they were
moving southeast. It was a mystery to him how anyone could mark directions
without seeing the sun.

Zecus and Broedi began to move with the rearguard, marching through the
thick, early morning mist. Those at the back of the column were expected to
keep an alert eye and a quiet tongue as they traveled, something Zecus had
welcomed and the reason he had volunteered for the position. While the
Sentinels were friendly and welcoming, he still felt out of place in their presence.
The silence and solitude of the rearguard was nice.

It was difficult to see much more than a couple dozen paces in any
direction, meaning the chances were high that someone might inadvertently
become separated from the group. Zecus made sure to keep the same three
soldiers in sight at all times as they moved through the forest, weaving around
the massive tree trunks.

As they passed a particularly giant specimen of the black-barked trees, he
looked to Broedi. "Great lion, what are—?"

"Uori," rumbled Broedi, cutting him off. "I have asked you several times to stop calling me that. Please. Broedi will suffice."

Zecus shook his head, protesting, "I cannot do that. In my home, people of high honor are never called by their name. It is disrespectful."

"I am aware of how things are done in the Borderlands," said Broedi. "Were you aware that among *my* kind, the way you honor someone is to use his or her full name?"

Zecus frowned, trying to reconcile the conflicting mores. Thinking it might be better to honor the White Lion in his fashion, he asked, "What is your full name?"

Broedi looked over and, wearing a slight smile, said, "Broedikurja Kynsipitka."

Zecus tried to wrap his mind and tongue around the unfamiliar sounds and syllables, but after a few incorrect attempts, he said with some amusement, "I see why people call you Broedi."

"And I would be honored if you would call me that as well. Titles make me uncomfortable. Some of the Lions enjoyed such notoriety. I was not one of them."

"I will do as you ask," said Zecus, "because you ask. However, should we meet another soul from the Borderlands, do not be surprised if I begin calling you 'great lion' again."

"Understood," rumbled the hillman. Zecus swore he almost chuckled. "Now, what were you going to say?"

After taking a moment to recall his question, Zecus said, "These giant trees." He tilted his head back to stare up one of the nearby trunks. "What are they called? I need a name for them."

"You *need* a name for them?"

"Yes, for when I return home and tell my family of this place. I doubt they will believe me unless I provide as many names and details as I can."

Broedi eyed him for a few heartbeats, seemingly on the verge of asking something, but then turned his stare upward at the towering pines. "The people here call them ebonwoods. I have heard others names in the past, but ebonwoods seems most fitting. It a remarkable tree, to be honest. The timber, when treated with a certain resin, hardens to rival tempered steel. Locals carry weapons made of such."

Yesterday, Zecus had spotted a man carrying such a sword in one of the occasional settlements they came across. The homesteads were tiny, no more than a few families living together in homes of stacked logs.

"Why wooden swords?" asked Zecus.

"Iron is rare in the Southlands, expensive enough that only nobility can afford to purchase iron goods. Truth be told, most metals are scarce here."

Over the next couple of miles, the White Lion shared a wealth of information about the area with Zecus: details about the wildlife and flora, a brief lesson on the history of nearby baronies, the geography of the region. Soon, Zecus suspected he knew more about the Southlands than anyone in their group besides Broedi.

The hillman was in the middle of explaining the medicinal properties of a particular purplish-green vine that grew up the sides of some of the ebonwoods, when he stopped talking mid-sentence.

Zecus continued for another half-dozen horse-lengths before realizing the hillman was no longer beside him. Pulling on the reins, he halted Simiah and swiveled in his saddle. Broedi stood still as a statue, his nostrils flaring, his eyes shifting back-and-forth, wide and alert.

Laying the reins against Simiah's neck, Zecus turned his horse around to face the hillman. "What is it?"

Broedi lifted his right hand; the request for silence was clear. Zecus scanned the mist and the trees, wondering what had alarmed the White Lion. The fog had lessened some since earlier, but in patches. Some stretches of the forest were clear, while others were still thick and opaque with gray mist. Ebonwood trunks rose from the haze like thick, black fingers clawing up from a blanket of smoke.

A dozen paces beyond where Broedi stood, a cloud of vapor curled and twisted, allowing Zecus a fortuitous glimpse into the forest. At the furthest edge of his vision, he saw a quick blur of motion, moving left to right.

His heart stopped.

The fog thickened again and the gap was gone.

His heart started again, pounding twice as fast a moment ago.

Zecus whispered, "Broedi!"

The White Lion looked at him and Zecus pointed into the fog, indicating that he saw something. The giant man hurried toward him, reaching Zecus in four long and impossibly silent strides. Standing on Simiah's right side, Broedi spoke, his voice hushed yet urgent. "What did you see?"

Zecus hesitated.

"*Uori,*" demanded Broedi, "what was it?"

"A bullockboar," whispered Zecus. He had only captured a glimpse—a pink, brown, and black streak dashing through the trees—but he was certain it had been the terrible, part-wolf, bear, and boar creature oligurts used as mounts. "And it was carrying an oligurt."

Broedi peered at him, his eyes calm yet intense. "You are sure?" He did not sound surprised.

"I am."

A soft crack of a stick drifted through the forest.

As one, Zecus and Broedi twisted their heads, seeking the source. The mist drifting through the tree trunks played havoc with Zecus' vision. Every curl and wisp of haze looked like a bullockboar now.

Zecus suddenly noticed just how quiet the woods were. Birds that had been singing all morning had gone silent. Worry wrapped its fingers around him, squeezing tight, when he realized the rest of the company was gone. The other soldiers had continued their march. He and Broedi were all alone.

As quietly as he could, Zecus drew his longsword, all the while looking to Broedi for guidance. The White Lion continuously sniffed the air, cocking his head in different directions. After a few agonizingly long moments, Broedi raised a hand and held up two fingers, pointing to the north first, then to the west. Gesturing with both hands, he indicated that whatever was out there was coming together, toward them.

A thick lump lodged itself in Zecus' throat as the hillman crept away from Simiah, slinking into a clearing spotted with waist-high bushes. Broedi bent his knees, lowering himself into a crouch.

Knowing he would be wholly ineffective fighting in saddle, Zecus removed his right foot from the leather loop—a stirrup, he had learned—lifted his leg over the back of the horse, and lowered it to the ground. He half-expected Broedi to order him to stop, but the White Lion remained silent and alert.

A soft, nervous nicker slipped from Simiah.

Zecus froze—halfway dismounted—and patted his horse's neck, trying to sooth him. The horse ignored his comforts and loosed a single, short snort of fear. Zecus' worry deepened threefold. If the typically stalwart Simiah was bothered, whatever was coming was bad.

He began to remove his left foot from the other stirrup when a low growling rumbled through the mist behind him. Simiah spooked, quickly sidestepping away from Zecus. His foot got snagged in the stirrup, forcing him to hop along the ground twice on his right until he was able to free his foot. Off balance, he dropped his sword and fell into a mixture of fallen leaves, pine needles, and soft dirt. As he tumbled, a second growl shot across the glade, nearer to Broedi than him. Simiah whinnied, the cry sharp and loud. Zecus prayed the soldiers heard that.

Rolling over, he spotted a gray oligurt running toward him—on foot, without a bullockboar—only fifty paces away.

The gray-skinned monster was just as he remembered from the camp in Midiah, bald and hideous, its yellowed tusks jutting up from its lower jaw. It carried a large, spiked club in its right hand as it ran toward him, thudding through the forest. Taking a quick glance to his left, through the prancing legs of Simiah, Zecus spotted another oligurt already on top of Broedi. The hillman was struggling with the beast, fighting hand-to-hand. Zecus wondered why the White Lion did not turn into the bear or lynx.

Spotting his sword a few paces away, partially covered with dried leaves and pine needles, Zecus scrambled on hands and knees and grabbed the hilt along with a handful of needles. Despite a dozen sharp, pricks of pain stabbing his palm, he squeezed tight. He was not letting go of his sword again.

He hopped up, spun to face the oligurt, and assumed the proper defensive position. As the beast thundered toward on him, it struck him just how unprepared he was for this. Two weeks ago, he had never held a sword. Now he was about to battle a giant, snarling oligurt carrying what looked like the trunk of a small tree. His slow, measured-pace lessons with Sergeant Trell had never covered this.

When the monster was a dozen paces away, it lifted its club high into the air and roared. Zecus raised his sword, preparing to block the blow, but realized in an instant that the oligurt's strength would drive through the parry as easily as if Zecus were holding a fistful of Borderlands' grass. Abandoning his attempt to block the assault, he instead decided to attack.

As the massive monster began to bring the massive club downward, Zecus dashed forward and to his left. He felt and heard the club whoosh past his back and thud into the ground where he had just been standing. Continuing past the off-balance oligurt, he lashed out with his sword, slashing wildly as he ran past the monster. The blade sliced deep into the oligurt's meaty thigh and struck something solid within. Caught off-guard by the resistance of flesh and bone, the hilt flew from his hand as his momentum carried him past the oligurt. Trapped pine needles fell to the ground.

Suddenly weaponless, Zecus stumbled forward a few steps before whirling around to face his foe. The enormous oligurt let out a loud, bellowing roar of pain and reached for the sword that protruded from its upper thigh. The beast ripped the blade from its leg and glared at Zecus. Oily, black blood ran down its leg. It roared again—more in anger than in pain it seemed—and tossed Zecus' sword away. The bloody blade soared through the air, spinning, and landed in the forest's undergrowth.

Zecus reached down to retrieve the new boot-knife he had purchased as they had left Fernsford. He had been an accomplished knife-thrower in Drysa, but the blades he had found at the Fernsford market were longer and thicker than those to which he was used. He had practiced a bit with the weapon in the evenings, but most of his time was spent on the sword now lying thirty paces away.

He held the unfamiliar dagger in his hand, squeezing the leather cord handle tightly, waiting for the oligurt to make a move. With a sneer and a growl, the beast began limping toward him. With a quick, underhand flick of his wrist, Zecus tossed the knife at the monster. The strange weight and shape of the dagger disrupted his throw, and he watched helplessly as the handle struck the oligurt in the chest and bounced off.

The bald oligurt slowed its approach, sneering and growling as it lurched closer. With Zecus defenseless, it seemed content to take its time.

Zecus scanned the ground around him for a stick or branch—anything that he could use as an improvised weapon. There was nothing but small stones, dead leaves, and pine needles. Looking across the clearing, he found Broedi—still as a hillman—atop the other oligurt, pinning the monster to the ground, pressing the creature's giant club down on its neck. Zecus was on his own.

He looked back to the oligurt to find it wearing a terrible, sneering smile. At least Zecus assumed it was a smile; the yellow fang-tusks jutting up from the lower jaw twisted it into a painful looking scowl.

"You lose, fleshling."

Zecus did not want to die today. He bent to the ground, grabbed a large stone, and heaved it at the oligurt. The stone smacked into the creature's flat nose with a sickening thud and fell to the ground. The oligurt growled in pain but continued its steady approach. Zecus thought he might have broken the oligurt's nose, but there was no way to tell. It was the same misshapen hunk of flesh as it was a moment ago.

As he bent to retrieve another rock, a soft whisper of air whistled past him, followed a moment later by a bellow of pain from the oligurt. Glancing up, he spotted a crow-feathered arrow embedded in the monster's right shoulder. Clearly enraged, the oligurt threw back its head and clasped its left hand to where the shaft pierced its chest.

Another arrow whipped past Zecus and ripped through the back of the oligurt's hand, pinning it to the beast's chest. The monster roared again, dropped its club to the forest floor, and tried to grab the new arrow. Zecus wondered from where the arrows were coming, but did not waste time finding out. The shafts were in the oligurt now and that was good enough for him.

Eyeing the oversized club lying the leaves and needles, he scurried forward, towards the oligurt's weapon. Preoccupied by the arrows, the oligurt paid no attention to Zecus as he ran up. He tried to retrieve the spiked club but was unable to lift it with a single hand. The weapon was much too heavy.

A third whistling sound, followed by a wet, squishy thunk, announced the arrival of another arrow. The oligurt screamed again, its deep, fury-filled cry swelling through the forest. Zecus was relieved to hear the anxious shouts of soldiers drifting through the mist in reply yet worried as they did not sound close.

Using two hands, Zecus lifted the spiked club, grunting with effort. He dropped the weapon as much as he swung it, slamming it square atop the oligurt's foot with a satisfying, solid crunch. He felt bones crack.

The oligurt roared louder as the metal hooks at the club's end dug into its flesh. Black blood splattered Zecus' face, smelling of metal and sour milk.

"No, uora!" shouted Broedi. "No Strands!"

Sneaking a quick look behind him, Zecus found Kenders astride her horse, watching the battle with wide, anxious eyes. Sabine was beside her, sending yet another arrow in his direction. The shaft flew over his head, tearing into the oligurt's cheek, turning the flesh into shredded meat. The monster's black eyes swelled wide as it gave another gurgling roar.

Baffled as to how the beast was still upright, Zecus hefted the spiked club again and whirled around, driving the full force of his spin into the side of the oligurt's right knee. Something gave way in the monster's leg as it collapsed in a heap, crashing to the leaves and pine needles.

Without hesitation, Zecus raised the club, intending to smash the oligurt's skull open. Loosing a vengeful scream, he brought the weapon down with all his might. Inexplicably, his blow stopped halfway. Surprised, he looked up to find Broedi holding the club's midpoint.

Through ragged breaths, the hillman ordered, "Not yet."

Zecus stared back down at the grayskin, his heart pounding. With each beat, a lusting pulse to take this monster's life thumped through his palms, urging him to crush the oligurt.

Looking back to the White Lion, Zecus demanded, "Why not?"

"Because she cannot tell us what we need to know if she is dead!"

Zecus glared at the oligurt, only mildly surprised to learn he had been battling a female. The monster stared up at him, sneering, "Kill me, fleshling!" Black blood covered her tusks.

Shaking his head, Zecus muttered, "No." He let the club slip from his hands. The great lion was right.

Broedi tossed the massive club into a nearby bush with ease. "Thank you."

Zecus took a few steps back and plopped down on the ground like a mushy sack of turn-old potatoes. The entire ordeal had been brief, but he was exhausted.

The sound of horses' nervous nickering caused him to look up and find the two young women riding nearer. Kenders was openly gaping at the oligurt on the ground. A sharp contrast to Kenders' open shock, Sabine was a visage of calm. With cool, unemotional eyes, she stared at other oligurt, the one with whom Broedi had struggled. The gray beast was on its back with its arms splayed to its sides.

"Dead?"

"Yes," rumbled Broedi. The hillman hovered over the living oligurt, his gaze alternating between the beast and the forest.

Sabine nodded once. "Good."

Zecus turned his eyes upward to peer at the young woman. "I have never seen a finer shot with the bow. Thank you."

Pulling another arrow from the quiver hanging from her saddle, she replied in a steady, composed tone. "You're welcome." She was acting as if she had done nothing more than bring him a mug of water when he had said he was thirsty.

Kenders, her eyes even wider than even a moment ago, asked, "Zecus? Are you all right? You're not hurt, are you?" The concern on her face and in her voice warmed his heart.

He gave her a kind smile, shook his head, and said, "No, beautiful one, I am fine." As Kenders' cheeks bloomed pink, he instantly regretted his words. He had been much too brazen.

An angry, pain-filled grunt ripped his attention away from the women and back to the oligurt. She was attempting to crawl away, through the leaves and underbrush. Zecus wondered where she thought she was going. She had a sliced-open thigh, crushed knee and foot, and three arrows sticking out of her chest. The fourth shaft that had struck her cheek was gone, but had left a nasty looking gash.

Unhurriedly, Broedi moved to Kenders' horse, removed a length of rope tied to the saddle, and returned to the oligurt to begin securing her legs. Once bound, Broedi ripped out the arrow pinning the oligurt's hand to her chest, prompting another roar of pain, and tied her wrists. The grayskin resisted, but stopped when Broedi drove his elbow across her jaw, grazing the arrow wound. The blow surprised Zecus. It was quite unlike the gentle giant.

As the echoing shouts of men drifted through the forest, getting ever closer, Zecus eyed Broedi and asked, "Why did you not become the great bear or cat? They could not have matched you."

"These are advance scouts, sent to search for us." He lifted his gaze to stare at the misty forest. "Which means our pursuers do not know exactly where we are. Any use of the Strands would have been a beacon to the right kind of mage."

"Scouts?" repeated Zecus. "Then there are more coming?"

"I would assume many more, uori."

Zecus exchanged a worried look with the two young women. Sabine nocked her arrow and lifted her bow a few inches, readying it.

"Do not worry, uora. I doubt their larger force is close. It is not their way. What concerns me at the moment is they typically scout in threes." The hillman stared down at the oligurt. "And we have but two." The oligurt on the ground glared at Broedi with hate in her black eyes.

Scanning the forest, Zecus asked, "Where's the third?"

"I expect riding back with details on our whereabouts."

"Riding to whom?" asked Kenders.

Broedi looked up to her atop her horse. "Is that a question that needs to be asked, uora?"

Kenders sighed, muttering, "I suppose not..."

Broedi stared back down at the oligurt. "Where is your ohraeg?" The last word carried the guttural twist of the oligurt language.

The grayskin turned her eyes away, ignoring him.

"How did you get here?" pressed Broedi.

The oligurt glared at him, sneered, and spat. Black, bloody spittle shot from her mouth and splattered on the dirt. Zecus winced. The action had to be painful considering the open wound in the side of her cheek.

Kenders said doubtfully, "I don't think he's going to answer you."

"Yes, she will," rumbled Broedi.

"She?" said Kenders, eyebrows arched.

"Yes, uora," answered Broedi, looking past the pair of young women as soldiers began to emerge from the forest mist. "This is a she-gurt."

Zecus scanned the ranks of the Sentinels, looking for Kenders' brothers, Sergeant Trell, or the tomble. Not seeing any of them, he prayed there had not been another attack somewhere else.

When the soldiers saw the oligurts, they pulled up short and stared. This was the first time any of them had seen one, meaning that besides Broedi, he was the most experienced of the group when it came to oligurts. It was not a comforting thought.

Broedi crouched beside the oligurt and stared at her. For a long time, the White Lion simply stared at the sneering creature in perfect silence.

Zecus noted that the wound on the oligurt's thigh was oozing copious amounts of black blood. A pool had already gathered on the needles and leaves underneath her leg. If Broedi wished to learn anything, he would have to hurry.

Finally, with a short, disgusted growl, the oligurt dropped her eyes. Broedi spoke an instant later. "Fallid ograg imshadok gol vrong illuth ruaukk?"

To an inexperienced ear, it might sound as though the hillman were clearing his throat in the form of a question. However, Zecus' short time in the Sudashian camp helped him recognize the grunting as the oligurt language. He was beyond impressed that the White Lion could speak the tongue.

The oligurt looked at Broedi, turned her head, and spit more blood out along with a low, spiteful word. "*Thargh!*"

Broedi lashed out with his huge right hand, grabbed the oligurt's chin, and directed the beast's gaze to his face. "Imshadok gol vrong illuth ruaukk? Uelag garok Ohraeg Urazûd? Uelag garok Jhaell Myrr?"

The oligurt's eyes widened at the mention of the demon's name, yet she remained silent.

Again, Broedi grunted, "Uelag garok Ohraeg—" He cut off, tilted his head to the side, and then turned to stare into the mist. After a moment, he released the oligurt and stood, peering over Zecus' head and into the trees.

Zecus swiveled around to stare into fog. Seeing nothing, he was about to ask Broedi what he was looking at when a mix of growls and snarls emanated from the trees. Nikalys entered the clearing, pulling the reins of an uncooperative bullockboar. The hideous beast dwarfed the soldiers' shying horses, yanking and jerking its head in all directions in a futile attempt to free itself from Nikalys' iron grip. The great warrior held tight, however.

"I found this…thing tied to a tree," said Nikalys through gritted teeth. Even with the strength granted by a god, he strained to hold this massive beast in place.

Broedi ordered, "Hold it there!" Nikalys nodded and stopped at the edge of the clearing. Looking back down at the oligurt, the White Lion rumbled, "Kuurag ugruthil yurgh hurgard?"

Her eyelids drooping, the oligurt sneered, "Thargh, tuhka kotiv-aki!" Her gray skin had turned pallid. She did not look well.

Broedi sighed, moved to Kenders, and asked, "May I have your beltknife?"

Kenders drew the dagger from its sheath and handed it to Broedi, her eyes brimming with unspoken questions.

Instead of turning back to the oligurt as Zecus expected, Broedi began to march toward the bullockboar purposefully, beltknife in hand. "Hold its head to the ground, uori!"

Nikalys wrapped the leather straps around his forearm, shortening the length of the reins, and kneeled low, effectively pinning the snarling bullockboar's head to the forest floor. As Broedi reached the creature, he lifted the blade up, preparing to sink it into the pink and black skin on the neck.

The oligurt shouted, "Shurr rog!"

Zecus—everyone, truthfully—jumped, startled by the outburst. Broedi halted his strike. Knife still raised, he looked back across to where the oligurt lay. "You will answer my questions, she-gurt. In Argot."

Zecus looked back to the oligurt. Fear filled her eyes as she stared at her mount. She nodded once and grunted, "Agreed."

Broedi lowered the knife to his side, whispered something to Nikalys, and then returned. After handing the knife back to Kenders, he crouched beside the oligurt again. "Your clan is shamed, she-gurt. You dropped your eyes, yet you did not submit."

"It does not matter," snarled the oligurt. "You are not one of us." Her words were slurred and muddled. Zecus wondered if it was due to the arrow-gash in her cheek or the loss of blood.

"You promised me answers. And you will give them else I will slice open your hurgard and force you to watch it bleed before you pass to Maeana's arena."

"What do you know of the great arena, tuhka kotiv-aki?" growled the oligurt.

"I am not tuhka kotiv-aki," rumbled Broedi. "I am without a tribe. *I* choose my own path. You, however, do not." He paused before asking, "Am I wrong?"

The oligurt glared at the White Lion, remaining silent.

Zecus spared a glance at Kenders and Sabine and found them as absorbed by what was happening as he was. Beyond the young women, Zecus saw that Sergeant Trell and the tomble had arrived to stand with the rest of the soldiers some distance away. Everyone seemed content to let Broedi handle this situation as he seemed to know great deal more about oligurts than anyone else here.

"Is Urazûd your ohraeg?" asked Broedi. "Your ruler?"

"Yes," growled the oligurt, her tone weaker than before. "The danurgalak leads us." The rush of oncoming death had robbed the oligurt's voice of its strength. Only Broedi, Zecus, Sabine, and Kenders could hear her speak.

Broedi frowned. "Why do you follow a danurgalak?"

An angry, bitter sneer spread over the oligurt's ruined face. "Because we must."

"Why must you?"

The oligurt dropped her head to the needles and leaves. "The choice…is not ours…" Her eyes fluttered shut. She was not long for the mortal world.

Clearly recognizing that, Broedi moved to the most important question of the moment. "How many of you are here?"

The oligurt began to shake. For a moment, Zecus thought she was going into her death throes before he realized the beast was chuckling. The laughing quickly morphed into choking as frothy blood bubbled from her lips, spurting into the air with each hack.

"How many…?" repeated the oligurt. Through the gagging, she managed to lift her head, open her eyes, and grin over her blood-smeared yellow tusks. "More than you."

His voice turning harsh, Broedi demanded, "How many, she-gurt?"

A touch of defiance returned to the oligurt's eyes as did the cruel sneer to her lips. "Rolgluth." The muscles in her face twitched and she muttered the strange word again. "Rolgluth." Her head fell back to the ground. The previously fierce, black eyes went vacant and air wheezed from her throat as Maeana claimed her.

A few quiet moments passed before anyone spoke.

"Broedi?" mumbled Kenders. "What does 'rolgluth' mean?"

Broedi remained crouched, unmoving.

In a louder, more insistent voice, Kenders said, "Broedi! What does 'rolgluth' mean?"

The hillman peered up to her, his eyes haunted. He sighed before quietly murmuring, "Hundreds." The great lion stared north. "It means hundreds, uora."

CHAPTER 63: NIGHT

Broedi stood as still as a statue, peering into night's blackness, watching. The air had cooled enough that the forest's mist had begun to form, making an already difficult task nearly impossible. Sergeant Trell had suggested a cold camp this evening and Broedi had agreed. Fires were a sour idea this night.

Tiny spots of bluish light dotted the faint vapor blanketing the forest floor as the thick ebonwood canopy blocked all but a few rays of moonlight. The soldiers currently keeping watch with Broedi were lucky if they could see five paces in front of them. Even Broedi could see but twenty-five in the gloom.

Mostly, he listened, wishing he could shift into the kisa and take advantage of the cat's heightened senses. However, he did not dare do so. Jhaell Myrr could weave Soul and Will, and Broedi needed both to take any animal form.

Outwardly, he appeared a picture of calm. On the inside, however, he was a boiling pot of worry. Very little of this journey had gone as he had wished, with one difficulty after another presenting itself. Yet he, the Progeny, and this unexpected collection of good souls had overcome every challenge laid before them. He prayed that string of success would continue.

There was a chance a contingent of Southern Arms might intercept and defeat their pursuers, but Broedi was not counting on it. Typically, oligurt scouts rode within a day's journey of the main host, meaning the Sudashians had made it to the cover of the Blackbark Forest unchallenged.

After the second oligurt scout had died, he had spoken with the group. As was typical, their questions outnumbered his answers.

Sergeant Trell wanted a more accurate count of their enemies' number.

Nundle worried if oligurt mages were with them.

Zecus asked if there were razorfiends as well. Or mongrels.

Sabine wanted to know if they could make it to Storm Island before they were found.

Nundle wondered if a limit existed to the number that Jhaell could move in a port.

Sergeant Trell wanted to know what type of tactics he could expect from oligurts.

They lobbed question after question at him, all of which he would have happily answered if he could.

Throughout the firestorm of questioning, the three Isaac siblings had remained solemn and quiet. He suspected knowing that the person responsible for the destruction of Yellow Mud—and their previous life—was so near had caused a fresh surge of emotions.

While they debated the best course of action, Broedi had the Sentinels slay the oligurt's hurgard—or bullockboar, as Zecus had called it. He loathed killing any beast, but the hurgard would be a terror to the people of the Blackbark Forest if freed. Hunsfin and Blainwood reported that they, along with a handful of other soldiers, had already encountered the other scout's mount tied to a tree and had disposed of it.

Their company had not troubled with burying or trying to hide the bodies of the oligurts or their mounts. Any capable scout—and oligurt scouts were very good—would have found evidence of the fight anyway. The time would be better spent putting as much distance as possible between themselves and their pursuers. Sergeant Trell had ordered a much tighter formation for the soldiers, and the company had set off at a quick pace.

Throughout the day, every branch that cracked sent a ripple of alarm through the group. Soldiers rode with bows in one hand and arrows in the other.

Broedi reached up to rub his eyes and allowed himself a quiet sigh.

Storm Island was still a week away. No amount of hurried marching would get them to the enclave before their pursuers caught them. Unfortunately, Broedi had no means by which to contact the enclave for help. As the day went on, try as he might, he could not come up with a plan that would enable them to evade Jhaell Myrr.

When Broedi had quietly shared his gloomy conclusion with Sergeant Trell, the soldier had agreed with his assessment. He then aggressively questioned Broedi about the terrain of Blackbark Forest, looking for any place that might offer a tactical advantage against an opponent with greater number of soldiers. Broedi told him of a lone, large hill about a day's ride due east. The mount loomed over the road that ran south from Masons Bay to the land bridge leading to Storm Island.

The pair reluctantly agreed that it was as good a place to make a stand as any.

Unable to reach the hill by nightfall, they had stopped for the evening with the camp under orders to remain dark, silent, and alert. The Red Sentinels had obeyed without question. Broedi had barely heard a whisper since darkness gripped the forest.

A soft rustling of leaves and pine needles behind him sparked a flash of alarm before a familiar scent wafted over him. Admonishing himself for letting his mind drift, he forced himself to relax. Everyone was on edge, including himself. No matter what, though, he could not let any of them see how nervous he was. Especially the children.

"It's me, Broedi," whispered Kenders.

Keeping his tone quiet and calm, he rumbled, "I know, uora."

He listened as Kenders moved closer, each hesitant footstep crunching against the forest floor. Forcing his tone to remain light, he whispered, "You make as much noise as a wounded horse walking on crushed sea shells."

In an annoyed, hushed whisper, she said, "If I could blasted see, I might pick my way better." She slipped around to stand on his right and faced the same direction as he was. He doubted she could see much more than a few paces in front of her.

Without looking over, he said, "I am surprised you found me."

"It was not easy," murmured Kenders. "Gods, but I wish there were a Weave to help me see in the dark."

"There is," replied Broedi softly. "Are, actually. Using Fire—or Charge—you could create a ball of light and bind it to a stick or pole. Add Soul, and the light would simply hover over your head. An even more complex Weave including Life could grant the ability to see in the dark. Much like a cat."

"Is that how it works for you, Broedi? When you're the lynx?"

Only after he shook his head did he realize there was a good chance she might not see it. "No, uora."

"How is it you have such tremendous eyesight, then? And hearing?"

"And smell. My sense of smell is much better than yours."

"Is that something that all hillman have? Nundle said tombles' eyesight is better than all of ours—except yours, apparently. Although, even he needs some light to see by." She chuckled quietly before adding, "When I stumbled upon him, he was looking in the wrong direction. Should our own camp attack us, Nundle will be the first to know."

Broedi smiled at the thought. "My senses are something I gained once I became Thonda's champion. I believe the part of him inside of me is responsible."

"A part of Thonda is…inside you?"

"I do not know how else to describe what I feel. It is…" He trailed off, searching for the correct word. It was not the first time he had struggled to put a name to the sensation. "'Vomakasti elosa' is how I would describe it in my native tongue. 'Fiercely alive' is as close as I can get in Argot. I have always thought of it as Thonda's Strand. Before the Assembly, it was not there. After, it was."

Kenders was quiet for a few heartbeats before finally responding. "Truly?"

Broedi knew it sounded odd. It had taken him time to get used to the idea himself. "Yes, uora."

Kenders remained silent, this time, for a much longer period. When she spoke, her voice was strong and curious. "Does that mean I have a piece of a god in me? I mean, if *you* have one, I'm assuming my mother did from Gaena. And my father from Horum. Did they pass it to Nik and me? Could they?"

Broedi looked over and down at Kenders. "I do not know. The two of you are…unique. Only the Celystiela know the answer to that question." He looked back into the dark, misty forest and sighed. "And truthfully? I wonder if even they know."

Silence stretched out between them. A soft fluttering of wings overhead drew his attention upward. He listened for a moment and concluded it was a small bat, no bigger than his fist.

Kenders muttered, "You haven't seen Nikalys or Jak recently, have you?"

"Actually, I have."

The two young men had stumbled past earlier, announcing their well-meaning intention to keep watch. Broedi had thanked them for their diligence and then sent the pair in a direction to keep them away from the camp's perimeter.

"How long ago?" pressed Kenders. "They missed eveningmeal."

Hearing the worry in her voice, Broedi smiled. "Not long. I am sure they are safe." He hoped he was right. "Was that the only reason for your visit, uora?"

"More or less."

Another round of oppressive silence filled the forest. A squirrel ran up a tree a few dozen paces to the east.

"Broedi?"

He glanced over at Kenders. She seemed reluctant to go. "Yes?"

"Have you given any more thought to what Helene did in Fernsford?"

Frowning, Broedi rumbled, "Some, uora."

The truth was that he had thought about the little girl often. They had been very lucky that she had not exposed them all. Should they escape Jhaell and reach the enclave's safety, he would need to speak with Helene. Now was not the time for that, though.

Kenders muttered, "I'm worried about her, Broedi."

The hillman turned to stare at her. "Why is that, uora?"

"I don't know," whispered Kenders. "I just am."

Broedi eyed her for a few moments before turning away. Were he not concerned about an imminent attack, he might probe more. For now, the fog and forest—as well as what might be lurking in them both—demanded his attention.

"She has a good soul. She will be fine."

"If you say so," murmured Kenders She shivered.

"Are you cold, uora?"

"A bit."

Broedi reached out his arm and put it around her.

Kenders whispered, "Thank you."

They stood in silence again, listening to the muted sounds of the nighttime forest.

"Broedi?"

"Yes?"

"Will they kill us if they catch us?"

He was unsure how to best respond to the question. After a long pause, he chose the truth. "They will try."

He felt her take a deep breath and expected her to say something. However, she exhaled and remained silent. Broedi patted her shoulder and stared into the forest.

CHAPTER 64: APPLES

"Jak?" Sabine made sure to keep her voice low as she stepped through the dark forest, arms outstretched before her. She had already walked headfirst into one tree. "Nikalys?"

The soldier named Bedwin had seen the brothers in this direction, but all she had found to this point was bushes, trees, and fog. She kept her back facing the camp as she moved through the forest, knowing that if she veered even the slightest, she might never find her way back in the blackness. Should she get lost, her only true option would be to sit down and wait until morning's light to find her way back. Sergeant Trell had made it clear they were to be silent.

She shook her head, muttering, "Why am I doing this?"

Shortly after making camp this evening, the Isaac brothers announced their intentions to help the Sentinels keep watch. Kenders and Sabine argued they should stay, but they did not listen, moving off to look for Broedi. Kenders remained, sitting with Zecus and Sabine as they attempted to keep Helene distracted from the tension that filled the camp. Hushed conversation during eveningmeal—dried boar meat and fresh apples bought from the Fernsford market—centered on happy moments from their pasts. No one wished to discuss the dark uncertainty facing them over the next few days.

Zecus shared a humorous tale about when a goat had wandered into the Alsher family's home one night. By morning, the goat had gnawed holes in his father's breeches, setting the entire family laughing. She was surprised to learn that he had a brother and two sisters, something about which he never spoke. When Kenders asked about them, his mood quickly darkened. He sounded heartbroken as he told them about how he had left them—and his mother—in Demetus when he had returned to defend his home.

By the time night came, which was early in the gloomy forest, neither Jak nor Nikalys had returned. Worried about her brothers, Kenders excused herself to go check with Broedi to see if he had seen them, giving Sabine the opportunity to sing Helene to sleep. Once her sister was gently snoring in a tent, she returned to sit with Zecus.

The pair stayed silent, listening to the strange nighttime sounds of the forest. The chirps, creaks, and cracks of this strange place unsettled her. She actually missed the quiet rustling of the prairie and the sweet, heady scent of grass. The air here smelled of fresh-turned mud. It reminded her of digging her father's grave.

Unable to sit still, she had stood, grabbed a canvas sack, and stuffed it with a half-dozen apples. She asked Zecus to keep an eye on Helene and moved off, intent on finding the Isaac brothers to bring them something to eat. At the time, it seemed a sweeter option than sitting around in the dark, waiting and thinking. Now, however, she was reevaluating her decision.

"I should have let them go hungry…"

Bumping into another tree, she whispered a short curse, felt her way around the trunk, and resumed walking. Two steps later, she stubbed her toe on what was either a rock or exposed tree root. Drawing in a hissing breath, she dropped the bag of apples, fell to one knee, and grabbed her right boot. Her toe throbbed.

"Blasted forest."

Once the ache subsided a bit, she began searching for the sack of apples. Running her hands through leaves, needles, and dirt, she sought the rough cloth of the bag. At one point, her hand swept through a pile of wet, gloppy mush. Grimacing, she wiped her hand in the leaves and resumed her search. She wondered what she had touched, but figured she was better off not knowing.

"It's a good thing you're so noisy, else I might have taken you for a deer and shot you."

Sabine's head snapped up. "Jak?" She peered about the darkness, but could see only the vaguest shapes in the misty dark.

"Behind you."

She looked over her shoulder and stared. It was like trying to see through a windowless, smoke-filled room with only a lit firestick to light the way. Her gaze settled on a nebulous black shape that was about the size of a person. "Is that you? Or a pine tree?"

A light chuckling came from the black shape. "A pine tree. A talking pine tree. And I want to know what you strange people are doing in my forest."

A tiny smile graced her lips. Shaking her head, she resumed her search for the sack of food. "Well, talking tree, I'd appreciate it if you would get over here and help me search."

Still laughing softly, Jak traipsed through bushes and brush, coming up behind her and dropping to his hands and knees. "So? What are we looking for exactly?"

"Apples. In a bag. At least I hope they're still in the bag."

"And why are you out here looking for a bag of apples?"

Crawling forward a couple paces, Sabine said, "I thought I'd bring you and Nikalys something to eat."

After a moment's pause, Jak said, "Thank you." The teasing was gone from his voice.

She slowed her search for a moment and glanced at the dark hump that was Jak. "You're wel—Ouch!" Something sharp had dug into her knee. After checking that nothing had pierced her skin, she shook her head, and sighed. "Don't expect me to do it again the next time you go wandering off into the forest. My generosity has earned me nothing but a stubbed toe and sore knee so far."

"That's only the sour, Sabine," murmured Jak. "You're forgetting the sweet."

"What's the sweet? That you didn't shoot me?"

"No matter," said Jak, a smile in his voice. "You already found it."

She grinned and continued searching. A few moments later, Jak let out a quick, restrained whisper. "Ah-hah!"

Sabine turned toward him and murmured, "Did you find the sack?"

The dark hump that was Jak rose from the forest floor. "Why else would I whisper 'ah-hah?'"

"Ever the jester, aren't you?"

Hopping up from the ground, she strode toward him, intent on retrieving her bag, doling out Jak's two apples, and continuing to look for Nikalys. Or perhaps head back to the camp, dragging Jak with her. That was probably the more prudent course.

After two steps, she tripped over an exposed tree root and stumbled forward, crashing into Jak. He attempted to catch her, but the sudden fall took him by surprise and they both tumbled to the ground. Jak let out sharp hiss as she landed on top of him, her elbow jamming into his stomach.

Rolling off him immediately, she apologized, "Oh, gods, Jak! I'm so sorry. Are you all right?"

For a moment, Jak simply lay there, making sounds that were a mix between pain and laughter. Through gritted teeth, he muttered, "I sat on a very sharp stick."

Sabine could not hold back the small burst of laughter that slipped from her lips.

"And I dropped the apples."

Her laughter grew even though she tried to restrain it.

Sitting up, Jak quipped, "This time, how about you find the sack and I tackle you?"

She slapped a hand over mouth to hold in her snickering. For a while, the pair sat in the dark forest, laughing. Sergeant Trell wanted them to be quiet. This was not quiet.

Considering their dire situation, the levity was wholly out of place. Nevertheless, Sabine laughed. And it felt wondrous.

"Are we mad, Jak?"

"What do you mean?" asked Jak, moving back to his hands and knees and resuming the search for the apples.

"We have an agent of the Cabal, hundreds of oligurts, and a demon tracking us right now. Perhaps razorfiends and mongrels, too. Yet here we are laughing like fools."

Jak's searching stopped, along with his laughter.

Her own quiet chuckling came to a halt a moment later. After letting out a short sigh, she said, "I'm sorry. I didn't mean kill the mirth."

"You didn't. It's just that I was trying to think when I last laughed like that. It's been weeks. Since before any of this started."

Sabine sighed again and moved to her hands and knees. "Let's just find the apples…"

The pair scooted around the forest floor in silence, their search literally fruitless. Sabine was moments away from announcing that she was willing to concede the sack as lost when an eerie, mournful cry pierced the forest night.

Her head snapped up as the hairs on her arm and neck stood on end.

The shriek rose, climbing quickly to a shrill pitch before cutting off in an instant.

Neither she nor Jak had been on the bridge the night the Tracker had died, but they had heard the cries. While the others had rushed toward the unnatural sounds, Jak had stayed with her and Helene in the camp.

Sabine leapt to her feet—Jak did, too—without saying a word. He ran his hand down her arm, seeking her hand. Upon finding it, he slipped his fingers between hers and gripped tight. "Do *not* let go." His voice was firm.

"You either."

As the two rushed back to the camp, it was impossible to tell who led whom.

CHAPTER 65: SOULWRAITH

What-Had-Been-Latius had watched the camp from afar for what seemed like an eternity. The sliver of his soul that had not yet succumbed to insanity wanted to warn them, to scream at them to run. Yet the Soulwraith had remained silent. The magic suppressing the urge to caution them was much too strong.

The wraith had moved about the outskirts of the camp in perfect silence, watching the soldiers peer into the forest, searching the night. It had discovered the tomble all alone, but had done nothing. It had spotted the White Lion and the girl earlier, but had done nothing. It had seen the boy wandering about the forest alone, but had done nothing.

The master's orders were clear. What-had-been-Latius was to observe, nothing else.

It had been watching the brother and the farm girl crawl about the forest floor when it sensed the master's call to return. Latius' soul managed to push through to the surface for a moment to call out a warning to the pair, but the cry turned into a long, mournful shriek slicing through the quiet of the woods. The bonds that held his soul clamped down tight, cutting off the screech in an instant.

What-Had-Been-Latius knew that they heard his warning, but doubted they understood it.

The wraith ran west for a few miles before turning north, dashing through the trunks of the ebonwoods, nothing more than a shadow of a shadow. Drawn by the master's beacon, it ran to the Sudashians' camp, past the oligurt guards and the fires roasting the remains of a family from a nearby homestead, and around the temporary burrows of the razorfiends.

As the Soulwraith neared the center of the camp, the horned demon-man standing beside the master glanced up and eyed the shade. A sneer spread over his lips. "It's back, Jhaell."

Immediately, the white-haired saeljul turned to stare at the wraith with wide, anxious eyes. "Did you find them?"

The Soulwraith screeched, "Yesss."

A large smile spread over the master's wide lips as he looked over at the demon-man. "I told you it would." Peering back to the wraith, he said, "Tell me everything."

The Soulwraith shared every detail it had learned from its observations. When the demon-man heard the distance that remained to the reach their prey, he let out a howl that rivaled the Soulwraith's and jabbed a fist at the Soulwraith's master. "Blast it, Jhaell! It will take us another day to catch them!"

"Then we push harder," said the wraith's master. "And we catch them by tomorrow evening."

"You had better hope we do," growled the demon. "I cannot stay away from my charge much longer. The bond weakens."

"You will be back tomorrow night."

Snarling, the demon-man spun around and began to pace. "We should start marching now."

"Give the order, then." As the demon-man turned to head to the main encampment, the master said, "Come back immediately, though. We should take some time to discuss our plan."

Stopping in place, the demon looked back and growled, "Again? They have but a hundred men. They do not stand a chance."

"I don't care if they had but ten soldiers with them!" snapped the master. "We are facing those destined to halt Tandyr!"

"You said they are children."

"But Thonda's champion is not!" The master advanced on the demon, pointing an elongated finger at the spawn. "Need I remind you what he and the rest of the Lions did to your kind the last time Tandyr marched?"

The demon-man's snarl slipped away. Dropping his gaze, he growled, "You do not."

"Then let us discuss the plans," said the master. "I have come *too* far for this to end wrongly." The part of the wraith that was still Latius heard a strange pleading in the master's voice. "I need this, Urazûd. I *need* this."

The demon-man peered at the master for a long moment, curiosity filling his blood-red eyes. "What exactly did Tandyr offer that has made you so desperate?"

The master's eyes narrowed to thin slits. "We are going to talk about the plans, Urazûd. Nothing else."

The corners of the demon's mouth turned upward. In a gruff yet soft, amused voice, he said, "Of course, Jhaell."

The pair talked long into the night as What-Had-Been-Latius stood idly by, listening, his soul in constant torment.

Chapter 66: Hill

16th of the Turn of Thonda

Nathan stood alone on the hill, peering down the slope and through the mesh of tree trunks and bushes. He drew in a deep breath, shook his head, and let the air slowly slip from his lips. The forest was thinner up here, the trees spread out and shorter. They might have the advantage of high ground here, but the enemy would have better cover below.

"This isn't much better than sitting in the open forest…"

When they had reached the rise earlier, Nathan carefully inspected the terrain as they marched to the top, looking for any advantage he could leverage. Seeing few, he had interrogated Broedi again about oligurt tactics, but had learned little of use. He had then pressed Zecus for every detail the young man could remember about the Sudashian camp, seeking some sort of edge. However, Zecus had been unable to offer anything that would help Nathan. In the end, he was forced to prepare for a battle knowing only that their enemy was—in Broedi's words—"very big and very strong."

Unwilling to remain ignorant, Nathan had stationed Blainwood, Hunsfin, and Cero at different points as the company had headed east today, hoping the trio might be able to gather something useful. Once the men had spotted the enemy, they were to get a force count and then ride to the hill as fast as their horse could run. So far, none had returned.

The company had reached the hill early in the afternoon and had set to preparing defensive fortifications at once. With no idea how much time they had to prepare, and absent any true tools, Nathan did not waste time ordering earthen boundaries. Instead, he had the men collect dead brush, fallen logs, and rocks in order to build small walls that he hoped might slow the enemy's advance. He ordered strategic holes in the makeshift fortifications that would—with any luck—funnel the enemy into the places he wanted them to go.

Nikalys had been a tremendous help, able to move a large numbers of trees and other material in a very short amount of time. Jak, Sabine, and Zecus had worked as diligently as any of the soldiers, shoring up defenses wherever Nathan directed them. Even little Helene had dragged sticks around, although she seemed to think this was all some sort of odd game. Broedi and Nundle had spent every moment since arriving with Kenders, giving her a series of rushed lessons about magic, tailoring their instructions to what they knew to be Jhaell's capabilities.

In all, everyone was doing everything he or she could, but Nathan had a hunch it would not be enough.

He dipped his chin to his chest and mumbled a quiet prayer to the god of War. "Mu, we could use some help today." After a moment, he added, "Ketus, you, even more." Some luck would be good, too. A lot of it.

Sighing, he tilted his head back and peered at the sky, visible now that the forest had thinned out. The clouds were growing dark again. Thunder rumbled, soft and distant, rolling through the forest and over their hill.

"Wondrous," he muttered with a frown. "More blasted rain."

A torrential storm had arrived with dawn and remained throughout the morning, forcing the company to travel in a thick, soupy mess of mud and leaves. The thick treetop canopy caught the rain as it fell and funneled it into streams that poured to the forest floor. The storm had ceased before they reached the hill, but these new, fresh rumblings of thunder seemed to indicate another was on its way.

A distant, jagged flash of lightning briefly lit up the clouds and Nathan waited for the thunder to come, counting. "…twenty-one, twenty-two, twenty—" The boom rumbled, rolling over his hill. "Four miles, then."

The darkest clouds were south and moving east, not toward them. After sending one last plea to Saewyn the Untamed, goddess of Sea and Storms, to keep the rain at bay, he studied the hillside, judging their accomplishments to this point.

The defenses focused on the northern, western, and southern slopes. The lone blessing granted by the terrain was that the eastern side of the hill was incredibly steep, almost a cliff. Any attack from that direction would require the Sudashians having wings. Recalling the way Kenders, Broedi, and Nundle had practiced holding rocks in the air with magic, Nathan amended that assessment. Suddenly, he was rather uncomfortable with their eastern flank being so exposed. He stood in the mud, rethinking everything he knew about tactics, attempting to account for how magic changed it all, when a shout interrupted his thoughts.

"Sergeant!"

Looking south, he found Jak running up the hill, slipping and sliding on the mushy ground.

Due to the rain, the hill was a muddy mess. If anyone tried to move faster than a steady walk, the leaf-covered ground gave way. Footing during the battle would be terrible. As the oligurts were the ones who had to charge up the hill, the slippery ground would be more of a detriment to them more than his men.

Mentally comparing that one bit of good fortune against the long list of things stacked against them prompted yet another low sigh.

Putting on a brave face, he smiled at the eldest Isaac sibling. "How goes things, Jak?"

The young man stopped before Nathan and shrugged his shoulders. "As well as can be expected."

Jak looked tired, bags beneath his bloodshot eyes. Sleep had been hard to come by last night after the bone-chilling wail that had echoed through the forest. No one had seen the Soulwraith, yet the consensus was the cries belonged to the creature.

"Do you have a moment?" asked Jak. "There's something I want to show you."

"Sure. Lead on."

Jak nodded and headed south. Nathan followed, walking across the wide summit of the hill while keeping an eye on preparations.

Jak led him to a small grove of stunted oaks on the slightly raised southern section of the hilltop. Nikalys was there, arranging large, broken branches from other trees between the oaks' trunks, creating a layer of sticks that shielded one side from view of the other.

Intrigued, Nathan asked, "What's this?"

"Well," began Jak, "I saw these trees and thought that if we could cover the spaces between them, we could make a blind."

"A blind?" asked Nathan. "Like for hunting?"

Nodding quickly, Jak said, "Every summer, Nik and I would help Father build one just like this to hunt deer." He paused, tilting his head while staring at the massive blind. "Although, this one's much bigger than those ever were." He glanced back to Nathan and gave small smile. "And we were hiding from deer. Not oligurts."

"I'm thinking they'll eventually find you, Jak."

Jak shook his head. "You've misunderstood." He nodded to the open space between the trees. "There's room enough here to fit twenty or so horses."

Crossing his arms, Nathan said, "So we hide twenty horses here. Then what?"

"Well, if they come from the west and get past that set of fortifications down there—" Jak turned, pointing down the hill to the piles of branches, logs, and ripped up bushes "—we can charge their flank from here. We'd surprise them, perhaps kill a few. Or at least cause some confusion. That's good, right?"

Nathan nodded slowly, impressed by Jak's idea and initiative. It was a nice addition to their meager defenses and one to which he was ready to agree. Still, he was curious how much thought the young man had put into this. "And what happens if they come from the south? Or the north?"

Jak smiled. "Already thought of that." He faced south and pointed again. "If they come up through there, the men can circle out of the grove and join the rest of us. Then this screen becomes just another impediment for the oligurts." Looking in the opposite direction, he said, "And if they come from the north…well, then this was a waste of time, but we're not at a disadvantage."

Nathan looked over to Nikalys. The young man had not slowed his stacking of brush and branches. "Did you have anything to do with this?"

Without pausing in his work, Nikalys said, "Not at all. Jak thought this up on his own." The smile he wore showed that he was proud of his brother. He had good reason to be.

Nathan eyed Jak. The young man appeared a touch apprehensive as he waited for Nathan's blessing or criticism. With a short nod, Nathan said approvingly, "It's a worthy idea, son. A very worthy idea. Good job." As Jak beamed, Nathan stepped forward and clapped a hand on his shoulder. "I'll give you your twenty horsemen." He glanced around the incomplete blind. "I hope you all fit."

Jak's smile faded as his eyes widened. "You'll give *me* twenty horsemen? As in—"

"As in you'll be in charge," interrupted Nathan. "Follow the plan you laid out. It's a good one."

After a few moments of stunned silence, Jak shook his head. "But I'm no soldier."

"You are today, son." Nathan patted him on the shoulder again. "Now, I need to go check on the rest of the preparations." He glanced one last time at the grove and blind. "I'll send up a few men to help with this."

"Yes, Sergeant," mumbled a still-surprised Jak.

As Nathan turned away, he heard Nikalys issue a quiet, teasing jest. "Congratulations, *Corporal* Isaac."

Nathan chuckled as he walked away from the pair, heading back north. While Nikalys' words were spoken in jest, they were not far from the truth. With the proper training, Jak would make a good soldier someday. Of course, he had to live through this one first.

As Nathan crossed the hill, he happened to glance to where Broedi and Nundle were working with Kenders and stopped in his tracks. "What in the…Nine…?"

An amorphous, translucent humanoid figure stood amongst the trio. Half the height of Nundle, it looked like a tiny man made of pure water. The White Lion and tomble were staring at Kenders while she peered at the watery figure, her gaze intense. Suddenly, the little man lost its shape and collapsed to the ground with a splash. Kenders smiled wide and looked to Broedi, clearly pleased with herself. The figure reformed an instant later Nathan heard Broedi rumble, "Again, uora. Faster."

When Nathan had stopped by the lessons earlier, Nundle had tried to explain what they were doing—something about unraveling the magic. Nathan had watched a few moments, listening to Nundle's excited mutterings about Strands and Weaves, and then excused himself. Magic still made him uncomfortable. A lifetime of distrust could not be swept aside in a couple of weeks.

Shaking his head, Nathan resumed walking toward the western set of fortifications when men's shouts came from the north. "Riders incoming!"

He began jogging toward the cries, slipping in the slick mud, scrambling, almost falling, down the hill. Reaching the edge of the stacked branches, he saw Cero and Hunsfin riding up the muddy slope. As they moved past their fellow soldiers, men called out, asking for details about the enemy, but the pair remained silent as they moved toward Nathan. He had been specific in his instructions earlier: only he was to hear their report.

The soldier and Tracker halted a few paces from Nathan and dismounted, their boots squishing as they landed in the rain-softened ground. Deep furrows lined both men's foreheads, their lips so tightly pressed they were white. Nathan's face mirrored their grim expressions. "Gentlemen."

They both gave silent nods in response. The other Sentinels started to gather round them, anxiously anticipating some particulars. Based on the scouts' expressions, Nathan did not think he wanted the rest of the soldiers to hear what the pair had to say. He sighed, unsure he wanted to hear, either.

Eyeing the pair, he mumbled, "Follow me, please." Looking at the other Sentinels, he ordered, "The rest of you, back to work." The men frowned, but complied, moving back to their tasks, murmuring and staring at the scouts.

Nathan marched up the hill with Cero and Hunsfin, toward an open area where no other soldiers were near. Stopping, he faced the pair. "So?"

The scouts shared an apprehensive look and Hunsfin motioned for Cero to talk. With a worried scowl, Cero stared Nathan in the eye. "Four hundred, perhaps more."

Nathan fought hard to avoid showing dismay at the figure, biting the inside of his cheek hard enough that he tasted blood. After a moment, he swallowed his surprise and asked quietly, "You are sure?"

Cero nodded, running his hand through his thick black hair. "Yes, Sergeant. After I saw them and counted, I rode ahead and stumbled across Hunsfin. We waited for them together and he confirmed my number."

Nathan glanced at Hunsfin. The crag-faced man gave a short, simple nod. "I marked four hundred and twenty four."

Nathan dipped his chin to his chest and muttered, "I suppose that's better than *nine* hundred and twenty four." A long, silent moment later, he lifted his gaze back to the morose pair. "Either of you see Blainwood?"

Blainwood had been the first scout Nathan had left behind on the trail and should have been the first to return. The fact he had not come back most likely meant he never would.

Both men shook their heads. Cero murmured, "Sorry, Sergeant."

Nathan sighed and then gave a quick, almost formal nod. Blainwood would not be the only one to die today, he just happened to be the first. Nathan swallowed his sorrow and focused on what he could to do to keep as many others alive as possible. Careful to keep all emotion from his voice, he said, "I need details, please. What did you see?"

Cero crossed his arms over his chest. "Well, close to fifty oligurts on those ugly wolf-pig beasts, two hundred fifty more marching on foot, and a hundred of those short, bladed creatures. Razorfiends." He paused for a moment before adding, "I have to tell you, Sergeant, those things terrify me. Their blasted arms are covered with knives."

"You forgot the demon-man and the ijul," said Hunsfin.

"Right," muttered Cero. "Them, too. Not sure how I forgot the demon."

Nathan sighed and reached up to scratch at his beard. "How far away are they?"

"They'll be here by early dusk," answered Cero.

Nathan stared up at the gray sky and dug his fingernails into his whiskers and skin. "That does not give us much time."

"No, Sergeant," sighed Cero, "it does not."

Nathan remained silent, thinking. Thunder rolled through the forest, louder this time. It would seem that Saewyn had ignored his pleas. The storm sounded as if it were edging closer.

Behind Nathan, a low rumbling voice joined with the thunder. "Did any of the oligurts have markings on their heads?"

Nathan turned to see Broedi approaching. Nundle and Kenders still sat together some distance away near the ridge and staked horses. The hillman stopped beside Nathan and stared hard at the two scouts. "Any sort of colored markings on their heads? Or necks? Anything at all?"

Eyes narrowing, Cero shot a quick glance at Hunsfin before answering, "Yes. A few. How'd you know?"

"How many of them had them?" asked Broedi, dismissing Cero's question. "Guess if you must."

After Cero and Hunsfin exchanged another look, Hunsfin said, "Fifteen or twenty."

Nodding along, Cero added, "Perhaps a few less, perhaps a few more."

"What did the markings look like?" demanded Broedi. "Describe them."

Cero shook his head. "They were too far away for me to see." A short, dry laugh escaped from him. "And I wasn't about to get any closer."

"Could you at least see the colors used?" asked Broedi.

"Red and yellow," said Hunsfin without hesitation.

The hillman glared at the man. "You are sure?"

While Hunsfin nodded, Cero said, "He's right. Without a doubt, red and yellow."

Broedi let out a slow, pensive sigh. "Laurr-Othraul, then."

Nathan asked, "And that means…?"

"'Desert Fire' in Argot. They are a sect of mages in northern Sudash who specialize in Fire, Charge, and Soul." He frowned and stared back to where Kenders and Nundle sat. "We must amend our lessons."

The White Lion turned and began to trudge up the hill, his steps long and quick. Nathan watched him go while trying to think up a defense that gave them at least a slim hope of victory.

Fifty oligurts mounted on bullockboars.

Two-hundred-fifty more on foot.

At least fifteen mages, perhaps twenty.

A hundred razorfiends.

Plus a demon-man and Jhaell Myrr.

Besides the Progeny and the White Lion, Nathan had a hundred men and horse, a lone tomble mage, and two farm girls, one of whom was a mere child.

He did not see how they could survive.

A sharp intake of breath from both scouts pulled his attention from the mossy log at which he had been absentmindedly staring. Glancing up, Nathan saw both men peering past him, their eyes wide and fixed on something behind him. A mournful shriek pierced the relative quiet of the hilltop.

Whirling around, Nathan reached for his sword's hilt and squeezed the leather-wrapped hilt. Staring west, he spotted a smoky, night-black figure running at an incredible rate up the slope, straight toward him.

"Bless the gods…"

He whipped his blade from its sheath, preparing to defend himself—if that were even possible against this thing—when the Soulwraith halted a few paces in front of him. The foul creature stared at him, its glowing, silver-orbed eyes pulsating, the only points of light in the lanky black void. Nathan lifted his blade and waited for it to attack but it never did. It simply hovered a few inches above the ground, staring at him.

Glaring at the wraith, Nathan asked, "What do you—"

A shriek, full of torment and despair, howled from somewhere deep within the creature, sounding as though it came from the bottom of a cold, empty stone well.

Nathan winced and covered his ears in a futile attempt to shut out the terror-stricken screech. After a moment, he realized the wraith seemed to be saying something and not simply screaming.

It went abruptly silent, its silver eyes snapping to stare back west. An instant later, it sprinted away, loping down the hill, entirely unhampered by the slippery mud and leaves. Within moments, it was gone, nothing but a series of shadowy black streaks dashing through the tree trunks.

Cero muttered, "Was that…was that Latius?" He sounded ill.

Nathan whispered, "I think so."

"What was he—" Cero stopped and corrected himself. "What was it saying?"

Nathan suppressed a shudder. "Run."

CHAPTER 67: FIENDS

Nundle stared down the tree-strewn slope, a deep frown affixed on his face.

Hundreds of oligurt voices roared in unison, grunting and chanting. Unintelligible phrases in the choppy, barbaric tongue joined to form a wild, thunderous cacophony that reverberated through the forest. The atonal song would swell, rising in both pitch and volume, hover at a feverish plateau for a brief moment, then drop down into low, rugged grumbles and snorts before beginning anew. It reminded Nundle of waves repeatedly crashing upon the shore.

A while ago, during their rushed Fire and Charge lessons with Kenders, Broedi had lifted his head, stared west, and rumbled, "They will be here soon."

Not long after, the rest of the company heard the first echoes of the rhythmic chanting. Since then, the roars had steadily increased in volume as the Sudashians drew close. When it sounded as though the thundering voices had stopped advancing, Nathan had sent Hunsfin down the hill. The longleg returned to report that the Sudashians had indeed stopped their march even though their grunting continued unabated.

"Not very subtle, are they?" asked Kenders.

Nundle peered up and to his right. He and Kenders stood apart from the others on the slope. She wore her now-ragged, green riding dress and had her straw blonde hair pulled into a simple, long braid bound by the new, bright crimson cord he had bought for her in Fernsford. A few curly wisps had escaped and hung free, tickling her ear in the light breeze. As she reached up to tuck them away, she glanced down at him and gave him a wide and brave smile.

Nundle respected the attempt, but he could see the fear and uncertainty lurking beneath the grin's surface. He searched for something to say that might calm her. When nothing worthy came to mind, he sighed and stared back down the hill.

Fifty Sentinels stood a hundred paces in front of them, strung out in a long line across the hillside. Each soldier had a bow in hand and arrows stuck in the soft ground before him, ready to be plucked and fired. The trio of Broedi, Nikalys, and Nathan stood together between Nundle and the line of fifty soldiers, watching and waiting like everyone else.

Two hundred paces to Nundle's left and right—standing even with him and Kenders—waited two sets of horsemen. Nathan's plan called for holding the mounted longlegs in reserve and using them to ride into any gaps that might open up. However, with only fifteen longlegs in a group, Nundle could not imagine how the small forces could be effective at plugging holes in the line. Truthfully, the line was more holes than soldiers already.

To Nundle's far left, Jak and Zecus hid in the oak grove on the southern section of the ridge with another twenty mounted soldiers. If an opportunity presented itself to charge the flank of the Sudashians, Jak was to lead it.

Sabine and Helene were huddled on the far eastern edge of the hill, near the cliff and the remainder of the staked horses. Sabine had begged to fight, but a group effort by the Isaac siblings had convinced her to stay with Helene.

Nundle had checked on the pair before coming to stand with Kenders and found Sabine softly singing to the terrified girl. As he had left them, Broedi approached the sisters and crouched down to speak with them. From afar, Nundle watched the hillmen talk with Sabine while pointing eastward. He had been surprised to see a flicker of hope dash over her face.

When the White Lion had passed Nundle on his way to join Nikalys and Nathan, the tomble asked what he had said to Sabine. Broedi glanced at him, remained silent, and walked past him, down the hill.

Still wondering about the odd exchange, Nundle turned to stare back at the Moiléne sisters. Sabine was standing at the edge of the ridge now, cradling Helene in her arms, and staring east. The little girl had her eyes shut tight and hands pressed to her ears. While Nundle had half a mind to go ask Sabine what the hillman had said, he needed to remain at Kenders' side to guide her through the coming battle.

Sighing, he faced downhill just as Nikalys looked back at them and gave them an encouraging smile. Like his sister, Nikalys was attempting to appear brave, but Nundle could see the mettle did not reach the boy's eyes. Kenders offered a short wave back.

As Nikalys turned back around, Kenders muttered, "I've never seen him so afraid."

Nundle stared up at her and frowned. For them to have a chance at surviving today, Kenders needed to be cool, collected, and focused. Fortifying his voice with grit he did not feel, he said, "Of course he's afraid, dear. He'd be a fool to not be."

She turned to look at him. "Pardon?" She sounded surprised.

Glaring hard at her from beneath the brim of his hat, he said over the din of the oligurt chants, "If you are waiting for me to tell you that everything is going to be perfectly all right, you will be waiting a long, *long* time. Things will *not* be all right. Maeana will be very busy today."

Visibly startled by his directness, Kenders simply stared at him, her lips parted.

Nundle pointed down the hill to the line of Sentinel bowman. "Many of those soldiers—perhaps all of them—will suffer a terrible death today. They know this, yet they are *still* willing to fight for the hope you and your brother offer."

"I don't want more people to die because of me."

"Too bad. Because they will."

Kenders lifted her head and stared at the line of soldiers. A heartbeat later, her gaze drifted to the mounted horsemen, then to where Jak and the others hid in the oak grove. Nundle had heard her pleading with him earlier not to ride with the Sentinels.

"Everyone on this hill has made their decision," said Nundle. "*Everyone.* Respect that. Honor that. And do your blasted best to help keep as many of them alive as possible."

She peered back down at him. The nervous uncertainty that he had seen in her hazel eyes only moments ago was gone. By no means was fear absent, but it was at least no longer the dominant emotion. She reached over, patted his head, and said gratefully, "Thank you."

"You are welcome." As her gentle tapping continued atop his wide-brimmed hat, he added gently, "And please stop that. I am not a cat."

She pulled her hand back as the corners of her mouth curled up into a tiny, wistful smile.

Nundle was about to ask the reason behind the slight grin when, suddenly, the oligurt chanting ceased. He and Kenders turned as one to stare down the hill.

A too-quiet moment later, Kenders muttered, "Why'd they stop?"

Nundle shook his head, his gaze darting about the forest below. "I have no idea." After listening to the persistent, strident roar for so long, the instant silence was unsettling.

In a voice just loud enough to be heard across the hill, Nathan called, "Everyone, remain quiet."

A distant, low rumble of thunder rolled over their hill and slowly faded. The storm that had threatened earlier had never come, instead drifting south and leaving heavy gray skies behind. The air was so moist, so thick that Nundle felt as if he could reach out and grab a handful of it.

After a long, agonizing period of heart-thudding silence, Broedi tilted his head and pointed to the northwestern set of fortifications. Nundle scanned the slope but did not see anything.

Nathan called in a quiet, calm voice, "Bows, arc twelve. Hold fire."

All fifty soldiers of the line turned, facing the direction that Broedi had pointed while readying an arrow on their bowstring.

They waited.

The only things that broke the silence were the soft, wet squish of mud when someone shifted their weight. After a while, Nathan turned to stare at Broedi, his eyebrows raised. The White Lion ignored him, his gaze never leaving the area he which had indicated.

Nundle leaned towards Kenders and whispered, "What do you think—?"

A muffled chittering suddenly surged from the area, a sound that reminded Nundle of rocks grinding against one another. The ground near where Broedi had pointed rose a bit, lifting like the thick skin atop a long-cooking stew when pressed with a bubble of air. A moment later, the ground came alive as dozens of creatures emerged from the ground, flinging mud as they climbed from the earth, already past the first line of sticks and brush,. Sharp, pointed quills covered the monsters from head to toe.

Nundle muttered, "Razorfiends…"

The monsters in Zecus' tale had been a variety of iridescent colors mixed with glossy black, but these were a mucky brown. The mud coating them obscured any shine.

The fiends paused briefly to shake off muck and leaves before rushing toward the line of shocked soldiers, hissing and clicking as they ran, the quills on their feet digging into the slippery mud.

"Hold!" shouted Nathan. "Wait until they are closer!"

The soldiers fidgeted, clearly nervous, but followed their sergeant's order nonetheless.

Nundle shot Kenders a quick glance. Her wide eyes were fixed on the shrieking fiends. "Are you ready?"

She nodded quickly. "I am."

"Just like we practiced," said Nundle. "Keep calm." He took a deep breath, reached for Strands of Air, and began to weave them together. Kenders, as Broedi's plan called for, did nothing. Her task was to wait.

The razorfiends rushed closer, brandishing their bladed arms like the weapons they were. When they were but a few dozen feet from the nearest stack of branches, Nathan's voice boomed across the hilltop. "Bows! Steady fire!"

Fifty arrows launched across the fortifications and into the charging razorfiends. Some shafts sunk deep into the softer, fleshy sections of the creatures: their stomachs, upper legs, and pinched faces. Yet any arrow that struck a quill simply bounced off and fell to the ground. Soldiers grabbed a second arrow and most were able to get another volley off before the fiends reached the fortifications and leapt into the air, trying to jump the walls of brush.

Nundle directed the Weaves of Air he had crafted down the hill, grabbing a dozen razorfiends in midair and holding them in place. Broedi aided him in the effort; a blessing as Air was not one of Nundle's strengths.

Throughout, Kenders remained motionless, her head tilted back as she stared into the sky.

The razorfiends suspended in midair met a quick death as soldiers stabbed them with hand-held arrows, piercing the fiends in their soft, vulnerable places. Not one of the creatures made it over the fortifications.

As Nundle watched one of the longlegs rip a bloody arrow from a fiend's stomach, he felt a massive surge of bright yellow crackling. He looked to Kenders and shouted, "Here it comes!"

A brilliant flash exploded overhead, paired with a deafening, teeth-rattling clap of thunder. A second, third, and fourth bolt of lightning chased the first in quick succession. None reached the ground however as the searing bolts came apart a few dozen feet above the treetops, exploding in dazzlingly bright, jagged, spider-webbed patterns. The worst part of the assault was the thudding boom that came with each flash.

After a handful more of the failed strikes, the lightning stopped. Nundle studied the sky, waiting, searching for more Strands of Charge, but he did not feel or see any. Smiling, he peered up at Kenders. He was ecstatic to see her completely alert. "Wondrous job, dear."

"Thank you," she said while wearing a tiny, satisfied grin. "It's much easier when I know what I'm doing."

"Don't get overconfident. Broedi expected this from the oligurt mages. They will not remain predictable forever."

From below them, Nikalys shouted, "Good job, sis!"

More than a few soldiers were staring back at her with expressions of open wonderment on their faces. Beyond the longlegs, on the other side of the brush wall, dozens of dead razorfiends littered the ground. As far as Nundle could tell, not a single Sentinel was injured. After doing a quick count of the dead or dying fiends, he said, "Looks like they lost forty in the attack.

"And have nothing to show for it," said Kenders.

Shaking his head, he muttered, "I don't see how this could have started better."

Everyone remained alert, expecting an immediate follow-up attack. Soldiers held their bows by their side, arrows nocked. Nundle strained, searching for any flicker of gold, yellow, green, white, or black. There was nothing.

After a while, the company relaxed somewhat and resumed their patient waiting. The Sudashians were certainly not going to go away.

Kenders asked, "Why did they stop?"

"Perhaps they are reassessing the situation?"

"That's not what I meant." She pointed to the disturbed earth to the northeast. "The razorfiends. Why did they stop there? If they can burrow like that, why not go under all the defenses and come up behind us?"

A pensive frown spread over Nundle's face. "That's a good question…"

Turning in a slow circle, he inspected the hilltop. There were certainly fewer trees here than in the forest below, but for the first time he noticed they were also shorter, their growth stunted for some reason. It reminded him of a ridge near his home in Deepwell, a small rise called Rockbump Hill. The reason for the name was obvious to anyone with a shovel who tried to dig more than a few inches into the soil.

Dropping his gaze to the mud at his feet, he pulled his dagger from his belt, bent to the ground, and sunk the tip into the ground. A few inches into the soft, wet earth, and he met resistance. He tapped the knife against what he had hit. Solid rock. "Huh."

He withdrew the dagger from the ground, moved to a spot a few paces away, squatted down, and repeated the probe with the dagger. Again, he met stone.

Kenders asked, "What is it?"

Looking up to her, he said, "Well, they may be able to burrow through dirt, but not stone. I think this entire hill is one giant rock."

"Lucky for us."

"Let's hope Ketus can spare a little more." Standing from his crouched position, Nundle called his findings to the group below. Nathan repeated the ground-probing exercise with his own steel longsword. He, too, met resistance after a few inches. Soon, most of the soldiers were doing the same, all with the same results.

A raucous, booming roar halted any further investigation as the oligurt chanting began anew. Nundle hurried back to stand next to Kenders and looked down the hill, wondering what was coming next.

The voices quickly fell into a too familiar, steady rhythm. After a few anxious breaths, Nundle realized the sound was getting closer. He shot quick glance at Kenders. "Felt anything?"

She shook her head once, her gaze fixed downhill. "Not since the lightning."

"Good. Stay alert."

Between the trunks of the ebonwoods and oaks, Nundle spotted flashes of gray skin and dusty red, hairy hide tunics. Dozens of hulking figures emerged from the forest, stomping up the hillside, their line stretching across the hill, three rows deep. Nundle estimated nearly two hundred oligurts—no razorfiends—marching toward them, led by the demon-man.

The description that Zecus had given of Urazûd mostly held true—the spiral horns were terribly unsettling—yet the demon-man appeared to be at least as tall as the oligurts. According to Zecus, he had looked the demon-man eye-to-eye only weeks ago. Nundle was not sure exactly what happened when a demon soul inhabited a mortal's body, but rapid growth seemed to be one of the effects. Urazûd wore a blood-red metal chest piece with matching greaves, and carried a long, curved sword that ended with a barbed, hooked point. Nundle cringed, thinking what that weapon would do if plunged into a person.

Nathan's voice rang out and over the chanting of the oligurts. "Steady, men! We have the high ground!" The soldiers did not appear reassured by their tactical advantage. A moment later, he added, "And we are much better looking than that lot down there!"

Despite the gravity of the situation, Nundle smiled. He noticed he was not the only one, as longlegs up and down the line grinned.

The oligurts moved slowly, purposefully, up the hill, knowing their prey had nowhere to go. Each oligurt carried a simple club with wooden or metal spikes on the end. None had a shield or wore any sort of armor besides their tunic. Their strategy clear and lacking any sort of subtlety: march forward and hit hard.

The moment they were in range, Nathan called, "Bows! Steady fire!"

Fifty bowstrings twanged, sending the first volley flying through the air.

As the hail of arrows struck the Sudashians, Nundle's stomach dropped. Only two fell, both from lucky shots that had pierced their face. Those struck in an arm, leg, or chest simply snapped off the shaft or ignored it altogether.

Nundle watched the advance with growing unease. The Sentinels kept up a steady cycle of shooting: fire, pluck an arrow from the dirt, nock it, draw back the string, and fire again. Yet the repeated volleys were not slowing the Sudashians down. By his estimation, all but a couple dozen of the lumbering beasts would breach the first row of fortifications. When they reached the second line and the Sentinels, he guessed well over one hundred fifty of the huge, incredibly strong beasts would still be standing.

"Nundle?" said Kenders. "I'd like to try something."

He looked up at her, about to ask what and he realized she was informing him, not asking for permission. Her eyes were shut tight and her face a taut mask of concentration.

"Be careful!" he urged. "We cannot afford to have you faint."

"I know. I'm only trying something small." Her forehead creased as she frowned. "I hope."

Nundle watched, full of worry. Whatever she was doing, it did not involve Will, Charge, Life, Void, or Air. He sensed nothing.

Two new sets of bowstring twangs joined the first fifty soldiers as both groups of mounted soldiers began to fire now that the oligurts were in range. A thunderous voice bellowed over the chanting of the oligurts, trembling with unearthly power, as Urazûd urged the Sudashians to move faster.

Sensing movement behind him, Nundle spun around and found Sabine running forward with her bow, arrow nocked and drawn. Her cold-eyed gaze fixed downhill, she loosed the shaft at the horde and immediately pulled another from her hip quiver. Nundle watched as she began to fire arrows at an incredible pace, faster than the soldiers were. One arrow had barely left the string before she was nocking the next.

Looking eastward, he spotted Helene's tiny form huddled in a ball beside a tree trunk, her legs drawn to her chest, her head buried between her knees. As he stared at the frightened child, the ground shook and shuddered. A massive chunk of soil exploded further up the slope, between him and Helene, forcing him to shut his eyes against the blast of dirt. When he reopened them a moment later, he found a hole the size of his horse in the earth. The smell of wet mud filled the air.

"What in the—?"

Behind him, down the slope, there was a solid, ground-shaking thud, accompanied by dozens of deep, guttural screams. Whipping around to face downhill, he spotted a muddy boulder in the middle of the Sudashian line with oligurts crushed beneath. When the enemy's advance slowed, Urazûd bellowed at them to hurry and the line resumed its steady march forward. They were only fifty paces from the first row of makeshift fortifications.

"Blast," said Kenders. "I thought that might work."

Nundle glanced up, stunned. One of Sabine's arrows zipped over his head. While accomplished Stone mages could do what she had done, he would never have expected Kenders capable. Not yet, at least. Neither he nor Broedi had taught her anything about Strands of Stone. They could not. They were both deaf to that type. She must have relied on her gift.

As Sabine loosed another arrow, he peered back to Kenders. "How do you feel?"

"Fine, I suppose. A little tired."

Another of Sabine's shafts whistled downhill.

"Can you do it again?" asked Nundle. "*Without* passing out?"

Kenders peered down at him, hesitated a moment, then nodded. "I think so."

"Then do it." He stared down the hill. Some of the oligurts had breached the first row of fortifications. "And hurry, please."

As Sabine loosed another arrow, she asked, "Is this wise?"

"Perhaps not," said Nundle, "but we have little choice. We either stop them or we—" He stopped, startled as another chunk of stone ripped forth from the ground, soared high into the air, over the Sentinel line, and came crashing back to earth with a sickening crunch, landing on more oligurts. The ground shook and the advance faltered. Again, Urazûd's threatening shout drove the beasts forward.

Nundle caught Broedi's warning eye and could guess what the hillman was thinking. Nikalys was staring up the slope, visibly concerned as well.

Sabine fired another arrow.

Looking back to Kenders, Nundle asked, "Do you still feel strong?"

"Mostly." She stifled a yawn.

Taking a gamble, Nundle said, "One more might break them."

Kenders nodded and set her jaw. A few moments later, four large stones exploded from the ground, one right after another, each the size of a bullockboar. They tumbled through the air, hurtling straight toward the line of oligurts. Four successive, thudding crashes later, the Sudashians broke. Nundle did not blame them. Giant boulders falling out of the sky would intimidate any army.

The oligurts turned and ran down the hill despite Urazûd's violent cursing and shouting. Nundle watched, abhorred, as the demon-man chased down some of the fleeing oligurts, cutting them down from behind, howling for them to return.

As he decapitated a number of his warriors with his wickedly curved sword, Nundle muttered, "Bless the gods..."

Sabine lowered her bow. "If he wants to help our side, that's fine by me."

Soon, the thick cover of trees at the bottom of the slope swallowed the fleeing oligurts. A great cheer exploded from the soldiers, one that quickly evolved into a chant of "Kenders! Kenders! Kenders!"

Smiling, Nundle turned to look at the hero of the moment. While Kenders was still standing, she was visibly woozy. Sabine reached out to grab Kenders' elbow to help steady her.

"Four?" said Nundle. "One probably would have been enough."

"I know...but they just came. I didn't—"

"Uora!"

Nundle spun around to find Broedi striding up the hill, glaring at them, a hot rage simmering in his eyes. "Uh-oh..."

Upon reaching them, Broedi demanded, "What are you three doing back here?"

Kenders started to explain, saying, "I was just trying to—"

"Stop! Do not 'try' anything. If you are unconscious when Jhaell and the other mages attack, we will be defeated. We need you to hold them at bay! Do not do that again!" Typically, the hillman's eyes were as calm as a stagnant pond's surface. Now, they raged like a white-capped sea during a spring tempest.

"I'm sorry, Broedi," mumbled Kenders. "You're right."

"Yes, I am," growled the White Lion. "We are lucky they do not seem to have Stone mages in their ranks. If they had, you would have accomplished *nothing* other than nearly passing out! Those boulders may have even fallen atop our own men."

Nundle frowned. He had not thought of that.

Broedi shifted his glowering gaze to Nundle. "And you! If you do not stop encouraging her foolishness, I will put you on the line with the soldiers!"

Nundle decided not to point out the boulders were originally Kenders' idea.

With one last, low growl, the hillman turned and strode back to where Nathan and Nikalys stood to resume his watch for the next advance. Kenders, Sabine, and Nundle all stared at his back in silence.

After a few moments, Sabine muttered, "A short 'thank you' would have been nice."

Kenders shook her head. "No...he's right. I need to be more careful." Looking down at Nundle, she added, "Sorry I got you in trouble."

"I'll take being in trouble and alive over dead and in good-standing any day." He smiled up at her. "You did well. Take a moment to rest." His gaze drifted back to the forest below. "You'll need it, I think."

CHAPTER 68: LEADER

Jak's heart would not stop pounding.

He had been but a breath from ordering a charge into the Sudashian flank when the hill had exploded. Like the twenty men with him, he had watched in awe as boulders flew through air to land amidst the oligurt line.

Now, with the oligurts gone, he stared with widened eyes through the screen of stacked brush at where Kenders and Nundle stood. Broedi had just marched away—the hillman did not look pleased—and Sabine was rushing back to Helene. The little girl's faint sobs drifted through the forest, mixing with the painful moans oligurts caught under the boulders who were still alive.

"Your sister is quite impressive."

Jak turned to stare at Zecus. Like every man here, the Borderlander sat in his saddle, watching and waiting. "Yes, she is." He looked back to where she stood. "I just hope she knows what she's doing."

Zecus gestured in the direction of the boulders. "Those seem to indicate that she does."

"Yes, well….apparently, there's more to it than that."

Zecus shrugged his shoulders. "If you say there is."

Looking over his shoulder, Jak checked the soldiers behind him and found twenty surprisingly calm and determined faces staring back at him. If they were anxious, they hid it well.

For reasons he still could not fathom, Sergeant Trell had placed these well-trained, capable soldiers under his authority, none of whom had batted when told that Jak was their commander. When Jak had asked Hunsfin how he felt taking orders from an olive farmer, the cragged-faced man had said, "If the sergeant thinks you can do it, you can" and moved on, helping with the final cover of the grove.

Jak stared to the rear of the group and whispered, "Cero!" He had assigned the sharp-eyed Tracker to watch their southern flank.

Cero looked at Jak and gave a quick headshake. Jak nodded, relieved there still was no visible threat from that direction.

"Urazûd is going to be a problem," mumbled Zecus.

Jak turned back to the Borderlander. "Pardon?"

"The demon-man. He is our biggest problem."

A mocking snort slipped from Jak. "Him and his few hundred of oligurts and razorfiends. Oh, and the mages that can call down lightning, the fifty bullockboars we have yet to see, and the blasted saeljul who destroyed my village."

Ignoring Jak's sarcasm, Zecus said, "All problems, yes. But Urazûd is the leader. He drives the fiends and the grayskins."

Sergeant Trell shouted an order to his line, drawing Jak's attention back to the hillside. Soldiers moved down the hill and retrieved any loose arrow they could. The sergeant went with them, keeping a watchful eye on his men. As Jak stared through the blind, he could not help but note the stark contrast between Urazûd and Sergeant Trell. One was a cruel tyrant, the other a respected commander.

"I can't understand why they follow him," muttered Jak. "Urazûd, that is." He pointed down the hill to where one of the decapitated oligurts lay. "Look what he did to his own."

"Perhaps that is why they follow?" suggested Zecus. "Fear and coercion can be a powerful motivator. After what he did, I doubt they will ever run again. Not as long as he lives."

Jak's eyes narrowed. The Borderlander's words had given birth to an idea. A very dangerous idea. Nodding slowly, he muttered, "You know, I think you're right. Those beasts won't run." Turning to Zecus, he gave his new friend a long, level stare and added with purpose, "As long as Urazûd *lives*."

Zecus' eyebrows drew together. "Are you suggesting we—?"

"I am," said Jak, cutting him off. "What do you think?"

"That you are mad."

"I'd have to be a little to consider this."

The Borderlander pressed his lips together before letting out a long, heavy sigh. "Mad or not, it is a worthy idea." He gave Jak a slight grin. "It certainly would be an honorable way to die."

Wearing a thin smile of his own, Jak said, "I'd prefer to live."

"Ketus himself will need to ride with us for that to happen."

Zecus' comment was not far from the truth. To survive what Jak had in mind would require every shred of luck the Shrewd Fox could spare.

After one last glance down the slope to ensure it was clear for now, Jak maneuvered his horse around in the grove's close quarters to face the Sentinels. As his gaze met the eyes of the men behind him, he frowned. He was about to ask these soldiers to do something that would likely get them killed. Nevertheless, Jak set his jaw and readied himself to do just that. Nikalys and Kenders must survive. If he, Zecus, and these men died so his siblings lived, so be it.

When Jak had promised his father to keep his brother and sister alive and safe, he never imagined it would lead to something like this.

"Gentlemen, we are going to do something very brave, very necessary, and very, *very* brainless…" As he explained his plan, the men's expressions turned as severe as Jak's own. Nevertheless, they began to nod in agreement.

Chapter 69: Battle

Nikalys scanned the hill below, searching for any movement whatsoever. The scene was unchanged. Oak and ebonwood trunks. Thick bushes and brambles. Moss-covered logs. Six muddy boulders lying atop dead or dying oligurts.

And nothing else.

Nothing at all.

After the oligurts' retreat, the enemy had remained silent and unseen for what seemed an interminable amount of time. The only sound filling the woods had been the cries of the injured oligurts pinned by the stone blocks. Most of them had gone quiet now.

Nikalys sighed, reached up, and ran a hand through his hair. He almost wished the blasted chanting would start again. Then at least he would know where the enemy was. "What are they waiting for?" he muttered, glancing at Broedi to his left. "Perhaps they left?"

The hillman drew in a deep breath through his nose. A distasteful grimace spread over his lips. "They are still here."

Standing on the other side of Broedi, Sergeant Trell said, "Then I would like to reiterate Nikalys' question. What are they waiting for?" Both he and Broedi were staring downhill, their eyes alert and faces taut.

"I suspect they are formulating a new plan," replied Broedi. "Their first two proved ineffective."

At least forty dead or severely injured oligurts lay on the slope below them, crushed by Kenders' boulders or felled by Sentinel arrows. Add to that the forty or so razorfiends they had repelled in the first attack, and they had dealt a severe blow to the enemy already while avoiding any casualties on their side.

"Things have gone well, haven't they?" asked Nikalys.

"They have," conceded Sergeant Trell. "Yet they still have us outnumbered by more than three to one. And based on the way the demon cut down his own, he doesn't much care if his soldiers live or die." A troubled frown split the man's dark beard. "*That* makes this a very dangerous situation for us."

While the sergeant's cool-headed assessment was accurate, it was not what Nikalys wanted to hear. "What can we expect next?"

White Lion and soldier turned to stare at one another for a moment before they both faced downhill again without ever giving any sort of response.

A deep frown spread over Nikalys' lips. "You don't know, do you?"

"I do not," rumbled Broedi.

Nikalys looked past the hillman. "Sergeant?"

The soldier reached up to scratch his beard and sighed. "Well, were *I* leading them, I'd attack with everything I have. Subterfuge did not work. A partial assault did not work. Any decent tactician would stop dallying and just attack with a full force. They certainly have the numbers." He paused a moment. "Then again, I'm *not* leading them. A demon-man is. And as my experience facing demons, oligurts, and razorfiends is extremely limited—as in this is my first—I'm afraid to say I have no idea what in the Nine Hells comes next."

Nikalys reached up to rub his eyes. "Wondrous."

Broedi rumbled, "It troubles me that they have not used the Laurr-Othraul again. Almost as much as why Jhaell Myrr has not made his presence known."

"Perhaps he's not here?" suggested Nikalys.

"Oh, he's here," muttered Sergeant Trell. "He's just a blasted bannockcat." The comment drew curious stares from both Nikalys and Broedi. Meeting their inquisitive gaze, he asked, "Surely you two know what a bannockcat is?"

Nikalys nodded. "Of course." Bannockcats were wild felines, thrice the size of a barncat, smart, quick, and incredibly cunning. "A few years ago, one terrorized Yellow Mud all summer. A dead chicken turned up missing every week. The Turners lost a horse."

"And how do they hunt?" asked Sergeant Trell.

"They lurk for days around their prey," answered Nikalys, "watching and waiting until they know exactly...how to..." He trailed off and frowned. "I see what you mean."

Sergeant Trell stared back down the hill. "I'd bet every last coin Nundle has that Jhaell is simply trying to discover everything we have at our disposal before he shows his face."

Broedi eyed the soldier, a pensive expression on his face. With a quiet sigh, he nodded and faced west, down the slope. "I believe you are right, Sergeant."

"It's odd, though," muttered the sergeant, a frown in his face. "He always struck me as the impatient type. I have to wonder where the sudden caution has...come..." He trailed off and stood a little taller, his gaze focusing on something in the forest below as a soft chattering arose from the Sentinel line. "Hold a moment..."

As Nikalys faced downhill, his hand flashed to his sword hilt.

When he had last seen Jhaell Myrr, the saeljul had been standing on a distant bluff overlooking the ruins of Yellow Mud. The crimson robes were gone, replaced with a simple tan traveling shirt, breeches and leather boots. Nevertheless, Nikalys recognized the long-limbed figure's white-blond hair at once, along with the graceful manner in which he moved as he climbed the slope, alone. Jhaell stopped and stared up at their company, scanning, searching. His gaze flicked to where Nikalys stood with Sergeant Trell and Broedi, briefly pausing on the White Lion before locking onto Nikalys. An anxious, excited grin spread over his wide lips.

For a long moment, the two glared at each other across the battlefield.

Nikalys shifted his gaze a fraction, staring at a spot immediately beside the ijul. Perhaps he could move there and kill Jhaell right now. Nikalys drew the Blade of Horum, the sword flashing as bright as though it was a sun soaked day.

Broedi's low voice rumbled, cautioning him. "Hold, uori."

"I can end this now," growled Nikalys. The venom in his voice surprised him.

"No, you cannot," replied Broedi firmly. "You might—*might*—end Jhaell now. But there are over three hundred Sudashians in the forest. Killing him will not make them go away."

Nikalys pressed his lips together. "You don't know that. They might flee."

"And they might not."

"I'll risk it," growled Nikalys, the muscles in his neck and face twitching.

"Then you are a fool," rumbled Broedi, fierce yet quiet. "What happens if *he* kills *you*, uori? You will doom not only the men standing on this hill today, but countless more. I know you are upset. I can *smell* your anger. But right now, you need to put that aside. Think with your head, uori, *not* your heart."

Nikalys glared at the saeljul, wanting nothing more than to see Jhaell answer for his crimes, to pay for what he did to Nikalys' family and to Yellow Mud. Yet Broedi was right. To try to kill Jhaell now would be as selfish as it would be foolish. Now was not the time. He took a deep breath, held it for a long moment, and then exhaled through his nose, forcing himself to relax.

"Fine."

As he lowered the Blade of Horum to his side, Jhaell's gaze left him, danced over Broedi once again, and then traveled up the hill to where Kenders and Nundle stood. The excitement in his face fled as an angry sneer spread his lips.

Sergeant Trell muttered, "I don't think he's too happy to see Nundle…"

A few breaths later, the ijul's stare shifted to the front line of Sentinels. Raising his arms in a supplicatory gesture, he called out in a clear, crisp voice, "Soldiers of the Great Lakes, drop your weapons now, give me the children—*and* the tomble—and I shall leave you unharmed. I give you my word."

A minute flicker of worry ran through Nikalys that they might accept the ijul's offer. Their situation was dire. As Broedi said, over three hundred oligurts and razorfiends were still waiting to kill them. Jhaell was offering them a way to be free, although he severely doubted the ijul's trustworthiness on following through. Nikalys eyed the soldiers carefully, running his gaze along the line. For a few moments, nobody moved or spoke.

Nikalys was about to shout out that they could not trust Jhaell, that he was beholden to the Cabal and wicked when he heard a soft snicker drift up the hill. Looking to the Sentinel line's left side, he spotted Wil openly chuckling. A few nearby soldiers joined in with the young swordsman and, soon, the entire hill of Red Sentinels was laughing outright.

Sergeant Trell called out, "Take your offer back to the Hell you came from, you demon-loving son of a bullockboar!"

A raucous cheer arose from the men. Nikalys joined in, his anger at the ijul fueling his shouts. For a few moments, he forgot that they were facing a very dangerous mage. He was quickly reminded however when Broedi drew a sharp, hissing breath and rumbled a single word.

"Water."

The soldiers' cheering faded as leftover rainwater leeched from the ground, rolled off the leaves of trees and bushes and flew through the air and towards the saeljul. Thousands of tiny water beads quickly coalesced together until, within moments, a giant, roiling ball of water had formed, half as tall and wide as the fifty-man line.

Nikalys stared, stunned. "Hells..."

The giant orb of impossibly clear water began to tumble up the hill toward them, but after only a twenty paces, it lost its shape and splashed to the ground, releasing a muddy torrent of water and cast-off leaves that rushed down the slope, back toward Jhaell, soaking the ijul's boots and breeches.

Broedi whispered, "Excellent, uora."

A grim smile touched Nikalys' lips. He was proud of his sister.

Jhaell's elongated features twisted in anger. He lifted one of his long, willowy arms into the air, and waved his hand forward. Other figures began to appear, stepping from the tree trunks and bushes to stand beside Jhaell, stretched in a long line across the hill.

"See?" grumbled Sergeant Trell. "Bannockcat. They're all just out of bow range."

The new arrivals were oligurts, but quite unlike the others who had charged earlier. These were bare-chested and wore a long skirt of leather that dragged along the ground, collecting mud and dead leaves. Each had a large, blood red and harvest-leaf yellow symbol either painted or tattooed on its bald head. Nikalys counted twenty in total, arranged ten on either side of Jhaell. Each carried a lit torch in its right hand.

"The Laurr-Othraul," rumbled Broedi.

"What are they wearing?" asked Nikalys. The leather skirts were unusual, made of irregularly shaped patches of strange browns, tans, and sickly grays all stitched together.

"The skin of those they have killed," answered Broedi. "Tanned and strung together with sinew."

"Skin?" asked Nikalys. "The skin of what?"

"Oligurts from rival clans," rumbled Broedi in his deep baritone, "As well as people, nascepel, kur-surus…they do not discriminate."

Fighting back the bubble of bile that rose in his throat, Nikalys asked, "Why do they have torches with them?"

"The flames make it easier for them to weave with Fire. However, I do not feel—" His eyes narrowed sharply as he called out, "Be ready, uora!"

A sizzling, crackling sound washed over them, prompting Nikalys to stare upward, looking for more lightning. However, the sky was clear.

Confused, he dropped his head, peered back at the oligurt mages, and spotted dozens of fist-sized orbs of fire and lightning flying through the air. He watched as one crackling yellow ball pierced the trunk of a tree, blasting through the other side in a shower of splinters, leaving behind only a blackened, smoking hole. The cascade of spheres rushed up the hill toward the soldiers. Yet before he could panic, the balls began to disappear, each one giving a soft, fizzing pop as it did.

Nikalys glanced over to Broedi and found the hillman staring down hill, his face lined deep in concentration. A look back to Kenders and Nundle revealed the same. The trio were tearing the balls of fire and lighting apart.

At first, they seemed to be holding back the magical assault, but after a time, the orbs began to get closer before dissipating. Nikalys stared downhill at the bare-chested oligurts. He needed to do something. "Broedi, let me go down—"

"Go!" interrupted Broedi through gritted teeth. He apparently had the same idea. "Move quickly. They will only be surprised for so long. Come back the *instant* they are aware of you."

With the Blade of Horum still in his hand, Nikalys scurried down the hill, sliding in the mud, and skidded to a stop at the edge of the fortifications. He felt Jhaell's gaze track him the entire way. He stood beside Wil and drew a deep breath, steadying himself.

"Keep the point up and your wrist tight," murmured Wil. Apparently, his tutor and friend had also guessed what he was planning.

"I will."

"Ketus be with you, Nik."

"Thanks," muttered Nikalys. He looked toward the mage on the far left—
Shift.

—and sliced open the back of the beast towering over him, easily cutting through the monster's flesh. The glimmering white blade bounced along bone as black blood gushed forth. Roaring in pain, the oligurt dropped its torch and clawed at its back. Before the burning flame or a single drop of the thick, oily blood hit the ground, Nikalys looked to the next oligurt—

Shift.

—leaped into the air, and whipped the sword around, severing the creature's head from its shoulders. The cut was so swift and clean that the head remained in place briefly, before it slipped from the oligurt's neck. The monster remained upright a moment, almost as if the body did not realize it should collapse now that it was absent its head.

Nikalys turned his gaze to the next in the line—

Shift.

—and stabbed the oligurt's back, twisted and jerked up, ripping the beast's insides, and then withdrew the sword. It remained white and gleaming, not a drop of blood on its sharp blade.

He looked to the next oligurt—

Shift.

—spun and severed the oligurt's torch arm at the shoulder, slicing through ligaments and arteries as easily as an over-stewed potato.

Without thought, driven by instinct and his gift, Nikalys moved from oligurt to oligurt, felling them with swift and lethal strokes. Six of the Desert Fire mages lay dead or dying before the others began to react to his presence. As Nikalys sliced the seventh's neck open, he looked to the next in line. The beast's black eyes were wide and fixed on him. The element of surprise was gone.

Nikalys knew he should return to the Sentinels' line, but instead, he eyed the ground behind the eighth beast—

Shift.

—and again sliced an oligurt's head from its shoulders. Unlike the last, however, this one collapsed immediately, its eyes remaining wide open as the bald head rolled down the hill.

Readying himself for the next one, Nikalys whirled around and was surprised to find the last two oligurts gone. Nothing but several dozen paces of open forest separated him from Jhaell Myrr. The saeljul stared at him, a wide smile of anticipation on his face.

Hot, blistering rage surged from deep within Nikalys, burning his veins and searing his soul. "It's time to answer for what you did!"

The ijul's smile grew even wider. He lifted his elongated arms out to his side, spreading them as though he were hawk taking flight, and taunted, "Come for me, then."

If Jhaell wanted to die, Nikalys would happily grant the monster's wish. Squeezing his sword's hilt so tight that he thought the metal might give way, he fixed his eyes on a spot to the left of the ijul. The air before Jhaell appeared to flutter, like waves of shimmering heat rising from sunbaked dirt on a hot day.

Suddenly, a twisting whirlwind of air surrounded him, lifting him from the ground, and whisking him away from Jhaell. He flew through the air, spinning, unable to see where he was going. It was all he could do to hold onto his sword.

A few stomach-lurching moments later, he crashed to the ground, slamming into mud and leaves. He scrambled to his feet immediately, but was unsteady, the world continuing to circle around him even though he had ceased moving. He shook his head, attempting to clear the dizziness, and found Nundle and Kenders standing before him, both staring past him and down the hill.

"What just happened?"

Nundle said, "You were about to go somewhere I didn't think you'd want to go."

"What does that mean?"

Pointing downhill, Nundle said, "Look."

Nikalys twisted around. While the fire and lightning attacks were ongoing, the orbs were vanishing almost the moment they appeared. The bodies of the eight oligurts he had attacked lay in crumpled heaps on the left. While the remaining two from that side were nowhere to be seen, in their place was the same strange shimmering he had noted near Jhaell. It looked as if the forest was painted on a piece of canvas that had been sliced down the middle with both sides flapping in the wind.

"What is that?"

"*That's* a port," explained Nundle. A few evenings ago, the tomble had explained the concept of ports after Nikalys had remarked about how long it was taking to reach Storm Island. "The last two oligurts saw you coming, turned, and ran straight into it. I doubt they knew it was there."

Nikalys eyed Jhaell. The saeljul stood a few paces from the disturbance, glaring up the hill at them, an expression of pure hatred gripping his face.

"Where's the other side?" asked Nikalys.

"Only the preceptor knows," said Nundle. "But as it was meant for you, I'm guessing nowhere pleasant. And as I have no idea how to unravel the Weave and Kenders and Broedi were busy, I simply decided to get you out of there."

Nikalys regarded the little man and gave a grateful nod. "Thank you, Nundle. Truly."

"You're most welcome."

Nikalys looked back down the hill to find the assault of fire and lighting orbs had stopped. Curls of black smoke drifted from dozens of holes in the trunks of trees. The forest was silent again. "Are they done?"

Nundle murmured, "With that tactic? I'd say yes. With only ten of them, we can undo them faster than they can craft them." He stared up at Nikalys. "Your sister is *very* talented."

Nikalys glanced back at Kenders and found her still staring intently down the hill. "You all right?"

"Perfectly fine," replied Kenders. She spared a quick glance at him. "You?"

"I'm a little dizzy."

A tiny smile touched her lips. "In that case, I'm a little tired." She nodded downhill. "Get back with Broedi. It's not over yet."

"Be careful, sis."

"You, too."

He gave another quick thanks to Nundle and hurried down to where Broedi and Sergeant Trell stood. As he arrived, the hillman looked over. "*Well done, uori.*"

"To a point," said Nikalys. "Jhaell laid a trap and I almost sprung it."

"'Almost' is the important word there."

"The only reason I didn't is because Nundle saved me."

Arching a lone eyebrow, the hillman rumbled, "How fortunate he is here today, then."

Turning his gaze to Broedi, Nikalys asked, "So, what's next?"

Broedi nodded at Jhaell and rumbled, "*That* is a question for him."

Nikalys again locked eyes with the saeljul and tried to mirror Broedi's calm stoicism. It was harder than it looked. With a bitter, angry sneer affixed on his face, Jhaell spun around and strode down the slope with the remaining oligurt mages in tow.

The wait began anew.

CHAPTER 70: SAELJUL

Kenders kept her gaze locked on Jhaell's back as he swept down the slope. Once he disappeared into the cover of the trees, she exhaled, releasing a breath she had been unaware she was holding.

For weeks, she had wondered what she would feel if she ever faced the ijul. She had anticipated some combination of fear and anger, but oddly enough, her initial reaction had been one of quiet surprise. Excusing the fact that he was a saeljul, he had looked ordinary. For a brief moment, she wondered if it was the same soul. However, the moment he locked his gaze on her, all doubt fled. His eyes burned with a clear, unadorned desire to see her dead.

When Jhaell had directed the roiling ball of water up the hill, she had hesitated for only a moment before reaching into the Weave and unraveling it with ease. Yet rather than feeling any sort of elation over what she had done, a paralyzing mixture of regret, sorrow, and guilt washed over her. She stared at the muddy water rushing down the hill, wondering if she could have done the same thing to the fibríaal that had destroyed Yellow Mud.

She had little time to feel sorry for herself, however, as the crackle of magic returned and the balls of Charge and Fire started flying up the slope. Holding back the barrage had been difficult. Unraveling the individual Weaves was easy, but tracking such a large number of them at once took immense concentration. She felt Nundle and Broedi helping, but knew the orbs of fire and lighting were getting ever closer.

When the oligurt mages started to scream, she spared a quick glance downhill and saw Nikalys cutting through their line, a blur of man and sword. A surge of black and white Strands surprised her as did a second burst of pure white when Nikalys came rushing up the hill in a twister of air. After Nundle had explained what Jhaell's Weave was, she felt sick. She had no idea the danger in which her brother had been.

Now that all was quiet once again, Kenders glanced at the tomble beside her. He was staring downhill, his red hair peeking out from under his hat. "Nundle?"

"Yes, dear?"

"Thank you."

Nundle looked up, smiled, and said, "You're most welcome." He did not ask the reason for her gratitude. He knew.

They both turned their gaze to the trees below and waited.

She stared at the twisted, broken bodies of the oligurts beneath the boulders she had tossed and frowned. She had expected taking a life might bother her, but strangely, it did not. Either she died, or they did. The choice was easy.

Letting out a tiny sigh, Kenders glanced at the sky. The clouds were breaking up, allowing a few rogue rays of sunlight to stream through the gray to light up the forest's canopy. Countless water drops sparkled and glistened. She would have enjoyed the striking vista were it not possible she might still die today.

Hearing hurried footsteps behind her, she looked back to find Sabine rushing down the hill with Helene cradled in her arms. Spinning to face them, Kenders said, "It's not safe up here." She glanced at Helene. "Especially for her."

"I know," replied Sabine. "But she didn't want me to leave her again."

Helene stared at Kenders with wide, brown eyes. As Kenders summoned a reassuring smile for the little girl, Nundle turned and asked, "What's wrong?"

"Broedi told me to come and tell him if we saw anything in the woods to the east." She paused, glanced between them, and then added, "Well, we did. Actually, Helene did. I was too busy watching the fire and lightning."

"What?" asked Kenders, suddenly worried. "More oligurts?"

Sabine shook her head. "I don't know. All I could see through the branches was movement." A frown spread over her lips. "*A lot* of movement."

Kenders stared down at Nundle. The concerned frown resting on the tomble's face likely matched her own. She started to turn, preparing to call out to Broedi, but stopped short. The hillman already halfway up to them, his strides long and quick. Kenders caught an almost hopeful glint in his eyes.

When he was still a few paces from them, the White Lion rumbled, "Nundle, go down with the Sergeant, please."

"Why? What—"

"*Now*, Nundle."

The clearly curious tomble miraculously swallowed his questions and scampered down the hill to where Nikalys and Sergeant Trell stood, repeatedly looking back as he did.

Studying the hillman's intense expression, Kenders asked, "What is going on?" Her gaze shot to the eastern ridge. "What's down there?"

Without stopping, Broedi rumbled, "I do not have time to explain." Taking Sabine by the shoulder, he headed back up the hill to the cliff's edge. "Tell me what you both saw and where. Quickly, please."

Sabine tossed Kenders a curious look as Broedi half-dragged her back to the ridge. Helene peered over Sabine's shoulder and gave Kenders a tiny smile and wave. Kenders lifted her hand and waved back, muttering to herself, "What is going on?"

Putting aside her irrational fear that he was abandoning them, she twisted back around to check down the hill. As she turned, she glanced at the grove where Jak was hiding and froze. Earlier, she had been able to see the rear ends of a few horses sticking from the blind. Now, there was nothing. She held very still, hoping to be able to see some movement in the grove, but there was none. Jak and the twenty soldiers were gone.

"Blast it, Jak. Where did—"

A burst of silver, green, and gold Strands surged behind her. Recognizing the combination, she looked over her shoulder, expecting to see the familiar lynx or bear. Her eyes went wide as an enormous, golden-brown hawk leapt from the cliff's edge and spread its wings, unfurling an impossible twenty-five-foot wingspan.

Mouth agape, Kenders muttered, "Bless the gods…"

Giant, sharp talons hung from the bird's belly as the hawk swooped down, dipping below the hill's summit to disappear from view. Sabine stood at the ridge's edge, clutching Helene and staring into the forest below them.

At that exact moment, the oligurts' war chants resumed.

Spinning around, Kenders stared down the slope, listening as the shrill hisses and clicks of the razorfiends joined the oligurt roars and rolled up the hill. It took only a moment for her to realize the thunderous sound was growing louder. And quickly.

"Here they come!" shouted Sergeant Trell. "Hold fast!"

A shiver ran up Kenders' spine. Based on sound alone, the entire Sudashian force was coming. The demon-man emerged from the tree trunks with hundreds of oligurts and razorfiends on his heels, every one of them running up the hill, charging the soldiers. The Sentinel line looked pitiful compared to the onrushing horde.

"Bows! Steady fire!" bellowed Sergeant Trell. "And fire fast, blast it!"

Arrows filled the air.

Kenders scanned the surging Sudashians, looking for Jhaell and the oligurt mages, but they were not among the crowd.

A different sort of snorting howl pulled Kenders attention to the northwestern side of the hill. A few dozen oligurts mounted atop the horrid bullockboars had crested the rise and were thundering toward the Sentinel flank.

Sergeant Trell spun around, pointed at the mounted attack, and shouted, "Right horse! Charge!"

The order was almost unnecessary as the northern group of horsemen were already inching forward. Corporal Holb pointed his sword at the bullockboars and shouted something Kenders lost in the roar of battle. Men and horse launched forward.

Kenders watched as the two groups converged, shaking her head as they drew near. "No…"

This was going to be a massacre. The Red Sentinel horsemen were outnumbered three-to-one. Those fifteen soldiers were rushing to their deaths. Kenders did not know whether to help them or direct her attention elsewhere. The battle scene before her was pure chaos. Men shouting, oligurts roaring, horses whinnying.

A surge of green, yellow, and white pulled her gaze down the hill. Nundle was facing the charging bullockboars whilst knitting a pattern she had never seen. Guessing it was helpful, she did her best to mimic the Weave, twisting her Strands to look like his. It was terribly difficult—she had never combined three different types of Strands before—yet, somehow, she remained but a step behind him, intertwining dozens of the magical strings into an intricate design. When Nundle finished, he flung the completed Weave at the charging bullockboars. Kenders did the same with hers a heartbeat later, having no idea what to expect.

A pair of explosions, one right after the other, sent two quick, brilliant spark-fueled flashes over the hillside. Blinking against the remnant flares, Kenders spotted two creatures, twice as tall as a man and made of pure lightning, rushing towards the oligurts and their hulking, snarling mounts. Despite her heightened anxiety, Kenders could not help but feel a flicker of awe at what she had crafted as the beings lashed wildly at the Sudashians. The moment a sizzling limb touched an oligurt or bullockboar, the victim would go rigid, crash to the ground, and go sliding through the mucky hillside with smoke curling from their charred wounds.

Howling in fear, bullockboars began to scatter just as the charging Sentinels crashed into their flank. The northern section of the hill became a tangled mess of men, horse, oligurts, bullockboars, and two fibríaals of lightning.

Sensing the orange of Fire, Kenders shifted her attention back west. Her eyes went round.

A sphere of flame the size of her home in Yellow Mud was speeding through the air, charring trees it engulfed as it flew up the hill. Just before it reached the first line of fortifications, Kenders reached out, grabbed a number of the Strands within the globe, and unraveled the Weave. The fire dissipated in an instant, blasting the Sentinels with a gust of hot, dry air.

Looking down the hill, she spotted Jhaell and the oligurt mages marching behind the rest of the host. As she glared at the ijul, the Sudashian mages crafted another colossal ball of fire and sent it flying up at her. Wearing a tiny smile, she immediately unwound the Weave. As the globe of flame disappeared with a great whoosh, she noticed something about arrangement of the Strands.

Her smile grew a fraction and she said a silent prayer the Desert Fire mages would try again. They obliged by sending two burning spheres her way, sizzling, rolling through the air toward the Sentinels. Instead of instantly unraveling them though, this time she let the fire fly.

Oligurts had breached the first line of fortifications on the southern side and were pouring through a gap. Only fifty paces of open ground stood between the Sentinels and dozens of grayskins.

Waiting until the fireballs were above the breach, Kenders then reached into the tangled Strands, twisted the pattern, and yanked. The two balls of fire changed course, dropping straight down on top of the oligurts, roasting dozens of the enemy on impact. The flames must have been especially hot as they managed to set the rain-soaked fortifications on fire. Thick, black smoke spewed into the sky. Oligurts screamed.

The fireballs stopped after that.

Scanning the hill, she spotted other sections of the branch-and-log barriers failing. Her stomach clenched tight when she saw some oligurts had already reached the northern section of Sentinels. Close quarters combat was underway, the soldiers' bows and arrows discarded and replaced with swords and small round shields.

Skirmishes quickly broke out all along the line. Sergeant Trell, no longer shouting orders, was with his men, fighting the oligurts himself, his sword flashing in the sunlight. Nikalys was dashing around the battlefield, slicing and stabbing as many oligurts and razorfiends as he could reach. Yet even with his skill and speed, he could not singlehandedly stave off the Sudashian assault. There were simply too many of them.

Nundle had been reduced to using quick, simple bolts of Charge to repel some of the enemy, trying to strike down as many as quickly as possible. Unfortunately, most of his Weaves were being undone by the Desert Fire Mages before they struck their intended target.

Whether or not an order had been given, the group of horsemen on her left charged headlong into the crowded mess of oligurts and razorfiends, punching a hole in their line briefly before the Sudashians swarmed the Sentinels.

Mimicking the same Weave of Air that Nundle had used against the first wave of razorfiends, Kenders began to lift Sudashians into the air and toss their flailing bodies back down the hill. She had flung a dozen away before her Weaves stopped working. As soon as she would pick up a foe, the pattern fell apart, letting the monster drop straight back to the ground.

The hopelessness of their situation set in. "We're losing…"

Oligurts bellowed, swinging their spiked clubs with abandon, smashing men to the ground. Razorfiends leapt about the hill, blades outstretched to slice any blue and gold clad soldier that they could reach. Urazûd, no longer leading the charge, stood on the hillside with a crooked, evil grin affixed on his face. Jhaell stood beside the demon-man, his long arms crossed, his expression one of joyful anticipation.

As she stared at him, the memory of her hiding beneath the yellow-leafed bush, watching the ijul atop the bluff over Yellow Mud washed over her. The remembered anger of that moment shoved aside her despair. A surge of resolve exploded inside of her.

Kenders set her jaw. If she continued to remain cautious, she would die. They all would.

Drawing her beltknife, she glared at Jhaell and—bypassing any attempt to weave the Strands properly—willed that the saeljul was standing with her.

She wanted him here.

Beside her.

Now.

Strands popped into existence around her—thick, pure black mixed with brilliant, glowing silver—fully arranged in an incredibly complex pattern. She tottered on the hillside as a wave of bone-weary fatigue rushed through her. Her eyelids drooped shut against her will. She wanted to lie down and sleep for a week. Her knees began to buckle when a whispered word of angry determination slipped from her lips. "*No.*"

She refused to faint and compelled her eyes to open.

Jhaell Myrr stood a few paces from her, glancing around with wide eyes. "How did you do that? That Weave is imposs—" He cut off as his gaze locked on the knife in her hand. His eyes narrowed and he took a few quick steps backwards. Puffs of acrid black smoke from the burning fortifications below drifted between them.

Afraid that if she used the Strands again, she would pass out, Kenders advanced toward him, lifting the knife up despite having no idea what she was doing with it. She took two steps, stumbled over a rogue rock, and almost fell.

Jhaell halted his retreat and smiled a wicked, wide grin. "You are not as strong as you appear, are you?"

She hissed, "I'm strong enough!"

"You weren't strong enough to save your village."

Rage saturated her soul, overwhelming any rational thought. "Ahhhh!"

She rushed the ijul, lifting the beltknife over her head when she felt the crackling of Water and Air. Blinded by fury, Kenders did not react quickly enough to repel the blue and white Weave he tossed at her.

Suddenly, inexplicably, her mouth was full of water. She tried to spit it out, but could not. Panicking, she stumbled to a stop, dropped the knife, and instinctively grasped her throat. Her eyes went wide as she realized the water sloshing in her mouth filled her throat and lungs, too. She fell to the ground, collapsing to her hands and knees. She sensed a Weave of Air covering her nose and mouth, but could not focus enough to unravel it. Her chest burned inside. She was drowning, mere moments from passing out and dying.

Her braid fell to the side of her head and draped before her. Through tear-blurred eyes, she stared at the crimson cord binding her hair as it danced back and forth with each jolting, silent hack.

A single, whispered word slipped from Jhaell. "Syra…"

The barrier over her lips disappeared. Jets of water exploded from her mouth and nose. Deep, hacking coughs wracked her chest.

A soon as she could, Kenders lifted her head, wondering why Jhaell had released the Weave. The ijul was staring at her, his eyes vacant. The maliciousness was gone from his face. He almost looked sad.

She did not understand the sudden shift in attitude, nor did she care. She reached for Charge, swiftly knitted a simple Weave, and lashed out with it. A hissing bolt of lightning leapt toward Jhaell and struck the saeljul in the left shoulder, spinning him around and tossing him to the ground.

As Kenders continued to choke up water while keeping an eye on Jhaell, Nikalys' panicked voice rose over the din of battle. "Jak! No!"

Kenders whipped her head around and peered down the slope.

Jak rode at the head of twenty horsemen thundering across the hill, his sword over his head and mouth opened wide in a battle cry. Zecus was at his side, sword out and screaming as well. Kenders' gaze shot across the hill to rest upon their apparent target, the demon-man. Upon seeing the charge, Urazûd turned toward the horsemen, lifted his massive sword, and loosed a roar of challenge that filled the hillside, his voice echoing with a strange, throbbing power that she felt more than heard.

"Gods, Jak, no!"

Without warning, a wall of solid air slammed into her, lifting her from the mud, and tossing her back a dozen paces. As she crashed to the ground, the back of her head sunk into the mushy mud, ricocheting when it struck the solid rock just below the surface. She let out a short, sharp cry of pain.

Lying on her back, she cracked her eyes open. Everything was blurry. Tasting blood in her mouth, she ran her tongue around and found a gash on the inside of her cheek. She slowly lifted her head from the mud, blinking, trying to clear the webs choking her thoughts.

Jhaell was upright and moving toward her, clasping his shoulder with his long, thin fingers. Bloody, charred flesh peeked out from beneath his smoking shirt. The hateful glint in his eye was back.

Kenders needed to do something, but the blow to her head and the image of Jak rushing to his doom made it difficult for her to concentrate. Closing her eyes, she let her head fall back into the mud as despair returned with vengeance. Jak must be dead by now.

As she lay there, listening to Jhaell grunting in pain as he shuffled closer, a wholly unexpected sound filled the air, mixing with the clamor of the yelling, screaming, and fighting.

Cheering.

Joyous, relieved cheering.

She listened, thoroughly confused. The voices fueling the jubilation were not oligurts or razorfiends. It was the Sentinels. She clearly heard Sergeant Trell's voice among the shouts.

A hawk's piercing cry sliced through the air.

When she opened her eyes to look at the sky, she found Jhaell standing over her yet staring downhill, an angry scowl spread across his face. Peering down at her, he said with disdain, "They're too late to save you." He bent down and started to reach for Kenders' face.

Smacking his hand away, she growled, "Don't touch me!"

Jhaell's sneer turned vicious. She felt a flicker of white and suddenly both arms were pinned flat to the ground. As she gathered her wits to try to unravel the Weave of Air, Jhaell bent down again with his long fingers outstretched.

"Leave me alone!" she screamed, watching as he reached for her hair. He grabbed her braid, ripped the crimson cord from it, and tossed it aside.

Managing to gather her thoughts, she reached out and unraveled the Weave of Air pinning her to the ground. As the pattern fell apart, she felt Jhaell reaching for Void and Air. It only took moment for her to recognize the black and white pattern as the one he had tried to use earlier against Nikalys. He was weaving a port.

She lifted a leg and tried to kick him, but she had no strength. Jhaell grabbed her foot and shoved it to the side. She tried to sweep his legs from under him, cracking her shin into his ankle. He stumbled yet kept his balance, although the blow broke his concentration as the Weave fell apart.

"*Beelvra!*" He glared at her, growling, "Hold still and die!" He dropped suddenly, driving a knee into her stomach.

Her eyes went wide as every bit of air in her lungs burst from her lips. She lay there gasping, trying to breathe, as Jhaell rose to his feet and began to weave again. Weak, weary, and wheezing, it was all she could do to bat aside the Strands as he pulled them to the pattern. They struggled, tugging the strings in opposite directions. Jhaell was clearly an accomplished and highly skilled mage, however, and crafted the Weave faster than she could unravel it. She had no way to measure how long she fought against him. Time was either flowing incredibly fast or had slowed to a halt.

As Jhaell neared completion of the Weave, he stared down at her, triumphant. He was going to win today, and everyone on this hill was going to die. Herself included. It did not matter that she was the Progeny, that Indrida had foreseen her leading the charge against the god of Chaos. This was Kenders' fate. The words of the prophecy were simply that. Words.

The throb of despair turned into a soul-aching misery. A scream of anger and anguish shot from the deepest depths of her soul, tearing at her throat as it burst forth.

"Aaaaaahhh!"

She was determined to fight until the moment Maeana claimed her soul. She clawed at the Strands, ripping at them, yanking them from Jhaell. She would not quit. She refused to quit.

Suddenly, Jhaell stopped weaving. The Strands stopped coming.

Lying in the mud on the hillside, Kenders reached into the unfinished pattern and pulled at the center of the Weave. The tangle of Strands fell apart. Void and Air faded.

Shifting her gaze to Jhaell, she found the ijul's eyes impossibly wide, his lips parted in a silent scream. Sticking from his chest was the shimmering Blade of Horum. Blood swelled from the wound, the crimson blooming over Jhaell's tan shirt like a spring flower.

Jhaell dipped his chin and stared down at the tip of the white blade. He reached down, wrapped his long fingers around the sword, and tugged at it as though he could somehow pull it free. Instead, the clean, white metal retreated slowly, back into his chest, slicing open his hands and fingers as it went.

After the blade disappeared, a stumbling Jhaell turned to face his attacker.

Nikalys stood there, pointing the sword's tip at Jhaell's torso. "Don't move."

Kenders barely recognized her brother. The hard glint in his eye. His readied and tense posture. The twitching muscles in his jawline.

Jhaell lurched forward a bit, no longer graceful, and reached out to Nikalys. "You don't understand." He reached to his hip, grabbed a dagger's handle, and pulled it free. Nikalys did not see the knife as his eyes, burning with red-hot hatred, remained locked on the ijul's face.

As Jhaell began to bring his arm up to plunge the dagger into Nikalys' gut, Kenders shouted, "Nikalys!" She had already had lost one brother today. She would not lose another.

She stared at the dagger and wanted it gone, anywhere but in Jhaell's hand. A small Weave of pure black and white popped into existence, surrounded the dagger, and, with a soft pop, the knife disappeared. The expected tiredness filled her but she did not care.

Jhaell's empty hand struck Nikalys' stomach and bounced off. He dropped his head to stare down at his bloody palm just as Nikalys plunged the Blade of Horum into his chest. The shining white blade ripped through the ijul's back, paused briefly, and then retreated, twisting as it went.

The saeljul staggered a few steps down the hill before collapsing to the mud and leaves. He landed with a soft squish, his head turned toward Kenders. His eyes were vacant, still and lifeless.

From somewhere in the woods came the piercing shriek of the Soulwraith, carrying with it the unmistakable tone of relief. As the cry faded away, she looked up to find Nikalys standing over her, the Blade of Horum at his side. He was staring into the western woods, listening to the final echoes of the Soulwraith's call of deliverance.

As he turned to stare down at her, fear and concern filled his eyes. Crouching beside her, he asked, "Are you hurt?"

Her head throbbed, her stomach hurt, and she had yet to catch her breath, but she was alive. "I'm fine." Blinking repeatedly, she stared into the heavens above. The clouds had completely broken up and were colored rose by early dusk. Rolling her head to the side, she looked at the lifeless body of Jhaell. "You did it, Nik."

"We did it."

Beyond Jhaell's corpse, further down the slope, she spotted the Sentinels' blue and gold uninforms and tried to stand. Jhaell was dead, but there was still a battle going on. The Desert Fire mages were still out there somewhere and she needed to make sure they did not hurt anyone.

Nikalys placed a gentle hand on her shoulder, restraining her. "Relax. It's over."

"Over? What do you mean it's over?" As he helped her to a sitting position, her eyes shot open. "Jak!" Pushing Nikalys aside, she scrambled to her feet. The moment she stood, her head felt thick and heavy, the forest began twirling around her. She shut her eyes and grabbed Nikalys' shoulder for support. Her stomach lurched.

"The brave fool's fine," said Nikalys. "Zecus, too. They're out there somewhere with Broedi." He paused for a moment before adding, "Along with—if I had to guess—some of the Shadow Manes."

After taking a steadying breath, Kenders opened her eyes and scanned the western slope. At least two hundred men and women on horseback filled the hillside, all in mismatched clothes and armor. A few of the Sentinels rode with the new arrivals, across the battlefield and down the hill, chasing down the fleeing oligurts and razorfiends.

Kenders watched the scene for a few heartbeats before muttering, "I'm a little confused, Nik." Her gaze settled on a one body in particular that lay on the hill. Two spiraling, black horns rose from the corpse's head. Urazûd was dead. "Make that very confused."

"Me, too," said Nikalys as he stood.

"How did this happen? How did they find us?"

"I don't know and don't care. We're alive and the Sudashians are on the run." He stared hard at her, his gaze evaluating. "Are you sure you're all right?"

"I said I'm fine."

"Well, if that's the case…" He trailed off, his expression darkening as he peered downhill again. "Nundle could use some help…"

Kenders looked down the hill again and spotted the tomble kneeling beside a blue and gold clad body amidst what was a pile of razorfiends, oligurts, and men. Injured soldiers up and down the line were crying out in pain. With the fog beginning to clear from her head, she realized that she could feel and see the verdant Strands of Life hovering near the tomble. Without saying a word, Kenders pushed away from Nikalys and scampered down the slope as quickly as her pounding head would allow. The army of the White Lions needed her help.

CHAPTER 71: VICTORY

As Kenders rushed down the slope, Nikalys took one last look down the hill to see if he was needed anywhere. The Sudashians, however, were clearly on the run, the Shadow Manes and Red Sentinels riding them down from behind using arrows, magic, and sword.

The battle was more or less over.

Nikalys shook his head and closed his eyes. Somehow, they had won, which was a miracle considering how poorly things had been going.

The Sudashians had been overrunning the Sentinels when Nikalys spotted Jak and Zecus leading the twenty Sentinels across the hill, thundering toward on the demon-man. Nikalys had wanted to help his brother, but if he left the soldiers to fight the Sudashians alone, they would have died.

He continued cutting down as many of the beasts as he could while stealing quick glances down the hill to watch his brother. When Jak and his men reached the demon-man, Urazûd skewered Hunsfin with his massive sword, lifting the man from his saddle and tossing him aside like a sack of flour. Hunsfin's sacrifice allowed Zecus to stab the demon's neck, and Jak and the remaining men surrounded the spawn.

The piercing cry of a hawk pulled Nikalys' attention to the sky as a colossal, golden-brown bird of prey swooped down to the field. As the hawk dove, it shifted to Broedi's hillman form briefly before morphing into the hill lynx and landing softly on the hillside. Broedi joined the fight, leaping onto the back of an oligurt, clamping his jaws on the monster's neck. A moment later, a water creature appeared in the midst of the remaining Desert Fire mages and began thrashing the oligurts.

Dozens of men and women—many with weapons, some without—rode forth from the northern woods and charged straight into the flank of the oligurts and razorfiends. In a matter of moments, the battle had turned from impending, hopeless defeat to resounding victory. Jak's mad charge was impossibly successful. He and Zecus not only managed to kill Urazûd, but they survived, as well, although many of the other Sentinels did not.

When the demon-man fell, the remaining oligurts and razorfiends fled.

With the enemy in full retreat, Nikalys had stood on the hillside, sword at the ready but without an opponent to fight. He was starting down the slope, looking for Jhaell when a raw, knife-like scream cut the air. Recognizing the all-too-familiar voice, he spun around and spotted Jhaell standing over his sister. A blink of an eye later, Nikalys was behind him.

And, now, it was over.

Nikalys stared at the lifeless body of Jhaell. The deviant responsible for his parents' death and Yellow Mud's destruction was dead at last. One of the ijul's long arms was splayed out, pointing downhill, the other one bent at an odd angle. Leaves and muck muddied his once-lustrous, white-blonde hair. His tunic was soaked red with blood, absurdly matching the bright crimson cord that lay next to the ijul. Peering downhill, Nikalys noted Kenders' braid unraveling as she rushed about.

Looking back to Jhaell, he sighed and shook his head. It was hard to equate the harmless lump of flesh with the merciless monster that had destroyed Yellow Mud.

Nikalys lifted his sword and stared at it. Its metal gleamed and glowed as bright as the first time he had set eyes on it, not a speck of grime or gore on it. He wished he could say the same for the rest him. The byproducts of death coated his arms, chest, and—by the foul taste in his mouth—his face.

Sighing, he slipped the sword into its scabbard and dropped to the ground, not caring that he was sitting in mud. For a time, he simply sat there, entirely unsure of what to do with himself, alternating between staring at Jhaell's corpse and the dead Sudashians littering the hill.

He wondered how many of them were by his hand. At the height of the battle, he had been keeping count but had stopped when he realized he was marking bodies, not crates of olives being delivered to the river warehouse. These were living, breathing creatures and he was slaughtering them. At that point, an icy numbness filled him and, so far, it had yet to go away. He had ended dozens of lives today.

Hearing soft footsteps approached from behind, his right hand drifted toward his sword's hilt.

"Nikalys?"

Relaxing, he looked over his shoulder. Sabine stood a few paces away, cradling Helene in her arms. He locked eyes with the young woman. The grime of travel coated her, yet her beauty was such that it shone through.

A worried expression rested on her face. "Are you alright?"

Nikalys held her gaze a moment before turning to stare back downhill. "Go away, please." He did not want to talk. Not now.

A few moments passed before she moved. He frowned when he realized she was drawing closer rather than walking away. Sabine placed Helene on the ground and kneeled in the mud beside him.

Without looking back, he said tersely, "Truly, Sabine. Just leave—"

He stopped as she wrapped her arms around his shoulders and laid her head on his back, her soft hair brushing his neck. Helene moved around to his front, crawled into his lap, and curled up into a little ball. Neither sister said a word.

He wanted to scream at them both to go away. If he could clear this hill of everyone and be here alone right at this moment, he would do so. He longed for solitude.

Yet, he did not yell. He did not shout. Instead, he slowly draped his arms around Helene, rested his chin on her soft, black hair, and stared at a dead oak leaf on the ground, studying the little lines fanning out from the stem and through the yellowing foliage.

At some point, while sitting there, he began to cry. The numbness he felt revealed itself for what it truly was: a roiling, swirling mixture of relief, anguish, despair, and a multitude of other emotions he could not name nor understand. Sabine silently stroked his head as tears rolled down his cheeks and dripped on Helene's head. The little girl did not seem to mind. Rather, she reached out with her tiny fingers, took his blood-covered hand, and held it, clutching tight.

The trio remained that way for a long time. No one approached them. No one asked for anything. Amidst the sea of post-battle chaos, Nikalys and the Moiléne sisters were a tiny island of calm.

When the tears stopped coming, Nikalys drew in a deep breath, reached his free hand over to Sabine, and gently patted her leg. "Thank you."

Sabine's only response was to squeeze him tighter.

Helene tilted her head back and stared up at him with her big, brown eyes. She gave him a tiny, fragile smile and muttered, "We're safe." Nikalys tried to smile back, but failed. After a moment, she dropped her gaze and whispered, "For now."

Nikalys stared at the dead bodies on the hill and sighed. He suspected Helene was right.

Chapter 72: Hope

17ᵗʰ of the Turn of Thonda

Nikalys stood alone on the hill, staring at the thick, black clouds of acrid smoke rising from the burning pile of corpses, billowing into the night and choking the stars from the sky. A constant, popping staccato exploded from the fire as razorfiends' quills burst open due to the blaze's heat. An awful odor filled the air, a mixture of roasting meat, charred filth, and death. The soft easterly breeze carried most of the stench from the ridge top, but it could not take it all.

A continuous succession of Shadow Manes moved past him, dragging or carrying Sudashian corpses to the inferno, tossing them into the pile, and then heading back down the hill to collect more. Too heavy for men to carry, dead oligurts were draped over horses' backs and brought to the fire. Razorfiends, their blades too sharp to risk anyone picking them up, were maneuvered onto makeshift stretchers with sticks and then dragged to the blaze.

Most every person who passed Nikalys during their grim task stole a glance or two at him. At first, the staring had bothered him. Every one of their expectant gazes felt like another yoke dropped around his neck. Having so many look upon him with hope, awe, and respect was unnerving.

Until recently, his days were filled with chores in Yellow Mud's groves and vineyards or afternoon swims in Lake Hawthorne. Life had been good. It had been simple. It had made sense.

These Manes knew nothing of that life, of that Nikalys. When they stared at him, they saw the Progeny of the White Lions, the son of Aryn Atticus and Eliza Kap, here to lead the fight against the god of Chaos and the Cabal. To them, he was a hero whose return they had been anxiously awaiting for fifteen years.

As he stood there, staring into the pyre without truly seeing it, he battled himself, trying to reconcile who he was: the middle child of farmers or the eldest son of two legendary heroes. It had taken time, a long time, but he eventually concluded he was not one or the other. He was both and always would be.

At once, his nerves settled. The Shadow Manes' gazes still bothered him, but less so.

What should have bothered him was the scene—and smell—before him now. Two turns ago, a bonfire of burning bodies would have made him sick to his stomach. Tonight, he felt nothing. The cold, empty numbness had engulfed him once again. It was easier to feel nothing.

A pair of men hefted an oligurt off a horse and tossed it into the burning pile. As they moved away, on their way to retrieve another, Nikalys eyed the new corpse. For a moment, the flames did not touch the oligurt, seemingly pausing as though unsure whether or not they were supposed to char the beast's flesh. Curls of white smoke seeped from crevices between the newest body and the others already burnt beyond recognition. The fire toasted the edges of the oligurt's hide tunic for a moment before fully committing to their purpose.

Nikalys wondered if this particular beast had perished at his hand. He was staring at a long, fleshy wound across the beast's chest, straining to recall if he had inflicted it when a deep voice rumbled behind him.

"You did what had to be done, Nikalys."

Nikalys blinked, startled. He had not heard anyone approach him. Turning to look over his shoulder, he found Broedi standing a few paces behind him, staring at the bonfire as well. With quiet wonder, he muttered, "You called me by my name."

The hillman's gaze shifted to Nikalys' face. "I know." As Broedi studied him, a small frown spread over the White Lion's face. The hillman let out a quiet sigh, stepped forward to stand between Nikalys and the fire, and clasped his hands behind his back. "Have you never wondered why I have not before?"

"I've wondered plenty, Broedi."

"Yet you never asked."

Nikalys shrugged. "I didn't ask because I didn't expect I'd get an answer."

Broedi was silent for a moment, nodding slowly, before rumbling, "When aki-mahet reach their fifteenth year, they lose their given name and are called 'uora' or 'uori' by the tribe until they prove themself worthy of their name. Dozens of people are alive tonight because of you, Nikalys. Your fathers—both of them, I believe—would be proud of you."

Not knowing how to respond, Nikalys simply stared up at the hillman, watching the bonfire's light dance around the edge of his hair and face. When the silence between the pair stretched long, the hillman nodded as genuine concern spread over his normally stoic face. "Aryn was very quiet after battle as well. He would stand alone for hours. 'Thinking,' he said."

Nikalys dipped his chin, dropping his gaze to the muddy ground, unsure what Broedi wanted him to do with that bit of information.

Broedi rumbled softly, "You would do well to remember his advice."

Nikalys looked back up. "Pardon?"

"His letter. Remember his words to you."

Nikalys had read the letter countless times since that first night by the campfire. By now, the scrawled words were burned into memory. Reciting it to himself in his mind, he stopped when he realized to what Broedi must be referring. In a quiet, reserved tone, he said, "'Do what you must, when you must. Move on as best you can, as soon as you can.'"

"It is good advice."

Nikalys looked past the White Lion to the glowing pyre. "He said it took him a long time to realize that."

"Decades, I am afraid."

Without looking away from the fire, Nikalys asked, "How long have I been standing here?"

"Longer than I would have had hoped."

Nikalys nodded slowly. Aryn was right. Standing here, dwelling on his actions was not helping anything or anyone. Pulling his eyes from the blaze, he stared up at Broedi. "Let's go."

A slight smile graced the hillman's face. "Come with me, please." Turning south, he began to stride from the burning bodies.

Nikalys followed, asking, "Where are we going?"

Lifting a hand, Broedi pointed toward the southern hillside and the grove of trees in which Jak and his men had hidden. "There."

A roaring campfire burned amongst the oaks where Nikalys' family and friends had set up for the night. "Good." He needed to be with them more than with his thoughts.

As the pair walked across the hillside, the people they passed would stare at him and, for the first time, he met their gazes without reservation. Most gave a silent nod of greeting, but some offered a quiet "hello" or even a "good evening, Progeny." He smiled and politely nodded back, trying not to cringe when someone addressed him with the title.

Halfway to the grove, they came across a section of ground with at least a dozen freshly dug, still-empty graves. Dozens of Sentinels were hollowing out more, using whatever they could to shove the muddy earth aside, trying to find places where solid rock was not inches below the surface. Nikalys spotted Cero and Wil on their knees, using their bare hands to dig. Wil looked ten years older than he had this morning.

Soldiers' bodies were lined up nearby, on their backs with arms folded over their chests, waiting to be placed into the unfinished graves. Nikalys might not have known many of them well, but he recognized every face and knew most of their names. Two, however, stood out. When he reached the bodies, he stopped and stared down at the pair of men.

Corporal Holb had suffered a crushing blow to the back of the head from an oligurt's club during the charge into the bullockboars. His face was untouched, and if it were not for the sunken, bloody skull Nikalys had seen earlier, he would swear that the man was sleeping. To the corporal's right lay

Hunsfin. Without the scout's sacrifice and those of ten other men in that charge, Jak would be dead. Staring at the dead man, Nikalys murmured, "Thank you for my brother."

If Broedi heard his quiet whisper—and he probably did—he showed no sign. The hillman stayed by his side, offering his mere presence as comfort.

Looking up, Nikalys spotted Sergeant Trell walking among the graves and dead soldiers. The sergeant glanced up, saw Broedi and Nikalys, and strode over to them, pushing aside the haunted expression on his face. Halting before the pair, Sergeant Trell examined Nikalys closely. The concern in his eyes was clear. "How are you doing, son?"

Nikalys stared at the man in quiet awe. The sergeant was burying dozens of his men and here he was, inquiring as to Nikalys' wellbeing. After a stunned moment, he managed to reply in a quiet, restrained tone. "I'll be fine."

Sergeant Trell shot Broedi a quick, questioning look. After a slight nod from the White Lion, the soldier glanced back to Nikalys and nodded. "Good to hear."

He accepted Nikalys' answer, whether or not he believed it was another matter. Nikalys wondered what the sergeant's instinct was telling him right now.

Glancing at the line of bodies, Nikalys murmured, "Do you have a final number, then?"

Sergeant Trell failed to hold back the sorrow in his face or voice as he answered. "Thirty-nine."

Nikalys' gaze drifted to the sky, coming to rest on White Moon. He took a deep breath and exhaled. Thirty-nine Sentinels dead.

"I'm sorry, Sergeant," rumbled Broedi. "They were good men."

With pride in his voice, the sergeant said, "Yes. They were."

Nikalys dropped his head and stared back to the dead soldiers. "So many…"

Sergeant Trell looked to the oak grove where the other campfire burned. "It would have been more if not for Nundle and your sister. At least twenty men owe them their lives."

Nikalys supposed that was some solace. "Is there anything I can do to help, Sergeant? Perhaps dig graves?"

Sergeant Trell held up a hand of protest. "No, thank you. I appreciate the offer, but I think the men want to do it themselves." He looked at the soldiers who were digging, a sad scowl spreading over his face. "It helps them, I think."

Nikalys nodded. "I understand."

Reaching out to pat him on the shoulder, Sergeant Trell said, "Go. Be with your brother and sister."

"Yes, Sergeant."

A weary smile touched the corners of the soldier's mouth. "Truly, son, you are going to have to stop calling me that."

Giving the man a tired grin of his own, Nikalys said, "Not until you pick your new rank. Have you chosen yet? Shall it be lieutenant or captain?"

"Don't start with that nonsense." His tone was jovial but definitely muted by the day's events. He gave Nikalys a gentle shove. "Go on, now. Get out of here."

Nikalys made sure to walk past where the injured were resting in order to check on their recovery. Most of those on the ground were Sentinels, although a few Shadow Manes lay among them, having been hurt while chasing down the fleeing Sudashians. Many were sleeping, healing quicker than was natural due to the magical aid given them.

Both Broedi and Nikalys stopped to talk with those who were awake, thanking them for their bravery and offering condolences for the loss of their friends and fellow soldiers. It was a difficult experience for Nikalys, but he did what he could to keep the grief he felt from reaching his face.

As they strode away from the final soldier, Broedi leaned close and murmured, "You did well. They will remember you care the next time they fight for you."

Nikalys let out a long, low sigh. "The next time, huh?"

Broedi eyed him, but said nothing. Nikalys knew there would be more battles, more injured, and more deaths. And it sickened him.

The pair finally reached the small grove where his family and friends waited. The brush that had covered the areas between the tree trunks now lay in a large pile off to one side. A huge fire roared at the camp's center, fueled by logs and branches from the nearby mound.

As he approached, Nikalys judged the fire unnecessarily large. The evening was chilly, but not cool enough that it warranted such a sizeable blaze. The bright, warm light that illuminated the grove was welcome, though, and effective in chasing away the gloom of night. As he stepped closer, the pungent wood smoke from this fire filled his nostrils, masking the odor of the roasting oligurts and razorfiends. His opinion changed in an instant. This fire was wholly necessary.

Zecus was the only one standing. Furthest from the fire and with his back to Nikalys, the Borderlander was staring westward into the night, as if he were keeping watch, waiting for one last charge from the Sudashians.

Between Zecus and the roaring fire, Nundle lay on his back with his eyes closed, more than likely sleeping. What with his constant feats of magic during the battle and then his tending to the injured, he had to be exhausted.

Sabine sat on the ground with Helene sleeping in her lap, stroking the little girl's black hair while softly singing. As Nikalys stared at toddler, he felt a tiny smile touch his lips. Helene was a sweet, funny, and inquisitive little girl for whom Nikalys would give his life. He wondered if this was how a father feels about a daughter or son.

He lifted his gaze to Sabine's face and the smile slipped away as a set of confusing emotions swelled inside him. Sabine was clever, brave, and fiercely protective of her sister, all qualities he admired. And her beauty was undeniable. Nevertheless, at times he felt uneasy around her, the image of her slicing the unconscious bandit's neck flashing through his mind unbidden. As wondrous as Sabine was, something inside her chilled him.

Sabine met his gaze and gave him a wide, brilliant smile, obviously happy to see him. The grin, like Sabine herself, both pulled him in and pushed him away. He looked away from her quickly without returning her smile.

His brother and sister were resting near Nundle. Jak was sitting upright, his back against an oak trunk and eyes closed while Kenders lie beside him, her head resting on his left leg as if it were a pillow. She, too, had her eyes shut, yet her face was taut, tense. Nikalys wondered what was going through her mind.

He had yet to say much to either of them since the battle. Jak and Zecus had ridden off with Broedi and the Shadow Manes to hunt down the scattered oligurts and razorfiends while Kenders had helped Nundle tend to the soldiers. By the time Jak had returned and Kenders was done, Nikalys had already taken up his position before the funeral pyre. Kenders had left him alone entirely, but Jak stopped by once, gave him a silent hug, and then walked away.

As Broedi and Nikalys stepped into the circle of firelight, Jak opened his eyes a crack and gave the pair a tired smile. "Hey, you got him to stop staring at that pile of dead things."

Jak's careless tone bothered Nikalys, his earlier thoughts about the lives he had taken still resonated within him. He almost said something, but stopped short. Such a comment could start an argument. Now was not the time for that. He was too tired. Everyone was.

Eyeing his brother, Nikalys said, "I'm here now..."

"Good. I'm glad."

Kenders pushed herself from the ground to settle into a sitting position and gave him a tiny, weary smile. "Me, too."

Nikalys strode over to an exposed, flat rock between Kenders and Nundle with the intention of sitting on the stone. As he approached, the tomble— apparently not sleeping—murmured, "Please don't sit on me." Nundle's eyes remained closed, his hands folded on his chest. He had removed his hat and was resting his mass of bright red hair on it.

Glancing down, Nikalys asked, "Why not? You're about the right size for a stool."

A tiny smile crept across the tired mage's lips. "Oh, come now. That's not very nice."

"I'm only jesting," said Nikalys as he settled on the stone.

"Of course, my Lord Progeny."

Nikalys smiled at the return jab. "I deserved that, I suppose."

Broedi retrieved his leather satchel and moved to sit on the ground between Jak and Sabine. The camp remained quiet as the hillman reached into the pack, pulled out his bone pipe, and began to pack it with smoking-leaf.

Nikalys watched him for a few moments before asking, "How do you still have any of that left?"

The hillman smiled his slight grin. "I purchased some in Fernsford. It is not anywhere near as good as Five Boroughs' Sweetbush cut, but it will suffice."

With eyes still closed, Nundle mumbled, "Everything about the Boroughs is better, you know."

"Is it, now?" rumbled Broedi. "How so?"

"Well, for one, I was never chased across the countryside by demons, oligurts, and razorfiends intent on killing me. See? Better."

The jest earned at least a light chuckle from everyone around the fire, including Nikalys. Smiling felt good. Broedi eyed him across the flames and gave a silent nod. The hillman had been right. This was better than staring at burning bodies.

The soft laughter slowly faded as a comfortable silence fell over the group.

Kenders put her head on Nikalys' shoulder and he wrapped his right arm around her. After a time, Zecus walked over and offered to get the "great warrior" something to eat, but Nikalys turned him away, thanking him without bothering to correct the silly title. He was not hungry. The remembered smell of the burning bodies was still thick in his nose despite the fire nearby.

For a time, the only sound in the grove was the crackling of the fire, Sabine's soft humming, and the sounds of digging down the slope. While Nikalys had dozens of things he wanted to ask Broedi, right now, he was content to be silent—and alive—with his friends and family.

His restful quiet was doomed, however. Too many questions begged asking. As soon as he heard Sabine stop humming, Nikalys knew the respite was over.

Speaking in a soft, quiet voice, almost as if she were ashamed to be the one to break the tranquility, Sabine murmured, "Broedi...?"

Nikalys opened his eyes—he did not remember closing them—and regarded the raven-haired woman. Her brown eyes shone bright with the fire's flickering light.

Keeping his gaze locked on the flames, Broedi pulled his bone pipe from his mouth. "Ask your question."

Sabine sat a little taller, shifting Helene in her lap. "How do you know I want to ask a question?"

One side of Broedi's mouth turned up ever so slightly. "So you do not wish to ask a question?"

"Well…yes. I do."

"Then ask."

Sabine's eyes narrowed a bit. "Fine, then. Mind telling us how the Shadow Manes found us? Not that I'm complaining they did, but I don't understand how."

"I have one, too," mumbled Nundle. "How did you know they were coming?"

Nikalys felt Kenders shift her head on his shoulder as she asked, "And why didn't you tell us?"

Nikalys stared at the White Lion and waited. All three questions had drifted though his mind a number of times when standing before the bonfire.

Without looking away from fire, Broedi let a slow stream of smoke drift from his parted lips before saying, "To be clear, I did not know they were coming."

"Pardon?" said Jak. He sounded surprised.

Broedi's gaze shifted to Jak briefly before returning to the fire. "I did not know they were coming. I thought the chance was good they might, though."

Nikalys was no longer restful upon hearing that. He had assumed Broedi had reasons for not telling them about the Manes and had been content to leave it at that. However, to learn that their arrival had not been assured was more than disconcerting.

"They weren't coming to find us?" asked Jak. Now he sounded surprised and disturbed.

Broedi shook his head. "No, they were not."

Incredulous, Nikalys asked, "We won today because of luck?"

"Luck?" replied Broedi, lifting a lone eyebrow. He gave a short shake of his head. "No. Luck had nothing to do with what happened today. Or any of the past few weeks." He placed his pipe back between his lips and took a long draw as everyone else stared at one another in clear confusion.

Jak said, "I don't suppose you'd care to explain what you mean by that?"

With little curls of smoke drifting from his mouth, Broedi said, "Luck is happenstance. Luck is random. Luck dances through life, helping fate to play out its intended course." He paused a moment. "The Manes are *not* here because of luck."

Nikalys asked, "Then how did they just happen to be out there at the *perfect* moment when we needed them? You said the enclave is a week away."

"It is."

From behind Nikalys, Zecus said, "Then I am confused, great lion." A tiny frown crossed Broedi's lips. "How is it they were here to aid us?"

Broedi pulled his bone pipe from his mouth and stared at it while answering. "I suspect they are here today thanks to a few helpful nudges by someone." He tilted his head to the side, pondering. "Or rather something. I have never decided how to name them."

Kenders sat tall and shook her head. "Broedi, you are making even less sense than usual."

"I have to agree," said Nundle. The tomble had propped himself up on his elbows and was eyeing the hillman with suspicion. "What are you saying?"

A number of frustratingly silent moments passed with Broedi staring at his pipe when Jak muttered, "Water from a blasted rock."

The comment drew Broedi's gaze. "You will have your water, Jak. This rock is merely trying to decide the best manner in which to share it."

Jak was quiet for a moment. "Know about our little saying, do you?"

"Of course," rumbled Broedi. He pointed to his ear. "Remember. Good hearing."

An embarrassed grimace spread over Jak's face. "Sorry."

"Do not be. You are not the first to feel that way about me."

"Broedi," said Kenders, her tone firm. "While I'm glad—very glad—you plan to tell us, could you speak plainly when you do for once? I'm tired and don't want to puzzle out riddles and half-answers."

Nikalys smothered a smile. The impatient, demanding outburst reminded him of the old Kenders.

The White Lion smiled slightly and nodded. "You want it plain?" His gaze unexpectedly shifted to Nikalys' left. "Tell me, Nundle, do you not find it incredibly fortuitous you are here?"

"Well, of course." The tomble pushed himself up further until he was sitting with legs crossed. "I mean, I thought for sure that we were about to be overrun by the Sudashians. We all did, I think."

Everyone nodded his or her heads. Defeat had seemed imminent.

Broedi gave a short, dismissive wave of his hand. "You misunderstand the breadth of my question. What I mean is: do you not find the sequence of events that brought *you*, an acolyte of the Strand Academies in the Arcane Republic all the way to this hilltop tonight rather unusual?"

"I suppose so," muttered Nundle, a frown on his face. A moment later, he continued with more conviction, saying, "Now that you mention it, it all does seem a little improbable."

"A little improbable?" rumbled Broedi. "That is like saying water is a little wet. You *happened* to be in Jhaell's office at the right moment to find that letter.

You find your way to the duchies where you *happen* to stumble upon Jhaell and the Sentinels. Then, the sergeant *happens* to decide to look—"

Putting his hands up to stop Broedi, Nundle said, "Yes, fine. I see your point. The list of coincidences is long."

Broedi lifted a single eyebrow. "Ah…but what if they are *not* coincidences?"

"You promised to speak plainly," said Jak.

"But I am. Do you remember the story of the White Lions I shared with you? The true tale?"

Nodding, Jak asked, "What of it?"

"The Assembly of Nine involved themselves in mortal affairs because the threat posed to order and balance was too great to ignore. Yet once the Demonic War was over and Norasim defeated, they retreated to their seats and temples, leaving us mortals to our own devices. All of us. Including the White Lions."

Sabine, keeping her voice quiet, said, "I fail to see how that has anything to do with the Shadow Manes arriving at the perfect time."

Staring at Sabine, Broedi asked, "No?"

The elder Moiléne sister shook her head firmly. "No."

Broedi looked around the fire, peering from face to face. "I believe the Celystiela—or some of them, at least—have deemed our current situation worthy of their involvement again. I think they have been subtly arranging things to aid us as we have made our way south. With their guidance, we were brought together to stand on this hill today. All of us, including the Manes."

"Hold a moment," said Nikalys. "You're saying the gods brought us here?"

"More or less," rumbled Broedi. "More for some, less for others."

Nundle asked, "Are you saying my choices, the decisions I made that brought me here…were not mine to make?" He sounded rather disturbed by the notion. Nikalys sympathized.

"Not at all," said Broedi. "The choices were yours. I am merely saying that you might have suffered a bit of inspiration at opportune moments, gentle nudges to ensure that you were in the right place at the right time."

The tomble's face bunched up. "I don't know…I mean, how would that even work?"

"The barrel," mumbled Jak. Nikalys, along with everyone, turned to look at him. He was staring into the fire, eyes distant. "The barrel I jumped in during the attack on Yellow Mud." He looked up, his voice gaining strength. "I had given up. I had accepted my fate. Then the idea of hopping in an empty barrel just popped into my head. I remember thinking where in the Nine Hells that had come from."

"Taken by itself, I may say inspiration," rumbled Broedi. "Or perhaps your own cleverness. Each and every event that has brought us together might seem a chance happening, but line them up, one after another?" He shook his head. "Coincidence only goes so far."

"What are you saying?" asked Kenders.

"The Celystiela meddled with countless lives during the Demonic War," answered Broedi, a grim frown on his face. "I believe they are doing so again. I have thought so ever since the night in the fort."

Zecus took a quick step forward. "I am here at a god's urging?" He wore a troubled expression.

Broedi stared up at the Borderlander. "With you, Zecus, I am convinced of it." He paused and draped his arms over his knees. "Why did you leave your family in Demetus?"

Zecus' expression turned hard. "I wanted to stop the invaders."

Staring intently at the dark-skinned man, Broedi asked, "In the Borderlands, nothing is more honorable than protecting one's family. *Nothing.* Yet you leave your mother, brother, and sisters alone? With no money and their safety in doubt?"

Zecus' eyes narrowed sharply. "I am *not* proud of that."

"Of course not. You have a good heart, a worthy soul. Learning what kind of man you are has convinced me the Celystiela are interfering again. Would you have *ever* thought to leave them on your own?"

Zecus glared at Broedi for a long, quiet moment before answering. "Unlikely." He looked and sounded angry.

Nikalys glanced at Kenders and found her peering back at the Borderlander with sympathetic eyes. A second, closer look revealed there was more than simple compassion in her gaze.

"What about me?" murmured Sabine. "And Helene? Did my father die because the gods meddled?" Her tone rivaled Zecus' angry one, yet was colder somehow.

Broedi's face clouded. "Perhaps. Perhaps not. Your fate might simply have crossed paths with ours. I do not pretend to know everything."

Sabine's expression hardened. Nikalys' uneasy feeling returned as he stared at her.

Kenders asked, "So, the gods and goddesses are involving themselves. Is this a sweet thing? Or sour?"

Broedi tilted his head, pondering the question. "Both, I believe."

"That's a half-answer, Broedi," said Kenders. "You promised."

Broedi held up his hand. "Let me explain. The sweet is that we may be able to turn to them for aid. The sour is that their interest means that the Cabal's threat is imminent."

Jak murmured, "Sounds mostly sour to me."

"I was thinking the same thing," said Nikalys.

Broedi tilted his head and sat tall. "If you require further proof the Celystiela are inserting themselves in mortal affairs, let us talk with them."

"Talk with them?" asked Nikalys, confused. "The gods?"

"No," rumbled Broedi. He pointed north. "Them."

Nikalys stared into the night beyond the campfire's glow to see a man and woman walking toward them with purpose. While standing by the funeral pyre, he had spotted the pair speaking with Broedi earlier. Both were members of the Shadow Manes and, from the little he had observed, they were in charge.

The man looked to be a couple decades older than Sergeant Trell, had short gray hair, a few days' stubble, and eyes sunk deep in their sockets. Based on the way he carried himself, his hand always resting on his sword's hilt, Nikalys marked him a soldier.

The woman was younger, perhaps in her mid-forties, with straight, blonde hair that hung to her shoulders. Her features were sharp and pristine: green eyes, an angular nose with a perfect, rounded tip, and a pair of full lips currently pressed together in a thin, straight line. She would be attractive if she smiled, but something about her made Nikalys think such an occasion was rare. While she seemed suited to wear the fashionable dresses of a noblewoman, she currently had on a light blue shirt, tan breeches, and brown leather boots. As she strode near, an aura of power and expectation moved with her.

The pair moved into the glow of the camp and stopped before Broedi. As one, they bowed to the hillman and said in unison, "Great honor to you, White Lion."

Broedi grimaced, clearly uneasy with the greeting. "Please do not do that. I am trying to break him—" he pointed at Zecus "—of the habit and this does not help." While the soldier cracked a smile at Broedi's minor admonishment, the woman's pressed lips grew ever thinner. Turning his gaze to the woman, Broedi said, "And I believe that might be the first time in ten years you've bowed to me, my Lady."

Nikalys' eyebrows arched as he exchanged a quick, surprised look with Jak and Kenders. 'My Lady' was a title reserved for noblewomen.

"As everyone is watching," said the woman quietly, "I felt I needed to make a *rare* exception."

Broedi's gaze drifted to where members of the Shadow Manes were walking about the hill, staring over at the campsite. "I see."

The woman turned to face Kenders and Nikalys and—for the briefest of moments—the hard lines on her face softened and the faintest of smiles touched her lips. As quick as it arrived, it fled, as though afraid of getting caught somewhere it should not be. "It has been fifteen *very* long years since I have laid eyes on either of you."

Nikalys gawked at the woman, unsure of what to say or do. He was still trying to figure out why or how a noble was a member of the Shadow Manes. Regardless, she was nobility and he decided he should at least be standing in her presence. He scrambled to his feet, as did Kenders and Jak. Nundle rose, as well, albeit much slower, while wearing a curious expression.

Once on their feet, Nikalys and his siblings stood motionless and silent, unsure what to do next. Thankfully, Broedi intervened.

"Introductions are in order, I think." After rising from the ground, Broedi moved to stand between the Shadow Mane pair and the Isaac children. "Nikalys, Kenders, Jak, this is Baroness Vivienne of the coastal Argolles Barony, and this is Jules Aiden, former Knight-Lieutenant in the Southern Arms and current commander of our forces at the enclave."

After a momentary pause, the three siblings began to speak at once.

"Good days ahead..."

"My Lady and...sir, I guess...?"

"It is an honor to meet..."

None of them completed their greetings, rather they all trailed off, jointly embarrassed at their fumbling. Nikalys caught an amused chuckle from Sabine.

Continuing with the introductions, Broedi said, "Lady Vivienne, Commander, I would like to re-introduce you to Nikalys and Kenders, as well as present to you their brother in all but blood, Jak Isaac of Yellow Mud."

The Shadow Manes both bowed in their direction, Lady Vivienne's gaze remaining fixed on Nikalys or Kenders throughout. Since first laying eyes on them, she had not looked away, even when Broedi had introduced Jak. Commander Aiden, on the other hand, after politely acknowledging Nikalys and Kenders, settled to staring almost exclusively at Jak. Deep furrows split his brow suggesting a very confused man.

Broedi went about presenting the others in their circle. Nundle and Zecus first, both of whom handled themselves with infinitely more poise than the Isaac children. Next, came Helene and Sabine, who profusely apologized for not rising as Helene was sound asleep. Wearing a kind smile, the commander insisted she stay seated while Lady Vivienne barely acknowledged her, giving only a quick nod in her direction. After each introduction, Commander Aiden would return to staring at Jak. He seemed intent on boring a hole into Jak's head with his gaze alone.

Eventually, Jak leaned close to his siblings and whispered, "Do I have something on my face?"

Nikalys was about to respond in the negative when the old soldier stepped forward and, with round eyes and a wide smile, exclaimed, "I've got it! Thaddeus! Thaddeus Karryl!" Nikalys, Jak, and Kenders turned as one to gape at the commander as he continued, relief washing over his face. "Gods, that was bothering me! Sorry for staring, young man, but Nine Hells if you don't look just like a blacksmith I knew years ago in Claw. The best blasted smith the Manes ever had. He and his wife...ah...oh, what was her name...?" He trailed off, his brow furrowing in thought.

Nikalys, Kenders, and Jak answered in unison. "Marie."

"That's it! Marie! Hells, I haven't seen them in—" He stopped suddenly and stared at the trio through narrowed eyes. "Hold a moment..." Lady Vivienne finally gave Jak more than a passing glance.

Nikalys ran through everything he knew about his parents—all four of them—in his head. His blood parents needed someone to watch over him and Kenders while they attempted to thwart a prophecy. It only made sense Aryn and Eliza would choose people who both knew the importance of the task given them and the risks they were taking. Thaddeus and Marie had been members of the Shadow Manes.

Broedi stared at the three siblings with the most open and honest expression Nikalys had ever seen hillman wear. He was shocked. Shifting his gaze to rest solely on Jak, he shook his head. "I am sorry, Jak, but if you look as much like your father as the commander says, I do not remember him."

"Hells," said Commander Aiden. "Why would you? What use did you have for a blacksmith?" He looked back to the siblings. "Aryn, on the other hand, spent countless afternoons in Thaddeus' workshop. He and I both." A smile spread over his face. "Him mostly because he enjoyed Thaddeus' company and stories, me because of all of the dents Aryn put in my armor from sparring." Looking back to Broedi, he asked, "You remember how Gamin and Sevan came to us?"

"Vaguely," rumbled the hillman. "They were found wandering the forest, I believe."

Commander Aiden nodded. "That, they were. Well, there was another pair with them. A husband and wife."

"I'm sorry?" interjected Nikalys, baffled. "Who are Gamin and Sevan?"

Kenders said, "Gamin is the head mage with the Manes."

Nikalys and Jak both turned to their sister. Jak beat Nikalys to the obvious question. "How'd you know that?"

Kenders pointed at Broedi. "He told me. On our way through Fernsford."

Broedi rumbled, "Gamin and his brother both left the city after the great fire destroyed much of the market district. They were accepted into the Manes that winter."

"As were Thaddeus and Marie," said Commander Aiden. "Although, I knew them as Karryl..." His gaze shifted to Jak as he shook his head with obvious wonder.

Kenders let out a heavy sigh and looked between her brothers. "I guess what they told us about the Fernsford fire was true."

"Only they went south afterwards," muttered Nikalys. "Not north." As he set to reorganizing his past yet again, he looked over at Jak, worried how he was taking this.

Jak's eyes darted back and forth, dancing around without truly seeing anything. After a few moments, a sly smile crept across his face and he looked over to Nikalys and Kenders. "I suppose this means I was a member of the Shadow Mane before you."

After letting out a quiet sigh of relief, Nikalys wondered aloud, "Why didn't they ever say anything to us?"

"Perhaps they didn't know where to begin?" suggested Jak. "And, Hells, even if they had said something, would any of us have honestly believed them?"

Jak was right. They would never have swallowed such a tale on words alone. Perhaps if Thaddeus and Marie had presented them with the teardrop necklace and Aryn's sword, they might have, yet there was no way to know that now.

Commander Aiden crossed his arms over his chest. "You know, now that I think on things, Thaddeus and Marie left Storm Island shortly before Eliza and Aryn disappeared. Perhaps only a turn or so." He stared at Jak, a fond smile on his face. "Thad said they wanted to settle somewhere safer to raise their son. I didn't blame them. We lost a number of good people for the same reason at the time. I never gave a second thought about the timing of their departure until now."

Lady Vivienne, who had remained quiet and stone-faced throughout the exchange, now stepped forward and gave a dismissive wave of her hand. "Wondrous. A grand enigma has been solved. Perhaps we can now focus on the present and not the past? The boy's parents served their purpose. Now let us worry about what is important."

The baroness' exceptionally callous comment stunned them all. Nikalys bit down, grinding his teeth to keep from saying something rude in retort. Kenders glared at Lady Vivienne while Jak looked as though he wanted to punch the noblewoman. Broedi's face tightened in bitter disapproval, but he remained silent. Commander Aiden winced and looked away while Nundle and Zecus simply stared in quiet disbelief.

The lone person who did not shrink from the baroness was Sabine. She leaped to her feet—jostling Helene as she did so—and stalked over to stand in front of Lady Vivienne, an angry scowl on her face. In a voice tempered only by the fact Helene was asleep, she hissed, "How dare you! That *man's* parents protected your precious Progeny for fifteen years, and all you can say is they 'served their purpose?' I don't care if you are the lady of some barony I've never heard of, you should be ashamed of yourself, you ice-hearted witch!"

Despite Sabine's efforts to remain as quiet as possible, Helene stirred, lifting her head up to stare at Sabine. Nikalys was trapped, wondering if he should do something to stop Sabine from berating Lady Vivienne or perhaps go collect Helene so Sabine could let her true anger show. Curious what his brother and sister thought, Nikalys glanced over and found Jak gazing at Sabine with open admiration. Looking closer, he realized there was more behind Jak's stare. Much more. Nikalys was not sure how he felt about that.

Kenders looked over, glanced between them both, and then stared at Nikalys alone, a tiny, sympathetic smile gracing her lips. Apparently, she recognized they were both developing feelings for Sabine. In fact, she would have bet good coin she knew before either of them had.

Nikalys sighed and looked back to Jak. A very awkward conversation faced him in the future, a talk that was for a later time. A much later time. Setting his jaw, he faced the baroness and Sabine.

Only a few moments had passed, moments filled with nothing more than steely, chilly glares thrice as cool as the Blackbark Forest's nighttime air. The creases radiating from the corners of Lady Vivienne's eyes lengthened as she finally responded.

"My dear, surely you are aware how serious our situation is. We have been waiting a decade and a half for *them*—" she glanced at Nikalys and Kenders "—to return, knowing all along that it was likely the god of Chaos was moving ahead with whatever his—or her—plans were." She nodded to Zecus. "Now I discover that the rumors about the Borderlands are not only true, but are *much* worse than I had heard. Moreover, it would seem the Cabal managed to sink their claws into at least *two* of our nation's sovereigns. Gods know if there are more."

Lady Vivienne paused, her eyes aglow with fierce determination. When she resumed speaking, her words were crisp and her tone pointed.

"As of this moment, we have *no* idea what the end goal of the Cabal is. *None!* We are blindly stumbling about a dark room, without candle or torch, and the *best* chance we have ever had at discovering some clue as to what Chaos is planning—or who he or she *even is*—is fueling that pyre." She jammed a finger in the air, pointing to the bonfire to the north.

Nikalys' eyes narrowed as he realized the noblewoman was speaking about Jhaell. Glaring at the woman, he protested, "I had no choice. He was about to kill Kenders."

The baroness' hot gaze snapped to him. "And you could not have simply knocked him over the head? Did you have to skewer him like some hunk of lamb roast on a blasted spit?"

Nikalys remained silent, not wanting to admit the thought had never occurred to him.

Scowling at him, the baroness hissed, "We know nothing, young man. *Nothing*! Other than we are severely outnumbered and cruelly pressed for time we do not have."

The picture she painted was beyond bleak. The tiny sliver of pride Nikalys had felt at their victory today slipped away.

After a moment's silence, Lady Vivienne's harsh gaze softened a bit. "Now, while all of that surely prompted my boorish behavior, it does not excuse it." Facing Jak, she inclined her head. "I apologize for my thoughtlessness, young man. Truly, I do. The young woman is correct. I acted every bit the 'ice-hearted witch.'"

Jak nodded slowly and muttered through tight lips, "I understand." Nikalys noticed he did not accept the apology.

Lady Vivienne turned her gaze to Sabine. "And you, my dear. I certainly admire your spirit, sense of loyalty, and commitment to your friends. You will fit in well with the Manes. Thank you for pointing out my discourtesy."

Clearly taken aback by the apology, Sabine offered a sedate and confused, "You're welcome." Helene was half-awake now, her head resting on Sabine's shoulder as she stared at Lady Vivienne.

The baroness' stare turned cold again. "However, there are ways to point out one's failings that do not involve loudly chastising them before the people they lead. I will forgive you for now, as I know you have never been more than a short walk away from your farm. Yet should you *ever* speak to me that way again within earshot of the Manes, I will take you and your sister to the Constables myself. Is that understood?"

Sabine's expression shifted in an instant, rivaling the icy hostility of Lady Vivienne's glare. Nikalys was relieved that Sabine was holding Helene at the moment and not a weapon of some sort.

"And if you try to do that, my Lady, the last thing you will see before striding through Maeana's hall will be an arrow shaft quivering in your chest."

The baroness studied Sabine for a long, silent moment, her gaze digging into the young woman, picking her apart. Eventually a slight smile touched one corner of her mouth. "Hold onto that determination, dear. You'll need it for what's to come." She motioned to where Sabine had been resting on the ground. "Now, sit. We have other things to discuss."

Sabine glowered at the noblewoman a moment longer before turning to retreat to her spot by the fire. Once sitting, she set to humming a soft and melodious tune while gently rocking Helene, trying to get the little girl back to sleep. Her scowling gaze never left Lady Vivienne.

Ignoring Sabine's stare, the baroness turned to Broedi. "There is something I neglected to ask you earlier. Whatever made you think to contact me at Mason's Bay? Why not Freehaven or the enclave?"

"*That's* what you were doing in Fernsford!" exclaimed Kenders. "When you left us in the tavern?"

Broedi eyed her and gave a short nod. "It was."

"Why didn't you just tell us that was what you were doing?" asked Jak.

"After the incident with the Soulwraith the previous night, I was afraid to do so." He shook his head. "I should have *never* shared anything about the enclave with any of you. My mistake had put the Manes in terrible danger. Admittedly, I was trying to put the rain back into the clouds, but I chose to err on the side of secrecy again."

"Could you not have told us something, great lion?" asked Zecus.

"What would you have had me tell you?"

"I don't know," mused Jak. "How about, 'Hey, we might have help when the ijul, the demon, and the oligurts attack us?'"

"I did not tell you that we might have help, because I did not ask for any. The missives I sent were simple and short should they fall into the wrong hands." He glanced at Nundle. "We have all seen firsthand what might happen should one stumble across something they are not meant to see."

Nundle nodded. "Excellent point."

"What did you say, then?" asked Nikalys.

"The message I received was but six words," said Lady Vivienne. "'I have found them. We return.' And no signature." She stared at Broedi. "Nevertheless, I knew it could only be from one person."

"I assumed you would," said the hillman. "What surprises me—rather, what *should* surprise me—is that the one I sent to Mason's Bay found you there. To your earlier question, I did send missives to the enclave and Freehaven as well. The one to Mason's Bay was on the chance you might have returned home for some reason." Eyeing the commander, he added, "Although why you were there, Commander, *with* two hundred Manes is a mystery to me."

Commander Aiden lifted his eyebrows. "Unusual, isn't it?"

"A turn ago," began Lady Vivienne, "Jules asked to take our soldiers north for drills. It was not easy to arrange, but I did so. We dressed them as Southern Arms and had them skirmish with true Southlands soldiers."

The hillman shifted his gaze back to the soldier. "What made you think to do something like that?"

Commander Aiden shrugged his shoulders. "I had the idea one day during morning drills in the courtyard. Figured we could benefit from facing someone other than ourselves."

Broedi cocked an eyebrow and looked back to the baroness. "And you agreed to such a maneuver, my Lady? It was a rather large risk."

"Be grateful I took it," conceded the noblewoman. "Else, we would have never arrived in time today."

Nikalys shook his head. Yet another coincidence. Broedi's theory about the gods' intervention in events was beginning to sound unnervingly plausible.

Nundle stepped forward, his red hair flashing in the fire light. Nikalys had almost forgotten the tomble was there. He had been unusually quiet.

"How is it you arrived in time?"

Lady Vivienne eyed the tomble for a moment before answering. "After I received Broedi's message, we left at once to hurry back to the enclave. Imagine my surprise when some of the mages and I felt the use of the Strands as we marched." She glanced at Broedi. "Then we saw you in the sky and—"

"Hold a moment," interrupted Kenders. "You're a *mage*?" A half a heartbeat later, she added, "My Lady?"

Lady Vivienne answered as though Kenders had just asked her if the sun was bright. "Of course." She looked to Broedi, frowning. "You and your secrets."

Nundle stared across the fire to Broedi. "I suppose you want us to believe this is the gods' doing, as well?"

"What more evidence do you require?" asked the hillman. "There have been too many lucky coincidences for Ketus not to have a hand, too many flashes of inspiration for Ashana not to be the source, and too much coordination for Nelnora not to be watching it all. Perhaps even Greya has lent her blessing over their meddling. If not, she will be rather unhappy to learn they are playing with fate."

"While I appreciate the fact that they're interested," chimed in Jak, "a little more assistance with the oligurts and razorfiends would have been nice."

Broedi shook his head. "One Celystiela alone, or even a handful, cannot deliberately aid the mortal world. An Assembly must be called before they lend assistance."

"Pardon me for asking the obvious," said Nundle, "but what exactly would you call what they have been doing to this point?"

"Everything and nothing," said Broedi.

"You promised, Broedi," muttered Kenders. "No riddles."

Wearing a slight smile, the hillman rumbled, "Our string of 'coincidences' may seem definitive to us, but I am sure the Celystiela would claim they have done nothing. What proof do we have of their involvement?" He stared around the fire at each of them. "None. None at all."

"It is not right," grumbled Zecus, his tone decidedly bitter. "Gods interfering with my life? My *family's* life!?"

"What is 'right' is of no consequence," rumbled Broedi. "Not to the Assembly of Nine. The Celystiela that comprised the Assembly were all of the Neither. Right and wrong? Good and evil?" He shook his head. "*None* of that matters to them. They strive for equilibrium, for stability. And they will do *whatever* is necessary to achieve it. If either evil or good gains too large a foothold in the mortal world, they insert themselves."

"How do you trust someone if you don't know where they stand?" asked Nikalys.

Broedi turned his gaze to Nikalys and remained quiet for a long moment before answering. "I have been asking myself that for two hundred-fifty years. Yet that is not the question of the moment."

"Then what is?" asked Jak.

"Why," muttered Kenders, drawing the attention of those gathered around the fire. Looking up, she asked, "Why have they chosen *now* to interfere?"

Broedi nodded slowly. "Precisely, Kenders. And that is what I intend to ask them when I travel to the Seat of Nelnora."

Nikalys was unsure he had heard correctly. "The Seat of Nelnora?" His eyebrows climbed high "In the Celestial Empire?"

Broedi met his incredulous gaze and nodded. "Once we reach the enclave and you two are settled, I intend to travel there and try to gain some answers. Somehow, I doubt I will be turned away this time." Turning to Nundle, he added, "And you are coming with me."

Nundle's eyes went round. "Me?"

"Yes," rumbled Broedi. "You. There is a mage at the enclave who can teach you the Weave for a port. Once you have practiced it quite a bit—I do *not* want to end up at the bottom of a lake—we can begin our journey. It will take us a while to reach the Seat of Nelnora overland, but I would like to return quickly."

Nundle's eyes shone with excitement. "You have someone who can teach me how to weave a port?"

"We do," replied Broedi. An amused glint danced in his eyes. "And I believe you will be quite surprised who that will be."

"What about the rest of us?" asked Kenders, concern in her voice. "You're just going to leave us there?"

"For a time, yes. You and Nikalys will be in excellent hands."

Kenders frowned. It was clear she did not want Broedi to go. Neither did Nikalys, which he found rather ironic, as not too long ago, all he had wanted was for Broedi to leave them alone.

Broedi faced the Moiléne sisters and rumbled, "If you would like, Sabine, you can learn to use what gifts you have at the enclave. I am sure Gamin will be happy to craft a set of lessons for you, should you desire. If not, you are welcome to live in Claw as a member of the Manes."

A small, relieved smile touched Sabine's face, and she gave Helene a gentle squeeze. "Thank you."

"You are welcome." His gaze shifted to Helene's sleeping form. "However, I do ask you allow your iskoa to spend time with our mages. It would be best for everyone that she learn to control her ability."

Sabine nodded at once. "Of course."

Looking across the fire to Jak and Zecus, Broedi said, "And for the two of you, Sergeant Trell and the commander have something else in mind."

Commander Aiden stepped forward. "I've had the opportunity to talk with Nathan, an impressive man in his own right. He had some very good things to say about you both. To charge a blasted demon with but twenty men? Gods, but that was brave. Utterly brainless, but definitely brave. The sergeant seems to think you would both make good soldiers. Care to find out?"

Jak nodded at Nikalys and Kenders. "I already told them I'd do whatever I can to help them. If that means playing soldier, so be it."

Kenders reached out, grabbed his hand, and squeezed. Nikalys grinned, reached around Kenders, and patted Jak on the back.

The commander shifted his gaze to Zecus. "What say you, Borderlander? We'd be honored to have you join us as well."

Zecus stood in silence for a long moment, a solemn expression affixed on his face. He glanced west, sighed, and then looked back to the commander. "I will stay and help as I can. For now." His gaze shifted to rest on Kenders. "Perhaps I *am* meant to be here."

A touch of color bloomed in Kenders' cheeks. Nikalys caught Jak's eye and the brothers exchanged a slight grin. They were normally protective about young men's interest in their sister, but Zecus was a good soul.

Broedi turned and looked to the northwest, his profile lit by flickering firelight revealing a worried frown. "Then, it is settled. We march for the enclave in the morning. The Cabal surely plot even while we stand here. They have had centuries to prepare. We have mere turns."

The task before them was daunting but Nikalys was determined to see it through. He glanced at Kenders and found the same expression of resolve that he knew was etched his face. Jak, too. With complete confidence and conviction, Nikalys said, "We will be ready."

Epilogue

19ᵗʰ of the Turn of Thonda

An icy wind lashed the mountain's peak, whipping and clawing at the black robes of the lone figure standing upon the rocky summit. The cloth fluttered and flapped in the blustery blasts, adding an arrhythmic snapping to the air whistling between the jagged gray rocks jutting from the ground.

Three black cords bound Tandyr's blond hair into a long ponytail, doing their best to refute the wind's power. His wide, frosty blue eyes stared eastward, down into the plains below. The vast range of mountains upon which he stood stretched north and south, clear to both horizons. Tall, leaden gray peaks, each one topped with white snowcaps, stretched into the azure sky. Thousands of tents and burrows dotted the valley below. A layer of hazy smoke from the countless campfires lay like a thick blanket over the sprawling camp.

As was typical, Tandyr was the first of their group of four to arrive. He tried to suppress his irritation at the others' tardiness, but he allowed himself one tiny sigh of exasperation.

An abrupt ripping sound, utterly distinct from his flapping robes, caused him to turn his head. A dozen paces away, a slit had appeared in the fabric of the world. "Finally."

A stunning erijul emerged from the port, stepping onto the rocky mountaintop. She paused a moment to glance around the barren landscape before striding towards Tandyr. The mountain wind tore at the thin, gauzy dress she wore.

Lifting an eyebrow, Tandyr queried, "Cold, Raela?"

Visibly shivering, the erijul used a quick Weave of Air to wrap herself with a small, invisible barrier to hold back the icy wind. "Not anymore." She eyed him and shook her head. "I do not know how you can stand it."

Tandyr did not mind the chilly gusts. In fact, he welcomed the cold sterility the wind added to the delicious barrenness of the mountaintop. It helped keep his mind clear and calm, allowing him to repress the bedlam churning inside his being.

He turned his gaze back to the eastern plains as Raela joined him. Without preamble, she spoke.

"I have looked everywhere. He is nowhere to be found."

"I am unsurprised," sighed Tandyr. "I suspect he has tried to clean up after his mistakes."

"That or he is hiding, afraid of what we would do should we find him."

"I doubt that."

She peered at him with curious eyes. "You say that with confidence."

"One of my demon captains is missing," replied Tandyr, his tone as cool as the wind. "Along with four hundred Sudashians." He shook his head, calm yet angry. "The fool demon left the rest of his charge alone. A thousand of which had killed one another before I arrived to put a stop to it." A bitter frown spread over his elongated lips. "Utterly reckless. He knows the binding weakens if he does not remain near."

"How long was he gone?"

Tandyr's scowl grew. "At least a week."

Deep furrows appeared in Raela's forehead. "Where would he go?"

"How I wish I could answer that question. Unfortunately, the one I can is 'with whom.'" He turned to meet Raela's inquisitive stare. "I learned that he left with a saeljul."

Raela dropped her chin to her chest and sighed. "Jhaell believes he can kill them on his own?"

"It would seem so, yes."

"He is a fool, then."

"*Was* a fool," corrected Tandyr. "Had he been successful, I would have certainly heard about it, bombarded by his petty demands I reunite him with his beloved at once." He shook his head. "No, Raela. We must assume that he failed and is dead." A tiny smile graced his lips. "At least he got his wish to be with his love, something that would have never happened despite my many promises." He peered over at Raela. "Maeana was *not* pleased with me after that stunt. She has held tightly onto that one's soul."

Raela's eyes narrowed a fraction. "You are remaining quite calm about this."

"Only because I must."

"I suppose I am still not used to your new demeanor." She gave a slow, wondering shake of her head. "I do not know how you do it."

"It is a challenge," admitted the god. The others did not believe he could keep his nature in check forever. Yet he had done so for over three hundred years and needed to for a little while longer. His plan was too ambitious for him to lose control. That had always been his downfall in the past.

Raela sighed and stared down at the Sudashian camp below. "You should have left Jhaell alone on that beach."

"Come, now, Raela. He was not entirely useless. Without his help, we would not have found two of the Suštinata. For all of his faults, he was good at what he did." He sighed and gave a tiny, careless shrug. "Without winter, there would be no spring, I suppose."

Raela mumbled, "He should have stayed in the libraries."

"Yes. He should have."

"So...what now?" asked Raela, staring back to him. "It would seem the Progeny do exist. And live. Indrida was right." A disappointed frown crossed her face. "Yet again." Peering eastward, she asked, "Do we hold and wait until we can find them?"

"No!" snapped Tandyr as a quick surge of wild, bitter anger swelled inside him.

Raela raised an eyebrow at the intensity of his response. A tiny, smug smile touched her lips. Ignoring her haughty stare, Tandyr forced himself calm and then spoke.

"We cannot afford to postpone. Word of our invasion is already spreading. Freehaven will be slow to react, but they will do so eventually. If we move quickly enough, no one, not the First Council, not even the blasted Progeny, will be prepared to counter." He stared at the world below him and frowned. "So, no, Raela. We do not wait. We have waited long enough."

Appendix

The Gods

The High Host

Name	Other Names/References	Sphere
Ceruna	The Hammer of Innocence	Purity, Hope, and Justice
Khanos	The Vital Soul	Life
Luraana	The Villager	Community and Song
Mu	The Bright Blade	Light, Sun, Honor, War
Rheoc	Delver of the Deep	Earth, Mines, Smiths
Roden	The Rebellious One	Change and Freedom
Sormina	Graceful Guider of Hearts	Beauty and Love
Sutri	Guardian of Eras	Summer and Time
Tirnu	The Ruler of Rules	Law

The Neither

Name	Other Names/References	Sphere
Ashana	The Inspired One	Ideas and Innovation
Chalchalu	Filler of Purses	Commerce and Wealth
Duryn	The Great Artisan	Industry and Crafters
Gaena	The Master Weaver	Magic
Greya	Cold Twister of Fate	Winter and Fate
Horum	The Strong Arm	Strength and Athletic Skill
Indrida	The Enlightened Oracle	Knowledge and Prophecy
Lamoth	She Who Walks the Woods	Forest and Wild Nature
Maeana	The Final Friend	Death
Nelnora	Watcher of the World	Civilization and Balance

Ketus	The Shrewd Fox	Shadows, Cunning and Luck
Rintira	Dodgy Gatherer	Autumn and Trickery
Saewyn	The Untamed	Spring, Sea, and Storm
Sarphia	Eternal Queen	Immortality
Thonda	The Great Tracker	Beasts and Hunt

The Cabal

Other Names/References	Sphere
The Eternal Anarchist	Chaos
The Great Quarreler	Strife
The Bringer of Misery	Sorrow
Agony's Friend	Pain
Immortal Teller of Lies	Deception
The Mad One	Madness
Bearer of Grudges	Vengeance
Terror's Maiden	Fear
The Loather of All	Hate

THE CALENDAR

The calendar of Terrene is symmetrical. Scholars suggest the gods altered the world and the moons to facilitate such a perfectly aligned set of dates. A year on Terrene is exactly three-hundred-sixty days, divided into twelve turns of twenty-eight days per turn. A week is seven days long; four weeks make up a single turn.

Between each turn is a two-day period that belongs to neither the turn before nor the turn that follows. They are commonly referred to as Days of Leisure, and throughout the year are used for feasts and other celebrations.

The turns of the year and the Days of Leisure between are as follows:

Turn of Khanos: Days of Leisure for Khanos and Indrida
winter in the southern hemisphere, summer in the northern hemisphere
Turn of Greya: Days of Leisure for Greya and Sarphia
Turn of Duryn: Days of Leisure for Duryn and Ketus
Turn of Roden: Days of Leisure for Roden and Rheoc
Turn of Saewyn: Days of Leisure for Saewyn and Nelnora
Turn of Sormina: Days of Leisure for Sormina and Tirnu
Turn of Lamoth: Days of Leisure for Lamoth and Horum
winter in the northern hemisphere, summer in the southern hemisphere
Turn of Sutri: Days of Leisure for Sutri and Mu
Turn of Thonda: Days of Leisure for Thonda and Gaena
Turn of Rintira: Days of Leisure for Rintira and Chalchalu
Turn of Luraana: Days of Leisure for Luraana and Ceruna
Turn of Maeana: Days of Leisure for Maeana and Ashana

THE MOONS

Two moons circle Terrene with two very different cycles. White Moon has a twenty-four day full moon-to-full moon cycle while Blue Moon has a thirty-six day cycle. This creates a very uneven pattern of light/dark cycles at night. One of the moons is always visible in the sky; at no point are both moons at the new stage. Five times every year, though, both moons are at the full stage. These are known as Nights of the Two Moons. Nights of the Two Moons occur every year on these dates:

First Night of Two Moons – 27th of Turn of Khanos
Second Night of Two Moons – 9th of Turn of Roden
Third Night of Two Moons – 21st of Turn of Sormina
Fourth Night of Two Moons – 3rd of Turn of Thonda
Fifth Night of Two Moons – 15th of Turn of Luraana

www.ingramcontent.com/pod-product-compliance
Lightning Source LLC
Chambersburg PA
CBHW052342020726
47503CB00001B/75